"A WINNER...
A FIRST-RATE
SUSPENSE STORY"

—*Newsweek*

In this riveting nine-month international bestseller, master storyteller Irving Wallace creates an unforgettable cast of characters who come to life against a continent-spanning canvas of courage and cowardice, scandal and intrigue.

"Exciting and provocative . . . brimming with suspense" —*Washington Star*

"Lots of story, suspense, sex, and details" —*National Observer*

"What a story! He maintains the suspense of his tale to the last page!" —*King Features Syndicate*

"A whopping good story!" —*Detroit Free Press*

Books by Irving Wallace

THE WORD

Irving Wallace

PUBLISHED BY POCKET BOOKS NEW YORK

Portions of this book have appeared
in *The Ladies' Home Journal*.

POCKET BOOKS, a division of Simon & Schuster, Inc.
1230 Avenue of the Americas, New York, N.Y. 10020

ISBN: 0-671-47926-1

First Pocket Books printing March, 1973

15   14   13   12

POCKET and colophon are registered trademarks
of Simon & Schuster, Inc.

Printed in the U.S.A.

For
Sylvia
With Love

In the beginning was the Word, and the Word was with God, and the Word was God.

—The Gospel According to John 1:1

And the Word was made flesh, and dwelt among us . . .

—The Gospel According to John 1:14

If God did not exist, it would be necessary to invent Him.

—VOLTAIRE (1770)

I

JUST AFTER he entered John F. Kennedy Airport, and as he was having his ticket to Chicago verified, he was handed the urgent message by the attendant at the airline's desk.

Call your office. Important.

Fearing the worst, heart thumping, he hurried to the nearest telephone booth and dialed his office in Manhattan.

His switchboard operator answered. "Steven Randall Associates—Public Relations."

"This is Mr. Randall," he said impatiently. "Let me speak to Wanda."

A moment later the connection was made, and he was on the line with his secretary. "What is it, Wanda? Is it my father?"

"No—no—oh, I'm sorry, I should have made that clear —forgive me. No, there's been nothing more from your family. It was something else, a business matter I thought you'd want to know about before you took off. The call came in just after you left for the airport. It—it sounded important."

He was at once relieved and annoyed. "Wanda, what else can be important after what I've been through today? I'm in no mood for business—"

"Boss, don't take my head off. I just thought—"

"Okay, I'm sorry. But make it fast or I'll miss the damn plane. Now, go ahead. What's so important?"

"A possible new account. The client himself called in, personally. When I explained you had to leave town on an emergency, he said he understood, but still he in-

1

sisted he must see you the first moment you're free and within the next forty-eight hours."

"Well, you know that's impossible. Who was it?"

"Have you ever heard of George L. Wheeler, president of Mission House?"

He recognized the name instantly. "The religious book publisher."

"Right," said Wanda. "The biggest. A very fat cat. Honest, I wouldn't have bothered you at a time like this, except it sounded so unusual, mysterious—and, like I said, he insisted it was important. He pressed me hard. Said I must get hold of you. I told him I couldn't promise anything. Only that I'd try to reach you and relay his message."

"What message? What does Wheeler want?"

"Believe me, boss, I tried to find out exactly, but I couldn't. He was very guarded. He said it was a top-secret matter of international importance. He did explain finally it concerned your representing a hush-hush project involving the publication of a brand-new Bible."

"A new Bible?" Randall exploded. "That's the big deal, the big important deal? We've got a billion Bibles already. What do we want with another one? I never heard such crap. Me playing shill for a Bible? Forget it."

"I would, boss, only I can't, because of Mr. Wheeler's message—what he wanted me to pass on to you. It was so odd, really strange. He said to me, 'If Mr. Randall is a Doubting Thomas, and wants to know more about our secret project, you tell him to open his New Testament to Matthew 28:7. That will give him a clue to what our project is all about.' "

Totally exasperated, Randall said, "Wanda, I have no intention of reading that passage now or ever. So you just call him and—"

"Boss, I looked it up," Wanda interrupted. "The passage in Matthew reads, 'And go quickly, and tell his disciples that he is risen from the dead; and, behold, he goeth before you into Galilee; there shall ye see him. . . .' That's the passage about Christ's Resurrection. That's what intrigued me—made me curious, and made me decide to try to catch you. What makes it doubly strange is the last thing Wheeler said to me before he hung up. I wrote it down. Here. He said, 'And after Mr. Randall reads that passage, tell him we want him to handle the Second Resurrection.' That's it."

This was enigmatic, and eerie to hear on a day like this, considering what had happened and what he must soon face. His exasperation subsided, and he began to wonder what this Wheeler was up to. "He wants me to handle the Second Resurrection? What's he talking about? Is he some kind of religious nut?"

"He sounded very sober and serious," said Wanda. "And he made the project sound like—like something world-shaking was going on."

Randall's memory had groped backward into his past. How familiar it was to him. The Tomb is empty. The Lord has arisen. He has appeared. The Resurrection. In memory, it had been the most meaningful and secure time of his life. Yet, he had spent years ridding himself of this crippling voodooism.

The public address system was intruding, beckoning to him through his partially open booth.

"Wanda," he said, "they're announcing the last call for my flight. I'd better run."

"What should I tell Wheeler?"

"Tell him—tell him you haven't been able to locate me yet."

"Nothing else?"

"Nothing else, until I know what's waiting for me in Chicago and Oak City."

"I hope it'll be all right, boss."

"We'll see. I'll call you tomorrow."

He hung up, and still puzzled and vaguely unsettled by Wanda's call, he hastened toward his plane.

THEY HAD BEEN in the air for almost two hours, and he had long since put Mr. Wheeler and his new Bible and his enigmatic Second Resurrection out of his mind.

"We're about to land," the stewardess reminded him. "Please fasten your seat belt, Mr.—Mr. Randall."

She had hesitated over his name, as if trying to remember whether she had heard it before and whether he was Somebody. She was a big full-bosomed girl, Texas pretty, with a stamped smile, and he supposed that out of uniform she could be fun, unless she was one of those girls who told you after two drinks that she was really a very serious person and did not make it a practice to go out with married men and was just starting to read Dostoevski. Probably another Darlene, he told himself. But no, Darlene had been reading Kahlil Gibran when he first met her a year and a half ago, and to the best of his knowledge she had read nothing else since.

He was tempted to tell the stewardess that he was Somebody, yet he was certain that he was not her kind of Somebody, and besides, it didn't matter, not tonight, especially not tonight.

He gave her a nod, and dutifully he began to fasten his seat belt.

No, he was not considered a Somebody, he reflected, except by certain people who wanted to become celebrities or remain celebrities, and by powerful people who had a product or even a country to promote. His name, Steven R. Randall, rarely was seen in print or mentioned on television, and his picture never appeared anywhere. The public out there saw only what he wanted them to see, while he himself remained unseen. And he did not mind —even with stewardesses—because he was important where it counted, and those who mattered knew that he was important.

This morning, for example. He had finally met, face to face, with Ogden Towery III, who mattered and who knew that Steve Randall was important, a couple of million dollars' worth of important. They had come to final terms on the take-over of Randall Associates, Public Relations, by Towery's international conglomerate, Cosmos Enterprises. They had bargained as equals on all— well, on almost all points except one.

That single compromise—Randall tried to soften his capitulation by calling it compromise—still made him uneasy, even ashamed. Anyway, the meeting this morning had been an early beginning for what promised to be one of the most miserable days in his life. And he was miserable because, important personage though he might be, he felt utterly helpless about his life and about what was waiting for him at the termination of this flight.

To end this introspection, he tried giving his attention to the activity on the plane. The stewardess, no girdle, nice ass, was returning to the front of the cabin, being cordial to those other bodies also locked inside seat belts. He wondered about those others. They appeared moderately happy, and he wondered whether they could detect that he was unhappy. At once, he was grateful for his anonymity, because he was in no mood to speak to anyone. In fact, he was in no mood for the reunion with Clare, his younger sister, who would be waiting for him at O'Hare Airport, tearful and ready to drive him from Chicago across the state line to Wisconsin and Oak City.

He felt the plane lurch and sink, and he knew that the jetliner was almost home.

Home, literally. He was coming home for a while, not dropping in or passing by, but coming home after being away—how long?—two years, two or three years since his last visit. The end of his short-long flight from New York. The beginning of the end of the past. It was going to be rough, coming home. He hoped that his stay could be brief and merciful.

The stewardess had paused in the aisle beside him. "We're just landing," she said. She appeared to be relieved, and more human, less plastic, an earthling with earth thoughts. "Forgive me, but I've been meaning to say, your name is familiar. Haven't I seen it in the newspapers?"

A Somebody collector, after all, he thought.

"Sorry to disappoint you," he said. "The last time I was in the papers was under 'Birth Notices.' "

She offered an embarrassed laugh. "Well, I hope you had a pleasant flight, Mr. Randall."

"Just great," said Steve Randall.

Real great. Fifty miles away his father lay in a coma. And for the first time since becoming successful (but sure-

ly it had occurred to him before in recent years), Randall
realized that money could not buy off every trouble or
solve every problem, any more than it could any longer
save his marriage or make him fall asleep at three o'clock
in the morning.

His father would say—Son, money isn't everything—
as he took his son's money. His father would say—God
is everything—and he would look to God and give his love
to God. His father, the Reverend Nathan Randall, was in
the God business. His father took his orders from the Big
Conglomerate in the sky.

Not fair, not fair.

Randall stared out the rain-splattered plane window at
the landscape and buildings caught crazily by the airport
lights.

Okay, Dad, he thought, so money can't buy you and
Mom out of this one. So now it is strictly between you
and your Maker. But level with me, Dad: If you are
talking to Him, do you think He is listening?

Then, he knew again that this was unfair, also, an old
lingering childhood bitterness, a remembrance that he had
always competed unsuccessfully with the Almighty for his
father's love. And it had always been No Contest. It surprised him now, that this strange pseudo-sibling jealousy
still rankled. It was blasphemous—he evoked the old-
fashioned brimstone pulpit word—on a night of crisis.

Also, it was wrong, he was wrong. Because there had
been good times between his father and himself. Instantly,
he was able to conjure up more fairly the stricken old
man—that foolish, impractical, warm, wonderful, decent,
dogmatic, misguided, sweet old man, his old man, and
suddenly he loved him more than he had in years.

Then he wanted to cry. It seemed impossible. Here he
was—big man from the big time and big city, with cus-
tom-made suit, Italian shoes, manicured fingernails, credit
cards, booze, women, Rolls, flunkies, best tables—a
sophisticated, worldly, jaded, hardened, image maker, and
he wanted to cry like that little kid in Oak City.

"We've arrived in Chicago," the stewardess's voice was
announcing. "Please check your personal belongings. All

deplaning will be done through the front door of the aircraft."

Randall blew his nose, found his leather briefcase, stood up shakily, and eased into the line shuffling toward the exit—the exit that would lead him home and to whatever lay ahead.

IT WAS NOT until O'Hare Airport was three quarters of an hour behind them, and the illuminated highway sign indicated they had entered Wisconsin, that Clare finally exhausted herself of the sobbing and blubbering and vain litany of regrets to lapse into humane silence behind the wheel of her car.

In the airport terminal, Clare had fallen into his arms in a half faint, weeping and moaning. No modern-day Electra had ever matched her public grief. Almost harshly, Randall had ordered her to control herself long enough to tell him his father's physical condition. He could learn only—Clare avoided medical terms, always had, as being threatening—that his father was in poor shape, and that Dr. Oppenheimer would make no predictions. Yes, there was an oxygen tent, and yes, Daddy was unconscious inside it, and oh God, Daddy looked like he had never looked before.

After that, in her car and driving at last, Clare's snifflings had continued to punctuate her incessant verbal catharsis. How she loved dear Daddy, and poor Mom, and what would happen to Mom and herself and Uncle Herman and the rest of them? They had been at the hospital the entire day, since it had happened early this morning. Everyone was still there, and they were waiting for Steve. Mom was there, and Uncle Herman—who was Mom's brother—and Dad's best friend, Ed Period Johnson, and the Reverend Tom Carey, all there, everybody waiting for Steve.

Waiting for him, Randall thought, the success in the family, the success from New York who always performed miracles with his checkbook or through his connections. He wanted to ask Clare whether anyone was waiting for the One who meant the most to Dad, the One whom Dad had given everything to, depended upon, invested in against Judgment Day, the Creator, the Jehovah, Our Father in Heaven. This Randall wanted to ask, but he had refrained.

"I guess I've told you everything I can," Clare had said. Then, eyes on the rain-slicked highway ahead, knuckles white on the steering wheel, she had imparted what he already knew. "It won't be long. We're almost there." With that, she had sunk into silence.

Leaving his sister to consort with her private guilt-demons, Steve Randall slumped back in the seat and closed his eyes, welcoming this interlude to be alone.

He could still feel, inside himself, the lump of agitation that he had carried along the entire day, but now he could better analyze it, and what was curious was that the smallest part of this unhappiness came from grief over his father. He tried to rationalize his unfilial reaction, and decided that grief was the most intense of the emotions and therefore the shortest-lived. The very intensity of grief made it so self-destructive that one's survival instinct rose up to draw a sheet over grief and hide it from mind and heart. He had drawn the sheet, and he was no longer thinking of his father. He was thinking right now of himself—realizing how heretical his sister Clare would find this, if she could know—and he was thinking of all his own recent dyings.

He could not number the day he had lost interest in his prosperous and booming public relations business, but it had happened at some time in the last year or two. This loss of interest had begun to occur about the time, just before or just after, he and his wife Barbara had faced their final showdown and break, and she had taken their daughter Judy and gone to San Francisco, where she had friends.

He tried to pinpoint when that had come to pass. Judy had barely turned thirteen then. She was fifteen now. So it had been two years ago. Barbara had spoken grimly of divorce, but had not acted upon it, and so it had remained merely a separation. Randall had not minded this suspended state, since he could not accept the finality of a divorce. Not because he feared losing his wife. Their relationship had gone stale. He cared for Barbara only as he cared for his own ego. He had not wanted a divorce because it would have meant admitting a failure. More important, the finality of it might have severed Judy from him completely. And Judy, although he had never seen much of her or given her much of his time, was a person, a person and an idea, an extension of himself, that he valued and cherished.

His career and business, upon which he had lavished so much energy and devotion, had finally become monotonous and boring, as boring as his marriage had been. Each day seemed simply a Xerox of the day before. You entered your lavishly decorated reception room, where the young receptionist, sexy and overdressed, was forever drinking coffee with two other girls and discussing jewelry. You saw your bright young promotion men, carrying their briefcases the same way, draping their trench coats over their arms the same way, going in to work, burrowing toward their plush holes like groundhogs. You conferred with them in their expensive modern offices, their desks always filled with a superabundance of pictures of their wives and children, so that you knew that they cheated.

There was no more excitement in capturing new clients, now accounts. In the job, you had handled everyone and everything—the rising black singer, the latest rock group, the crazy British actress, the miracle detergent, the fastest sports car, the emerging African nation that wanted tourist trade. There was no more thrill in promoting renowned personalities or promising products. There was no more creative challenge, and no more money motive. Whatever you did, you'd done before. Whatever you earned made you richer, but not rich enough.

It was far, far from the hopeless middle-class prison, Randall knew, but this sentence to life seemed almost as empty and inhuman. Each day ended for him as it had begun, with self-hate, and hatred for his treadmill existence. Inevitably, his private, wifeless, Judyless, distaste-for-the-rat-race life not only went on, but intensified. There were more women to possess without love, more booze, more uppers and downers, more insomnia, and more lunches, bars, nightclubs, openings, each one populated by the same traveling circus composed of the same faces of men and the same bodies of women.

Recently, he had begun to escape more and more frequently into an old daydream, a goal once sought but from which he had been detoured. He wanted a refuge, some place with green trees and only water to drink and no shop to repair your watch, a place where *The New York Times* came two weeks late and you had to hike into the village to find a phone or a girl you could sleep with and with whom you wanted to have breakfast in the morning. He wanted to write not exaggerated or half-phony handouts, but scholarly and truthful history books on a manual typewriter, and never think of money again, and find out why it was important to stay on this earth.

Yet, somehow he could not find the bridge to that dream. He told himself that he could not change his life because he did not have keeping-money. So, he tried to make do. For weeks he would busy himself, compulsively, with good health. No drinking, no pills, no tobacco, no late hours. Lots of handball.

He was thirty-eight years old, five feet eleven, with bloodshot brown eyes already a bit baggy, a straight nose set between flushed cheeks, a strong jaw that revealed the first inklings of a double chin, and a husky frame. In his good health period, when he began to feel twenty-eight instead of thirty-eight, and the brown eyes began clearing and the circles smoothing out below them, and the round face was becoming square, the chin gaining definition and becoming noticeable, and the stomach was becoming flat and the biceps almost brawny, when that happened, he would lose the incentive for maintaining his Spartan regime and clean living.

He played this losing game twice a year. He had not played it in recent months. Also, in trying to regularize his life, he had tried to confine himself to one woman. A sustained relationship. That was how, he remembered, Darlene Nicholson and Kahlil Gibran had been brought into his two-level brownstone Manhattan apartment.

It was in his work, which occupied the greater part of his time, that it was most difficult to make do anymore. Wanda Smith, his personal secretary, a tall black girl with a modified natural and a size-forty bust, worried about him. Joe Hawkins, his beetle-browed protégé and associate, worried about him. Thad Crawford, his graying, soft-spoken attorney, worried about him. He constantly reassured them that he was not going to crack, and to prove it, he did his day's work every day. But it was dark and joyless, that work.

Yet, sometimes, so rarely but sometimes, there was a shaft of light. A month ago, through Crawford, Randall had met a brilliant and original young law graduate who was not practicing law but practicing a profession new to a competitive capitalist democracy, a profession, a social science really, called Honesty. This young man, in his late twenties, with fantastic walrus moustache and burning eyes like a John Brown at the Ferry, was Jim McLoughlin. He had established something called The Raker Institute, with offices in New York, Washington, Chicago, Los Angeles. The organization was nonprofit, staffed by young fellow attorneys, by business school graduates and former professors, by rebellious journalists and professional fact-finders and bright errant fugitive sons of America's affluent industrial community. Quietly busy for several years, Jim McLoughlin's Raker Institute had been investigating, as its first project among the many that were expected to follow, an unspoken, an unwritten conspiracy by America's big business, its industries and corporations, against the public at large and the common good.

"What it amounts to is this," McLoughlin had told Randall during their first meeting. "For decades, our leaders in private enterprise, virtual monopolists, have suppressed new ideas, inventions, products that would have lowered the cost of living for the consumer. These new inventions, ideas, died stillborn, or were suffocated by big business, because if they had ever reached the public, they would have destroyed the huge profits made by private enterprises. We've done an incredible detective job these many months. Did you know that someone once invented a pill that could produce high-quality gasoline for automobiles?"

Randall said he had heard rumors of such things as long as he could remember, but had always assumed such discoveries were pure fancies, more sensational wish than fact.

Jim McLoughlin had gone on intently. "It's always been the job of big business to make you think such findings are, as you say, pure fancies. But you can take my word for it, such wonders have existed and still exist. A perfect illustration is the gasoline pill. An unknown genius of a chemist came up with a formula for a synthetic gasoline, and compressed the chemical additives to the size of a small tablet. You merely had to fill your gas tank with ordinary water, drop the pill in your tank, and you had eighteen or twenty gallons of pollution-free gas at a cost of maybe two cents. Do you think the mammoth oil companies would let that get out on the market? Not on your life—not on *their* life—it would have meant the end of the trillion-dollar petroleum industry. That's only one case. What about the so-called perpetual match? Was there really a single match that could give you fifteen thousand lights? You bet there was, and you bet it was suppressed quickly by big business. Then we found more, much more."

Randall had been definitely intrigued. "What else?" he had demanded.

"We learned of a textile—yes, I mean cloth—that never wears out," said McLoughlin. "We learned of a razor blade, one blade, that can last a lifetime, and never even needs sharpening. There have been several examples of a rubber tire that could go two hundred and fifty thousand miles without wearing out. There has been a special light bulb that could burn for ten years without being replaced. Do you realize what these products could mean to the struggling low-income family? But big business won't allow it. Through the years, inventors have been bought out, blackmailed, destroyed—in two cases they simply disappeared, and we suspect they were murdered. Yes, Mr. Randall, we have it well documented, and we're exposing the whole filthy suppression in a white paper—a black paper, if you prefer—to be called *The Plot Against You.*"

Randall had repeated the title, savoring it. "Great," he had murmured.

"The minute our white paper is released," McLoughlin had gone on, "big business will use every conceivable means to keep our exposé from being seen by the public. Failing that, they'll try to discredit it. That is why I've come to you. I want you to handle The Raker Institute and its first white paper. I want you to communicate our discoveries to the public—through interested congressmen, television and radio newsmen, the press, printed pamphlets, sponsored lectures. I want you to overcome every effort to gag us or defame us. I want you to drum our story across the land until it's as well known as 'The-Star-Spangled Banner.' We won't be clients who will make you rich. But hopefully, after you see what we're doing, we will make you feel you are part of a meaningful people's lobby which will exist for the first time in American history. I hope you will do it."

Randall had found himself coming alive as he considered the project. Do it? And how he would do it! He was ready to work out details, start meetings, as soon as Jim McLoughlin and his crusaders were ready. McLoughlin had said that they would be ready soon, certainly before the end of the year. With a veteran study team he would be off, for some months, looking into a highly secret prototype of a nonpolluting, low-priced steam-engine automobile that had been suppressed for two decades by the internal-combustion people in Detroit. In addition to that, he would be checking with his field men who were evaluating future projects that involved other powerful legal racketeers, abusers of the American dream, and included among them were the insurance companies, the telephone monopolies, the packinghouse combines, the loan associations.

"Don't expect to hear from me or my staff for a while," young McLoughlin had said. "Our whereabouts will be confidential. We have to work undercover. I learned that early on. Otherwise, the big business lobbies, and their

puppets in various branches of government, they'd have
their goons tailing us, anticipating and thwarting us. I
used to believe such police-state activity impossible in a
government of the people, by the people, for the people.
I thought talk of such harassment was sheer juvenile paranoia, melodramatic nonsense. Not so. When profit is made
synonymous with patriotism, any means seem justified to
preserve that profit. In the name of the public, the public
be damned. So to protect the public, to expose lies and
frauds, we have to operate like guerrillas. At least for the
present. Once we can come out into the open, through
you, honest practices and the people will prevail, and
we'll have support and safety in numbers. I'll keep in
touch with you, Mr. Randall. Or I'll try to. But anyway,
be prepared for us to go ahead—with your help—in six
or seven months, like in November or December, and
that's definite."

"Okay," Randall had agreed, feeling genuine excitement,
"in six or seven months come back to me. I'll be ready
and waiting, and away we go."

"We'll be depending upon you, Mr. Randall," Mc-
Loughlin had said at the door.

The waiting period for The Raker Institute account
had hardly begun when a far greater prospect of change
had come to Randall out of the blue. Cosmos Enterprises,
the international multibillion-dollar conglomerate presided
over by Ogden Towery III, burst into Randall's life. Like
a colossal magnet, Cosmos Enterprises was combing the
United States and the world, attracting and collecting relatively small, successful businesses to enhance its diversi-
fication program. Searching for footholds in the area of
communications, Towery's team had settled on Randall
Associates as a promising public relations firm. Preliminary
talks on the lawyer level were conducted. Progress was
made swiftly. All that had remained, before papers were
drawn, was a meeting between Towery and Randall.

It was this very morning, early, that Towery had
appeared at Randall Associates in person, inspected the
premises with his aides, and finally closeted himself with

Randall, alone, one to one, in Randall's office, with its eighteenth-century Hepplewhite furniture.

The remote Towery, a legend in financial circles, had the rangy look of a prosperous rancher. He was an Oklahoman, who kept his modified Stetson hat in his lap as he settled in the deep-tufted leather chair and who spoke crisply like a man who was used to being listened to.

Randall had listened, because he saw his visitor as freedom's angel. By the grace of this billionaire, Randall could possess, in short years, his long-held fantasy, that haven, that happiness, with green trees and no telephone and a manual typewriter and security for the remainder of his lifetime.

If was near the end of Towery's monologue that the only bad—the only truly horrendous—moment came.

Towery had been reminding Randall that although Cosmos Enterprises would own Randall's firm, Randall would be in complete charge of his company under a five-year management contract. With expiration of the contract, he would have the right to exercise an option to stay on or leave with enough extra cash and stock to make him wealthy and independent.

"This will still be your business as long as you're with us, Mr. Randall," Towery was saying. "So you will continue to run it as you have in the past. It would make no sense for us to interfere with a successful operation. My policy, in whatever I take over, is always hands off."

That moment, Randall ceased listening. A suspicion had come to him. He decided to test freedom's angel. "I appreciate your attitude, Mr. Towery," he said. "What I understand you to be saying is that my office can make its own decisions about which accounts it will take on, the clients it will handle, without any screening by Cosmos."

"Absolutely. We've seen your contracts, your list of clients. If we didn't approve. I wouldn't be here."

"Well, not every client is in the files you've seen, Mr. Towery. There are some new ones who haven't been formalized yet. I just want to be sure that you're going to let us go on handling whomever we wish."

"Of course. Why not?" said Towery. Then his tanned brow wrinkled slowly. "Why should you even imagine we'd be concerned?"

"Sometimes we take on a client, an account, that might be regarded as controversial. And I wondered—"

"Like what?" Towery quickly interrupted. "What kind of account?"

"About two weeks ago I made a verbal agreement with Jim McLoughlin to handle the first report of The Raker Institute."

Towery sat up, ramrod-straight. He was very tall, even when sitting. His face seemed suddenly cast in bronze, hard and bronze. One split-cowhide boot pushed the ottoman aside. "Jim McLoughlin?" he said, as if mouthing an obscenity.

"And his—and The Raker Institute."

Towery stood up. "That bunch of Commie anarchists," he said harshly. "That McLoughlin. He's getting his from Moscow, you know that. Or maybe you didn't know."

"That wasn't my impression."

"Listen to me, Randall, *I know*. Those radicals, I wouldn't pee on them. They don't deserve a country like this. The second they start fomenting trouble, we're going to drive them out of this country. I promise you." He squinted at Randall, and then a small thin smile crossed his face. "You just don't have the information we have, Randall, so I can understand your being taken in. Now I've given you the facts. Now you won't have to sully yourself by taking on scum like that."

Towery, pausing to inspect Randall, observed his troubled reaction. Instantly, dropping his attack, Towery became placating. "Don't worry. It will be as I promised you. No interference in your business—except when we find someone trying to subvert you, and subvert Cosmos in the process. I'm sure the problem won't crop up again." He extended his large hand. "Settled, Mr. Randall? Far as I'm concerned, you're part of the family. Our lawyers can take over from here. We should be signed and sealed in eight weeks. Then I want you to dinner." He winked. "You're going to be a wealthy man, Mr. Randall, wealthy and independent. I believe in spreading it around. Congratulations."

That had been it, and as he sat alone in his high-back swivel chair, Steve Randall had known that there had never been a choice. Good-bye, Jim McLoughlin and Raker. Hello, Ogden Towery and Cosmos. Absolutely no choice. When you are thirty-eight, and feel like seventy-eight, you don't play in the honesty league at the price of giving up your one chance in the big time. And there is only one big time: freedom with money.

It was a bad moment, though, one of his worst, and he had been left with a nauseating aftertaste in his throat. He had gone to his private bathroom and thrown up, and then assured himself it was something he'd had at breakfast. He had returned to his desk, feeling no better, when Wanda buzzed him on the intercom to tell him that Clare was telephoning long-distance from Oak City.

That was when he had learned that his father had just suffered a massive stroke, and was on his way to the hospital, and nobody knew whether his father would live.

In the hours following, the day had become a kaleidoscope of whirling activity, of appointments to be canceled, of reservations to be made, of personal things to be put in order, of informing Darlene and Joe Hawkins and Thad Crawford what had happened, of innumerable calls to Oak City, and then the rush to John F. Kennedy Airport.

And now, he realized, it was night in Wisconsin, and he was in Oak City, and his sister had glanced at him.

"Have you been sleeping?" she asked.

"No," he said.

"There's the hospital," she said, pointing. "I can't tell you how I've been praying for Dad."

Randall pulled himself upright as Clare turned her car into the crowded parking lot that stretched alongside the Oak City Good Samaritan Hospital. Once she had located an empty slot, and guided her automobile into it, Randall got out of the car and eased his tight shoulder muscles. Waiting behind the car, Randall became aware for the first time that it was a gleaming new Lincoln Continental sedan.

When Clare joined him, Randall gestured toward the Lincoln. "Quite a wagon, Sis. How do you manage that on a secretary's salary?"

A frown shrouded Clare's broad, shiny face. "I got it from Wayne, if you must know."

"You have quite a boss. I hope his wife is half as generous—toward her husband's friends."

Clare glared at him. "Coming from you, that's a laugh."

She started stiffly up the circular drive that led between flanking rows of oak trees toward the hospital entrance, and Randall, sorry to have thrown a stone from his glass house, slowly followed her.

HE HAD BEEN in the private room, to which his father had been moved from the intensive-care ward earlier, for almost an hour. He had been sitting in the straight-back chair, beneath the unplugged television set on the shelf above him and the framed sepia reproduction of Christ, facing the metal bed. By now, almost drained of emotion, one leg crossed over the other, he knew that his right leg was falling asleep. He uncrossed his legs. He was beginning to feel restless, and he ached for a smoke.

With effort, Randall tried to involve himself in the activity around his father's bed. But as if he were hypnotized, his gaze was drawn to the oxygen tent and to the mound covered by a blanket inside the tent.

The worst of the experience had been his first glimpse of his father. He had entered the room still carrying an image of his father as he had last seen him. His father, the Reverend Nathan Randall, even in his seventies, had been an imposing figure. In his son's eyes he had resembled nothing less than one of those magnificent patriarchs who might have just stepped out of Exodus or Deuteronomy. Like Moses in his great age, "his eye was not dim, nor his natural force abated." His thinning white hair covered a great dome of forehead, and the long, open, perpetually forgiving face had calm blue eyes and regular features, except for the somewhat sharp nose. Randall had never seen his father without the deep lines that now marked that face, but these only heightened his appearance of authority, although he was not authoritarian. The Reverend Dr. Randall had always possessed about him an air, difficult to define, but something private, secret, mystical, suggesting that he was one of the select who were in constant communication with Our Lord, Jesus Christ, and that he was privy to Our Lord's wisdom and counsel. His Methodist parishioners, some of them at any rate, believed this of their Reverend Nathan Randall, and therefore believed in him and his God.

It was this stained-glass image of his father that Randall had brought into the hospital room, and it was this image that was instantly shattered. For what Randall saw behind the transparent oxygen-tent wall was a ruin, a mockery of a human being, like those wizened heads of Egyptian mummies or those ghastly bags of bones in Dachau. The shining white hair was matted, dull, yellowish. The veiny eyelids were closed over eyes lost in unconsciousness. The face was emaciated, sunken, mottled. The breathing came labored and rasping. To every limb, it seemed, were taped tubes or needles.

For Randall, it had been frightening to see one so close, of the same blood and the same flesh, one so invulnerable, so certain, so believing, so trusting, so good and deserving of good, brought down to this vegetable condition and helplessness.

After a few minutes, Randall had turned away, fighting back tears, and groped for the chair, and he had not stirred out of it since. There had been a diminutive, slavic-looking nurse, perhaps Polish, working steadily at the perimeter of the bed, busy with overhanging bottles, and pendent tubes, and wall charts. After an indeterminate passage of time, perhaps thirty minutes or more, Dr. Morris Oppenheimer had come in to join the private nurse. A solid, chunky man past middle age, he moved with an easy efficiency and self-confidence. He had met Randall with a quick handshake, a sentence of sympathy, and a promise to deliver the latest report on his patient's condition shortly.

For a while, Randall watched the physician examine his father, and then, exhausted, he closed his eyes and tried to summon up an appropriate prayer. He could think only of *Our Father which art in heaven, Hallowed be Thy name,* and then he could remember no more. His mind, wandering back through the events of this day, unaccountably rested on his secretary Wanda's fantastic breasts, and then went back to the night before when he had been kissing Darlene's very real breasts, and then, ashamed, he sought his father in the present. He remembered the last time that he had visited his father and mother, more than two years ago, and the time before that, which had been more than three years ago.

He still felt the sting of what he had sensed during those two visits: his father's disappointment in him. The reverend had plainly been displeased with his son's broken marriage, his mode of living, cynicism, and lack of faith.

Recalling the parental disappointment and disapproval, Randall still challenged it in his head: Who was his father to judge him, when by society's standard his father was the failure, and he himself the success? But then, he thought again: He himself had succeeded only materially, hadn't he? His father was measuring his son by a different standard, a standard by which the good reverend measured himself and all men, and by this standard he had found his son wanting. Randall understood. His father possessed the one human component that his son lacked: faith. His father had faith in the Word, and therefore in humanity and in the purposefulness of life. His son had no such blind faith.

That's right, Dad, he thought. No faith. No belief. No trust in anything.

How could one believe in a God of Good? Society was unjust, hypocritical, rotten to the core. Men, most men, were beasts turned loose to savage and survive or hide and survive. And nothing man could fabricate, from the myth of some hallelujah heaven above—hell need not be fabricated, it already existed on earth—to false gods who cared, could change the reality of the present and the nothingness that was the end for all human animals. It was like that old Yiddish proverb a Jewish client had once quoted to him: If God lived on earth, people would break His windows.

Dammit, Dad, can't you see?

Stop arguing with him—he'd almost made it Him—Randall told himself. Stop arguing with the past.

Randall opened his eyes. His mouth was parched and his lungs were laboring and his lower spine was beginning to ache. He was sick of the room's smell—medicinal and antiseptic and dying flesh—the smell of hospital white and green. He was tired, too, of inner rage and sorrow, of doing nothing and being able to do nothing. He was frustrated by his role of spectator. This was no spectator sport. He decided that he had had enough.

He got out of the chair. He meant to speak to the physician and the nurse, to explain that he was leaving and would be with the others in the waiting room. But Dr. Oppenheimer was absorbed in studying his patient's chart, as a technician entered rolling a portable cardiograph machine toward the bed.

Walking lamely, since the blood hadn't yet circulated in his numb right leg, Randall left the hospital room, went up the corridor, avoided a young man in white garb who was mopping the floor, and approached the visitors' waiting room. At the entrance, he halted to light his favorite British briar pipe and enjoy its soothing narcotic for a few seconds, before reentry into the land of the mournful living. Bracing himself, he stepped into the vestibule, but at the threshold of the waiting room he held back again.

Within the fluorescent-lit room, enlivened by gay floral-patterned curtains at the windows, and furnished with a sofa, wicker chairs, outmoded television set, tables with ashtrays and thumbed magazines, were only the members of his family and his father's friends.

Hunched in a chair, hidden behind a movie magazine, was Clare. Near her, at the pay telephone on the wall speaking in an undertone to his wife, was Randall's old college classmate and his father's chosen successor, the Reverend Tom Carey. Not far from them, at a table,

Ed Period Johnson and Uncle Herman were engaged in a gin rummy game.

Ed Period Johnson was the Reverend Nathan Randall's best friend. In another age, he had founded the *Oak City Bugle,* the community newspaper which appeared six days a week, and he was its publisher and editor still. "The way to run a small-town newspaper," he had once told Randall, "is to see that everyone in town gets his name in the paper at least twice a year, and then you don't have to worry about competition from those slick snobby Chicago newspapers." Johnson's given name was not actually Ed Period but either Lucas or Luther, as near as Randall could remember. Years before, one of his reporters had started calling him Ed for Editor, and since it was an abbreviation, some conscientious grammarian had added the Period. Johnson was a hulking Swede, with a pocked face and a ski nose, and he was never seen without his heavy trifocal spectacles.

Across from Johnson, clumsily fanning his cards, was Uncle Herman, Randall's mother's younger brother. He had a vacuous Kewpie countenance, and gave the impression of a tub of butterfat. Randall could recall only one job that Uncle Herman had ever secured. He had worked for a while in a liquor store in Gary, Indiana. After he was fired, he had moved into the guest room of his sister's house. That had been when Randall was in high school, and Uncle Herman had lived there ever since.

Uncle Herman was the lawn sprinkler, loose-shingle fixer, errand runner, football-game viewer, and home-made-pie consumer. Randall's father had never minded his presence. Uncle Herman was a visible charity, a practicing of what the reverend preached: He that hath two coats, let him impart to him that hath none; and he that hath meat, let him do likewise. So—the reverend did likewise, and amen.

Now, Randall's gaze lighted on his mother. He had embraced her and consoled her earlier, but only briefly, for she had urged him to go to his father. At the moment, she was dozing in a corner of the sofa, sedated and asleep. She seemed strangely incomplete without her husband beside her. She had a kind, pudgy face, almost unlined, although she was in her late sixties. Her body, which seemed shapeless, was covered by one of her familiar clean faded blue cotton dresses and she wore the same clumpy corrective shoes that she had worn for years.

Randall had always loved her, and he loved her still, the patient, gentle, background creature for whom he could do no wrong. Sarah Randall, the adored preacher's adoring wife, had stature in the community, Randall supposed. Yet, to her grown son, she appeared hardly a separate individual, but instead only his mother. He could barely evoke a picture of her as an identity with opinions, ideas, prejudices, except for what he remembered of her from his boyhood. As a man, he had known her largely as someone who listened, who echoed her mate, who did chores that needed doing, whose prime job was to be there. She was forever confused and bewildered, but instinctively pleased by her son's alien success and big-city ways. Her love for her son was steadfast, blind, unquestioning.

He decided to sit down beside her and wait until she awakened.

As he crossed the room, Clare's head popped up over the magazine she was reading. "Steve. Where have you been all this time?"

"I was in with Dad."

Ed Period Johnson swiveled in his chair. "The Doc say anything?"

"He's been too busy. We'll see him as soon as he comes out."

Suddenly awakening, Sarah Randall pushed herself away from the arm of the sofa, at the same time straightening her dress. Randall kissed her cheek and put his arm around her. "Don't worry, Mom. Everything will turn out right."

"Where there's life, there's hope," said Sarah Randall. "The rest is up to the good Lord." She looked at Tom Carey, who had just hung up the wall telephone. "Isn't that so, Tom?"

"It's absolutely so, Mrs. Randall. Our prayers will be heard."

Steve Randall saw Carey's eyes go to the entrance of the waiting room, and he followed them, and immediately came to his feet.

Dr. Morris Oppenheimer, pulling on his suit coat, distracted by whatever was on his mind, had appeared. Fumbling through his pockets for a cigarette, he found one, and as he brought it to his lips he seemed to become aware of the others and the increased tension that his arrival had generated among them.

"I wish I had something new to tell you," he said to no one in particular, "but I don't have, not yet."

He gestured for Randall to sit, reached back and dragged a chair to a position across from the sofa, and plumped down, finally lighting his cigarette, while Clare, Johnson, Uncle Herman, and the Reverend Tom Carey gathered around.

"Now, medically speaking, here is what we are contending with," said Dr. Oppenheimer, addressing himself mainly to Randall and his mother. "Nathan suffered, this morning, an intracranial blockage of uncertain origin. The stroke was brought on by the clogging of an artery—a blood clot in an artery of the brain. The usual result of this sort of cerebral accident is loss of consciousness, usually followed by at least temporary hemiplegia."

He paused to inhale his cigarette. Steve Randall said, "What is hemiplegia?"

"Paralysis of a side—the face, arm, leg, usually—the side opposite the part of the brain where the episode occurred. In this case, it is the left side. Before Nathan lapsed into a coma, his left side showed indications of paralysis, but the vital organs are functioning. There has been no worsening of his condition." He surveyed the circle of worried faces. "That about sums it up for now."

"Dr. Oppenheimer," said Randall impatiently, "you haven't told us where my father stands. What are his chances?"

The physician shrugged. "I cannot predict. I am not in the Nostradamus profession, Steve. It's simply too early to tell. His condition is critical, no denying that. We are doing everything we can. As long as this stroke is not complicated by a heart attack, well, I would give him a fair chance to pull through."

He leaned closer to Sarah Randall. "Sarah, your husband has a good constitution. He has a will to live. He has faith. Those are considerations not to be taken lightly. But I cannot hide reality behind rose-colored glasses for you. His situation is grave. We must know that. However, there are many pluses, also. For the time being, we can only be vigilant and watch and wait. Many persons, many well-known ones, have had similar cerebral accidents, and survived them, and lived useful lives afterwards. Like Dr. Louis Pasteur. When he was forty-six, Pasteur suffered a stroke and paralysis not unlike your husband's. Yet, he recovered, and in the years that followed he was sufficiently alert to resume his career. He went on and isolated the fowl cholera germ, researched anthrax, pioneered vaccinations, discovered a treatment for hydrophobia, and he lived to the age of seventy-three."

Dr. Oppenheimer stubbed out his cigarette, and rose. "So, Sarah, we can hope for the best."

"I will pray," said Sarah Randall firmly, as Clare and Randall helped her to her feet.

"You'll do more than that," said Dr. Oppenheimer. "You will go home now and you will get some sleep. The important thing is to conserve your strength. . . . Clare, you see that your mother takes a sedative, one of the tablets I prescribed, before she goes to bed. . . . Steve, I am sorry that we must have our reunion under such circumstances as these. But as I said, we will hope for the best, and I'll keep in close contact with the desk and the special. If there are any changes during the night, I'll be in touch, you can be sure. Otherwise, well, I'll see you here in the morning."

The physician took Sarah Randall by the arm and led her out of the waiting room, speaking to her in a soothing undertone.

The others stayed behind briefly. Uncle Herman had

waddled up alongside Randall. "What are you going to do, Steve? We can make up the bed in your old room."

"Thanks, but no," said Randall quickly. "My secretary reserved a room for me at the Oak Ritz Hotel. I've got a lot of calls to make, and I don't want to keep all of you awake." Actually, he had promised to phone Darlene at his New York apartment, and he had wanted to speak to his attorney, Thad Crawford, about the sellout to Towery and Cosmos Enterprises, but it had been a battering day and night and now he felt too tired. "Besides, I want to phone Barbara and Judy in San Francisco. They've always been close to Dad, and I feel I should—"

"My God, I forgot to tell you," interrupted Clare, pushing in beside her brother. "They're here, Barbara and Judy are right here in Oak City."

"What?"

"I forgot, Steve. Forgive me, I'm so mixed up. I can't remember anything. I phoned them in San Francisco just after my first call to you in New York. They were both terribly upset. They caught the first plane East. Uncle Herman told me they got here at dinnertime, came straight from the airport to the hospital. They looked in on Dad, and waited around a while for you, but Judy got so jittery that Barbara finally took her back to the hotel just before I brought you in from O'Hare."

"Where are they staying?"

"At the Oak Ritz, where else? Is there another decent hotel here?" said Uncle Herman. "And let me see, Barbara said for me to tell you—if it wasn't too late—she'd like to see you when you left the hospital."

Randall looked at his watch. Not yet midnight. It wasn't too late. Barbara would be up and waiting. He wished the goddam horrible day were over with. He was in no mood for a reunion with his wife, after so long, after so much, but there was no way to avoid it. Besides, his Judy would also be there, and tonight he wanted to see her.

"Okay," he said, "who'll give me a lift to the hotel?"

THE door to her hotel suite opened, and there she was.

"Hello, Steve," she said.

"Hello, Barbara," he said.

"I'm sorry about Nathan," his wife said. "I love him the way I loved my own father. It always happens to good people, doesn't it? . . . Well, let's not just stand here. Come in, Steve. I'm glad you could drop by."

She had offered him no kiss, and he made no effort to kiss her. He entered the sitting room after her. The room was clean but drab, a clutter of nondescript chairs, two coffee tables, a couch, an open cabinet doubling as a bar with glasses sitting on the shelf above it, next to a new bottle of Scotch. Obviously, his wife had expected him.

Barbara, who had moved to the middle of the room, was strangely quiet and contained. Her appearance had not altered much since their parting. If anything, she looked a little better, sleek coiffure, more careful grooming. She had brown hair and small, hurt brown eyes in a plain face, and at thirty-six her figure was adequate, small breasts, slim waist. She was wearing a tailored suit, a copy of something expensive. She looked very San Francisco, and not at all distraught, which was unusual.

"We went in to see Nathan the second we got to the hospital," she was saying. "I can imagine how you must feel, Steve. Seeing him, it just about broke our hearts. Judy just came apart and wept. We love him so."

Maybe Randall's ears deceived him, but he thought that he had detected an emphasis placed by her on the *we*—*we* looked in, *we* love him so. Now Judy had been fused into the *we* of mother and daughter, and goodbye stranger-husband-father. Barbara knew him well, knew where he was most vulnerable, and either she was turning the knife of *we* into him to get even, or it was a stratagem to remind him that mother and daughter belonged together, or maybe it was nothing but his imagination.

"It's lousy," he said, "the whole scene." He considered her. "A long time. You seem to be surviving."

She smiled. "Somehow."

"What about Judy? How is she?"

"Right now she's in bed. She was worn out by the flight, the hospital, she just wanted to get some rest. She's probably asleep by now. But she did want to see you. Maybe tomorrow."

"I want to have a look at her right now."

"Whatever you like. Do you want me to make you a drink?"

"I thought maybe you'd join me in a nightcap at the bar downstairs. It's still open."

"If you don't mind, Steve, I'd rather stay here. It's more private. I hoped we could have a little talk. Very brief, I promise you."

She wanted a little talk, he thought. He remembered their little talks in the past. Who was it—some German philosopher—who'd said that marriage was one long conversation? He wished it had been that, one long conversation, which sounded placid, and was not what it had been, a reality of furious little talks in which he knew that he was being orally castrated and she believed that she was enduring a verbal hysterectomy.

"Whatever you want," he said. "Make it Scotch on the rocks."

He opened the bedroom door quietly, and went inside. There was a dim light filtering through a fluffy lampshade on the dressing table. Adjusting his eyes to the semidarkness, Randall finally made out his daughter in the twin bed to his right.

He went to the side of the bed and knelt on one knee. She was deep in the pillow, blanket drawn close to her neck, flowing silky, cornsilky, hair spread around her on the pillow. She was asleep, and she was beautiful, this fifteen-year-old part of him, this angel, the only proud-making thing he had ever produced on this earth. He observed her in silence, the pure smooth face, tiny nose, half-parted lips, and he heard her shallow breathing.

On impulse, he bent closer, brushing her cheek with his lips. As he backed away, her tightly lidded eyes parted.

"Hi," she murmured.

"Hello, darling. I've missed you. I'll treat you to breakfast tomorrow."

"Ummmm."

"You sleep now. We'll be together tomorrow. Good night, Judy."

As he rose to his feet, he saw that she was already asleep again. He lingered over her a moment, and then he left the bedroom. The sitting room was brighter than before, and he realized that Barbara had turned on the wall lights. He wondered why.

Barbara was resting on the couch, both elbows sunk in a pillow on her lap, and she was holding a highball glass with a drink in her cupped hands.

"Your drink is there," she said, nodding toward a tumbler of Scotch on the far side of the coffee table.

"What are you having?" he asked lightly. "Seven-Up on the rocks?"

"I'm having what you're having," she said.

This was not promising, he decided, as he circled to take the empty chair opposite her. Barbara had not shared liquor with him in years. She would have one or two drinks at parties, but whenever they had been alone, she would refuse to join him in a highball. It had been her way of rebuking him, letting him know that she hated his kind of drinking, the kind of drinking that took you away, put you away, helped you escape any relationship with your wife. Yet, here she was with a Scotch. Was this a healthy sign or was it ominous? He chose ominous, and remained on guard.

"Was Judy asleep?" she was inquiring.

He took up his drink, as he sat down. "Yes. She woke for a second. We're having breakfast in the morning."

"Good."

He sampled his Scotch. "How's she doing in that new private school, the one outside Oakland you were so sold on? Is she—?"

"She isn't," Barbara cut in. "She's not doing, she's not there any longer. She hasn't been there for a month."

He did not hide his surprise. "Well, where is she then?"

"She's home. That's one reason I wanted to see you tonight. Judy was thrown out of school a month ago."

"Thrown out? What are you talking about?" There was no precedent for this. She was perfect, his Judy, she'd always been perfect, a dedicated student with straight A's. "You mean the school dropped her?"

"I mean they threw her out. No probation. No reprieve." She paused to emphasize her next words. "It was a drug bust."

He felt his face redden. "What in the hell are you talking about?"

"I'm talking about speed. I'm talking about bennies, bombitas, dexies, crystals, jolly beans, meth. I'm talking about amphetamines, Steve, the kind you pop in your mouth and the kind you inject. Judy was caught walking on the ceiling, and after the headmaster got her down on the carpet, and talked to her and talked to me, they simply dropped her."

"You mean they didn't give her a second chance? Those bastards, any kid is liable to get off base these days, get influenced by someone, experiment—"

She stopped him. "Steve, she wasn't experimenting. She was on speed regularly, hooked. And she wasn't being influenced by any of her classmates. In fact, she had influenced a couple of them."

He shook his head. "I can't believe it."

"You'd better."

"Barbara, this doesn't happen to a kid like Judy. Where were you?"

"Where were you, Steve?" It was said utterly without viciousness, just matter-of-factly. "Forgive me. Where was I? Why didn't I see it? Because you don't at first. It's too unexpected. So you don't look for it. You don't *see*. There were some changes, but I put them down to a new school, the burden of work, the difficulty of trying to make friends. At first she seemed very bright and alert and sure of herself when I saw her weekends, and then a few times I noticed that she was irritable, jittery, depressed—crashing, they call it—and toward the end, she was withdrawn. Then suddenly, I was called to the school, and there it was."

"Why didn't you let me know, call me?"

Barbara stared at him. "I was going to, Steve, but I decided there was no point. There was nothing you could do immediately, and certainly there was nothing you could do in the long run. I saw no point in getting our lives entangled again. I saw no way Judy would gain by it. I decided that I could manage it by myself, and I did."

Randall gripped his highball glass, and he finished his drink. "Is she still on the stuff? She seemed fine just now. She didn't seem loaded or abnormal——"

"She isn't, Steve. She's on her way back. We believe she's kicked it. Through friends, I got Judy the best help available. It was rough, it was terrible, but she's coming out of it now. I'd guess she's down to a little marijuana—a few joints at parties occasionally—but no big deal, and certainly no more hard stuff."

"I see." Randall examined his empty glass, and stood up. "Never mind, stay where you are. I need another one."

"I'm sorry, Steve, all this, after the kind of day you've had. But I had to grab the chance to speak to you personally."

He poured himself half a glass of Scotch. "Of course, you had to tell me." He returned to his chair. "How'd you get Judy off it? Sanitarium?"

"As a matter of fact, it was—and is—one man. A psychologist in San Francisco, a specialist in drug abuse cases. His name is Dr. Arthur Burke. He's written——"

"I don't care what he's written. Is she still seeing him?"

"She is. And, I meant to say, he has a clinic, also. Anyway, Judy likes him. She relates to him. He's young middle-aged, moustache, beard, absolutely no double-talk. Dr. Burke is confident he can not only cure her but make it stick."

Randall sat drinking, and he was beginning to feel the alcohol. "And now I suppose it turns out it was all my fault. Busy father. Ergo. Speedy daughter."

"No, Steve, it's not your fault, and it's not mine, and maybe it is both our faults. It's the fault of the way life is, what happens to parents, what's there or isn't there for the children—and even then, it's more—what no set of parents can control—the style of today's society, and the kind of future or lack of future waiting—and rebellion, and escape, and a desire to find a better world by expanding the mind, finding another level of consciousness, finding a perfect planet in the head. So you become a speed freak, take that space trip, become spaced out, and if you're lucky, somebody pulls you out of orbit— before you're lost forever. Well, Dr. Burke pulled Judy out of orbit. She's a member of the human family again, and rethinking her whole value system."

Randall had put his empty glass up against his nose, was rubbing his nose with the coolness of the glass, and now peering through it he realized that Barbara was no longer across from him. He lowered his glass and looked blankly at the empty sofa.

"Steve—" she said.

He turned his head, and saw her coming back with her second drink.

"Hey, you're really belting," he said.

"Only tonight," she said, sitting. "Steve, there's something else I want to tell you tonight."

"Haven't we had enough for one night? You've already told me about Judy—"

"In a way, this still has to do with Judy. Let me get it out and over with fast, Steve, and then I'll be done."

"All right, shoot." He put down his glass. "Go ahead, what else is on your mind?"

Barbara took a sip, and looked directly at him. "Steve, I'm going to get married."

He felt nothing. In fact, he was amused. "You get married, and you'll get arrested." His mouth was distorted into a crooked smile. "I mean, sweetie, you *are* married. Another husband, and that's bigamy, and the hoosegow for our Babs."

Her features were rigid. "Steve, don't joke. This is serious. This is really serious. I told you once on the phone, after you asked me, that I saw some men from time to time. But actually, lately, I've been seeing only one. That's Arthur Burke."

"Arthur—you mean—you mean Judy's psychologist?"

"Yes. He's a wonderful man. You'd like him very

much. And I—I happen to care for him very much. And, as I told you, so does Judy." She looked down at her drink, as she went on. "Judy needs a home, a family, stability. She needs a father."

Randall deposited his glass noisily on the coffee table. He articulated each word carefully. "News for you, sweetie pie—Judy has a father."

"Of course she has a father, you're her father. She knows that. Arthur knows that. But I mean a practicing father, one who's under the same roof, in her home, one who is always there. She needs the quality of life, attention, love she can have only in a conventional and going household."

"I get it now," Randall said. "I hear the sounds of brainwashing. The quality of life, attention, love—bullshit. That's his language, his con job, his cheap way of trying to pick up a family, a daughter, without earning it. If he wants a daughter, let him make one. He's not getting my little girl—no, ma'am, not my Judy."

"Be reasonable, Steve."

"So you're doing all this to save Judy? That's the ploy, eh? You want to marry this guy for Judy, because Judy needs a father."

"That's not the main reason, Steve. I want to marry Arthur because I need a husband, a husband like him. I'm in love with him. And I want a divorce, so that I can marry him."

"Divorce?" He felt drunk and angry. He pushed himself out of the chair. "Forget it, you're not getting one."

"Steve—"

He retrieved his glass and started for the bar. "No," he said. "I'm not giving up my daughter because her mother needs someone in the hay."

"Don't be stupid. I can't stand it when you get drunk and stupid. I don't need someone in the hay. I've already got someone in the hay. I've got Arthur, and I intend to make it legal. He wants a wife, a marriage, and he deserves a family life, and so does Judy. If Judy is what you're concerned about, you'll cooperate, agree to a settlement, and not make it hard for us. You've had plenty of chance to ask us to come back. You've never lifted a finger. But when we want to go, you try to obstruct us. Please let us go."

He poured his drink. "You telling me Judy wants this hotshot of yours for her father?"

"Ask her."

"Don't worry, I will. And you're already rolling in the hay with him? Now isn't that something?"

Standing at the bar, absently running his finger around inside the rim of his glass, he watched Barbara rise and go searching for her pack of cigarettes. His eyes followed her, the movements of that female body he had known so well. She was giving that body to another man.

Unaccountably—or was it countably—yes, he must be drunk—he was picking back through the wreckage of their marriage to one broken moment that had long been buried in memory. It had been their last trip abroad together, a night in Paris, a bad, bad night, very late. They had gone to bed, a large double bed, the headboard against the wall of some luxury hotel in Paris. The Plaza Athénée. The George V. The Bristol. He could not remember which. They had been lying on the bed, coldness and resentment rising like a bundling board between them, while each pretended to sleep. Then, past midnight, from the next-door room through the wafer-thin wall, had come the muffled sounds of voices, one male, one female, the words indistinct, and after a while the squeaking of a bed, and then the outcries of the female and her moanings, and the male gaspings, continual moanings and gaspings and the squeaking of the bed—the sounds excited, passionate, quick.

As he lay listening, every sound sank into him like a dagger, and he had bled envy and jealousy for that muffled pleasure, and he had bled wrath mingled with guilt because of the Barbara-body on the bed beside him. He could not look at her, but he knew that she was also listening in the darkness. There was no retreat for either of them. The next-door sounds mocked the apartness of their own cold bodies and underlined their empty years. Randall had hated the woman beside him, hated the two behind the wall with their interminable coupling and one-ness, and most of all he had hated himself for his in-ability to love his partner. He wanted to leap from the bed, be rid of the Barbara-body, the horrible room, the taunting carnal sounds. Yet, he could not. He could only wait. And when the last moan and gasp, the last sighs of pleasure, had been heard, there remained the silence of fulfillment behind that wall, which was even more un-bearable.

In the night that followed what drifted through his mind first was the fragment of a poem by George Meredith, and it chilled him: "Then, as midnight makes/ Her giant heart of Memory and Tears/ Drink the pale drug of silence, and so beat/ Sleep's heavy measure, they from head to feet/ Were moveless, looking through their dead black years,/ By vain regret scrawled over the blank wall./ Like sculptured effigies they might be seen/ Upon their marriage-tomb, the sword between;/ Each waiting for the sword that severs all."

And in the continuing blackness, he knew that they lay on their marriage-tomb. What dominated his mind, be-fore the oblivion of sleep, was total comprehension of the void in his own marriage and the impossibility of sus-taining their life together. There was no future for them, he knew that night. He could never again honestly enter and love that body on the bed beside him. He could fake it, maybe. He could imitate love, maybe. But he could not make spontaneous love to her, or even want her. Their relationship was hopeless. And she must know it, too. And that night, before sleep, he realized it must end soon—the sword that severs all must drop—and he prayed that she would be the one to end it. Several months later, she had moved out of their New York apartment and, taking Judy with her, had gone to live in San Francisco.

Blearily, he studied her across the room, smoking, pac-ing, avoiding his eyes. He followed the outline of her thighs against her skirt. Mentally, he stripped off her skirt to expose the familiar flesh on sharp bones, and tried to imagine how that secondhand, inflexible, ungiving body could stimulate passion in someone named Arthur, how it could excite gasps and wild passion. Apparently, it did. How odd, how very odd.

He swung away from the bar and started toward her. Her eyes held on him.

She was pleading. "Steve, one last time, don't oppose the divorce. Please let me have it without making problems. You don't want me. You'll never pick up your option on me. Why not let me be free without any fuss or trouble, the way that civilized people do? Why fight? It can't be Judy alone. You'd still see her as often as you have time for her. It would be written into the settlement. What is troubling you? It must be something else. Is it the finality? Is it that you can't face the idea of failing at something? What is it?"

"It's Judy. Nothing else. Don't be ridiculous. It's just that I won't have another man, some stranger, raise my daughter. That's my decision. That's it, at least till she's twenty-one. No divorce now, that's it." He hesitated. "Maybe you and I—we—maybe we can make some arrangement together, figure out something."

"No, Steve. I don't want you anymore. I want a divorce."

"Well, you're not getting it."

He had started to turn away, but she grabbed at his arm, to make him face her.

"All right then, all right!" she exclaimed in a shaking voice. "You're forcing me to do what I never wanted to do. You're forcing me to sue you for a divorce."

"You sue, and I'll meet you in court," he said. "I'll fight you, and I'll have a damn good case. You walked out on me. You couldn't control our daughter. You let her get hooked on drugs, let her get thrown out of school. You've been shacking up with another man, doing that with a fifteen-year-old in the house. Don't make me take you to court, Barbara."

He waited for her outburst. To his amazement, her features were calm, self-assured, and in her eyes was something frighteningly akin to pity.

"Steve," she said, "you'll lose. I won't have to make an effort to smear you. I wouldn't do that. But my lawyer will turn you inside out in court, in public, for the record, and the court will see the truth—your performance record with me, with your daughter, your role as non-husband, non-father. Your behavior in the past and the present. Your irregular life. Your drinking. Your affairs. The young girl you're keeping in New York. You'll lose, Steve, and you may even lose the chance of ever seeing Judy. I hope you're not angry and stubborn enough to let that happen. It would be ugly for all of us, bad for Judy, a horror, and in the end you'd lose her completely, no matter what the court says."

He despised her these minutes, not for what she was saying, but for her assurance, her confidence, possibly for her righteous rightness. He said, "You're blackmailing me. When I prove in court that this lover of yours, this Arthur whatever, used his professional relationship with Judy to insinuate himself into your life, take you and our daughter over, the judge will never let you have custody."

Barbara gave a sorry shrug. "'We'll see.'" Then she said, "Think about it, Steve, when you're—you're fully sober. Let me know, before we leave. If you haven't changed your mind, if you're determined to contest it, I'll have to go back and initiate divorce proceedings and go to court. I pray you don't let that happen. I'll also pray tonight—" She stopped, abruptly. "Get some sleep. You may have another hard day tomorrow."

She slipped past him toward the door. He refused to follow her. He said belligerently, "What did you start to say? What else will you pray for tonight? Tell me."

She opened the door for him and waited. He put down his glass and went to her.

"Tell me," he insisted.

"I—I'll pray for your father, of course. And for Judy, as I always do. Most of all, Steve, I—I'll pray for you."

He despised this superior, sanctimonious bitch.

"Save your supplications for yourself," he said, voice trembling. "You'll need them—in court."

Without another look at her, he went out the door.

* * *

HE WOKE in the morning with a hangover, and he saw at once that he had overslept.

Showering, drying, dressing, he realized that the hangover had not come from his drinking last night. Normally, he drank much more, yet awakened clearheaded. No, this hangover came from deep inside, from the residue of shame that suffused him, the shame over his performance with Barbara last night.

With objectivity, he could see that her request for a settlement and divorce had been reasonable. He could also justify his own resistance. There was no question but that if she remarried, he would lose his only child. Such a loss was untenable, especially when his emotional attachments were so few. Still, he had given Barbara no alternate choice. He supposed there was a compromise. She did not have to marry this Arthur and make Judy his child. She could simply live with Arthur, as she was doing —and why not? This was the twentieth century—and Judy would not have a new father, would know her father in fact was himself.

Oh, he would fight Barbara in court, he certainly would.

Nevertheless, what hung over, grown of shame, was his immature, perfectly childish, petty behavior. He had made it an ugly scene. An outsider, observing it, would have regarded him as a heel and a son of a bitch, and this galled him, because he was better than that. His gut knew it. Somewhere down there he was better than that, better than the way he let people see him, know him, better than the way he had shown himself on the last visit before this one to his father, last night to his wife, and as he would soon be seen by that good Jim McLoughlin of The Raker Institute. At the same time, the rat race was like a horse race—you were rated by your performance, not your feelings, and he was bumping and fouling everyone he came in contact with from wire to wire.

Nor was he delivering on a social level, either. At work, fine. He delivered. In off-work hours, in contacts with persons who mattered, he was not being responsible. He had promised his daughter—what could be more important?—that he would have breakfast with her this morning. He had forgotten it the evening before when he left word at the desk that he was not to be disturbed by any calls except one from Dr. Oppenheimer, and he had neglected to set his alarm, and so he had overslept.

Before calling room service, he had rung Barbara to find out whether Judy was still there. No one had answered the phone. Now, unhappily, he sat down to his bacon and eggs and coffee, and had breakfast alone. Then he became aware that, under the morning paper, there were some messages. The boy, bringing his breakfast, must have found them at the door and scooped them up.

He opened the messages. The first reported that a Miss Darlene Nicholson had telephoned from New York. There had been a message from her last night, also. He had been in no mood to return her call after the Barbara scene, and now he was too harried to return her second call. He promised himself that he would catch up with Darlene later. There was a message from Uncle Herman. He had come by in the family car to pick Randall up and take him to the hospital, as agreed, but he had not been permitted to phone Randall's room. That had been three hours ago. Dammit. The only thing for which Randall could be grateful was—there had been no emergency call from Dr. Oppenheimer.

Hastily, he finished his breakfast, pulled on his Burgundy-checked sport jacket, and took the elevator down to the lobby. He was certain that he would find Judy at the hospital, but to make doubly certain that he did not miss her again, he went to the reception desk, scratched out a note apologizing for missing her at breakfast, and asking her to save lunchtime for him. Requesting that the note be left in Barbara's mail slot, Randall hurried outside into the muggy late May morning, signaled the cabstand, and in a minute was on his way to the Oak City Good Samaritan Hospital.

Arriving, he took the concrete steps in front two at a time, rode the elevator to the second floor, and turned right, and went down the corridor. To his dismay, he could see his mother, his sister, and Uncle Herman, clustered about Dr. Oppenheimer in front of his father's room. Ed Period Johnson and the Reverend Tom Carey were standing apart from them, some yards off, engaged in a conversation. Approaching them, Randall suffered a shiver of apprehension. Everyone congregating in the corridor—this was unnatural, and it spoke of emergency or change. Something had happened.

Drawing nearer to them, seeing their faces enlarge and their features become plainer, Randall tried to detect any reactions of grief or mourning. There were none. He wondered, and also wondered why neither Barbara nor Judy was present.

He broke in on the group without apologies, interrupting the physician's discourse to ask, "How's Dad? What's happening?"

Dr. Oppenheimer's pinched mouth offered the best smile it could. "Good news, Steve, the most we could have hoped for. Your father recovered consciousness at—it must have been near six o'clock this morning. His cardiogram shows a decided improvement. His blood pressure is close to normal. His left side is partially paralyzed, and his speech is a little thick. In all, however, a remarkable comeback. Assuming no unexpected complications, every sign points upward from this day on."

"Oh, God," said Randall with relief. "Thank God." He felt limp, as if just unfettered and released from tension, and he sagged over his mother, and kissed her, and kissed Clare, who was crying again, and he grinned at Uncle Herman. Swinging back to the physician, Randall gripped Dr. Oppenheimer's hand. "It's wonderful, a miracle," he said, "and I can't tell you how grateful we are to you."

Dr. Oppenheimer nodded appreciation. "Thank you, Steve, but your father deserves all the credit. I was just explaining to your mother that the speed and degree of his recovery will be largely in his hands. Medicine can go only so far. After he is sent home—maybe two, three, even four weeks—there will be a program of physiotherapy. It can be arranged to take place at home. If he co-operates, this can lead to a surprising degree of rehabilitation. The goal is to make him ambulatory and independent again. As I was telling your mother, the key factor remains your father's spirit, his will, his desire to live."

"He's never lacked that," said Randall.

"True," Dr. Oppenheimer concurred. "But remember, he's never had a stroke before. His mental attitude may be altered, yet his future depends upon its staying the same."

"Jesus felt abandoned on the Cross." It was Sarah Randall, speaking softly. "He died. Still, He rose again to save us all."

"With God's help," piped Uncle Herman.

Sarah Randall glanced at her brother. "Nathan will also have God's help, Herman. Nathan has earned it."

Embarrassed by pious mumbo-jumbo, even when it came from his mother, Randall separated himself from her and stepped closer to the physician. "I'd like to see Dad. May I?"

"We-ll, he should be resting as much as possible right now. However, if you'll stay only a minute and no more, you can go in. By tonight, perhaps, you can spend more time with him."

Randall went inside the hospital room.

The transparent oxygen tent was parted, and the private nurse, who was straightening out the blanket, shielded the patient from view. When she heard Randall approach, she backed off.

"I just want to look at him," explained Randall. "Is he asleep?"

"He's dozing. Doing fine, though. We are very proud of him."

Randall walked over to the bed. The old head was there on the pillow, skeletal, but not so shocking as last night. The eyes were closed. Color had been restored to the skin. His father was snoring peacefully.

"He looks much better than he did yesterday," Randall whispered over his shoulder.

"Much better," agreed the nurse behind him.

When Randall turned back to his father, he was surprised to find his father gazing up at him blankly.

"Hello, Dad. It's Steve. You're getting better. You're going to be fine."

A flicker of recognition touched the old man's eyes and his lips quivered. Quickly, Randall bent over him, kissed his forehead.

The eyes closed and opened, a kind of nod of acknowledgment.

"You're on the way back, Dad," Randall said. "We've been praying for you, and our prayers were answered. I'm going to keep praying for your—"

Randall's voice trailed off as he saw a corner of his father's mouth curl, ever so little, curl upward, and he could not go on because he was less sure about his father's nick of a smile—whether it had been appreciation for prayer or doubt that his son could pray for anyone. He guessed that his father could still see through him, as always, as ever, and accept what was sincere concern but question any sudden piety.

The smile, as enigmatic as the smile on the face of the Mona Lisa, was gone, yet its motive and meaning remained unexplained. Had it been a pitying smile, finally? Pity not for a son's fake piety, but pity (from one who knew that belief, faith, allegiance to something had triumphed) for a child who had nothing but godless skepticism and would never know the ultimate passion of love and loving and peace.

Randall wanted to speak of this, probe for an explanation, but the veiny eyelids had closed and the snoring had resumed.

Wordlessly, Randall left the bedside and returned to the corridor. The doctor had gone on to make his rounds. The others were in a circle, near the waiting room, cheered, chattering animatedly.

Randall asked Clare about his wife and daughter. They had come by early, heard the good news, looked in upon Dad, and had left a half hour ago. When Randall's mother interrupted to invite him home for lunch, Randall explained that he was having lunch with Judy, but promised to be by for a home-cooked dinner before they visited the hospital again this evening.

Since there was no need to go back to the house, Sarah Randall decided to stay on at the hospital a little longer, with Uncle Herman. Clare thought that she had better get back to her job, but assured her mother that she would leave work early to help prepare dinner.

"Anyone want a lift anywhere?" Clare asked.

Ed Period Johnson thought that he had better return to the newspaper. His oldest son had gradually been taking over the editorial chores, but Ed Period liked to be on hand to supervise things. The newspaper building was such a short walk that he needed no ride. As for Tom Carey, he had to get back to the church. There were appointments with parishioners, a backlog of correspondence to tackle, a sermon to write.

"I could use some fresh air and exercise," Carey was saying. "Thanks, Clare, I think I'll do it on foot." He looked at Randall. "What about you, Steve? Up to a medium-long walk? You remember. The church is only a few blocks from your hotel."

Randall consulted his watch. He still had forty-five minutes before he was to lunch with Judy, presuming that she had received his note. "Okay," said Randall, "I'll join Pedestrians Anonymous."

THE THREE of them had been walking for ten minutes, and it had been pleasant. The humidity had dropped, and the air was clear beneath a high, dry, early afternoon sun. The towering elm trees and hoary oaks were budding or full and presented a rich variety of greens, small children were out on their bikes, dogs were chasing cats, and a fat woman with her mouth full of clothespins was hanging the wash and waving to Johnson and Carey.

Contrasting this place with his dark stone canyon in mid-Manhattan, the small Wisconsin town seemed to Randall an Elysian paradise. But this was looking with his heart's eye, blurred by nostalgia. His mind's eye was more trustworthy. It knew better. It reminded Randall that he had been too far, seen too much, lived too much, to adjust to the monotony and limited choices of a back-fence community again. This was an in-between compromise life. He could survive in one extreme or the other, but not here. He could have running room for his restless soul in New York, among the crushing millions, or retreat alone, alone or with one other, to some isolated French hillside, there to soar freely with his creative imaginings, this destination to become a reality in five years when Towery and Cosmos gave him the two-million-dollar ticket.

He strode in step with Ed Period Johnson and Tom Carey, and was attentive to Johnson's lively monologue. Johnson had been recalling the beginnings of his close friendship with the Reverend Nathan Randall, and the best times in this friendship, and their glorious weekend fishing trips at the lakes.

Now, Ed Period Johnson was reminiscing about some of Nathan's creative do-gooding.

"Most people, you know, they get ideas to do good works, but somewhere along the line they get bogged down," Johnson was saying. "Not Steve's pa. No, sir. Our fine reverend was always unique in that respect. If he got an idea for good works, no matter how unusual or bizarre, by God, he would take off and do it. I mean he'd find a way of doing it. Nathan's one of those who's always practiced as well as preached."

"That's Nathan exactly," Carey chimed in.

"Like when he got the notion one day to compete with me in the newspaper business. Remember that time, Steve? Remember his weekly—what the devil was it called?—let me see—"

"Good News on Earth," said Randall.

"Right you are, son. *Good News on Earth,* he named it, after the original meaning of the word *gospel,* which derives from the Anglo-Saxon word *godspel*—meaning 'good news.' Now that was beautiful, just plain beautiful. That took courage, one thing Nathan's always had. Remember that paper of your father's, Steve?"

"Yes, I remember."

Ed Period Johnson was addressing himself to Carey, as they ambled on in the warm afternoon. "This is a true story, Tom, sure as I live. Steve here will vouch for it. Tells more about my friend `Nathan than anything else could. This was a good many years ago, but we were listening one day to the radio set. We were listening to some program, part of a series, about little-known clergymen in history, who had accomplished unusual things in the secular world. So on this particular program they were retelling the life of Dr. Charles M. Sheldon, of the Central Congregational Church in Topeka, Kansas. You ever hear of him, Tom?"

"I may have. The name sounds familiar."

"Well, I'd not be surprised if you hadn't heard about him," said Johnson, "because that day Nathan and I hadn't, either. But Dr. Sheldon was real. You can look him up in the library, if you don't believe me. Dr. Sheldon came to Kansas from New York to found this church in Topeka. Around 1890—Sheldon being maybe thirty-three, I think—he became worried about his evening church attendance on Sundays. Then he got an idea. Instead of giving sermons, he would put together twelve fictional chapters of a story, each ending on a note of suspense, and he'd read one a week to his congregation. The idea went over big, real big."

"That's clever," said Carey. "What kind of story was it?"

"About a young minister, shocked by world conditions and the way people behave, who asks his congregation to promise that for one year they will act as Jesus would have acted in all their relationships. This series was such a hit that Dr. Sheldon published it as a novel in 1897. He called it *In His Steps*. Some estimates say it sold thirty million copies, including the forty-five foreign translations. Became the greatest best-seller in history, except for the Bible and Shakespeare."

"Fantastic," said Carey.

"You bet, fantastic. Now comes something more fantastic. Three years after that book was published, the owner of the *Topeka Capital*, a daily newspaper with a circulation of around fifteen thousand, went to Sheldon and asked him, 'How would you like to edit the *Capital* for one week the way Jesus might have edited it?' Dr. Sheldon accepted the challenge. He wanted to prove a newspaper could be decent, honest, play up good news instead of sensationalism, and still be a success. So Dr. Sheldon took over the managing editor's desk, as proxy for Jesus Christ, for one week."

Randall shook his head. "I always thought that pretty sensational in itself."

"Not really," said Johnson. "A stunt, but one on the side of virtue."

"What happened?" inquired Carey.

"Well, Dr. Sheldon saw the practical problems, of course," Johnson went on. "He realized that Jesus had never seen an automobile, train, telephone, power press, electric light, newspaper, printed book. He realized that Jesus had not ever seen a Christian church or Sunday school or peace society or democracy. But Dr. Sheldon knew Jesus had seen something else that has never changed. Dr. Sheldon realized, as he put it, that the inward world Christ saw and understood was exactly the same in its pettiness and sordid scorn of goodness as in Sheldon's day. So as editor playing Jesus Christ, Sheldon set some new rules. Scandal, vice, crime would be played down. Editorials and news stories would be signed. And for the first time, stories of virtue and good will would be featured on the front page. That was only for starters. Dr. Sheldon announced that he would refuse all liquor, tobacco, and immoral entertainment ads. Furthermore, his reporters were told that there was to be no smoking, no drinking, no profanity in the city room. You asked what happened, Tom? What happened was that the circulation of the *Topeka Capital* jumped from fifteen thousand to three hundred sixty-seven thousand copies daily by the end of Dr. Sheldon's week of experiment. He'd proved that good news could sell as well as bad news."

Randall placed his hand on Johnson's shoulder and spoke past him to Tom Carey. "That's not the whole story, Tom. Actually, the experiment was considered a flop in the newspaper world. They said the paper had been too watery, too dull, too preachy, and the circulation rise was a temporary fluke stimulated by novelty and publicity. Besides, simultaneous editions had been published in Chicago and New York to sell extra copies. If Sheldon had gone on a couple of more weeks, he'd have bankrupted the paper."

"Pure speculation," said Johnson good-naturedly. "The fact is, for whatever reason, it worked. Readers did not resist the emphasis on morality instead of immorality. Which brings me back to the point. Namely, that when Nathan Randall heard about Sheldon, he was inspired to try the same thing on his own."

"He was?" said Carey. "I don't remember that."

"Well, you were away in California or somewhere at the time," said Johnson. "Yup, the idea stayed with Nathan for a long time, and finally, busy as he was, Nathan started a weekly newspaper called *Good News on Earth,* and he announced that he would publish and edit it as Jesus Christ might have published and edited it. Nathan started it off—using my presses, some of my people—aimed at parents of Sunday school kids, and then advertised it for the general public. You know, he got a circulation up to—let me see—up to around forty thousand copies a week. Got letters from readers as far away as California and Vermont, even some from Italy and Japan. It was a great thing, and it could have been greater, except Nathan just didn't have the time and strength to play Jesus-as-editor and still keep up his obligations to his congregation."

They had come to a halt at a street corner. Ed Period Johnson gestured off. "Here's where I leave you," he said. He nodded at Randall. "Anyway, Steve, whenever I think of the dedicated things your father has done in his life, I remember *Good News on Earth* and the success he made with it. He could have been successful at anything. And the best news on earth today is that he's going to be with us a long time to come, thank the Lord, and each of us— everyone in Oak City—is going to benefit from it." He pumped Randall's hand. "Great having you home again, Steve. See you—you, too, Tom—at the hospital tonight."

He was off, in his loping gait, up the side street toward the reddish brick building housing his newspaper. Randall and Carey watched a moment, then crossed the intersection, and resumed their walk toward the center of town and the Oak Ritz Hotel.

They progressed in silence for a brief time, before Tom Carey finally spoke. "That was quite a story Ed Period told about your father, Steve."

"It was sheer bull," said Randall without a trace of anger.

"Bull?" repeated Carey, disconcerted. "You mean Ed Period made it up—all that about your father and *Good News on Earth?*"

"He didn't make it up," said Randall patiently. "It's true that my father did publish that damn newspaper. But the last part, about the operation being such a success, was absolute baloney, as they say in Oak City. Sure the circulation reached forty thousand. But they were free copies—my father gave them away for nothing. I don't think a hundred people in the country paid for their copies of that ridiculous weekly. And nobody advertised in it. The few that wanted to, my father turned down because Christ wouldn't have taken their ads. No one wanted to read just good news, and they still don't. Because that's not the way the real world is. Dad's paper was full of people loving people, giving to charities, having prayers answered. Vomitous pap. Hell, Christ himself wouldn't have edited a paper in Galilee that way. Nor would any of His disciples or the gospel writers. Those ancient Jewish and Christian writers—they laid it on with adulterous women, violence in the temples, floggings, crucifixions, the works, life, both sides of life, not just goodies. *Good News on Earth* was bad news in our household. It folded after five or six issues. Not because my father was busy, as Ed Period romanticized it, but because it was bankrupting the family. My father lost every cent in the family kitty on the project."

Carey appeared worried. "Was the money—was it his money?"

"No," said Randall. "It was mine."

"I see."

Randall glanced at his friend. "Don't get me wrong. Tom. I'm not complaining about the project. It's just that I've reached a stage in my life where I'm sick and tired of listening to fairy tales perpetuated as truth. I'm tired of lies, half-lies, exaggerations. Hell, that's been my business for half my life. Now, more and more, like a reformed pimp who's become a puritan, I'm becoming interested in fidelity to fact, utmost veracity. I've come to detest phoniness and phonies. It takes one to know one, and I've been one for a very long time. So I'm trying to change my spots."

"Aren't you being a little hard on yourself?"

"No. And I wasn't being hard on my father, either. I respect my old man, I really do. I know his good side, just as well as you do. He hasn't a mean bone in his body. He's an honestly decent human being, something I've never been able to be. But my father, he is and always has been the most impractical human alive—living in a special state called Euphoria—responsible only to some big—forgive me, Tom—some big bag of ooze in the sky, to the neglect of many of his responsibilities to the children of the earth."

Carey smiled. "I forgive you, but—"

"Wait. Don't tell me the Reverend Nathan Randall has something none of us have—that he holds the secret to happiness, to peace—while the rest of us are miserable. Sure, in a way it's true. He's always been content, and his son, for example, has not been. But why? Because Dad has had faith, unquestioning trust and belief—but in what?—in an unseen Divine Author of Good News, Forgiveness, and Happy Endings? I can't play that self-deluding game. I was figuratively taken by the scruff of the neck at an early age—by H. L. Mencken, that scoffer at all *mythos*—and inculcated with Mencken's abbreviated version of the Decalogue. 'I believe that it is better to tell the truth than a lie. I believe it is better to be free than

to be a slave. And I believe it is better to know than to
be ignorant.' Ever since, I've believed in what I can see
or what others can prove they've seen, and in this I can
believe. That's been my credo, and I'll tell you what, Tom,
it stinks. But I can't change my attitude at this point,
Tom. I'm stuck with it. And I'll tell you something else—
I don't mind telling you either—I envy my father. Blind
faith, that's a better game."

He turned to observe Carey's reaction, but Carey was
looking straight ahead, his face wearing a thoughtful
frown, as they continued to walk.

Randall wondered what lay unspoken in his friend's
mind. Although they had taken different paths in the many
years after college, and had little in common anymore,
Randall's affection for Tom Carey had never abated. They
had been on the track team together in high school and,
for a period, roommates at the University of Wisconsin.
Following their graduation, Randall had gone to New
York City, and Tom Carey had heard the call and been
accepted by Fuller Theological Seminary in California.
After three years in the School of Theology, Carey had
emerged with his Bachelor of Divinity degree. Later, more
graduate studies behind him, he had married the very nice
brunette from Oak City whom Randall had taken to the
junior prom in high school, and had become pastor of a
small church in southern Illinois.

Because Carey was often in Oak City to visit his widowed mother and his in-laws, he had maintained his ties
with the Randall family, especially Steve's father, whom
he admired. This affection was reciprocated by the Reverend Nathan Randall. Then, three years before, as the
demands of the older man's prospering church and congregation continued to increase, and as his energy
decreased with age, the Reverend Dr. Randall had summoned young Carey and offered him a post as associate
minister at a greater salary than he had received in Illinois.
Carey was to take over some of the senior minister's more
routine duties, as well as expand the First Methodist
Church's involvement in social works among the disad-

vantaged. In addition, Carey had been promised that he
would replace the old man after his retirement.

Tom Carey had accepted the offer at once and, with his
wife and six children, returned to his home town. Now
he would succeed the Reverend Dr. Randall. He appeared
almost too young for a minister of God. Carey was slight
of build but athletic, with close-cropped hair, pug nose,
pale complexion, a kind of walking billboard for the Boy
Scouts of America. He was square, straight, serious, well-
read, intelligent, socially aware. He did not preach with
God at his elbow—the Reverend Nathan Randall at his elbow, maybe, but not God. He disdained fire and brimstone.
He was an understater.

He was speaking again, quietly, hesitantly.

"You mentioned your father's blind faith, Steve, his unquestioning faith, and how you envied him it. I was just
thinking about that—actually, debating with myself,
whether I should discuss that with you." He moistened
his dry lips. "You remarked you had come to prefer the
truth about things. So—so maybe you won't mind hearing
the truth."

Randall slowed his pace, and inquired, "The truth
about what, Tom?"

"Your father's blind faith. You know how close I've
been to him these recent years. Well, to be honest, I've
detected a gradual alteration in his outlook. You might
not have noticed it the last time you were out here, but it
was starting to happen. Your father has never lost his
faith. That would be unthinkable. I would say, rather,
that these recent years, the events on earth, the behavior
of men, have tended to shake—to shake just slightly—his
faith."

This was the last thing that Randall had expected to
hear. He could not hide his perplexity. "His faith in what?
Surely not in God and the Son of God? So in what?"

"It is difficult to be explicit. I'd say—not precisely his
faith in Our Lord—but in the literal truth of the New
Testament canon, in the dogma of the church, in the
relevance of Christ's ministry on earth to today's problems, in the possibility of applying some of Our Lord's

teachings to these intensely scientific and rapidly changing times."

"Tom, you *are* saying you feel my father has lost faith in the Word, aren't you? Or at least some of his faith?"

"It is a suspicion I've recently harbored."

Randall was distressed. "If that's true, it's terrible, absolutely terrible. It would mean he knows his life amounts to nothing, nothing but ashes."

"He may not have come quite to that, Steve. He may not have even understood or faced within himself his uneasy feelings. I'll put it simply. Employing the traditional wisdoms, your father was trying to solve the multitude of new problems of twentieth-century man in this microcosm of our society. Not only wasn't the method working, but more and more people were turning their backs on the message. I think in these last few years he has been baffled, confounded, a little defeated, and finally, discouraged and restive. I think Dr. Oppenheimer, precise and unimaginative though he sometimes seems, has some understanding of this. Yesterday noon, after your father suffered his stroke and was hospitalized, Dr. Oppenheimer was taking a coffee break and I joined him. Just the two of us. I wondered whether your father's stroke had been brought on by overwork. Dr. Oppenheimer looked at me and he said, 'Cerebral accidents like coronaries do not come from overwork. They come from frustration.' Need I say more?"

Randall shook his head. "No, that tells a lot. What concerns me is—without that lifetime-guaranteed unbreakable crutch—blind faith—how will my father ever be able to stand up again?"

"Perhaps his recovery may strengthen his faith. I repeat, the foundation of his faith is there, strong. Only now, a few cracks might be visible."

Randall could see the outline of the Oak Ritz Hotel in the distance. He took out his pipe, packed and lit it. "What about you, Tom? Any cracks visible in you?"

"Not in my faith in the Supreme Being. Nor in His Son. It's something else." He massaged his smooth chin, and picking his words slowly, he went on. "It's—well, what is troubling me is the representatives, the messengers of the Saviour. They've bought and sold the whole idea of materialism. How do you establish a kingdom of heaven on earth, when the keepers of the kingdom idolize wealth, success, power? Equally discouraging, our churchmen have failed to reinterpret, modernize, make useful a faith born in an ancient time. They've taken too little cognizance of social upheaval, a world of instant communication, a world teetering on a hydrogen bomb, a world that has sent men to the stars. In this new world where the cosmos becomes a fact seen on television, where death becomes a biological certainty, it is hard to keep one's faith in an amorphous heaven. Too many adults are too educated to reality—you yourself for one—to accept a creed that demands belief in Messiahs and miracles and a hereafter. Most of the young are too independent, knowledgeable, doubting, to look with respect upon a religion that seems mythic, old-fashioned, a mere opiate. Those among the young who want the supernatural have found more wondrous wizardry in astrology, witchcraft, Far Eastern philosophies. The idealistic dreamers seek better opiates in drugs, and they reject the materialism of urban communities in favor of the commune."

"But, Tom, there has been a dramatic revival of interest in religion among the young in recent years. Thousands of Jesus People, Jesus Freaks, turned on to the old familiar father figure, turned on to His ideas about love and brotherhood. I've seen them, and all the rock operas, musicals, records, the books, newspapers, banners, all celebrating Christ. Doesn't that show promise?"

Carey smiled wanly. "A little, a little, but not much. I've never counted on that revival. It's as if the young—some of them anyway—are on a new trip. But a short one, I'm afraid. Because the trip is backwards in time to seek peace in a nostalgic antique—instead they should be seeing that the antique is remodeled, modernized, and transported out of the past to those in the present. Their trip has nothing to do with long-term faith. This Christ of theirs—He's a Beatle, He's a Che, and finally, He's Old Hat. No, Steve, a more durable Christ and a better

church are needed. Any revival could have staying power
and grow, and be meaningful, but only if it could connect
with the established church."

"Well, why can't it?" Randall wondered.

"Because the established church does not relate to those
people, or indeed to most people these days. The church
is simply not keeping pace, is not reaching and holding
enough human beings. The rigidity of the Christian
church, its slowness to recognize and grapple with immediate earth problems, deeply disappoints me, too. I
confess sin. I find myself beginning to question what I am
selling."

"Do you see any hope whatsoever, Tom?"

"One slight glimmer of hope. But it may be too late. I
suspect the one hope for the survival of organized Christianity lies in the growth of the reform or radical or so-
called underground church movement worldwide. The
future of orthodox religion may depend on the rise to
power of a clergyman like the Reverend Maertin de
Vroome—he's the Protestant revolutionary in Amsterdam—"

"Yes, I've read about him."

"A minister like de Vroome is not chained to the past.
He believes the Word has to be reread, then revised,
revived, resold. He believes we must stop emphasizing the
idea that Christ was once not only a reality but the Son
of God, the Messiah. He feels this Jesus, as well as the
superstitions about miracles and the Ascension, the events
after the Resurrection, destroy the effectiveness of the New
Testament and limit the church in its activity. The only
thing important in the gospels, de Vroome insists, is the
basic wisdom of Christ. Son of God or of Man or merely
myth, no matter—it's the message that was His or attributed to Him that must be yanked out of the first century and be revitalized and applied practically in twentieth-century terms to the twentieth century."

"How does one possibly do that?" Randall wondered.

"I'm not sure," Carey admitted, "but de Vroome feels
it can be done. I think he goes along with Dietrich Bonhoeffer, who, despite his conservatism, tried to put the

church into the real world, tried to give it a program of humanistic action and social involvement. De Vroome says that the Word, in modern terms, in modern language and performance as well, must be taken into the world's ghettos and palaces, into the United Nations, into nuclear plants, into government offices, into prisons, dispersed from the hierarchy of all Christian churches down through the pulpits of the earth to the congregations of millions. This done, the Word will work, and religion and faith will live, and civilization will survive. Without this ecclesiastical revolution, de Vroome sees the death of religion, faith, and finally, humanity. He may be right. But he represents the minority, and the Establishment—the World Council of Churches in Geneva, the Catholic Church as represented by the Vatican—resists drastic change, tries to stamp him and other rebels out and maintain the status quo. Churchmen feel safer in the first century. Their congregations don't. There is the problem. That is why your father saw, and I now see, reports of more vacant pews in many churches every year. In a decade it may catch up with us and I may be preaching to an empty house."

"Tom—is there nothing you can do?"

"Within the system, probably not. Outside the system, maybe—but I'm too—too conditioned to the old ways, and too timid, to become a radical. For me, for many of us, who feel religion is stagnant and stale, there is only one possibility, and I keep thinking about it. I keep thinking of getting out of the church. I feel sometimes I might do more good surrendering my pulpit and entering secular teaching or social work and reform. I feel that I might really come to grips with human needs, as they are, and perhaps stumble on a few human solutions of the moment. I don't know. I just don't know what I'll do."

Moved, Randall said, "I hope you don't quit, at least not now. Selfishly, I'm afraid that it would break my father's heart."

Carey shrugged. "Steve, can one break a heart that may already be broken? Never mind. If I were to consider resigning seriously, it would only be after I knew your father was strong and well."

They halted at an intersection. Carey continued speaking. "If the church can't reform, there's only one thing that can save it. A miracle. Just as the Jews, at Christ's birth, awaited a Messiah to save them from oppression under the Romans, and ignored a Christ who failed to save them and merely died on a cross, unable even to save Himself, we need an authentic Messiah. If a Christ, or the Christ, could appear again, and reiterate His message—a message that was unheard of when He first brought it to Judea—"

"What message do you mean, Tom?"

"Have faith. Be forgiving. Two new concepts in the first century and two concepts that should be renewed in the twentieth century. If Christ returned to earth with that message—well, I think governments and people might look at one another and start doing something meaningful about slavery, poverty, misery, materialism, injustice, tyranny, nuclear Armageddon. The Second Coming, or some sign of it, might restore hope and save the world. But, as I said, that would be a miracle, wouldn't it? And who believes in miracles in the age of computer science, television, rockets to the moon? . . . There's your hotel, Steve. Sorry to have bent your ear like this. Thanks for listening. It was therapeutic for me, and you're one of the few agnostics I would trust. I'll see you this evening."

He was gone, and Randall's exuberance over his father's survival had now vanished. He felt helpless, the more so when he remembered the lunch date that he hoped to have with his daughter. Judy was another of the lost, without faith, with nightmares instead of a dream, and she probably needed more than a mere father to save her. Judy, too, needed a miracle. But who could make out a miracle in this time of speed?

THEY HAD BEEN in the booth of the half-empty coffee shop, located beneath the lobby of the Oak Ritz, for nearly a half hour.

After reaching the hotel, Randall had telephoned Barbara's suite, and Judy had answered, saying she had been looking forward to lunch. He had waited for her in the coffee shop, and she had apologized for being late, but she had been inquiring about an organic restaurant that served unadulterated foods. Her friends were into that, and into wheat germ, soybeans, carob puddings, herbs, honey, and she had recently gone along and liked it. Not unexpectedly, she had found no such health-food restaurant in Oak City, but she supposed a few meals of tainted food would not destroy her altogether.

By now, Randall had finished his hot roast beef sandwich, and he watched his daughter munching the last of her egg salad sandwich and sipping her lemonade. She was, in his eyes, an absolute beauty. Her skin was without a blemish, and her radiant eyes, tiny upcurved nose, full lips gave her the appearance of an absolutely virginal creature, unused by life. But her mature, shapely figure, in a tight white blouse and blue jeans, contradicted the initial appearance of adolescence.

It was impossible to believe that this new young being, this only-fifteen-years-on-earth girl, this pure nature child who refused to corrupt her body with food poisoned by additives or preservatives or emulsifiers or pesticides, had fed her body and mind intravenously by hypodermic with a hard and vicious drug. He considered discussing it with her.

In the half hour that had elapsed since their meeting, when she had briefly returned his hug but not the kiss, she had been curiously distracted, nervous, remote. Their conversation had gone haltingly. She had rambled on about the cleansing effects of organic foods, and had gone from that to her discovery of the writings of Alan Watts, and then (a morsel for him, he was sure) she had mentioned how much she enjoyed her groovy French teacher in her new school.

At one point, having run out of uncommunicative talk, Judy had asked him about his work. Since he knew that she was not really interested, he had told her little, mostly describing a name rock group—The Spare Tires—that his office was publicizing. It had been on the tip of his tongue to tell her about his meeting with Jim McLoughlin, and the work of The Raker Institute, because he sensed that this would have intrigued her and given her father more merit in her eyes, but he had refrained in the nick of time. He had refrained because he had recalled, with a sinking feeling, that he was going to reject McLoughlin and the Raker account, and there would be no way of justifying that to his Judy.

Judy had pushed aside her plate and was bringing the paper napkin to her lips.

"Now, how's about a dessert?" he asked with feigned enthusiasm.

"I wish I could," said Judy, "but I'd never get into those new jeans I bought. I'll tell you what. I'll have some chocolate milk, if *you* will."

He tried to remember whether it was chocolate milk he used to share with Judy on Sunday mornings when she was nine or ten years old and they had breakfast together. He simply could not remember. "Just what I was thinking about," he said, and he slid to the end of the booth and called out their order to the waitress.

He worked himself back opposite her, and he knew that it was his turn. He had wanted this lunch not only to see her, but also to probe her feelings about her mother's determination to obtain a divorce and to remarry. It was difficult to get into this now, great risks, but if he avoided it, there might not be another chance. He had to find out. Then there was the unbelievable drug thing. That, too.

Not more than an hour ago he had told Tom Carey that he had become increasingly interested in truth.

So truth it must be.

"Judy, we haven't talked about your new school yet, and—"

She had been picking at her burlap purse, but now she looked up warily.

"—and I want to know what happened there," he said. "I heard they busted you because of some drugs."

"I knew Mother would tell you. If there was a Wailing Wall around, she'd go and tell it to that, too."

"Well, do you want to talk about it?"

"What's there to say? I happened to get caught. Most

of them don't get caught. The fatheaded pigs on the faculty board were afraid I might corrupt the others—funny—me corrupt them—nine tenths of them are really ripped, spaced out. So the faculty board told me to leave, even though I was the smartest one in my class."

He tried to keep Stern Father and Disapproving Parent out of his voice. "But why the hard stuff, Judy? Why was that so important?"

"It wasn't a big deal. It was like—well—like it was an experience, that's all. It was something of my own, that's all. I wanted to explore my perceptions. You know—light up my head. Some of the others can't handle it. I felt I could. I'd have kicked it without the big hassle."

Randall hesitated. Now more dangerous terrain. He decided to enter it. "What about this Dr. Burke you've been seeing? How is that going?"

He could almost see her defenses rise. "I don't know what to tell you," she said lightly, "except he's a shrink. Doesn't that tell it all?"

"It doesn't tell me whether you're making progress with him."

"If you mean the speeding—Mother'd say he's slowed me down to thirty miles an hour." She met her father's eyes briefly, and dropped the note of flippancy. "If you want to know where I'm at—I'm clean."

"I'm glad to hear that."

The waitress had finally brought their chocolate milk, and Judy took a sip and with winning good cheer announced that it was delicious.

Randall would not be put off. "This Dr. Burke," he began casually, "do you like him personally?"

Judy's eyes seemed to brighten. "Old Arthur? Oh, he's a groove. I mean that beard, it's enough to kill you. I don't understand him half the time, but he tries. He's a good guy."

Randall felt weak and hurt, betrayed. "Do you know your mother intends to marry him?"

"She'd better. I think he's balling her half the time." She came up from her chocolate milk, and saw his face, and at once retreated. "I didn't mean—I'm sorry if you—"

"Never mind," he said curtly. "I'm just not used to hearing that kind of language from you."

"Well, I'm sorry—I said I'm sorry. I—I know they want to get married."

The big one remained, the big question. "What I'm interested in is how you feel about it. How would you feel about your mother's marrying this Dr. Burke?"

"At least it would get Mother off my back."

"And that's all you feel, Judy?"

She appeared puzzled. "What else do you want me to say?"

The interrogation was futile, he saw. And there were no more risks. "Judy," he said, "how would you feel if I objected to your mother's marrying Burke?"

The smooth brow had creased. "That—that's a heavy question. I mean, like what's supposed to be my answer? I mean, why should you object? You and Mother have been separated ten million years. I didn't know you cared anymore one way or the other about her."

"Even if I didn't care about her, Judy, I do care about you. You're my main concern in whatever happens."

"I—" She was unable to find words, and she seemed both troubled and pleased. "I'm glad."

"You sound as if you don't know how much you matter to me."

"I guess I know, only—like—I mean I hardly ever see you, so that—it's like you're so far away and I've been with so many new people."

He nodded. "I understand, Judy," he said. "I just wanted you to know how I felt. The problem that your mother and I have is our problem, not yours, and we'll work it out. I have only one interest—to see that you're happy."

"I'll be happy," she said quickly. She clutched her purse. "I'd better go now. Thanks for the lunch and—"

"Why the rush?"

She moved to the edge of the booth. "Mother's packing.

Now that Grandpa is sort of better, she wants us to get back to San Francisco. We've got a flight from Chicago in a couple of hours. She doesn't want me to miss too much time with Arthur—I mean—the shrink."

"I guess she's right."

Judy stood up. "Well, good-bye," she said awkwardly, "and—uh—thanks for the lunch again—and I'm glad Grandpa's going to get well."

He stared at her wordlessly. Absently reaching for the check, he said, "Yes, good-bye, Judy."

There was nothing more. She had started away toward the coffee shop exit, and he numbly counted out his change. Suddenly, from the corner of his eye, he saw her slow down, whirl around, and hurry back.

She leaned into the booth toward him, as he lifted his head, bewildered.

"No matter what, Pop," she said in a breaking voice, "you'll always be my father." She bent closer, her long hair brushing against his face, and she kissed him on the cheek.

His hand had gone up to her face, and he felt choked. "No matter what, darling," he whispered, "you'll always be my girl. I love you."

She straightened, eyes brimming. "I love you, Pop. I always will."

She backed away, then ran toward the exit and disappeared from his sight.

He sat on in the booth, alone, for five minutes more. Finally, he lit his pipe, left the coffee shop, and climbed the stairs to the lobby. He was not sure whether he wanted to go to his room or take another walk. Then, he heard his name being called out.

He spun toward the reception desk.

"Mr. Randall," the clerk called out again, holding up a telephone receiver. "We were just about to page you. A Miss Wanda Smith is phoning you from your New York office. She says she must speak to you. You can take it in the phone booth at the end of the lobby, if you like. I'll have the operator transfer the call."

* * *

HE WAS in the booth, waiting, and when he heard his secretary's voice, Steven Randall demanded, "What is it, Wanda? They said you had to speak to me about something."

"That's right. Some urgent calls came in, but first, everyone here wants to know how your father is and how you are."

He adored this buxom black girl who had been his devoted secretary and confidante for nearly three years. At the time he had hired Wanda, she was taking diction lessons with the intention of becoming a stage actress, and she was just losing her Southern drawl and replacing it with a faint theatrical accent, but she had enjoyed her job with Randall Associates so much that she had soon given up any thoughts of the stage. And she had never quite lost her charming drawl. Nor had she surrendered her independence. This sometimes made her exasperating, as right now on the telephone. She must know about his father and about himself, before she would proceed to business matters. He knew her, and he knew that he could not divert or change her. He also knew that he would not wish her any other way.

So he related to her the results of his visits to the hospital last night and this morning.

Now, several minutes later, still enclosed in the stifling telephone booth, he was finishing his recital. "That's about it, Wanda. Unless something unforeseen happens, Dad has passed the crisis. He will recover. To what degree, I can't say."

"I'm happy for you, boss. Do you want me to pass along the news to anyone else?"

"I guess you'd better. I haven't had a chance to call anyone. You can ring Darlene at the apartment and tell her. Also—" He tried to think. There were Joe Hawkins, his assistant, and Thad Crawford, his legal wizard. They would want to know. "—I guess you can also inform Joe and Thad. Oh yes, and tell Thad I'll definitely firm up the Towery and Cosmos deal the minute I get back. Tell him I should be back in maybe two or three days. I'll let him know."

"Will do, boss. Except I was hoping we could get you back to New York by tomorrow. That's why I'm calling."

At last, he thought. Wanda was ready.

"By tomorrow?" he said. "All right, honey, out with it."

"I have two urgent messages for you, boss. At least, the parties who left them considered them urgent. I didn't want to burden you with them if your father was still in a critical condition. Now that you say he's better, I feel I can pass them on."

"I'm listening, Wanda."

"One is from George L. Wheeler again—you remember? —the religious book publisher I reported to you about yesterday when you were at the airport. When I told Wheeler I was still trying to get hold of you, he insisted I contact you immediately. Have you had time to give him any thought?"

"Frankly, no."

"Well, if you can find the time, he might be worth thinking about," said Wanda. "His credentials are the best. I've already done some checking for you. *Dun and Bradstreet, Who's Who in America, Publishers' Weekly.* Mission House is number one in the Bible publishing field. Way out in front of Zondervan, World, Harper and Row, Oxford, Cambridge, Regnery and all the rest. Wheeler owns it lock, stock, and Bible. He sponsored the Reverend Zachery's revivalist tour to Australia, and he was recently at the White House to get some kind of award. He's been married thirty years to a Philadelphia socialite, has two sons, and is fifty-seven years old, according to *Who's Who.* He took over Mission House from his father about twenty years ago—they have an office building right here in New York, and branches in Nashville, Chicago, Dallas, Seattle."

"Okay, Wanda, enough already. So he phoned you again. This time did he tell you exactly what he wants?"

"He wants to see you tomorrow morning, early as you can make it. He was so obstinate, I finally had to tell him where you were and more about what was going on. He was sympathetic, but he kept repeating that it was vital you meet with him in the morning. He begged me to run you down and ask if you couldn't fly back just for this meeting, and he assured me everything could be settled by noon, and then you could rejoin your father. I did what you instructed me to do yesterday—told him I would try to locate you, but I couldn't guarantee I'd succeed."

"Wanda, this meeting—did Wheeler finally tell you what it's supposed to be about?"

"Well, he talked a little more about having you promote that brand-new Bible—"

"Just that?" Randall cut in sourly. "Big deal. More of the same. Who needs it?"

There was a brief silence on the other end of the line, then Wanda's voice once more. "I was thinking, maybe you need it, boss," Wanda drawled. "I've just been reviewing my notes. Wheeler gave me a few more details on this call. He would want your representation for a full year. He said it would be for top money, more than any industrial account ever paid you. He said there would be a considerable amount of prestige for you. He also said he'd want you to go to Europe for a month or two, expenses paid, and you'll find the trip fascinating. The only catch was you'd have to leave for Europe almost immediately."

"What does an American Bible publisher need a public relations man in Europe for?"

"That occurred to me, too. I tried to find out, but he clammed up. Wouldn't even tell me where in Europe you'd have to go. But Joe Hawkins and I were discussing it, and Joe agrees with me. Considering the pressure you've been under lately, you could stand a change."

Randall snorted. "Ballyhooing a Bible—some change. Honey, I grew up with the Bible, and I've been up to my ears in it since last night. I don't find any pleasure in going back to where I came from."

Wanda was persistent. "All of us here have a hunch it's not the same old thing, that it could be something different. George L. Wheeler reminded me to be sure to pass on to you that clue to what his project is all about."

"What clue?"

"Matthew 28:7 in the New Testament." She paused.

"I guess you don't recall, with all you've been going through. Remember I told you yesterday, the passage in Matthew that reads, 'And go quickly, and tell his disciples that he is risen from the dead; and, behold, he goeth before you into Galilee; there shall ye see him. . . .' And Wheeler again reminded me to tell you that you'd be handling the Second Resurrection."

Randall remembered. It all came back to him. Wheeler's enigmatic crack about wanting Randall to promote the Second Resurrection.

As before, Randall was puzzled: What in the devil was Wheeler trying to tell him?

Randall had given over a good part of a lifetime to shedding himself of the effects of the First Resurrection. What did he need with a Second—whatever that could possibly be?

Yet, there had been his father this morning, barely conscious, with his pitying eyes. How pleased his father would be to learn that his son was going to become involved in the Good Book and good works. How much strength this might give to his father. And there was something more. What a salve to an uneasy conscience such a religious project might be, a conscience still ashamed of his agreement to sell out another good work, The Raker Institute, in favor of the selfish gain offered by Cosmos Enterprises.

He wavered, but only briefly. He had no heart for promoting this nonsense. With all the problems that beset him, he could never become absorbed in making a pitch to the world on something so irrelevant today as the Bible, even a new Bible.

"I'm sorry, Wanda," he found himself saying into the mouthpiece, "but I simply can't find one practical reason for wasting time on that meeting with Wheeler tomorrow morning. You'd better call him and explain—"

"I can give you one practical reason, boss," Wanda interrupted. "A real practical reason. Which brings me to the second message I have here for you. Right after Wheeler called, there was another call. It was from Ogden Towery III of Cosmos Enterprises."

"Oh?"

"Mr. Towery wanted you to know that George L. Wheeler is a close friend of his, and that he, Towery, had personally recommended our firm to Wheeler. Mr. Towery told me to pass this on to you immediately—that he feels this account, Mission House's new Bible, is just the kind of account he would like to see you take on— as a great favor to him. Mr. Towery sounded like he meant it, boss, like this was very important to him, too." Wanda paused. "Is that a good, practical reason to see Wheeler tomorrow morning?"

"It's the only reason that makes sense," said Randall slowly. "Okay, I guess there's no choice. You call George L. Wheeler and let him know I'll meet him in his office at eleven o'clock tomorrow morning."

Hanging up the receiver, he hated himself more than ever. It was the second time in two days that he had allowed Towery to twist his arm. It should be the last time. After seeing Wheeler, after he had made his deal with Towery, no one would ever be able to twist his arm again. Maybe it was worth it, enduring these small humiliations, making these little blackmail payments, to attain his future freedom.

He left the booth. He tried to think what next. Barbara and Judy were leaving. He would notify his attorney to be prepared to contest any divorce action. No second father named Burke was going to take over his little girl, not if he could prevent it. As for the rest of this day, he would definitely have dinner with his mother and Clare and Uncle Herman. Following that, they would look in on his father at the hospital, and check with Dr. Oppenheimer once more. If the report was favorable, and he felt sure it would be, he would take the latest scheduled red-eye flight from Chicago tonight, and head back to— what had Wheeler said it was about?—ah—the Second Resurrection.

He speculated upon the so-called secret project to be revealed to him at Mission House. He sought to recall Wheeler's cue. Yes. "And go quickly, and tell his disciples he is risen from the dead."

Now what in the hell did that mean? No matter. The head of Cosmos Enterprises had said that it was important. So it was important. Besides, for the first time, his curiosity had been aroused. He was interested in anything, anything at all, that promised—Resurrection.

SEATED THERE at the large antique oak table, which occupied the center of the conference room on the third floor of Mission House, Steve Randall found himself no longer able to concentrate on the business at hand.

He listened to the muffled rubbery whir of New York City's traffic on Park Avenue far below the large picture window across the table from him. His eyes rested on the Early American grandfather clock against one wall. It was eleven forty-five in the morning. This meant that they had been talking—more accurately, he had been listening —for over half an hour. In that time, he had heard nothing to excite him.

Pretending to be attentive, Randall surreptitiously took in the rest of the conference room. The setting more closely resembled a converted apartment living room than the center of an office complex. The walls were tastefully paneled. The carpeting was a rich dark cocoa. Along the lower half of one wall ran bookshelves filled with expensively bound Bibles and volumes on religion, most published by Mission House, as far as Randall could make out. In a corner, a glass case displayed a variety of crucifixes, medallions, and religious articles. Not far from it, atop a table, stood a pot of coffee on its own warming tray.

Randall had come to this meeting alone. George L. Wheeler, his host and the president of Mission House, was attended by five of his employees. Directly across from Randall was one of Wheeler's elderly lady secretaries, whose presence exuded such goodness, whose being was so churchlike and Salvation Army, that you felt unworthy and sinful. The secretary busily jotted her shorthand notes on a pad, rarely raising her head.

Next to the secretary was another woman, much younger, more interesting. Randall remembered her name. She

was Miss Naomi Dunn, Wheeler's administrative assistant.
Her brown hair was pulled straight back and severely
bunned. She had a sallow complexion, grayish eyes, thin
nose, compressed mouth. She had a dedicated, fanatical
look, like that of a person who dislikes you for not being
a minister or missionary or something devout and useful,
so that you felt frivolous for simply being a plain secular
citizen. She wore horn-rimmed glasses, and she hung on
Wheeler's every syllable as if he were speaking from the
Mount, and she had not once met Randall's eye.

The three other Mission House employees around the
table were young men, one an editor, one a book design-
er, one the trade-book sales manager. They were indis-
tinguishable, one from the other, each with conservative
haircut, each clean-shaven, each with a serious, bland,
washed-out visage. In common, they wore agreeable
seraphic smiles. None had spoken a word throughout
Wheeler's lengthy discourse.

A few feet from Randall's elbow was seated the considerable bulk of George L. Wheeler, his lips still moving.

This was the powerful Towery's close friend, this was
the giant of American Bible publishing, and now Randall
scrutinized him more carefully.

Wheeler was an impressive two-hundred-pounder with
a receding hairline and a comb of white hair above it. He
had a ruddy moon face, and the two matching circles
within that circle were the gold rims of his spectacles.
His bulbous nose sniffed a lot as he spoke, and he had the
habit of unconsciously scratching himself, scratching his
head, behind an ear, beside his nose, beneath his armpit,
a gesture as natural as Randall's own habit of pushing his
overgrown hair out of his eyes even when it was not over
his eyes.

Wheeler wore an expensive, lusterless suit, and only his
necktie betrayed the promoter, the seller. It was a satiny
tie, a tie with a metallic cast, and one that door-to-door
salesmen who tried to push themselves into your living
room often wore.

Randall had ceased listening to Wheeler, not only because what the publisher had been saying struck no responsive chord in him, but because Wheeler's manner of speech and the loud monotony of his voice wore a listener down. He spoke like one not used to conversation but interested only in giving dictation. His voice, tiring—what was it like?—well, his voice was like the incessant braying of a dromedary.

There was a movement at the table and Randall realized that Wheeler had signaled to Naomi Dunn, who had instantly risen and was making her way to the coffeepot. Welcoming any diversion. Randall watched her. He had not noticed Miss Dunn's legs before. They were shapely. She had a tight-assed provocative little walk. As she came toward him with the coffee, he could see that she had tiny, ripe apple breasts securely brassiered beneath her linen blouse.

She hovered over him. "May I refill your cup, Mr. Randall?"

"Just a little," he said.

She performed her duty, next filled Wheeler's cup, and went on around the table. Randall wondered what she would be like in bed. Those prissy middle-thirty ladies could sometimes be the wildest, the best. Yet, he doubted it. She was too formidable, too career-oriented. It was suddenly impossible to imagine her ever without her clothes, just as it was almost impossible to imagine Darlene with her clothes.

He had flown back to New York last night and had not arrived until one o'clock in the morning. His Rolls-Royce and driver had been waiting. On the way back to the city, he had hoped that Darlene would be sound asleep. He had been utterly exhausted by the tensions of the past two days, the crisis at the hospital, the contact with his wife and daughter, his family and father's friends, and he wanted only to shut his eyes and sink into slumber. But upon his return to the brownstone, he had found Darlene wide-awake, perfumed and nude beneath the blanket, in their bed. So there had been little sleep, but instead an hour or two of her incessant chatter about missing him, and her playing hands, and her long young legs around him, and arousal finally, and the going into her, and the geisha acrobatics from her, and his coming at last so that he had been left juiceless, empty, almost deathly worn out.

Earlier this morning, refreshed slightly, made nervously alert by his curiosity about the Wheeler account and its mysterious promise, he had arrived at Mission House with all senses alive. What had transpired since had dulled him, and weariness was beginning to curl through his bones. What had transpired since, Randall knew, was that he had heard nothing except a dreary exposition on a specialized field of book publishing and a routine new project.

The past forty-five minutes boiled down to something about as animated as a dead halibut. Five publishers—Wheeler in the United States, and the leading Bible publishers in Great Britain, France, Germany, Italy—were combining their resources to bring out a brand-new international Bible—no, not the complete Bible, but a New Testament, actually. This New Testament would be freshly translated and contain exclusive information never before published, on some unrevealed archeological discovery. It would be the definitive New Testament, the most perfect one in the history of Christianity, and, on publication, it would not only render the King James Version of the New Testament obsolete, but would also surpass and make obsolete the Revised Standard Version, the New English Bible, the Jerusalem Bible, and every other Bible in existence.

This latest version of the Christian Scriptures—Randall tried to remember its name, and with effort he did—this International New Testament, as Wheeler had called it—had been in the process of preparation for six years. Wheeler's American-language edition alone would cost at least $2,500,000. This represented the costs of translation, setting type, three sets of plates, proofing, lightweight India paper stock, the variety of bindings from cloth to morocco leather, and soon there would be advertising and promotion. When the firm of Thomas Nelson & Sons had brought out the Revised Standard Version in

1952, $500,000 had been spent on advertising alone. With his International New Testament, Wheeler planned to spend double that amount.

The advance copies of the International New Testament—copies for the religious-book critics, for ministers, for theologians, for opinion makers and heads of state (including the President of the United States)—were now in production, in the process of being printed in Mainz, Germany. Now, after six years of toiling in absolute secrecy, the time had arrived for the final step—the mounting of a gigantic publicity campaign, one based on hard news rather than puffery, that would guarantee the success of the International New Testament. Since this Bible would be published in late July or early August, only two months or less remained for the setting up of the promotion campaign. Each of the international publishers was contributing a specialized service, and the publishers had agreed that their American partner should retain the public relations head, inasmuch as Americans were admittedly expert in handling publicity.

"Now, Mr. Randall—" George L. Wheeler was saying, and with difficulty Randall tried to become attentive to the Bible publisher once more. "—before we entered this room, I mentioned our terms to you, the largest fee for publicity ever offered in this field, I believe, and you indicated that the fee was satisfactory. In return for it, as I said, I would want you in our headquarters in Europe for two months, working with an extremely select staff we have there, creating the formula for publicity that could be used with modifications in all five countries. When that is done, you would return to New York and use your company, Randall Associates, to concentrate on the American edition only, just as the European publishers will then use their own publicists to work from the master blueprint you've laid out. But time, as I have indicated, is of the essence. It would be necessary for you to get your affairs in order immediately, and leave with me for Europe as soon as possible. A week from today, on Friday, June seventh, there is a sailing of the S.S. *France* from here to Southampton. We need that time on the ship, those five days, so that you can be briefed on every aspect of what lies ahead. There you have it, Mr. Randall. Do you have any further questions?"

Randall pushed himself up straight, fiddled with his pipe a moment, and met the publisher's gaze. "One question," he said, "just one key question, Mr. Wheeler."

"Yes, certainly."

Randall felt all eyes around the table upon him, but he had to get it said and done and over with. "I should think there are enough versions of the Bible around. Why would anyone ever want to publish a new one?"

Wheeler sniffed, scratched his temple, and said, "I thought I'd already made that sufficiently clear to you. Allow me to recapitulate. The Bible is the revelation of Our Lord. Yet, it must never be permitted to become an antiquated piece. It must be kept alive for every new generation. Up-to-date translations are required because contemporary languages are constantly changing, old words take on new meanings, and new words are brought into common usage by the masses. Furthermore, archeology is steadily making astounding discoveries of ancient papyri, parchment, pottery, inscribed stone, which give new meanings to and understanding of the Greek Scriptures in existence, and which shed fresh light on early Christian times. As discoveries and scholarship bring us closer to the gospels as originally written in the first century, we are moved to retranslate and continually to update, for increased accuracy, our versions of the New Testament. Legibility is yet another factor, of course. Most people own several Bibles or buy any number for gifts. So we are encouraged to bring out different versions of a New Testament because we want to improve the typography or the format or the commentary or change the binding."

"To get more sales," said Randall.

"Why not?" said Wheeler, shifting his bulk uncomfortably. "You must understand that while we believe in the Good Book, we are also in the highly competitive business of promoting and selling it. Yes, of course there are new versions brought out in order to obtain new sales, so that we can stay in business."

"Fair enough," said Randall. "I'm still not completely satisfied with your answer to my question. It may be my fault. Perhaps I didn't frame my question clearly. Let me get to the nitty-gritty. Why are you spending a fortune to publish this International New Testament? What's the reason for it, for this costly New Testament, the specific reason for it? Is the motive behind it merely to offer a better translation, or is the motive to present fresh information to support an accompanying concordance or center reference? Or because you've invented a better typeface or more esthetic binding? If that's all there is to motivate your publishing a new Bible, then frankly I don't see anything I can sell. I don't see my role at all. I don't see anything unusual about this longtime secret effort. Why would anyone out there give a damn about another edition of the New Testament, especially in times like these, with growing turmoil and social unrest and change? You mentioned that the publication of this Bible could be sold as hard news, would not be merely press-agentry. I'm sorry, Mr. Wheeler, but I haven't heard a single fact that adds up to hard news. I want to be honest with you, I don't want you to waste your money. There is nothing I can do for you, or for this New Testament of yours, based on what you've told me. You don't need me, and I don't need this kind of account. So I've got to tell you—I must decline your offer."

A damp silence fell over the room. Randall did not bother to look for the reaction of Naomi Dunn and the others. He was certain that they were horrified at this *lèse majesté*. Well, to hell with them.

George L. Wheeler sat nonplussed, scratching himself steadily. "Mr. Randall, I was told—Ogden Towery assured me—that you would take on this account."

"He had no right to tell you that."

"But I understood he—his Cosmos Enterprises—owns your firm."

"Not yet," said Randall sharply. "Anyway, that's not an issue. I take accounts on their own merit. Perhaps I wasn't always able to do so. Perhaps at times I took anything that paid enough. But no more. Now I intend to accept only those accounts that are worthy of my effort and time, of my devotion, and I don't find any such motivating force in what you've told me."

He had begun to shove back his chair, prepared to rise and leave, when Wheeler reached out and clamped his arm to the table.

"One minute, Mr. Randall. I—I haven't told you—I really haven't told you everything."

"Why haven't you?"

"Because I'm pledged to secrecy—it's very secret, has been for six years—except to those now working inside the project. I'm not in a position to reveal the truth to you, have you know it, and then for some reason have you turn down the account. Once you agree to take us on, I can tell you the entire truth."

Randall shook his head. "No, I'm afraid I hold the opposite view. Until I know the truth, I can't agree to take you on."

For charged seconds, Wheeler stared at Randall, then he exhaled with a wheeze.

"That's your last word, Mr. Randall?"

"That's my absolute condition."

Wheeler gave a heavy nod of concession. "Very well." He turned his head toward Naomi Dunn, lifted a finger, and she acknowledged his gesture with a blink. Immediately, she touched the elderly secretary's shoulder, signaled the three men, and suddenly the five were on their feet.

Wheeler ignored their departure, but waited until he heard the conference-room door close tightly before he faced Randall once more.

"Very well, Mr. Randall. We're alone, just the two of us. I've decided to take the risk. I'm going to level with you."

His demeanor was transformed and his voice had changed, Randall noted. No longer was he the self-assured, self-styled holy man, the self-appointed Keeper of the Book of Books. Now he was the businessman, the salesman, the impresario down in the arena touting his wares. Gone, too, the dromedary bray. The voice was smoother, winning, more controlled and crisp, and the language no-nonsense.

"I've told you our project has been secret for six years," he was saying. "Didn't you wonder why?"

"Not after listening to you for a while. I thought it was a game, a publisher's in-game, to make something important out of what was routine and banal."

"You were wrong," said Wheeler flatly. "Dead wrong. Now I'm going to set you right. We've maintained secrecy because we knew we were sitting on a keg of dynamite, keeping the lid on the hottest, most tremendous news story of all time. I am not being extravagant, Mr. Randall. If anything, I am understating it."

This was the first time that Randall's early morning curiosity had been revived. He waited.

"If the truth leaked out," Wheeler went on, "it might ruin us and our enormous investment, or at least damage us severely. The press is onto us, but they don't know the truth. Churches throughout the world suspect something is going on, but they don't have an inkling of what it really is. And we have enemies, eager to know in advance of our publication day what we know, so they can distort and misrepresent the contents of the International New Testament and try to destroy it. So we are pledged to secrecy, and our co-workers throughout Europe are similarly pledged. When I reveal the truth to you now, you will be the first person outside the project who is uncommitted to it, who will know the essential facts."

Randall put down his pipe. "Why take such a chance on me?"

"First, because I want you with us, because you are the last link needed to insure our success," said Wheeler. "Second, after weighing the chances, I think I know enough about you to believe you are trustworthy."

"We've just met. What can you know about me?"

"I know a good deal about you, Mr. Randall. I know that you are the son of a Midwestern clergyman, a good man with a good family. I know you've rebelled against orthodox religion, and that you are an agnostic. I know that you have a wife and teen-aged daughter, and that you are living apart from them. I know where you live and how you live. I know you've had many lady friends, and that you have one now. I know that you drink heavily, but are not an alcoholic. I know—"

Randall frowned, and interrupted. "You're not describing a very good risk, Mr. Wheeler."

"On the contrary," said Wheeler quickly. "I am, because I happen to know one more thing about you. I know that despite your intimacies with women, despite your social drinking, you've never discussed your private business with outsiders or betrayed a client. You've handled some of the biggest accounts in the country, and you've treated their confidences with total secrecy. You've been a private man. You've isolated your personal life from your business life. You've never had a client who had reason to regret placing his trust in you. That's why I've decided to rely on you, also."

Randall was more annoyed than flattered. "I'm not used to having people pry into my private affairs, Mr. Wheeler."

The publisher inclined his head apologetically. "Under ordinary circumstances, it might be improper and unjustified, but this is that rare exception to the rule. Surely you understand that when a huge conglomerate prepares to buy out another business, perhaps at a cost of two million dollars, especially when the conglomerate is buying administrative and creative talent, it must take a close look before it leaps."

"Towery," Randall murmured.

"He is my closest friend. He wanted to reassure me, if I was forced to go this far. I had hoped that it would not be necessary to confide in you—yet. But if it proved necessary, as it has, I had to be reassured. Now I'm taking the gamble. I won't go into details, Mr. Randall. I'll tell you only what I have to tell you. It will take me less than five minutes. I think it will be enough." He eyed Randall speculatively, and inquired, "Mr. Randall, exactly what kind of account could really involve you, commit you, excite you, these days?"

"I can't be certain. I'm jaded, so—" His voice drifted

off, and then he said simply, "I could become involved in something I could believe in." He paused, and added, "Something I wanted the whole world to know about, to buy, because for once a product had genuine value."

Wheeler reacted with a satisfied half-smile. "Good," he said. "I told you that we were sitting on the greatest story of all time. I told you that I wasn't being extravagant when I said that. Well, could the greatest story of all time excite and involve you?"

He did not wait for a reply. "Some years ago, the top newspapermen in this country were polled by a leading public opinion firm. They were asked to speculate on what story, within the realm of scientific possibility or beyond it, could be the biggest story of this century. There were many varied answers. Some newspapermen voted for the discovery of a cure for cancer. Others voted for a treatment that could enable human beings to live to the age of one hundred. Yet others voted for the landing on earth of creatures from another planet, or our reaching another planet and finding civilized life on it. Some voted for a day when the United States of the World was announced as a reality. But do you know what the majority of newspapermen voted as the biggest possible story of our time? They voted for the Second Coming."

Confused, Randall asked, "The Second Coming?"

"Of Jesus Christ to earth. If Jesus Christ returned to our earth in person, in the flesh, if He proved the Resurrection a reality tomorrow—if He came down amongst us tomorrow—that, those reporters voted, would be the biggest story of our time."

Steve Randall felt a chill creeping up his arms. "What are you trying to say, Mr. Wheeler?"

"I'm saying to you, my friend, it *has* happened. Not literally, but figuratively. We have stumbled upon, we are in the possession of, the biggest story of our time."

Randall came slowly forward in his chair. "Go on."

"Listen," said Wheeler urgently. "Six years ago, a most respected Italian archeologist, Professor Augusto Monti, of the University of Rome, was digging near Ostia Antica—the ruins of the old town of Ostia, the great trading seaport of ancient Rome in the first century. Following years of research, Professor Monti was hoping to find something, anything, that would bring us closer to the truth of the story of the Saviour presented in the New Testament. Then, by perseverance or genius or luck, he found what he had hoped to find. He found it, the truth, the final truth."

Randall felt strangely dazed. "What—what final truth?"

"In a deep excavation he discovered the ruins of an ancient Roman villa, what must have been the home of a wealthy merchant of the first century, and in the crumbling walls of the *tablinum,* the study where the master kept his papyrus rolls and codices, Professor Monti made his incredible discovery. Theologians and scholars of the past have always said it was unlikely, even impossible, that such a discovery would be made in the wet climate of Italy, or in fact anywhere else. But it happened, this discovery, and it has been verified by every authoritative scientific test available to us. Professor Monti came upon an ancient block of Roman stone, actually the granite base of a statue which had been split, hollowed out, and then resealed with pitch. Inside it, surviving more than nineteen centuries, were two documents. The shorter one, in poor condition, consisted of five fragments of parchment of the kind the Romans wrote upon in the first century. Fitted together, the fragments turned out to be a brief official report in Greek from Pontius Pilate's captain of the guards in Jerusalem, one Petronius, to the head of the Praetorian Guards in Rome, one Lucius Aelius Sejanus, who ruled the Empire in the name of Tiberius Caesar. The longer document, better preserved, consisted of twenty-four fairly large fragments of papyrus, which were covered with writing in Aramaic. The contents apparently had been dictated in Jerusalem by the Jewish leader of the future Christian church just before his execution in the year 62 A.D."

Randall's excitement increased. He pressed against the table. "What—tell me—what was in those documents?"

Wheeler's eyes were shining. "The greatest story of our time, the one that will dazzle the entire Christian world, the one that will cause a rebirth in religion and a revival of faith. The papyri that were found—that we now possess—are the lost source for the Synoptic Gospels, the so-called Q document, a fifth but actually the first and original gospel—the Gospel According to James—written by James. James the Just, the younger brother of Jesus, to record the life of the real Jesus Christ as He walked upon the earth as a man among men, a human being as well as the Messiah, in the first century of our world. Now we have it all, all of it."

Wheeler waited for Randall's reaction, but Randall was speechless.

"When you read the translations of the manuscripts, you'll be even more astounded," Wheeler went on fervently. "The contents are enough to boggle the mind. Now we know truly where Jesus was born, where He studied, how He grew up, how He prayed over His father's grave after Joseph died, what He did for His livelihood before His ministry, the details of His missing years between twelve and thirty, everything, everything. Jesus existed, and if this fantastic Christian source, the oldest ever known, were not enough, were considered suspect because it was written by a Jew turned Christian, then we have the corroboration of Our Lord's ministry and existence and Crucifixion from a non-Christian source, a pagan source, from a Roman soldier reporting from occupied Palestine to his superior in Rome about this rebel, this so-called Messiah, in the Petronius Parchment. But even that is not the best of it, Mr. Randall. I've saved the best for the last. This part is the most remarkable."

Randall sat dazed, still speechless.

"Hear this," the publisher resumed with a tremulous voice. "Jesus did not die on the Cross in Jerusalem in 30 A.D." Wheeler paused, underscoring the next. "He survived and lived on for nineteen years."

"Lived on," Randall murmured, almost to himself.

"Petronius reported to his superiors that Jesus was crucified, declared dead, removed for burial. But James the Just found out that his brother had not expired on the Cross, that Jesus was alive and breathing. Whether He survived due to God's help or a physician's skill, James could not say. He could only say Jesus recovered, and clandestinely continued His ministry in Palestine, in other provinces, finally appearing and preaching in Rome —*in Rome*—in the ninth year of the reign of Claudius Caesar, in 49 A.D., a time when Jesus would have been fifty-four years of age. And it was not until then that the real Resurrection and Ascension occurred. Do you understand what I'm telling you? Do you realize the implications of this find?"

Steve Randall swayed slightly in his chair, too shaken to comprehend fully as yet. "Is it—can it be true? I can't believe it. There must be a mistake. Are you absolutely sure?"

"We are absolutely positive. Each and every fragment of each document is authenticated beyond question. We know the truth. We have the Word, at last. We are giving it to the world in the International New Testament. We are resurrecting for mankind the real Jesus Christ, the actual Saviour who once lived on earth and who lives on in us. That is why we've given our secret project in Amsterdam the code name which it bears. Steve, can you believe in Resurrection Two?"

Randall had closed his eyes. Behind them spun a bright pinwheel carrying images of both his recent past and his present. He visualized the human images on that pinwheel responding to this most sensational find in nineteen hundred years. He saw them electrified and aglow with renewed faith in the meaning of life. His father. His mother. His sister Clare. Tom Carey. Above all, himself. He saw those whose faith was cracked or riven and those who, like himself, had no faith left and were lost. And he saw, approaching this gyrating wheel of despair, the One who had so long been myth, make-believe, fairy-tale figure. The Son of God, Jesus of Nazareth, would be known finally to man. The Gospel of James would revive the Saviour's message of love and peace and would comfort and heal His human family.

Incredible, incredible. Of all the wonders that Randall

had seen and heard in his life, there had never been one as prodigious as this. *Good News on Earth.*

Could it really be?

What had Wheeler asked him? Yes. Can you believe in this project, this Resurrection Two?

"I don't know," he replied slowly. "It is something—something I'd like to believe in, very much, if I can believe in anything, anymore."

"Are you willing to try, Mr. Randall?"

"Try what? To sell the Word?" Randall considered it, and he came unsteadily to his feet. "Look, if He's here to save us, I guess I'm here to be saved. When do we start?"

II

SOMEHOW, every dream, whenever he had dreamt in the past week and a half, seemed to have had Jesus in it. As he struggled out of sleep now, the dream he had been living or embellishing in his emerging consciousness was still vivid behind his eyes—

The disciples saw Jesus walking on the sea, and they were troubled, saying, "It is a spirit." Straightaway Jesus spoke to them, saying, "Be of good cheer, it is I. Be not afraid." And Steven Randall answered Him and said, "Lord, if it be Thou, bid me come to Thee on the water." And Jesus said, "Come." And when Steven was out of the ship, he walked on the water to go to Jesus. But when he saw the wind boisterous, he was afraid. Beginning to sink, he cried, "Father, save me." And immediately the Reverend Nathan Randall stretched forth his hand, and caught him, and said to him, "O thou of little faith, wherefore didst thou doubt?" And Steven Randall was saved, and had faith.

Crazy mixed-up dream that was suffocating him.

He was finally awakening, opening his eyes, to find that what was stifling his breathing was Darlene's soft breast, her exposed left breast pressed against his lips. She was perched on the bed leaning over him, the upper part of her sheer pink negligee spread open, one naked breast rubbing against his mouth.

He had been awakened in many strange places and in many unusual ways, but he had never before been awakened on a ship in the Atlantic Ocean by the touch of a woman's breast. He was still on water, but suddenly Jesus

Christ and the Reverend Nathan Randall Christ were far away.

Darlene grinned down at him. "Well, admit it. You can't think of a better way to wake, can you? Name one pasha who gets better treatment."

One more of Darlene's young love games, he knew. He was in no mood for it at this hour, but he also knew that this was Darlene's stock in trade, the only goods that she had to offer, so he was kind. He performed the obligatory response. He kissed her breast gently around the crimson nipple until it began to harden and was drawn away from him.

"Naughty boy, Steve," she said with mock severity. "Let's not start anything now. I just wanted to be sure you got up smiling." She cocked her head, pursed her full lips, as if to appraise him. "But you are cute." She reached down, slipping a hand beneath his blanket and sliding it between his legs. She caressed him a moment, then quickly withdrew her hand. "Hey, you're not wasting time," she said.

He lifted his arms to bring her closer, but she squirmed away and jumped to her feet. "Let's behave, darling. I told the steward what we wanted for breakfast. He'll be here in a minute or two."

"In a half hour or two," grumbled Randall.

"You take your shower and get dressed." She started for the adjacent sitting room of their small suite on the Upper Deck of the S.S. *France*. "*L'Atlantique*, you know, the ship newspaper, it says there's a documentary movie in English on what to see in London. It's on Channel 8A. I don't want to miss it." Darlene delighted in the ship's closed-circuit television, which showed films throughout the day, and she would not let herself miss any of the luxuries of the voyage.

He looked across the stateroom at the porthole. The brown drape still covered it. He called after her, "Darlene, how's the weather?"

"The sun's trying to come out," she answered from the next room. "Sea is like glass."

Propped on an elbow, he surveyed their stateroom. It

was a functional double, with a long metal four-drawer chest between their beds, and on the chest a white telephone near his bed and a white-shaded lamp near hers. Strewn atop the striped brown armchair, her underthings —flimsy brassiere and panty hose. Near the foot of his bed, a stunted orange chair stood before the high mirror of the dressing table.

He listened to the sounds of the ship's throbbing engines, and the swishing liquid sounds of the sea parting before and closing around the ocean liner. Then he heard the crackling of the closed-circuit television from the next room, and the drone of a commentator's voice.

Randall fell back into his pillow and tried to bring himself into this fourth morning and fifth day of the crossing from New York to Southampton.

When he had agreed to become publicity director for the International New Testament and the project known as Resurrection Two, he had not intended to bring Darlene Nicholson along on the trip. He had wanted to go alone with Wheeler, and concentrate on the background that he must absorb and the work he had agreed to do. Darlene was too frivolous, too hedonistic, on a voyage to an undertaking such as this one. It was not that she was demanding of his time, but merely that she might divert him from his purpose with her inane lightweight chatter and ever-present sexuality. Moreover, her presence might prove an embarrassment. Wheeler and his people, and certainly those specialists and experts, scholars and theologians, connected with Resurrection Two in Amsterdam, would have nothing in common with a girl like Darlene. Randall guessed that she would be as suited to that company and scene as, say, a chorus girl or striptease performer at a Catholic raffle.

It was not that Darlene looked cheap, but rather that she was gaudy, showy, somewhat mindless, with no sense of occasion. As a matter of fact, she was attractive and she exuded sensuality. She was tall, with the flat, elongated, bony figure of a high-fashion model, except for her breasts, which were firm and pear-shaped and which were always evident in the low-cut gowns and blouses she wore and in the clinging sweaters she collected by the dozens. Her blonde hair was shoulder-length, her blue eyes set a shade too close together, her cheeks becomingly hollow, her skin fair, her mouth small with full lips. She walked in a kind of slithering glide, so that all the right parts of the body—breasts, hips, thighs, buttocks—moved in the right ways, or at least in ways that always provoked men to turn around. She had the longest legs that Randall had ever seen on a girl. Outside of bed, she was restless, useless, dumb, flighty. In bed, she was a mink, tireless, inventive, pleasure-giving, fun. The center of her intelligence, Randall once concluded, was entirely in her vagina.

She had given him what he needed when he had found her, but she was not the companion he wanted for the exciting and emotional journey into faith on which he was about to embark.

He had offered her every alternative. Since he would be abroad no more than a month or two, and would be too busy to give her any attention during that time, he had begged her to go back to Kansas City and visit her parents, family, high school friends. He would pay her way and her support while he was gone, and upon his return she could rejoin him in New York. She would not have it. He offered her a trip to Las Vegas and Los Angeles, or a month's vacation in Hawaii, or a six weeks' tour of South America. But it was no, no, no, Steve, I want to be with you, I'll kill myself if I can't be with you.

So he sighed, surrendered, and signed her on as his secretary, and he knew that no one was fooled, and finally he didn't care. As a matter of fact, there were some advantages. Well, one. He hated to go to bed alone. It was, after drinking, a time when he always felt sorry for himself. Darlene was a wonderful diversion. Last night she had been at her best, everything going, everything in motion, hands, legs, hips and ass, and when he had eventually erupted, he had thought he'd be blown straight out the porthole.

In the week before sailing, except for the decision to

take Darlene along, there had been few other personal
decisions to make, but somehow he had been occupied
daily, from dawn to midnight, setting his house and office
in order. Following Wheeler's thunderous revelation about
the Ostia Antica discovery establishing for the first time
the irrefutable historicity of Christ, he had been brimming with curiosity and impatient to learn every detail of
the secret find. Wheeler had put him off. There would be
plenty of hours for a more thorough briefing during their
ocean crossing, and full details would be waiting for Randall when he reached Amsterdam. Randall had been eager
to inform Wanda, Joe Hawkins, and his publicity staff
about their new account, but he had promised Wheeler
to hold back until advance copies of the International
New Testament were off the presses and until the board
of publishers gave permission. Most of all, Randall had
wanted to pass on the revelation to his father and to Tom
Carey, sensing what this earthshaking news would do for
each of them, yet he had given his pledge to keep his
silence, and he had kept it.

Each day he had telephoned Oak City, speaking to his
mother or to Clare, and he was reassured that his father,
although still partially paralyzed, was gradually gaining
strength and recovering. He had telephoned San Francisco once. With difficulty, he had explained to Judy that
his plan to have her in New York for two weeks during
the summer would have to be postponed. He had told
her that he would be going abroad on a special assignment,
but promised that somehow they would have their time
together in the fall. Then he had asked his daughter to
put her mother on the line. He had wanted to know
whether Barbara had changed her mind about filing for a
divorce. Barbara had replied quietly that she had not.
She would be meeting with an attorney next week. Very
well, Randall had told her coldly, he would instruct Thad
Crawford to contest the action.

The following morning, Randall had consulted with
Crawford and outlined his case, while his attorney had
tugged at his tufts of white sideburns and tried to dis-
suade Randall from challenging his wife. When Randall

remained adamant, Crawford had reluctantly started to take notes for the inevitable court appearances and agreed to file the counter suit. During the hectic week there had been several more conferences with Crawford and Ogden Towery's two attorneys, to iron out certain unresolved points concerning Cosmos Enterprises' take-over of Randall Associates. Painfully, Randall had de-termined to telephone Jim McLoughlin in Washington, D.C., and arrange a meeting. The least Jim deserved was a personal explanation of the reason why Randall was reversing himself and turning down The Raker Institute account. Jim would not understand, but the effort must be made. Unfortunately, Jim McLoughlin was already off somewhere on his highly confidential mission and could not be reached. He would not be back in Washington for several months. Randall left word for McLoughlin to tele-phone Thad Crawford. There was no other option. Mc-Loughlin would have to learn the bad news in the worst way.

When sailing day arrived, Steve Randall finally wel-comed it.

Now, lying on his stateroom bed, he rolled over on his side. Next to the telephone rested the pile of souvenirs and mementos Darlene had been collecting during the crossing. Randall groped past the telephone and picked up the sheaf of programs that scheduled each day's events since they had been on shipboard. There were five of these four-page leaflets, the first two pages in English, the last two in French. Four of them represented activities that had been available the past four days aboard, and the fifth one outlined today's program. There would be none to-morrow morning, for they were arriving in Southampton at daybreak.

Spreading out the programs like a hand of oversized playing cards, Randall could see how little they really represented his own activities on the crossing. Yet, each one jogged his memory. It had been a fine sea voyage so far, both restful and intellectually stimulating. Except for one uncomfortable experience on the very first day, shortly after boarding, just before sailing, it had been a perfect trip.

The first day. He studied the program, imprinted on top with the words S.S. FRANCE, and decorated with drawings of the Statue of Liberty, the Eiffel Tower, and the S.S. *France*. The first day.

EVENTS DU JOUR

FRIDAY, JUNE 7
CLOCKS ARE SET AHEAD 15 MINUTES AT 6 P.M.

AFTERNOON

2:30 P.M.   SAILING FROM NEW YORK

4:00 P.M.   TEA WITH MUSIC
Fontainebleau Lounge, Verandah Deck Amidships.

He laid the program aside, and relived what he could remember of his own first *Events du Jour,* relived it in flashes and glimpses again.

After going up the steep gangplank to first class, trailing behind Darlene, her get-up attracting the attention of other male passengers, ship's officers (she bra-less under a sheer blouse, with wide leather belt, short, short silk skirt, black stockings, high patent leather boots), they had been directed to George L. Wheeler's bon voyage party in a private room next to the theater entrance on the Verandah Deck.

Wheeler's wife was off with their sons at their Canadian summer house, so this was less a social than a professional and business bon voyage. The private room was packed with the seraphic men and Salvation Army sweet ladies from Mission House. Yet, there were some new faces that Randall had not seen before, definitely professorial or theological types, mostly with their middle-aged wives. Passing into the room with Darlene on his arm, accepting champagne being proffered by white uniformed stewards, but rejecting the hors d'oeuvres, introducing his "secretary" to anyone he recognized, Randall noticed Naomi Dunn standing not far from the ebullient Wheeler.

Randall had just started toward her when Wheeler spotted him and leaped over to pump his hand. "The beginning of a history-making trip, Steve, history-making!" he exclaimed. "And this pretty young lady—is she your secretary, the one you were telling me about?"

Nervously, Randall went through the introductions. The publisher was definitely intrigued by Darlene, whom he'd previously known only secondhand from Towery's dossier. "You are embarking on God's work, Miss Nicholson. In assisting Mr. Randall, you will be performing a service for mankind. I don't think you know anyone here. . . . Steve, do you mind if I introduce your lovely lady around?"

Wheeler was off with Darlene, and Randall found himself momentarily alone with Naomi Dunn. She stood taut and constrained, her back to a tapestry on the wall, sipping from her champagne glass.

"Hello, Naomi—may I call you Naomi?"

"Why not? We'll be working closely together."

"I hope so. Good of you to come and see us off."

She smiled. "I'm sorry, but I've not come to see you off. I'm traveling with you and Mr. Wheeler."

Randall did not conceal his surprise. "George hadn't mentioned it. I'm delighted."

"Mr. Wheeler never travels far without me. I am his memory bank, encyclopedia, and handy concordance to the New Testament. Mr. Wheeler knows all there is to know about publishing. When it comes to biblical background, he relies upon me. I am to be your mentor during much of this voyage."

"I'm pleased, most pleased," Randall said.

With faint amusement, Naomi examined his face. "Are you?" She peered past him. "I had better circulate. Lesson One begins tomorrow afternoon."

Five minutes later, Wheeler had Randall by the elbow and was drawing him to a corner of the room, whispering above the din, "Two personages you must meet. Extremely important to our future. They know our secret, of course, support it. They're really part of the project.

Without them we would be helpless. Dr. Stonehill of the American Bible Society, and Dr. Evans of the National Council of Churches."

Dr. Stonehill, a representative of the American Bible Society, was bald, somber, a trifle pompous. He was also enamored of statistics.

"Practically every church in the United States supports our work and contributes to our budget," he told Randall. "Our principal business is dispensing Bibles. Each year, we supply to member churches copies of the Scriptures which are printed without notes or commentaries. We publish Bibles, or biblical extracts, in twelve hundred different languages. Recently, in a single year, along with the United Bible Society, we distributed 150,000,000 copies of the scriptures around the world. In a single year, mind you. We are proud of that."

He appeared rooster-pleased, as if he personally had been responsible for those 150,000,000 Bibles. Randall did not know what to say. "Impressive," he mumbled.

"There is a reason for this universal acceptance," said Dr. Stonehill. "The Bible is a book for all men and all seasons. Perhaps this is because, as Pope Gregory put it, the Bible is a stream wherein the elephant may swim and the lamb may wade. From the sixth-century Gregory, you know."

Randall knew. His head swam.

"With the discovery, the New Testament will be enhanced," Dr. Stonehill went on ponderously, "and our Society's distribution will be increased tenfold, I predict. Until the present, there were 7,959 verses in the New Testament. But with the addition of—I dare not even mention the latest gospel by name yet—but with its addition to the canonical verses, enthusiasm for Our Lord will know no bounds. The King James Version, you know, has Jesus speaking 36,450 words. But now, now—"

Now, Randall wanted only to be rescued.

Minutes later, pleading thirst, he sought any oasis, but soon found himself again in the grasp of Wheeler and in the presence of Dr. Evans, head of the National Council of Churches.

Dr. Evans was better. He was only semibald, not at all somber, and rumbling with controlled ardor. He was likable, and what he was saying was more intriguing to Randall than Dr. Stonehill's statistics, especially in these distracting surroundings.

"The National Council of Churches," Dr. Evans was saying, "is the official agency for thirty-three church commissions—Protestant, Eastern Orthodox, one Catholic—in the United States. No new Bible venture in America can be totally successful without our full backing. We have been represented from the start in Mr. Wheeler's project, and we are fully satisfied that Professor Monti has made the most significant archeological find in the history of Christianity. There is no parallel to it. The importance of this fifth gospel discovery exceeds by far the discoveries of the Dead Sea Scrolls in Israel and the Nag Hamadi papyri in Egypt. The full import of this discovery cannot yet be imagined."

"What is the full import?" asked Randall. "Of course, for a start, it proves that Jesus actually existed."

"Oh, it's not that," said Dr. Evans. "After all, only a small school of skeptics, mainly in Germany, ever denied there was such a person as Jesus. Most Bible scholars, in truth, were never deeply troubled about the historicity of Jesus. We have always believed that Our Lord's life was as well established as were the lives of Socrates, Plato, Alexander the Great. The Assyrians and Persians left us much less information about their famous leaders, yet we've never questioned their existence. As for Jesus, we've always reminded ourselves that the area of His activity was relatively confined, that the length of His ministry was extremely brief, that His followers were primarily simple people. We could not expect temples built, or statues made, to honor One whom many seemed to regard as a mere rural evangelist, One characterized unfairly by Shelley as only a parish demagogue. Even the death of Jesus, in the context of His time, was of slight importance."

Randall had not thought of that before. "You really think it was ignored?"

"When it happened? Certainly. From the standpoint of the Roman Empire, the trial of Jesus in Jerusalem was purely a minor local disturbance, of which the Romans were having hundreds. Even the Petronius report of Jesus' trial—for all its value to us today—was merely another routine report in 30 A.D. In fact, Mr. Randall, most biblical scholars have always thought it surprising and fortunate that anything was written about Jesus by people who had picked up information from those who had known Him. Yet, in the gospels, we did receive such testimony. Law courts have usually depended upon the testimony of witnesses as evidence of facts. The gospels gave us such evidence. Scholars always understood that biographical details about Jesus were scarce because the witnesses with their oral accounts—whom the gospel writers later drew upon—were not interested in Christ's biography but in His Messiahship. His followers felt no need to record history because to them history was about to end. They were not interested in how Jesus looked, but in what He did and said. They could conceive no need for preserving a life or description of Jesus, because they expected His immediate return 'on the clouds of heaven.' But laymen, ordinary people, have never understood this, and so skeptics and doubters have grown in number. To people of our time, who are biography and history educated, Jesus has become unreal, the fictional figure of a folktale, like Hercules or Paul Bunyan."

"And now, with the new Bible, you feel their doubts will be put to rest."

"Forever," said Dr. Evans finally. "With the advent of the new Bible, universal skepticism will cease. Jesus the Messiah will be fully accepted. The proof will be as strong as if He had been preserved in photographs or on film. Once it is known that Jesus had a brother who anticipated doubt by taking care to set down firsthand facts about His life, once it is known that shreds of manuscript have survived that bear an eyewitness account of His Ascension, the world will be thrilled and unalloyed belief restored everywhere. Yes, Mr. Randall, what our Mr. Wheeler and his colleagues are about to introduce to the world will not only sweep away distrust but will also inspire a millennium of faith and hope among men. For centuries, human beings have wished to believe in a Redeemer. Now, at last, they can. You are embarking on a memorable journey, Mr. Randall. We all are. It is for that journey that I wish you bon voyage."

Dazed, still unable to absorb the implications of the find, Randall sought respite in another champagne and then simple reality in the person of Darlene Nicholson.

Searching, he located her near the door. A French officer had just bent closer to her, to whisper something. She nodded, and hastily followed the officer out of the private room. Curious about this sudden departure, Randall got a refill of champagne, and sipping it, he decided to find out where she had gone.

Pushing his way through the crowd of visitors, he emerged into the elevator area outside. Darlene was nowhere to be seen. Preparing to search for her in the Main Lounge, he saw her standing before the open windows of the Verandah Deck, and she was not alone. She was deep in conversation with a young man. Darlene was twenty-four, and the earnest young man could not have been more than a year or two older. A baggy seersucker suit did not hide his skinny frame. He had sandy hair, a bristling crew cut, and an undershot jaw. He seemed to be pleading with Darlene.

Then, from memory of a snapshot that Darlene had once teasingly shown him, Randall recognized the young man. This was Roy Ingram, her old boy friend in Kansas City. He was an accountant or at least planning to be one. Before Randall could speculate on his presence here, Darlene noticed Randall, waved jerkily, and started leading the young man inside to meet him.

Randall sought a means of escape, but it was too late. The two were upon him. Darlene was holding a gardenia corsage. Randall could not believe that they made those corsages any longer.

Darlene was wearing a pleased smile. "Roy, this is my boss, Mr. Steven Randall. . . . Uh, this is Roy Ingram, a friend of mine from Kansas City."

Randall shook his hand. "Yes, Miss Nicholson has told me about you."

Roy Ingram was ill at ease. "Glad to meet you, sir. Darlene wrote me about her job with you, and said she was going to Europe on this trip to work for you. I—I thought I'd just stop by to say—to wish her a good trip."

"That's gallant of you," said Randall, "coming all the way from Kansas to say bon voyage."

Ingram blushed, and stammered, "Well, I—I had some business in New York, also, but yes, thanks."

"I'll leave you two," said Randall. "I'd better get back to the party."

Once safely inside the private room, Randall recalled when he had first heard of this Roy Ingram. It had been the evening of the day he had met Darlene Nicholson. She had been one of several girls sent over by an agency as applicants for a secretarial opening. Randall had been working in his office, and he'd buzzed for Wanda to pick up some papers. Wanda had come in, and through the open door behind her, Randall had seen Darlene sitting across from Wanda's desk with her long legs crossed.

"Who is she?" Randall had asked.

"One of the girls applying for the job. I've been interviewing her. She won't make it."

"Maybe she's applying for the wrong position. Send her in, Wanda, and no cracks, please. And remember to shut the door."

It had been almost too easy, after that. Her name was Darlene, and she had left Kansas City two months earlier because it was smothering her creative bent. She had always wanted to be on New York television. There had been promises and prospects, but no performances, and she was almost out of money. So she had thought that she might like to work for a famous firm that handled famous people, because that might be fun. Randall liked her easy manner and those breasts and long legs. He had served her a drink and dropped a few names of clients and friends. He had told her that he was too impressed with her personality and intellect to let her waste her talents on office drudgery. He would find something better for her. And by the way, was she free for dinner this evening?

After dinner, she had gone back to his apartment with him. That was when he'd inquired whether she had a steady boy friend. She had admitted to a boy friend in Kansas City, a Roy, but she had broken off with him before leaving home for New York, because he was too immature and dull.

"Would you like someone steady here?" he had asked her.

"It would depend."

"Someone who'd take care of you?" he had persisted.

"If I liked him, why not?"

"Do you like me?"

She had spent the night with him. The next day she had moved in. He had always thought it a fair bargain. Darlene had desired leisure and luxury and glamorous people and expensive surroundings, and these she had. Randall had needed a female companion with a youthful body and no emotional involvement, and these he had. No question, a fair bargain. Yet, now that he had seen her with her loyal boy friend and contemporary, he suffered a pang of guilt.

A few minutes later she joined Randall in the private room where the party now was, if anything, noisier. She still seemed gratified and she was still carrying the silly gardenia corsage.

"I got rid of Roy," she said. "Were you jealous?"

Stupid baby, he thought. "What did he want?" Randall asked.

"He wanted me not to go on this trip with you. He wanted me to go back to Kansas City with him. He wants to marry me."

"What did you tell him?"

"I told him I wanted to go on this trip with you. Now, aren't you pleased, honey?"

His guilt had grown. He had nothing to offer her in the long run. Nevertheless, she was rejecting someone and something permanent and decent for this arrangement with him. It wasn't right. Still, it wasn't wrong, either.

After all, putting a penis inside a young woman who wants it was hardly an act of corruption. If there was any corruption, it was in using his image as a father figure, as well as his wealth and power, to take advantage of her neurotic weakness. She belonged with someone her own age who cared for her and would give her three children and a new washing machine and dryer for life. She belonged with someone like Roy Ingram. But she preferred a bon voyage party on the S.S. *France*. Well, it worked for her and it worked for him, and to hell with morality.

"Come on, Darlene," he said, "the champagne's on the house."

That was what he could recollect of the first day aboard. Then, the second day, a day at sea.

Lying on the stateroom bed, he picked up the second program and skimmed it.

EVENTS DU JOUR

SATURDAY, JUNE 8

MORNING

7:30 A.M. to 9:30 A.M.	BREAKFAST Chambord Dining Room.
10:00 A.M.	CALISTHENICS by the Swimming Pool, "D" Deck, with your instructor.

He tossed the program aside, and revived what he could of the second day.

Wheeler and Naomi Dunn, who had separate bedrooms in the luxurious Normandie Suite on the Upper Deck, came down and joined Randall and Darlene as they were finishing their light breakfast. After promising Wheeler and Naomi to begin working with them in an hour, Randall had taken Darlene on a brisk hike around the Verandah Deck, and then he had placed a ten-dollar bet for each of them on the distance that the ship would cover between noon today and noon tomorrow. They had ridden the elevator down to "D" Deck, and he'd changed into trunks and Darlene into the briefest bikini he had ever seen. They had gone swimming for thirty minutes. After that, Darlene was off, either on a tour of the ship or to see a movie or to learn clay pigeon shooting on the Boat Deck. She had no interest in his work or in serious conversation or in reading. She was satisfied with any activity that was physical, that and meeting famous people, if any could be found.

Randall made his way to a small secluded room, the Salon Monaco, just beyond the Library and Writing Room, and there Wheeler, coatless, tie loosened, was waiting at a card table with Naomi Dunn, who was removing research notes from an alligator portfolio.

Sitting with them, Randall soon forgot about the modern floating palace that surrounded him. Gradually, he found himself slipping backwards in time, backwards through the corridors of many centuries, to a rawer age, an ancient, primitive, turbulent age, to early first-century Palestine where Jews suffered the Roman occupation.

It was George L. Wheeler, peeling and cutting one of the Cuban cigars that he had purchased on shipboard, who had begun the briefing.

"Steve, to comprehend fully and appreciate the importance of Professor Monti's discovery at Ostia Antica, you have to realize how truly little we've known Jesus Christ until this discovery. Oh, if you accept the four gospels as something handed down by God, as revelation, and accept their every sentence purely on faith, then naturally you are satisfied that you know enough about Jesus. But most people have long ago refused to do that.

"Now, despite what Dr. Evans told you at the cocktail party about the majority of biblical scholars always having believed in the existence of Jesus, there has been less confidence in that likelihood among religious rationalists and secular historians. Understandably. The minute that you demand proof, a verifiable history of the life of Jesus set against His actual surroundings, you run into trouble. Ernest Renan tartly reminded us that the known facts about Jesus would fill less than a single page.

Many scholars believe the facts would hardly make up a single sentence. Other scholars—Reimarus and Bauer in Germany, Pierson and Naber in the Netherlands—felt not even one word of fact could be set down about Jesus because they insisted that He was a myth. Yet, in the last one hundred years, at least seventy thousand so-called biographies have been written and published on Jesus."

"But how could that be?" asked Randall. "On what were these biographies based? On the four gospels?"

"Exactly," said Wheeler. "On the writings of four disciples—Matthew, Mark, Luke, John—and on little else. These four gospel writers had not lived with Jesus, observed Him, seen Him in the flesh. They had merely collected oral traditions, some writings, from the early Christian community and transcribed them on papyrus decades after the supposed death of Jesus. All of this was frozen into the immutable canon that became our New Testament in about the third or fourth century."

George L. Wheeler puffed his cigar, picked through the papers Naomi had laid before him, and resumed.

"If we based our knowledge of Christ's existence and His life on purely Christian evidence, gospel evidence, what have we got? The New Testament story covers a span of no more than one hundred years. Of the twenty-seven books of the New Testament, only four really consider the life Jesus lived, and these four represent less than forty-five percent of the entire New Testament. But what do they tell us of an actual life? They sketchily report on the first and twelfth years of Jesus' being and then skip to the last two years or so, and that is the extent of it. Actually, nine tenths of His life was not reported. We are told little of His childhood or of His youth through His twenties. We are not told exactly when He was born, where He studied, what His trade was. We are given no physical description of Him. Based solely on Christian sources, what we know of Jesus could be compressed into one paragraph. . . . Naomi, read Steve what you have."

Randall turned his attention to Naomi Dunn. Her features were emotionless. Her eyes were concentrated on a sheet of paper she held before her.

Without meeting Randall's gaze, she said, "From the gospel writers, this is what we have in a capsule." She began to read aloud in a monotone. " 'Jesus was born near the end of the reign of Herod the Great in either Nazareth or Bethlehem. He may have been taken for protection to Egypt. He probably spent His childhood in a town of Galilee known as Nazareth. Only twelve words are devoted to His childhood, and these state that He grew, waxed strong in spirit, was filled with wisdom. Around the age of twelve, He went to Jerusalem and into the temple to meet with the doctors. After that, there is a void. No more information until Jesus is about thirty-two years old. Then we learn He was baptized by John the Baptist, who had been sent by God to prepare for the appearance of the Messiah. Once baptized, Jesus retired to the wilderness to meditate for forty days.' "

"That going off into the wilderness," Randall interrupted. "Did more than one gospel writer record it?"

"Mark, Matthew, and Luke did," said Naomi, "but not John." She concentrated on her paper again, and read, " 'Emerging from the wilderness, Jesus returned to Galilee to undertake His ministry. He made two tours in and around Capernaum, and in a third tour He crossed the Sea of Galilee to preach in Gadara and Nazareth. Later, He traveled north, to preach in Tyre and Sidon. Finally, He went back to Jerusalem. He withdrew to a place outside Jerusalem. He remained in touch with His disciples. On the eve of the Passover, He entered Jerusalem for the last time. He overturned the tables of the money changers in the temple. He taught in the temple. He took refuge on the Mount of Olives. With His twelve disciples, He had supper in the home of a friend. In the garden of Gethsemane, He was arrested, and found guilty of blasphemy by the council of the Sanhedrin. He was given a hearing before Pontius Pilate, the Roman governor, and sentenced to death. He was crucified on the hill of Golgotha.' "

Naomi lowered the sheet of paper.

She glanced at Wheeler. "That is the gospel history of Jesus the man, without the sayings, the miracles, and ifs and maybes. That is all hundreds of millions of Christians have been able to know of Jesus, as a person, in almost two thousand years."

Randall stirred himself. "I must admit, that was very little upon which to build a church and hardly enough to prove that Jesus was the Son of God."

"Or to keep millions as believers so long," said Wheeler. "And recently, since the onslaught of the rationalists and the coming of the scientific age, not enough, not enough to keep the faithful satisfied."

"Still, there were outside non-Christian writings about Christ," Randall recalled. "Josephus, for one, and some Roman scribes."

"Ah, Steve, but still not enough and not conclusive. Christian evidence is relatively detailed compared to non-Christian evidence. Our Roman evidence speaks of the existence of Christians, but gives no description of Christ. However, we can safely assume that if Christianity was acknowledged by its enemies, there must have existed a Christ. In fact, we do have two Jewish sources which speak of Christ." Wheeler placed his cigar stub on a tray. "You mentioned Flavius Josephus, the self-styled priest and Jewish historian who became a Roman. His life spanned the years 37 A.D. to around 100 A.D. If we could trust the extant manuscripts of his writings, we would have factual confirmation of the gospels. Josephus finished writing his *Antiquities of the Jews* in 93 A.D. He apparently mentioned Christ in two passages. . . . Naomi, do you have them handy?"

Naomi Dunn had already located her research. "The longer one of Josephus' two passages reads, 'There arose at this time Jesus a wise man, if it is right to call him a man. For he was the doer of extraordinary acts, a teacher of men who are glad to receive the truth, and he drew to himself many Jews and many of the Greek race. He was the Christ. And when Pilate at the instance of the foremost men among us had sentenced him to be crucified, those who had first loved him did not cease to do so, for on the third day he appeared to them again, alive, since the divine prophets had foretold this and ten thousand other marvels about him. And even now the tribe of Christians named after him is not extinct.' Next, the second passage, which—"

Wheeler held up his hand. "That'll do it, Naomi." He addressed himself to Randall. "Now, if Josephus had actually written that himself, that would be the earliest reference to Jesus in secular writings. Unfortunately, I don't know a single scholar who believes Josephus wrote that passage in its entirety. None consider it genuine as it stands, because it is too pro-Christian to have been written by an early Jewish writer. It's simply too much to swallow, a non-Christian historian referring to Jesus as 'a wise man, if it is right to call him a man' and stating, 'He was the Christ.' This latter is regarded as an interpolation by a Christian scribe in medieval times who was trying to create a historical Jesus. On the other hand, several of our consultants on Resurrection Two—among them Dr. Bernard Jeffries, whom you will meet—are convinced that Josephus did refer to Jesus twice, but they also agree that what Josephus wrote was evidently uncomplimentary and some centuries later was touched up by a pious Christian scribe who didn't like the passage."

"In other words, your scholars do feel Josephus himself acknowledged the existence of Jesus?"

"Yes. But they are only speculating, so it proves nothing. We are concerned with historical fact in secular writings. The other Jewish source on Jesus is the Talmud, which Jewish scribes began to put into writing in the second century. These rabbinical writings were based on hearsay and were, of course, unfavorable to Jesus, reporting that He practiced magic and was finally hanged on charges of heresy and leading people astray. More trustworthy are the pagan or Roman mentions of Christ. The first was—"

He scratched a white eyebrow, trying to remember, and Naomi said quickly, "The first was Thallus, in his three-volume history. Probably written the middle of the first century."

"Yes. The first was Thallus. He wrote of the darkness that settled on Palestine when Jesus died. He thought an eclipse caused the darkness, although later Christian authors insisted it was actually a miracle. Next, Pliny the Younger, when he was governor of Bithynia, in a letter to the Emperor Trajan—around 110 A.D.—spoke of contending with the sect of Christians in his community. He considered this Christianity a crude superstition, but wrote that the followers appeared to be harmless, gathering before daybreak to sing 'a hymn to Christ as to a god.' Next, there was Tacitus writing in his *Annals* sometime between 110 A.D. and 120 A.D. The Emperor Nero, to absolve himself of having burned Rome, had blamed the conflagration on the Christians. . . . Naomi, let me have that passage."

Wheeler took two typewritten pages from her, then said to Randall, "I want you to hear at least a portion of what Tacitus wrote about that event. 'Nero fastened the guilt and inflicted the most exquisite tortures on a class hated for their abominations, called Christians by the populace. Christus, from whom the name had its origin, suffered the extreme penalty during the reign of Tiberius at the hands of one of our procurators, Pontius Pilatus, and a most mischievous superstition, thus checked for the moment, broke out not only in Judaea, the first source of the evil, but even in Rome. . . .' "

Wheeler looked up. "Finally, we have that gossipy historian, Suetonius, in his *Lives of the Caesars,* written at some time between 98 A.D. and 138 A.D. Speaking of the Emperor Claudius, Suetonius wrote, 'He banished from Rome all the Jews, who were continually making disturbances at the instigation of Chrestus.' And that's the bulk of it, Steve, the only real non-Christian mentions of Christus or Chrestus or Christ, most of them between a half century to more than a century after Jesus was supposed to have died. So what we've inherited from Jewish and Roman history is that probably the catalyst of this new religion was named Christ. If we wanted more, we had to depend on highly biased sources, namely the four gospel writers. We simply did not possess an objective factual biography of Jesus Christ, written by one of His contemporaries. We had only a growing cult converted by their belief in a possible myth."

"Still," said Randall, "the lack of real biographical information is not necessarily suspect. As Dr. Evans pointed out to me, the period of Jesus' preaching was considered so brief, His death so unimportant to the Romans, that there was no reason to record any of this."

"True," Wheeler agreed. "I think Millar Burrows, the expert on the Dead Sea Scrolls, put it best. He pointed out that if Jesus had been a revolutionary with a wide following, had fought the Roman legions and tried to set up His own kingdom, there would certainly be coins and inscriptions on stone to report His revolution and its failure. But, said Burrows, Jesus was just a wandering preacher. He wrote no books, built no buildings, organized no institutions. He simply left to Caesar what was Caesar's. He sought only to establish a kingdom of heaven on earth, and hoped that some poor fisherman would carry His message to mankind by word of mouth. As Burrows said, Herod's reign left its testimony in tumbled columns. The beginning of Christianity has no such archeological proof, for Jesus left no monument but the Christian Church."

"And now, almost overnight, the world will learn otherwise," mused Randall. "The world will learn Jesus' biography was written by two persons—James and Petronius—who knew him in the flesh. George, it *is* a miracle."

"It's a miracle of chance, of wild luck," said Wheeler. "Jesus had a brother who was close enough to Him, who revered Him, who was sufficiently impressed by Him and His cause to commit the life of Jesus to writing. As a result, two months from now, the Gospel According to James will fall upon an unsuspecting world like a thunderbolt. But if James were not enough, the power struggle in Rome in 30 A.D. at the very time Jesus was crucified gave us proof of Jesus Christ's being and His last days in Jerusalem. And we have this from an unprejudiced pagan source."

Randall had finished lighting his pipe. "You haven't told me much about that yet, George."

"You'll get the whole story in the next weeks. For now, briefly, here is how the Petronius Parchment probably came into being. As you know, while Jesus was preaching in the Roman colony of Palestine, the emperor of Rome was the elderly Tiberius. For various reasons, Tiberius preferred to live on the isle of Capri. As his representative in Rome, he left the prefect of his Praetorian Guard, the ambitious Lucius Aelius Sejanus. Emperor Tiberius ruled through Sejanus, but actually Sejanus was the man who ran the Roman Empire and he planned to get rid of Tiberius and take over the throne for himself. In the colonies and provinces of Rome, Sejanus set up governors who would be loyal to him and he had a network of centurion captains who reported to him regularly on any disloyalties, defections, or rebellions in the Empire. It was Sejanus who gave Pontius Pilate his post in Palestine. And apparently, the officers of the Roman soldiers under Pilate were ordered to report regularly—sometimes secretly—to Sejanus by courier on every disturbance, trial, execution, no matter how minor, taking place in the province."

Randall was fascinated. "So when Jesus went on trial and was crucified, even though it was a small affair, a Roman officer routinely reported it to Sejanus in Rome?"

"Something like that," said Wheeler. "Either Pilate himself approved and sent the routine report of Jesus' trial to the governor of Damascus, who in turn sent it on to Sejanus in Rome. Or Pilate did not bother to pass the report along, but the captain of his personal guard, who led Jesus to the Cross and supervised His Crucifixion, wrote the report in Pilate's name and sent it by military courier to Sejanus. And this captain under Pilate was named Petronius. But here is the interesting thing. Sejanus probably never saw the report."

"Never saw it?" said Randall. "What do you mean?"

"According to the report, Jesus was supposedly executed on the seventh day of the Ides of April in the seventeenth year of the reign of Tiberius—that would have been 30 A.D. Well, by the time the report was ready to be sent, rumor had reached the colonies that Sejanus was in trouble with the emperor. This report on the Crucifixion of Jesus, along with other reports, was almost certainly held up until Sejanus' position could be assessed. Then, it must have been decided in Caesarea or Damascus that things had settled down in Rome and Sejanus was secure and still in power. So this report, with many others, was sent on. By the time the courier arrived by merchant ship at the port at Ostia in Italy, it must have been well into the following year, 31 A.D. The minute he landed, the courier learned from other soldiers and officers that Sejanus and all who communicated with him were under suspicion, and that Sejanus was truly on his way out."

"Was he actually?"

"Oh, yes," said Wheeler. "The emperor—Tiberius Caesar—had found out that Sejanus was trying to undermine his authority and take over, and so the emperor ordered Sejanus executed in October of 31 A.D. Realizing this was coming, fearful of delivering his confidential reports to Sejanus and taking the risk of incurring the emperor's wrath, the messenger probably left his reports, including the one on Christ's trial and Crucifixion, for safekeeping with some lesser officer of the Praetorian Guard or even with some civilian friend, and he returned to his term of duty in Palestine."

"I'm beginning to picture what may have happened," said Randall.

"We don't know with certainty," Wheeler reminded him, "but we can make some logical conjectures. The most likely one is that whoever was given the report on Christ held on to it after Sejanus was killed. Soon the report was put aside as outdated, and was forgotten. After the person to whom the report had been entrusted had died, a relative could have come across it, someone who was a secret Christian, and this convert would have preserved it along with the document that James wrote. Another and simpler theory is that the person who was originally given the report by the messenger became a Christian convert, and his most prized possessions would naturally have been

the Petronius Parchment and the Gospel According to
James. Either way, since Christians were being persecuted, these papers were sealed in the base of a statue
and hidden from the authorities, and with the passage of
decades and centuries, the base was buried under silt and
debris and lost—until Professor Monti excavated it six
years ago. Currently, the contents are leased to us, and
are still secret, but soon they will be made public and
become the property of the world in the pages of the International New Testament."

"Fantastic," said Randall. He scraped his chair closer
to the publisher. "Still, George, you haven't let me in fully
on the secret. The little you did reveal, at our first meeting, was obviously enough to make me set everything else
aside and go along with you. Now I'd like to be told the
rest."

Wheeler nodded understandingly. "Of course you
would, and you shall be told." He held up his forefinger.
"Not yet, though, Steve. We have reserved in Amsterdam
one galley proof for you. Once we arrive, you shall read
the Gospel According to James and the annotated material from the Petronius Parchment in their entirety. I'd
prefer not to spoil that first reading by dribbling out bits
and pieces of it. I hope you don't mind."

"I do mind, but I suppose I can wait a few days. At
least tell me this—What did Jesus look like?"

"Not as da Vinci, Tintoretto, Raphael, Vermeer, Ve-
ronese or Rembrandt depicted Him, I assure you. Not like
the figure on those store-bought religious crosses found in
millions of homes throughout the world. James, His brother, knew Him as a man, not a martyred matinee idol."
Wheeler smiled. "Patience, Steve—"

"What continues to haunt me," Randall interrupted,
"is what you told me about Jesus' surviving the Crucifixion.
Is that conjecture?"

"Absolutely not," said Wheeler emphatically. "James
was witness to the fact that Jesus did not die on the cross,
did not ascend to heaven—at least not in 30 A.D.—but
lived on to continue His missionary work. James gives

concrete evidence from eyewitnesses of Jesus' safe escape from Palestine—"

"Where did He go?"

"Caesarea, Damascus, Antioch, Cyprus, eventually to Rome itself."

"I still find that hard to believe. Jesus in Rome. It's incredible—"

"Steve, you will believe, you will have no doubts," said Wheeler with conviction. "Once you see the authenticated evidence with your own eyes, you will never question it again."

"And after Rome?" demanded Randall. "He was around fifty-four years old in Rome. Where did He go from there? When and where did He die?"

Abruptly, Wheeler lifted his huge bulk out of the chair. "You'll learn the answers in Amsterdam, at Resurrection Two in Amsterdam," Wheeler promised him. The publisher waved to someone in the doorway. "There's Miss Nicholson. I think it's time to take a break for lunch. The sitting is being announced."

That had been the second day on shipboard, what Randall recollected of it, and here he was, in bed, on the fifth and last full day on the S.S. *France.*

He heard Darlene's voice from the adjacent sitting room. "Steve, are you up? Breakfast is here!"

He sat up. Three of the ship's daily programs still lay on his lap.

EVENTS DU JOUR

SUNDAY, JUNE 9

That had been the third day, and at George L. Wheeler's insistence, a day of rest. At 11 A.M. Wheeler and Naomi and Darlene had attended the Protestant service in the ship's theater. Randall had avoided that to attend "Your French Lesson" in the Riviera Lounge. They had had a protracted lunch together in the Chambord Dining Room, the ship's mammoth restaurant. In the afternoon there had been bridge, wine tasting, cocktails in the

Cabaret de l'Atlantique, and after dinner in the Fontainebleau Lounge, the main one amidships, dancing and horse-racing games.

EVENTS DU JOUR

MONDAY, JUNE 10

That had been the fourth day, yesterday. Hours of questions and answers with Wheeler and Naomi Dunn on how previous new Bibles, from the King James Version to the modern Revised Standard Version, had been prepared, as indoctrination for an understanding of how the International New Testament had been and was being readied. The torrent of talk had left him fatigued, and he had drunk too much red wine and Scotch at the "Captain's Gala Dinner" in the evening.

EVENTS DU JOUR

TUESDAY, JUNE 11

Today.

He would learn, for the first time, the setup of Resurrection Two in Amsterdam, and he would be briefed on the consultants he would meet at the British Museum in London tomorrow, on his staff in Amsterdam, and on other consultants he was free to call upon for public relations copy in Paris, in Frankfurt and Mainz, and in Rome.

"Steve, your eggs will be cold!" Darlene's voice again.

He tossed aside the final daily program, and swung off the bed.

"Coming, honey!" he shouted.

The last day at sea had begun.

BY midafternoon, the three of them had moved outdoors and they were still talking. Darlene, when he had seen her a short time before, was playing Ping-Pong on the Verandah Deck with some oily Hungarian lecher. Now,

Randall was stretched on the pad of his deck chair, with Wheeler straddling the chair beside him, and Naomi shivering beneath a woolen maroon blanket in the third chair.

They were in the North Atlantic, nearing England, and except for a slight swell, the sea was smooth. Above them, dark mottled clouds had obscured the sun, and the air was cooler. Randall stared out at the horizon, mesmerized by the wake of white foam trailing the huge vessel. Idly, he fixed on the flagpole between the two masts, and wondered why the tricolor was missing, and immediately remembered that the flag was hoisted only when the ship was in port. Then, because Wheeler had resumed his orientation, Randall concentrated on what the publisher was saying.

"So now you have at least some idea of our headquarters situation in Amsterdam," Wheeler went on. "At this stage the problem that concerns us the most, and one I want to stress, is the problem of security. Picture our setup again. There stands the Grand Hotel Krasnapolsky, right on the busiest square of Amsterdam, right on the Dam, facing the royal palace. Resurrection Two occupies and controls two entire floors of the five stories of the Krasnapolsky. After we had renovated and occupied those two floors, the five of us directing the project—the five publishers—Dr. Emil Deichhardt of Germany, the president of our board, Sir Trevor Young of Great Britain, Monsieur Charles Fontaine of France, Signore Luigi Gayda of Italy, and yours truly, George L. Wheeler of the United States—we had to make our two fifths of the hotel airtight against leaks. After all, despite our two floors, it is still a public hotel, Steve. Believe me, once we were in full preparation, and then in production of our revised New Testament, we gave this problem of security an extraordinary amount of time. It was a formidable job to figure out how to plug the holes, shore up weaknesses, anticipate every conceivable danger."

"How well did you lick it?" Randall asked. "Is the Hotel Krasnapolsky absolutely secure?"

Wheeler shrugged. "I think so. I hope so."

Naomi inched herself up higher in her chair. "Steve,

you'll find Mr. Wheeler is unduly cautious and pessimistic about such matters. I can tell you, I have observed the operation in the Krasnapolsky. It is foolproof. It is an absolute fortress of security. The fact is that the operation has been in existence in that hotel for twenty months, and no one on the outside has the faintest notion of the magnitude of what has been taking place on the inside. . . . Mr. Wheeler, you must tell Steve your security record—not one word leaked to the press, or sold out to the television or radio media, or even gossiped about to the dissident clergy in this time."

"That's true," agreed Wheeler, scratching his neck. "Still, as we approach these last two crucial months, I worry. Secrecy becomes more important than ever. Despite the fact that we have the most experienced private security force ever assembled—guards and plainclothesmen recruited from those who have formerly been with the FBI, Scotland Yard, the Sûreté, this group headed up by a Dutchman, Inspector Heldering, a former officer at Interpol—I continue to worry. I mean, there have been rumors circulating about us, and tremendous pressure is building from the outside, in press and dissident clergy alike, to find out by any means what we are up to."

Something had caught Randall's ear for a second time. "The dissident clergy," repeated Randall. "I should think all the clergy, without exception, would want to cooperate with you in keeping this under wraps until the last minute. Clergymen, as a body, will benefit as much as the public when your New Testament appears."

Wheeler peered out to sea, and thought for a moment. "Have you ever heard of the Reverend Maertin de Vroome, pastor of the Westerkerk, that big church in Amsterdam?"

"I've read something about him"—Randall recalled his conversation with Tom Carey in Oak City—"and a friend of mine in my home town, a minister, is a great admirer of de Vroome."

"Well, I'm not an admirer of de Vroome, quite the opposite, but those young Turks in the clergy who want to overthrow the orthodox church, convert it into a com-

mune for social work and to the devil with faith and with
Christ—they are the ones who are backing de Vroome.
He's the big power in the Nederlands Hervormd Kerk—
the Dutch Reformed Church. And our Dominee de
Vroome—Dominee is his title—he is spreading his ten-
tacles everywhere, subverting and undermining Protestantism throughout the Western world. He is our biggest
threat."

Randall was bewildered. "Why should he be a threat
to you—to a group of Bible publishers bringing out a
revised New Testament?"

"Why? Because de Vroome is a heretic, a student of
form criticism, influenced by that other heretic, Rudolf
Bultmann, the German theologian. De Vroome is skeptical
about the events presented by the gospel writers. He believes the New Testament must be demythologized, shorn
of miracles—turning water into wine, feeding the multi-
tudes, raising Lazarus from the dead, the Resurrection,
the Ascension—before it can have meaning to modern
scientific man. He believes that nothing can be known of
the Jesus of history, he downgrades the existence of Jesus,
he even suggests that Jesus may have been invented as a
prop for Christianity's new message, and that the only
thing worthwhile is the message itself when made relevant and rational for modern man."

"You mean to say that all de Vroome believes in is
Christ's message?" asked Randall. "What would he like
to do with that message?"

"Well, based on his own interpretations of it, de
Vroome wants a social and political church, one interested mainly in our immediate life on earth, to the
exclusion of heaven, of Christ as the Messiah, of the
mysteries of faith. There is more. You will hear of it soon.
But you can see how such an anarchist as de Vroome
would view the Gospel According to James, the Petronius
Parchment, in fact our entire International New Testament
with its revelation of a real Christ. De Vroome would see
instantly that our revelation would reinforce the church
hierarchy and orthodoxy, and turn wavering clergymen
and congregations away from religious radicalism and

back to the solidity of the old church. This might bring
an end to de Vroome's ambitions and bring a halt to his
ecclesiastical revolution."

"Does de Vroome know about Resurrection Two?" Randall wondered.

"We have reason to believe that he suspects what we
are up to in the Hotel Krasnapolsky. He has dozens of
spies, more spies than we have security guards. We are
only certain that to date he does not know the details
of our discovery. If he did, he would have been heard
from months ago, undercutting us before we could give
the public our entire story and proof. But now, with
every day, it becomes more dangerous. For as the New
Testament comes off the presses, there are more pages
available, and some of them may fall into de Vroome's
hands before our publication date. If this happened, he
could harm us—perhaps even destroy us—through clever
advance misrepresentation and distortion. A leak to the
press or to de Vroome could kill us. I tell you of this,
Steve, because the moment that de Vroome knows of
your existence, your position with us, you will become
one of his prime targets."

"He'll get nothing from me," said Randall. "No one
will."

"I just wanted to warn you. You'll have to keep your
guard up every minute of every day." Wheeler was lost in
thought again. "Let me see whether I've omitted anything more you should know about Resurrection Two."

As it turned out, there was an hour more of information that Wheeler had omitted.

The publisher went on about the inner circle of personalities most directly responsible for the International
New Testament. There was the Italian archeologist, Professor Augusto Monti, who had made the sensational discovery. Professor Monti, connected with the University of
Rome, dwelt with his younger daughter, Angela Monti,
in a villa somewhere in Rome. Then there was the
Frenchman, Professor Henri Aubert, a profound and incomparable scientist who had authenticated the papyrus
and parchment fragments in his Carbon 14 Dating De-

partment of the Centre National de la Recherche Scientifique in Paris. He and his well-bred wife, Gabrielle, were charming company.

Next, said Wheeler, there was Herr Karl Hennig, the renowned German printer who had his presses in Mainz and his business offices in Frankfurt. Hennig, a bachelor, was a Gutenberg scholar and a benefactor of the Gutenberg Museum located in the neighborhood of his printing press. Finally, there was Dr. Bernard Jeffries, the aged theologian, textual critic, and Aramaic expert, who headed the Honour School of Theology at Oxford, as well as his young assistant and protégé, Dr. Florian Knight, who had been doing research for Dr. Jeffries in the British Museum. Dr. Jeffries had been director of the international team that had translated the Gospel According to James.

Eventually, Wheeler struggled out of his deck chair. "I am exhausted. I think I'll nap a few hours before we meet for dinner. Last night on board, so no dinner jacket. Look, Steve, our Drs. Jeffries and Knight are the first ones on our team you'll be seeing in London tomorrow. I think Naomi can brief you on them adequately." He half pivoted. "Naomi, I commend our eminent publicist unto thy hands. Carry on."

Randall watched the publisher march off, and then his eyes met Naomi's across the empty red-cushioned deck chair.

Suddenly, Naomi lifted her blanket and pushed it away. She sat straight up. "Another minute out here, and I'll be an icicle," she said. "If you need a drink half as much as I do, you'll offer to buy me one."

Randall rose to his feet. "Be my guest. Where shall we go? Would you prefer the Riviera Lounge?"

She shook her head. "Too big, too crowded, too much string music." Her normally rigid features softened. "The Atlantique is more intimate." She removed her horn-rimmed glasses. "Wouldn't you like something more intimate?"

THEY were in a booth of the Cabaret de l'Atlantique, near the postage stamp of a dance floor where a lone French pianist was playing the haunting Parisian song, *"Mélan-colie."* Each was finishing a second Scotch-on-the-rocks, and Randall was feeling relaxed.

As they made small talk, Randall took in the Cabaret de l'Atlantique once more. It had become his favorite refuge on the S.S. *France*. They were seated between the two bars. The drinking bar was the one up ahead, se-cluded in a dark recess. Three or four passengers were astride stools, and the handsome bartender, who looked as if he had been a leading man of the Comédie Française, was identifying for a customer the miniature flags of all nations which decorated the wall of the bar. Behind Ran-dall was the horseshoe-shaped food bar which opened at midnight and where a perfectly type-cast French chef dispensed onion soup, hot dogs on rolls, and similar de-lights, to the night people.

"Anyway, Steve, we put in at Southampton at six o'clock in the morning," he heard Naomi say. "After pass-port check, we disembark for customs around eight in the morning. I don't know whether Mr. Wheeler has a limousine and driver to take us to London or we're taking the boat train to Victoria Station. Once we get to London, we'll check you into the Dorchester. Mr. Wheeler and I are staying only long enough to take you over to the British Museum and get you started with Dr. Jeffries and Dr. Knight. When we're sure you're settled, we'll leave you. We have to get right over to Amsterdam. You can stay on with Dr. Jeffries and Dr. Knight, ask them what-ever questions you want, tape their answers, and remain overnight to pick up anything you still require the next day, before following us to Amsterdam. I'm sure you'll find the sessions with these gentlemen interesting."

"I hope so," said Randall. The two drinks had given him a fine glow, and he didn't want to lose it. He hailed the waiter, and said to Naomi, "What about a refill?"

She nodded benignly. "I'll keep you company as long as you wish."

Randall ordered another round, and focused on Naomi once more. "Those Britishers I'm to be with—

anything I should know about their backgrounds and exact functions in Resurrection Two?"

"Yes, I'd better fill you in fast—before I slide under the table."

"You don't look like—"

"I never look like I've had a drink," said Naomi. "I never do. But I'm beginning to feel giddy. Anyway, where were we? Yes. First, Dr. Bernard Jeffries. He is one of the world's foremost theologians, an expert on the languages of the first century in Palestine—you know, Greek, which the occupying Romans used, and Hebrew, which the Palestinian Jewish synagogue leaders used, and Aramaic, a form of Hebrew, which the common people and Jesus spoke. Jeffries is a big grizzly of a man, small head and features, pince-nez, Malacca cane, in his late sixties, a dear. He is the senior member of the School of Oriental Studies at the University of Oxford. To be more exact, he holds the chair of Regius Professor of Hebrew. But he is also head of the faculty of the Honour School of Theology. In short, he's the best there is in his field."

"His field being languages?"

"Actually, far beyond that, Steve. He's more than a philologist. He's a papyrologist, also. And he's an expert on the Holy Scriptures and comparative religions. He headed the international committee that translated Petronius and James. He'll tell you about that. However, although he's the senior member, he won't be as important in your life as his protégé, Dr. Florian Knight."

The third round of drinks had arrived, and Randall touched his highball glass to Naomi's and they both drank.

"Now," Naomi resumed, "Dr. Knight is another matter. He is what they call at Oxford a tutorial fellow. That is, he does—or has been doing—most of the actual lecturing and teaching for Dr. Jeffries in the School of Oriental Studies. He was handpicked by Dr. Jeffries to become Jeffries' successor. Dr. Jeffries must retire at seventy— he'll become a professor emeritus—and then, we think, Dr. Knight will be appointed to the chair as Regius Professor. At any rate, Dr. Florian Knight is as different from Dr. Jeffries as night is from day."

"How so?"

"Appearance, temperament, everything. Dr. Knight is one of those precocious and eccentric English geniuses. He's very young for what he is. Maybe thirty-four or so. Looks rather like Aubrey Beardsley. Have you ever seen a picture of Beardsley? Kind of Buster Brown haircut, deep-set eyes, nose like the beak of an eagle, pushed-out lower lip, big ears, long, thin hands. Well, that is Dr. Florian Knight. High-pitched voice, high-strung manner, nervous, but absolutely a marvel on New Testament languages and scholarship. So, what happened was this. Two years ago, Dr. Jeffries needed someone to do research for him—and for his translation committee—in the British Museum, where they have priceless early codices of the New Testament. He arranged for Dr. Knight to get a leave of absence from Oxford, so that he could move down to London and work in the museum as a reader—"

"A reader? What's a reader?"

"It's the name the British give to a researcher. Anyway, you'll meet Dr. Knight tomorrow, and then he'll follow you to Amsterdam as one of your consultants. You'll find him an invaluable source for material to be used in preparing your publicity campaign. I'm sure you'll get on with him. Oh yes, only one small difficulty. Dr. Knight is rather deaf—too bad, for a person so young—and he uses a hearing aid, which makes him very self-conscious and often testy. But you'll manage. You'll win him over. I think you're good at that."

She held up her empty glass, and gave him an inquiring look.

"Okay," said Randall. "I could stand another one too."

He signaled toward the bar, until the waiter saw him and acknowledged the reorder. He returned his attention to Naomi Dunn. The bunned brown hair, dark complexion, straight nose, thin lips still gave her an air of severity. Yet, somehow, after three Scotches, the gray eyes were more tolerant, and the dedicated, primly religious aspect had modified. His curiosity about her had heightened. She had revealed nothing of herself, as a woman, in the nearly five days on shipboard. He wondered whether she would.

"Enough of business, Naomi," he said. "Can we talk about something else?"

"If you like. What do you want to talk about?"

"First, me, and the way I look to you. That last remark you made. You said you thought I'd have no trouble winning over Florian Knight. You said you thought I was good at that. Now what is that supposed to mean? Is it sarcasm? Or is it a compliment?"

Before she could reply, the waiter appeared, setting down their fresh Scotches and removing the empty glasses.

When the waiter had gone, Naomi held her drink thoughtfully. She raised her head. "The first time I saw you, I didn't care much for you," she said. "I was prejudiced before I laid eyes on you. I detest publicity people. They're from a false make-believe world. They play sleight-of-hand with the public. They stand for nothing real or honest."

"For the most, that's true."

"Well, there you were. You looked too successful, too arrogant, too disinterested in human beings. I just resented you. You seemed so superior to us, as if we were a bunch of stupid religious kooks."

Randall could not help smiling. "Funny," he said. "The first time I saw you, I felt you disliked me for—for being a plain secular person, and not devout, not full of mission." He paused. "Well, do you still feel the same way about me?"

"If I did, I couldn't speak as I have," she said with candor. "Being thrown together with you on this voyage has given me another view of you. For one thing, I feel you are ashamed of your calling."

"In a way, that's true, too."

"And I've guessed you're more vulnerable and sensitive than I would have first imagined. As to my remark about your being able to win Knight over, your being good at that, it was meant as a compliment. You can be charming."

"Thanks, I'll drink with you to that."

They drank slowly.

"Naomi, how long have you been with Wheeler at Mission House?"

"Five years."

"What did you do before that?"

She fell silent, then gazed directly at him. "I was a nun, a Franciscan nun, for—for two years. I was known as Sister Regina. Are you surprised?"

He was more than surprised, but he tried not to reveal it. He took a long swallow of his drink, eyes still on her, and realized that in all his recent and surprising fantasies of undressing her—because she was so prim and tight-assed—he had always visualized her in a full-length nun's habit before she was disrobed.

He did not answer her question. Instead, he inquired, "Why did you leave?"

"It had nothing to do with faith. I'm as religious as I've ever been—well, almost. It was simply that I wasn't cut out for the stern routine and discipline of the convent. In fact, once I made my decision—this meant sending a letter to the Pope requesting a dispensation of release, which was automatically granted—I thought the step into the secular world would be easy. After all, I wasn't alone. There are about one million two hundred thousand nuns scattered around the world, and the year I quit the religious life, I was one of seven thousand nuns who had also quit. But it was difficult, the reentry crisis. No more orderly routine and rules. No more prescribed prayers, activities, dress, meals, periods of solitude. Overnight, I had to think for myself, fill my days on my own, cease feeling naked in very short dresses, get used to male games. I had been an English major in college, before the convent, and afterwards it seemed natural to get into some phase of publishing. The job at Mission House has suited me very well. So you see—"

She was interrupted by a shrill voice from the doorway of the cabaret. "There you are!" It was Darlene Nicholson's voice. Darlene, in a tight breast-filled pullover sweater and form-fitting pants, came rapidly toward them.

"I've been looking for you everywhere," she said to Randall. "Are you still working?"

"Just finished," said Randall. "Come on, join us for a drink."

"No, thanks, I'm still hung over from last night. I'm surprised you aren't, darling."

"I'm all right—"

"Just wanted to tell you where I'll be," said Darlene, searching through her purse for her daily program. "They're running that cute movie we both liked so much last month, the one we saw on Third Avenue, remember? About the young girl who gets involved with a married man, only he pretends to be a widower."

"Oh, yes," said Randall dully.

"I thought I'd see it again." She examined her program. "Dammit, it's been on forty-five minutes already. Well, I guess I'll catch the ending. That was the best part anyway." She stuffed the program into her purse, bent down and planted a wet kiss on Randall's mouth. "Ta-ta, see you when we change for dinner."

Both waited until she was gone. Randall took up his drink, and glanced at Naomi uncomfortably. "Anyway, Naomi, you were saying—?"

"Never mind. I've told you enough already." She swallowed the remainder of her Scotch, and studied Randall for a few seconds. "Maybe this is out of bounds, but I'm curious about something."

"Go ahead."

"I'm curious to know what a man like—like you—sees in a girl like Darlene." Before he could answer, she went on. "I know she isn't your secretary. I know she hasn't used her cabin on the ship even once. I assume she's been your—what is the old-fashioned word?—mistress, your mistress, for some time."

"Yes, that's right. I've been separated from my wife for two years. I met Darlene about six months after that. She lives with me."

"I see." Naomi compressed her lips. Not looking at him, she said, "Is it anything besides young sex?"

"Not much, I'm afraid. We can close the generation gap

only in bed. But, well, she's a decent kid, and it's nice to have someone around."

Naomi pushed her empty glass to the edge of the table. "I could stand an encore."

"So could I. We're going to feel very good tonight."

"I feel good already."

He ordered again, and the drinks were before them almost immediately.

Randall sipped his Scotch, and squinted over the rim of his glass at Naomi. "I—I wanted to ask you something personal. About after you left the convent. About what it was like with men."

"Lousy," she muttered, more to herself than to him.

"What I mean is—"

"Don't want to talk about it," she said thickly. "Tired of talking. Let's drink."

They drank in silence, and her glass was empty first. "One more, Steven, for the road."

He waved at the bartender and had just enough time to finish his drink before two new filled glasses of amber liquid materialized.

She stared at him through narrowing gray eyes as she continued with her Scotch. She said, "Mustn't forget. Have some material on how they did the translation. Should read it, you should, before we land. It's in my cabin. I'd better get it."

"You can give it to me tomorrow," he said.

"Now," she said. "Important."

She took a final swallow, worked herself out of the booth and stood up unsteadily.

He was beside her. He tried to take her arm, but she pressed her arm closely against her print dress, rejecting his grasp, and starting to walk straight and ladylike out of the bar. He followed her, feeling woozy and wonderful.

They took the small elevator near the Atlantique cabaret on the Verandah Deck down two stories to the Upper Deck. Naomi Dunn held on to the wooden corridor railing as she made her way ahead of him to the deluxe Normandie Suite.

She took out her key and let them into the first bedroom. It was spacious and attractive, dimly lit by the standing floor lamp. Under the gray bedspread was a real bed, not a studio bed, and this rested on deep carpeting. There seemed to be mirrors everywhere.

"Nice room," he said. "Where's George's room?"

She swung around. "What do you mean?"

"I mean he's in this suite, too, isn't he?"

"My room's private, locked. Next door is the big parlor. His bedroom's on the other side a mile or more off. We use the parlor, living room, to work." She turned away. "I'll get you the research." She started for a suitcase propped on a low metal stand. Opening it, she rummaged inside, came up with a folder. "Here." She held out the folder formally. "Sit down and look at it a minute, while I go to the bathroom. Excuse me."

He cast his eyes around blearily, and finally settled himself on the edge of the nearby bed. He opened the manila folder. There were three sets of papers. The three headings, in capital letters, referred to the translation methods for three different Bibles—the King James Version, the Revised Standard Version, the New English Bible. The typing blurred before his eyes. He listened to the sounds of Naomi Dunn moving around behind the bathroom door, heard the toilet flush, heard the faucet run. He tried to conjure up a vision of her in a heavy nun's habit, the ever-youthful smooth plastic nun look, the ever-present rosary dangling at her waist.

The bathroom door opened and Naomi appeared, looking exactly as she had before except for one difference. The mellowness had left her features, and her prim face was a forbidding shield again.

She planted herself before him. "Well, what do you think?"

Randall held up the folder, then dropped it on the bedside table. "The material—"

"Not the material. Me."

Involuntarily, his eyebrows went up as she moved closer and sat down beside him on the bed.

"You?" he managed to say.

She twisted away from him and offered him her back. "Do me a favor and unzip me," she said tightly.

He found the catch beneath her bun of hair, pulled at it, and ran the zipper slowly down to the small of her back. The nylon print dress fell open, revealing her bony spine and the light tan flesh. She wore no brassiere and he could not see the elastic band of her panties either.

Her back was still to him. "Does this shock you?" she said with a tremor in her voice. "I have nothing on underneath." She twisted around to face him squarely, her unfastened dress slipping off her shoulders as she did so. "Does this excite you?"

He was too astonished to be excited. And as he blinked at her in confusion, she began to pull her arms out of the sleeves of the dress. She freed her arms and brought them down to her sides. The top of her dress dropped to her waist. She drew back her bare shoulders and the two small exposed breasts became firmer, and the large circles of brown nipple seemed to cover most of the surface of each breast.

Randall felt the heat rising in his chest and running along the inside of his thighs.

"Do I excite you?" she asked breathlessly.

Her hand went down between his legs, and slowly her fingers rubbed the inside of his left thigh. He could feel his penis growing larger and larger under her hand. Her hand curled around his full erection.

"I love that," she whispered. "I love it. Do the same to me. Go ahead, do it."

He embraced her with one arm, bringing her against him, as his free hand slid under her skirt, touching her warm skin, massaging along her leg until his fingers reached the pubic hair. "Naomi," he murmured. "Let's—"

"Wait, Steve, I'll take off your clothes."

With her help, he quickly stripped. Throwing aside his jock shorts, he saw that she had stepped out of her dress and was naked. In a moment, they were lying on the bed together, facing one another. As he tried to bring her body in contact with his own, her back arched and she resisted him.

"Steve, what do you do with Darlene?" she asked.

"What do I do? I—you mean what do I—why, I go inside her, of course."

"Do you do anything else?"

"I—I've tried, but—if you must know, she's a little squeamish."

"I want you to know I'm not."

"All right, honey, that's good. Now let's—"

"Steve, I don't fuck. I don't like it. But I do everything else, anything you want to do."

He loosened his grip on her. "What do you mean?"

"Steve, I'm ready. Don't waste time. Let me show you."

She came up on her knees quickly, turned her knobby back and narrow buttocks toward him, straddled his chest, and then stretched out on top of him. Her hands cupped his testicles, and her tongue flicked around the tip of his penis, and then her mouth closed over it.

As she hung above him, he could see the protruding lips of her vulva. His fingers clutched at her buttocks, brought her down closer and closer to him.

She released him below, and began to groan and writhe. "No, no, no," she moaned, "don't—don't—more, don't stop, don't stop—"

Suddenly she froze, trapped his head tightly in the vise of her thighs, pressed her pubic mound harder and harder against his face. He heard the guttural cry escape her throat, felt her entire body shudder, and then she went limp.

Slowly, she rolled off his body. "Sorry, Steve, for not going on with you, but—"

"Relax, baby."

"I can't relax until you're relaxed."

He lay on his back unmoving. He felt her cool hand go around his flaccid penis, felt the contact of her lips again, felt his erection fill her hand and push out beyond her circled fingers. He shut his eyes and began to gasp, and his hand found and tried to hold her bobbing head.

He was going out of his skull. He was way up there, rising, spinning.

"Ohhh!" he cried, and could feel it all leaving him, emptying his mind, his gut, his swollen crotch. The sensation of complete relief engulfed him, and he allowed himself to sink down on the bed again, slack and deliciously at peace.

He was conscious of her leaving the bed, heard her dash into the bathroom, and he listened to the rush of the flushed toilet, listened to her returning. Reluctantly, he opened his eyes. She had seated herself on the bed beside him.

She was still naked and she was holding a hand towel. As she gently wiped him, her eyes held on his. She remained unsmiling, but the rigidity had gone from her features.

He did not know what to say. He had to fill the after-void. He said, "Well, anyway, if we sinned, it wasn't original—and it was pleasurable."

The transformation in her bewildered him. The pliant mien of her features instantly petrified into formal disapproval. "That's not very funny, Steve," she said.

"Naomi, come off it. What's with you?"

He reached for her, but she evaded him, leaving the bed and waiting in silence while he went into the bathroom. When he returned to dress, she started for the bathroom once more. At the door, she hesitated. "Thank you," she said. "The only favor I ask is that you forget this ever happened. I'll see you at dinner."

Five minutes later, having finished dressing, he left her cabin and stood in the corridor, lighting his pipe and reflecting upon the experience.

The residue of the sexual encounter was not a feeling of well-being after all. In retrospect, it had been an unfun act, and had left him with distaste, not for Naomi but for himself. Nor, he realized, was it the nature of their performance that disturbed him. He had gone down on women before, and they had gone down on him. If partners were consenting, and it happened naturally, if something was harmless yet wore a face of love, it was 'okay in his book. In fact, Randall knew, had he indulged in routine sexual intercourse with Naomi instead of oral-genital contact, he would still have felt self-loathing.

He wondered if he was flagellating himself without reason. But no, there was reason. Somehow, embarking upon this voyage toward Resurrection Two, attempting to ignore any doubts he might have about the truth of the project and its worth, he had hoped to alter the course of his life. His intentions had been the best. This change would be a beginning, an odyssey to ferret out the meaning of his life, to find something to believe in, to become the kind of person who was no longer ashamed of himself.

Yet, on that bed in the cabin behind him, he had once more abdicated even good intentions. He had performed as he always performed with women—sex without love, flesh contact without human warmth, release without meaning. It had been merely one more cynical cheapening of two naked bodies, animal coupling (of a sort) which enriched neither heart nor spirit. Nor could he evade guilt by telling himself that he had been the one seduced. Freud, Adler, Jung would have known better, and he knew better. Unconsciously, he had been on the make for Naomi from the moment that they had set foot on this ship. He had not wanted her from love, but because she had seemed so straitlaced and impregnable, and success promised a tawdry thrill. He had craved another crummy victory to divert his empty soul. He had exuded desire, and she, little tight-ass, had caught the vibrations.

Now it was done, and the pleasure of it was as pleasurable as a cheap gin hangover.

Yet, he told himself, as he started for the elevator, in an odd way it had not been for naught. A lesson had been learned. Or rather, he had been reminded of a lesson learned after he had been in the publicity business a few short years.

This: There are no saints, only sinners. From such crooked wood as that which man is made of, nothing straight can be fashioned. Emmanuel Kant had said that.

Naomi the ex-nun, the believer, the good ambassador

of a religious publishing house of goodness—a mere frail mortal, a human being, finally, with every weakness to which the flesh is heir. Like himself. Like everyone.

The lesson had been relearned. He must not forget it. Resurrection Two would not be peopled by gods and their angels, any more than the International New Testament would hide Jesus, the Son of Man. Inside those sanctimonious ones, inside each one of them, was a human biped, who tried to stand up to keep from falling.

He felt a little better.

Tomorrow and the day after he would not be confined to purgatory while the rest of them were in heaven. If truth be known, he was simply one more of them, and all of them were in hell together.

THEIR last dinner on the S.S. *France* was almost over.

The meal that George L. Wheeler had ordered in advance, from caviar to crêpes Suzette, had been a heavy one, but Randall had eaten sparingly and felt the better for his austerity.

Randall could feel the heat coming from behind him, where the crêpes were being prepared, and although Darlene would be delighted with such an elaborate dessert, he had no stomach for it. He had napped in his stateroom, despite the drone of Darlene's eternal closed-circuit television, and showered, and his hangover was mild. But he had no interest in food.

He glanced around their small table, situated in the rear of the glittering Chambord Dining Room, with its star-studded ceiling ringed by bright lights. At his left, Darlene was testing the good nature of a young table steward by addressing him in her terrible high school French. At his right, hands primly crossed on her lap, sat Naomi Dunn, cool, standoffish, speaking only when spoken to. He tried to revive her nudity, her mons veneris, her paroxysm at orgasm. He could not revive any of that. It was as impossible to imagine as violating a vestal virgin. Opposite him, the chair stood empty.

Not fifteen minutes earlier, George L. Wheeler had

been paged on the ship's intercom system. There was a ship-to-shore telephone call awaiting him from London.

Pushing back his chair, swallowing the last piece of his Chateaubriand, Wheeler had grumbled, "Who in the hell can be calling at this hour?" He had gone tramping between the tables, halloing this new passenger acquaintance and that, and climbing the two flights of carpeted stairs to the Communications Desk off the central elevators on the Main Deck.

As Randall idly watched the table captain serve Darlene her plate of folded crêpes, he heard Naomi speak out.

She was calling to the table captain. "Mr. Wheeler is returning. You can serve him now, too."

Indeed, the publisher was descending the staircase rapidly, and wending his way among the tables, looking neither right nor left. As he approached, Randall saw plainly that he was discomposed.

Wheeler plumped down in his chair with a snort of annoyance.

"Damn bad luck," he muttered, taking up his napkin. He sat brooding.

"What is it, Mr. Wheeler?" Naomi finally asked.

Wheeler acknowledged the presence of the others for the first time. "That was Dr. Jeffries from London. We may have a problem."

The table captain had come forward to serve Wheeler his crêpes personally, but Wheeler dismissed him brusquely. "I'm not in the mood for that now. Pour me some fresh American coffee."

"What kind of problem?" inquired Naomi tentatively.

Wheeler took no notice of her. He addressed himself to Randall. "Dr. Jeffries was agitated, I must say. He understands the limited time we've allowed you to prepare your publicity campaign. He knows we have no leeway for delays or postponements. If Florian Knight isn't available when we need him, we're in trouble."

It was not like Wheeler to speak in circumlocutions. Randall was puzzled. "Why shouldn't Dr. Knight be available?"

"Sorry, Steve. I should explain. Dr. Jeffries came down from Oxford today to meet with Florian Knight at the British Museum. Dr. Jeffries' purpose was to inform Knight that he was being assigned to follow you to Amsterdam and work with you there, work as one of your consultants on Resurrection Two. Of your many consultants, he would have been the most valuable. Dr. Knight's knowledge of New Testament background—not merely languages, but biblical lore of the first century—is wide-ranging and thorough. Well, apparently they discussed Dr. Knight's new assignment, and then Dr. Jeffries made arrangements for them to meet for dinner early this evening and carry on their talk. A few hours ago, as Dr. Jeffries was about to leave his club to keep the engagement, he received a telephone call from the young lady who is Dr. Knight's fiancée. I've met her once. Bright young thing. Miss Valerie Hughes. Well, she was on the phone informing Dr. Jeffries, on Knight's behalf, that the dinner must be canceled. Dr. Knight had suddenly been taken ill—quite ill, Jeffries gathered, for not only was Knight canceling out tonight, but he won't be able to see Jeffries or any of us tomorrow."

"That doesn't sound too serious," said Randall. "If I can't see Knight tomorrow, I can still—"

"Tomorrow's not the point," interrupted Wheeler. "The point is Miss Hughes told Dr. Jeffries that Knight had instructed her to say that he—Knight, that is—would not be well enough to work on our project in Amsterdam in the foreseeable future. Just that. Nothing more. Well, Dr. Jeffries was too befuddled to pursue the matter further this evening. He did ask when he would be able to call upon his protégé, but Miss Hughes was vague and muttered something about having to discuss this with Knight's physician first. And she hung up. Very strange. And disconcerting. If Dr. Knight is out of it, well, that would be a severe blow."

"Yes," said Randall slowly. "It sounds very strange indeed."

Darlene, who had been only half attentive, waggled her forkful of crêpe Suzette at the publisher. "Hey, if there's nobody to see in London, maybe we can take the ship right on to Le Havre?"

Wheeler glared at her. "There *is* someone to see in London, and we are *not* going to Le Havre, Miss Nicholson." He addressed Randall again. "I made an appointment for us to meet with Dr. Jeffries at the British Museum at two o'clock tomorrow afternoon. I'm going to insist that Dr. Jeffries exert his authority to make Knight rejoin the project as soon as he is recovered. This is vital to our immediate future."

Randall had been thinking. Almost casually, he spoke what was on his mind. "George," he said, "you haven't told us what is wrong with Dr. Florian Knight. What is his illness?"

Wheeler was startled. "By God, you know what—Dr. Jeffries never told me what was wrong with Knight. That's a good question to ask him tomorrow, isn't it?"

THE FOLLOWING DAY they had found London overcast and cheerless, and this had not improved their dispositions as they had ridden in the chauffeured Bentley S-3 from the Dorchester Hotel on Park Lane to the majestic British Museum in Bloomsbury. There had been three of them in the back seat. Darlene had gone off on a guided tour— Westminster Abbey, Piccadilly Circus, the Tower, Buckingham Palace.

As they arrived at the series of huge columns before the main entrance of the British Museum on Great Russell Street, Randall had suddenly been reminded of his only other visit to the museum—one made with Barbara when Judy was a little girl.

He had recalled the great sphere of a reading room, rings of books within rings of books with the main desk at the hub, and the treasures in the adjacent rooms and in the galleries on the upper floor. He had remembered the stimulation of the exhibits—the actual map, engraved in 1590, of Sir Francis Drake's journey around the globe; the First Folio edition of Shakespeare's plays; the early manuscript of *Beowulf;* Lord Horatio Nelson's logbooks; Captain Scott's Antarctic journals; the bluish T'ang dy-

nasty model of a horse; the Rosetta Stone, with its hiero-
glyphics carved in 196 B.C.

Now, having been greeted by their host in the front
hall, they were being led across the inlaid marble floor
by Dr. Jeffries, their destination the assistant keeper's
office upstairs, where Dr. Knight had been working. Dr.
Jeffries was very much as Naomi had described him on
the ship. He was under six feet, barrel-chested, with
shaggy white hair, a small head with rheumy eyes, pinkish
nose with large pores, an untidy moustache, wrinkled
face, striped bow tie, dangling pincenez, and a blue suit
in need of a pressing.

As the bemused Dr. Jeffries, with Wheeler abreast of
him, plodded ahead of Naomi and himself, Randall
wondered whether the publisher would bring up Florian
Knight's name. Then, as though Wheeler had got the
message by extrasensory perception, Randall heard
Wheeler inquire, "By the way, Professor, how serious is
Dr. Knight's illness? I meant to ask you yesterday evening. What's wrong with our Dr. Knight?"

Dr. Jeffries seemed oblivious to the question. He slowed
and stopped, lost in thought, and looked back over his
shoulder. "Umm—one thing, Mr. Randall, one thing you
should see while we are here on the ground floor. Our two
foremost New Testament holdings. The Codex Sinaiticus
and the Codex Alexandrinus. Umm—you will, you will
certainly hear them mentioned frequently in your discussions. If you have the time, I would suggest this brief
detour."

Before Randall could reply, Wheeler answered for him.
"Of course, Professor. Steve wants to see everything. Lead
on. . . . Steve, come up front and join us. Naomi won't
feel neglected."

Randall came up beside Dr. Jeffries as he swung off
to the right. "It's just through the Manuscript Saloon, in a
repository reserved for our rarest items, the Magna Carta
Room," said Dr. Jeffries. "You know, Mr. Randall, until
—umm—until the recent and most remarkable Ostia Antica find, our oldest fragment of the gospels was a scrap
of John's Gospel, 3½ by 2½ inches, in Greek, found in

a rubbish heap in Egypt and written prior to 150 A.D. It presently resides in the John Rylands Library in Manchester. After that, we have some New Testament papyri acquired by A. Chester Beatty, an American who had residence here in London, and the papyri acquired by Martin Bodmer, a Swiss banker, which may be dated around 200 A.D. Of course, one fragment, Bodmer Papyrus 2—" He slowed, and gave Randall an amused sidelong glance. "But that can be of no interest to you. Forgive me when I become frightfully pedantic."

"I'm here to learn, Dr. Jeffries," said Randall.

"Umm—yes, and you shall. Some of the younger scholars, like Florian, they will serve you better. However, let me say this. With the exception of the Ostia Antica fragments, James's Gospel, Petronius' Parchment—always excepting them, for no discovery in the biblical field has ever been comparable to them in importance—I should rank the most valuable biblical discoveries made in the last nineteen hundred years in the following way."

He halted at the entrance to the Manuscript Saloon, lost in thought, apparently ruminating upon the comparative value of historic manuscript finds.

"First," said Dr. Jeffries, "would be the five hundred sheepskin and papyrus scrolls, discovered in 1947 in the vicinity of Khirbet Qumran. These are familiarly known as the Dead Sea Scrolls. Second, the Codex Sinaiticus, found in its complete form in the Monastery of St. Catherine on Mount Sinai in 1859. This is a New Testament copied in Greek in the fourth century, and this is the one in our possession which I am about to show you. Third in importance, the Nag Hamadi texts discovered in 1945 outside Nag Hamadi in Upper Egypt. This find consisted of thirteen papyrus volumes, preserved in earthen jars uncovered by farmers raking humus for use as fertilizer. In these fourth-century writings were a hundred and fourteen sayings of Jesus, many never known before this Coptic library was revealed. Fourth, the Codex Vaticanus, a Greek Bible written around 350 A.D., which is housed in the Vatican Library. Its origin is unknown. Fifth, the British Museum's own Codex Alexandrinus, the text writ-

ten in Greek on vellum before the fifth century. It came
to London as a gift to King Charles I from the patriarch
of Constantinople in 1628."

"I hate to confess my ignorance," said Randall, "but
I don't even know what the word *codex* means."

"You are wise to ask for explanations," said Dr. Jeffries, pleased. "The word *codex*—umm—its root is the
Latin *caudex,* meaning the trunk of a tree. This refers to
the ancient writing tablets made of wax-coated wood. In
fact, the codex was the beginning of the bound book as
we know it today. At the time of Christ, non-Christian
writing was done largely on rolls of papyrus or parchment
—extremely cumbersome for the reader. By the second
century, the codex was being adopted. Papyrus rolls were
cut into pages and fastened on the left side. As I said, the
beginning of the modern book. Now then, how many—
how many important biblical discoveries have I mentioned as ranking behind our Ostia Antica find?"

"Five, Professor," said Wheeler.

Dr. Jeffries slowly resumed walking. "Thank you,
George. . . . Mr. Randall, I should mention four others, in
no particular order. It would be remiss of me not to mention—especially as a textual scholar and translator—the
findings of that young German pastor and Bible scholar,
Adolf Deissman. Until Deissman, translators of the Greek
New Testaments who realized biblical Greek differed
from literary Greek supposed it to be some kind of special
pure Greek, a sacred Greek employed only in New Testaments. In 1895, after studying the masses of ancient Greek
papyri discovered during the hundred years before—ordinary commonplace fragments of two-thousand-year-old
letters, household budgets, business bills, deeds, leases,
petitions—Deissman was able to announce that this every-
man's colloquial Greek, this Greek of daily life and the
streets—which is called Koine—was the very Greek used
by the gospel writers. This caused a revolution in the
translations that followed."

Dr. Jeffries cast another sidelong glance at Randall.
"The other three most valuable finds might include the
discovery of St. Peter's tomb in an ancient cemetery thirty

feet beneath the Vatican, presuming it is authentic. At any rate, Dr. Margherita Guarducci deciphered a coded stone inscription found beneath the basilica nave, and this inscription—which dates back to 160 A.D.—reads, 'Peter is buried in here.' Next, the discovery in Israel during 1962 of a building block used to dedicate a structure to the Emperor Tiberius before 37 A.D., a block inscribed with the name of Pontius Pilate followed by the words *prefectus Udea,* the very title we have authenticated in the Petronius Parchment. Then in 1968, in a stone casket at Giv'at ha-Mivtar in Jerusalem, a truly great find—the skeleton of a man named Yehohanan, his name inscribed in Aramaic on his coffin, who had had seven-inch nails driven through his forearms and through his heel bones. This two-thousand-year-old skeleton was the first physical evidence we've ever seen of a man who had been crucified in New Testament times in Palestine. Histories had told us it happened. The gospels had told us it happened to Jesus. But with the exhumation of Yehohanan's remains, the literary knowledge was finally confirmed."

Dr. Jeffries lifted his pince-nez and pointed it directly ahead. "Here we are."

Randall saw that they had already passed between the showcases in the Manuscript Saloon and were being led toward the entry of another room. At the doorway, placed on a stand, was a sign reading:

DEPARTMENT OF MANUSCRIPTS
TO STUDENTS ROOM
CODEX SINAITICUS
MAGNA CARTA
SHAKESPEARE DEED

The guard in the entrance, attired in black cap, gray coat, and black trousers, gave Dr. Jeffries a friendly salute. Immediately to their right was a long metal showcase, with two blue curtains covering two panes of glass.

Dr. Jeffries brought them to the covered display. He lifted aside one curtain, then mumbled, "The Codex Alexandrinus—umm, no, we needn't bother about that one now. It's of lesser importance." With tenderness, he drew back the second blue drape, tucked his pince-nez on his nose, smiled broadly at the ancient volume lying open behind the glass panel. "There you have it. One of the three most important manuscripts in Bible history. The Codex Sinaiticus."

Steve Randall and Naomi stepped forward and peered down at the brownish vellum pages, each bearing four narrow columns of neatly hand-printed Greek.

"You are looking at a portion of the Gospel of Luke," said Dr. Jeffries. "Note the card of explanation in the corner here."

Randall read the typing on the small card. The Codex Sinaiticus was open to Luke 23:14. At the foot of the third column on the left page were verses that described Christ's agony on the Mount of Olives, verses many earlier authorities had not known about before the discovery of this Bible and so they had not used them in their own translations.

"In its original state, this manuscript," said Dr. Jeffries, "probably contained 730 leaves. What has survived are 390 leaves—242 of them devoted to the Old Testament and 148 leaves representing the complete New Testament. The vellum, you see, is made from both sheepskin and goatskin. The printing, all in capitals, is in the hands of three different scribes, most likely done before 350 A.D." Dr. Jeffries turned toward Randall. "That this much of the Codex Sinaiticus was salvaged makes quite a thriller of a story. Have you ever heard the name Constantine Tischendorf?"

Randall shook his head. He had never heard the odd name before, but it intrigued him.

"Briefly, here is our thriller," said Dr. Jeffries with evident relish. "Tischendorf was a German biblical scholar. He was always poking about the Middle East in search of ancient manuscripts. On one such trip, in May of 1844, he went climbing up to the walled Monastery of St. Catherine on Mount Sinai in Egypt. As he made his way through a corridor of the monastery, he noticed a rather large trash basket heaped full of what appeared to be tattered pieces of manuscript. Poking through the trash basket, Tischendorf saw that these were leaves of ancient parchment. Two similar baskets had already been burned as rubbish, and this one was about to follow them. Tischendorf persuaded the monks to turn the contents over to him for examination. Sorting out the waste, he found 129 leaves of an ancient Old Testament written in Greek. The monks, now aware of their value, permitted him to keep 43 leaves, and these he took back to Europe and presented to the king of Saxony."

"Those were not part of this codex?" said Randall.

"Wait," said Dr. Jeffries. "Nine years later, Tischendorf returned to the monastery for another hunt. The monks proved uncooperative. Tischendorf did not give up. He bided his time. Six more years passed, and in January of 1859, the persistent German returned once more to Mount Sinai. More cautious this time, he did not solicit the monks for old manuscripts. But on his last evening, Tischendorf engaged the monastery steward in a discussion about ancient Bibles. To prove his own erudition, the steward boasted that he had studied one of the oldest Bibles known. Whereupon, he reached up to a shelf above his cell door on which he kept his coffee cups, and he brought down a thick parcel wrapped round in red cloth. He unwrapped it, and there before Tischendorf's eyes was the Codex Sinaiticus, containing the oldest complete New Testament known to man."

Dr. Jeffries chuckled. "One can imagine Tischendorf's emotions, akin I am sure to those Columbus felt on sighting the New World. After many months of effort, Tischendorf convinced the monks that they should present this codex as a gift to the patron of their church, none other than the czar of Russia. The Codex Sinaiticus remained in Russia until the 1917 revolution and the advent of Lenin and Stalin. The Communists had no interest in the Bible. To raise money, they tried to sell it to the United States, but without success. In 1933, the British Government and British Museum raised the hundred thousand pounds necessary to purchase the codex, and here you see it before you. Quite a story, what?"

"Quite a story," Randall agreed.

"I've gone into it at length," said Dr. Jeffries, "so that you will appreciate a better story—Dr. Monti's excavation and discovery of the Gospel According to James at Ostia Antica, a New Testament find older than the Codex Sinaiticus by almost three hundred years, a find older than any of the canonical gospels by possibly a half century, a writing attributed to a relative of the Christ and an eyewitness to the major portion of Christ's human life. Now, perhaps, Mr. Randall, you can appreciate the stupendous gift you are about to herald to the wide world. And now, perhaps, we had best go to Dr. Knight's office upstairs and deal with the practical aspects of your immediate mission. Please follow me."

With Wheeler and Naomi Dunn behind him, Steve Randall followed Dr. Jeffries up two steep flights of stairs, until presently they came upon a plain door. As Dr. Jeffries opened it and led them inside, he announced, "The assistant keeper's office which Dr. Florian Knight uses for his headquarters."

It was a messy, lived-in, worked-in, scholar's cubicle. There were jammed bookshelves from floor to ceiling. Reference volumes, papers, packages were stacked on the tables and on the carpet. There seemed barely space for the old desk near the window, the locked file cabinets, the sofa, and a chair or two.

Puffing after the climb and walk, Dr. Jeffries settled himself behind the desk. George Wheeler and Naomi Dunn had already found places on the sofa. Randall pulled a chair in close to the others and sat down.

"Umm, perhaps I should have taken you to the staff canteen so we could chat over tea," said Dr. Jeffries.

Wheeler held up his hands. "No, no, Professor, this will be fine."

"Splendid," said Dr. Jeffries. "I did think that the nature of our conversation might best be suited by privacy. I must say, to begin, that I have little new to offer about our young don—umm, Florian—Florian Knight. His mystifying behavior, as well as his inaccessibility, has distressed and embarrassed me. I have not been able to reach him, or indeed, his fiancée, Miss Valerie Hughes, since my call to you on the ship last night. You asked me something—I forget what—forgive my absentmindedness —you made some inquiry about Dr. Knight downstairs, did you not?"

Wheeler rose from the sofa and moved to a chair nearer the desk. "Yes, Professor. I neglected to ask you one last thing last night. What is this sudden illness that Dr. Knight is suffering from? What is wrong with him?"

Dr. Jeffries plucked at his moustache nervously. "George, I wish I knew. Miss Hughes was not specific, and she gave me almost no opportunity to question her. She said Florian had come down with an extremely high fever and had been put to bed. His physician had remarked that what he required above all was a protracted period of rest."

"Sounds like a nervous breakdown to me," said Wheeler. He nodded his head at Randall. "What do you make of it, Steve?"

Randall considered the possibility unlikely but he answered seriously. "Well, if it were a breakdown, there would have been signs of it, warning signs, in little ways, for some time. Perhaps Dr. Jeffries can tell us." He looked at the Oxford professor. "Did you note any signs of irrationality in Dr. Knight's behavior, or deterioration in his work in recent months?"

"None whatsoever," Dr. Jeffries replied emphatically. "Dr. Knight fulfilled every assignment I gave him conscientiously, even brilliantly. Dr. Knight is an expert in Greek, Persian, Arabic, Hebrew—and Aramaic, of course, the language we were largely working in. As a reader here, what he produced was flawless, precisely what I required. Understand this. A young man as knowledgeable as Florian Knight does not have to translate the Aramaic on a fragment of papyrus word by word. Usually, he reads it straight off, easily, naturally, as if it were his own native language, as if he were reading the morning *Times*. At any rate, Dr. Knight's performance in rendering Aramaic, Hebrew, and Greek into English for our committee of five at Oxford was always high, always as accurate as could be desired."

"In short, he made no errors, especially in the past year?" Randall persisted.

Dr. Jeffries eyed Randall for a moment before speaking. "My dear chap, human beings are fallible, and their work is always subject to error. It is past error—as well as the new knowledge gained through archeology and from our advances in philology—that motivates scholars to make new translations of the Bible. I had better explain, if you are to understand the pitfalls that Dr. Knight faced. Take the word *pim*. It appears only once in the Bible. It appears in the Book of Samuel. Translators had always thought *pim* meant tool, and so considered it as a kind of carpenter's file. Recently, translators found *pim* really meant a measure of weight like the word *shekel,* so the latest Bibles have used it correctly. Another example. The older English Bibles always had a line in Isaiah 7:14 read, 'Behold, a virgin shall conceive.' For years this was regarded as a prophecy of the birth of Christ. Then the translators of the Revised Standard Version came along and changed the line to read, 'Behold, a young woman shall conceive.' They were translating from the original Hebrew and in this the word *almah* means 'young woman.' Earlier Bibles had been translations of inaccurate Greek texts that had used the word *parthenos,* which means 'virgin.' "

"Wonderful promotional material," Randall exclaimed appreciatively.

Dr. Jeffries inclined his head, then lifted a finger of caution. "But, Mr. Randall, on the other hand, translators can sometimes go too far when trying to modernize, and they incorrectly alter meanings. For example, Paul quotes Our Lord as saying, 'It is more blessed to give than to receive.' That has always been considered a perfectly literal translation from the Greek. Yet the translators of the New English Bible were so eager to put their new work into British idiom that they altered the quotation to read, 'Happiness lies more in giving than in receiving.' Now that was not only a weak translation from a literary point of view, but it changed the meaning. It reduced a firm statement to a lazy, casual reflection. It sacrificed a strong phrase for a weak one. Moreover, there is a considerable difference between being happy and being blessed. As for Dr. Knight, he was never guilty of such innovations. Thinking back, I cannot fault Dr. Knight's work in any way. Let me elaborate—"

Dr. Jeffries was thoughtful, as Randall waited for him to go on, hoping for some clue that might solve the enigma of Dr. Knight's illness.

"While I directed a team of senior scholars in the English translation of the new discovery for the International New Testament, Dr. Knight performed as my reader here in the museum. He never failed to dig deep for contemporary meanings of language. Most scholars forget that Christ lived and moved among farmers. Too often, scholars neglect to delve into the usage of words by farmers in the early first century in Palestine. Our team had translated a phrase as 'ears of grain.' Dr. Knight was not satisfied. He burrowed way back and learned that in Christ's time farmers said that wheat, oats, and barley had 'heads,' not 'ears,' and he proved to us that 'ears of grain' was incorrect. He also challenged our use of the word *cattle*. He proved that in biblical times *cattle* did not mean bovine but meant all animals in general including donkeys, cats, dogs, goats, camels. Had we used *cattle* in the translation, it would have been frightfully misleading. Dr. Knight saved us from the inaccuracy." Dr. Jeffries considered Wheeler, then Randall. "Gentlemen, a mind so alert hardly seems a candidate for a nervous breakdown."

"I guess I'd have to agree with you," Randall conceded.

"You can be certain I am correct in this," Dr. Jeffries said amiably. "Because if ever a man worked under circumstances that invited a mental breakdown, that man was Florian Knight."

Randall knitted his brow. "What were those circumstances?"

"Why, in these many long months the poor chap was never told precisely what he was working on. Remember, we were pledged to secrecy. While Dr. Knight and our other readers were as trustworthy as their seniors, nevertheless we were advised that the fewer people who knew about the Ostia Antica find, the better. So we kept our secret from Dr. Knight, as well as from the others."

Randall found himself utterly perplexed. "But how could he work for you if you didn't show him the newly discovered fragments?"

"We never showed him or anyone else *all* of them. We assigned certain crucial bits and pieces to Dr. Knight to work on, and different verses or phrases to others. I told Dr. Knight that I had some fragments of an apocryphal New Testament codex, and that I planned to write a paper on it. I was forced to withhold the truth from him. The scraps of material I gave him were so incomplete, so difficult, so confusing, that he must have wondered what the assignment was all about. Yet, he was decent enough never to question me."

Randall was becoming intrigued. "Are you telling me, Dr. Jeffries, that your researcher, Florian Knight, does not know about Resurrection Two?"

"I'm saying he didn't know about it—until yesterday afternoon. When I came down from Oxford to meet with him, to prepare him for becoming a consultant to you in Amsterdam, I felt it was finally safe to reveal the truth in its entirety. Indeed, the Bible is on the presses, and to render Florian useful to you, I had to disclose every fact about Professor Monti's momentous discovery. That is why I came to the office here and told him about the Gospel According to James and the Petronius Parchment for the first time. I must say, he was overwhelmed."

"Overwhelmed? In what way—?"

"Umm—stunned would be more accurate, Mr. Randall. Stunned, and speechless, and finally extremely excited. You can understand. He has made the Bible his entire life. A revelation such as the one I made to him—it *can* be overwhelming."

Randall's curiosity was fully aroused. "And he became ill after that?"

"What? No, he did not become ill in my presence—"

"But after he left you, he went to his home, and then he fell ill?"

Dr. Jeffries was plucking his moustache again. "Why yes, I suppose that is what occurred. We were to meet once more in the evening for dinner. I wanted to discuss in detail his new assignment as your consultant. Not long before dinner, I had that cryptic telephone call from his young woman, Miss Hughes. He could not make it for dinner. He could not take on this next assignment. His physician advised against his even considering it. Moreover, he must have no callers, no one, for a week or two." Dr. Jeffries shook his head. "Too bad, too bad. Baffling. But no use trying to learn more, at least for the time. We can no longer depend upon Florian Knight. What shall we do? I suppose there is but one alternative. Find a replacement for Dr. Knight." He addressed himself to Wheeler. "I have two or three other readers who've worked for us. Stable young men. I suppose we could send one along after Mr. Randall and hope for the best. Unfortunately, not one of them is up to Dr. Knight, who is rather a wizard."

Wheeler rose with a grunt, and Naomi also came to her feet. "I hate to settle for second best, Professor," he said. "I suppose it is unavoidable, but there is so much at stake that we simply must obtain the best information possible, and present our International New Testament in the most stimulating way. Well, I barely have time to catch my plane to Amsterdam. I'll tell you what. Why don't you and Steve here discuss the possible substitutes for Knight? Steve can stay over—he's registered at the Dorchester. Perhaps he can interview the other candidates and choose one tomorrow."

Dr. Jeffries rose to escort the publisher and Naomi to the door. "Beastly luck, but I shall do anything I can to help," Dr. Jeffries promised. "Have a good flight. I'll be joining you in Amsterdam shortly."

Wheeler sighed. "Yes. Too bad about Knight, though. Well, do your best. . . . And, Steve, give me a ring tomorrow. Let me know when you'll be arriving. I'll have a car meet you."

"Thanks, George."

Randall was on his feet, waiting, when Dr. Jeffries ambled back into the office. "Umm—this business of a replacement—I will have to give it a little thought. It's a brute, getting the right man. Let me mull it over, possibly make a few inquiries around. We could discuss it more clearly in the morning, arrive at some decision. Is that satisfactory?"

"Perfectly," said Randall. He shook the professor's hand, then, as they moved to the door, he asked casually, "By the way, Dr. Jeffries, this girl friend of Knight's— Valerie Hughes, isn't it?—would you happen to know where she lives?"

"I'm afraid not. However, she's employed in the book department at Sotheby and Company—you know, the auction house in New Bond Street. Matter of fact, I recall Florian's telling me once that that's where he first met her. He's always haunted the place to have a view of new biblical materials coming up for sale, on the chance that he might find a rare bargain. He collects in the field, as best he can on his wages. Yes, Sotheby's is where he met his young lady." Dr. Jeffries opened the office door. "If you are just rattling around, Mr. Randall, and would like someone to dine with, I'd be pleased to have you join me at my club."

"Thanks ever so much, Dr. Jeffries. Maybe another time. I expect to be tied up—there are a few people I had better see—this afternoon and this evening."

AT FOUR THIRTY in the afternoon, Steve Randall reached his destination in New Bond Street.

Between an antique shop and a W. H. Smith and Son newsstand were the double doors that led into the oldest auction house in the world. High above the entrance was the black basalt head of an Egyptian solar goddess. Randall had read that the ancient piece had once been auctioned off, but had never been picked up by its buyer, and so the proprietors finally mounted it over their doorway and employed it as their trademark. Beneath the goddess was a sign that told him this was Sotheby & Co., and on either side of the firm's name was the street address, a No. 34 and a No. 35.

Randall hurried inside, across the tile hallway floor, across the doormat with the woven legend—SOTHEBY 1844—and through the second set of doors. Taking hold of the wooden banister, he started to climb the green carpeted stairway to the New Gallery.

Upstairs, the display rooms were crowded and seemed to be populated only by males. There was a gathering of men around a jewelry collection, and several others were studying individual items through loupes. There were guards in blue uniforms and gold braid hovering near onlookers who, holding their green catalogues open, were studying paintings soon to be auctioned. There was an elderly gentleman at an open showcase examining several rare coins.

Randall scouted about for any female employees, but there were none. He was beginning to wonder whether Dr. Jeffries had been mistaken about Valerie Hughes's job, when he realized someone was speaking to him.

"May I assist you, sir?" The middle-aged speaker, a slight cockney accent to his voice, was some kind of official wearing a long gray coat. "I'm one of the porters. Is there anything in particular you wish to see?"

"There is *someone* I'd like to see," said Randall. "Do you have a Miss Valerie Hughes employed here?"

The porter's face lit up. "Yes, yes, certainly. Miss Hughes is in the Book Department right next to the Main Auction Room. May I direct you?"

They made their way through an adjacent auction room, walls covered in red felt, and filled with visitors.

"What does Miss Hughes do in Sotheby's?" Randall inquired.

"Very clever young lady. For a while she was a receptionist at the Book Department counter. When a private party brings in books to put up for sale, he is received by a receptionist. She, in turn, summons one of our eight book experts to place a value on the individual item or bulk lot. Miss Hughes evidently knew as much about rare books as most of our experienced experts. When there was an opening available, she was promoted to book expert. This, sir, is the Book Room."

It was a fair-sized auction room with busts of Dickens, Shakespeare, Voltaire, and other immortals gracing the topmost shelves. The shelves themselves were packed with bound-book lots soon to go on sale. In the middle of the room was a U-shaped table at which the main buyers sat during an auction, and at the open end of the table was a wooden rostrum for the auctioneer. Alongside the rostrum rested a Bob Cratchit-type desk with a high stool, for the use of a clerk collecting the money from successful bidders, Randall guessed.

Randall became aware of two older men and a young lady busily sorting books, perhaps in preparation for new catalogue listings.

"I'll get her for you," said the porter. "Who may I say is calling?"

"Tell her Steve Randall, from America. Tell her I'm a friend of Dr. Knight's."

The porter, coat flapping, had gone to summon Valerie Hughes. Randall watched him whisper to her, saw her glance up puzzled. Finally, she nodded, put aside her notebook. As the porter disappeared, she advanced toward Randall. Quickly, he met her halfway, beside the U-shaped table.

She was small and on the plump side. She had stringy short hair, outsized spectacles, a cute nose and mouth, and peach-fair complexion. "Mr. Randall?" she said. "I— I don't recall that Dr. Knight ever mentioned you."

"He heard my name for the first time yesterday from Dr. Bernard Jeffries. I've just arrived from New York. I'm the one who was to meet with Dr. Knight and work with him in Amsterdam."

"Oh—" she said, and her hand went to her mouth. She seemed frightened. "Did Dr. Jeffries send you?"

"No, he has no idea that I'm here. I found out where you worked, and I determined to see you on my own. I introduced myself as a *friend* of Dr. Knight's, because I want to be his friend. I need his help. I need it very much. I thought if I could let you see me, let you know what I plan to do, and how much Dr. Knight's assistance would mean—"

"I'm sorry, it's no use," she said unhappily. "He's too ill."

"Nevertheless, hear me out. I'm sure he's told you about the—the secret project—well, I guess it's safe to mention it by name—Resurrection Two—he heard of just yesterday?"

"Yes, he told me a little," she said tentatively.

"Then, listen to me—" said Randall with urgency. In an undertone, he began to tell her about himself and his profession. He explained to her how Wheeler had involved him in the project. He told her of Dr. Jeffries' call to the ship the preceding night, of Dr. Jeffries' bewilderment at this afternoon's meeting, and of everyone's disappointment that Florian Knight could not undertake the new assignment. Randall went on, as winning, as sincere, as sympathetic as he could make himself.

"Miss Hughes," he concluded, "if Florian Knight is really as seriously ill as you assured Dr. Jeffries he was, then believe me, I won't bother you anymore about this. *Is* he seriously ill?"

She stared at Randall, and her eyes began to fill behind her big glasses. "No, it's not that," she said with a break in her voice.

"Can you tell me what it is?"

"I can't, I truly can't, Mr. Randall. I've given my word, and Florian means everything to me."

"Don't you think he'd be interested in Resurrection Two?"

"It's not what I think that matters, Mr. Randall. If it were up to me, I'd have him on your project in two minutes. Because the project is just his sort of thing. It is what he's so good at, what interests him more than anything else in life. It would be helpful for him, too, seeing this work to its conclusion. But I can't tell him what's best for him."

"You can try."

Valerie brought a handkerchief from her smock pocket

to her nose. "Oh, I don't know. I don't know whether I dare."

"Then let me try."

"You?" She seemed astonished by the suggestion. "I —I doubt if he'd see anyone."

"He wouldn't see Dr. Jeffries. He may have his reasons for that. But I'm someone else. I'm someone who respects Dr. Knight and who needs him."

She blinked at him from behind her glasses. "I suppose there is nothing to lose," she said hesitantly. "I certainly want him with you in Amsterdam. For his own sake." The decision formed on her chubby face. "Yes," she said. "I'll try to make him see you. Do you have a pencil and paper?"

Randall extracted a calling card from his wallet and handed it to her along with his gold pen.

She jotted something on the back of the card and returned it to him together with the pen. "That's Florian's address in Hampstead—Hampstead Hill Gardens, off Pond Street. It'll probably be a waste of time, but anyway, come to Florian's flat at eight o'clock this evening. I'll be there. If he won't see you, well, you'll know I tried and had no luck."

"But maybe he will see me."

"Nothing would make me happier," said Valerie Hughes. "He's really a wonderful person, once you get beneath the surface. Well, fingers crossed until eight." She offered a sad dimpled smile for the first time. "And God bless us, everyone."

HE HAD DROPPED an irritated Darlene off at the movie theater near Piccadilly, and continued on in the taxi on the seemingly endless drive to the address at Hampstead Hill Gardens.

From the dim street, Steve Randall had surveyed the intricately gabled three-story Victorian house, red brick with a gingerbread canopy over the ornate front door. Inside, and ascending the communal staircase, Randall guessed that the house had been divided into five or six modest apartments.

Dr. Florian Knight's flat was located past the head of the first flight of stairs. Unable to find a doorbell, Randall knocked, got no response, and knocked again more vigorously. The door finally opened, and a troubled Valerie Hughes, in blouse, skirt, low-heeled shoes, squinted at him through the owl spectacles.

"Has God blessed us?" he asked lightly.

"Florian has agreed to see you," Valerie half whispered. "Only for a few minutes, though. Follow me."

"Thank you," he said, and he followed her through the musty living room, with its drab, shabby furniture, its heaps of books and file folders occupying the armchairs, and now they entered the cramped bedroom.

He had to adjust his eyes to the subdued light of the bedroom. One table lamp beside the brass bedstead provided the only illumination in this dingy, gloomy cubicle.

"Florian," he heard Valerie Hughes saying, "this is Mr. Steven Randall from America."

Immediately, she faded back against the wall behind Randall. He could make out a figure propped up in the bed against two pillows. Florian Knight did resemble Aubrey Beardsley, as Naomi had suggested. Only he looked more so, more the esthete, more the eccentric. He was sipping what Randall supposed was sherry from a wineglass.

"Hullo, Randall," said Dr. Knight in a dry and somewhat supercilious voice. "You've quite an advocate in dear Valerie. It was only because I was curious to set eyes on such a paragon of sincerity that I consented to receive you. I'm afraid it will come to naught, but here you are."

"I'm pleased that you've allowed me to come by," said Randall with determined affability.

Dr. Knight had put aside his sherry and waved a limp hand toward a chair near the foot of the bed. "You may sit down, if you won't take it as an invitation to stay forever. I think we can cover whatever we have to say in five minutes."

"Thank you, Dr. Knight." Randall went to the chair and sat down. He could see now that the young man in the bed was wearing a hearing aid. He was not certain where to begin, how to penetrate the young don's hostility. He began with an amenity. "I was sorry to hear you'd been ill. I hope you're feeling better."

"I was never ill. It was a lie. Anything to be rid of our vain, deceitful friend, Jeffries. As to feeling better, I am not feeling better. I am feeling worse than ever."

Randall perceived that he would have no time for amenities. He would have to be as frank and direct as possible. "Look, Dr. Knight, I haven't the faintest idea why you feel as you do. I'm an outsider. Plainly I've walked into something I know nothing about. Whatever it is, I hope it can be resolved. Because I need you. I have been given very little time to prepare promotions for what appears to be a remarkable new Bible. While I am a clergyman's son, I have no more than a layman's knowledge of the New Testament or of theology. I need help desperately. I was advised, from the start, that you were the one person who could give me the help I require. Surely, whatever you have against Dr. Jeffries need not stand between our collaborating in Amsterdam."

Dr. Knight clapped his thin, nervous hands in mock applause. "Pretty speech, Randall. Not enough by a long way, be sure. But you can bloody well bet I'll not let myself be involved in anything that bloody bastard Jeffries is involved in. No amount of sucking up to me is going to swing it. I am through truckling to that pompous son of a bitch."

There was nothing more to lose, Randall could see. He spoke out. "What have you got against Dr. Jeffries?"

"Ha! What haven't I got against that filthy swine." Dr. Knight looked past Randall. "We could tell him a mouthful —right, Valerie?" He pushed himself higher in the bed with a pained expression. "Here is what I have against Jeffries, dear fellow. Dr. Bernard Jeffries is a beastly, bloody liar, who has used me for the last time. I'm damn tired of being put out among the dustbins, cleaning up behind him, while he goes on higher and higher. He lied to me, Randall. He wasted two years of my precious life. I'll forgive no man for anything like that."

"For what?" persisted Randall. "What did he—?"

"Speak up, for God's sake," Dr. Knight said loudly, fiddling with his hearing aid. "Can't you tell I'm deaf?"

"Sorry," said Randall, raising his voice. "I'm still trying to find out why you are so furious at Dr. Jeffries. Is it that, until yesterday, he didn't tell you the truth about the research he was having you do?"

"Randall, put yourself in my boots, if you can. I know it's not easy for a prosperous American to get inside the hide of an impecunious and malformed theology scholar. Yet, try it if you will." His voice was trembling. "Two years ago, Jeffries enticed me into leaving my comfortable situation at Oxford to come down to this petrol-foul city and live in this scruffy flat to do work for some earthshaking paper he was preparing. In return, he made certain promises to me. He has not kept them. Nevertheless, I have trusted him. I did not sulk. I've slaved for him, and did not mind doing so. I love the arena of our work, always have, always shall. I gave my bloody all. Then to learn yesterday, to learn overnight, that it had been a sham. To learn that this man I had put my trust and faith in had neither trusted nor believed in me. To have had it revealed to me, for the first time, that all my bloody toil had not been for what I thought, but rather for the translation of a new gospel, a revolutionary new Bible. To have been treated with such disrespect, contempt even— it drove me stark mad with rage."

"I can understand that, Dr. Knight. Still, you've admitted you loved the work. And taking an overview of it, you did great work—as Dr. Jeffries sincerely admitted in praise of you—you did important work for an important cause."

"What cause?" Dr. Knight snarled. "That bloody papyrus and the scraps of parchment from Ostia Antica? The revelation of the human Jesus Christ? Do you expect me to believe such a story on Dr. Jeffries' word?"

Randall frowned. "It's been thoroughly authenticated by leading experts in both Europe and the Middle East. I'm certainly ready to accept—"

"You don't know a damn thing about it," snapped Dr. Knight. "You're an amateur. And you're in their pay. You believe what you're told to believe."

"Not quite," said Randall, trying to control his temper. "Not even slightly. But from the evidence I've seen and heard, I have no reason to doubt or disparage the work of Resurrection Two. Surely you're not suggesting that this find—"

"I'm not suggesting anything," interrupted Dr. Knight, "except this. No scholar on earth knows more about the historical Jesus Christ and his time and his land than I— not Jeffries, not Sobrier, not Trautmann, not Riccardi. I'm stating that no one deserved to be at the forefront of that project more than Florian Knight. Until I have seen their bloody discovery with my own eyes, examined it to my own satisfaction, I'm not accepting it. Everything so far is just hearsay."

"Then join me in Amsterdam and put it to the test, Dr. Knight," said Randall.

"Too late," said Dr. Knight. "Too little, too late." He fell back against his pillows, fatigued and pale. "I am sorry, Randall. I've nothing against you. However, I shan't lend myself to being a consultant on Resurrection Two. I am neither that self-destructive nor that masochistic." He passed a limp hand over his forehead. "Valerie, I'm perspiring again. I feel beastly awful—"

Valerie had come up alongside the bed. "You've tired yourself enough, Florian. You must have another sedative and some rest. Let me show Mr. Randall to the door. I'll be right back."

Offering his thanks to Florian Knight for giving him time, but feeling great reluctance at leaving without gaining his objective, Randall followed Valerie Hughes out of the bedroom to the living room door.

Disconsolately, he had gone out into the hall and started toward the top of the stairs, before he realized that Valerie was coming after him.

"Wait for me at the Roebuck," she whispered hastily. "That's our local, the pub round the corner on Pond

Street. I won't keep you waiting more than twenty minutes. I—I think there is something I had better tell you."

HE WAS STILL waiting for Valerie at nine forty-five.

He sat on the wooden bench against the wall, close to the glass-paned doors of the entrance. Although he was not hungry, he had ordered a veal-and-ham pie to fill the time rather than his stomach. He had consumed the hard-boiled egg, some of the cold pressed veal and ham, and all of the pastry crust.

Lazily, he watched the younger of the two women behind the bar of the Roebuck draw a glass of beer from the spigot of a keg labeled Double Diamond, wait for the froth to dissolve, then fill the glass to the brim. She took it to the lone customer at the bar, an older man in laborer's clothes, munching a hot sausage on a stick.

Randall speculated again on what Valerie had meant outside Florian's flat: *There is something I had better tell you.*

What could there be left to tell him?

He wondered, also, what was keeping her so long.

That moment, he heard the entrance door of the Roebuck open and close, and Valerie stood before him. Randall leaped to his feet, took her arm, and steered her behind the table to the bench. He settled down across from her.

"I'm sorry," she apologized. "I had to wait until he fell asleep."

"Will you have something to eat or drink?"

"I wouldn't mind a small bitter. If you'll join me."

"Of course. I could stand one, also."

Valerie called off to the matronly barmaid. "Two orders of Charrington! Make it a pint and a half pint!"

"I'm sorry if I agitated Dr. Knight," Randall said.

"Oh, he was worse last night and most of today, before you came. I'm glad you spoke frankly to him. I listened to every word. That's why I wanted to talk to you in private."

"You mentioned, Valerie, that you had something to tell me."

"I have," she said.

They waited for the barmaid to serve them. The pint of draft beer was placed before Randall. Valerie was already drinking her half pint. Finally, she lowered her glass.

"Did you notice anything curious about the things Florian told you?"

"I did," said Randall. "I've been thinking about them while I waited. He spoke of promises that Dr. Jeffries had made to him, and not kept. He spoke of not joining Resurrection Two because he was not that self-destructive or masochistic, whatever that means. He spoke of being ill-used, not trusted, yet I can't believe he'd become so enraged that he'd withdraw from everything, merely over a matter of bruised vanity. I felt then and still feel there must be more to it."

"You are absolutely right," said Valerie simply. "There is much more to it, and what there is I feel I have to tell you, if you will keep it in confidence."

"I promise you I shall."

"Very well. I don't have much time. I must look in on Florian again, and get some sleep myself. What I'm going to tell you, I'm revealing for Florian's own good, for the sake of his survival. I don't feel I'm betraying him."

"You have my word," he reassured her. "This is between us."

Her pudgy face was solemn, her tone both solemn and urgent. "Mr. Randall, Florian is deafer than he lets on. The hearing aid helps make communication possible, but it's not truly effective. Florian manages only because he taught himself to lip-read long ago. He can do anything he undertakes to do. I honestly believe he is a genius. Anyway, as far as can be learned, both of Florian's middle-ear areas were damaged by an infection just after adolescence. The only possibility of a cure involves surgery and transplantation—maybe a series of operations. The surgery is called tympanoplasty."

"But can his hearing be fully restored?"

"His otologist has always thought so. The surgery, the

possible series of surgical operations, is costly. The one
surgeon recommended to do the job is in Switzerland.
It's always been far beyond Florian's purse. He barely manages to grub along. Also, he supports his widowed
mother. She's in Manchester, and entirely dependent on
him. I've offered to help Florian—little enough that I
can do—but he's far too proud for even that. You saw
how he lives. His three-room flat costs him eight pounds
a week. He needs a car, any kind, but can't afford one.
For all his brilliance, being a don and being so invaluable
to Dr. Jeffries, he makes only three thousand pounds a
year. You figure how far that can go. Consequently, Florian has been determined to earn more. His deafness
haunts him. Not only the actual difficulties it creates for
him, but the psychological part of it as well. The handicap has embittered him. So his major goal has been to
earn enough money for the surgery. After that, he—well,
he would like to be able to marry me and have a family.
You see?"

"Yes, I see."

"His one big hope was that Dr. Jeffries, his superior,
would retire before the mandatory age of seventy, which
would give Florian a chance at the Regius chair in Hebrew. It was a hope, but two years ago it became a
promise. Dr. Jeffries actually promised Florian that if
he would go down to the British Museum as a reader, he
would be rewarded, rewarded with Dr. Jeffries' early retirement and a recommendation that Florian be appointed
to replace him. The promotion would mean sufficient salary for Florian to have his surgery and eventually be able
to marry. With this understood, Florian was pleased to
dedicate himself to Dr. Jeffries' affairs in London. All too
soon, Florian heard a disquieting rumor—from a responsible source—that Dr. Jeffries had changed his mind about
retiring. The reason was selfish political ambition. According to what Florian heard, Dr. Jeffries was being discussed as the leading candidate to head the World
Council of Churches in Geneva. To promote his candidacy,
Dr. Jeffries had decided to retain his chair at Oxford as
long as he could."

"As a showcase?"

"Exactly. Poor Florian was most upset. But he could not verify the rumor, so he kept some faint hope alive that Dr. Jeffries would retire, as he had promised. Still, knowing he could not depend upon that, Florian undertook another scheme to raise money. He had always intended to write and publish a new biography of Jesus Christ, to be based on what is known of Jesus today—from the gospels, from non-Christian sources, from speculations by theologians—as well as on original deductions that Florian himself had made. So beginning two years ago, working mornings and afternoons for Dr. Jeffries, slaving every evening until past midnight, every holiday, almost every weekend, even during vacations, Florian did his research and wrote his book. A marvel of a book which he entitled *Christ Plain*. Several months ago, Florian showed a portion of it to a leading British publisher. The publisher was tremendously impressed. He agreed to give Florian a contract and a rather large advance of money—enough to take care of his surgery, even enough to let us marry—upon delivery of the completed book. Well, Florian had completed the book, and he was just doing the final revision. He planned to deliver the manuscript in two months, sign his contract, and be comfortable—or, let us say, solvent—after what seemed an eternity. I cannot tell you how happy he was. Until yesterday."

"You mean when Dr. Jeffries told him—?"

"When Dr. Jeffries revealed the secret of the Ostia Antica find, revealed that the International New Testament was on the presses, revealed all the hitherto unknown facts about Jesus Christ which are about to be made public. For Florian, it was as if he had been hit on the head with a mallet. He was crushed, in absolute shock. Every ounce of his energy, because of his dreams and hopes, had been poured into *Christ Plain*. Now, with this new find, this new Bible, Florian's precious biography was made obsolete, unpublishable, without meaning. What was most embittering was that had he been told of this new find two years ago, he would not have wasted his energies and hopes on this particular book. Worse, he realized that Dr. Jeffries had, unknowingly, used him to help research and translate the very work that destroyed his own book and his own future. Can you appreciate what happened to Florian yesterday, and understand why he was too overwrought to see you and too embittered to agree to go to Amsterdam?"

Steve Randall sat staring helplessly at his beer. "That's dreadful, a terrible thing to have happened," he said at last. "I can't tell you how sorry I am for Dr. Knight. If it had happened to me—why—I'd want to kill myself."

"He tried," Valerie blurted out. "I—I wasn't going to tell you—but—it makes no difference. He was so ill with despair yesterday, after leaving Dr. Jeffries, that he came back to his flat and swallowed a dozen, maybe two dozen, sleeping pills, and threw himself on his bed to die. Luckily I had promised to come by and make him dinner. I had a key, let myself in, and found him unconscious. The minute I saw the empty bottle, I rang up my mother's physician—he brought me into this world—I knew he could be relied upon—and he rushed over in time, and he saved Florian. Thank the Lord. Florian was quite ill throughout the night, but he began recovering his strength today."

Impulsively, Randall reached out and covered the young girl's hand. "I honestly can't tell you how bad I feel, Valerie."

She nodded. "I know how you feel. You're a decent man."

"I'm sorry I bothered him tonight. I can't blame him for not wanting anything to do with our project."

"Oh, but you're wrong about that, Mr. Randall," said Valerie with sudden animation. "If you hadn't come tonight, I couldn't be here to tell you what I'm going to tell you next. You see, I believe this is the very time that Florian must have a diversion, keep occupied, lose himself in work. I feel he must—absolutely must—become a part of your Resurrection Two. Before your visit, I thought there would be no chance. But when you brought the subject up, I was watching Florian's face, listening to him speak. I know every nuance of his voice. I know him so intimately that, whatever he may say, I know what he is

truly feeling. I heard him say he wasn't rejecting the
Ostia Antica discovery completely. I also heard him say
that he would believe it only if he could see it firsthand.
I know Florian, and I know the signs when he is piqued
and when he is coming to life. The signs were there. Only
he was too angry to allow himself to admit it."

"Do you mean—?"

Valerie offered her rare sad dimpled smile. "I mean
that Florian puts the greatest trust and confidence in me.
I can influence him to do almost anything, when I have
to. Well, I want him there with you on Resurrection Two.
I believe, beneath his pride, he wants to be there. I'm
going to see that he joins you in Amsterdam. I can almost guarantee that he will. Let's say in a week. He'll
need a week to get on his feet. After that, you'll have
him beside you, embittered, resisting, unforgiving, but
loving every moment of it and doing the job you need
done. You'll have him, I give you my word. Thanks for
your patience—and—and the half pint. I'd better dash."

It was only later—after he had found the cab in Hampstead, and reminded himself that he must telephone Dr.
Jeffries and say that he already had a translator-consul-
tant—that Randall unfolded the evening edition of the
London Daily Courier.

On the front page, the three-column headline leaped
up at him:

MAERTIN DE VROOME HINTS AT
STARTLING NEW TESTAMENT FIND;
BLASTS NEED FOR ANOTHER BIBLE.
CALLS PROJECT "USELESS AND IRRELEVANT"

The dateline for the news story said Amsterdam. The
byline read: "Exclusive From Our Staff Correspondent,
Cedric Plummer. First of Three Parts."

All the secrecy, thought Randall, and now this.

Heart pounding, he skimmed down the column in the
faint light of the cab.

Plummer had obtained an exclusive interview with the
increasingly popular Protestant church revolutionary, the

Reverend Maertin de Vroome of Amsterdam. The august cleric had stated that he was party to inside information that, based on an archeological discovery recently made, a fresh translation of the New Testament was in preparation. It would soon be foisted upon the public by an international syndicate of publishing profiteers, who were being supported by the greedy orthodox elements of the crumbling world church.

"We do not need one more New Testament to make religion relevant in this changing world," de Vroome was quoted as stating. "We need radical reforms within religion and the church itself, changes in the clergy as well as interpretations of the Scriptures, to make religion meaningful once more. Faith in this uneasy time requires something beyond new Bibles, new translations, new annotations based on yet another archeological discovery, to have real value for mankind. Faith requires a new breed of men of God working on behalf of men on this earth. Let us ignore or boycott this continuing commercialism of our Belief. Let us resolve to resist another useless and irrelevant Holy Book, and instead make relevant the message of the symbolic Jesus already familiar to suffering people everywhere."

And there was more and yet more of the same.

But nowhere in the news story was there a single concrete fact. No mention of Ostia Antica, no mention of Resurrection Two, no mention of the International New Testament by name.

The Reverend Maertin de Vroome had only the first rumor, and this was his opening warning to the members of the church establishment that he was arming to do battle.

Randall closed the paper. Wheeler had not been exaggerating the need for security, after all. With a power like de Vroome already onto them, the future of the project could be in utmost danger. As a part of the project, Randall himself felt threatened and unnerved.

And then one more thought unnerved him.

He had just been responsible for arranging to bring to Amsterdam an angry and embittered young man named

Florian Knight. If Maertin de Vroome was an enemy of Resurrection Two, then this cleric might find in Dr. Knight an ally who hated the project even more than he did.

As yet, de Vroome had not penetrated the inner defenses of Resurrection Two. But any day, with the presence of Dr. Knight in Amsterdam, the radical reformer might have his Trojan Horse at last.

Randall wondered what he should do.

He decided that he would watch and wait and try to learn whether the Trojan Horse was fated to remain an empty shell or was to become a carrier of destruction for what had become Randall's own last hope on earth.

III

FROM HIS aisle seat in the KLM Dutch jetliner, Randall leaned across Darlene in time to catch a passing glimpse of the capital of the Netherlands far below. Amsterdam resembled a gray-and-rust irregular checkerboard, with the squares occupied by spired towers and Humpty-Dumpty buildings, and marked off by gleaming liquid lines that were the old city's canals.

In his dark age during the time with Barbara, he had been in Amsterdam once, for two days, and had seen it routinely, impatiently: the principal square known as the Dam, the shopping area called Kalverstraat, the Rembrandt House, and the Van Gogh paintings in the Stedelijk Museum.

Now, in his plane seat, he looked forward to his return. What waited for him promised a new life. Even the lingering threat implicit in that London newspaper last night, the interview by someone named Plummer with the formidable Reverend Maertin de Vroome, added an air of hazard and uncertainty, and therefore stimulation, to his visit. Within the checkerboard below, two forces, antagonists, were moving in secrecy against one another: the orthodox legions of Resurrection Two, out to save and reinforce existing faith, pitted against a revolutionary named de Vroome, who wanted to assassinate the living Jesus Christ and bring down a church that had existed since the first century.

Randall was inwardly amused at the black-and-white simplistic way he had lined up the goods and bads, like matching a manufacturer-client against his competition,

like dashing off a press release. Still, he had long been
conditioned to be loyal to a client, and this was the way
he still felt.

He wondered whether Wheeler and the others had
seen Plummer's front-page story, and if so what the reactions had been. He wondered whether he should mention
the interview when he met Wheeler, who would be waiting with a car at the Schiphol Airport. He decided he
was wasting his time. Of course, Wheeler and the rest
would know about the Plummer story.

Five minutes later their plane landed smoothly on one
of the jetways, rolled up to a terminal apron, and Randall
and Darlene exited through the covered mobile gangway.
Standing on the rumbling travellator, they moved the distance of almost three football fields into customs. The
yellow glass sign over the Italian-made electronic computer, saying SOLARI 5, directed Randall to the location
of his luggage just arriving on the conveyor belt. The
uniformed Dutch customs officer came across the tile floor.
His open countenance beamed at Randall and Darlene.
"Americans?" He noted their customs questionnaires.
"Ah, Mr. Randall, we were notified to expect you.
Please go right on."

As they followed their porter, Darlene sighed with relief. "I was afraid they'd take away all my extra cigarettes."

Emerging into the arrival hall, Randall was momentarily lost. It seemed that he was within a small glass cage
encompassed by a larger glass cage.

Darlene was tugging at the sleeve of his sport jacket.
"Should we change our money?" she wanted to know,
pointing to a money-changing machine.

"Wheeler will take care of that," he answered. "Where
in the devil is he?" He signaled a radiant-faced KLM
girl wearing a navy blue outfit and white gloves. "Where
would we find a friend who is expecting us?" She directed
them to the nearest of four doors leading through the glass
wall into the outer area.

Wheeler, big and blustering, was already striding toward them. "Welcome to Amsterdam!" he bellowed. Then,

lowering his voice, he said, "I want you to meet the president of our publishing board, the head man at Resurrection Two, the distinguished Munich religious publisher—he insisted on coming along—"

Randall became aware of another presence which dwarfed Wheeler, a dignified gentleman at least six feet four in height. The gentleman had removed his hat, to reveal slicked-down silver hair outlining a bullet head. He wore rimless spectacles over his quick eyes, had a pointed nose, large yellow teeth.

"Dr. Emil Deichhardt," announced Wheeler, introducing Steven Randall and Darlene Nicholson.

Dr. Deichhardt went through the gesture of kissing the back of Darlene's hand without touching his lips to it, engulfed Randall's hand in a pawlike grip, and said in guttural but correct English, "We are so pleased to have you in Amsterdam, Mr. Randall. With you, our team is complete. Now we shall be able to put our effort of so many years before the entire world in the most effective way possible. Yes, Mr. Randall, your reputation precedes you."

Wheeler began to herd them out of the arrival hall. "No time to waste," he said. "We'll take you straight to the Amstel Hotel, the best in the city, where most of our executives are staying. Soon as you've dropped off your baggage, we want you right over at our headquarters. We want you to get your bearings there, meet some of the key personnel. After that—one o'clock, Emil?— you'll have lunch with all five of the publishers, as well as their theologian advisers—these will be present, too, excepting Dr. Jeffries, who arrives in a few days. Sa-ay, your wire promised quite a coup, your almost certain recruitment of Florian Knight. Later, you'll have to tell me how you managed it. You *are* a salesman, aren't you? Here we are, here's the car."

Before a huge pot of flowers, the sleek Mercedes-Benz limousine waited on the elevated driveway. The Dutch chauffeur had both doors open. Randall followed Darlene into the back seat, and Dr. Deichhardt joined them. Wheeler had taken the front seat.

They left Schiphol's giant radar control tower behind them, passed an unidentifiable modern black statue, rode through a well-lit tunnel, and attained the highway to Amsterdam. There was inconsequential talk, mostly between Wheeler and Deichhardt about publishing plans, and some directed to Darlene about the sights, but Randall hardly listened.

He preferred to contain himself, conserve his energies, before the strangeness of the alien place and new people and first day swept over him. It proved to be a thirty-minute trip to Amsterdam. The day was warm, the countryside and housing developments bathed in sun. An IBM factory loomed in sight, and after that they were off the highway, and there were street signs flashing past the windows, signs reading JOHAN HUIZINGALAAN, POSTJESWEG, MARNIXSTRAAT, and at a busier corner one read ROZENGRACHT.

He heard Deichhardt speaking to Darlene: "The house of Anne Frank is nearby. This canal is thirteen feet higher than the airport. Did you know the airport—indeed, most of the city—is below sea level? A most industrious people, these Dutch. Rozengracht—*gracht* means canal, and for your information *straat* and *weg* mean street—and *plein,* a word you will become familiar with, means square, or if you wish, plaza, such as Thorbeckeplein, which means only Thorbecke Square. *Bitte,* you see the tram ahead of us? You see the red-painted box on its rear?"

Randall, peering ahead, observed the cream-colored slender streetcar that had slowed them down.

"That is a mailbox," continued Deichhardt. "The Amsterdamers run up to deposit their mail on the back of the streetcar. Convenient, yes?"

The Mercedes had turned, and was going along Prinsengracht, and soon alongside the Amstel River. Randall took in the low-slung, glass-topped sightseeing boats in the canals, the Dutch crowding the thoroughfares on bicycles and motorbikes and in their compact cars, mostly the Dutch-made DAFs or Fiats or Renaults. Randall felt as if he were driving inside a tank. He watched the sturdy gabled brick houses go past. It was as if he had never been here before.

They were traveling over a sizable bridge, their speed decreasing, their chauffeur having eased into a left turn.

"Finally arrived," said Wheeler from the front seat. "Number One Professor Tulpplein. That's the address. The Amstel Hotel's tucked into the little cul-de-sac. One of the finest establishments in Europe. Nineteenth-century building. Elegant. When Queen Juliana and Prince Bernhard had their twenty-fifth wedding anniversary, with the royalty from the whole Continent attending, they had it right here in the Amstel. Now we have a surprise for you. Dr. Deichhardt and I got you the best suite in the hotel, the royal suite, the one the queen uses whenever she has need for it. Dr. Deichhardt and I are living in servants' quarters compared to yours."

"Thanks, but you shouldn't have," said Randall.

"Well, we're not all that altruistic, are we, Emil?" Wheeler gave the German publisher a stage wink and said to Randall, "There's method in our sacrifice. From this moment on, only one thing counts, above and beyond the paramount need for absolute secrecy. And that is your preparation of the most mammoth promotion campaign in history. We expect, the moment the news is out, you'll be receiving hundreds of representatives of the international press and television. We want you to receive them as if they are royalty and you are royalty, and meeting them in these regal surroundings will be very impressive and seductive. So you've got the queen's royal suite, Numbers 10 and 11 and 12. Miss Nicholson has a room adjacent. Anyway, we hope this setting will put you into a creative mood, so you'll get off to a flying start."

"I'll do my darnedest," said Randall.

They had drawn up before the stone steps and pillars and revolving door of the Amstel. The doorman was holding the car's rear door open, while the chauffeur was setting the luggage on the sidewalk.

Randall had stepped out of the limousine and helped Darlene down, when Wheeler beckoned to him. Randall bent back into the car.

"You're already registered, Steve," Wheeler said. "You can check the reception desk for your mail, which we had delivered here, but there should be no local messages. Except for customs at the airport, which was alerted to pass through a VIP we were expecting, no one else knows you are in Amsterdam. Outside of Resurrection Two, and some of the hotel personnel, no one knows or is to know you are here and connected with us. This is vital. If it got out, there are certain elements who'd do anything —*anything*—hide in your suite, bug your phone, bribe room service—to get whatever possible out of you. As our public voice-to-be, you are the most vulnerable of all of us. Keep that in mind and tell your—your secretary—"

"She knows nothing," said Randall. "As for caution, from this point on I'm the invisible man."

"Can you be ready in forty-five minutes?" asked Wheeler. "We'll send the car back for you. Tell you what, phone me just before you leave your suite. I'll be waiting downstairs at the Krasnapolsky to get you in. We've got a lot ahead of us."

Randall watched while the Mercedes limousine slowly circled the curve of the dead-end street—taxis and the private vehicles of hotel guests were parked in the center of it—and disappeared from sight. Darlene and the porters with the luggage had already gone into the hotel. Randall hurried after them.

Inside the lobby, he paused a moment to absorb his surroundings. Beyond the Oriental rug laid on marble was a magnificent brown-carpeted staircase leading upward to a landing, and then, winging off from the landing in two directions, tiers of steps led to a kind of mezzanine-balcony which could be seen from below. Off to the right, the two porters were waiting with the luggage, and near them, in a vaulted corridor, Darlene was inspecting a display of handbags in a lighted glass showcase. To Randall's immediate left was the tiny reception desk, and next to it a counter belonging to the cashier, where dollars could be exchanged for guilders and from which cables could be sent.

Randall approached the reception desk. "I'm Steven Randall," he said. "I understand I've been registered—"

The concierge gave a half bow. "Yes, Mr. Randall. We've been holding your mail."

He handed Randall a packet of thick envelopes. Randall thumbed through them. Office, office, office, all from Randall Associates in New York, from Wanda Smith, Joe Hawkins, and one from Thad Crawford, triply thick, no doubt a draft of the Cosmos Enterprises contract.

He had started away, when the concierge called out, "Mr. Randall. I almost overlooked this in your box. A message was left for you—"

"A message?" Randall was startled. Wheeler's recent words still rang in his ears: *There should be no local messages. . . . No one knows you are here.*

"A gentleman left it an hour ago. He is waiting for you in the bar."

The concierge handed Randall the message. It was in the form of a calling card. Randall looked at the delicate embossed printing. In the center of the card, a name: CEDRIC PLUMMER, ESQ. At the lower left: LONDON. At the right, handwritten in purple ink, one word: *Over.*

Randall turned the card over. In a neat hand, in more purple ink, was the message:

"Dear Mr. Randall—Greetings. Good luck with Resurrection Two. They do require public-relations counsel. Please join me in the bar to discuss briefly an urgent matter of mutual interest. Plummer."

Plummer!

Shaken, Randall slipped the card into his pocket. He could conjure up clearly—as if it were still last night—the front page of the *London Daily Courier*. Exclusive From Our Staff Correspondent, Cedric Plummer. June 12, Amsterdam. The interview with the Reverend Maertin de Vroome about the rumor of a new Bible.

How in the hell had Plummer known he was arriving in Amsterdam today? And in Plummer's message, something that he had not mentioned in his story last night, the code name Resurrection Two?

Randall prided himself on his cool, but momentarily, he verged on panic. His survival instinct told him to telephone Wheeler immediately. But Wheeler would not be at their headquarters yet. Randall's next instinct was to retreat to the safety and isolation of his suite. At the same time, he knew that he could not hide there forever.

He began to calm down. When there was an enemy, you confronted him with every appearance of strength. If possible, you used him. Forewarned, forearmed. Too, he was curious to see and know the face of the enemy.

He hurried over to Darlene. "Look, honey, there's someone I've got to meet in the bar for a minute. Business. Go up and unpack. I'll be with you in a jiffy."

She began to protest, then surrendered cheerfully, and accompanied the porters carrying their luggage toward the elevator. Randall returned to the concierge. "Where's the bar?" he wanted to know.

The concierge directed him leftward through the lobby, adding, "He is wearing a boutonniere."

Randall made his way to the bar, and went inside. It was a glassed-in room and spacious. Visible through a window was an outdoor restaurant directly below, where some couples were having late breakfast in the sun. Ahead, beyond the glass, he could see a portion of the canal, with a barge plowing through the water. The hotel bar was at his elbow. Above the exotic counter, and partially shielding it, was a latticework heavy with vines, while a decorative webbed mat covered the lower half. Randall went around it. The bartender, a jolly Dutchman humming to himself, was drying glasses.

Randall scanned the bright room. It was occupied by only two customers at this early hour. Nearby, a fat man sipped an orange juice and pored over a guidebook. At the far end, settled in a blue upholstered chair, at a table beside the draped window, was a well-dressed youngish man. A flower grew from his lapel. The enemy.

Randall started across the room.

The enemy was a dandy.

Cedric Plummer had thin dull hair, dark and combed sideways to cover a bald spot. He had beady ferret eyes above a bony nose, pinched-in cheeks, a small Van Dyke beard. His complexion seemed oyster-white. He wore a maroon cravat, jeweled stickpin, and a pinstriped suit of a conservative cut. An enormous turquoise ring encircled the finger of one hand. No frayed-cuff journalist from Fleet Street, thought Randall.

Catching sight of Randall, the staff correspondent of the *Courier* dropped the newspaper he had been reading, uncrossed his legs, and rose to immediate attention.

"I am honored, Mr. Randall," he said in a high-pitched voice, smiling mechanically to reveal buckteeth. "Do please sit down, Mr. Randall. May I offer you a drink? I was in bloody need of a Bloody Mary, but have what-ever—"

"No, thanks," said Randall curtly. He seated himself and Plummer dropped into the chair opposite him. "I've only a minute," resumed Randall. "I've just checked in."

"I know. What I have to discuss shan't take more than a minute, believe me. You read my message?"

"I read it," said Randall. "It was cutely contrived to bring me in here."

"Exactly," said Plummer with his unwholesome smile. "Precisely, my dear chap. That I knew you were arriving today, that I knew you were assuming the public relations post at the Grand Hotel Krasnapolsky, that I knew you would be working on Resurrection Two—all were intended to excite your curiosity and elicit your respect. I'm delighted that I have done so."

Randall detested the man. "Okay, what do you want?"

"Your cooperation," said Plummer.

"How?"

"Mr. Randall, it must be obvious to you that I have fairly dependable sources of information at my beck and call. I had no trouble learning of your appointment to this job, of your visit to London, of your arrival time here. As to Resurrection Two, well, as an opening gun, there was my exclusive story featured in the *Courier* yesterday. Certainly you read it."

Randall sat quietly, deliberately drumming his fingers on the table. He did not speak.

"Very well, play your strong and silent American role," said Plummer. "But be practical. You can hardly expect to publish an entire Bible—or New Testament—and have a couple of hundred people involved in its production, without the secret becoming unsecret sooner or later. Truth will out, my dear chap, always does, you know. My associates are familiar with all the people coming and going from and to your headquarters on the Dam. I know a lot, an awful lot, about your project already—"

Randall pushed his chair back. "If you know about it already, you don't need me."

"A moment please, Mr. Randall. Let's not play games. Admittedly, I don't know everything yet. But I shall, I shall, long before you are prepared to release the story officially. When I have learned the contents of your Bible, I'll know exactly what I need to know. I guarantee you, I'll have every detail, every fact, within two weeks. But I am in a highly competitive business, Mr. Randall. I must be first with the entire—the exclusive—story. I shall be. However, your cooperation can save me a great amount of effort, and hasten my exclusive by days. Understand this, I merely wish the story. When I possess it, I shall be favorable to your Resurrection Two—that is, *if* you've cooperated."

"And if I don't cooperate?"

"We-ll, I just might feel resentful, and what I write for the world might reflect how I feel." A note of nastiness had crept into his tone. "You wouldn't want that, would you? Of course not. Now I have studied your background, Mr. Randall, with special emphasis on the clientele your public relations firm has handled in recent years. You appear to be businesslike and unsentimental about the persons and organizations you've represented. You don't seem inhibited or stifled by high-mindedness or ridiculous morality. If people pay, you take them on. More power to you. Most admirable." He paused. "Mr. Randall, we —my associates and I—are prepared to pay."

Randall wanted to punch him, wipe the smirk off that oyster-white face. He contained himself, because there was one more thing he had to know. "You are prepared to pay," repeated Randall. "For what? What do you want?"

"Better, much better. I knew you would be sensible. What do I want? I want to see the advance page proofs of that—that supersecret New Testament. You'd have no trouble getting them. No one at the Krasnapolsky would be the worse off for it. You could go on with your proper announcement at the proper time. I only want a beat on my competition. I'm ready and empowered to talk business with you. What do you say, Mr. Randall?"

Randall stood up. "I say—drop dead, Mr. Plummer."

He spun on his heel and quickly headed for the exit, but not before the squeal of Plummer's parting shot reached his ears. "I'll not drop dead, my friend, until long after I've exposed Resurrection Two—and I am sure of doing just that, absolutely sure, as sure as I am that you and your ridiculous project are the ones who'll be dead in a fortnight!"

AFTER ARRANGING for Darlene, despite her objections, to go it alone on a sightseeing bus tour of Amsterdam by day and a Candlelight Tour of the canals in the evening, Randall had telephoned George L. Wheeler that he was on his way to the Hotel Krasnapolsky. Randall had also reported the unexpected encounter with the British journalist Plummer, and this drew a salvo of anxious questions from the publisher. Hanging up, Randall had girded himself for his entry into the protected and mysterious retreat where Resurrection Two operated.

Now, attentive beside a rear window of the chauffeured Mercedes-Benz limousine as it arrived inside a sprawling plaza area, he heard his chunky, middle-aged Dutch driver, who had given his name as Theo, rasp, "The Dam. Our central square. It is our hub, with the main streets of Amsterdam going out from it like the spokes of the wheel."

This was among the few sights of Amsterdam that Randall fully recognized. Clear memory of it from his previous trip, refreshed by Darlene's reading to him about it from a KLM guidebook fifteen minutes ago, helped him identify the landmarks they were passing. In the center of the square were two islands of people. One was around the Monument to the Liberation, the memorial of the Dutch to their countrymen who had died in the Second World War. When he had seen it several years ago, the monument steps had abounded with freaky-looking students of every nationality, who had generally been stoned on pot in the daylight and had often been caught copulating there in the dark. This morning there were as many young tourists lolling on the steps as ever, but they appeared more alive, engrossed as they were in conversations with one another or by reading in the early sun. Nearby was the second island of the Dam, a flat cement rectangle like a grassless park, with a hurdy-gurdy, a puppet show, an ice cream stand surrounded by children, and here numerous older citizens were resting on benches or feeding pigeons.

"To left, the Koninklijk Paleis," rasped Theo from behind his wheel. Randall obediently inspected the massive royal palace, which occupied an entire side of the square. "Our shrine, like Englishmen's Westminster Abbey," Theo went on. "Built on marsh, so there are thirteen thousand wooden piles underneath. The queen does not live in it. She lives outside city, only using palace for official receptions, the state occasions."

"Does it have a special throne room?" Randall wondered.

"Throne room? *Troonkamer? Ik versta het niet.*" Then he understood. *"Ja, ja, ik weet wat u zegt. Natuurlijk, wij hebben het."*

"Theo, can you please speak—"

"Excuse, excuse," the driver said quickly. "Throne room—yes, absolutely, of course we have one—a very big-size ceremonial great hall, very fine."

Randall pulled a yellow note pad from his pocket, and jotted down a few words. He had just had his first public relations idea since arriving in Holland. He would try it out on his employers. He was beginning to feel better again.

"Ahead, de Bijenkorf," Theo announced. Randall

recognized Amsterdam's largest department store, de Bijenkorf or Beehive, a six-story madhouse of customers. This moment, dozens of shoppers were streaming through the chrome-framed swinging and revolving doors.

"There, on the side next to it, where you go," said Theo. "The Kras."

"The what?"

"Grand Hotel Krasnapolsky, where is your headquarters. No one can speak such a name easily, so to us it is the Kras. A Polish tailor, A. W. Krasnapolsky, he quit his tailor shop and put there in the Warmoesstraat in 1865 a café, with wine and pancakes à la Mathilde made by his sister-in-law. After, he made a billiard room, and after the Wintertuin, the winter garden, then bought houses all around, and put extra floors on top, and made one hundred rooms for a hotel. Today three hundred and twenty-five rooms. The Kras. See, there is Mr. Wheeler. He is waiting for you."

George L. Wheeler was, indeed, waiting beneath the glass canopy that projected over the sidewalk.

When Randall stepped out of the limousine, Wheeler bounded forward to shake his hand. "Good to have you here, safe and sound," said Wheeler. "Sorry about that nasty run-in you had with Plummer. How in the devil he ever knew you were in Amsterdam, I can't figure out."

"We'd better figure it out," said Randall ruefully.

"Yes, we'd better. It's something we'll be taking up today. I warned you, they're cunning, they're sparing no expense or effort to destroy us. Never you mind, we'll be ready for them." He gestured grandly over his shoulder. "Here it is. The Kras. Our fortress for at least one more month, maybe two."

"It looks like any ordinary deluxe hotel."

"We prefer it that way," said Wheeler. "We've leased a small part of the ground floor for full staff meetings, and our employees can use any of the drinking and eating facilities at reduced rates—the American Bar, Palm Court and White Room for dining. However, Resurrection Two is really barricaded upstairs on the first and second floors. We've taken them over completely, mainly because we can secure them that way. For publicity work, Steve, we've assigned you and your staff two conference rooms up on the first floor. For your private office you'll have Zaal F, with a secretarial room next to it. You will have two more rooms—actually hotel rooms, Rooms 204 and 205. We haven't converted them into offices. That's where you can receive people or interview them privately. Or even have seclusion if you want to think or grab a nap. Although I doubt whether you'll find much time to nap this month."

"I doubt it, too," agreed Randall. "Well, where do we start?"

"By going right in," said Wheeler. He took Randall's arm, but he did not move. "One more thing. We have several entrances here on Warmoesstraat. You can use any one. You can use the main hotel entrance behind us. If you do, you always run the chance, as you go through the lobby, of someone like that Plummer person jumping out of the Prinses Beatrix Lounge, or the Prinses Margriet Zalen, or the American Bar, and delaying or accosting you before you reach the elevators. Of course, when you get out of the elevator, you'll be checked by our security guards. Actually, Steve, I'd prefer that anyone with a red card use another entrance."

"What do you mean—red card?"

"You'll see. The best entrance is just up Warmoesstraat a short way." He gripped Randall's arm more firmly, and propelled him up the street with the department store on one side of them and the hotel on the other. They arrived at a sign reading: INGANG KLEINE ZALEN. The revolving door was framed by two green-black marble columns.

"Right through here," said Wheeler.

They went into a narrow entry hall between a tiny room to the left and a larger room to the right, both with doors wide-open. A husky guard, wearing cartridge belt and pistol and a khaki summer uniform, blocked the doorway to the larger room.

"Up ahead," said Wheeler, "is the corridor leading directly to an elevator. Very well, now we'd better clear you with Inspector Heldering." Absently, Wheeler greeted the guard, and told him, "Heldering is expecting us."

The guard stepped aside, and Wheeler pushed Randall toward the security office. There were six people in the room. Two amply built young girls were busy with some file cabinets. Two suntanned young men in plainclothes appeared to be examining a map at a table. An older man in shirt sleeves, who was fussing over a small switchboard, was seated inside a semicircle of equipment that included microphones, banks of push buttons, and a low-slung television set whose four screens seemed to be picking up activity in the halls and corridors of the upper two floors.

Near them, at a brass-trimmed rosewood desk-table, a wiry man in his fifties, wearing the stern Dutch face of a Rembrandt town burgher, was completing a telephone conversation. At the front of his desk a brass sign identified him as Inspector J. Heldering.

Immediately upon hanging up, Heldering was on his feet, taking Randall's hand, while Wheeler made the introduction.

As the three men sat down, the publisher said to Randall, "I think you'll want to arrange some interviews with Inspector Heldering, Steve, once you're settled. He's colorful, and his operation here and in the city is fantastic. After we've announced our International New Testament, the public may be curious as to how we managed to keep it hushed up so long."

"They very well may be," said Randall, "that is, if we do continue to keep it hushed up." He smiled at Heldering. "No offense meant, Inspector, only—"

"Only you are worried the Cedric Plummers may penetrate us," said Heldering dryly. "Have no fear."

Randall was taken aback. "Mr. Wheeler told you of my encounter with Plummer?"

"Not a word," said Heldering. "In fact, I did not know Mr. Wheeler was informed about your meeting with Cedric Plummer in the Amstel Hotel bar. I was about to have a report of the incident prepared for him. In any event, you handled yourself admirably, Mr. Randall. I believe you told him to drop dead—and he replied that he would see this project dead first."

"Touché," said Randall with an embarrassed smile. "How did you know?"

Inspector Heldering brushed the air with one hairy hand. "No matter. We try to know always what our people are doing. Perhaps we do not always succeed—after all, the Reverend de Vroome seems to have learned something about our operation—but we try, Mr. Randall, we certainly try."

"You *will* make a good story," said Randall.

"Steve, you don't know half of it," said Wheeler. "Inspector Heldering was hired by the International Criminal Police Organization—Interpol—when it was reactivated in Paris in 1946 after the war. He was still with Interpol, in fact he had been promoted to a position just under Interpol's secretary general, when we succeeded in luring him away from his beautiful office in Saint-Cloud to head up security for Resurrection Two."

"It was not a difficult decision to make," said Inspector Heldering. "With Interpol I was doing man's work. Important. With Resurrection Two I am doing God's work. More important."

God's work with a gun, Randall thought. He said, "I guess I know very little about Interpol."

"Very little to know," said Heldering. "It's an organization of police from twenty nations giving mutual assistance to trap international criminals. I was with Interpol's main office in a suburb of Paris, but there are branch offices in over one hundred countries—the branch office in the United States is associated with your Treasury Department, the bureau in Great Britain is at Scotland Yard, and so on.

"At Saint-Cloud, we had one million identity cards of criminals on file. Each file listed nearly two hundred characteristics of a criminal we were hunting, these under headings such as nationality and race, complexion, gait, vices, tattoos, deformities, habits, and so on. In a lesser way, I've introduced the same identity system into Resurrection Two. My files have everything that we should know about everyone employed here. Also, similar information about those members of the press, about those religious revolutionists, extremists, competitors, who might have the desire and the opportunity to sabotage our effort."

"Very impressive," admitted Randall.

Heldering nodded courteously. "In fact, I had to know everything possible there was to be known about you, Mr. Randall, before I could issue you a pass from this office. It was most important to know your weaknesses—the degree of your drinking or taking of drugs, the types of women with whom you cohabit—as well as your vulnerabilities—could you be blackmailed if something damaging were known about your daughter Judy, or if someone revealed personal information about your sister Clare, or if someone seduced Miss Darlene Nicholson into revealing bedroom intimacies."

I'll be a son of a bitch, Randall thought, *le grand frère* —Big Brother—is watching. He said, "I see nothing is private, nothing sacred."

"Only Resurrection Two," said the unruffled Heldering.

"Well," Randall inquired with a trace of annoyance, "have I earned an A?"

"Not quite," said Heldering seriously. He opened a table drawer, extracted a small card. "You have earned a B, a red card, Grade B, but this is still a high priority, extremely high. You see—"

"I'll explain," Wheeler interjected. "Based somewhat on Interpol's system, the inspector has five security classifications for everyone in Resurrection Two. The red card, Grade A, means accessibility to everything, and has been given only to me, to the other four publishers, and to Mr. Groat, the curator. The red card, Grade B, insures accessibility to everything except holdings in one restricted area. Cards of other colors are for employees with fewer access privileges. So, you see, the inspector considers you a good risk at that, Steve. You have the second-highest priority."

Randall glanced across the desk-table at Heldering.

"And that restricted area Mr. Wheeler mentioned," said Randall, "what is it?"

"The steel safety vault beneath this hotel," said Inspector Heldering, "where Mr. Groat is the curator."

"What's in the vault?"

"The original papyri of the Gospel According to James written in 62 A.D. and the original pieces of the Petronius Parchment written in 30 A.D., as well as our five translations of them. They are more priceless than all the jewels and gold on this earth." Inspector Heldering rose from behind his desk, came around it, and handed Randall his identity card. "Here is your pass to Resurrection Two, Mr. Randall. You are free to go inside and begin your work."

TWO HOURS LATER, when Steve Randall returned to Zaal F, his private office on the first floor, he settled into his leather swivel chair, highly stimulated and charged by the first people he had met at Resurrection Two.

After Wheeler had shown him his office—heavy L-shaped oak desk, Swiss electric typewriter, several side chairs grouped before the desk, an imposing green fireproof file locked with a security bar down the center, rows of fluorescent lights above—Naomi Dunn had materialized to start him on his rounds.

Naomi had been assigned to introduce him to the scholars, specialists, and experts on the first floor, men who had spent years producing the International New Testament. Now, returned from meeting them, he awaited the arrival of Wheeler. In twenty minutes, the publisher would come by to escort him to Zaal G, the private executive dining room down the hall, where he was to attend a luncheon presided over by Dr. Deichhardt so that he could meet the syndicate of publishers and their advisory experts in theology. Following the luncheon, Naomi would return to take him up to the second floor where he would be introduced to the members of his own public relations staff and hold his first promotion meeting in preparation for the busy weeks immediately ahead.

Meanwhile, his mind was on the scholars he had visited in the past two hours. He knew that he would need the help of these specialists to mount his many-faceted publicity campaign for the International New Testament. He knew, also, how difficult it would be to sort out and remember the strange faces, those voices, those beings, their jobs, their infinite amount of intriguing knowledge. One of his sport coat pockets held a yellow note pad already filled with hasty scribblings and jottings made whenever he had trudged up one hall and down another to a new cubbyhole and its occupant.

To fix each specialist in his mind, he had decided that he must write down thumbnail impressions of every personality. This start of a condensed dossier of the Resurrection Two staff would be his handy hidden reference and guide to memory.

Randall rolled his chair up to the typewriter. He inserted a sheet of bond paper in the machine, sifted through his notes, and rapidly he began to type:

June 13
RESIDENT EXPERTS AT RESURRECTION TWO

HANS BOGARDUS . . . Has long blond hair, heavy-lidded eyes, flat features, effeminate voice. Rather slender. Had worked as librarian for the Netherlands Bijbelgenootschap--check spelling-- the Netherlands Bible Society. Joined Resurrection Two at outset as librarian in reference room, which is the hotel's Schrijfzaal or writing room, or used to be. Room now filled floor to ceiling with books, all cross-referenced. Every important Bible manuscript or codex in facsimile edition, and printed Bibles as reprints or in the original issues, and in all languages, available. Don't like Bogardus. Seems warm as an eel. Humble and sniveling and secretly feels superior. Naomi says he has a mind like a computer. Can find anything we require.

Can communicate it to us. So I need
him and will get along with him.

REV. VERNON ZACHERY . . . The big
preacher-orator from California who has
filled stadiums in New Orleans, Liver-
pool, Stockholm, Melbourne. Fundamental-
ist with booming voice and theatrical
features. Hypnotic eyes. Speaks with
the authority of a grandson of God.
Friend of President of U.S.A.--and of
George L. Wheeler. Sat me right down on
sofa of Consultants' Room and, as if
I were some Amazon Indian or cannibal,
began to convert me. Anyway, he is
considered a valuable salesman for International New Testament and I'm supposed
to think of how best to program him.

HARVEY UNDERWOOD . . . The American
public opinion pollster whose Underwood
Associates has branches throughout
Great Britain and Europe. Quiet, medita-
tive, factual gentleman. Has been doing
private survey for Resurrection Two on
religion and the public's attitude toward
it today. He's also been retained as an
adviser, and is contracted to be on
hand in Amsterdam one week out of every
month until publication. I felt a kinship
with him, and we had an amiable chat in
a corner of the Consultants' Room.
Underwood is to feed me poll results
which I will use as guidelines for
slanting my publicity pitches. Told
me his latest polling shows that whereas
50 percent of people attended church
once a week ten years ago, now attendance
has declined to 40 percent of population. Loss of attendance by far greatest

among Roman Catholics in United States
for first time. Polls shows Lutherans,
Southern Baptists, Mormons have best
attendance record. Among Protestans, the
Episcopalian attendance has declined most.
Decade ago 40 percent of Americans felt
religion losing its influence. Today, 80
percent feel religion losing influence.
Underwood said poll of college campuses
showed 60 percent of students feel church
and religion are not relevant to their
lives, while the rest feel they definitely are. Underwood and I agreed that
publication of new Bible could reverse
trend, possibly save organized religion.

     ALBERT KREMER . . . Met him next
door in the Copy-editing Department. Four
persons there, and Kremer is head copy
editor. According to Naomi, the most
important editorial job in preparing
new Bible, next to job of translating,
is that of proofreading. Kremer dwarfish,
hunchbacked, dedicated, sweet, diffident,
with hyperthyroid eyes bugging out like
binoculars. He's a native of Switzerland, from Berne, descended from a long
line of proofreaders. His father,
uncle, grandfather, great-grandfather
and other ancestors were all proofreaders of Bibles and other religious
works. He told me that exactness has
been a Kremer family fetish ever since
an immigrant Kremer ancestor, copy-
editing a new King James Version of the
Bible in London during the time of
Charles I, carelessly overlooked the
fact that the printers for the Station-
ers' Company had omitted the word <u>not</u>

from what was probably called the
Seventh Commandment, so that Exodus
20:14 read, "Thou shalt commit adultery." When this edition appeared in
1631, it became known as the Wicked
Bible or the Adulterous Bible, was much
in demand among gleeful libertines of
the period. The Archbishop fined the
printers 300 pounds, gave the money to
Oxford and Cambridge for printing
equipment, and ordered the Wicked Bible
destroyed. All but five copies in stock
were destroyed. However, the real responsibility and failure had been that
of Kremer's relative, who lived under a
cloud for the rest of his life. Ever
after, the contrite Kremer descendants
made a cult of accuracy. "You will find
not one error in the International New
Testament," Kremer promised me.

PROFESSOR A. ISAACS . . . I met him
in the remaining partitioned section of
the Terrazaal, called the Honored Guests'
Room, where visiting scholars and
theologians do their work. Only Professor
Isaacs, on leave from the Hebrew University, Israel, was on hand. He is
an expert on ancient Hebrew, and is
highly regarded for his efforts in
translating the Dead Sea Scrolls. Among
other things, he pointed out how a lack
of knowledge of the finer shadings of
Hebrew could transform an ordinary act
into a miracle. "An example I give
you," said Isaacs in his mellifluous
singsong voice. "The Hebrew word al
was always translated as on, so that the
Scriptures tell us that Jesus walked on
the water. However more, the Hebrew word

al also has another meaning, which is by.
Therefore, the translations could have
as correctly read that Jesus walked by
the water, in short, took a stroll by the
seaside. But perhaps the early Christian propagandists deliberately sought
a miracle maker instead of a pedestrian."

Steve Randall halted his typing, checked over the four
pages he had written, and surveyed his yellow note pad.
His scratchings reminded him how much the meetings
with those experts and specialists on the first floor had
inspired him. For the most, they had been men of direction and purpose. Unlike himself, each one of them
seemed to have love for his work and to have found
meaning in it.

About to consider his notes once more, Randall was
interrupted by a sharp rapping on his door.

Immediately, the door opened, and George L. Wheeler
put his head in. "Glad to see you working, Steve. Very
good. But it's time for lunch. Now be prepared to meet
the big guns."

THE big guns.

There were ten of them at the oversized oval table,
and their speech was a mixture of English and French.
While Randall's conversational French was rusty, faulty,
he had found that he could understand almost everything
he heard in French. And what Randall heard he found
tantalizing.

The lunch served by two waiters—mainly turtle soup
and fillets of turbot with asparagus tips—had not hindered
the conversation. There had been constant talk, much
verbal electricity, before and during the meal.

Now the fruit compote and coffee were being served,
and Randall sought to distinguish each guest from the
other and clearly identify each in his mind. Seated between George Wheeler and Dr. Emil Deichhardt, Randall
once more surveyed the big guns. Just as Wheeler had
the Reverend Vernon Zachery at his elbow, each of the

foreign publishers at the table except one had his adviser theologian at his side.

Next to Dr. Deichhardt, there was Dr. Gerhard Traut-mann, a professor of theology at Die Rheinische Fried-rich Wilhelms-Universität in Bonn. Randall suspected, and was amused by the suspicion, that Dr. Trautmann trimmed his monkish half-moon of hair to give him the look of Martin Luther seen in all those familiar prints. In the chair beside Trautmann sat Sir Trevor Young, the British publisher, a rather youngish fifty, aristocratic, fond of the low-keyed deflating comment and the understatement, whose theologian adviser, Dr. Jeffries, was still in London or Oxford.

Randall's eyes continued around the table. There was Monsieur Charles Fontaine, the French publisher, thinly handsome, foxy, witty, addicted to the epigram. Wheel-er had whispered that Fontaine was wealthy, also, with a splendid residence on the Avenue Foch in Paris and with political entrée to the highest circles in the Élysée Palace. Close to Fontaine was his theologian adviser, Professor Philippe Sobrier, from the faculty of the Collège de France. Sobrier appeared faded, withdrawn, part of the wood-work, yet listening to him, Randall suspected that this unobtrusive field mouse, reincarnated as a philologist, pos-sessed fangs.

Then there was Signore Luigi Gayda, the Italian pub-lisher from Milan who so strikingly resembled Pope John XXIII. He had either a goiter or four chins, and a bubbling, outgoing manner, and he referred with pride to the countless periodicals he owned in Italy, to the private jet plane he used to travel about his financial empire, and to his belief in American business methods. It was Signore Gayda who first had learned of Professor Monti's discovery at Ostia Antica, and had brought it to Dr. Deich-hardt in Munich, who in turn had organized this Bible-publishing syndicate. Finally, there was Gayda's Italian theologian, Monsignore Carlo Riccardi, a churchman of high intellect whose keenly chiseled features, aquiline nose, and severe cassock made him seem formidable. Associated with the Pontifico Istituto Biblico in Rome, he was present at Resurrection Two to serve as unofficial representative of the Vatican.

With his gaze still holding on the two Italians, a question occurred to Randall.

"Signore Gayda," he said, "you are a Catholic publisher. How can you bring out a Protestant Bible, and, in fact, how do you expect to sell it in a Catholic country like Italy?"

The Italian publisher lifted his shoulders in surprise, and his chins jiggled. "But it is perfectly natural, Mr. Randall. We have many Protestants, respected people, living in Italy. Actually, Protestant Bibles were among the earliest ones published in Italy. How can I do it? Why not? Catholic publishers need an imprimatur—official sanction to publish—on their Bibles, but of course the Vatican does not interfere with a Protestant Bible."

"Dear Gayda, permit me to elaborate for Mr. Randall, if I may?" It was Monsignore Riccardi who had spoken up, and he now addressed himself to Randall. "Perhaps what I say will also make clear my presence on this project." He seemed to formulate what he wished to say, and then he resumed. "You must know, Mr. Randall, there is very little difference between the Catholic and Protestant versions of a Bible, except in the Old Testament where we admit most of the Apocryphal books as sacred and canonical, and our Protestant friends do not. Otherwise our Biblical texts are largely the same, without differing theological overtones. In fact, a common Catholic-Protestant Bible already exists in France, as my friends Monsieur Fontaine and Professor Sobrier will verify, and two of our Catholic theologians collaborated with the French Protestants on the edition. You are surprised?"

"I am indeed," admitted Randall.

"But it is so," said Monsignore Riccardi, "and there will be more of the same cooperation in the future. Of course, that particular French Bible does not have our imprimatur, any more than this first edition of the International New Testament will have our imprimatur. But we remain interested. And we remain involved. Because—well —I daresay that ultimately we will prepare our own edition of the International New Testament, and that version will have to be newly translated to conform to our own doctrines. There is one critical point upon which we differ with our Protestant friends."

"And what is that?"

"On the relationship of James the Just to Jesus, of course," said Monsignore Riccardi. "James refers to himself as the brother of Jesus, just as Matthew and Mark referred to the brothers and brethren of Jesus. Our Protestant friends have suggested that we interpret *brother* to mean blood brother, implying—not stating so outright, but implying—that Jesus and James and their siblings were conceived as a result of a physical union between Mary and Joseph. For Catholics, this is quite impossible. There can be no ambiguity. As you know, we believe in the perpetual virginity of Mary. From the time of Origen and the early Church fathers, Catholics have held that James was an older stepbrother of Jesus, the child of Joseph by a former marriage, a stepbrother or perhaps a cousin. In short, we hold that the Virgin Mary and Joseph had no conjugal relationship. However, arriving at an acceptable interpretation presents no difficulty, since the word *brother* in Aramaic and Hebrew has no precise or single definition, and can mean a half brother, a brother-in-law, a cousin, a distant relative, as well as a blood brother. Regardless, we will ultimately have a Catholic version of the International New Testament. His Holiness is far too understanding to ignore future implications of the Gospel of James and its value to our multi-nation Catholic community."

Satisfied, Randall retired to his role of listener, as the others went on talking. Gradually, Randall began to discern with growing interest that the conversation was divided and separate. During one prolonged period, the theologians—the Reverend Vernon Zachery, Professor Sobrier, Dr. Trautmann, Monsignore Riccardi—fell into a discussion of the need to preserve the orthodoxy of the church.

Dr. Zachery felt that a revival in religion inspired by the new Bible would create an opportunity that the organized church must take advantage of to strengthen its position of authority. "Until now, we have been allowing ourselves to go slack, give in, compromise with the devils of radicalism and dissolution," Zachery insisted. "No more. No more softness and no more compromise. Our flock needs the authority of tradition, of discipline. We must again stress doctrine and dogma. We offer an expanded New Testament now, and we must be emphatic about its infallibility. In our sermons we must reinterpret the Resurrection on the basis of St. James, making it clear it was an act of God, an incarnation, and we must assert the need for brotherly love, forgiveness of sinners, the promise of a hereafter."

Professor Sobrier agreed, but less bombastically. He said, "If I may quote a countryman of mine, the French philosopher, Marie Jean Guyau, 'A religion without myth, without dogma, without cult, without rites is no more than a bastard thing. . . . Religion is a sociology conceived as a physical, metaphysical and moral explanation of all things.' "

Dr. Trautmann interjected his views, and they were even more conservative. "I concur that ceremony and ritual are of the utmost importance. But I have come to believe that the church should give higher priority to liturgical music and chanting, and that readings from the Bible during the service should be in Latin and not in any modern vernacular tongue. I hold that this, like the repetition of the Hindu or Buddhist mantras, can offer a mystical experience, encourage meditation, bring our worshipers more by feeling and less by reason to a Oneness with the Supreme Being. In short, although the Gospel According to James will offer a new picture of Our Lord that rationalists can accept, we must not permit Him to be reduced to a passing secular historical figure— but must remind our parishioners that through Him, and His church, may be found the answers to our birth, our being, our passing, the ultimate mysteries."

Randall could detect that the publishers, who had been listening attentively, were faintly concerned. Monsieur Fontaine, the French publisher, interrupted the exchange among the theologians. "Gentlemen, if I understand you correctly, you expect to reshore entirely the bastions of the old church. But if you use the impetus that the International New Testament will give to religion by going totally backwards to traditionalism, you may be making a serious mistake. The activist factions in the church will not be satisfied, and soon the ground you have gained will be lost. Of course, reinstate orthodoxy with the revealed Truth, if you will, yet serve it up with a modicum of relevancy."

The discussion went back and forth for a while, but before long the publishers fell silent, and the theologians were again deeply involved in their own conversation, this time over the value of the symbolism in the newly discovered sayings of Christ, as recorded by His brother, James the Just.

For a while, Randall noted, several of the religious publishers listened, but their attention span was short. They became increasingly restive. They seemed to regard their churchmen as loons engaged in counting how many angels might be able to dance on the head of a pin. Gradually, Deichhardt, Wheeler, Fontaine, Sir Trevor, and Gayda began to monopolize the conversation. Their exchanges were purely business, commercial, and involved their problems of publishing and promoting their great investment.

Sir Trevor Young voiced some concern. "This discovery will have a profound effect on the churches, but what I fear is that it may cause clashes between one church and another. The majority of churches will accept our New Testament, as we know, but others may not. It may take a generation for our revised Bible to take its full effect, and this worries me, for any controversy may bankrupt every one of us. We need solidarity. We must overwhelm all churchdom, before any opposition can form and cause trouble."

Dr. Deichhardt chided Sir Trevor in a friendly way for having any concern about a commercial success in Great Britain. "You, Sir Trevor, and George Wheeler in America, you do not have to overcome the obstacles we face in

Germany. You can go directly to the public with your advertising and stories in your hundreds of religious weeklies and monthlies. In Germany, we have two entrenched obstacles. First, the Lutheran Bible, which is used in most of our eleven states. Second, the Lutheran Bible is published only by members of our Union of Bible Societies. To make these publishers accept our International New Testament, I must ask them to give up their own profitable venture. We may have to arrange some profit sharing partnership with the Union, to avoid trouble."

"You're a needless worrier, Emil," the British publisher replied. "You won't have any trouble in Germany. Once your public learns of the new gospel, the new discoveries, they'll clamor for the International New Testament. They'll consider the Lutheran Bible superseded, incomplete and therefore obsolete. Your Union of Bible Societies will have to distribute and sponsor your edition. Mark my word. Once the publicity drums beat— and Mr. Randall will see to that—public demand for our product will overcome every obstacle. Perhaps even the dissenting churches that give me so much anxiety."

Fontaine and Wheeler then turned the talk toward costs, pricing, distribution, advertising.

Finishing his coffee, Randall sat back, fascinated. Now he was certain of what he had sensed—a definite rift between the theologians and the publishers. The theologians were as annoyed with the publishers' dollar-pound-mark-franc-lire talk as the publishers had been impatient with their theologians' spiritual talk. Randall had a heightened feeling of an old ongoing conflict. To himself, he tried to summarize the clear-cut difference: He guessed that the theologians felt genuine passion for the International New Testament, with its words from the brother of Jesus and from the centurion who had recorded the results of Christ's trial. In these theologians he perceived real faith, real belief, in the newly revealed Resurrection of the real Christ. The publishers, on the other hand, while paying lip service to this Resurrection, to its potential in giving men everywhere faith and hope, seemed interested mainly in their profits. They were business tycoons who happened to be in the Bible production trade. They could as well have been producing automobiles or packaged food or oil, and spoken no differently.

Unsettling, this schism. But understandable.

Dr. Deichhardt had resumed speaking of his apprehensions about a commercial failure. "And don't forget we have had accentuated in Germany an obstacle some of you also suffer from strongly. We have been the center of church reform from Luther to Strauss and Bultmann. Now we are a hotbed for what verges on the heretical, for what goes beyond the demythologizing of the gospel stories, for what amounts to more than mere skepticism about Our Lord's existence and His message. We are an exceptionally virulent hotbed for the growth of the revolutionary and radical de Vroome movement. This madman is not only the enemy of our established churches—but clearly the enemy of our sacred collaborative effort to rescue mankind with our International New Testament. Think of what I must overcome in Germany, gentlemen."

"No more than any of us will have to contend with in any of our countries," insisted Wheeler. "De Vroome's reform converts are everywhere. But I do believe once our Bible is released, the truth and power of it will drown out de Vroome and his adherents, overcome them, eradicate them from the face of the earth. Our surprise revelation will stun them, leave them helpless and unable to retaliate."

"Since the element of surprise is the key to your success," Randall interrupted, "are you positive that you're doing everything possible to keep the contents of the International New Testament from the Reverend Maertin de Vroome?"

Immediately, everyone spoke up at once, describing new protective measures being taken to keep their secret from de Vroome and his fanatics who lurked not far away in the city surrounding the Dam.

For the first time during the luncheon, businessmen publishers and spiritual advisers were as one in their cause and their belief.

Interesting, Randall thought. Give the inhabitants of the

Tower of Babel a common fear, and they learn to speak a common tongue.

THIS WAS even better. Randall was among his own kind, and he felt comfortable and relaxed.

Naomi had brought him to Room 204 of the Hotel Krasnapolsky—an ultramodern room, white walls, cubist-style white lacquered furniture, shining chrome lamps, a box of fluid and moving kinetic art hanging over a red couch—and she was introducing him to his public relations assistants for the first time.

Drink in hand, Randall was chatting with Paddy O'Neal, a native of Dublin who looked like an Irish lorry driver and had been employed by publicity organizations in London and New York. O'Neal had a winning sort of irreverence toward the Bible. "I'll write about it," he promised Randall, "but don't expect me to believe in it, unless there's a bonus involved. I'm an Oscar Wilde man. Remember what Oscar said about the Crucifixion of Jesus and Christianity? 'A thing is not necessarily true because a man dies for it.'"

Next, Randall was led to a young man slouched in a chair who, in profile, looked like a question mark. As it turned out, he also knew all the answers.

"Elwin Alexander is our planter of oddity items," Naomi explained.

Puzzled, Randall asked, "What do you mean by oddity items?"

Naomi nodded to Alexander. "Tell him, Elwin."

Alexander cocked his head at Randall. "You really want to know? Okay, if you're willing to suffer cruel and unusual punishment. This is what I feed to hungry newspaper columnists and editors." He inhaled deeply, and exhaling, he began speaking a mile a minute like a tobacco auctioneer. "Do you know the shortest verse in the English language text of the New Testament contains only two words, 'Jesus wept.'? Do you know that the apostles addressed Christ as Rabbi, for Teacher? Do you know that the New Testament credits Jesus with exactly forty-seven miracles? Do you know that the Old Testament makes no mention of a city called Nazareth, and that the New Testament makes no mention of Jesus' being born in a manger, worshiped in a stable, or crucified on Mount Calvary? Do you know that in the gospels Jesus refers to Himself eighty times as the Son of Man? And now, Mr. Randall, do you know what a planter of oddity items is?"

"I didn't, but I do now, Mr. Alexander," Randall laughed.

After that, there were more faces, more lively exchanges. These were his people, and Randall appreciated them and tried to file away information on each one. The consumptive-appearing and reedy gentleman was Lester Cunningham, who had gone to a Baptist divinity school in the South to escape the United States Army draft, and become genuinely devout. Previously, he had worked as an advertising man for *Christian Bookseller, Christian Herald, Christianity Today*. The stout bourgeois Dutch maiden from Rotterdam, the one with bangs and no makeup, was Helen de Boer. According to Naomi, of the 325,000,000 practicing and nonpracticing Protestants on earth, none knew more about their religion than Helen. Protestantism was her major; Luther, Melanchthon, Calvin, Wesley, Swedenborg, Eddy, Bonhoeffer, Schweitzer Niebuhr were her minors. The attractive dark-eyed girl with semi-shingled hair, lithe torso, wearing a trim suit, was Jessica Taylor, whose parents were American and who had been raised in Portugal. Biblical archeology was Jessica's specialty, and before coming to Resurrection Two she had worked on the Tell Dan excavation north of the Sea of Galilee near Lebanon.

Finally, Randall found himself face to face with Oscar Edlund, a melancholy Swede from Stockholm who had been hired to do the artwork for the project. If Edlund was the most unprepossessing person in the room, he was also the one with the most impressive credentials. He had carroty hair, squint eyes, acne-marked cheeks, and a Rolleiflex dangling from a strap around his neck which seemed part of his anatomy. A longtime student of Steichen, he was now considered one of the world's foremost photographers.

"We should get maximum press coverage through your photographs of the original papyri and parchment," Randall told Oscar Edlund. "The one thing that worries me is the quality of the reproductions. How did they turn out?"

"First-rate," said Edlund, "when you consider what I had to work with." He shook his head. "Those bits and pieces of papyrus and parchment were pretty worn and brittle after being buried for more than nineteen hundred years. Before anyone could work with them, specialists had to humidify the fragments to a critical degree, moisten them enough so that they could be flattened under glass, yet not get them so moist that they would liquefy. Of course, the ancient Aramaic writing by James or his scribe and the Greek printing on the older parchment pieces required that I use infrared photography to bring out, to make legible, the dim ancient words. But you'll like what you see."

"How many sets of prints did you make?"

"Only three," said Edlund. "Strict orders. The three sets went to Dr. Jeffries for use by his translating teams, although sometimes the translators were permitted to examine individual original fragments in the vault. When the translations were completed, the three sets of photographs were returned to the Krasnapolsky. Two of the sets were destroyed, and the remaining set, the only existing one, well—you have it, Mr. Randall."

"I have it?"

"It was placed in the fireproof file cabinet in your office only yesterday, in a folder along with many other publicity pictures behind a security bar and lock. Valuable cargo, Mr. Randall. Handle with care."

"You bet I will," said Randall.

"Of course," added Edlund, "I still have my negatives —I've just moved them from the vault to the darkroom we built, so that I'm ready to run off hundreds of sets of prints for the press any day before Resurrection Two is announced. In case you have any worries about it, the negatives are safe enough. This darkroom of mine—it was constructed under the supervision of Inspector Hel-

dering—is well protected from intruders, I assure you.
I'm prepared to go ahead the moment you give me the
signal."

"Great," said Randall. "Those pictures will make a
tremendous impact. . . . Well, I guess we ought to start
our first staff meeting and find out where we stand."

Where they stood, Randall quickly learned, was dismay-
ing.

Earlier, Dr. Deichhardt had ordered members of the
staff to develop some publicity ideas, make notes on such
fragmentary materials as they were familiar with, but he
had not permitted them to write full stories. Deichhardt's
concern was that any advance stories floating around might
leak out and thus endanger secrecy. This meant that
little had been accomplished to date. It also meant that
there was a fantastic amount of work to do in short
weeks.

As the meeting proceeded, Paddy O'Neal volunteered
a suggestion. He felt that one thing that might be done
immediately would be to write advance interview features with the key personalities responsible for the International New Testament. He suggested they start with a
series of dramatic stories about Professor Augusto Monti,
of Rome, who had dug up the Gospel According to James
and the Petronius Parchment at Ostia Antica. Then, several pieces might be written on Professor Henri Aubert,
the radiocarbon wizard in Paris, who had authenticated the
age of the papyri and the parchment. Next, there could
be a few articles on Dr. Bernard Jeffries, who had supervised the three committees translating the Aramaic and
Greek finds into four languages (plus an Americaniza-
tion of the English translation). Finally, a number of
colorful features could be readied on Herr Karl Hennig,
who was now printing the various language editions of the
Bible in Mainz, in the very place where Johann Gutenberg had invented movable type and produced the first
mechanically printed book in history.

Conceding that these personalities behind the Bible
should be tackled first, Randall requested copies of the

staff's research files so that he might study them in the next few days.

"I'm going to speak to Deichhardt and Wheeler tomorrow about giving us the green light on publicity material," Randall said. "I'll promise them we'll be careful. I know the risks involved. In fact, I had a dangerous run-in this morning."

Randall told the staff briefly about how Cedric Plummer had tried to bribe him. Immediately, Cunningham and Helen de Boer chimed in with their own experiences. Since Plummer's interview with de Vroome had appeared, they had each received threatening anonymous phone calls, but had hung up before they could learn exactly what the callers wanted. And yes, they had reported this to Heldering's security office.

"Okay," said Randall. "I'm sure there'll be more of the same. But let's assume we reach publication safely, with our secret intact. The next question on the agenda: How do we release the story of the International New Testament to the public?"

Everyone in the room thought that there should be a huge press conference for newspaper, television, and radio representatives of all nations.

"Agreed about the press conference," said Randall. "However, since this is, in my opinion, absolutely the biggest news story in modern times, I think the press conference should be the biggest one in history. I have two wild notions. I'd like to see the opening announcement made from a stage in the Netherlands Royal Palace on the Dam. And I'd like it made not only to the press, but simultaneously to the world's viewers around the globe. I'd like to transmit our press conference—the announcement of the discovery, the announcement of the new Bible containing it—to every country on earth via Intelsat, the communications satellite system. How's that?"

The staff reaction was unanimously enthusiastic.

Helen de Boer volunteered to investigate discreetly the possibility of using the royal palace on Friday, July 12, the date for the publication announcement. Lester Cunningham offered to speak in confidence to the heads of the International Telecommunications Satellite Consortium and to the European Broadcasting Union to learn the chances of using satellites to relay to over seventy member nations the first news of the Word.

"Finally," said Randall, "I've saved discussion of our real story, our number-one story, our most sensational story, for the last. That, of course, is the story about the complete Jesus Christ, the real Christ, as revealed in our International New Testament. Into the preparation and popularizing of our story of Christ Returned will go our greatest combined effort. Now, I'll confess I know only sketchy details about the contents of the new Bible. I know that from this Bible we'll learn of Christ's physical appearance for the first time. We'll be filled in on His missing years. We'll be told by His brother that Jesus survived the Crucifixion and continued His ministry as far away as Rome, and died in His fifty-fifth year. Since I'm so new to this project, I haven't had time to learn much more than that. But I hope one of you has somehow had a look at the actual Gospel According to James and the Petronius Parchment, and knows what is really in it and can—"

Randall was interrupted by protests from almost everyone in the room. The protests added up to one complaint: "No. They wouldn't let any of us read the discoveries."

Again, security was keeping them all dumb—and helpless.

Randall was infuriated. "To hell with that," he told the others in the room. "If they want us to publicize their new Christ, they've got to let us meet Him. Okay, the next move is clear. I'm going to get my hands on those page proofs and find out exactly what we have to work with. And I promise you, I'll see that you get copies as soon as possible. Let's adjourn now—and reconvene tomorrow, when I expect to have news for you."

BACK IN his office, Randall rested only briefly. Dazed as he was by meeting so many people in the past six hours, he knew that there was still one major task that needed doing.

But first, he must not forget his homework. He went to the heavy fireproof file cabinet, unlocked it, and removed the security bar. Opening the top drawer, he located the thick folder marked PHOTOGRAPHS OF PAPYRI AND PARCHMENT—ONLY COPY—RESTRICTED.

He carried the folder to his desk, lifted his already bulging black leather briefcase atop the desk, and shoved the folder alongside the other manila folders containing information on Monti, Aubert, Jeffries, and Hennig that he had just collected from his staff members.

Only one item was missing from his briefcase—the most important one—and he meant to get his hands on it right now.

He sat down in his swivel chair, and he was about to pick up the telephone, when a knock on the door brought him around. Before he could say *Come in,* Naomi Dunn had come in. Shutting the door behind her, she examined him impassively.

"You look as if you'd been through a washing machine," she said.

"A brainwashing machine," he corrected her, "a whirlpool machine that spun me in with maybe a hundred other people. You ought to know. You led me into it." He sighed. "Quite a day."

"Only the beginning," Naomi said unsympathetically. She dragged a chair to the front of his desk, and sat on a corner of it to indicate that her visit was going to be brief and businesslike. "I saw you making notes wherever you went."

"I always do," he said defensively. "Especially when I'm thrown up against so many different names. I wanted a record of who's who and what."

"Well, it's inefficient, a person in your position, having to do all that. You should have had a secretary along to take care of that for you. It's my fault. I should have seen to it the second you arrived. We'd better settle the business of a secretary before you do another thing." She paused. "Do you have any preferences? I mean to say, are you thinking of using Darlene Nicholson? Because if you are, Inspector Heldering will have to—"

"Cut it out, Naomi. You know better than that."

She shrugged. "I like to be sure. Now that you're formally installed, your importance to the project has grown. We want you to be satisfied in every way. You need a confidential secretary, one conversant with religious publishing, one you can completely trust."

He placed his elbows on his desk and looked straight into her eyes. "What about you, Naomi? I'd trust you. We've been close."

She flushed. "I—I'm afraid not. My loyalties are entirely to Mr. Wheeler."

"Mr. Wheeler? I see." He thought he did see. He saw that perhaps the model American religious publisher had an ex-nun on the side. "Okay, what do you suggest, Naomi?"

"I think you need someone who's already involved in the project. I have three girls who've been with us for over a year. Each one is highly qualified. Each has been screened and awarded a green card, which is a step up since the other girls hold black cards. You can interview these three before you leave."

"No, thanks. I'm too tired. Besides, there's something else I've got to do. I'll take your recommendation. Can you recommend one?"

She stood up. Her tone was brisk. "As a matter of fact, I can. Just on the chance that you might want my advice, I brought along one of the girls. She's in the outer office. Her name is Lori Cook. She's American. I felt that might make it easier for you. She's been abroad two years. Complete stenographic know-how. Exceptional skills. She's been working on this floor for a year and two months. She's fanatically devoted to the project—and to religion."

"Oh?"

Naomi Dunn's eyes narrowed. "What does that mean? You want someone who's a believer, don't you? It helps. When an employee of ours feels she's doing God's work, the clock has no hands for her." Naomi paused. "One more thing. She has a physical deformity. A crippled leg. I've not questioned her about it, because she gets along fine. As I said, she has everything a secretary should have,

but I might warn you"—Naómi gave him a crooked smile
—"Lori is hardly a sex object."

Randall winced. "You really think that's a big thing
with me?"

"I just wanted you to know. I think you'd better see her
for a minute, before you make up your mind."

"I'll take her. And I'll see her—for a minute."

Naomi had gone to the door and opened it. "Lori,"
Naomi called out, "Mr. Randall will see you now."

As Naomi stepped aside, Lori Cook came into the
room. Hastily, Naomi introduced her and then took her
leave.

"Come in, come in," Randall said, "and have a seat."

Naomi had spoken the truth, of course. Lori Cook
was hardly a sex object. She was birdlike, a tiny gray
sparrow. She limped toward his desk, sat nervously,
brushed back her wispy hair, and placed her folded
hands carefully in her lap.

"Miss Dunn says you're a whiz," Randall began.
"You've been working in another office, I understand.
Why would you want to leave it to be my secretary?"

"Because I was told that this is where everything will
be happening from today on. Everyone says the success
of the International New Testament depends on you and
your staff."

"Everyone exaggerates," said Randall. "It'll be a success
anyway. But we can help. The success of this new Bible
is very important to you?"

"It's *everything*. None of us knows what's in it, but
from what I've heard, it is something incredibly miraculous. I can't wait to read it."

"Neither can I," said Randall dourly. "What is your
faith, Lori?"

"I was a Catholic. Recently, I've left the Church and
been attending Presbyterian services."

"Why?"

"I'm not sure. I guess I'm searching."

"I'm told you've been abroad a few years. I'm interested
in why you left whatever you're from."

He could see Lori Cook clench her hands. Her little

girl's voice, barely audible, quavered. "I left Bridgeport, Connecticut, about two years ago. After high school I worked and saved my money so I could travel. When I was twenty-two—I thought I should do it then. So—I went on this pilgrimage."

"Pilgrimage?"

"To find—don't laugh at me—to find a miracle. My leg. I've been crippled since birth. Medicine could never do anything. So I thought maybe the Lord would. I made a pilgrimage to all the holy shrines and places I'd heard about, the famous ones where there had been authentic cures. I traveled, and took jobs along the way to travel some more. I went to Lourdes first, of course. Since Our Lady was seen by Bernadette, I prayed that she would appear to me, too. I knew that two million pilgrims went there every year, and nearly five thousand reported cures in a single year, and the Church declared fifty-eight of the cures—blindness, cancer, paralysis—miraculous."

Randall was tempted to ask what had happened to Lori at Lourdes, but she was so intent on her recital that he refrained.

"After that," Lori Cook was saying, "I went to the Shrine of Our Lady of Fátima in Portugal, where in 1917 the three shepherd children first saw the apparition of the Blessed Virgin standing on a cloud, shining brighter than the sun. Next, I visited the shrine at Lisieux in France, and Turin Cathedral in Italy, where the Holy Shroud is kept, and then Monte Allegre, and then Sancta Sanctorum Chapel to pray to the portrait of Our Lord which was not painted by mortal hands, and there I tried to mount the twenty-eight holy steps on my knees, but they wouldn't let me. After that I traveled to Beauraing in Belgium, where five children had visions in 1932, and finally I went to Walsingham in England, where there had been cures reported. And—and then I stopped."

Randall swallowed hard. "You stopped—a year ago?"

"Yes. I guess Our Lord did not hear my prayers anywhere. You see my leg, it is still crippled."

With a pang, Randall remembered when, during a summer vacation while in high school, he had first read W.

Somerset Maugham's *Of Human Bondage*. The hero,
Philip Carey, had been born with a clubfoot. At fourteen,
Philip had become religious, and he convinced. himself
that if God willed it so, faith could move mountains. He
had decided that if he believed strongly enough, prayed
to God long enough, the Lord would make his clubfoot
whole. Philip believed and he prayed and he set the date
for the miracle. The night before the date of the miracle,
he said his prayer naked to please his Maker. He went to
bed and to sleep with confidence. He woke in the morning
filled with joy and gratitude. *His first instinct was to put
down his hand and feel the foot which was whole now,
but to do this seemed to doubt the goodness of God. He
knew that his foot was well. But at last he made up his
mind, and with the toes of his right foot he just touched
his left. Then he passed his hand over it. He limped downstairs* . . .

With that passage, Randall supposed, he too had become a cynic.

And Lori Cook? He listened.

"I've never blamed Our Lord," she was saying. "So
many people pray, and I've supposed that when I prayed
He was too busy. I still have faith. I was going to go
home a year ago, but I heard of a religious project that
needed secretaries. Some instinct told me to go for the
interview in London. I was hired, and sent to Amsterdam.
I've been with Resurrection Two ever since, and never
regretted it. Everything here is mysterious, but exciting.
I'm doing my job and waiting to learn what good work
we've accomplished."

Randall was moved. He said, "You won't be disappointed, Lori. Okay, you're hired."

She was genuinely thrilled. "Thank you, Mr. Randall.
I—I'm ready to start this second, if you have anything."

"I don't think so. Besides, it's almost going-home time."

"Well, if you have nothing special, Mr. Randall, I'll just
stay on a bit and move supplies from my old desk into
my new one."

She had limped toward the door, opened it, ready to
go out, when Randall remembered there *was* something,

something important that he had been about to do when Naomi had sidetracked him.

"One second, Lori. There is a matter you can help me with. I want to get my hands on an English-language copy of the International New Testament immediately. I understand that Albert Kremer in Copy-editing has galley proofs. Will you get him on the line for me?"

Lori left hurriedly to undertake her first assignment on the new job.

Randall sat back a few seconds, waiting, and picked up the receiver when Lori's buzz came through.

"I'm sorry, Mr. Randall," she said. "Mr. Kremer has left for the day. If I may suggest someone else, sir. The librarian, Hans Bogardus, has a record of where every copy is kept. He usually stays late. Shall I try him?"

A moment later, Randall was connected with the librarian.

"Mr. Bogardus, Steve Randall here. I'd like to get hold of a proof copy of the International New Testament that I can read and I—"

From the other end came an amused effeminate giggle. "And I'd like to get hold of the Kohinoor diamond, Mr. Randall."

Irritated, Randall said, "I'm told you have a record of where every copy is at any time."

"No one in possession of a copy would be permitted to let you see it. I'm the librarian for the project and I haven't been allowed to see it."

"Well, *I've* been allowed, my friend. Mr. Wheeler promised me I'd see it when I got to Amsterdam."

"Mr. Wheeler has left for the day. If you will wait until tomorrow—"

"I want a copy tonight," said Randall with exasperation.

Bogardus' voice had become more serious, more solicitous. "Tonight," he repeated. "In that case, only Dr. Deichhardt can be of assistance to you. There is one English copy in the vault below, but only he could authorize having it removed. I happen to know Dr. Deichhardt is still in his office."

"Thanks," Randall said and abruptly hung up.

He left his chair and strode out of his office. In the alcove, Lori was sorting more supplies for her desk.

As he hastened past her, Randall called back, "Ring Dr. Deichhardt for me and tell him I'm on my way to see him. I'll need only a half minute. Tell him it's important."

He plunged into the corridor, ready to do battle.

TWENTY MINUTES LATER, he was settled in the rear seat of the Mercedes-Benz limousine, and the chauffeur, Theo, was driving him across the Dam in the darkness of early evening.

He had won his battle.

Dr. Deichhardt had agreed with great reluctance that if the cooperating publishers wanted their International New Testament publicized, then their publicity director must have an opportunity to read it. But there had been explicit conditions appended to the loan of the Bible. Randall could have the copy for one night only, at this stage. He must read it within the confines of his room. He must not make notes. He must return the copy to Dr. Deichhardt in the morning. He must not disclose to anyone, not even to members of his staff, what he had read. He must confine his use of the contents to outlining publicity ideas, and he must retain these ideas in his security file cabinet.

In two weeks, Herr Hennig would arrive in Amsterdam from Mainz with finished copies of the Bible. Then, and only then, would Randall and the members of his staff receive their personal copies. From that moment on, Randall would be free to discuss the ideas that would result from tonight's private reading, and the entire publicity staff would be free to prepare its promotional campaign.

Randall had instantly agreed to these arrangements, and had pledged himself to observe every precaution. After that, he had waited with anticipation until the vault curator, Mr. Groat, had appeared with the American edition of the page proofs.

Mr. Groat proved to be a short, broad-beamed Dutchman, who seemed as unreal as a figure in Mme. Tussaud's waxworks. He sported a flat, ill-fitting toupee, the tiny moustache of a dentist, a deferential minor bureaucrat's manner, and an oversized pistol of a strange make (Randall had asked and learned it was an F.N. 7.6, of Belgian manufacture), the latter carried in an armpit holster which was revealed by his unbuttoned, skimpy black suit coat. He had handed the Bible—the page proofs bound between elongated pure white cardboards stamped with a large blue cross—to Randall stiffly, formally, as if conferring upon Randall a hand-delivered message from the Maker.

Now, with the bursting briefcase containing the International New Testament, the photographs of the Ostia Antica find, the papers from his staff, on the seat beside him, and with his first full day at Resurrection Two gradually receding, Randall was able to settle back and enjoy this interlude of relaxation.

Through the car's rear window he could see that they were leaving the Dam, and had entered a wide, tree-lined thoroughfare called Rokin. Soon, Rokin merged into Muntplein, and they were driving along Reguliersbreestraat, and soon Theo slowed the limousine as they began to travel through a noisy plaza. This was Rembrandtsplein, one of the city's more popular squares, which the Dutch liked to call their Broadway, and lining the small central park Randall could make out the Hotel Schiller, the Hof van Holland with its terrace, and a queue of youngsters before the box office of the Rembrandtsplein Theater.

Once the square was left behind, the city suddenly fell quiet around them. Except for the passage of a few automobiles, there was little movement, and the street they were on seemed pleasant. Randall squinted into the dark to locate the name of the street—he wanted to remember to take a walk here one day—and he finally made out that it was called Utrechtsestraat.

Immediately, he was overwhelmed by a desire to walk, to stretch his legs and get some air. He was not hungry yet. Even though he was eager to read the New Testament in his briefcase, he did not mind putting off that excitement a little longer. The very idea of moving from one enclosure, the Krasnapolsky, to the confines of a second enclosure, this Mercedes, to yet one more enclosure, his suite in the Amstel Hotel, was oppressive. Definitely—providing he maintained Heldering's precautions —he would allow himself a walk and a breath of the clean fresh Dutch air.

"How far are we from the Amstel Hotel, Theo?"

"Wij zijn niet ver van het hotel. Near, not far. Six, seven blocks maybe."

"Okay. Stop right there at the corner, Theo, the corner at the canal intersection."

The driver half turned in his seat, puzzled. "You want me to stop, Mr. Randall?"

"Just to drop me off. I want to walk the rest of the way to the hotel."

"My instructions, Mr. Randall, are not to let you from my sight until I have delivered you safe to the hotel."

"I know your instructions, Theo. I intend to see that you follow them. You *can* keep me in your sight. You can tag right behind me, follow me all the way to the hotel. How's that?"

Theo looked uncertain. "But—"

Randall shook his head. These automatons following their goddam instructions, programmed, literal, forever inflexible. "Look, Theo, we're adhering to the rules. I want to as much as you do. You'll have your eye on me all the way. It's simply that I haven't been out in the city since I arrived. I need a little exercise. So please drop me here, and you can stay fifty feet behind."

Theo, emitting an audible sigh, swung to the side of the street and pulled up. He leaped from his seat to open the back door, but Randall had already stepped out of the car with his briefcase. "Just tell me where I am," he said. "Point me in the right direction."

Theo pointed to the left along the canal. "You walk straight beside this canal, the Prinsengracht, to the end. You are at the Amstel River then. You go right for one, two, three blocks until Sarphatistraat, and next left across the bridge, and the first next small street is Professor

Tulpplein where we reach the Amstel Hotel. I will honk my horn if you go wrong."

"Thanks, Theo."

Randall remained where he was standing until Theo had got behind the wheel of the idling Mercedes-Benz. Then, offering the driver a short, appreciative wave, Randall started ahead. Feeling free for the first time since his arrival, he inhaled deeply, filling his lungs with air, exhaled, took a comfortable grip on his heavy briefcase and sauntered up the middle of the narrow road that ran alongside the Prinsen canal.

After a minute or two, he glanced over his shoulder. Dutifully, some fifty feet back, Theo kept the Mercedes-Benz creeping after him.

Okay, instructions, rules, he conceded. Meanwhile, the walk felt wonderful and he felt revived.

It was lovely here, restful, peaceful after the turmoil of the day, and the tension was leaving the muscles and nerve ends in his arms and back. A scattering of midget cars was parked before meters for the night. On one side of him, shadowy in the dim street lighting, were rows of quaint houses, with short stairs leading up to old front doors, houses mainly drapeless and unilluminated and with almost no signs of life behind their windows. The good burghers of Amsterdam, Randall guessed, went to bed early.

On the other side of him, visible through the milky blue of evening, not far below the narrow street, were the still waters of the canal. He could see boats at anchor, and some of these were attractive houseboats, with lights inside, and once there was a child in a nightgown going past a window. The reflection of the boat lights shimmered across the water.

As he slowly walked toward the end of the Prinsen canal, Randall's mind wandered backwards across the day. He thought of Darlene, and hoped that she had enjoyed her tours of the city. He thought briefly of the meeting with his staff, so many alert young people, and of the luncheon with the powerful religious publishers and their theologians, so much conflict below their common purpose, and he thought of Lori Cook. This led his mind further backwards to his daughter Judy, and how much he wished that she could be beside him now, and how troubled she would be over the divorce contest. Yet, the profiles of those in his life—Judy, Barbara, Towery, McLoughlin, his father, mother, Clare, Tom Carey—all seemed vague and distant this quiet night.

He halted briefly, as a meowing calico cat meandered in front of him, and just as he resumed his walking, the bright lights of an automobile hit him in the face, momentarily blinding him. Instinctively, he protected his eyes, and was able to make out the shape of the vehicle that had swung into this street from the direction of the river and was bearing down upon him at an accelerated speed.

Paralyzed for mounting seconds by the unexpected, he watched the black sedan rushing at him, looming larger, enlarging to crush him beneath it. Didn't the damn fool see him? Or see Theo behind him? The monster was almost upon him, when his stilts of legs came to life. He began to edge crabwise, out of the path of the speeding vehicle, but the relentless beams of yellow light were following him. Then he saw that the car had swerved straight toward him, was closing in fast, about to run him down. Wildly, he scrambled toward the canal, to save himself, and then he stumbled and began to go down, the briefcase escaping his grip as his palms opened wide to protect his body from the rising pavement.

He fell flat. Knocked breathless, hurting, he waited for the car to pass. Instead, there was a grinding and screeching of brakes and rubber tires on cement, and he rolled on his side in time to see that the compact sedan had skidded so that the Mercedes now faced it broadside, forcing Theo to slam to a sudden stop.

From his prone position, Randall could make out someone, a man wearing a cap, the driver, leave the sedan and yank open Theo's door. Immediately, Randall's attention was diverted to another figure, a second man, as the door on the passenger side was flung open. A man, no hair, no face—it was grotesque, frightening—a man with a skintight stocking pulled down over his head—had leaped from the car and was hurrying away from it, not toward Randall but toward some object in the street behind the car.

That instant, Randall's heart froze.

The object lying out there was his briefcase.

Every nerve in his body sent off impulses, urging him to rise. He pushed himself up, and regained his feet. He staggered, his knees folding like hinges, and he grabbed for a parking meter to maintain his balance.

The outlandish and repellent figure with its bizarre skull bagged in a nylon placenta had snatched up the briefcase and was wheeling around to return to the car.

Randall's eyes sought his protector behind the wheel of the Mercedes. But Theo was not there. Theo was nowhere to be seen. The other attacker, the driver with the cap, was inside the black sedan once more, unblocking the road in front of the Mercedes limousine and heading his car down the empty street. And his accomplice, with the briefcase, had almost arrived at the sedan.

"Drop that!" Randall shouted. "Police! Police!"

Then he bounded forward. The other had reached the open door, pausing to get inside, when Randall swiftly closed the gap between them, catapulting himself at the man, tackling him behind the knees. He felt the impact of the thief's rough cords and hard legs against his cheekbone. Randall could hear the thief's gasp as they careened into the car door and fell to the street.

Frantic, Randall abandoned his adversary, scuttling on his hands and knees to retrieve the briefcase. As his hand touched the smooth leather, a crushing force hit him square on his back, and fingers were at his throat, choking him. Randall ripped at the claws, and began to call out to hammer at the figure behind him, he became dimly aware, high above the sounds of their panting, of a strange piercing sound.

It was a whistle, growing louder, nearer, louder.

He heard an urgent low cry from inside the car. *"De*

politie—de politie komt! Ga in de auto! Wij moeten vlug weggaan!"

Suddenly he was released and, lightened, he pitched forward on his face. The claws were at his throat no more, the fists had gone. Forcing himself to his knees, he snatched up his briefcase, hugging it to his chest. The car door slammed behind him. The motor raced, the gears ground, and rubber spun against the pavement. Reeling slightly, still on his knees, Randall looked over his shoulder. The car had taken off like a rocket, evaporating, swallowed up by the night.

Head swimming, Randall tried to rise and failed. Then, gradually, he realized that a pair of strong arms had grasped him under his armpits and someone was helping him to his feet. He turned to find the person assisting him was wearing a navy blue officer's cap with a black visor, and had a wide, concerned, flushed face, a slate-blue jacket, dark blue trousers, a whistle on a chain, a badge, a truncheon, and a pistol such as the one Mr. Groat had worn. The badge. A Dutch policeman. And another policeman, same uniform, coming up on the run. The police were exchanging words that Randall could not understand.

Randall was swaying on his feet, when he saw Theo at last, breathless and pale, rubbing his bruised neck as he elbowed between the police, speaking rapidly to them in Dutch.

"Mr. Randall, Mr. Randall," Theo cried out, "you are hurt?"

"I'm fine, perfectly fine," said Randall. "Just scared out of my wits, that's all. What happened to you? I looked for you—"

"I tried to help—tried to get the gun from the glove compartment—but the lock jammed and before I was able—one of them grabbed me from behind, clubbed me so hard I was knocked out, flat on the seat. You have your briefcase? Ah, good, good."

Randall became aware of a white Volkswagen, with a blue light above the roof and the police badge painted on the door, drawing up across the way from Theo's Mercedes. An officer called out to the policeman who was holding Randall by the arm, *"Vraag hem wat voor een auto het was en hoe veel waren daar."* The policeman turned to Randall, and said in perfect English, "The sergeant wishes to know the make of the car, and how many of them there were."

"I don't know the car," said Randall. "Maybe a Renault. It was a black sedan. There were two. One with a cap went after my driver. I never got a clear look at him. I saw only the one who tried to get my briefcase. He had a stocking over his head. Maybe he was blond. Turtleneck sweater. He was a little shorter than I am, but huskier. I—I don't remember anything else. Possibly my driver, Theo, can tell you more."

The policeman questioned Theo closely, then relayed the descriptions in Dutch, and the sergeant waved his acknowledgment and the white Volkswagen screamed off into the darkness.

In the next ten minutes there were formalities. As onlookers from the neighboring houses and from the Amstel River bridge curiously gathered and watched and listened, all with apologetic countenances, Randall showed his passport. The first policeman made notes from it. Randall was politely questioned. He related exactly what had happened. As to his business in Amsterdam, he was deliberately vague. A vacation, merely some visits to some business friends, nothing else. Could he think of any reason why anyone might want to waylay or harm him? He could think of none. And he was not injured, except for the scraped knee? No, he was absolutely fine.

The police were satisfied, and the first closed his notebook.

Theo stood before Randall. He said seriously, "I think, Mr. Randall, you will drive with me the rest of the way to the hotel."

Randall was weakly amused. "I think I will."

The crowd of onlookers parted as Randall, carrying the briefcase, and accompanied by the two policemen, followed Theo to the limousine. He stepped into the car, and sat on the edge of the back seat as Theo slammed the door. The rear window was down, and the first policeman, his friend now, leaned in through it.

"*Wij vragen excuus,*" he said. "*Het spijt mij dat u verschrikt bent. Het—*" He broke off, shook his head. "I forget and speak Dutch. I was saying our apologies to you for your trouble. I am sorry you had this fright, and the inconvenience. It was plainly an attempt at robbery by two hoodlums. After all, they only wanted your briefcase. Petty thieves."

Randall smiled. Only his briefcase. Only petty thieves.

The policeman had one more thing to add. "We will be in touch with you, to identify them, if we catch them."

You won't catch them, not in a million years, Randall wanted to say. Instead, he said simply, "Thank you, thank you very much."

Theo had started the car, and as the policeman straightened to stand aside, Randall had a clear view of his oval badge. On the metal badge was depicted a book, with a sword above it, pointing upwards, protecting it. Around the edge of the badge were the words: *Vigilat ut quiescant.* He guessed the legend to mean: They watch, so that you can be safe.

The sword protecting the book.

Yet, he knew, he could never again be sure that he was safe.

Not so long as the book must be kept a secret.

IV

MANY YEARS FROM NOW, he was sure, when he looked back on his life, he would remember the last two hours of this evening, the last hour of this evening, really, in the living room of the royal suite of the Amstel Hotel in Amsterdam. He would remember that hour of this evening as a landmark, a milestone, a turning point in the course of his personal odyssey on earth. He had arrived at this place, and at this point in time, a being rudderless and without direction. Tonight, for almost the first instance in memory, he felt that he had guidance, a light that might direct him toward whatever life he chose to live.

And there was something infinitely more, something you could not touch or hold but that you knew was alive inside of you as tangible and real as the organs of your body.

What he felt inside was a sense of peace. It was also a sense of security. It was, above all, a sense of purpose, although to what end he was not certain, and somehow that did not matter.

There was one thing this feeling was not, and this he also knew for certain. The feeling that had possessed him had nothing to do with religion in any strict or orthodox way. He still felt with Goethe that mysteries are not necessarily miracles. No, it was not religion that had possessed him. Rather, it was a belief, a strength difficult to define. It was as if he had discovered that the meaning of his life, and its goal, was not mere nothingness. Instead, there had appeared this belief that his existence, like that of all men, had been created out of some

reason, some larger purpose. He had become conscious
of a continuity, of his linkage to a past where he had, in
a way, lived before and to a future where he would live
on and on, again and again, through mortals unknown to
him who would come into being as he had come, and
they would perpetuate his reality throughout eternity.

What pervaded his being, he was aware, could not
yet be called by the name of faith—that is, unquestioning faith in an unseen and divine master or master
planner who provided humans with motivation and purpose and was the explanation for the inexplicable. What
had overcome him, and could be more easily understood
by him, was the beginning of a belief, a belief that his
being on earth had a meaning, not only for himself but
also for those whom his life brushed against or touched.
In short, he was not here by accident or chance, and
therefore he was not expendable, a waste, a cipher dancing in a void until the ultimate darkness.

He remembered his father's once quoting the terrible
and suffocating St. Augustine to him: *He who created us
without our help will not save us without our consent.*
With an old regret, Randall knew that such was not yet
part of his belief. He could envision nothing to which he
might offer consent for salvation. Nor could he believe,
with the Book, that we walk by faith, not by sight. He
himself required sight—and yet, tonight, he had seen
something.

Seen what? He could not describe it further. Perhaps
time would bring it into focus. For now, the discovery
of belief within him, belief in a design, in a human aim,
was enough, an excitement, a hope, almost a passion.

With determination, he released himself from this co-
coon of introspection, and tried to reenter the more
prosaic world around him and retrace the steps that had
brought him on this journey to the alien land of belief.

Two hours ago he had come back to the royal suite he
occupied, but had hardly seen, on the first floor of the
Amstel Hotel. He had still been shaken by his experience in the street. In this safe and disarming city of open
and friendly people, he had been attacked, waylaid by two

strangers, one of them masked. The police had written off the incident as a minor crime, a routine attempt at robbery by a pair of hoodlums. Randall, setting his scuffed briefcase on the enormous, ornate bed, knew better. He carried in that briefcase not merely a book but what Heine had called a Book containing sunrise and sunset, promise and fulfillment, birth and death, the whole drama of humanity, large and wise as the world, the Book of Books.

Yet, Randall reflected, this very Book that Heine had spoken of had become, in the eyes of many readers, a stale object, obsolete, unrelated to a new era, like a dusty, useless heirloom relegated to civilization's attic. Now, almost overnight, by chance, it had been infused with life, given youth, and the Book—like its Hero—had been revitalized. Once more, its sponsors promised, it would be the Book of Books. But even more, this one held the password, the key, the Word, that would usher in a faith supported by James's fresh picture of Jesus, and therefore justice, goodness, love, unity, and finally eternal hope would enter a materialistic, unjust, cynical, machine world spinning closer and closer toward Armageddon.

In the street, two men had been ready to maim, even kill, to obtain this password. Until that frightening experience, Randall had paid only lip service to the warning that he had joined a dangerous game. He would not have to be warned again. He had been thoroughly convinced. From this night on, he would be ready for anything.

He had reached his suite burning to read the Word, but he had determined to put it off until his nerves had settled. He had gone back into the huge living room, where a tray of bottles, highball glasses, and fresh ice rested on the marble-topped coffee table, which was surrounded by three deep-lemon-colored armchairs and by a long modern sofa upholstered in blue felt.

On the tray he had found a note from Darlene, its tone slightly peevish. She hadn't liked being on her own all day—but the bus tour had been a success, and she had reserved a place on the last Candlelight Tour of the canals, since the maid had told her that was the most romantic, and she would be back around midnight.

Randall had poured himself a double Scotch-on-the-rocks, poked around the regal living room, sat down at the modern desk with its morocco leather top, studied the three sets of French doors that led to a balcony overlooking the river, and finished his drink. He had then summoned room service, ordered the *salade* and the *filet-steak* and a demi of Beaujolais, and then he had gone to the bathroom to take a leisurely shower.

He had just finished pulling his Italian silk bathrobe over his cotton pajamas, when the waiter had rolled in his late dinner. He had avoided the temptation to read the International New Testament while he ate, but he had not lingered over his salad, steak, and wine.

At last, an hour ago, brimming with expectancy, he had unlocked his briefcase, extracted the white-covered page proofs, and taken the book to the sofa. He had arranged the cushions and sunk back into them, and examined the book.

On the title page, beneath the title, *International New Testament,* there was stamped in ink the reminder: UN-CORRECTED PAGE PROOFS. Below, on a label pasted to the sheet, was the reproduction of a typed interoffice memorandum from Karl Hennig, K. Hennig Druckerei, Mainz. Hennig pointed out that the proof-sheet paper was common stock, but that the initial two printings of the Bible would be on the best quality of paper available—the first printing a limited edition for the press and clergy to be called the Pulpit Edition and done on imported India paper, and the other printing the popular trade edition for the public to be done on vellum. The pages would be ten inches in height and six inches wide. Since this Bible would be used primarily by Protestants, although available to Catholics as well, the annotations had been kept at a minimum and arranged as a special supplement immediately following each New Testament book.

The contents of the Petronius Parchment had been placed as an appendix between the Gospel According to

Matthew and the Gospel According to Mark, and this appendix included annotations on the background of the parchment's discovery in Ostia Antica, its authentication, its translation from the Greek, and its relationship to the story of Christ.

The newly discovered book by the brother of Jesus had been entered as part of the canon and had taken its place between the Gospel According to John and the Acts of the Apostles. All of the New Testament had been newly translated in the light of the latest discoveries. Ultimately, an International Old Testament would be published as a separate volume, and it would also be newly translated to take advantage of the linguistic advances provided by the Ostia Antica find. Tentative publication date was July 12th.

In his childhood and youth, Randall had read the New Testament, and reread portions of it, endlessly. This evening, he did not have the patience to reread the Synoptic Gospels—Matthew, Mark, Luke—or the fourth gospel, John's, with its symbolic discourses—again. He wanted to get straight to the new discoveries, to Petronius, to James.

Immediately following Matthew, he had found the page bearing the boldface heading.

REPORT ON THE TRIAL OF JESUS BY PETRONIUS. *An Appendix.*

The text of the report by Petronius, written in the name of Pilate, covered two pages. The annotations following it covered four pages. Randall began to read.

To Lucius Aelius Sejanus, Friend of Caesar. Report on the sentence pronounced by Pontius Pilate, governor of Judea, that one Jesus of Nazareth shall be punished by crucifixion. On the seventh day of the Idles of April, in the sixteenth year of the reign of Tiberius Caesar, in the city of Jerusalem, Pontius Pilate, governor of Judea, condemned Jesus of Nazareth for acts of insurrection and sentenced him to death on the cross [Annotation: the *patibulum*].

Moved by this dry, cold, pagan verdict reverberating up through the corridors of centuries, Randall sat transfixed as he read on to the end of the official report written on Friday, April 7, in the year 30 A.D.

Without spending time to examine the text again, or even to think about it, Randall flipped through the pages that followed until he arrived at the last page of the Gospel According to John. He held his breath and turned that page also.

There it was in simple splendor, a reality, a fact, the password to faith, the long-awaited Resurrection.

THE GOSPEL ACCORDING TO JAMES

I, James of Jerusalem, brother of the Lord Jesus Christ, heir of the Lord, eldest of the Lord's surviving brethren and the son of Joseph of Nazareth, am soon to be brought before the Sanhedrin and the head priest Ananus charged with seditious behavior because of my leadership of the followers of Jesus in our community.

Herewith, as a servant of God and of the Lord Jesus Christ, and while time is left for me to perform this necessary act, I set down a brief testimony of my brother Jesus Christ's life and ministry, to prevent growing distortions and calumnies and to give guidance to the disciples of the faith against manifold temptations and to restore fortitude to our followers among the persecuted twelve tribes of the Dispersion.

The other sons of Joseph, the Lord's surviving brethren and mine own, are . . . [Ed.: Portion of fragment missing] I remain to speak of the firstborn and best beloved Son. This testimony is my witness and recollection of the life, and the testimony of the apostles of The Disciples of Jesus who also witnessed the life where I could not witness it, and I put forth the truth of the Son who spoke for the Father so that the messengers may bring the tidings to The Poor everywhere. [Ed.: The earliest followers of Jesus

were known as The Disciples of Jesus and also as
The Poor.]

The Lord Jesus Christ was born of his mother
Mary, who had been overshadowed by a oneness
with the Creator, and he was delivered in the courtyard of an inn in the place called Bethlehem in the
year that witnessed the death of Herod the Great,
and some years before Quirinius was proconsul of
Syria and Judea, and Jesus was taken to be circumcised . . .

The Word.
The Sign. The Light. The Manifestation of God.

Dazzled, his forehead damp, his temples throbbing,
Randall read on, and then on and on, the entire thirty-
five pages, absorbed and shaken by the voice of the brother speaking out from the year 62 A.D., little more than
thirty years after the unconscious, bleeding Jesus had been
removed from the barbaric Cross and revived. This was
James speaking out to countless generations yet unborn
just months before he himself would meet his own brutal
death.

Randall had finished the Gospel According to James.
The end.
The beginning.

He was drained by the wonder of it. The wonder was
that he felt as if he had been there, had seen and heard
the man from Galilee, had touched and been touched by
Him. He believed. Man or God, it did not matter. He,
Steve Randall, believed.

It was difficult to leave these pages, turn to the annotations, the background, the explanations, but he did it, and
his attention was gripped by each of the seven added
pages.

Still, he would not allow himself to think. He felt, but
he refused to think.

Quickly, he went back to the start of the Gospel
According to James and swiftly he reread it. Then back to
the earlier appendix, the Report on the Trial of Jesus by
Petronius, and he reread that.

At last, placing the International New Testament gently on the coffee table, he had slumped back into the cushions of the sofa and permitted himself to think as well as feel.

And it was then that Randall had realized the extent to which this newest Word, The Word, had penetrated his cynicism and awakened an emotion inside him that he had not felt since he was a youngster in Oak City.

His life had been created so that it could mean something, to himself, to others.

He had examined the feeling over and over again.

And now, after a passage of two hours since he had entered the suite, and almost an hour since he had opened the International New Testament, he sat on the sofa, trying to control his feelings and deal with what he had read as a rational and intelligent person would.

He stared at the bound pages of the book, and tried to conjure up and turn over in his head what he had so recently experienced.

The Petronius Report was a relatively short and routine official document. The very flatness of its tone, the terseness of it—an unpolished Roman centurion or captain describing the sentencing of a minor crackpot criminal to his superior, to the prefect of the Praetorian Guard in Rome—made it a hundred times as real, far more believable and chilling than Luke's more beautiful and literary account.

Luke had written:

And Pilate gave sentence that it should be as they required. And he released unto them him that for sedition and murder was cast into prison, whom they had desired; but he delivered Jesus to their will.

Petronius had written:

At sunrise, the trial was held before Herod's palace. As witnesses, the Pharisees and Sadducees were uncooperative, insisting that the accused was being

tried for undermining civil law, not Mosaic Law.
Witnesses who came forward before the tribunal
were friends of Rome, those who desired peace, most
of them being citizens of Rome. These accused Jesus
of crimes and gave forth their evidence that Jesus
claimed himself to be King of Israel and claimed
authority higher than that of Caesar, and was one
who taught and preached sedition and disobedience
in cities throughout the land, and who attempted to
stir our subjects to rebellion.

Randall recalled more in this report signed by Petronius,
sent over the signature of "Pontius Pilate, praefectus
Udea," to "Lucius Aelius Sejanus, Friend of Caesar," in
Rome.

Petronius had brought to life, in two sentences, that
awful final scene in the Praetorium, with Pilate on his
raised dais, and the man Jesus standing quietly before
him:

The accused appeared in his own defense, denying
all charges put against him except the charge that he
claimed authority higher than that of Caesar. The
accused Jesus affirmed that his mission was given
him by his god and it was to establish a kingdom of
heaven on earth.

Petronius had reported the sentence of death, and
Pilate's order to his first centurion to carry out the execu-
tion at once. After being flogged with three-pronged whips,
Jesus had been led by Roman guards to the place of
Crucifixion. Petronius had concluded:

He was so executed beyond the Sheep Gate. His
death came, as was verified, in the ninth hour. Two
friends of the criminal, both members of the Sanhedrin, petitioned Pilate for the body, and they were
permitted to receive the body for burial. The case of
Jesus was thus disposed.

But what had moved Randall even more was the narrative of the Gospel According to James. The biography had been broken here and there where words or phrases were missing only because certain portions of the papyrus leaves had dissolved to dust or because the ancient printing, the printing in primitive ink, had become illegible on the discolored fiber. But by using deductive logic, eminent scholars had filled in most of the missing words and phrases, and although enclosed in a forest of brackets, these in no way obscured the view of the real Jesus.

To read James was to believe, without a single doubt.

Not only did the words of James ring with truth—carrying the same pungent forthrightness of the General Epistle of James in the standard New Testaments—but they clearly indicated that this was the history of one human being who had been close to another human being. The narrative, crude in its simplicity, was unembellished by the propaganda of the gospel writers or the later Christian salesmen who had skillfully doctored or rewritten the four gospels early in the second century, before they had become the canon of the New Testament in the fourth century.

James, as leader of the followers of Jesus in Jerusalem, had written of Jesus as a Jew who wanted to alter and improve Judaism. His account was uncluttered by the theology of the organized Christians who came later, and who wrote of events they had not seen. These Christians set out to change drastically and eventually supplant Judaism. They borrowed the best of its morality and history, but they altered its God from one of righteousness who had a chosen people, into a God who believed in love for Jews and Gentiles alike, and they laid exclusive claim to the Messiah Returned. The gospel authors had devoted themselves to heralding not merely a man and his life but an idea upon which could be built their Christian Church.

Moreover, James had absolved the Jews of any responsibility for the death of Jesus Christ, and, in flat contradiction to the apologetics of Matthew, Mark, Luke, and John, had squarely placed the blame on the Romans, and

James's version was confirmed by the Petronius Report. Modern biblical scholars had long suspected that the whole idea of a reluctant Pilate being forced by Jewish authorities to condemn Jesus to death had been a tampering with truth by the gospel writers for political reasons.

An annotation had quoted the French scholar Maurice Goguel, Paris, 1932:

> The One whom the Christians presented to the world as the messenger of God and the Saviour had been sentenced to death by a Roman tribunal. This fact created difficulties for the preaching of the Gospel in the Roman world, for it might give the impression that to be converted to the Christian Faith meant taking the side of a rebel, and therefore to be in revolt against the Imperial authority. Hence the Christians were anxious to prove that the Procurator who had sent Jesus to execution had been convinced of his innocence, and that he had publicly announced that he had been forced to yield to the irresistible pressure of the populace and of the Jewish authorities.

Another annotation had quoted the German scholar Paul Winter, Berlin, 1961:

> Writing probably in Rome, [Mark wished] to emphasize the culpability of the Jewish nation for the death of Jesus, particularly of its leaders; they, not the Romans, are to be held responsible for the crucifixion. It is not to be assumed that the Evangelist was moved by positively anti-Jewish sentiments; his tendency was defensive rather than aggressive. He was concerned to avoid mentioning anything that would provoke Roman antagonism towards, or even suspicions of, the ideals for which he stood. . . . No grounds must be given for the inference that Jesus was in any way connected with subversive activities such as those which had resulted in the recent uprising. The Evangelist therefore contrived to con-

ceal that Jesus had been condemned and executed
on a charge of sedition. The argument runs that he
was not arrested by Roman troops, not sentenced for
political reasons by a Roman magistrate; but that his
condemnation and subsequent execution was due to
some obscure cause of the Jewish Law.

Now, at last, that historic lie had been put to rest forever by James the Just.

But above all else, first and foremost, was the astonishing revelation that Jesus Christ had survived His Crucifixion—whether by the will of God or a mortal physician's hand—and had not merely shown Himself but had
gone off to tread the earth and extend His earthly ministry
for another nineteen years before ascending to heaven.

James on Jesus.

Incredible, yet totally credible.

It was an earthquake that would rock the gospel
canon of centuries and at the same time secure its place
as an edifice that housed a teacher of genius, wisdom,
foresight, a believable prophet, one whom a rational and
scientific age could relate to, interpret, and follow. It
would cause an international sensation, a sensation and
a thrill of hope that might inspire men to veneration for
centuries to come.

James on Jesus.

It was an ancient memoir, shorn of fable, reviving a
man, not an unnatural puff of heaven, perhaps not a
walker on water nor a raiser of the dead, and not a Son
of God alone, but a son of all men in all times who
knew suffering and joy, and who taught kindness and
understanding and fellowship and inveighed against cruelty and hypocrisy and greed.

Search the scriptures, the disciple John had advised in
his gospel. Steve Randall had searched a new scripture,
and now he tried to recollect what had inspired and animated him and lifted him so high.

James on Jesus. The images and visions danced and
sang in Randall's head.

The birth of a child in the courtyard of an inn in

Bethlehem, of course. Whether born to a fifteen-year-old virgin who had conceived by the Holy Spirit or born to an adolescent female who had been impregnated by an earthly mate—this left unclear, either by James or by his translators. However, a hint of Virgin Birth through James's use of the word "Overshadowed." [Annotation: The implication in James is that Jesus was conceived by the Holy Ghost, born of the Virgin Mary. As Justin Martyr explained in 150 A.D., "The words 'Behold the virgin shall conceive' signify that the virgin conceived without intercourse; for if she had had intercourse with anyone whatever, she would no longer be a virgin. But the power of God coming upon the virgin overshadowed her and caused her to conceive though she was a virgin." On the other hand, since James unequivocally calls himself brother of the Lord Jesus Christ, the argument may be made that Jesus was born of a union between Mary and Joseph, as James would seem to have been later. The gospel writer John had, in fact, stated that Jesus had been born "according to the flesh."] And following the birth, Jesus had been circumcised on the eighth day, yes.

The flight to Egypt, confirmed by James. There had been a King Herod who had feared the birth of a Messiah and had prepared to slay all the children under two years of age in the area of Bethlehem. [Annotation: Herod's cruelty was well known in his time. Although observing the Mosaic Law, refusing to kill pigs and eat pork, he had put to death his onetime favorite wife and his two stepsons. This provoked Augustus Caesar to remark in Rome: "I would rather be Herod's pig than Herod's son."]

In order to protect their child from infanticide, Joseph and Mary had taken Jesus and fled to Hebron on the coastal plain, gone on to Gaza and Raphia, and then—by means unknown, the words were missing—they reached Pelusium in Egypt. There were a million Jews in Egypt and Jesus had been sheltered with Jewish relatives in Alexandria until Herod the Great was dead. After the reign of Archelaus had begun, Joseph and Mary and the child had returned to Palestine and made their home in Galilee.

The hitherto unknown years of Jesus' youth, sketchily yet brilliantly illuminated by James. Jesus studied in a *beth ha-sefer,* a house of the book, a primary school, and before the age of thirteen (His age deduced in the annotated material) He studied the Law of Yahweh, the Book of Jonah, the tales of various Messiahs, and commentaries of the preachers. Several times He visited the nearby ascetic Essene community and had conversations with certain scholars and discussed the Enochan books. From them He gained the desire to abolish slavery and the making of weapons and the offering of sacrifices. From them, too, He gained the wish to see the Messianic kingdom fulfilled. For a period, He was tutored by a Pharisaic teacher in Jerusalem, and in the temple the priests were much impressed by His learning, precocity, and holiness. James was present at his brother Jesus' confirmation.

Their father, Joseph, had indeed been a worker of wood [Annotation: There was no Hebrew or Aramaic word for *carpenter* in Jesus' time.] and felled cedars and cypresses in the forests, and repaired building beams and made chests and plows and kneading-troughs, but the eldest son, Jesus, had not been a worker of wood, except to assist Joseph occasionally in the fashioning of a wooden object. Jesus had given His adolescent years to toiling as a farmer and a shepherd, first sowing the small family plot of wheat, caring for the vineyard, and when older tending the flock of sheep. Joseph's family had lived austerely, in a one-room clay-brick dwelling, half given over to the animals.

Upon Joseph's death (the fragment indicating the time had crumbled, but the annotators thought it to be three years after Jesus' bar mitzvah), Jesus had stirred the family and neighbors with His prayer over His father's body: "Father of all mercy, seeing eyes and hearing ear, oh listen to my plea for Joseph, the old man, and send Michael, the chief of your angels, and Gabriel, your messenger of light, and the armies of your angels, so that they may march with the soul of my father, Joseph, until they bring him to you on high."

Thereafter, Jesus headed the household consisting of

His mother and brothers and sisters, and worked the farm and vineyards, and studied deeply the ancient writings. At last, divinely inspired, He gave over the farm to James, and began to preach quietly a doctrine of love and union and hope in the villages of remote Galilee. He knew Koine, the common Greek of the cities, but He addressed the Jewish communities in the everyday language of Aramaic.

In the eleventh year of the reign of Tiberius Caesar [Annotation: when Jesus was twenty-nine years of age], Jesus sought out the one known as John the Baptist and was baptized. He retired, in the days that followed, to the forests and hills to meditate on His course and seek guidance from His God in heaven. When He returned among men, His mission was clear and His preaching became bolder and more intense.

And then, from the reed pen of James, a description of his elder brother as He undertook His ministry of salvation of the oppressed, of the common people who were burdened by the irrelevant legalisms of the Jewish orthodoxy and crushed by the Roman occupation legions. Jesus was of slightly more than normal stature. [Annotation: Normal stature of his countrymen was about five feet four inches in that time, so Jesus was probably five feet six inches in height.] Jesus wore His hair to His shoulders, with curling locks below His ears, and had a generous moustache and was thickly bearded. His hair, the color of chestnuts, was parted in the middle of his head. His scarred forehead was high, His eyes gray and sunken, His nose overly large and bent or hooked, His lips full. His countenance was covered with sores, and His body was also ulcerated: "The Lord was disfigured of the flesh, but beautiful of the spirit." His look was commanding, yet often He was withdrawn and introspective. His manner was kindly, but sometimes this was clouded over by severity. His voice was deep and musical and it gave comfort to His growing band of followers and disciples. His posture was slightly stooped. His gait was uneven due to a bodily deformity, a lameness in one crippled leg which had become evident the year before His Crucifixion in Jerusalem and gave Him much difficulty. [Annotation: In 207 A.D., the early church writer, Tertullian, born in Carthage, converted to Christianity in Rome, noted that Jesus had been a cripple: "His body was not even of honest human shape."]

He traveled with an ass, which carried His skin of water, His gourd, His scrolls rolled on cylinders, His spare sandals, and He walked ahead of the ass, sometimes wearing a wool cape, and a linen waistcloth held fast by a girdle, and thonged leather sandals, and carrying His bag and His staff.

To Jesus' message, James gave what now filled seven pages in the International New Testament. Jesus addressed Himself to the poor and suffering, and He awakened them. He would kiss each who was a friend, and say, "Peace be with you," and say to them He was from their Father in heaven, and say, "Those among you who believe in me, though you be dead, you will live on." He would say He had been sent to introduce a new kingdom on earth of peace and love.

"All who saw and heard him, equally they knew his compassion." All were as one in His eyes. He spoke of the tyranny, brutality, poverty, and chaos on this earth which must fall before His promise of justice, kindness, sharing, peace. Those who believed would triumph over death and in the kingdom to come would know happiness for eternity.

Often, James wrote, Jesus was specific in His preachings. He demanded equality for women. "A daughter has the right to inherit share for share with her brothers." James authenticated John's story of the woman taken in adultery, except that James's account differed from the later one. Jesus had gone to teach in the temple on the Mount of Olives when the Pharisees, in an effort to entrap Him, confronted Him with a betrothed woman found in adultery. "They said to him, 'Teacher, this woman has been found in adultery. It was commanded to us that such a woman suffer strangulation. What say you to this?' And Jesus said to those who had tried to trick Him, 'Whichever of you is free from sin, let him strangle her.' Thus,

convicted by their consciences, each left the temple.
Jesus touched the woman's brow and asked, 'Has any man
condemned you?' She replied, 'None, Lord.' And Jesus
said, 'Nor do I condemn you. Go, and henceforth sin no
more.' "

James had set down numerous sayings of his brother
Jesus that had uncanny relevance to the world today, sayings concerning exploitation of the poor by the wealthy
and the ruling class, sayings concerning the need for a
compact among nations to end war and colonialism, sayings on the necessity of education for all, sayings that
disapproved of superstition, dogma, ritual, and two sayings that actually prophesied that one day men would
stride the planets of heaven at a time when the earth
verged on self-destruction.

Throughout, James had recollected precepts, aphorisms,
maxims, adages of Jesus that had been heretofore unknown, as well as some that had obviously served as the
original source material for the writers of the four
traditional gospels and for the writers of the many apocryphal gospels.

According to James, "Our Lord Jesus said to them that
he who has a morsel of food in his basket and wonders,
'What shall I eat tomorrow?', such a one is of little faith."
According to James, "And Jesus reminded them, 'Remember this, no servant can serve two masters. If you desire
to serve God and Mammon, it will give you no profit in
either case.' " According to James, "The anointed one
told his followers, 'Renew yourself by seeking communion
with the nature of life and with the maker. Go into the
forest and into the meadow, and breathe long and fully,
and know the air and the truth, and meditate on truth,
casting out all that defiles man, all that is unclean in the
body and evil in the mind. Thus, by the air and by the
holy Father, you will be born again.' "

There was more.

There was this, the germ of the Golden Rule: "Jesus
said, 'The sons of God must become the sons of men,
each man comforting and aiding the other, each a brother
to the other. All sons of men will be sons of God if they

love not only those who love them, but if they love their enemies and return love for hate. Any two who make peace with one another in this house, they shall say to the mountain, Be moved, and it shall be moved. Deal you with others as you would yourself be dealt with. Do nothing to your neighbor that you would not have him do to you thereafter. Those who obey shall make the earth like the heaven, and they shall inherit and know the kingdom of God.' "

There was this, a way of life: "Then Jesus said, 'Despise hypocrisy and that which is evil. Seek truth and that which is good. Let not the kingdom of heaven wither, for the kingdom is like a palm branch whose fruits fall about it, and the fruits are goodness that must be salvaged and again planted.' "

There was this, a philosophy for the present: "And Jesus gathered them about him, saying, 'Forget not how long the world existed before your birth, and know how long it will be after you, and with this know that your earthly life is one single day and your sufferings one single hour. Therefore, live not with death but instead with life. Remember my word, which is to have faith, to give love, to do good works. For blessed shall they be who shall be saved by belief in this word.' "

On several occasions, James had been witness to his brother's healing of the ailing, yet he had never been witness to the divine miracles that were rumored on so many tongues. James had seen the intervention of Jesus on behalf of Lazarus. Although John had later embellished the event and made it a miracle of raising the dead, James had been a personal witness to the actual happening. "Then Martha and Mary had sent for Jesus after their beloved brother, Lazarus, had fallen gravely ill and lay unmoving. I went with Jesus to the house of Lazarus on the slope of the Mount of Olives, and went with him into the house, where Jesus looked down upon his friend, and touched his fevered brow, and called out, 'Oh, Lazarus, rise up,' and Lazarus rose up and thereafter was well."

Twice, in His ministry, Jesus had undergone rough

handling by Roman centurions, once in Capernaum where He suffered a broken leg. (The leg was reset poorly, and from that time Jesus walked with a pronounced limp.) Both times, the centurions had threatened Him with arrest and punishment if He did not desist in His agitation of the populace. Yet, on neither occasion had He actually been arrested, and at no time did He desist in His preachings.

In the sixteenth year of the reign of Tiberius [Annotation: when Jesus was thirty-four years of age], Jesus had brought His creed of charity and mercy and peace—and obedience to no authority other than God and Himself as the Word of God—to the heart of Jerusalem. The occupying Romans warned Him that His preachings could foment another rebellion, and both James and the hierarchy of the Jewish Sanhedrin begged Jesus to take His preachings elsewhere so that the Romans and the violently anti-Semitic Pontius Pilate, a protégé of Sejanus in Rome, would not be further antagonized.

Jesus had refused to heed the warnings or the advice He had received. Although His every move was observed by paid spies, He continued to preach, and during the Passover holiday, He dared deliver His message to a multitude in the very shadow of the palace of Herod. Enraged, Pilate conferred with Herod Antipas, governor of Galilee, who had just arrived in the city. That evening, Jesus celebrated the Seder supper with His closest disciples at the house of Nicodemus, where He retold the story of the Exodus of the Children of Israel and answered questions asked by the youngest one present, and broke unleavened bread, or matzoth, and had bitter herbs and wine. Finally, persuaded by James and the others to depart from Jerusalem for a time and to take His message elsewhere, Jesus set off that night through the Valley of Kidron, when an unnamed spy led a detachment of Roman soldiers to Him. Jesus was intercepted and placed under arrest.

The following morning, before Herod's palace, Jesus was placed on trial before Pontius Pilate. Charged with defying authority and fomenting unrest, Jesus stood await-

ing judgment. The witnesses brought against Him had
been Romans or persons upon whom Roman citizenship
had been conferred, since the Jewish Sadducees who ran
the temple refused to bear witness against Jesus (for fear
of alienating His followers or incurring the hostility of the
Jewish community by siding with the Roman authorities).
Pilate had been implacable during the brief trial. [Anno-
tation: King Agrippa I informed Caligula Caesar that Pilate was always "inflexible, merciless, and obstinate."]
Pilate's verdict was terse. He said to Jesus, "You shall be
crucified." And Jesus replied, "Behold, your house is left
desolate."

After a severe scourging—two whips tipped with dogs'
bones were used to lash Jesus more than one hundred
times—He and two criminals named Dysmas and Gestas
were led by a contingent of Roman soldiers out of the
Sheep Gate to a small hillside near the walls of Jerusalem.
There, Jesus was crucified. No iron nails were driven
through His hands or feet. Rather, His wrists were bound
to the crossbar with cord and His ankles were strapped to
the olivewood post of the cross. Writhing in agony,
bleeding still from the lacerations of the whip, thirsty,
delirious, He hung there in the sun to die. To hasten His
end, a soldier stabbed Jesus in the side with a short
sword, and laughingly said, "Now let Elijah come to save
him!" As the blade was drawn from His body, Jesus lost
consciousness.

In the ninth hour [Annotation: three o'clock in the
afternoon], the centurion looked up at Jesus, touched Him,
found Him cold, and pronounced Him dead. Then, friends
of the deceased, Nicodemus and Joseph of Arimathea,
invoking the Roman law that permitted an honorable
burial for those executed for political reasons, besought
Pilate to allow them to take the corpse and give it a decent burial. Their wish was granted.

Before nightfall, Nicodemus directed the disciples,
Simon and John, to take down the body and carry it to his
private family tomb and there prepare the corpse for
burial. While the men went to summon James, and find
winding linen as well as myrrh and aloe powder to anoint

Him, Mary of Magdala sat in watch over the body lying on the floor of the antechamber of the tomb. When the men returned, with the bereaved James in their fold, Mary met them with the astonishing words, "Brethren, a miracle! *Rabbuli*—the Master—he lives!"

And according to James, his brother was indeed alive, in a coma, breathing faintly. Immediately, James and the disciples spirited the unconscious Jesus to the safety of a cave, while a messenger was sent in secrecy to summon an Essene physician to minister to Jesus as He still clung to life. Upon examination, the physician stated that the soldier's sword had missed Jesus' vital organs, and that the Romans had prematurely pronounced Him dead. After a week's care, during which He was attended daily by the Essene physician, Jesus was healed but left weakened by His suffering.

According to James:

There were two accounts of his rising from the dead. Mary of Magdala testified that our Jesus had been resurrected by his Father in heaven. The physician claimed that Jesus had survived the crucifixion as a mortal, because by chance his wound had been shallow. [Annotation: This was not the only recorded survival of a crucifixion. Reporting on a similar case that occurred forty years later, the historian Flavius Josephus wrote: "and when I was sent by Titus Caesar . . . to a certain village called Thecoa, in order to know whether it was a place fit for a camp, as I came back, I saw many captives crucified; and remembered three of them as my former acquaintances. I was very sorry at this in my mind, and went with tears in my eyes to Titus, and told him of them; so he immediately commanded them to be taken down . . . yet two of them died under the physician's hand, while the third recovered." See Josephus: *The Life of,* 75] Whether my brother and our Lord had died and been resurrected by God, or whether he had recovered in the flesh through medicine and God's will, I am unable to say. But once I was certain of my brother's survival, I hastened to inform the others who believed him dead, and to say to them, *"Maranatha*—the Lord has come," and they accepted his return and rejoiced and were renewed in their faith.

All agreed as one that whatever had happened had been a miracle. Jesus lived on. Then, one night, when he had healed and was strong, Jesus summoned me, as well as our uncle, Simeon Cleophas, to his hiding place and he spoke, saying, "You are the beloved ones, and you shall be the cause of life among many. Proclaim the good tidings of the Son and the Father." Then he said he must take his leave, and when I asked where he would go, he replied, "There are many mansions in my Father's house, and I must visit them and spread the message of salvation until I am summoned to ascend to the Father." Before the cock crowed, we accompanied our Lord to a hill near Bethany, and he bade us remain, and blessed us, and with his staff in hand he went off and disappeared in the mist and the darkness. Then we knelt down and gave thanks and lifted up our hearts to the heavens.

Amen, He lived on, James affirmed, and all else that James recorded he had heard from those who witnessed firsthand Jesus Christ's continuing pilgrimage.

The physical appearance of Jesus had been altered by His suffering, and there were few upon meeting Him who recognized Him at once. Jesus went on to Caesarea, to Damascus, to Antioch, and made a journey to Parthia, and another to Babylonia, and returned to Antioch, and moved on to Cyprus, to Neapolis, to Italia and Rome itself.

That He was in those places, and others, James heard from the disciples whenever they returned to Jerusalem. *Maranatha*, they would say in Aramaic, and James would know then that the Lord had come to them and they had seen Him in the flesh.

The witnesses to His second ministry were numerous.

In the village of Emmaus, seven miles from Jerusalem, Jesus was seen by Cleopas and Simon, and He broke bread with them. On the shore of the sea of Tiberias, He came upon Thomas, Simon Peter, and Simon, son of Jonas, and revealed Himself to them and dined with them. On the road to Damascus, five years after the Crucifixion, Saul of Tarsus—renamed Paul after his conversion—was approached by a stranger in the night, and asked the stranger who he was, and the stranger replied, "I am Jesus."

Long after the Crucifixion, Ignatius of Antioch, when a boy, heard Jesus preach at a meeting place in Antioch, and when Ignatius was grown, he reported to the disciples, "He is in the flesh, I have seen him." Later, after Jesus had taken a trading vessel to Italy, and was walking on the Appian Way on the road to Rome, He encountered the apostle Peter, and Peter was dumbfounded. Jesus said, "Touch me and see that I am not a bodiless demon." Peter touched Him and believed He was flesh. "Where are you going, Lord?" Peter asked. Jesus replied, "I have come this way to be crucified again." [Annotation: James confirms the statement of the theologian, Irenaeus, who wrote between 182 and 188 A.D. and was the first to mention the four canonical gospels, that Jesus did not die until the age of fifty. James also confirms the statement by an unknown author in Acta Pilati, or the Acts of Pilate, also known as the Gospel of Nicodemus, probably written in 190 A.D., that Jesus died not in 30 A.D. but sometime between 41 and 54 A.D. during the reign of Claudius Caesar.]

But only a relative handful who had known Him before ever recognized Him in the flesh. The rest of His disciples and followers believed He had ascended to heaven near Bethany. And this story was encouraged by James and Simeon Cleophas and the handful. For these apostles had, out of a desire to protect the life of Jesus in His renewed ministry and to prevent His arrest and second Crucifixion, agreed not to speak further of what had actually occurred. And so Jesus safely continued His ministry as a humble and holy teacher, revealing Himself to only a few.

In Rome, James had learned, his brother Jesus was often seen at the Pincian Gate, there in beggary among the poor and ailing, giving them aid and comfort. In the ninth year of the reign of Claudius Caesar, all sixty thousand Jews in Rome were driven from the city and Jesus was among them. "And our Lord, in his escape from Rome with his disciples, had that night walked across the abundant fields of Lake Fucinus, which had been drained by Claudius Caesar and cultivated and tilled by the Romans." Jesus was then fifty-four years of age.

James wrote:

It was told to me by Paul that when Paul arrived in Corinth, and dwelt with a Jew named Aquila and his wife Priscilla, both workers of leather, he learned of the final agony and the true resurrection and ascension of Jesus. Aquila and Priscilla had been driven from Rome with other Jews at the command of Emperor Claudius, under strict edict not to congregate or to practice their outlawed creed while on Roman soil. Aquila and Priscilla had left Rome in the company of Jesus, and made the arduous journey south to the port of Puteoli. In the port city, while awaiting an Egyptian grain vessel to take him to Alexandria, and thence to Gaza, Jesus gathered up the refugees in the Jewish quarter and spoke to them of maintaining steadfast faith in the Father and in the coming kingdom of God and the Son. And he revealed himself as the Son. An informer in the congregation, for the reward of 15,000 sesterces, reported to the local authorities that Jesus had disobeyed the command of Caesar. Forthwith, a company of Roman soldiers garrisoned at a *statio* outside the port was dispatched to arrest Jesus for the crime of treason.

Without trial, Jesus was condemned to death. On a rise of land outside Puteoli, he was scourged, bound to a cross, and his bleeding body covered with inflammable matter. The soldiers secured him to the cross, put a torch to Jesus, and departed. No sooner had they left than a great rush of wind came up from the harbor, extinguishing the flames that engulfed our Lord. When Aquila and other disciples removed his seared body from the cross, Jesus was lifeless. His corpse was temporarily secreted in a cave to await the fall of night and proper burial. In the night, returning with shroud and spices to embalm our Lord, Aquila and Priscilla and seven witnesses found the cave empty. Among the disciples there was consternation and confusion. As they speculated upon what had become of the corpse, a circle of light with the incandescent glow of a million lights filled the mouth of the cave and revealed to them Jesus raised in full glory. He beckoned to them, and they followed him, Aquila and Priscilla and the seven witnesses followed him, to the summit of a distant hill above Puteoli. Then, as day broke, Jesus gave them blessing, and immediately he was lifted up on high and enveloped by a cloud that carried him out of their sight toward heaven, and the witnesses knelt in awe and wonderment and gave their thanks to the Father and to the Son.

Behold, so did my brother Jesus ascend to his Maker. This, Aquila and Priscilla told to Paul in Corinth, who passed it to me. Now, our Lord is exalted and enthroned in heaven by the right side of the Father.

James concluded his narrative on a personal note:

My faith in the divine purpose of my brother Jesus has grown upon me daily, and upon all of his disciples, and his message has been sent forth. I have practiced the law of the Jews—have eaten no meat, drunk no wine, kept but one garment, and my hair and beard have remained unshorn—I have also headed his Church in Jerusalem. The tidings continue

to be spread among the receptive Jews of the Dispersion, and among the Gentiles from Damascus to
Rome, and among the converts in Samaria, and
among those in Caesarea, Ephesus, and Joppa, where
we do baptize the circumcised and uncircumcised
alike.

The authorities suspect me, and my earthly time
nears its end. I therefore am giving one copy of this
narrative of our Jesus to Matthew for Barnabas to
use in Cyprus, and one copy to Mark for Peter in
Rome, and this copy I shall send off with another. . . . The salutation of James with mine own
hand.

[Annotation: James, the brother of Jesus, author
of this lost gospel, was put to death by the high
priest of Jerusalem in 62 A.D.]

[Further Annotation: Several months after James
recorded his gospel, during a period when there was
a vacuum in authority due to a change in Roman
procurators of Judea, the high priest of Jerusalem,
an insolent man named Ananus, took on authority beyond his right. He determined to dispose of James
the Just, leader of the Christian community in Jerusalem, on charges of blasphemy. The blasphemy,
Hegesippus wrote in the second century, was that
James insisted Jesus had survived Crucifixion.
According to the historian Josephus, "Ananus assembled the Sanhedrin of judges, and brought before
them the brother of Jesus, the so-called Christ, James
by name, together with some others; and when he
had formulated a charge against them as breakers of
the Law, he delivered them to be stoned." According to other witnesses, when James was being prepared for execution, he went down on his knees and
prayed, "I entreat thee, O Lord God and Father, forgive them for they know not what they do." A
friendly priest stepped forward to prevent the killing,
telling the executors, "Stop! What are you doing?
The Just One is praying for you!" But a member of
the execution squad shoved the priest aside, and

brandishing a club used to beat out cloth, he smashed James on the head and killed him instantly.]

Thus did the brother of Jesus die.

And his legacy, prepared only months before in that year of 62 A.D., had been this.

The Word.

[Final Annotation: Any discrepancy between the canonical four gospels and the Gospel According to James is clarified by evidence that Mark, writing around 70 A.D., Matthew writing around 80 A.D., Luke writing around 80–90 A.D., John writing around 85–95 A.D., did not know of the second ministry of Jesus, of his visit to Rome, of his second Crucifixion. The small circle of apostles who knew the secret kept it secret to protect the continuing evangelism of Jesus. The three copies of the life of Jesus that James wrote in 62 A.D. never reached the public—because one copy, that was sent to Barnabas in Cyprus, was lost with the death of Barnabas in Salamis, and Peter's copy perished when he was crucified "head downward" in Rome in 64 A.D., and the third copy was the one hidden and buried in Ostia Antica. Consequently, the four responsible for the canonical gospels—Matthew, Mark, Luke, and John —had no information beyond the limited oral reports that Jesus had died, been resurrected, and ascended to heaven outside Jerusalem in 30 A.D. The four gospel writers, forty to sixty-five years later, did not know of the extended years of Jesus Christ's life. What they set down took Jesus' story up to a point. After that point, there remained only the Gospel of James to supplement and complete the story, and this gospel was lost for more than nineteen centuries until the present day.]

And now, Randall realized, it was found, the truth, the whole truth, the Word in its entirety.

Then Randall remembered something else. In another

gospel, he remembered, that recorded by John, there had been a curious promise, and it was this: "And there are also many other things which Jesus did, the which, if they should be written every one, I suppose that even the world itself could not contain the books that should be written."

Now the world contained all the books that should be written—now, at last, in a single book.

And here was that book. Here, the Word.

It was an astounding narrative, and it would electrify the wide world. For the first time since he had read and reread it, Steve Randall sat up on the sofa and saw that it was in his hands to pass on this miracle of discovery to that waiting world.

Certainly, it was the greatest find in the history of biblical archeology. In fact, had there ever been a discovery in any field of archeology the equal of this one? Had Schliemann's discovery of ancient Homeric Troy been the match of this? Or Carter's uncovering the tomb of Tutankhamen? Or the finding of the Rosetta stone? Or the excavations of the Neanderthal man, the missing link? No, nothing that had come before was the equal of Dr. Augusto Monti's find near Ostia Antica in Italy.

Randall knew that he was thinking like a press agent once more, and if he opened the floodgates, a hundred ideas to promote this find, this new Bible, would rush into his head. Yet, somehow, he kept the gates closed. He was selfish. He was still absorbed by the power of the discovery to move and shake him personally.

How he envied those others out there, the believers, the faltering believers, the backsliders, the ones who needed the Word and would be even more emotionally receptive to it than he himself had been. Instantly, he thought of those dear to him—his stricken father, his lost mother, his disillusioned friend Tom Carey, even his sister Clare— and he tried to imagine how this revelation of Christ reborn might affect each of them.

At once, he thought of Judy, and then of his wife Barbara in San Francisco and the freedom that she had pleaded for, and the love that she needed, and the hope she had of a better new life for Judy and herself.

He left the sofa, walked slowly into the bedroom, and sat down on the side of the bed, staring at the telephone.

It was late evening here, therefore still early afternoon there, six thousand miles away.

He considered his second thoughts. Finally, he lifted the receiver off the hook, and began to place a long-distance call to San Francisco.

FIFTEEN MINUTES LATER the connection was made. There were several operators—Amsterdam, New York, San Francisco, Randall wasn't sure—but they had his party on the other end, at last.

"Hello, Barbara?"

"Who is this?"

"It's Steve. How are you, Barbara?"

"Steve? I can't hear you very well. Where are you?"

"I'm calling from Amsterdam."

"Amsterdam? My God, what are you doing—oh, I remember, you mentioned it to Judy—some kind of new account."

"Yes. By the way, how is Judy?"

"She's not here now, or I'd let you speak to her. Oh, she's fine, doing very well."

"Still seeing the shrink?"

"She's seeing Arthur, yes. And her school took her back. I think she's writing you about that."

"Good."

"She wrote your father the sweetest letter. I had a long talk with Clare the other day. I gather he's slowly improving."

"You still haven't told me about yourself, Barbara. How are you doing?"

"Well—well, Steve, what am I supposed to say?"

"I guess I'm the one who's supposed to say. First. I'm sorry, I'm damn sorry about the way I behaved the last time we were together, up in your hotel room in Oak City."

"Never mind. You have your—"

"I do mind. Look, Barbara, I'll tell you why I'm calling you. I've given the whole thing some thought. I mean, your wanting a divorce so you can marry Arthur Burke, and my telling you I was going to fight it. Well, I'd like you to know I've had a change of mind and heart. You deserve to be free to marry again. I want that for you. It's the right thing. So this was—anyway, you're free, you can file for divorce, and I won't contest it."

"Steve! I—I don't know what to say. I can't believe it. I was praying you'd do it for Judy's sake."

"I'm not doing it for Judy's sake. I'm doing it for your sake, Barbara. You deserve some happiness."

"I—dammit, I'm choking up. Steve, I can't tell you how I feel. This is the nicest thing you've done in years. I can almost say—I will say—I love you for it."

"Never mind that. There's not enough love anywhere to spread it around that easily. You just love that fellow you're going to marry. And you love our daughter. And know that I love her, too."

"Steve, dear, remember this. Judy is your girl as much as mine. You'll be able to see her whenever you wish. I promise you that."

"Thanks. I'll just have to hope she wants to see me."

"She does. She loves you."

"All right. Anyway, I'll phone Crawford in New York in the next day or two—tomorrow, if I can—and tell him we've come to an agreement on the divorce. I'll have him get in touch with you, and then he can work out the property settlement, whatever else, with your attorney."

"There'll be no problems, Steve. . . . Steve, you haven't told me—how are you?"

"I'm not sure yet. Better, definitely better. I'm sorting out a lot of things. I may be a little crazy, letting you go."

"I wish it could have worked, Steve."

"I wish that, too. But it didn't. I'm glad you're on the right track now. Anyway, you have my best, both of you. Maybe I'll drop in on you one year when I'm out in your direction."

"You'll always be welcome, Steve."

"Okay, be sure to give Judy my love. And, whatever's left of it, love to you, too."

"Our love to you, Steve. Good-bye."

"Good-bye—Babs."

Gently, he returned the receiver to its cradle. He felt—
what?—decent. He hadn't felt that way in a long time.
He also felt sad, which was more familiar.

He wondered what had inspired him to cut the bond.
Had he been softened by that goddam Christ stuff? Or
had a lingering and nagging bad conscience impelled him
to surrender? Had he subconsciously planned to give in
all the time? No matter, it was done.

Then, he became aware that he was not alone.

He looked up, and in the entrance between the living
room and the bedroom stood Darlene.

She was attractive in the transparent white blouse that
revealed her net brassiere, and the form-fitting pale blue
short skirt that accented the shapeliness of her long legs.
She was smiling broadly at him, he could see. In fact,
she seemed elated.

She gave a cheerful toss to her shoulder-length blonde
hair and came into the bedroom toward him. "How's my
honey?" she purred.

Her presence surprised him. "I thought you were on
that canal tour."

"It's over, funny." She bent and kissed his nose, and
sat on the bed snuggling close to him. "It's almost midnight already."

"Is it?" Something crossed his mind, and he glanced at
her joyous face. "When did you get back?"

"Five minutes ago, I guess."

"Where were you? In your room?"

"I was here in the living room. I let myself in. You
were just too tied up on the phone to hear me." Her
smile remained broad. "I couldn't help it."

"It doesn't matter. How was your—?"

"But, Steve, it does matter, it matters very much. I
can't tell you how happy I am."

"About what?" he asked suspiciously.

She pretended amazement. "It's obvious, isn't it? I'm
happy you finally got up the guts to split from that bag.
I thought you'd never shake her. Now you've done it,
thank God. You're free, you're absolutely free. It's taken

long enough." She kissed his cheek. "We can be together, at last."

He eyed her, and said carefully, "We are together, Darlene."

"Silly, you know what I'm saying."

He changed his position on the bed, to confront her. "No, I'm not sure. Exactly what are you saying, Darlene?"

"We can get married, and it's about time. As long as you had that wife tied around your neck, I never bothered you or brought it up, did I? I went along because I cared for you. I knew if you could, you'd marry me. It's what every girl wants. Now, honey, you can, and I've never been more excited." She leaped to her feet and began unbuttoning the front of her blouse. "Wow. Let's get into bed—no more wasting time. Let's celebrate."

Randall came to his feet fast, and grabbed her wrists to prevent her from undoing her blouse further. "No, Darlene."

Her smile vanished. She looked down at his hands. "What are you trying to do?"

He released her wrists. "We're not celebrating getting married. I'm not marrying anyone, at least not right now."

"You're not—what? You must be kidding me."

"Darlene, marriage was never part of our arrangement. Think back. Did I ever promise to marry you? From the start, I made it clear to you, if you simply wanted to move in and live with me, that was fine, that was great. We'd live together. Have some fun. I never spoke of anything more."

Her smooth brow had wrinkled. "But that was before, ages ago, because you were tied up. I mean, like—well, that was it, and I understood. You always said you loved me. I figured you did, and if you ever got a divorce, you'd want to be together with me. For real, I mean." She tried to revive her good humor. "Steve, listen, it could be great for us. It's been swell up to now. It could be ten times greater. I heard the part on the phone, when you were talking about your daughter. That's fine, caring for her, but she's growing up and she's out of your life, and you don't have to think about it. Because you'll have me.

I'm twenty-four, and I'm ready and willing to give you as many kids as you want. Out the window go the pills. You and I, we can produce as many sons and daughters as you want, and have a ball doing it. Steve, you can start all over again."

He shifted uneasily from one foot to the other, and stared down at the carpet. "Darlene, you can believe it or you don't have to," he said quietly, "but I don't want to start all over again. I just want to resolve this first start I'm stuck with, and find out what I can do next. I've got some plans, but marriage isn't one of them."

"You mean marriage to me isn't." Her voice was getting shriller. He looked up, and saw the tightening of her features. "You mean I'm not good enough for you," she went on. "You don't think I'm good enough."

"I never said that, and I never would, because it's not true. I'd put it another way. Having an uncomplicated arrangement, such as we have—that's one thing. Marriage is quite another. I know. I've been through it. We're not right for each other, not for the long haul. Certainly, I'm wrong for you. I'm too old for you, and you're too young for me. We don't have the same interests. And a dozen other things. It wouldn't work."

"Bullshit," she blurted. She was angry and she was letting it show, something she had never dared do in front of him before. "Don't con me, Steve, like you con everyone else. I see through you. It's what I said. You don't think I'm good enough for hotshot you. I'm going to tell you something. Plenty of men would crawl to marry me. Plenty have asked me. When Roy came to the ship to see me off—Roy Ingram, remember?—he came all the way from Kansas City to beg me to marry him. You know that, and you know I turned him down. I was being loyal to you. So if I was good enough for Roy, why the hell am I not good enough for you?"

"Dammit, being good enough has nothing to do with it. How many times do I have to repeat it? Being right for each other is the name of the game. I'm not right for you, and maybe Roy is. You're not right for me, but maybe you are for Roy."

"Maybe I'm going to find out," she said loudly. She began buttoning her blouse. "Maybe I'm going to find out if Roy is right for me."

"Do whatever you want, Darlene. I'm not going to stand in your way."

She met his eyes evenly. "Steve, I'm giving you your last chance. I'm through whoring around with you. I'm a nice girl and I want to be treated with respect. If you're ready to do that, to do what you should do, I'll stay. Otherwise, I'm leaving you this minute, this very minute, and taking the first plane out of here, and I'm never coming back. You won't ever see me again. It's up to you."

He was tempted. He wanted to rip her clothes off, and throw her on the bed, and fuck her until her ears bled. He wanted her. And he did not want to be left alone. Yet, he held back. The price tag she had put on herself was too high. Another lousy marriage. He simply could not face it. Especially, he could not imagine it now, now when he was groping for a road, a path that would lead him to a better place. Darlene wasn't the way. Darlene was a dead end. Even worse, viewing her as she was, seeing her as a young human being with a life ahead of her, he knew he would destroy that life, destroy it for lack of love and communication. It was impossible. United, they would be victims, he of suicide and she of murder.

"I'm sorry, Darlene," he said. "I can't make it the way you'd like."

Welts of anger distorted her young face. "Okay, you no-good dirty bastard, then you're not making it any way at all with me anymore. I'm going to my room to pack. You can make the flight reservation, and you can pay for it. Tell them I'll pick the ticket up at the desk in the morning."

He started to follow her out to the entry hall. "If you're sure that's what you want," he said lamely.

She whirled around. "I'm sure I want a one-way ticket to Kansas City, you hear? And don't you ever come near me again!"

She banged out of the suite.

After a while, he went to mix himself a strong drink, and find out whether he could do any more work that night.

AN HOUR and three drinks later, Randall was still too engrossed in the research to feel self-pity.

He had gone through the manila file folders containing interviews and background material on Dr. Bernard Jeffries, expert in translation, textual criticism, papyrology; on Professor Henri Aubert, expert in radiocarbon dating; on Herr Karl Hennig, expert in book design and printing. He had saved the last folder until he could reread the translations of the Petronius Parchment and the Gospel According to James once more. He had reread the texts in the page proofs, and had been as thrilled this time as he had been before by the discoveries. Now he was eager and ready to learn what he could about the discoverer.

He took up the final folder supplied by his publicity staff. This one contained the facts on Professor Augusto Monti, archeologist.

Randall opened the manila folder. Inside, to his dismay, there were only five pages of typescript held together with a paper clip. Quickly, Randall read the five pages.

There was a colorless biography of Professor Monti. Sixty-four years old. Widowed. Two daughters, Angela and Claretta, one of them married. The archeologist's academic history, his positions, his awards. Currently, Director Istituto di Archeologia Cristiana, Professor of Archeology, University of Rome. A list of various excavations in Italy and in the Middle East in which Monti had participated or which he had supervised. Finally, two pages, crammed with dates and abstruse technical archeological terms, devoted to the dig at Ostia Antica six years ago. Period.

This was a publicity file?

Randall was incredulous. Professor Monti had made one of the most momentous finds in world history, and all that was reflected of this was some information that was about as exciting as a railroad timetable.

Frustrated, Randall finished his Scotch and reached for the telephone.

It was almost one o'clock in the morning. He had been told that Wheeler always worked late. It was worth a try, calling the publisher, Randall decided, even if he woke him up. Monti was the key personality to publicize in promoting the International New Testament. Randall had to know the reason for the absence of information, and by what means more could be obtained at once.

He rang Wheeler's suite, and waited.

A feminine voice answered. He recognized the voice. It belonged to Naomi Dunn.

"This is Steve," he said. "I wanted to talk to George Wheeler."

"He's out of town," Naomi answered. "I've been assembling some of the loose papers in his room. Is it anything I can help you with?"

"Maybe you can. I read the Petronius and the James tonight. First time. Tremendous. I was shook up good."

"I expected you would be."

"I was so turned on by the discovery, that I tried to find out about the genius responsible. Namely, Professor Monti. I happened to have his file along. I just read it. Next to nothing. Flimsy. No color on the man. No details about the discovery—"

"I'm sure Mr. Wheeler and Signore Gayda can fill you in."

"Not enough, Naomi. What I want should come from the heart and gut of the archeologist himself. How he hit upon where to look. What he was looking for. How he felt when he found what he found. Not only what he did, but what was going on inside him before, during, and after. This is a fantastic story, and we can't blow it."

"You're right," said Naomi. "What do you suggest we do about it?"

"To begin with, has anyone on this project ever personally interviewed Professor Monti?"

"Let me think. Some of the publishers in the beginning, then all five of them met with him several times, in Rome, after they leased the rights to the papyri and parchment from the Italian government. They've had no reason to meet with Professor Monti recently. However, I do remember something. When the publicity staff was taken on, before you were hired to head it, one of the girls on your staff, Jessica Taylor, felt she should meet Monti to get more material. Also Edlund tried to make an appointment to go down to Rome and shoot some pictures of him. Neither one got to see him. On each occasion, he was off in some remote place, representing the Italian government at various digs. One of his daughters told Jessica, and later Edlund, that she'd let them know when her father returned to Rome. But we've never heard from her, I'm afraid."

"When was that?"

"Maybe three months ago."

"Well, old Monti should be back in Rome by now. I want to see him. In fact, I must see him. We don't have much time. Naomi, can you call him in Rome and set up an appointment for the day after tomorrow? No, wait. That would be Sunday. Make it for Monday. And when you call, if he's not there, you tell his daughter I'll go and find him wherever he is. I won't take No for an answer."

"It's as good as done, Steve."

He felt tired and suddenly dispirited. "Thanks, Naomi. And while you're about it, you might as well throw your weight around to line up appointments to follow with Aubert in Paris and Hennig in Mainz. I should see all the top people behind this Bible as soon as possible. I can make time for it now, by working evenings. Besides, I'd like to keep myself as busy as possible."

There was a brief silence on the other hand, and then he heard Naomi's voice again, less impersonal. "Do I detect the slightest note of—of self-pity in your tone?"

"You do. It finally caught up with me. I've been drinking, and feeling a little sorry for myself. I guess—I don't know—I've never felt quite as alone as I feel tonight."

"I thought Petronius and James had you occupied. They can be good friends."

"They can be, Naomi. They've helped me already. But I'll have to give them more time."

"Where's Darlene?"

"We broke up. She's going back home for good."

"I see." There was a long pause before Naomi spoke again. "You know, I hate for anyone to be lonely. I know what that's like. I can endure it. But I can't stand it in anyone else. Especially someone I'm fond of." There was a second pause, and then Naomi said, "Would you like company, Steve? I can stay the night, if you want."

"Yes, that would help."

"Just tonight. Not again. Just because I don't want you to be alone."

"Come on down, Naomi."

"I'm coming. But only because I don't want you to be alone."

"I'll be waiting."

He hung up the phone, and he began to undress.

He had no idea why he was doing this. Naomi would never know it, but making love with her was like— like being alone.

Still, he needed someone, something, anyone, anything —just for now, for this brief now, before he came close to the true passion and the full revelation of the Word in Rome.

V

As it turned out, it was not in Rome, but in Milan, that Steve Randall arrived this hot and humid late Monday morning for his meeting with Professor Augusto Monti.

Three days earlier, Friday in Amsterdam, Randall had been awakened at daybreak by the sounds of Naomi's dressing and leaving his suite. Remembering all that he had to do, Randall had not remained in bed either. After a light breakfast, he had tested Darlene's door, found it still securely locked, and with his briefcase in hand he had gone down to the Amstel Hotel lobby to arrange her jetliner reservations from Amsterdam to Kansas City. He had left for her, in a sealed envelope, a parting note and cash for incidental expenses, and explained to the concierge that he wanted this sent up to her room with her tickets when they were ready.

After that, even though the time difference meant he had to rouse his lawyer from sleep, Randall had placed a transatlantic telephone call to Thad Crawford. Their talk had been a lengthy one. Randall had repeated his conversation with Barbara, and Crawford had sounded clearly relieved that Randall was not going to contest his wife's divorce action. They had discussed terms for a reasonable settlement. With the marital matter resolved, they had discussed the Cosmos deal. Various compromises had been made with Ogden Towery, and the final papers would soon be drawn. As for the uncomfortable business of dropping The Raker Institute account, Jim McLoughlin had still not been located nor had he responded to any message.

By ten o'clock in the morning, Randall had checked into Zaal F, his office in the Hotel Krasnapolsky, with his precious briefcase. There had been no walking that morning in Amsterdam. He had permitted Theo to drive him straight to the Kras entrance. The effort to waylay him the night before was still on his mind, and he had summoned his secretary so that he might dictate a memo about the assault. Lori Cook's eyes had widened, and stayed wide, as she had taken down details of the attack. He had instructed her to see that Inspector Heldering got the memorandum, with copies to go to the five publishers.

This done, Randall had decided to return the page proofs of the International New Testament to Dr. Deichhardt, as he had promised. Preparing to leave his office, he had received a call from Naomi, who said she had to see him immediately about his forthcoming appointments with Professor Monti, Professor Aubert, and Herr Hennig. She had said that she was on her way over with her notes.

Randall had summoned Lori again, and handed her the page proofs. "Put the book in a manila envelope. Show it to no one. Hand it to Dr. Deichhardt personally. Don't leave it with his secretary. And don't let yourself get abducted."

Minutes after Lori had limped out of his office, Naomi had entered it with her news.

There had been no trouble setting appointments for Randall with Aubert in Paris and Hennig in Mainz.

"Strange people, those Montis," Naomi had said. "The professor's daughter, Angela, took my call. I guess she acts as her father's secretary. She admitted her father had returned to Italy. As to seeing anyone from Resurrection Two, she insisted that he was tied up now, and kept trying to postpone it. I simply wouldn't let her off the hook. I explained that it was imperative that our publicity director obtain more material from Professor Monti. I told her about you, Steve, and how you felt the most important personality to be publicized was Professor Monti. I even told her we're publishing in a few weeks, so there could be no delay. When she continued to be vague about an appointment date, I threatened her. I said you were going down to Rome this coming week and would just camp on Professor Monti's doorstep until you saw him. That did it. She capitulated and promised her father would see you. But not in Rome. He was on his way from Rome to Milan by car on some private business, but he'd make time to see you Monday morning in Milan. I told her you'd be at the Hotel Principe & Savoia, and we agreed that Professor Monti would be up in your suite at eleven o'clock in the morning."

So here Steve Randall was, in the small, overfurnished sitting room of Suite 757 of the elegant Hotel Principe & Savoia in Milan at five minutes to eleven on Monday morning.

Removing his miniature cassette tape recorder from his suitcase, Randall checked it to see whether it was in working order, then laid it on top of the television set and went to the window. He pressed a button and the electrically driven blinds rose upward, baring the window and the Piazza della Repubblica below. The neighborhood beyond the driveway entrance, beyond the lawns and trees, was quiet, almost deserted in the late morning heat. Randall thought about what he would ask Professor Monti, and he prayed the archeologist was a good subject and that his English would be understandable.

A series of short, sharp raps on the door brought Randall around fast. Professor Monti was on time. A happy omen.

Randall went quickly to the door, pulled it open, determined to greet the archeologist with enthusiasm and warmth—and then his face fell.

A young lady stood in the doorway.

"You are Steven Randall from the International New Testament group?" she said in a low voice that bore the faintest soft trace of a British accent.

"Yes, I am," he said, confused.

"I am Professor Monti's daughter. I am Angela Monti, from Rome."

"But I was supposed to see—"

"I know. You were expecting my father. You are surprised and disappointed." She smiled briefly. "Do not be disappointed. I will explain, if you will allow me. Also, I will help you for my father, if you wish." She peered past Randall. "May I come in?"

"Oh, I'm sorry, forgive me," he said, flustered. "Do come in, of course. I'm afraid I was thrown off balance for a minute."

"It is understandable," she said, going into the living room of the suite. "My father sends his apologies for being unable to appear in person. The circumstances were beyond his control, as you will learn."

Randall closed the door and followed her to the center of the room.

She circled gracefully, taking in the surroundings, then gazed at him with frank amusement. "At least they gave you air conditioning. Perhaps that will keep you cool. Seriously, this is a relief. It is twenty-nine outside—centigrade, of course. That would be in the eighties for you—which is not enough to melt one, but the humidity is suffocating."

His immediate surprise and disappointment, as well as his annoyance over Professor Monti's not keeping his word, had rapidly modified as he observed the girl.

Angela Monti was, literally, breathtaking.

She was, he guessed, five feet six inches in height. She wore a broad-brimmed Italian straw hat, outsized lavender-tinted sunglasses, a low-cut sheer yellow silk blouse that revealed two wisps of bra which did little to contain the overflow of her provocative breasts. A wide leather belt hugged her slim supple waist, and a rust-colored summer skirt enhanced the curves of her voluptuous hips.

He was unable to take his eyes off her, as she put down her brown leather handbag, surely Gucci, and removed her straw hat and sunglasses. Her tousled bobbed hair was soft and raven-black, the wide-set almond eyes jade-green, the broad-bridged nose pert with delicate nostrils, the generous carmine lips moist, and there was a beauty mark beneath one high cheekbone. A thin gold chain around her neck held a gold cross that nestled in the deep cleft between her breasts.

She became aware of his stare. "You are angry to have me here instead of my father?" she asked.

"No, no, of course not. Frankly, I was admiring you. Are you a model or an actress?"

"Thank you," she said without coyness. "I am much too serious for that." She appraised him. "You are not what I expected."

"What did you expect?"

"I was told only that you are a famous publicity maker, and now the press director from America for the Bible project. I suppose we all think too much in stereotypes. To me the word *publicity* is one I associate with a big trumpet—no, I mean tuba—which makes a big noise. I did not expect someone who would be restrained and gentlemanly and look so—how should I say?—American, yes, brown hair, eyes, strong frame—but so sophisticated."

She is softening me up, he thought, or else she is utterly without guile. No matter. He liked it.

"Why don't we sit down?" he said. He joined her on the sofa. "Believe me, I'm pleased to have you here, Miss Monti—"

"Angela," she corrected him.

"Very well, I give you Steve for Angela."

"Yes, Steve," she said with a smile.

"My problem is one of pressure," he went on. "I was brought into this project late. It's a tremendous project and it deserves the best promotional campaign possible, perhaps the best and biggest in history. That can't be done unless everyone cooperates with me. To my mind, the most dramatic and most exciting role in the entire new Bible story is the one Professor Monti has played. I feel he should receive the credit he deserves. Yet, members of my staff tried to see him recently and failed. Now, I've made up my mind to see him, and I've been frustrated. Can you explain just what is going on?"

"Yes," she said. "I will explain and will reserve nothing from you. It is all a matter of politics and jealousies in the Roman archeological community. When my father determined to make his dig, he had to apply for permission to the archeology superintendent of the Ostia Antica region. The one in charge—he was so seven years ago, though recently he was promoted—is Dr. Fernando Tura, who has always disagreed with my father's ideas about biblical archeology as being too radical, and who has always been a rival of my father. Only Dr. Tura's approval can send an application on to the Higher Council of Antiquities and Fine Arts in the Via del Popolo in Rome. Then, if the Council of three finds the application valid, it recommends the application to the Director of Antiquities, who gives the formal permission. But Dr. Tura was difficult—"

"You mean he refused to approve your father's application to dig seven years ago?"

"He ridiculed my father's theory that any valuable original manuscript, one that predated Mark or Matthew, could be found right here in Italy. Dr. Tura not only ridiculed, but he made delays. He instigated bad propaganda against my father in official circles. But my father would not be stopped by such pettiness. Through unofficial means, my father appealed to a friend and colleague on the Higher Council. This made Dr. Tura furious, but he was forced to pass along the application for the excavation, which was then approved. Later, after my father made his brilliant discovery, and it was proved to be authentic, Dr. Tura was beside himself with envy and anger. He set out to keep my father in the background and to keep him from receiving credit for the find he made. Also, Dr. Tura began to take credit for the discovery by spreading the word that he had directed Professor Monti to Ostia Antica and had encouraged him to excavate, as if he, Tura, was the genius, and Professor Monti really only the one who used a spade. Furthermore, so that he could not be contradicted, Dr. Tura goaded the Ministry of Instruction to send my father outside the country to instigate or supervise new digs in faraway places."

"Did the Ministry have the authority to assign your father to those places?"

"Not actually," said Angela. "But you know, in life, only the people who make the law can safely break the law. That is the privilege of power. Dr. Tura advised his close ones in the Ministry that it would be best if his associate, Professor Monti, were sent abroad, quietly, secretly, so that he would not detract from the department by taking all the credit for himself for the discovery. Well, in fact, no one can send an archeologist anywhere if he does not wish to go. An archeologist selects his own digs. But since my father is not a tenured professor at the University of Rome, it was made clear if he did not do as he was told, he could lose his teaching position. Despite a modest inheritance from my mother, which my father has always insisted was for Claretta—she is my older sister—and for myself, he has only a modest income to live on. So he had to do as he was told, to keep his position and salary."

"But didn't Professor Monti make a good deal of money on the Ostia Antica discovery?" Randall wondered.

"All discoveries belong to the Italian government. He was given a percentage of the money the publishers paid to the government to lease the papyri and parchment. But it evaporated. My father had borrowed, indebted himself deeply, to make the long excavation. This he had to repay with usurious interest. Most of what money he had left he shared with our needy relatives in Naples. So anyway, he must do now as he is ordered. When Miss Taylor and Mr. Edlund from your staff called to meet him, my father was in the Middle East making a survey of the site of Pella—it is where the ancient Ebionites fled after the first Jewish revolt against Rome—for a future excavation. When my father returns to Rome after each assignment, he is warned not to participate in the publicity of commercial publishers at the penalty of being dismissed."

Randall was still not satisfied. "What happened today? Professor Monti was on his way to Milan. He did agree to meet with me."

"He agreed to meet with you because I advised him if he received much publicity, he would be more famous than the Ministry people, and need not be afraid of them any longer. But somehow, I do not know how, Dr. Tura learned my father was on his way to meet you in Milan. Dr. Tura had my father intercepted in Florence and commanded him to return to Rome immediately for an urgent new assignment to Egypt. My father was afraid to resist. He returned to Rome, and by tomorrow will be in Egypt. For me, this was the last straw. I made up my mind to drive to meet you myself, if my father would not. I know everything he knows. I can tell you anything he would tell you. I am determined he must receive the international credit he deserves. That will make him more powerful than those jealous politicians in Rome who keep him frightened and silent. That is what brought me here. I pledge you my cooperation for today and for as long as you wish."

Randall rose and took his tape recorder. "I'm grateful, Angela. I need you. I have some basic questions to ask you."

"I will answer everything. You can put it on the tape."

"My first question is—what about having lunch with me?"

She burst into laughter. He could see that she was even more beautiful than he had thought. She said, "You are so charming, Steve. Of course, I would like to have lunch. I am famished."

"I made a reservation downstairs in the Escoffier Grill. But now that you're here, not your father, you might prefer something livelier. I don't know Milan. Do you have any favorite restaurants?"

She stood up. "You have not been in Milano before?"

"Never. I was in Rome once for a week, and in Venice and Florence for a quick day or two, but never Milan."

"Then I will take you to the Galleria."

"The what?"

"The Galleria Vittorio Emanuele. It is the most wonderful arcade in the entire world. So silly and unusual and romantic. Come, I will show you."

She took his hand quite naturally, and the touch of her hand, her nearness, instantly excited him.

"Angela," he forced himself to say, "this place we're

going to—is it a place where I can interview you? It's
something I have to get done."

"But of course," she said gaily. "We are in Milan, not
Rome. Here it is always business before pleasure. I shall
not seduce you." Her fingers tightened between his. "At
least, not yet," she concluded lightly.

Once downstairs, they got into her low-slung vintage-
year red Ferrari. Shortly, they were rolling through the
Piazza della Repubblica ("where they hung Mussolini and
Petacci by their heels," she was explaining), and
swerved left into the broad Via Filippe Turati.

Randall was curious to know more about her. Angela
was quite willing to talk about herself. During their short
ride, she spoke openly if briefly of her background. Angela had been fifteen years old when her mother, part Italian, part British, had died. Angela had attended the
University of Padua, and spent two years at the
University of London. She had majored in Greek and
Roman art. She had a sister, Claretta, older by five
years, who was married and had two young daughters
and made her home in Naples. Angela herself had been
engaged to marry only once. "It couldn't work. He was
spoiled and arrogant in that typically Italian male
way, and I was too independent to become a second-class
citizen, a shadow in a man's world." She gave most of her
time to assisting her father with his writings, editing his
scientific papers, running the family villa in Rome, and
teaching the history of Italian art twice a week in a private
school for foreign students. She had recently turned twenty-six.

About himself—for Angela was curious about him—
Randall was guarded. He spoke of his Midwestern American beginnings, and of his father's recent illness. He
revealed a little about his public relations operation in
New York, and touched lightly on the life he led. He
mentioned Barbara and Judy, and his decision last week
to give Barbara a divorce. He said nothing about Darlene.

Angela had been listening closely, her eyes on the street
ahead, but she had been noncommittal.

Now, she spoke. "May I ask, how old are you, Steve?"

He hesitated, unwilling to be twelve years older than she. Finally, he said, "I'm thirty-eight."

"You are young for one so successful."

"For one successful in business, you mean," he said, and could see that his self-deprecation was not lost upon her.

Then she was pointing past him. "The Teatro alla Scala, the best-known opera house in the world."

The exterior of La Scala was ordinary and it disappointed him.

"You are displeased?" she said. "La Scala is like so many people. It cannot be judged from the outside. Everything is inside. A place for three thousand people. Acoustics perfect. Music perfect. . . . We are in the Piazza della Scala. I will find a place to park."

After she had parked the Ferrari, and locked it, she led him to the Galleria Vittorio Emanuele.

As they entered, she said, "If you are like me, you will not believe it."

They were inside, and he was like her, for he could not believe it.

The Galleria resembled a miniature city within a city. Encapsulated beneath a vast and glorious glass dome, the most enormous skylight that Randall had ever seen, was an endless row of fine shops, to his immediate right the huge Rizzoli bookstore, to his left boutiques, travel agencies, a day hotel for transient businessmen. There were restaurants, and open trattorias filled with well-dressed Italian gentlemen and fashionably attired women, eating, drinking, chattering away, and here and there persons engrossed in Milan's elite morning newspaper, *Corriere della Sera.* "And most are reading the *terza pagina,* the third page, which has cultural news, interpretive stories. The paper has six hundred special correspondents in Italy and twenty-six in foreign cities. It is our national newspaper, and important for your work."

"I know," said Randall. "We have them on our Italian press list along with *L'Osservatore Romano, La Stampa,*

Il Messaggero, and your news agency, Agenzia Nazionale Stampa Associata."

"They will all carry the announcement of the International New Testament?"

"And stories about Professor Monti, as well—if you cooperate."

"I will cooperate," she said. "Let us go to the other end of the Galleria."

What she wanted to show him, from the opposite entrance, was the Duomo, the cathedral, the fourth-largest in the world, with its belfries and gables, with its 135 delicate pinnacles and 200 statues of saints.

"Now we will eat and talk," she said, leading him back into the Galleria.

"I'd always thought of Milan as an unromantic, commercial city," Randall confessed. "I never expected this."

"You have read Henri Beyle, Stendhal?"

"One of my favorites. Perhaps because he was so introverted, self-analytical, involved with his own ego, even as I am."

"He came here, and after that he wished to have inscribed on his tomb 'Henri Beyle, Milanais—Henri Beyle, a man of Milan.' I am a Roman in my heart, but I can understand."

They had arrived at the center of the Galleria, at the intersection of the two main pedestrian thoroughfares bathed in filtered sunlight from the dome above.

Angela chose the Caffè Biffi, and they found an outside table that was relatively isolated. Randall trusted Angela to order lunch for both of them. She selected *risotto milanese,* a rice cooked in butter, chicken broth, saffron, and *osso buco,* braised veal shanks, and she debated between two wines and settled upon Valtellina, a Sondrino red wine.

Then, although he was not ready for business, he knew that he must begin. He placed his tape recorder near her, pressed the start lever, and said, "Okay, Angela, let's discuss your father, Professor Monti. Anything you can think of, beginning with when he became an archeologist."

"It will take much more time than our lunch."

"Well, give me a little of everything, right up to his discovery. Mostly concerning his career. I'll have an opportunity to determine what's best for our promotion, and develop those aspects in more detail another time with you."

"There will be another time?"

"Many times, I hope."

"Very well. My father's career. Let me see—"

Augusto Monti had been a student at the University of Rome, and received his degree in the Facoltà di Lettere, the liberal arts. For the next three years he had gone to several schools that specialized in archeology, to the Institute of Archeology at the University of London, and to the Hebrew University of Jerusalem. After that, competing with other graduate honor students, he had participated in Rome in the *concours,* an examination before five professors. The foremost competitor would himself become a professor and be awarded the first vacant chair available in archeology. Augusto Monti had exceeded all the others in the test, and was shortly thereafter installed as a professor of Christian Archeology in the University of Rome.

Except for the fact that he eventually rose to the position of Direttore of the Instituto di Archeologia Cristiana, Monti's routine inside the university and outside differed little in his early years from what it was today. Four days a week, from the podium of the Aula di Archeologia, backed by maps and a blackboard, he gave his lecture courses before as many as two hundred students. Often, late in the day, or between courses, he would climb upstairs, cross the marble floor to his office beside the library, and sit in the green leather chair behind his polished bleached-wood desk to receive visitors and to write his papers for archeology journals.

Professor Monti directed field excavations every summer vacation, and sometimes when on special leaves of absence. His earliest reputation was gained by his discovery of several new sections of the fifty catacombs that encircled Rome, underground corridors and crypts in which six million Christians from the first to the fourth century had been buried, Monti's greatest and most persistent interest was in searching for an original document, written during the time of Jesus or shortly thereafter, that preceded the appearance of the four gospels.

Most scholars agreed that such a document—commonly called the Q document, after the word *Quelle* in German, which meant "source," the source or first document —had existed. They pointed out that the gospels written by Luke and Matthew have many identical passages that are not in Mark. Obviously Luke and Matthew drew these passages from a single earlier source. Perhaps the source had been oral, and if so it was lost to history. More likely, as Monti believed, the source had been written, and anything written, and copied, might still survive.

A decade ago, based on his studies, field work, deductions, Professor Monti had published a sensational but scholarly paper in *Notizie degli Scavi di Antichità,* a Rome-based journal devoted to current archeological excavations in various countries, and an expanded version of the same paper in *Biblica,* an Italian Jesuit journal of international renown which was devoted to scientific Bible treatises. His paper had been entitled "A New Direction in the Search for the Historical Jesus Christ." In it, he had contradicted most of the prevailing notions about the possibilities of retrieving the Q document.

"Like what, Angela?" Randall wanted to know. "What did the scholars believe, and how did your father contradict them?"

Angela set down her glass of red wine. "I will make it simple. The theologians, the biblical archeologists, the ones like Dr. Tura, the ones who were faculty colleagues of my father in the University of Rome, in the Pontifical Institute of Christian Archeology, in the American Academy in Rome—they held that the Q source had been oral. They believed that the apostles of Christ had written nothing down. They argued that, for eschatological reasons, there had been no motive or purpose for the apostles to write anything. The apostles were convinced the end of the world was near, the kingdom of heaven at hand, so they did not bother to leave written records. Only later, when the world had not ended, did the gospels come to be written. But these writings were not historical reporting. They represented Jesus as seen through the eyes of pure faith."

"And your father disagreed?"

"My father held that other records had been put down in writing before the time of Jesus, as witness the Essene library revealed by the finding of the Dead Sea Scrolls. My father felt that the disciples and friends of Jesus had not been just unlettered, illiterate fishermen and tentmakers. Some, like James, had even become leaders of the Christian sect. One of these, less certain that the world would end, must surely have dictated or written the sayings of Jesus or something of His actual life and ministry. My father would often joke that the greatest find would be a diary kept by Jesus. He had no such serious hope, of course. His real hope was for an original version of Mark, not doctored like the existing one by later church writers, or an original source—testimony book, collection of sayings, parables—the missing M source used by Matthew. Also, my father saw the possibility that some Roman document on the death of Jesus might have been written."

Randall, aware of his tape recorder, persisted. "How else did Professor Monti contradict the establishment?"

"The others, unanimous, contended that new first-century manuscripts could be found only in Egypt, Jordan, or Israel, where the dry climate and soil would preserve ancient papyrus or parchment. Italy, they said, was almost impossible because our climate is moist, and if manuscripts had ever been transported here they would have rotted long ago or certainly have been destroyed in the countless fires that swept through Rome in early days. My father argued that many holy papers and objects had been smuggled or shipped from Palestine to Italy in the first century, to save them from destruction in the revolts and for use in sustaining the many secret Christian converts in and about Rome. Also, my father argued that second-century papyri had survived and been found in the ancient ruins of Dura-Europus on the Euphrates River, and at

Herculaneum, which were not exactly dry climates. And since these documents received by early Christian converts from Palestine were precious, the Christian converts would enclose them in leather and seal them in airtight jars and place them in underground tombs, as my father had found bodies, perfumes, and vases filled with writings, preserved in the catacombs. But what created the biggest uproar was my father's theories about what might be learned about Jesus in this Q document."

"Your father had new theories about Jesus?"

"Oh, yes, radical ones. If you go down into the Catacombs of St. Sebastian on the Appian Way outside Rome, you will see carved on the wall, from maybe the second century, many pictures. Among them you will see ancient carved drawings of Jesus as a shepherd, carrying a lamb, or leading a flock of sheep. These were always regarded as symbolic. My father theorized that they may have been literal evidence that Jesus had been a shepherd and not a carpenter. That was my father's first heresy. The second, scholars believed that Jesus had limited His travels to a small area of Palestine no larger than the area of Milan or perhaps Chicago in your country. They believed that if He had traveled outside Palestine, the early church bishops would have made much of it in their writings to prove Christ was the Saviour of the whole world. Yet, the church writers rarely spoke of such travels."

"And what did your father say?"

"My father insisted that if Jesus had traveled more widely, it still could have been known to very few and was kept secret to protect Him. Indications that Jesus had been outside Palestine, even to Italy, had been found in writings by Paul, Peter, Ignatius, and others. The third heresy concerned His life span. My father did not believe that Jesus had died in His thirties, but many years afterwards. For this my father cited a number of sources, such as the writings of—I forget if it was Papias or Tertullian—which said Jesus was a young man to save the young, a middle-aged man to save the middle-aged, and an old man to save the old—and old in those days meant maybe fifty years of age."

Randall finished his wine, reversed the tape on his machine, and continued his questioning. "Did Professor Monti specify where, in Italy, such an original document might be found?"

"Yes, in his first paper, and several times in later papers. He suggested exploring further certain catacombs near Rome, or houses that had been secret meeting places of Christians in or around Rome, or the Palatine Hill. Ideally, one might hope to find the home library of a wealthy Jewish merchant such as those few who lived in the vicinity of Ostia Antica. These Jews were the original Christians, and the ones near seaports would have had earliest access to imported materials."

"That was what led Professor Monti to dig at Ostia Antica?"

"It was something more precise," said Angela Monti, recollecting it. "It was a theory and a fact my father brought together seven years ago. His theory was that the author of the source gospel in Jerusalem could have sent a copy by a disciple, to some wealthy Jewish family in some seaport of Italy. If this family had secretly been converted to Christianity, they could have hidden it in the family library. As to the fact, my father found in a newly opened St. Sebastian catacomb a crypt that preserved the bones of a young Christian convert of the first century, with indications that this convert had either been in Jerusalem once or had had a friend in Jerusalem who was a centurion, possibly at the time of Pilate. The family name was on the catacomb crypt. Like a detective, my father tried to trace the family of the young man, and he found that the father had been a prosperous Jewish shipping merchant who owned a great villa on the coast near Ostia Antica. My father made a survey of the topography of this area—especially one hilly section which had eroded and become level through the centuries—and he was satisfied there were early ruins in the layers beneath the ground, and he applied to Dr. Tura for permission to dig."

After overcoming political obstacles, Professor Monti had borrowed enough money to acquire the land where he was prepared to excavate. According to Italian archeological law, if you own or purchase land where a dig is to be made, you can receive 50 percent of the value of whatever you find. If you lease the land from a property owner, you have to give the owner 25 percent and the government 50 percent, and you can keep only 25 percent. Professor Monti had purchased the plot of land outright.

Assisted by a team he had hired—surveyor, engineer, architectural draftsman, photographer, cryptographist, pottery and coin expert, bone expert—Professor Monti had brought all the necessary archeological equipment to the site at Ostia Antica. He had brought electronic detectors, surveying instruments, drafting instruments, photographic supplies, and a hundred other items to the dig. The excavation had proceeded. The site was worked in squares, and the team dug up only ten square meters at a time, going downward through the stratum, slicing and trenching and clearing.

"The excavation took twelve weeks," said Angela. "My father figured out that he had to remove from most trenches one foot of debris for each century from now backwards to the time of Jesus, to reach the layers that contained the Roman merchant's house. As he dug deeper through the soil and subsoil of rubble and alluvial material, my father was surprised to come upon layers of porous tufa rock which had been formed by deposits of underground springs—very similar to the rock in the nearby catacombs that he knew so well. The first finds were many, many coins from the times of Tiberius, Claudius, and Nero. Then, when my father found four coins imported from Palestine, three of Herod Agrippa I, who died in 44 A.D., and one minted under Pontius Pilate, his hopes and excitement knew no end. And finally, that glorious morning of our lives, he discovered the stone block containing the jar with the Petronius Parchment and the papyri of the Gospel According to James inside it."

"What happened next?"

"Next?" Angela shook her head. "So much, so much. My father flew his discovery to the laboratory at the American School of Oriental Research in Jerusalem. The brown fragments were so brittle they had to be put in humidifiers, then smoothed clean with alcohol applied with camel's-hair brushes, and flattened and studied close-ly under plates of glass. The Petronius one was in poor condition, although the parchment had been official and top-grade. The James gospel, pieces of it dark brown or almost black, flaked at the edges, with eaten-out holes in many leaves, had been written with reed pen, and ink of soot and gum and water, on the poorest quality of papyrus, on sheets five by ten inches. James wrote with misspellings in his Aramaic, no punctuation, and his vo-cabulary was figured out to be eight hundred words. The textual critics in Jerusalem confirmed the authenticity of the writing, and even issued a veiled announcement of the discovery in the confidential newsletter they period-ically distribute to scholarly circles. These experts sent my father to see Professor Aubert in his laboratory in Paris to learn if the parchment truly came from the period of 30 A.D. and the papyri from the time of 62 A.D. You will hear the rest from Professor Aubert, Steve. It was almost a supernatural occurrence, the whole find."

"Sounds more like the result of your father's astuteness, Angela."

"The discovery, yes. But not the survival of the text. That was a miracle from the hand of God." She paused, and fixed her green eyes on Randall. "They have allowed you to read the text, Steve?"

"The other evening in Amsterdam, I read it. I was profoundly affected."

"How?"

"Well, for one thing, I phoned my wife and agreed to give her the divorce she wanted."

Angela nodded. "Yes, I understand. It happened in another way to me, but it did happen. I hated Dr. Fer-nando Tura for obstructing and maligning my father. I vowed to have a vendetta with him, take real revenge for my father's sake. I looked for something to blackmail him with, to expose him, to hurt or ruin him. It was not difficult. I found it. Dr. Tura, a respectable married man, sanctimonious even, keeps for a second mate a young boy on the side. When I mentioned to my father what I had learned and intended to use against Dr. Tura, he told me not to proceed but have charity in my heart and turn the other cheek as he had done. For the first time, he showed me the translations into Italian of the Petronius Parchment and the Gospel According to James. That night, Steve, I wept and knew compassion, and put aside forever my ammunition for revenge. I turned the other cheek. Since then I have felt we can achieve more of serenity and peace through understanding, kindness, and forgiveness than by striking out and doing harm."

"I'm not as sure as you. I wish I were. I'm still trying to—well—find my way."

Angela smiled. "You will, Steve."

He reached over and shut off his tape recorder. "First session completed. I gather there's much more to your father's story?"

"Much more. Far too many details to relate in a single afternoon. And photographs, we have many photographs of the dig. You must see them. Can you stay in Milan tonight, or another day?"

"I wish I could. But I'm on a tight schedule. I'm off to Paris tonight. Then to Frankfurt and Mainz tomorrow night. Then back to Amsterdam the next night or morning after." He regarded Angela with frank affection. He had no desire to leave her. "Angela, what you've given me— it's absolutely what I require—it'll be useful to us and it'll give your father the credit he deserves. But I must see you again. I have one suggestion. I happen to have an open-end promotion budget. I can hire anyone I wish. I could use you as a consultant on salary, with expenses paid. Can you come to Amsterdam?"

The generous carmine lips curled into a smile. "I was wondering if you'd ever ask me."

"I've asked you."

"And I've answered you. When do you want me there?"

"When I'm there. Three days from now. As for your salary, Angela—"

"I wish no salary. I like Amsterdam. I desire to help my father's name. I want to assist this Bible to be in every hand. And—"

He waited, restraining himself, and then he prompted her, "And what else?"

"E voglio essere con te, Stefano, è basta."

"Meaning?"

"And—I want to be with you, Steve. That's all."

STEVE RANDALL had arrived in Paris from Milan early last night, after a flight during which he was preoccupied with mental pictures of Angela Monti and himself, and he had wondered how he could be so enthralled by a girl he had just met and hardly knew.

He had checked into L'Hôtel, a lively hostelry in the Rue des Beaux-Arts on the Left Bank. It had attracted him once during a stroll through the area simply for the reason that it bore a plaque beside the entrance commemorating the fact that this had been Oscar Wilde's last lodging and the place where he had died in 1900.

Because both the patio and cave restaurants were noisy, filled with jazz and chic young people, and he had been in no mood for that, Randall had walked to Le Drugstore, across from Café Flore on the Boulevard St.-Germain looking out over the Place St.-Germain-des-Prés, and found a booth upstairs, and the upstairs was filled with jazz and chic young people also, but this time he had not minded. He had consumed his hamburger steak *avec oeuf à cheval* and enjoyed his *vin rosé*, and continued fantasying his reunion with Angela in Amsterdam.

Not until he had returned to his single room in L'Hôtel, and opened his research folder on Professor Henri Aubert, renowned director of the Radiocarbon Dating Department of France's Centre National de la Recherche Scientifique, was he able to put Angela out of his mind.

Now it was morning. A half hour ago he had taken a taxi to the new stone building that housed the Centre National de la Recherche Scientifique in the Rue d'Ulm,

which was in the 5th arrondissement and down the block
from the Institut du Radium de la Fondation Curie.

Alighting from his taxi before the CNRS building in the
still cool, sparkling Paris morning, Randall had a brief misgiving. Angela Monti, a lay person speaking on archeology, had been one thing. Professor Aubert, a scientist
briefing him on authenticating the Ostia Antica papyri
and parchment, might be quite another thing. Although
Randall had primed himself on the carbon-14 dating
process, he was dense on anything scientific, and he
hoped that Aubert would treat him as patiently as he
might an inquiring child.

His apprehensions had been groundless. In the last ten
minutes, Professor Henri Aubert had indeed treated him
as patiently as he might an inquiring child.

At first, Randall had considered the Frenchman formidable. He proved to be a rather tall, well-proportioned,
fastidiously attired man in his middle forties. He wore his
hair in a pomaded pompadour, possessed a beaky Gallic
face, eyes narrowing and gestures stiff when he spoke in
impeccable English. His façade of aristocratic aloofness
was quickly dispelled by Randall's interest in his work.
For Aubert, the work was the meat of his being. Everything else was fat, to be cut away. When he perceived
that Randall meant business, and had real curiosity, Aubert was at once easier and more charming.

After Aubert had made a half-apologetic complaint to
Randall because his wife Gabrielle, who fancied herself
a decorator, had transformed his utilitarian metal-furnished
director's office into a showcase for Louis XVI antiques,
the scientist had led Randall from the office up a corridor
into the nearest laboratory of the Radiocarbon Dating Department.

Along the way, as Randall flipped on his tape recorder,
Aubert started to explain, in simplest terms, the carbon-
14 dating process.

"It was a discovery made by Dr. Williard Libby, an
American professor, and for it he was awarded the 1960
Nobel Prize in chemistry. By use of this extraordinary
device, for the first time ancient bones, pieces of wood,

fragments of papyri can be fairly closely dated as to their time of existence, going back as far as sixty thousand years. It was known that ever since there was life on this earth, everything alive in the world, every living organism in the world from human beings to plants and trees, has been bombarded by cosmic rays from outer space. Because of this bombardment, nitrogen was being changed into radioactive atoms of C 14. Everything alive, one way or another, absorbed this C 14 until the time it died.

"With death, the death of a person, animal, or plant, the carbon atoms inside its tissues began to decay, to diminish, at a rate that could be predicted. It was known that after an organic object died, it lost half the carbon 14 inside it in a period of 5,568 years. Possessed of this knowledge, Dr. Libby had the theory that if the amount of C 14 and its decay products inside a dead substance could be somehow measured, then, *voilà*, the amount of radioactive carbon that had decayed or disappeared could be calculated. By this means, by figuring the amount of loss, it would be known when the object had last absorbed carbon and been alive. Thus, Monsieur Randall, it would be known how much time had gone by since the death of the object and thus the object's age and the date when it had been alive could be determined."

Randall had a glimmer of understanding of the process. "And Dr. Libby invented the means to make this measurement?"

"Oui. He created the so-called carbon-14 clock, the Geiger-counter device which revealed how much carbon had been lost by the object since its life had ended. This gave science the dating system it so long needed. Now we can know, finally, the year a piece of charcoal burned in a fire for a prehistoric caveman or when a fossil was actually a living animal, or the age of an ancient house from a piece of its wooden beam. Dr. Libby, I am told, tested ten thousand items. His process once proved that a pair of Indian sandals found in an Oregon cave were nine thousand years old. A large sliver of wood from a funeral boat found in an Egyptian pharaoh's tomb proved that the pharaoh had died about 2000 B.C.

A piece of linen wrapping taken from a Dead Sea Scroll found in a Qumran cave proved that the scroll had been written between 168 B.C. and 233 A.D., probably around 100 B.C. On the other hand, the bones of the Piltdown man, discovered in the gravel pit of a Sussex moor, were believed to be those of a prehistoric being until fluorine tests conducted by Dr. Kenneth Oakley showed, and tests by Dr. Libby's carbon-14 method confirmed, that the Piltdown man was not ancient but modern in origin and merely a fake or hoax."

They were inside the laboratory where burners on tables were heating bubbling test tubes and where the clicking sounds of Geiger counters continued steadily.

"Now, Monsieur Randall," said Professor Aubert, "you known the means by which we authenticated the age of the Petronius Parchment and the Gospel According to James from Ostia Antica. Permit me to show you, briefly, how this was done."

He had brought Randall before two separate yet connected metal machines, one twice the width of the other, standing before several bookcases. To Randall, these resembled a pair of metal storage cabinets furnished with mysterious and incomprehensible equipment. The smaller metal machine had an instrument panel on top and a shelf holding two timepieces below. From it, tubes appeared to tie it to the wider machine, which was open in the center, and held a complex type of Geiger counter.

"This is the radiocarbon dating apparatus used to test Professor Monti's discovery," said the French chemist. "When Professor Monti arrived here five or six years ago to have me perform the definitive test, he had already been informed that he must bring me very small samples of the actual parchment and papyri he had excavated. Dr. Libby had required around thirty grams—that is one ounce—of the flax fiber, or linen, from the Dead Sea Scrolls to fix its date. Our carbon-dating process had become more sophisticated and improved since that time. Dr. Libby originally used solid carbon, which he smeared inside a cylinder like this one as you smear a coat of paint. That method required a good deal of priceless ancient material.

Since those days we had, as I said, improved the procedure and we required far less."

"Professor Aubert, how much parchment and how much papyrus did you need from Professor Monti?"

The French scientist gave a slight smile. "Fortunately, very little, since we must burn it. I doubt that Professor Monti would have given us more. For a piece of charcoal, I can work with three grams. For a piece of wood, I need ten grams. To test Professor Monti's discovery, I requested fifteen grams—about one-half ounce—of the parchment, and twelve grams from one fragment of papyrus and twelve grams from another."

"And you burned them?" said Randall, holding his tape recorder closer to the scientist.

"Not at once," replied Aubert. "To begin with, each sample must be pure, freed chemically and physically of any outside carbon that may have contaminated it since its cells died."

"Do you mean contaminated by radiation from hydrogen or atomic bomb tests?"

"No, that has no effect on matter already dead," said Aubert. "I took each of Professor Monti's specimens and I cleaned it thoroughly to eliminate foreign elements like roots, or traces of any other deposit that could pollute it and influence the test. This done, I burned each sample of parchment and papyrus under oxygen current, until it was reduced to ashes. The carbonic acid emanating from the combustion was purified, dried, and introduced into this Geiger measurement counter. The counter has a volume of one liter—"

"Less than two pints?"

"Correct," said Professor Aubert. "Above all, as you can observe from the way this apparatus is built, we must shield off any outside radiation that might interfere and give us a false count and wrong date. *Voilà.* We placed Professor Monti's parchment and papyrus ashes into the tubes and we began our test."

Carried away by his subject, Professor Aubert launched into an intricate explanation of the testing process. He spoke of the amplification chain surrounded by a cylinder of mercury, and of the Geiger counter impulsions placed in anticoincidence with the proportional counter impulsions, and of cosmic rays and gamma rays.

Randall was completely lost, but Aubert's words were recorded on the cassette tape, and Randall promised himself that once Lori Cook had transcribed it, he would find someone in Amsterdam to explain it further. "Yes, I see," he brought himself to say. "And how long did the entire test take, Professor?"

"Two weeks. But that was nearly six years ago. Today we have a remarkably advanced counter that can make the test overnight. But Monti's test took two weeks."

"What did you learn at the end of that time?"

"That we could date the grams of parchment and the grams of papyrus to within twenty-five years of the time when they had existed, been written, been used."

"And what were those dates?"

"Happily, I was able to inform Professor Monti that the measurement of our radiocarbon dating apparatus does not dispute the date of the Petronius Parchment as 30 A.D. and the Gospel According to James as 62 A.D. In short, I was able to assure Professor Monti that the most advanced scientific apparatus of the twentieth century had confirmed the fact—the *fact*, monsieur—that the parchment could come from the period when Pontius Pilate had passed sentence on Jesus Christ, and that the papyri could come from the period when the brother of Jesus was alive to write the true story of the Messiah. The Ostia Antica discoveries were absolutely authentic ones."

"No question about that?" said Randall.

"None whatsoever."

Randall shut off his tape recorder. "What you've contributed, Professor, will help us promote the International New Testament throughout the world."

"I am pleased to cooperate." Professor Aubert was looking at his wristwatch. "I have an errand, followed by a luncheon engagement with my wife. Are you free for lunch, Monsieur Randall?"

"I wouldn't want to impose—"

"No imposition. We can talk more. I would enjoy it."

"Thank you. As a matter of fact, I am free until this evening, when I take the train to Frankfurt."

"*Ah, bon.* You go to see Herr Hennig. You will find him less obscure than I have been." Aubert had begun to guide Randall out of the laboratory. "If you do not mind, then, we will stop by Notre Dame Cathedral to leave the results on chips of a painting of Christ I have tested. Next, we will be joined by Madame Aubert at the Café de Cluny. It will be pleasant to have a snack together."

After that, in Professor Aubert's late-model Citroën, Randall had suffered a harrowing drive, his feet braking against the floorboard all the way across the Seine to the esplanade before the Cathedral of Notre Dame. A guard, recognizing Aubert, promptly located a parking slot for him.

At the main entrance of the cathedral, to the west, Aubert left Randall, telling him, "I will be no more than a minute or two. I have only to drop off this report with one of the priests."

Randall considered going inside, but decided that Aubert would be back soon, and so he remained standing in the sun, observing tourists of every nation parading in and out. In no more than a few minutes, Aubert was beside him once more.

"Have you seen the stone carving above the portals?" said the Professor. "I find it of special interest since my involvement with the International New Testament. You know, of course, no painting or sculpture of Jesus, made of Him in His time, exists. It could not exist, because it could not have been done. The Jews—and the first Christians were Jews—believed it a sacrilege to produce pictures or graven images. All portraits were forbidden by Jewish law. Of course, there is a picture of Jesus in the Vatican which legend says was drawn by Luke and filled in by angels. But that is nonsense. I believe the earliest picture representing Jesus was one found in a catacomb, and that was done around 210 A.D. Now if you will look up there—"

Randall followed the direction of Professor Aubert's finger. He made out a sculpture on the wall of Notre

Dame showing the praying Virgin being crowned by an angel, as Christ stood beside her, a crown on His head, a scepter in His left hand, blessing her.

"That is called the Coronation of the Virgin," Aubert went on. "It is from the thirteenth century. It is typical of the absurdity of the portrayal of Jesus in art. No artist knew what He looked like, and so they painted Him ridiculously handsome and glorified. It will be a shock to people, after they read the James gospel, to learn how He actually looked. What will they do with all that misleading art? Perhaps they will do what people did during the French Revolution. The revolutionaries thought that those statues of Old Testament kings on Notre Dame were French kings, and they tore them down. Perhaps that will happen again later this year. Then those unreal representations of the Lord will be replaced by statues of the real Jesus as He was, Semitic nose, disfigured features, and all. It will be better. I believe in truth."

Randall and Professor Aubert returned to the Citroën, and drove across the Pont de l'Archevêché and turned into the traffic of the Quai de la Tournelle. When the Quai de la Tournelle became the Quai de Montebello, Randall observed and envied the unbusy French who were browsing among the *livres* and *affiches* in the bookstalls on the Seine side. To his left he had a glimpse of a shop called Shakespeare and Company, the old haunt of James Joyce at another site, he remembered.

Soon, they had swung into the broad Boulevard St. Michel, and ten minutes later, having finally found a parking place, Professor Aubert led Randall to a smart café on the corner of the Boulevard St. Michel and the Boulevard St.-Germain, which seemed to be a convergence point for all vehicle and pedestrian traffic on the Left Bank. Across the border of the green café awning, lowered to protect the three rows of citron-colored wicker chairs and round marble tables from the sun, Randall read the words: CAFÉ DE CLUNY.

"One of my wife's favorite cafés," said Professor Aubert. "The heart of the Left Bank. Youth everywhere. Across the street—see the black grillwork fence?—there is a park with some Roman ruins built here in Paris only three hundred years—less, according to James—after Christ. Well, now. Gabrielle is apparently not here." He glanced at his wristwatch. "We are a bit early. Where do you prefer to sit, Monsieur Randall, inside or outside?"

"Definitely outside."

"I concur." Most of the tables were empty, and Aubert picked his way among them, selected a table with three wicker chairs in the rear row, and gestured Randall to the seat beside him. Once settled, Aubert snapped his fingers for a white-coated waiter. "We will wait for Gabrielle before we order lunch," he told Randall, "and when we do, if you prefer light fare, I recommend the *omelette soufflée à la saucisse*. Now let us have an aperitif."

The waiter had arrived. "I will have a Pastis Duval," Aubert told Randall. *"Un Pastis Duval, garçon."*

"Make it two," said Randall.

"La même chose pour lui," Aubert said to the waiter.

Aubert offered Randall a cigarette, but Randall declined, holding up his pipe. Aubert inserted his cigarette into a long holder, and when they were both smoking, the scientist stretched his legs, watched the foot traffic with mild interest, and appeared fully relaxed for the first time.

After an interval, rubbing his sharp nose, exhaling smoke, he turned his head toward Randall. "I was thinking just now," said Professor Aubert, "how odd the circumstances that I should have been the one to authenticate those two documents, and be responsible for giving them as fact to the world."

"How so?" asked Randall.

"Because I was never a really religious person, in fact quite the opposite," confessed Professor Aubert, "and even today, whatever religion I have is not particularly orthodox. Yet, I will admit, all that has happened—I refer to my minor role in the preparation of the new Bible— has had a profound effect upon me."

Randall was hesitant but curious. "Do you mind explaining in what way, Professor?"

"It has altered my outlook. It has with certainty affected

my relationship with those close to me. If you are really interested——?"

"I am."

Aubert looked off. "I was raised in Rouen, raised loosely as a Catholic, very loosely. My parents were teachers, and they paid the minimum obeisance to the Church. In actuality, they were free-thinkers, rationalists, that kind. I always remember that next to our copy of Challoner's Rheims-Douai Bible was a copy of *Vie de Jesus*—the *Life of Jesus* by Ernest Renan—*un livre qui a fait sensation, mais qui est charmant.* Forgive me—I am saying that it was a sensational book that charmingly stated that the four gospels were mere legends, the miracles of Christ could not stand the scrutiny of science and were only myths, and the Resurrection story had been dreamt up by Mary Magdalene. There you have the picture of my youth. The Bible *and* Renan. But at one point, I could no longer continue in this ambivalent and schizophrenic posture."

"When was that?" asked Randall. The aperitifs had been served, and he drank his pastis and waited.

"The change occurred when I enrolled in the Polytechnique, the university where I studied radio-electricity, before I concentrated on chemistry. When I became a full-fledged scientist, I departed from my faith completely. I decided religion was *merde*. I became a cold bastard. You know how it is when one finds something new, a new attitude. One is inclined to go overboard. Once I had settled upon my unfaith, my scientific approach, I would only give my respect and belief to that which came out of a laboratory, in effect, to that which one could see, feel, hear, or logically accept. This condition persisted after I left my schools. I worked and lived for the now, the present, this time on earth. I was not interested in the future and the hereafter. My sole religion was Fact—and God was not Fact, the Son of God was not Fact, and neither hell nor heaven was Fact."

Aubert stopped, sipped his drink, and chuckled almost to himself.

"Speaking of heaven, I was now recollecting that I

even assaulted heaven with my scientist's logic. Once, some years ago, for our alumni periodical, I wrote a brief pseudoscientific paper analyzing the possibility of going to heaven. As I recall, I submitted the only statistic that exists on the actual size of heaven. It comes from John, in Revelation, when he wrote, 'and he measured the city with the reed, twelve thousand furlongs. The length and the breadth and the height of it are equal.' In other words, heaven is a perfect square, fifteen hundred miles in length, width, height. I figured—I will use your American measurements—this made heaven about five hundred quintillion cubic feet in area. If each human who went to heaven required ten cubic feet to stand upright, then there was room in heaven for only fifty quintillion people. Yet, since the time our Bible author John gave us the measurement, there have been three hundred six sextillion humans who have lived and died and hoped for heaven —far, far, far more than heaven is ready to hold. In fact, heaven was filled to overflowing centuries ago. You see?"

Randall laughed. "Devastating. Very clever."

"Too clever. Because in the end I was the one who was devastated. While my scientific approach was admirable, my knowledge of the Bible left much to be desired. In the very next issue of our alumni periodical, there appeared a caustic letter from a professor of theology at the Institut Catholique, in Paris, who chastized me for not reading my New Testament with care. For what John was describing was not heaven on high, but heaven on earth—'And I saw a new heaven and a new earth'—and this vision of heaven, the new Jerusalem, the true Israel, with its twelve gates and its rivers, would accommodate only 'the twelve tribes of the children of Israel.' In short, quite adequate in size for its purpose, and a city not likely to suffer overpopulation. Well, it was a lesson to me to avoid trying to apply scientific standards to the Bible. Nevertheless, I remained unconvinced that such a place as heaven could exist."

"Nor, I suspect, do a great many people think it exists," said Randall. "After all, not all the people in the world are fundamentalists. A large number of persons, including some of the religious ones, can't possibly take the Bible literally."

"Still, too many believe in heaven, in an afterlife, in a personal God, in the old superstitions. They believe not through reasonable faith, but through fear. They are afraid not to believe. They dare not question. Monsieur Randall, I always questioned. I refused to believe and give myself to that which my scientific and rational mind could not accept. This skepticism caused me grave trouble after my marriage and throughout my married life."

"How long have you been married, Professor Aubert?"

"Nine years last month. My wife, Gabrielle, comes from an extremely orthodox, rigid, God-fearing Catholic family. Like her parents, who are both alive, she is an unquestioning believer. Her parents, her father especially, dominate her. Her father is one of France's wealthiest industrialists, and he is among the secular hierarchy of the Roman Catholic Church in Europe. In fact, Gabrielle's father is one of the leaders of the Sociedad Sacerdotal de la Santa Cruz et Opus Dei. It is known in public as Opus Dei. It is also known, not so much in public, as Octopus Dei or as the Holy Mafia." He studied Randall. "You have not heard of Opus Dei?"

"I—I don't think so."

"Simply, then. A Spanish lawyer turned priest, José María Escriva, in Madrid during 1928, created Opus Dei. It has been characterized in print as an elitist, semisecret lay Catholic order with the avowed purpose to re-Christianize the Western world. It demands that its lay members—only two percent are priests—lead a Christian life and live up to the ideals of the gospels. It has fanned out from Spain through the world, into France, into the United States, into over seventy countries, until the Vatican has had to recognize and cooperate with it. Opus Dei has perhaps—who can know?—perhaps a hundred thousand members, perhaps twice that number. They try to influence business and economics, government and politics, education of the young everywhere. These secular Jesuits, as I call them, must take the vows of poverty, obedience, chastity—but these vows have been interpreted for the members, like my father-in-law, to mean that the rich must believe in the virtue of poverty but may remain rich; they must give obedience to God but many behave in ungodly ways when necessary; and they must adhere to the spirit of chastity while having marriages, even mistresses, and children—because they say, 'Chastity does not mean celibacy.' So now you have a picture of my father-in-law, and the atmosphere in which his daughter, my wife Gabrielle, was raised. You understand?"

"I understand," said Randall, and wondered why his host was revealing all of this to him.

"My Opus Dei wife setting up house with a Renan husband," Professor Aubert went on. "Bad chemistry. We were suited for each other, Gabrielle and I, except for this conflict. The big issue, more and more in recent years, became children. The Roman Church says propagate. Opus Dei says propagate. My father-in-law says propagate. Genesis says, 'Be fruitful, and multiply, and replenish the earth.' And so my otherwise sensible wife must have children, not one, not two, but many. I, in turn, remained still the scientist, with knowledge of the nuclear peril, with factual knowledge of the population problem, and added to this was a certain contrariness— I was not ready to permit any outside organization too stubborn to sanction birth control to dictate to me. So I refused to bring more children, not even one more child, into this world. The situation became increasingly serious a year ago. My wife, under pressure from her parents, insisted we have a child. I refused. My father-in-law instructed Gabrielle to apply to the Vatican to annul our marriage. Gabrielle did not want this, yet she wanted the child. I did not want this either, but I wished no child. Frankly, I rather disliked children. *Mon Dieu,* what an impasse, but one about to lead to an annulment—when something happened, in actuality happened to me, that resolved the conflict and saved my marriage."

Randall wondered what had happened, but he did not press. He maintained his passive role of listener.

In a few seconds, Professor Aubert resumed. "Ten months ago, the French publisher of the International New

Testament, Monsieur Fontaine, whom I know well, came to my office. 'Would you like to see the result of your authentication of our parchment and papyri?' he said. He left with me, while he attended to an errand in the neighborhood, a copy of the French translation of the Petronius Parchment and the Gospel According to James. Of course, Monsieur Randall, you must understand that while I had authenticated the parchment and papyri in my radiocarbon apparatus, I had never been told the contents nor was I able to read Aramaic, even if I had had the chance. So, I learned of the contents for the first time. Only ten months ago, I repeat." He sighed. "Can I even put into words how the report from Petronius and the gospel from James, especially James, affected me?"

"I think I can imagine," said Randall.

"No one can possibly imagine. I, the objective scientist, the skeptic of what is unknown, the seeker after truth, had come upon truth. It was a truth that by some inexplicable fate, some providence, I had been assigned to test. It was a trust I had affirmed in my cold laboratory. Now, I could not deny it. Our Lord was a reality. My reaction was—how can I put it?—it was as if I had been transformed. To me, plainly, the Son of God was a fact. Therefore, it was reasonable that God was a fact. For the first time, like Hamlet, I had an inkling that there might be more in heaven and on earth than we can know in our philosophies or sciences. For centuries, people had believed in the Christ with no evidence, only with eyeless faith, and their faith was finally about to be supported by fact. Perhaps then, there were more abstracts one could have faith in, the good will and the divine motivation behind creation and life, the possibility of a hereafter. Why not?"

His gaze met Randall's challengingly, but Randall merely offered a good-natured shrug, and said, "Why not, indeed?"

"Therefore, monsieur, for the first time, the very first time, I was capable of understanding how predecessors and colleagues of mine in the sciences had often been able to reconcile faith and religion with science. Blaise Pascal in the seventeenth century could affirm his faith in Christianity by stating, 'The heart has its reasons, which reason does not know.' "

"I thought Pascal was a philosopher," Randall interrupted.

"He was a scientist first," said Professor Aubert. "Definitely a scientist first. Before he was sixteen, Pascal wrote a treatise on conic sections. He originated the mathematical theory of probability. He invented the first computer, and sent one to Queen Christina of Sweden. He established the value of the barometer. Yet, he believed in miracles, because he had once experienced one, and he believed in a Supreme Being. Pascal wrote, 'Men have contempt for religion, and fear that it is true. To cure this it is necessary to commence by showing that religion is not contrary to reason; then that it is venerable, and worthy of respect; next to make it amicable, and make the good wish that it were true; and finally to show that it is true.' As Pascal put it—either God exists or He does not exist. So why not gamble? Place a wager. Bet that God does exist. 'If you gain, you gain all; if you lose, you lose nothing. Wager, then, without hesitation, that He exists.' That was Pascal. Of course, there have been others."

"Others?"

"Scientists who could live with both reason and the supernatural. Our beloved Pasteur could confess that the more he contemplated the mysteries of nature, the more his faith became that of a Breton peasant. And Albert Einstein—he saw no conflict between science and religion. Science was devoted to 'what is,' he would say, and religion to 'what should be.' Einstein could admit, 'The most beautiful thing we can experience is the mysterious. To know that what is impenetrable to us really exists, manifesting itself as the highest wisdom and the most radiant beauty which our dull faculties can comprehend only in their most primitive forms—this knowledge, this feeling, is at the center of true religiousness. In this sense, I belong in the ranks of devoutly religious men.' "

Professor Aubert tried to gauge the impression he was making on Randall, and offered a shy smile. "In this sense, I, too, became a devoutly religious man," he continued.

"For the first time I could be amused by Froude's remark that the superstition of science scoffs at the superstition of faith. Overnight I became a changed person, if not in my laboratory, then in my home. My attitude toward my wife and her feelings and desires, my attitude toward the meaning of family—these were transformed. Even the idea of having a child in this world—it was something I must at least reconsider—"

That moment, a feminine voice interrupted them. *"Henri chéri, te voilà! Excuse-moi, chéri, d'être en retard. J'ai été retenue. Tu dois être affamé."*

Aubert came hastily to his feet, beaming, and Randall also stood up. A youngish woman, possibly middle thirties, with a perfect bouffant hairdo, highbred and refined facial features, carefully made up, expensively accessorized, had reached the table and gone into Aubert's arms, accepting a kiss from him on each cheek.

"Gabrielle, my pet," Aubert was saying, "I want you to meet my American guest, Monsieur Steven Randall, who is with the project in Amsterdam."

"Enchantée," said Gabrielle Aubert.

As Randall shook her hand, his gaze dropped and he saw that she was fully and gloriously pregnant.

Gabrielle Aubert had followed his eyes, and with amusement she confirmed his unspoken realization. "Yes," she said, almost singing the word, "Henri and I shall have our first child in less than a month."

STEVE RANDALL had left Paris from the Gare de l'Est at 2300 hours—eleven o'clock on his watch—on the night train for Frankfurt am Main. In his private compartment, the bed had already been prepared, and he had undressed and gone to sleep at once. At 7:15 in the morning, the sounds of a buzzer followed by a sharp rapping had roused him. The Wagons-Lit conductor had delivered a tray of hot tea, *biscotte,* butter, a bill for two francs, and Randall had accepted the tray along with the return of his passport and rail tickets.

After dressing he had pulled up the shade of his compartment. For the next fifteen minutes there had passed

before his eyes new sights that resembled a colorful but
changing diorama—green forests, cement ribbons of auto-
bahns, tall sharply etched buildings, more and more railroad tracks with a red *Schlafwagen* on a siding and a
control tower with a sign proclaiming: FRANKFURT/MAIN
HBF.

Having exchanged a traveler's check for German marks
at a counter in the depot, Randall had taken a dirty taxi
to the Hotel Frankfurter Hof in Bethmannstrasse. Inside,
after registering, inquiring of the Fräulein behind the
Portier's desk if there were any mail or messages for him,
and buying a copy of the morning's *International Herald-
Tribune,* Randall had been shown to the two-room suite
that had been reserved for him. Restlessly, he had inspected his quarters, a bedroom with an outdoor terrace
and gay flowerpots on a stone rail, and a corner sitting
room with a high French window that looked out on the
Kaiserplatz where he could make out storefronts with
signs reading BÜCHER KEGEL and BAYERISCHE VEREINS-
BANK and ZIGARREN.

He was in Germany, all right, in Hennigland, and the
transition from Amsterdam to Milan to Paris to Frankfurt, in little more than fifty hours, was dizzying.

The time had been 8:15, and he still had forty-five
minutes before the car and driver that Herr Hennig was
sending to bring him to Mainz would appear. He ordered
a real breakfast, had his suit pressed, read the newspaper,
reviewed the publicity file on Herr Karl Hennig once more,
telephoned Lori Cook in Amsterdam to instruct her to
arrange a security pass and office space for Angela Monti,
and verified that Dr. Florian Knight had arrived with Dr.
Jeffries from London the day before yesterday, and finally
it was time to leave.

The drive from bustling Frankfurt to the quieter town
of Mainz had taken fifty minutes. His cigar-smoking,
elderly German chauffeur had guided the custom-built
Porsche into the four-lane autobahn where a sign advised
them: ANFANG 80 KM. There had been numerous hitch-
hikers loaded down by heavy knapsacks standing on the
side of the highway. There had been endless canvas-

covered trucks and occasional silver-helmeted motorcycle policemen on the road. There had been verdant sage-green forests, blue-painted gas stations, orange-yellow signs with black arrows pointing to hamlets like Wallu, several airfields, farms, gray factories belching smoke, and eventually the sign: RÜDESHEIM/MAINZ/BITTE. They had taken an off ramp, and presently, after crossing one brick bridge over railroad tracks, and a second bridge over the broad expanse of the river Rhine, they were in Mainz.

Five minutes later they had drawn up before a six-story, ultra modern corner office building with two revolving entrance doors.

"Das its die Hennig Druckerei, hier, mein Herr," the driver announced.

At last, Randall thought. Now, he would see the International New Testament in its final dress rehearsal, before it was offered to the public in full production. How he wished that either Professor Monti or Angela—Angela, really—could be here with him to see how a dream begun in the ruins of Ostia Antica had become a reality in up-to-date Mainz, Germany.

Randall had thanked Hennig's driver and opened the rear door to get out, when his eyes caught the figure of a man emerging from the revolving door farthest away, a figure that was faintly familiar. The man, slender, dandyish, not Germanic-looking, paused, sniffing the air, and began to remove a cigarette from a gold case. Randall remained poised, half out of the car, half in it, trying to place the face: the chalky complexion, ferret eyes, Van Dyke beard. Then, as the man brought the cigarette to his lips, his buckteeth were bared, and in that instant Randall knew, and immediately he fell back so that he was hidden in the rear seat.

The man was Cedric Plummer of the *London Daily Courier*.

Frozen, Randall waited. Plummer had exhaled a cloud of smoke, and looking neither right nor left, he strutted to the corner of the sidewalk, tarried for the light, crossed the street, and in seconds disappeared from view.

Cedric Plummer in Mainz, coming out of the very

fortress that protected the book, leaving the headquarters of the printer and producer of the Word.

What in the hell did this mean?

Randall wasted no more time. He hurried into the Hennig works, identified himself to the two young reception girls who were dressed in long blue coats, and one of them took him up in the elevator and along a wide marble corridor to the proprietor's private suite.

In an airy office that seemed to have been imported intact from Scandinavia, Randall found himself receiving a bone-crushing handshake from Karl Hennig, the printer for Resurrection Two.

"In German, first! *Willkommen! Schön, dass Sie da sind!*" Hennig rasped. "In English, now! Welcome! Good to have you here—in the city of Johannes Gutenberg, who changed the face of the earth, as Karl Hennig shall change it again." Hennig's voice was deep and hoarse, and it made one's eardrums vibrate.

Hennig had the look of a muscle-bound wrestler. His head was disproportionately large, with a close-cropped Prussian haircut, an apoplectic face that appeared to have been reshaped when a large fist had punched into it, almost concave, eyes way back in their sockets, mashed nose, discolored teeth, chapped dry lips, no neck that was apparent. Definitely, he resembled a squat Suma wrestler who had been draped in a rich gray silk suit. He welcomed Randall, not only as a colleague on their secret project, but as an American. He had affection for Americans, especially the smart business community, and he was proud that he spoke Americanese and not British, and without a German accent, regretting only that he'd had too little opportunity to use his Americanese lately.

"*Setzen Sie sich, bitte, setzen Sie sich*—please sit down," he said as he hustled Randall into a comfortable leather armchair between his desk and an office wall entirely covered by a gigantic relief map of Mainz, which bore on its thin silver frame a plate reading: *Anno Domini 1633 bei Merian.*

"*Wir werden etwas trinken,*" he rasped, and he tramped to a natural oak bureau and unlocked it, revealing the wet bar and miniature refrigerator inside. He poured Scotch over ice cubes, gave one glass to Randall, and took the other behind his desk, where he moored himself to the oversized executive chair. He talked steadily, once he had reminded Randall to turn on his tape recorder.

"My father founded this firm because the idiocy of German printers annoyed him," said Hennig. "One printer would turn out stationery for the shops, and a different printer would turn out envelopes that did not even match. So my father turned out stationery *and* envelopes together, and made a fortune. After his death—he had just started to print books before that—I took over. I didn't give a damn about stationery and envelopes, and I converted the entire operation into book printing. Today I have five hundred people working for me. Well, I must say, Karl Hennig hasn't done badly, not badly at all."

Randall made an effort to show that he was impressed.

"Fortunately—and I think this is what made Dr. Deichhardt insist that I take on the job—I used to be heavily in the Bible-printing business," continued Hennig. "Most of the Bible printing in Germany is done around Stuttgart. Junky stuff. I stayed away from there, stayed in Mainz under the eyes of Johannes Gutenberg—besides Mainz is a better location, handy to both Hamburg and Munich, so it makes it cheaper and faster to ship to all points. I stayed here and got together a crew of real printers, the handful of remaining ones who had respect for their work, who had printing in their ancestry and in their blood, and we did some of the finest handcrafted limited-edition Bibles known in Europe. But I was forced to give up the Bible business—too costly, unprofitable— but luckily, I'd held on to some of the old-timers, the veteran workmen, and when the International New Testament job came along, I had the nucleus of a crew to tackle it."

"How long will it have taken you to print this Bible?"

Hennig smacked his lips. "Let me see. Well, let me put it this way. The Bible is a damn big book. If you are doing the whole damn Bible—Old Testament and New Testament in one volume—you're printing about 775,000 words. That's about the length and size of six or seven ordinary books using regular-size type. Well, when we're not being rushed, to do a whole Bible requires maybe a year to design the typeface and format, and maybe two years for composition and proofing, and one year, a little less, for actual printing and binding. Four years, but that's the whole damn Bible. Here we're doing only the New Testament, a much shorter volume, less time-consuming, except we are trying to do it with care and artistry. We'll do the longer part, the new translation of the International Old Testament, with less pressure later—and besides, for the present, we're doing only a limited edition."

"A limited edition?"

"Yes, of course, I'm doing what we call the Advance Pulpit Edition, in four languages but limited to copies for pastors and churchmen around the world, the press, leaders, opinion makers, a small percentage of the public. Once this edition is out, each of the publishers will have a printer in his own country run off the cheaper trade editions for the general public, and then I'll confine myself to the popular German edition. Right now, well, I'd say I've spent at least a year on design. The actual printing and binding won't have taken more than six months."

"What would you say was your biggest problem?"

"Paper. For the Bible printer it is always paper. Of course, I mean for the popular edition. The Bible is so damn long, even the shorter New Testament part of it, that you can't use regular stock. You've got to find light paper, thin paper, yet thick enough so there won't be show-through from one side of the page to the other. You've got to have durable paper. Some people keep their Bibles for their entire lives. At the same time, it must not cost too much. But for this first edition, we're using the finest grade of India paper."

"When will you have bound copies ready?"

"In two weeks, I hope."

"What about security?" Randall asked casually. "It's tight enough at the Hotel Krasnapolsky in Amsterdam.

But how have you managed to hide an operation like this from prying eyes?"

Hennig's ruddy squashed features worked into a dark frown. "Not easy, not easy, a bitch," he muttered. "Security's been a bitch. It's cost me a fortune. Tell you what I did. We have several presses in the neighborhood, all short walking distance from here. I took one plant, our largest, segregated half of it from the rest of the building and the other plants, loaded it with guards, and put my best and most trusted old-time craftsmen in that half of the building. Even took over two entire apartment houses nearby for those workmen and their families, and set up those places with more guards and informers. There have been a few nervous moments, but that's the most of it. We've kept the lid tight on our entire operation. Not a whisper has got out. In fact, Steve—mind if I call you Steve?—it's been such a successful secret, thanks to my vigilance, that no one from the outside has been able to find out what we are up to."

"No one?" said Randall softly.

Hennig was momentarily taken aback. He scowled. "What do you mean?"

"I mean Cedric Plummer," said Randall. "I saw Cedric Plummer leaving this building as I was about to come in."

Hennig was clearly disconcerted. "Plummer? You know him?"

"He tried to bribe me the day I arrived in Amsterdam. He wanted me to smuggle out a copy of the Bible for him. He wants to serve it up to the public before we do, serve it up his way, and possibly damage our announcement."

Hennig, who had composed himself, blustered defensively. "Well, he's a separate case. He's the only one from the outside who got onto us. But believe me, that little bastard's not getting any copy from Karl Hennig. That I can promise on my father's grave."

"He was in this building," Randall persisted.

"Nobody asked him to come, and nobody that counts would see him," rasped Hennig. "Sure, Plummer's after a

copy, like a dozen others outside Germany are. He called
me three times from London and from Amsterdam. I'd
read his damn interview with de Vroome in *Frankfurter
Allgemeine*. I refused to take his calls. Yesterday, he
telephoned a fourth time, and this time I came on the
line myself to tell him to stop bothering me. He wanted
an interview. I warned him if he came within ten kilo-
meters of Mainz, I'd have him shot dead. Nevertheless,
he showed up today unannounced. I was enraged when
my secretary told me he was standing at her desk. I
wanted to go out and beat him up. Don't worry, I didn't
lose my head. I ordered my secretary to get rid of him.
I flatly refused to see him. I wouldn't let that bastard
through my door. So finally he gave up and left. Believe
me, Steve—"

He swiveled around in his chair and reached for a
framed photograph of a woman that stood on the cabinet
of a television set. Picture in hand, he rose and left his
desk.

"No man on the project has sacrificed more than I
have to make this Bible a success. You see this photograph?"

Randall saw a portrait of a sensuous, theatrical-looking
young woman, possibly in her late twenties. In the lower
right-hand corner was the flowing inscription, *"Meinem
geliebten Karl!"* and it was signed, *"von deiner Helga."*

"Recognize the face?" Hennig demanded.

Randall thought that he did. As he turned off his tape
recorder, he asked, "Isn't she the German actress who
starred in—?"

"She is," said Hennig. "You have seen her in many
films. This is Helga Hoffmann." Hennig returned the portrait to its original place and stood admiring it. "I'm a
bachelor. This is the only woman I've ever wanted to
marry. I've been seeing her off and on for two years. I
think she's too immersed in her career, too ambitious to
consider marriage. At least, right away. However, she has
made it clear that she might, under certain circumstances,
live with me." Hennig stared down at the photograph.
"Unfortunately, actresses come high. Her dream is to

have a villa and yacht of her own on the Riviera, at St.-
Tropez. She does not have the money for such excesses.
If I bought her what she wanted, she would be very
impressed. In fact, I could have whatever I wanted from
her." His concave mashed features crunched into a grim-
ace. "That will not sound like love to you. But it is
almost as good to me. I am not sentimental. I am practical. I've never wanted anything more than this woman.
That is, not until this damn Bible came along. Well, in
the end, I was not practical but vain. I chose to have my
name connected with the International New Testament. I
can't say why. Maybe to prove something to my father,
who is dead anyway. Or maybe to assure myself some
share of immortality. Anyway, to undertake the Bible
meant certain financial sacrifices that made it impossible,
at least for now, to provide for Helga also."

"Won't she wait?" asked Randall.

"I can't say. Maybe someone else, in Berlin or Hamburg, will offer her the baubles she desires. We shall see.
All I am explaining, Steve, is that once I made my choice
to become the printer of the most important Bible in
history, more earthshaking than the 42-line Bible for different reasons, I am not going to jeopardize this opportunity in any manner. Certainly, merely to obtain some
special publicity or attention, I am not going to give out
the contents beforehand to any of the Cedric Plummers,
no matter what they offer. Do you believe me?"

"I believe you."

"I hope you had that damn tape recorder off during
my personal aside."

Randall nodded. "It was off."

"You and I, we'll get along," Hennig grunted. "Let's
go. I'll show you our key plant, one of our three in the
area. This is the one, under security, where we are
printing our Bible right now. It's just past the Gutenberg
Museum, a block off the Liebfrauenplatz am Dom. We
still have a little time before lunch."

They left Hennig's office in silence. Once outdoors,
Randall automatically surveyed the street to see whether
Cedric Plummer was still around, waiting to accost the

printer. No one resembling the British journalist was anywhere in sight. The two of them began walking, and Hennig, in spite of his short legs, set a brisk pace, and at the end of two blocks Randall was beginning to perspire.

Before the courtyard of an intensely modern three-story building, Hennig slowed, and peered at his gold-cased wristwatch. "We have time for a short visit. Come inside."

"What is this?" Randall wanted to know.

"*Ach,* forgive me, I spend so much time here. This is our Gutenberg Museum. You can turn on your tape recorder again. I will give you information for your stories."

In the open courtyard, across from a glass-covered announcement board, a bronze bust stood on a pedestal. The bust revealed a rather somber, unhappy Johannes Gutenberg adorned with heavy moustache and cropped beard.

Hennig waved a stubby, disparaging hand at the bust. "Meaningless. Only there for tourists. Nobody has the slightest idea of what he really looked like. No contemporary picture of Gutenberg has come down to us. The closest is a print—it's in Paris—done sixteen years after his death. It's not like this. It shows a kind of angry man with a flowing moustache and forked scraggly beard like the Chinese sages affected. We know he was always frustrated, but damn tough. Once, because this city owed him some money, Gutenberg physically manhandled a city clerk and had him thrown into jail. We have evidence of that. But otherwise, we know little."

They moved to the entrance, opened one of the glass doors, and walked into the ground floor of the museum. Hennig greeted the ticket seller behind the counter and accepted the respectful salutation of a guard wearing a blue coat with red badges on the sleeves.

"I'm on the board of the museum," Hennig explained, "and a contributor. I collect rare Bibles. Did you know that? I own one of the existing copies of the 42-line Bible. I suppose I could sell mine for more than a million dollars and get Helga what she wants and have her. But I wouldn't do that. Look here—"

He brought Randall to a large map of the world on the wall. Beneath it was a board with seven buttons marked: *1450, 1470, 1500, 1600, 1700, 1800, Heute.*

"You press the button of any year," said Hennig, "and it shows you how much printing was being done in that year around the world." He punched the button marked *1450.* A single light glowed on the world map. "Only Mainz, you see." He pressed the button marked *1470.* Several lights glowed. "Printing was catching on," he said with satisfaction. "Now I'll press *Heute*—that's today— see." The map lighted up like an overloaded Christmas tree. "One of the things that held up mass printing so long was that so few people in the world could read. But with the Renaissance, necessity mothered the invention of printing. Once printing was made possible, there was no stopping the production of books. First, Bibles. Then, dictionaries and histories. At prices cheaper than the manuscripts turned out by hand by the copyists, the calligraphers and illuminators. That was Gutenberg's probable motive to create movable metal type—to undercut the copyists and make himself some money. But he was always in debt once he started his printing."

Hennig looked around. "There are some other exhibits on this ground floor. Down below there's a replica of Gutenberg's old workshop and handpress. But we don't know if it is accurate. No description of Gutenberg's original printing shop or press ever survived. I suggest we skip that, Steve. We can't waste time. Let's go up- stairs briefly. One thing you must see on the first floor. Keep your tape machine going."

They climbed the broad staircase. At the top, Hennig spoke to a guard in German, and had his answer.

"Good," said Hennig. "One of the girl guides has some tourists in there. I want you to see."

Randall followed the printer into a darkened but spa- cious vault. Four lighted windows had been cut into one wall. Through them Randall could see a display of hand- written Bibles, painstakingly prepared by monks before

1450. Hennig, lowering his voice, said, "It would take two scribes more than twenty-four months to copy out and produce four such Bibles. One of the first printers after Gutenberg took only two months to produce twenty-four thousand copies of an Erasmus book."

Hennig led the way deeper into the vault. Ahead of them, Randall could see a dumpy young lady, beside a glass showcase, lecturing to eight or ten visitors. Approaching the group, Randall made out the sign above the showcase. It read: DIE GUTENBERG-BIBEL MAINZ 1452–1455. A bright lamp shone down spotlighting the open Gutenberg Bible beneath the glass of the case.

The young lady guide had finished her talk in German, and immediately, in a monotone, looking directly at Randall, she repeated her lecture in English:

"It took monks thirty to forty years to prepare a lavishly illuminated special Bible such as you have seen through the windows at my right. In three years, Johannes Gutenberg produced by hand-press two hundred ten Bibles, one hundred eighty on handmade paper. Around the world there are forty-seven full copies or portions of this Bible extant—in New York, London, Vienna, Paris, Washington, D. C., at Oxford, Harvard, Yale. The Gutenberg Bible you see here is the second issue on vellum and it is worth one million marks or two hundred fifty thousand dollars. A complete one on vellum would be worth four million marks or one million dollars. There are forty-two lines to a column, and two columns on almost each page of this Gutenberg Bible. Gutenberg first started with a thirty-six-line Bible which he did not finish immediately. This one was finished, however, and in 1460 Gutenberg produced the world's first printed dictionary, in Latin, the *Catholicon* by Balbus."

She had now begun to repeat her lecture in French, and Randall's attention had strayed to examine the low blue ceiling of the vault and the walnut walls, when he felt Hennig tugging impatiently at his sleeve.

Randall accompanied the German printer out of the vault and into the light of the museum's first floor.

"That was interesting," Randall said.

"That was total nonsense," Hennig growled. "Not one shred of factual evidence exists that Gutenberg or any single individual invented printing as we know it. Based on circumstantial evidence, we can deduce that Gutenberg may have invented printing from movable type. I happen to believe he did. I couldn't prove it, though. Thirty accepted documents or pieces of paper exist from Gutenberg's time that mention that he was a living person. Only three of these papers indicate that he was involved in the art of printing. What do these papers tell us?" Hennig halted, as if addressing his rhetorical question to Randall's tape recorder, then looked up at Randall. "Your machine is recording?"

"Of course."

"Good. Because this information can help you. These papers tell us that Gutenberg came from a patrician family and his father's name was Gensfleisch—it was the habit then to go by the mother's family name. Gutenberg worked as a goldsmith. He was sued for breach of promise by a lady named Anna. He moved from Mainz to Strasbourg for ten years. During that period he ordered what was probably printing equipment to be built for him. He returned to Mainz, borrowed two thousand gulden from various parties for some big project, probably the 42-line Bible. There is evidence that he had borrowed money for equipment to print 'books.' But was the famous 42-line Bible one of those 'books'?"

"The young lady lecturing in the vault said it was."

"You forget her. You listen to Karl Hennig. Despite that young lady's patriotic lecture, there is not a bit of evidence that Gutenberg had any role in actually printing the great 42-line Bible associated with his name. That Bible was probably produced by Gutenberg's financial backer, Johann Fust, and another printer named Peter Schoeffer. As for Gutenberg, we know he died in 1467 or 1468 only because a man who had loaned him printing equipment applied to the archbishop for 'certain forms, letters, instruments, tools, and other things belonging to the work of printing which Johannes Gutenberg left after his death, and which were and still are mine.'

There you have the essence of it, Steve. Just slightly more than we knew of Jesus Christ before the International New Testament."

"Presuming that Gutenberg was the inventor," said Randall, "what exactly did he invent?"

"To make it simple, he invented the mold for casting type. His mold was copper, mine is more durable steel. He sculptured the letters of the alphabet. He cut punches. He raised the surfaces of the letters to put them in relief. He figured out that letters must be reversed to come out the right way. He invented the tray or form that held characters. Finally, he invented the means by which the type form could be pulled back to be inked and returned into the press to have the iron platen laid against it for the next impression. He made the press move and move again, producing one impression after another. He invented movable type. Because of him, I am here with you today, and our Petronius and James will inundate the literate world and maybe change mankind."

As they left the museum, and proceeded up the sunny street, Hennig reminded Randall to keep his tape recorder activated. "Before you visit my plant, I want you to know what I have going on in there," he said, as they strolled along. "For the special Advance Pulpit Edition I have created a typeface which I call fourteen-point New Gutenberg. I will explain. In preparing his original 36-line Bible, Gutenberg tried to cut his letters in imitation of the hand-printed Bibles made by monks. He used blackletter type which we Germans call *Textur,* meaning it appears to be woven into a page. Gutenberg's type would be unfamiliar today, although it is artistic and esthetically pleasing. Black-letter is too heavy, convoluted, too many pointed corners. It conveys a Germanic harshness, like our tongue. So I fashioned a type which only suggests the black-letter, but is more familiar, more rounded, more clear, more contemporary. Here we are at the plant. Let's have a quick look."

After passing through security—Randall had remembered to bring his red card from Amsterdam—they entered the huge noisy press-room, and ascended a spiraling metal stairway to a steel mezzanine running the length of the wall. There were four presses and a few dozen laborers in blue overalls below, and above the rackety sounds of the machines, Karl Hennig began to speak again.

"What you see are two letterpress sheet-fed machines, and at the other end are two web-fed machines, which are faster. The pages coming off are for the limited edition, the Pulpit one. As they leave here, the printed sheets are folded, assembled, sewn. The binding cases have already been prepared, already blocked out. The gathered sheets are then cased in, jacketed, and shipped off to warehouses for distribution. The finished books will be flown to New York, London, Paris, Munich, Milan, ready for distribution the day you announce the discovery and the new Bible."

Hennig squinted below and jovially waved to several elderly laborers. They gazed up at him and waved back good-naturedly. Hennig showed his pleasure. "My veterans, the most reliable ones," he said proudly. "The two presses below are printing the English language versions. The other two are printing the French version. In the next room of the building, the presses are turning out the last of the German and Italian editions."

A logistical problem came to Randall's mind, and he decided to speak of it. "Karl, after all the publicity we'll get in three or four weeks, there will be millions of people demanding copies of the International New Testament. If you and other printers are producing a different edition for the general public, how can you get it to them in great numbers while the demand is high?"

"*Ach,* of course, you have not been told," said Hennig. "For the popular standard trade edition, we must set the type all over again in four languages. We cannot do this before your announcement. We could not guarantee security. So the composition of the popular edition will begin the day of your announcement. Now, if we set the type the way the limited edition is being done, in the regular way, using linotype machines and human operators, it would take a month or two. But no, the popular edition will be done by electronic composition, the cathode-ray tube method, which is a phenomenon of speed. By CRT electronic method we can set type for a complete Bible, Old and New Testament, in seven and a half hours. Since the New Testament is one-fourth the length of the whole Bible, the CRT method can set the whole book in about ninety minutes—minutes, mind you, not one or two months. Overnight, we will be on the presses and a few million copies of the cheaper standard edition will be in bookstores around the world at least a month before Christmas. Come, let me show you the rest of my operation in this plant, the other half, the non-Bible section that deals with my ordinary commercial business."

Leaving the metal mezzanine, they went downstairs, and began to tour various smaller printing rooms, passing through corridors that led from one press to another. As they progressed, Randall became gradually aware of a strange and inexplicable resentment—almost an open hostility—in the air. When Hennig greeted his young foreman, the response was halfhearted and unsmiling. When Hennig tried to engage his pressmen in conversation, they casually turned their backs on him and pretended to be busy with their work or at best answered him in monosyllables. Once, leaving a group of laborers, Randall thought that he saw two of them making obscene gestures behind Hennig's back. He heard one of them mutter, *"Lausiger Kapitalist. Knauseriger Hundsfott."* Randall had no idea what the expression meant, but he suspected that the men did not mean Hennig well.

They had entered a corridor leading to the exit, when Hennig was intercepted by a worried guard, who spoke in an undertone to him.

"Excuse me," Hennig said to Randall. "A minor problem. I will be right back."

Randall used the interval to locate the men's room. Inside, there were two urinals and one was blocked by a white-collared office clerk. Randall joined him, using the unoccupied urinal. Standing there, Randall was startled to find a crude caricature of Hennig painted on the white wall above the urinals. The caricature depicted a naked

Hennig with a penis in place of his head and two bags of gold in his hands, and a laboring man's head being crushed under one boot. Beside the caricature was crudely printed an obviously angry slogan. It read: *Hennig ist ein schmutziger Ausbeuter der Armen und der Arbeiter!*

Randall glanced at the clerk next to him, who was closing his fly. "Do you speak English?" Randall asked.

"A little."

Randall pointed to the slogan. "What does that say?"

The clerk seemed hesitant. "It is not so kind—"

"Anyway—"

"It says, 'Hennig is a dirty exploiter of the poor and the laboring man.' "

Troubled, Randall left the lavatory, and walked up the corridor to search for his host. He found Hennig around a corner, a grim Hennig, hands on his hips, supervising a painter who was running his brush over another caricature and another protest slogan similar to the one Randall had seen in the men's room.

Hennig met Randall without embarrassment. "You know something is wrong, eh?" he said.

"I just saw the same drawing and words in the men's room."

"And you saw more, how the younger workers acted toward me?"

"I'm afraid I couldn't help but see, Karl. I also overheard some things."

"So you heard? You heard *lausiger Kapitalist,* right? You heard *knauseriger Hundsfott,* right? Yes, they called me lousy capitalist and sonofabitching tightwad. If you spent more time in the plant you'd also hear *Geizhals*—miser, and *unbarmherziger Schweinehund*—ruthless bastard. Now maybe you think Karl Hennig a monster, yes?"

"I don't think anything," said Randall. "I simply don't understand it all."

"I will explain for you," Hennig said gruffly. "Let us go. I have made a reservation for lunch at the restaurant of the Hotel Mainzer Hof. I don't want to be late. Someone will be waiting."

Once they were outside, in front of the plant, Hennig

stopped. "It is only six blocks. A short walk. If you are tired, we can take a car."

"We can walk."

"Better, because I must explain what you have observed. It is between us. First, please shut off your tape recorder."

Elaborately, Randall pushed the lever of his recorder, and fell in beside the German printer. They walked in silence for a half block. Hennig pulled out a large handkerchief, coughed and expectorated into it, stuffed it back into his pocket.

"All right, I will explain," he said in a gravelly voice. "I have always been, in my way—I do not hide it—a tough commercial boss. To survive in postwar Germany, it was necessary. We had been devastated by the war. After that it was survival of the fittest. The language of survival is money, hard money, lots of money. I went into Bible printing only because there was a big market for Bibles. There was wealth in the field, great wealth. Profits in expensive Bibles. In that way, I gained a reputation as a quality religious printer. Then something happened."

He was lost in himself briefly, and once more they walked silently.

"What happened was that here in Germany the interest in religion and the church dwindled," he resumed. "Not many years ago, the poor and oppressed and those oriented by science and technology declared that God was dead. Religion slid downhill, and with it the sales of Bibles. As a matter of survival, I saw that I must immediately make up my losses for the decreasing Bible sales. I could not leave all my eggs in the ecclesiastical basket. So gradually, then more and more, I began to bid for and win contracts to print cheap popular books, novelty books, and pornography. Yes, there was a rising market for hard pornography in Germany, and I was ready to print it, just to keep the money coming in. I wanted money, plenty of money, always. I would never let myself be poor and therefore helpless. Also, I confess, I was involved with many young ladies, expensive young ladies, and then Helga Hoffman, and that also took big money. Are you beginning to see?"

"I'm afraid not," said Randall.

"Of course not. You do not know the German craft mentality. In this drastic changeover I made from Bibles to pornography, I ran into strong conflict with my workmen and their Labor Council. The young workmen, like their seniors, came from long family traditions of fine printing, with pride in their craft, their trade, their production, that almost transcended their considerations of income. Their families had always worked for religious-book publishers, quality ones, and they had been proud to continue doing so for me. Now, when I almost abandoned Bibles, religious books, and converted to the printing of cheap books without merit, these laborers in my plants were dismayed. They resented the degradation they felt because of what they were printing. They resented much more than that, also. They resented the new mass production I had to impose. They resented the fact that I had to pressure them, squeeze and drive them for greater output. Little by little, they began to rebel, and speak of a strike. I had never been faced with a strike before, and most of my best men had never had a reason to strike. But now, even those who could not afford to be out of work began to prepare to strike. In fact, the first chairman of the Print and Paper Trade Union, Herr Zoellner, set a date. That was months ago. We negotiated, of course, but made no progress. I could not give in. Zoellner and his men would not give in. We reached a stalemate. And a week from today, I am confronted with the date of the strike. If only I could explain to them—"

"But, Karl," Randall said, "there must be some way to let them know you are doing the greatest Bible job in printing industry."

"No way whatsoever," said Hennig. "I will come to that. First, when Dr. Deichhardt approached me, he did not inform me of the contents of the new Bible he wanted printed. Only that it was radically new, different, important. After he outlined the project, I had to reject it. I turned it down because there would be too little profit in it for me. I refused to give up profitable work, no matter how low it was regarded, for more prestige. Still,

Dr. Deichhardt wanted me, because of my background. Do you know what he did?"

Randall shook his head, and listened.

"He swore me to secrecy," Hennig said, "and arranged for me to have a private meeting in Frankfurt with Dr. Trautmann. I was impressed. Dr. Trautmann is one of our foremost theologians. Dr. Trautmann handed me a manuscript. He suggested I read it to myself, at once, in his presence. What I had and what I read, for the first time, were the German translations of the Petronius Parchment and the Gospel According to James." He eyed Randall. "Did you read them?"

"Recently."

"Did they shake you up as much as they shook me?"

"I was deeply moved."

"For me, it was a spiritual awakening," said Hennig. "I could not believe such an inner transformation could happen to me, to me the businessman, commercial man, profiteer. Yet, it happened. It overturned my sense of values. *Ach,* what a soul-purging night that was. There was no question what I must do. I accepted the job to print the Advance Pulpit Edition. It meant abandoning certain highly profitable but shabby accounts. It meant much less income. It meant forgetting about Helga for the time."

"Well, didn't that satisfy your workmen?" Randall asked once more.

"No. Because the majority of them did not know of it, and could not be told of my new good works. Inspector Heldering flew in here from Amsterdam and imposed the most difficult security regulations. Only a limited number of my veteran workers could be placed on the job and permitted to know what they were printing. They are the ones who are segregated from the others, and they must keep their new job assignments secret. As for the majority of my laborers, they remain uninformed, unaware that I have returned to tradition and craftsmanship, and have sacrificed a great percentage of my profit, merely so that I could be part of a historic religious adventure."

"So they are going to strike next week?"

"I don't know," said Hennig with a sudden grin. "I will know in a few minutes. We are at the Mainzer Hof. Let us cross the Ludwigstrasse and go up to the top floor of the hotel to the restaurant and find the answer."

Puzzled, Randall followed the German printer into the hotel, where they took the elevator to the eighth floor.

It was a cheerful restaurant, Randall could see, with a wall of windows opening out on the vista of the Rhine River far below. The maître d'hôtel welcomed Hennig and Randall with a low, deferential bow, and quickly led them between the rows of white tables and brocade-upholstered chairs to a place along a window where a stout, rough-hewn man with unruly rust hair had buried his face myopically within a sheaf of legal-sized papers.

"Herr Zoellner, mein Freund!" Hennig cried out. *"Ich will schon hoffen dass Sie noch immer mein Freund sind? Ja, ich bin da, ich erwarte ihr Urteil."*

The stout man jumped to his feet. *"Es freut mich Sie wieder sehen zu können, Herr Hennig."*

"But first, Herr Zoellner, meet an American from Amsterdam who will promote a special book of mine. This is Herr Randall—Herr Zoellner, who is *der erste Vorsitzende,* the first chairman, of the Industrie Gewerkschaft Druck und Papier, our national printers' union." Hennig turned to Randall. "I greeted him as my friend. I told him I'm here, ready for his verdict." Hennig gestured for Zoellner to be seated, and dragged Randall into the chair next to him.

Hennig fixed his gaze on the union head. "Well, Herr Zoellner, the verdict—life or death for Karl Hennig?"

Zoellner's countenance cracked wide into a smile. *"Herr Hennig, es bedeutet das Leben,"* he boomed. "You live— we all live because of you. It is good news." He lifted the sheaf of papers, and said excitedly, "This counter offer you have made to our trade union is the best contract offered to the union in my memory. The benefits, the raises, the sick pay, the pension fund, the new recreation facilities—Herr Hennig, I am happy to tell you the board has approved and will submit this to the membership this weekend, and they will also approve unanimously."

"Delighted, delighted," rasped Hennig. *"Ich bin entzückt, wirklich entzückt.* So we forget the strike? We go ahead together?"

"Ja, ja, together," boomed Zoellner. He bobbed his head respectfully. "Overnight you will be a hero. Maybe not so rich, but a hero. What made you change your mind?"

Karl Hennig smiled. "I read a new book. That is all." He turned to Randall. "You see, Steve? It is sickening, so maudlin I have become. Imagine, being transformed from Satan to St. Hennig practically overnight. But suddenly I want to share with others. I am a fool, but a happy one."

"When did you make up your mind to do this?" Randall wanted to know.

"Perhaps it began the night when I read a certain manuscript. But the mutation took time. Perhaps it really happened last week, when my labor crisis approached its climax, and I sat down to reread some page proofs we had printed. What I read soothed me, gave me a degree of proportion, and made me decide that I would rather be the second Gutenberg than another Croesus and Casanova. Well, peace, it is wonderful. We must celebrate." He rapped his fork on a glass to summon the maître d'hôtel. "We will toast with a 1959 Ockfener Bockstein from the Saar. It is a cool, dry white wine with only eight percent alcohol. That will be enough when we are so heady."

The leisurely meal at the Mainzer Hof took two hours. After Zoellner left, Karl Hennig telephoned for his chauffeur and Porsche and insisted upon driving Randall back to Frankfurt.

During the journey, Hennig spoke cheerfully of the Olympic-sized swimming pool he intended to install under a domed enclosure for his workmen. He spoke wistfully of his affection for the actress Helga. He touched upon his social life, mentioning a box he owned at the opera house in the district. Once, he pointed out a field of green grapes that would produce a delicious Mainz wine.

Another time, as they passed through a quiet old village —brick walls, narrow winding streets, aged houses, a steepled church, a small square protected by a broken saint with fresh flowers in its arms—he identified the place as Hockheim, where some of his relatives lived. After they had entered the autobahn, they had gone faster, and Hennig lapsed into silence.

Abruptly, it seemed, although forty-five minutes had gone by, they were caught up in the vortex of Frankfurt. The police in short-sleeved shirts were on their pedestals directing traffic. The streets were clogged with trams, delivery trucks, Volkswagens, people doing last-minute shopping or returning home from work. Beneath the white and red umbrellas of the Terrassen-Café, customers were settling down for their *Teestunde*.

Hennig emerged from his reverie. "You are going back to the Frankfurter Hof, Steve?"

"Yes, to check out. I'm catching an immediate flight to Amsterdam."

In German, Hennig directed his chauffeur to the hotel.

As they reached the Kaiserplatz, Hennig said, "If you require more information, I expect to be in Amsterdam shortly."

"Do you know exactly when?"

"When I have the first bound Bibles ready. Probably in the week before you make the announcement."

As the car came to a halt before the Frankfurter Hof, Randall shook the printer's hand.

"I'm grateful for your cooperation, Karl," he said. "I just wish you hadn't put yourself out to make this drive with me."

"No, no, it's not that alone," said Hennig. "I had to come here anyway. I only regret I have no time to treat you to a drink. But I already have an appointment, a five-o'clock business meeting in the bar of the Hotel Intercontinental. Well, *auf Wiedersehen*."

Randall waited until the Porsche had left and only then started into the lobby of the Frankfurter Hof. About to go to the *Portier's* desk to learn if there had been any messages for him, he suddenly came to a dead stop.

A slender man, preoccupied as he stroked his Van Dyke, was crossing to the *Portier's* desk.

Cedric Plummer, here.

In Mainz, and now here.

The long-ago story from Maugham flashed through Randall's mind.

The merchant's servant in Baghdad: *Master, just now when I was in the market-place I was jostled by a woman in the crowd and when I turned I saw it was Death that jostled me. She looked at me and made a threatening gesture . . . now, lend me your horse. . . . I will go to Samarra and there Death will not find me.*

And later in the day, when the merchant found Death in the marketplace and asked why she had made a threatening gesture to his servant, Death replied: *That was not a threatening gesture, it was only a start of surprise. I was astonished to see him in Baghdad, for I had an appointment with him tonight in Samarra.*

Senseless, this recollection, yet not entirely.

Randall held back, watching.

Cedric Plummer had reached the *Portier's* desk and was crooking a finger at a clerk.

Quickly, Randall moved behind Plummer, past him, keeping his back to him and face averted, going swiftly in the direction of the elevator. Yet, trying to escape notice by the British journalist, he did not escape Plummer's imperious, high-pitched voice.

"Guter Herr," the journalist was saying, "I am Cedric Plummer—"

"Yes, of course, Mr. Plummer."

"—and if there are any calls for me, know that I shall be back in an hour. I have a five-o'clock business meeting in the bar of the Hotel Intercontinental. If any message is urgent, you can find me there."

A chill of apprehension crept through Randall. He continued to the elevator. Arriving, he paused, and glanced over his shoulder. Plummer was nowhere to be seen.

In the elevator, Randall did his arithmetic.

Karl Hennig had said to him: *I already have an appoint-*

ment, a five-o'clock business meeting in the bar of the Hotel Intercontinental.

Cedric Plummer had said to the clerk: *I have a five-o'clock business meeting in the bar of the Hotel Intercontinental.*

Add it up: coincidence.

Add it once more: conspiracy.

Subtract Hennig's words in Mainz: *I flatly refused to see him. I wouldn't let that bastard through my door.*

Add again. It didn't figure.

For the moment, Randall decided, he would leave it at that, unsolved. He'd get back to Amsterdam this evening and then—no more work tonight, he was seeing Angela, aching to see her—then tomorrow, tomorrow and in the days to follow, he would have someone keep Karl Hennig under close observation.

BOTH THE Mercedes-Benz limousine and Theo had been waiting for him, when Randall arrived at Schiphol Airport in Amsterdam after the short flight from Frankfurt.

He had gone to the Amstel Hotel, found the hoped-for message from Angela Monti saying that she had arrived in Amsterdam and had checked into the Hotel Victoria. She would be looking forward to seeing him.

He had hastily showered, dressed, and firmly put Hennig and Plummer out of his mind. Downstairs, he had directed Theo to drive him to the Hotel Victoria. There, he had rung Angela's room on the first floor, and waited at the foot of the green-carpeted curving staircase for her appearance.

When she had descended the stairs at last, he stood mesmerized and disbelieving. He had seen her only once before, one afternoon before, in her own country, and had parted from her knowing that he had not been so attracted to a woman in many years. Throughout the week he had carried with him this impression of a beautiful female. But here, this second time, he had been overwhelmed by her presence. To remember her as merely beautiful had been to do her a disservice. She was the most dazzling and desirable young woman he had ever seen. And there, in the lobby, when she had come so naturally and comfortably into his arms, her soft lips pressing warmly against his own, he had known that she was someone who had already become a part of him.

Theo had driven them to the Bali, a highly recommended Indonesian restaurant in the Leidsestraat. After dismissing the Dutch driver, insisting he would be perfectly safe since he had none of his work with him, Randall had taken Angela by the arm and led her through the revolving door, up two flights of stairs, and into the central dining room of the restaurant. A turbaned, dark-skinned waiter had guided them to one of the three smaller rooms in the rear.

They had sat at a table against the wall and ordered the *Rijstafel*—the rice-table, or Indonesian smorgasbord—and they had hardly been aware of the vast array of dishes that had been placed before them, the *sajor soto* or soup, the beef in Java sauce, the mixed soya beans, the jumbo prawns, the fried coconut. They had eaten and spoken sparingly, and consumed a bottle of dry Moselle wine, and made love with their eyes and the touch of their fingers.

Leaving the Bali, holding hands, they had strolled in the cooling summer's night. They had traversed the Leidseplein, pausing to listen to three gentle young boys strumming their guitars. From the bridge of the Prinsengracht, arms linked, they had peered out at the canal, toward a shimmering distant bridge where the hundreds of lights resembled rows of luminous pearls in the darkness. Presently, they had come to the wide bridge on the Singel, and below them the illuminated boats overflowing with flowers bobbed in the water.

Now, in the lateness of the seductive night, they were still on this bridge, and almost alone.

Angela had mentioned that Naomi had found her an office this afternoon, an office on the same floor as Randall's, and very close to his, almost next door.

"Yes," he said. "I arranged it."

She hesitated. "You wanted me so close to you every day?"

"I did and I do."

"Are you not afraid you will make a mistake, Steve? You hardly know me."

"I've been with you all week, every day, every night. Oh, I know you, I know you very well, Angela."

"I have felt the same," she said quietly.

He gazed out over the canal again, and when he turned back to her, he saw that her eyes were closed, her lips barely moving, her hands clasped together. When she opened her eyes, she smiled at him.

"What were you doing?" he asked. "Were you praying?"

She nodded. "I feel better," she said.

"About what, Angela?"

"About what I am going to do." Her smile remained. "Steve, take me to the hotel."

"Which one?"

"Yours. I want to see your rooms."

"You really want to see my rooms?"

Her palm slipped beneath his hand. "No," she said. "It's you. I want to be with you."

THEY WERE NAKED on his bed, side by side, facing one another, kissing, tongues teasing, her hand playing against the skin of his hip and stomach, his hand caressing the flesh of her thigh.

They had not exchanged a word since lying down together, and all they could hear now was their quickening breathing and the hurrying of their heartbeats.

His hand slid up across the moist long narrow and broadening triangle of her soft pubic hair, and his fingers found and touched the prominent bud of her clitoris, and ever so slowly, so lightly, his fingertips massaged it. Involuntarily, her hips began to rotate, and he heard her suck in her breath and emit a pleasurable sigh. Her free hand left his belly, dropped downward, groped for his erect penis, and her fingers touched it, rubbing it, loving it, until it expanded and stretched and he felt it would burst.

Then, a groan, low and imploring, rose from deep within her, like a distant cry for the fullness of love. Her hand came away from him, and she rolled on her back, arms behind her on the pillow, eyes closed, mouth open.

In the muted light from a single lamp across the room, he saw the naked Angela beneath him, the girl he would enter, become one with, totally possess. She was ready, the rumpled raven hair on the white pillow, the lids shut over the eyes, the lips of her mouth parted, the breathing harder, the two mounds of her breasts rising and falling, the moons of crimson around the firm red nipples, deepening in color, the sunken slash of navel, the wide hips and buttocks undulating.

She was ready for love.

And he was ready, too.

Her knees had come up and were separating, the rounded thighs opening, and he came over upon her, between her legs, and his penis found the vaginal passage giving way, tissue satiny and pliant and lubricated. And as his penis sank slowly inside her, the hot walls of her vagina closed over him, pulled him deeper and tighter inside, engulfed him.

He stroked her inside, he caressed her inside, he drew back and thrust deeper, until they both moaned with mingled pain and pleasure, and her legs left the bed and wrapped themselves around his back and her hands clutched his shoulders. He rode her with love, back and forth ceaselessly, and when she rocked and swayed, he held on, astride her, occupying her burning flesh as he was consumed by an ecstasy of passion he had never felt in his life.

She tore at his hair, and pressed her fists into his rib cage, and her buttocks rose and fell as she met his thrustings. Gradually her vagina, her hips, the whole lower part of her body gyrated, faster and faster, and he rotated in rhythm with her, his penis going round and round along with the supple vessel encompassing it.

"My God," he whispered, "oh, my God, my dearest—"

It was perpetual motion now, this coupling, and it was heightening, climbing, soaring.

Her fists drummed against his slippery back, and mindlessly he gripped her sides.

"Darling, darling," she gasped, "I'm coming—"

And as her hips lifted high off the bed and her thighs came together like a vise against his thighs, she sobbed and shuddered in the final convulsion of total orgasm, and he let go, utterly, entirely, filling her with his semen, coming and coming and coming again inside her.

"I love you," he whispered against her ear. "I love, I love you."

"Oh, Steve, never leave me, never."

Emptied, fulfilled, they lay locked and safe in each other's arms.

She slept, her sweet face, so dear and at peace, upon his chest.

Drowsily, he tried to think, still warm with her giving and her flesh. There had been many, but not another like this. Not Barbara, certainly not Barbara, whom he could remember with kindness and affection tonight, accepting now that their mechanical loveless bouts had been as much his failure as her own. Not Darlene, not all the Darlenes before Darlene, with their inanimate receptacle deadness or their practiced geisha acrobatics. Not Naomi, and the many Naomis before Naomi, with their limited servicings, their going down on, their sixty-nining, their mutual manual spasm-makings.

He had never, in so many nights in a life of so many grownup years, offered or taken, given or received, an orgasm born and released entirely of love, never once, until this night on this bed with this young woman in Amsterdam. He wanted to weep. For wasted years? For final joy? For the millions of others on the earth who would live and who would die without knowing this ultimate oneness?

He kissed Angela's cheek with love, and lowered his head deeply into the down pillow, and let the heavy lids close over his eyes, until he slept, too.

When he regained consciousness, he realized that it was a far-off bell that was summoning him. He struggled awake, saw Angela next to him still lost in sleep and, through the blinds of the windows beyond, the grayness of early morning.

The ringing was persistent and louder now, and he rolled over toward the bedside table, saw the hands on his travel clock pointing to twenty minutes after six in the morning, and realized that the steady ringing was from the telephone next to the clock.

Dazed, he fumbled for the receiver, managed to remove it from the telephone, and brought it to his ear and mouth.

"Yes, who is it?" he asked quickly.

"Steve? This is George Wheeler," the hushed but wide-awake voice announced from the other end. "Sorry to get you up like this, but I had to. Are you up? Can you hear me?"

"I'm awake, George."

"Listen. This is important. I want you at the Hospital of the Vrije Universiteit—that's the main hospital in Amsterdam, the Hospital of the Free University. I want you there in an hour, seven thirty latest. Have you a pencil? Better take this down."

"One second." He located the stub of a pencil and the note pad the hotel had placed on the table. "I have one," he said.

"Make a note. Hospital of the Vrije Universiteit. The address is 1115 Beolelaan. It's located in Buitenveldert—a new section of the city—the taxi driver will know it. Have the hotel get you a taxi. When you get inside the hospital, tell the woman at the information desk you want to be taken to Lori Cook's room on the fourth floor. I'll be there, we'll all be there."

"Hold it, George. What in the devil's going on?"

"You'll find out. I can't discuss it on the phone. Suffice it to say something absolutely extraordinary has happened. And we need you here. . . ."

VI

Once Randall's taxi, a Simca, left the city and entered the wide thoroughfare named Rooseveltlaan, it had accelerated, racing past open meadows and woods, slackening its speed only when they were on Boelelaan and approaching the hospital. Randall had offered the taxi driver an extra ten guilders if he could get to the hospital before seven thirty and the driver had been determined to earn the bonus.

Now, from the Simca's window, Randall could see the impressive complex of what appeared to be recently constructed hospital buildings. They swung into the curving driveway which was bordered by a flower bed, the only color visible on this overcast early morning.

The Simca skidded to a halt before the seven-story structure. On the wooden awning over the entrance were the words: ACADEMISCH ZIEKENHUIS DER VRIJE UNIVERSITEIT. "Six minutes early," the driver proclaimed with satisfaction. Randall gratefully counted out the fare plus ten guilders from his wallet.

Still mystified by the "absolutely extraordinary" happening that demanded his presence, Randall hurried up the stone steps of the hospital. Going through the revolving door, he found himself in a low-ceilinged lobby. There was a shop selling tobacco, candy, cookies, and near it the information desk that Wheeler had mentioned, with a matronly receptionist behind it.

Even as he started for the desk, the Dutch woman inquired, "You are Mr. Randall?" When he nodded, she said, "Please be seated a moment. Mr. Wheeler called to say he is on his way down to meet you."

Too restless to sit, Randall filled and lighted his pipe, and examined a lobby wall made up of modernistic mosaics—one representing Eve being born of Adam's rib, another depicting Cain and Abel, still another showing Christ healing a child. Just as he was becoming interested in the mosaics, he heard his name. He spun around as George L. Wheeler, polishing his gold-rimmed spectacles and setting them on the bridge of his meaty nose, came striding up to him.

The publisher placed a paternal arm around Randall's shoulders, and in his braying dromedary voice, he said cheerfully, "Glad you got back from your trip in time for this, Steve. Wanted you in on it from the beginning, even though you can't use the story yet. We have to keep it under wraps until we're sure. But the instant the doctors say okay, we'll let you bellow it to the wide world."

"George, what are you talking about?"

"I thought I told you. Guess I didn't. I'll give it to you quickly on the way up."

Leading Randall toward the elevator, the publisher lowered his voice but could not repress his excitement. "Hear this," he said. "Last night, I was out with Sir Trevor having late supper at Dikker en Thijs—actually, Signore Gayda, our Italian publisher, you remember, and his Monsignore Riccardi were our hosts—when I received an urgent call from Naomi. She gave me only a shorthand account of what was happening, and advised me, all of us, to come straight to this hospital. I've been here the entire night. You can see the bags under my eyes."

"George," said Randall impatiently, "will you tell me what in the devil is going on?"

"Sorry, yes, of course." They had arrived at the elevators, but Wheeler drew Randall away from the sliding doors. "As best as I can piece it together—information is still scanty, too much confusion—your girl, the one in your office who knows so much about archeology—I forget her name—"

Randall was about to say Angela Monti, when he realized that the publisher did not know Angela yet and he was speaking of a member of Randall's publicity staff.

"You mean Jessica Taylor? The American—"

Wheeler clapped his hands. "Right. Miss Taylor. Last night, just before midnight, she received a crazy, incoherent telephone call from Lori Cook, your secretary, the lame girl, the one who's been a cripple all her life. Lori was sobbing, kept saying she'd had a vision, seen a vision, and had gone on her knees and prayed to it asking that she be cured and be able to walk normally again—and when the vision disappeared, and she got up, her affliction was gone and she could walk just like you and me."

"What?" exclaimed Randall incredulously. "Are you serious?"

"You heard me, Steve. She could walk normally, and she kept saying on the phone she felt faint and feverish, out of this world, and she had to see someone right away. Well, you can bet, in a jiffy Jessica Taylor was off to see her. Jessica found Lori collapsed on the floor of her apartment, and revived her, but after listening to Lori's babblings, Jessica didn't know what to do, became unstrung herself, so she called me. I was out, but Naomi got the call, and immediately phoned for an ambulance to be sent for Lori. Then Naomi got hold of me, and I called the physician who treats the Resurrection Two staff, Dr. Fass, and told him what I knew. I made a few more calls to others, and everyone came posthaste to the Free University Hospital. What do you think of that, Steve?"

Throughout the recital, Randall had been recollecting his first interview with Lori, that wispy gray sparrow with her self-conscious gait, remembering her moving pilgrimage (as she called it) to Lourdes, Fátima, Turin, Beauraing, that odyssey of hope and despair in search of the miracle of normality.

"What do I think?" repeated Randall. "I don't know what to think. I'd like to know the facts. You see, George, I'm sorry, but I simply don't believe in miracles."

"Come now, you yourself have referred to the International New Testament as a miracle," Wheeler reminded him.

"I never meant a literal miracle. I was using hyperbole.

Our Bible was born of a scientific archeological excavation. It has a rational factual basis. But miracle healing—" He drifted off, recollecting something else that Lori Cook had said to him in their interview, something to the effect that the new Bible meant everything to her, and from what she had heard it was something incredibly miraculous. A suspicion entered his mind. "George, there must be more. Has Lori explained what might have brought on that vision and the—the so-called miracle?"

"ESP, because I was about to tell you," said Wheeler with continuing enthusiasm. "You're darn right something brought it on, and what brought it on was a security lapse on the part of our publicity director, namely Steven Randall. You were directly responsible, but considering what's happened, we forgive you."

"I committed a breach of security?"

"You did. Think back. Dr. Deichhardt loaned you our New Testament to read for one night. A condition was that you personally return the proofs to Dr. Deichhardt the following morning. Instead, you had Lori return them."

"I remember doing that. I was about to take them in to Deichhardt, and suddenly I got tied up with Naomi over the itinerary of my trip, and I handed the proofs to Lori. Well, I was sure she would deliver them. I probably should have done it myself—but still, what was so wrong with Lori's doing it?"

Wheeler grinned. "As your Lori confessed to Jessica last night, before the ambulance came, you'd ordered Lori to hand those page proofs to Dr. Deichhardt in person—to him and to no one else. Right?"

"That's right."

"So the kid took you at your word. She went to deliver the page proofs to Dr. Deichhardt. He happened to be out of his office. Lori refused to leave the envelope with Dr. Deichhardt's secretary. She decided to hold on to it until he returned. But the nearness of this—this holy object, as she called it—like having the Lord's shroud or the Holy Grail in hand without looking at them—the temptation was too much. Lori confessed that she pretended to take a late lunch, but instead hid herself in one of the storage rooms on our floor in the Kras, and she read the Petronius Parchment and the Gospel According to James. In fact, if she is to be believed, she read James four times before returning the gospel to Dr. Deichhardt himself later in the day."

"I believe she read it four times. What—what did she say happened next?"

"All she could think of throughout this week, all that dominated her mind and filled her heart, was what James had written down about Jesus. She began to imagine, awake and asleep, to act out in her head—Jesus treading this earth, His survival of the Cross, His daring visit to Rome, and James in Jerusalem, facing death, putting the story on papyrus. Last night, she was alone in her room with her hallucinations of that period, when suddenly she closed her eyes, placed her hands over her heart, and standing in the middle of her room, she prayed to James the Just to bring her to the fullness of life as he had brought Jesus to life for her. And lo, when she opened her eyes, a luminous circle of bright, almost blinding light, a ball of light, floated before her eyes, across the room, and there was the bearded and robed figure of James the Just and he lifted a knobby hand and blessed her. She says she was at once frightened and exalted, and fell on her knees and closed her eyes again, praying to James to help her. When she opened her eyes, the vision was gone, and when she came to her feet, she took a few steps and her lameness was gone. She kept sobbing and crying to herself, 'I am cured!' Then, she managed to call Jessica Taylor, who found her in a faint, or a trance —it's not clear—and well, Steve, you know the rest. Let's go upstairs now."

They took the elevator to the fourth floor and hurried past two six-bed wards toward a gathering in front of what was obviously Lori Cook's hospital room.

Nearing the group, Randall recognized Jessica Taylor, with a notebook, and the redheaded photographer, Oscar Edlund, a camera slung over his shoulder. Others in the group who were familiar to Randall were Signore Gayda,

Monsignore Riccardi, Dr. Trautmann, and the Reverend
Zachery.

Joining the group, Randall could see that they were
concentrating on the white-jacketed physician, who was
speaking to them. At his elbow was an attractive nurse,
trim in a blue uniform with white collar. Wheeler whispered that the physician was the project's own Dr. Fass,
a dignified, dry, precise Dutch internist, probably in his
early sixties.

"Yes, we X-rayed Miss Cook immediately upon her
admittance," he was saying in reply to someone's question. "When she was brought in last night—early this
morning, to be more exact—she was placed in a mobile
bed—we do not like to use stretchers—and brought to
this room. To expedite diagnosis, our Swiss beds are so
constructed that we can X-ray a patient right through
the mattress, and this was done at the outset. Now to
return to your other question. No, we cannot accurately
know what Miss Cook's condition was prior to the hallu-
cination—let me say the traumatic experience—she underwent last night. We are trying to locate the parents of the
patient, who are traveling in the Far East. Once we've
contacted them, we hope eventually to obtain medical
records of the disease that crippled Miss Cook in her
childhood. For the time, we have only her non-profes-
sional word to go by. From how Miss Cook has described
her affliction, it would seem to me that she suffered some
form of osteomyelitis as a youngster, perhaps fifteen years
ago."

Randall stirred himself. "Can you describe the disease, Doctor?"

"In Miss Cook's case, the symptomatic inflammation
occurred in the tibia or larger bone between her right knee
and ankle. It may have been an acute case and caused
bone destruction—our X-rays may confirm this—for she
has memory of swelling, pain, prolonged bouts of fever.
She was not treated properly for it, and neither did she
undergo surgery. In the years after, she was afflicted with
lameness."

"Dr. Fass." It was Wheeler who was speaking. "How

can you explain last night? After all, she was cured, wasn't she? She is walking normally now?"

"Yes, it would be reasonable to say she can walk normally now," said Dr. Fass. "She has already performed satisfactorily for our physiotherapist. Our medical director was witness to the tests. Our neuropsychiatrist will spend some time with her this afternoon. At the moment, she is being examined and questioned by Dr. Rechenberg and Dr. Koster, two consultants whose services I requested. As to last night, I doubt whether I am in a position to explain what happened. On the one hand, she may have suffered a psychic shock of some nature instead of an organic disease in her childhood, and last night her hallucinations could have counteracted the shock by triggering autosuggestion. In that event, we might classify her as a longtime victim of neurasthenia, and her recovery could not be regarded as miraculous. On the other hand—"

Dr. Fass surveyed his small circle of listeners, and his eyes twinkled.

"—if her lameness proves to have originated from an organic disease, and she was healed with no help from science, then we are dealing with another matter. As to that matter, I would refer you to a sixteenth-century surgical report made by the estimable Dr. Ambroise Paré after treating a certain patient. *'Je le pansay; Dieu le guérit'*—'I dressed him; God cured him.'" Dr. Fass made an apologetic gesture. "Now, excuse me, I must return to my colleagues. We may permit you to interrogate the patient in another day or two. Certainly, we will want her under observation here for a minimum of two weeks."

As Dr. Fass opened the door behind him, to go inside with his nurse, Randall pushed through the circle to the temporarily open doorway. He had only the briefest glimpse of what was going on inside.

Lori Cook, so tiny, so boyish, was seated on the edge of the rolled-up bed, her hospital gown pulled above her knees. A physician was bent over her, feeling the calf of her right leg. Two others were watching him with interest. Lori Cook appeared oblivious to those attending her. She was gazing upward at the ceiling, her plain face holding a secret smile. She looked positively beatific.

Then, the door to the hospital room swung shut and blocked her out.

Moving away from the door, lost in thought, Randall saw that the group behind him had dispersed and Wheeler, who had gone up the hall with two of the others, was beckoning him.

Randall went after Wheeler—whose companions proved to be the Italian publisher, Gayda, and the Italian Catholic theologian, Monsignore Riccardi—and seated himself near the others in one of the leather-upholstered chairs in the visitors' day room.

"What do you make of it, Monsignore Riccardi?" Wheeler demanded to know. "You Catholics have much more experience in these matters."

The Monsignore smoothed down the front of his cassock. "It is much too early to tell, Mr. Wheeler. The Church moves cautiously in these matters. We always counsel against immediate credulity."

"But this is so obviously a miracle!" Wheeler exclaimed.

"At first glance, Miss Cook's cure is impressive, most impressive," Monsignore Riccardi agreed. "Yet, we must reserve judgment. Since the time Our Lord wrought some forty demonstrative miracles, there have been additional signs visited upon His faithful, even in our very day. This we know with certainty. But precisely what, we must ask ourselves, is the nature of a true miracle? We hold it to be an extraordinary occurrence, one visible in itself and not merely in its effect, an event inexplicable in terms of ordinary forces, one that can only be explained as having happened through God's special intervention. It is through continuing miracles that God reveals Himself according to His will. Yet, not all cures seemingly credited to faith can be attributed to God's intervention. Remember this. Of every five thousand cures submitted from the shrine of Our Lady of Lourdes, the Church finds perhaps one percent are truly miraculous."

"Because so much is imaginary," said Gayda pedantically. "The imagination, the powers of suggestion, can show strong results. There is, for example, false pregnancy. The Mary who was Queen of England until 1558 wished to have a child so much, she was twice falsely pregnant although the symptoms appeared real. Recall the demonstration of the French neurologist in Paris in the thirties. He told a blindfolded patient that a flame had just been put to his arm and that he had been burned. Promptly, a blister appeared on the patient's arm. Yet, the patient had been deceived. He had not been touched by any flame at all. It had only been suggested. Or recall those who have received the stigmata, the bleeding from wounds such as those Christ suffered—how many such cases, Monsignore Riccardi?"

"In history, 322 verified cases of persons who bled from their hands and side as Christ had bled on the Cross. The first, St. Francis of Assisi in 1224, and the last renowned one, Theresa Neumann in 1926."

Gayda turned from the Monsignore to Wheeler. "So you see, George. Suggestion. They believed in the Passion. They suffered what He had suffered. Conversely, by the same power of suggestion, our Lori Cook wanted to be healed so much, and her belief in our new Bible was so intense, she was healed."

Wheeler spread his hands. "But that's a miracle, that's purely and simply a miracle."

Monsignore Riccardi rose, nodding at Wheeler. "It may be. We shall observe this case closely. This may very well be the beginning. Once our James spreads his new gospel to all peoples, belief in the Passion may spread, and with faith, belief, Our Lord will respond, and miracles will abound in every land. We will pray for it."

As Riccardi exited with the Italian publisher, Wheeler held Randall back. "We're in, Steve," he said with fierce jubilation. "I can tell. I can feel it inside. Those theologians know it's a miracle, the first divine miracle that can be credited to our International New Testament. Even if Protestants don't look upon miracles as the Catholics do, they can't ignore evidence like this. They've got to be impressed by the powers of our new Bible. And can you imagine how Catholics will demand an imprimatur for

our Bible. Once we get the go-ahead, I want you ready to
run with this, Steve. After the announcement is out, you
can pull the cork on Lori's story. Can you think of a
better endorsement on earth than this? No hard sell,
Steve. Just rightful missionary work. Think of the good
we can do."

The good we can do at ten dollars a copy, Randall
wanted to add. Yet, he held his tongue.

Because he *was* impressed.

Something had happened to a girl he knew, who had
been a cripple and was not a cripple any longer.

He had no answer for it. Apparently, neither did
science. So why not call it what it was—a miracle?

FIVE HOURS later, seated in a rattan chair opposite Angela
Monti, doodling with a spoon on the blue polka-dotted
tablecloth of the outdoor café table, Randall had been
relating to her his experience at the hospital.

They had met for lunch at de Pool, a café-restaurant
midway between the Victoria Hotel, where Angela had
been working on research notes the full morning, and the
Krasnapolsky, where Randall had been feverishly occupied after leaving the hospital with Wheeler.

Angela had heard out and accepted the story of Lori
Cook's miraculous cure without surprise or question. "Not
because I am such a good Catholic, although I do have
religious faith," she had explained, "but because I suspect
that in a seemingly rational world there is so much mystery that cannot be understood by our limited mental
capacities. In the rank of living things in the universe,
we may be on a scale not much above ants."

After that, holding his hand on the table, she had
wanted to know how he had spent every minute of the
morning since leaving the hospital. Before he could tell
her, a waiter had materialized to take their orders.

Randall took up the menu, a glossy card with color
photographs of four of the luncheon specials, each pic-
tured on an oblong cardboard plate like prepackaged
American TV dinners.

"You know this place," Randall said. "And now you know me. What do you suggest?"

Angela seemed pleased. "For people with much work to do, I suggest we eat little. Actually, the servings are light." She pointed to a picture on the menu, and addressed the waiter. "We will have the *Hongaarse goulash.*"

Once the waiter had gone, Angela turned back to Randall. "Now tell me the rest of your morning, Steve."

"Let me see. Before leaving the hospital, I phoned you, right? As I told you, anything you could type up from memory, from your diary, your notes, your father's papers, on the excavation and discovery, would be useful, and lead us into some further questions."

"I've already written a part of it for you to see."

"Wonderful. Okay, after the hospital, I went to the Krasnapolsky. Les Cunningham and Helen de Boer—they're members of my publicity staff and you'll meet them soon—were waiting for me with some good news. The Dutch government approved our use of the auditorium in the Netherlands Royal Palace for the announcement of our discovery and its publication on July 12th, and we got an okay to broadcast the event on worldwide television by Intelsat V, the communications satellite system. Then we drafted a confidential memorandum for the five publishers with extra copies to other personnel on the project who might be concerned with this, and we circulated it along with a note from me to the publishers suggesting a meeting by tomorrow to make the plans final. . . . Angela, didn't I tell you most of that when I called you again from the Kras for lunch?"

"You told me some of it."

"I hate to repeat myself. But there's so damn much going on—"

"I like you to repeat yourself. I love the sound of your voice. What happened next, Steve?"

"Well, then I called together my staff for a promotion meeting upstairs in Room 204—the room we use for publicity meetings, but it's so attractive I thought the two of us could set up light housekeeping there—"

Angela squeezed his hand. "You found time to think

of me during your work? I'm flattered. But you are really too busy to be domestic."

"I hope not," said Randall. "We are pressed for time, it's true. Anyway, we had the meeting and it went well."

"What do you discuss in a publicity meeting?"

"I told them everything—of course, Jessica Taylor was in on it from the start—but the rest of them, I told them about Lori Cook's sub-rosa reading of the Gospel According to James, and what happened after, and how she can walk normally now. That created quite a sensation. I assigned Jessica to write two features—one a first-person byline story I want her to ghost in Lori's name, recounting her life, her years of living with an infirmity, her long search for a miracle, and what took place after she read James and Petronius, and the other a story about Jessica herself, on her own experience with Lori last night. I assigned Paddy O'Neal to prepare a straight news story about the occurrence, with some solid plugs for our new Bible. Of course, this material will have to be held back from the press pending approval from the physicians and theologians. Once we have that, we can shoot the stories straight out. This will be just one of the features we'll release after the Intelsat announcement."

Angela shook her head in wonder. "I never knew about publicity. I thought newspaper and television reporters dug up their news, the way my father digs on his own."

Randall laughed. "Not quite, not quite. Oh, the press does dig and find news on its own. But editors depend on publicity people for a great share of it. If you want leaks or news on a war, politics, inventions, religion, education—you name it—most of it originates with public relations people representing a military command or a nation's leader or a church group or a school. It's not just entertainers or athletes or industrial products that have publicists. It's almost everyone. Even Jesus Christ. Didn't He depend on apostles and disciples to go out and sell the Word?"

"It sounds almost cynical," said Angela.

"Sometimes it is. Usually it isn't. There is so much going on in the world every day that the news media can't know all of it every minute. The media needs help. We give it to them, out of our own self-interest. And each of us tries to give the media something that we believe is more important to the public than the offerings of the competition."

"What else did you discuss in your meeting, Steve?"

"I passed on the added material I'd picked up from you in Milan about your father, and told the staff you were here to provide more archeological information. I promised the staff they'd have transcripts of my taped interviews with Aubert on the authentication process and with Hennig on the printing of the Bible. We kicked around ideas for stories. Oh yes. Dr. Florian Knight was there. Remember my mentioning him to you at dinner yesterday?

"The bitter young man from the British Museum?"

"Yes. But as his girl friend promised me in London, he came around. Still sour, but reluctantly cooperative. Dr. Jeffries was right. The young man is an absolute wizard on Aramaic dialect and textual criticism of the Bible— the kind of detective work on the Scriptures that further authenticates the text. It was a little difficult with the questions and answers, despite his using a hearing aid, but once he had an idea of what we needed, he was fascinating, and my whole staff took notes."

"About what? What did he talk about, Steve?"

"Mostly, he explained how Dr. Jeffries and his committees actually went about translating the International New Testament. Dr. Jeffries had finally filled him in on all that, and he related the details, including his own role in unwittingly assisting the translators. Dr. Jeffries followed the procedure used by the translators of the King James Version some three and a half centuries ago. Do you know how that was done?"

"I haven't the faintest idea," said Angela, "except that the Authorized Version—the King James one, which, as a Catholic, I read only in a course on classical books—is the most beautiful writing in the English language."

"And the only great work of literature ever to be produced by a committee. According to Dr. Knight, there was a lot of religious dissension in England in 1604, and in order to give the warring elements of the church a common purpose and project, King James accepted the proposal of a Puritan named Dr. Reynolds, president of a college at Oxford, and originally ordered fifty-four churchmen to do a new translation of the Bible. King James was apparently the last person you'd expect to instigate such a project. He loved books, but he also loved vice, and he was vain, and extremely effeminate. His subjects used to say of him that King Elizabeth had been succeeded by Queen James."

Angela burst into laughter. "Very clever. Your Dr. Knight told you that?"

"He can be amusing. Anyway, King James approved of forty-seven translators, a diverse and intriguing group. The oldest was seventy-three, the youngest was twenty-seven. They were preachers, professors, linguists, scholars. One knew fifteen languages, including Aramaic, Persian, Arabic. Another had tutored Queen Elizabeth in Greek. Another had been able to read the Bible in Hebrew at the age of six. One was a refugee from Belgium. Another, a drunkard. Another, who was wasting away from tuberculosis, worked from his deathbed. Another, a widower who died during the project, left behind eleven destitute children. Anyway, they were divided into six committees, two translating at Oxford, two at Cambridge, two at Westminster. One committee of eight at Oxford took on half the New Testament, and another committee of seven at Westminster did the other half."

"But, Steve, how could they translate together?"

"Because each committee was assigned a section of the Bible to translate from Hebrew and Greek into English, and each individual on the committee was responsible for one or more chapters of the section. Members of a committee read their translations to one another, took suggestions, made corrections, and when their whole section was done, they sent it over to a different committee for further rewrites. In two years and nine months they were

done. Then a panel of twelve went over the first draft
to revise and unify it. Finally, one man, a butcher's son
who'd graduated from Oxford at nineteen, Dr. Miles
Smith, did the final rewrite, with a bishop overseeing
him. The result? The fifteen-hundred-page King James Authorized Version, published in 1611, five years before
Shakespeare's death."

"And our International New Testament was prepared
in the same way?"

Randall nodded. "Dr. Jeffries created three committees
with five linguists, textual critics, first-century scholars on
each. Dr. Trautmann advised the committee at Cambridge, and they translated the four gospels and Acts.
Professor Sobrier was with the group at Westminster,
and they translated the books from Paul's Epistle to the
Romans through Revelation. Dr. Jeffries and his committee at Oxford did the translation of the Petronius
Parchment, the Gospel According to James, and the annotated material. An awesome job. . . . And Angela,
here's our lunch at last."

As they ate, the blue awning of the Café de Pool was
rolled back. There was no sun. The day remained gray
and overcast, and the weather was dank and humid. Randall and Angela diverted themselves by observing the
pedestrians on the street beyond the flower-filled red con-
tainers atop the protective iron railing.

Randall had just finished eating when a young man,
circulating among the tables, dropped an advertising handbill beside his plate. Randall glanced at it, then blinked
and held it up. "Angela, what in the devil is this?"

The handbill read in English: "ENJOY WIGNAND FOCK-
ING. Corner of Pijlsteeg and Dam."

Angela nodded. "Yes. It is a very old bar nearby, and
the object of much sophomoric humor from tourists. Focking is a famous Dutch cognac. Would you like to try
some?"

Randall discarded the handbill. "No, thanks. And no
jokes, I promise you. I think I'd better get back to the
office—clearheaded."

"And I'd better get back to my room and work some more, unless——"

"Unless what?"

"Unless you need my help as a secretary. If Lori Cook will be in the hospital for two weeks—your hardest weeks —who will you have for your secretary?"

"You," he said. "You can still keep on with your own work. Do you really want the job?"

"If you want me."

"I want you."

"I am happy. I'll go back to the Victoria and get my notes——"

"And I'll go with you, and help you carry your homework to school."

After paying the bill, Randall led Angela out into the busy thoroughfare. They walked up the Damrak to the Victoria Hotel, an aged six-story structure that stood on a corner, one side looking across a canal toward the Central Railroad Station and the other side facing the harbor known as Open Haven Front.

The humidity was oppressive, and by the time they came out of the elevator on the spacious first-floor landing and made their way to Room 105, Randall's shirt was wet and clung to him. Angela's room proved cooler. It was a comfortable double room, cream-colored walls, restful green carpeting, a broad inviting bed, a pale green armoire, and several chairs, one standing at a brown wooden desk on which Angela's portable typewriter and papers rested.

"Angela," he said, "while you're gathering together your things for the office, do you mind if I take a quick shower? I need one."

"There is no regular shower," she said, "only a hand one in the tub. But it has a good spray."

"That'll do fine." He kicked off his shoes, removed his sport jacket, and peeled off the rest of his clothes until he was down to his jock shorts. "What are you looking at?" he said.

"To see how you are in the daytime."

"And?"

"And you take your shower now."

He went through the bathroom door next to the bed. The floor tiles were cold, and he hastily pulled the thick fluffy pink bath mat off its towel bar, unfolded it, threw it in front of the tub. He took off his jock shorts, tossed them aside, removed the hand shower from its holder above the faucets, and started the shower going, adjusting the warm and cold until the spray was lukewarm.

Stepping into the tub, Randall drew the pink curtain across the tub to protect the floor from the spray. Turning the hard spray on his face, shoulders, chest, he immediately felt better. For several minutes, humming to himself, he reveled in the water beating and splashing against his flesh. Feeling refreshed, he sought the soap, and rubbed the bar across his body, until he was covered with a cloak of bubbling white foam.

As he put the soap back in its holder, he heard a metallic scraping, and swung around so quickly he almost slipped. The curtain had been pushed aside. Angela stood there, entirely nude, and he could only blink at this sight of the gorgeous face, abundant quivering breasts with their crimson nipples, wide hips enclosing the mat of pubic hair barely hiding the soft vaginal crease.

Wordlessly, she stepped into the tub across from him. She picked up the soap, smiled at him, and said, "I was hot, too, Steve."

She began to soap him some more, all down his body, along his hips, and the inside of his legs, and he turned the hand shower upon her. "How does it feel?" he asked.

"Oooh—good, good, good. Here, let me soap myself."

He directed the hand shower away, watched her cover herself with soap until she resembled an ethereal creature composed of a million bubbles.

As the bubbles slowly broke, dissolved, revealing the hardened nipple of one breast, then the other, and the rivulets of soap and water ran down her belly and converged upon the V formed by her legs, he felt the throbbing inside him and the swelling between his legs. He dropped the hand shower and grabbed for her, and she slithered into his arms and against his soapy body.

"Ummm, this is so good, Steve."

"I love you, darling."

She backed off slightly, because she had to, and she looked down his body. "It's beautiful," she said. "Let's not waste it."

With one hand, she tore aside the bathtub curtain once more, and they both stepped over the side of the tub. She dropped down to her knees on the deep fluffy rug, and pulled him down facing her. Hands behind her, she lowered herself backward, extending her legs, bringing her knees high. She was on her back now, glistening with her wetness and the patches of foam, and she wriggled forward on the rug, her legs parting wider to enclose his dripping, kneeling body.

It was crazy, spontaneous, wonderful, and both of them knew they needed no foreplay. He lowered himself between her slippery thighs, and as the last foam cleared from her legs to reveal the velvety red orifice waiting, he slid his penis into it, deep and then deeper and then deeper yet. He held himself inside her, as her hands massaged his drenched back.

"I've never had a mermaid before," he whispered.

"How do you like it?" she whispered back, almost inaudibly.

He couldn't answer her, because they were moving, and she would know, she would know as he knew.

His damp body slapped against hers, and paused, and slapped again, and then again faster and faster and harder.

This Focking was spelled the right way, he thought. And it made you more intoxicated and higher, much higher.

The wet flesh against wet flesh, harder, still harder, the wet applause of two bodies, finally one, joined, welded, one, like one hand clapping.

Ohgod, he called inside his head, I'm coming. "Angela," he cried aloud, "I'm coming."

He had never been so high—and so happy.

It was midafternoon when Randall returned to the Hotel Krasnapolsky. Immediately, he was brought back to earth.

He had entered the hotel, flashed his red security card, and the guard had frowned and said, "Mr. Randall, yes, they have been hunting for you everywhere. Inspector Heldering wishes you to go to Zaal C at once."

"Zaal C?"

"The private conference room beside the staircase on the first floor."

"Where is the inspector?"

"With the publishers in Zaal C."

"Thanks."

Randall hastened inside.

He had arrived feeling euphoric, relaxed, at peace. Behind him, in the Victoria Hotel, he had left Angela on the bed, where he had carried her and put her down, and where she had fallen asleep as he had dressed. Now, his state of mind had undergone a sudden change. Ahead of him, a group of men who had been hunting for him *everywhere* were waiting for him. It sounded ominous. Randall's instincts told him something had gone very wrong.

He continued past the elevator, took the stairs two at a time to the upper landing, and there paused to catch his breath and locate the room. He saw the door marked ZAAL C and went around the stairwell toward it. He twisted the doorknob to go inside, but the door did not give. Then, he saw for the first time that a tiny one-way door viewer was set above the room's marking. He rapped his knuckles sharply against the wood.

He waited. A few moments later, a muffled voice from behind the door asked, "Are you alone, Mr. Randall?"

"Yes," he answered.

He heard the dead bolt move, and the door opened to reveal a phlegmatic Inspector Heldering gesturing for him to come inside.

From his first sight of them, gathered in a tight cluster around the conference table, Randall knew that his instincts had not misled him. Something was definitely wrong.

Beneath a haze of smoke, the publishers sat—Deichhardt, Wheeler, Gayda, Young, Fontaine—and among them was Heldering's empty chair, and another chair, presumably reserved for Randall himself. There was one more person in the room. In a corner, shorthand pad in her lap, pencil poised over it, sat Naomi Dunn. The now familiar faces were individual, yet they appeared oddly the same. Randall divined that this was because they all bore a common expression. They looked deeply troubled.

Wheeler spoke first. "Where in the devil have you been, Steve?" he said testily. "Never mind." His impatient hand motioned Randall to the vacant chair between Deichhardt and himself. "We called this emergency meeting a half hour ago. We need your help."

Awkwardly, Randall took his place, watched Heldering bolt the door and return to the table. Since most of the others were smoking cigarettes or cigars, Randall sought his pipe nervously.

"Well," he said. "What's going on?"

He heard Dr. Deichhardt's guttural voice answer him. "Mr. Randall, to be certain of one point—" Deichhardt shuffled several papers on the table before him and held up a pink sheet of foolscap. "This is the confidential memorandum you circulated among us this morning, is it not?"

Randall squinted at it. "Right. The memorandum proposing we make the announcement of the International New Testament from a stage in the ceremonial great hall of the Netherlands Royal Palace, and that we broadcast our announcement and the press conference that follows by Intelsat. We have agreements to proceed, if you are willing."

"We are willing, we are willing, that is unanimous," said Dr. Deichhardt. "It is a brilliant idea and one worthy of our project."

"Thank you," said Randall cautiously, still wondering what was troubling them.

"Now as to this memorandum—" Dr. Deichhardt rustled it. "At what hour did you send it out this morning?"

Randall tried to recall the time. "Around—I'd say around ten o'clock this morning."

Dr. Deichhardt took a heavy gold watch from his vest

pocket, snapped it open. "And now it is not quite four o'clock. So." His eyes met the others around the table. "So, the confidential memorandum was circulated here six hours ago. Interesting."

"Steve." Wheeler had pulled at Randall's arm to obtain his attention. "How many copies of the memorandum went out?"

"How many? Why, nineteen, I believe."

"Whom did they go to?" Wheeler demanded.

"Well, I don't have the list handy. But those of you in this room—"

"That's seven of us," said Wheeler. "What about the other twelve copies?"

"Let me think—"

Naomi spoke up. "I have the list. I picked it up, in case you might want the names."

"Read it," said Wheeler, "the ones besides those of us in this room."

Reading from a slip of paper, Naomi intoned the names. "Jeffries, Riccardi, Sobrier, Trautmann, Zachery, Kremer, Groat, O'Neal, Cunningham, Alexander, de Boer, Taylor. Twelve plus seven present, nineteen in all."

Sir Trevor Young shook his head. "Incredible. The top security personnel. Mr. Randall, might we have overlooked anyone? Did you convey the information in this memorandum orally to anyone?"

"Orally?" Randall knit his brow. "Well, of course, Lori Cook, as my secretary, knew we were investigating the royal palace and Intelsat, but of course she never saw the memo itself. Oh, yes, I mentioned it to Angela Monti, who is here on behalf of her father—"

Dr. Deichhardt peered through his rimless spectacles at Inspector Heldering. "Did Miss Monti receive full security clearance?"

"Thorough," said the inspector. "No problem. Everyone named has been cleared and given full trust."

"And finally me," said Randall lightly. "But then, I wrote the memo."

Dr. Deichhardt emitted a grunt. "Twenty-one, excepting Miss Cook in the hospital," he said. "There were twenty-one, and no more, who read or heard the contents of this confidential memorandum. Each one is trustworthy. I am baffled."

"By what?" Randall demanded with slight irritability.

Dr. Deichhardt drummed his fingers on the table. "By the fact, Mr. Randall, that precisely three hours after you sent out this confidential memorandum this morning, its contents were in the hands of the Reverend—the Dominee Maertin de Vroome, Hervormd Predikant—pastor of the Westerkerk, which is a member of the Dutch Reformed Church. He is also leader of the RRCM—the Radical Reform Christian Movement throughout the world."

Randall sat up straight, eyes widening. His astonishment was complete. "De Vroome—he got hold of our confidential memo?"

"Exactly," said the German publisher.

"But that's impossible!"

"Impossible or not, Steve, he got it," said Wheeler. "De Vroome has learned the place, method, and date of our big announcement."

"How do you know he knows?" asked Randall.

"Because," said Dr. Deichhardt, "just as Dominee de Vroome has penetrated our security, we have recently managed to break through his own. We now have an informer in their movement, posing—"

Inspector Heldering came out of his chair, wagging a finger. "Careful, careful, Herr Professor."

Dr. Deichhardt nodded at the project's security chief, and addressed Randall again. "Details are not necessary for you. We have someone in the RRCM—the Radical Reform Christian Movement of de Vroome's—who a few hours ago telephoned me with the contents of a confidential message de Vroome himself had sent out to his own leadership. It was dictated to me on the telephone. You wish to see it? Here it is."

Randall accepted the white sheet of paper from the German publisher. Carefully, he read it:

Dear Brother in the Cause:
   In confidence, I report. The orthodox syndicate

will make announcement of their discoveries and new Bible from the ceremonial hall of the royal palace in Amsterdam, and will broadcast it by the Intelsat satellite system, on Friday, July 12. Preparations to anticipate this are in progress. You will be informed of a meeting to be held shortly in the Westerkerk. By then we shall have our hands on an advance copy of their Bible. We will discuss our own announcement for the world press which will precede theirs by two days. We shall do more than blunt their propaganda. We shall destroy and silence them forever.

In the name of the Father, the Son, and the Future of Our Faith,

DOMINEE MAERTIN DE VROOME

Hand trembling, Randall gave the paper back to Dr. Deichhardt. "How did he find out?" Randall wondered, almost to himself.

"That is the question," said Dr. Deichhardt.

"And what are you going to do about it?" Randall wanted to know.

"That is the other question," said Dr. Deichhardt. "As to this question, we have already decided upon our first step. Since Dominee de Vroome knows our announcement date, we have decided to change it to a new and earlier date, and keep the revised date a secret among those in this room—and a few others like Hennig—to the very last moment. We have moved up the announcement press conference from Friday, July 12th, to Monday, July 8th, four days earlier. You no doubt can rearrange our reservations for the royal palace and the satellite broadcast."

Randall shifted uneasily in his seat. "I'm not worried about that. It'll be done. I'm worried about the lack of time you're giving my department. You're giving me only until two weeks and three days from tomorrow to prepare the most comprehensive publicity campaign in modern times. I don't know whether it can be done."

"If you are a believer, anything can be done." The speaker was Signore Gayda. "Faith can move mountains."

"Or for the unbeliever," said Monsieur Fontaine, breaking his long silence, "a cash bonus might serve as a better bulldozer than faith."

"I don't need a bonus for myself or my staff," snapped Randall. "I need what apparently I can't have—time." He shrugged. "Okay, two and a half weeks."

"Excellent," said Dr. Deichhardt. "Another reason for moving up our announcement is not only to outmaneuver de Vroome, but to narrow the period in which something might go wrong. Another leak of our progress might be sprung. Mr. Randall, we've already alerted Herr Hennig in Mainz of the change and the necessity to have some of the bound Bibles here earlier. He will deliver them, and so your staff members will have adequate opportunity to read Petronius and James and prepare their work. But by so doing, we expose ourselves to the ultimate danger. You have read Dominee de Vroome's note. He promises his followers he will possess a copy of our International New Testament before we can give it to the public. His tone is one of arrogant certainty. He expects that the same traitor who turned over your secret memorandum to him will soon deliver to him our Book of Books. This brings us to both questions. How did de Vroome obtain your memorandum? How will he get hold of our Bible? In short, who is the traitor in our midst?"

"Yes, who is the damn Judas Iscariot in this building?" Wheeler exclaimed. "Who's selling us out to Satan for thirty lousy pieces of silver?"

"And how do we catch him," said Dr. Deichhardt, "before he helps destroy us?"

Randall looked around the table. "Have there been any ideas?"

Inspector Heldering, who had been making notes on a pad, lifted his head. "I have suggested the lie-detector test for all persons—the twenty-one—who received or knew of the memorandum."

"No, no," said Dr. Deichhardt firmly. "It would give away too much to too many, and disrupt and demoralize those who are loyal."

"But all are not loyal," persisted Inspector Heldering.

"Certainly there is one who is disloyal. I can think of no other method."

"There must be a better way," said Dr. Deichhardt.

Randall, half listening, was trying to fasten on to a fleeting thought that had passed through his head. His imagination had been awakened, and his mind was churning. The very means by which they had been betrayed might be used a second time to trap the betrayer. He tried to think it through, ignoring the helpless voices around him, and the notion developed in seconds, logical and foolproof.

Suddenly, he interrupted the others. "I have an idea," he said. "It might work. It is something we can try immediately."

The conference room hushed. He felt every eye upon him. He stood up, rubbing his pipe thoughtfully, and he paced a few steps behind his chair and returned to the table.

"It's almost too simple, but I can't find a flaw in it," he told the group. "Listen. Suppose we invent a second top-secret memorandum, a follow-up one concerning our promotion plans. What it contains does not matter. It must look like a piece of hard information about our promotion that would logically come right after the royal palace announcement. Say we send this memo to the same people who received the other memo—well, we don't have to include anyone in this room—you're in on it—but we'll send copies to every one of the others. Each copy of the new memo would be exactly the same, except for one word. In each memo there would be one word not in the others. We would keep a record of the person to whom we sent the memo—and beside his name we would jot the unique word that was in his memo. Do you see what I'm driving at? When the memo goes out, the person here who is betraying us will pass it on word for word to de Vroome, isn't that so? Your informer in de Vroome's headquarters would learn of it and report back to you. Since no memorandum would be precisely the same as the others, because of the single word change, you'd look for the different word in the memo de Vroome received.

and be able to find out the person who had passed on his copy of the memo. You'd know your traitor."

He paused to observe the reaction.

"Not bad, not bad at all," said Wheeler.

Dr. Deichhardt, as well as several of the others, appeared confused.

"I want to be sure I understand your plan," said the German publisher. "Can you give a concrete example?"

Randall's mind was alive, creating, and he already had a specific approach. "Okay. Let's take Christ's Last Supper. How many of his disciples were there with him?"

"Twelve, of course," said Sir Trevor Young. "You know —Thomas, Matthew and all the rest."

"Okay, twelve," said Randall. "That'll work nicely. Now I'll get up a list of twelve matching names of twelve people inside this project who received or heard about the last memorandum. No need to include anyone in this room, as I said before. There are eight of us here, including Naomi. That leaves thirteen possibilities. Subtract one I'll need to help me in preparing this. Subtract Jessica Taylor. I'll gamble on her. That leaves twelve names to get the baited memo. If one of those twelve doesn't sell us out, then the traitor has to be Jessica or Naomi or me or one of you around this table. But we're betting one of the twelve will repeat the business of passing the new memo along to de Vroome. . . . Naomi, give us the names of the twelve."

Naomi rose and read from her list. "Dr. Jeffries, Dr. Trautmann, Reverend Zachery, Monsignore Riccardi, Professor Sobrier, Mr. Groat, Albert Kremer, Angela Monti, Paddy O'Neal, Les Cunningham, Elwin Alexander, Helen de Boer."

Another thought entered Randall's head. Dr. Florian Knight, recently arrived. He considered adding Dr. Knight's name, but he was afraid. The young Oxford don, embittered by the project that had ruined his own book, could not be admitted to this game yet. Still, if he were that much of a risk, he should be included. Yet, knowing Knight's problem, Randall hated to tempt him. Randall told himself that it was not necessary, anyway. Dr. Jeffries would likely share his own memorandum with his protégé.

"Fine, Naomi," said Randall. "Those are the ones who'll get our new memo."

Dr. Deichhardt uttered a heavy sigh. "It is difficult even to imagine one of them betraying us. Each has been cleared, most of them have been with Resurrection Two from the outset, and all have a personal stake in the security of the new Bible."

"Someone did it, Professor," said Wheeler.

"Yes, yes, I suppose so. . . . Go ahead, Mr. Randall."

Randall resumed. "Okay, let's say the memorandum reads something like this: 'Confidential. It has been decided to follow the royal palace announcement of our publication—the announcement day dedicated to the glory of Jesus Christ—with twelve successive days dedicated to the twelve disciples the New Testament mentions by name. These days will be devoted to public affairs celebrating the new Bible. The first of the twelve days will be dedicated to the disciple Andrew.' Okay, we send that memorandum to Dr. Jeffries. The code name for Dr. Jeffries becomes Disciple Andrew. Now we prepare another copy of the memorandum, exactly the same contents except for the last sentence. This would read: 'The first of the twelve days will be dedicated to the disciple Philip.' We send this memorandum to Helen de Boer. The code name for Helen de Boer becomes Disciple Philip. The third memorandum, the same as the others, ends its last sentence with the disciple Thomas. We send this to the Reverend Zachery. Thereafter, the code name for Zachery becomes Disciple Thomas. And so on down the list, matching a different disciple to each different recipient of the memorandum. If word gets back to us tomorrow that de Vroome got his hands on one copy of the memorandum, it is likely he obtained it from the member of our group to whom it had been sent. If we learn de Vroome's copy has—let's say—the disciple Andrew in it, then we know that for whatever motives our weak link is Dr. Jeffries. Is that clear?"

There was a chorus of assent from the others, and Dr. Deichhardt muttered, "Too clear, and too frightening."

"Too frightening?" Randall repeated.

"To conceive of one of our twelve betraying us."

"If one of Christ's twelve disciples could betray Him," said Randall quietly, "why should we not believe one of our own could be ready to betray Him, also—betray Him and destroy us?"

"You are right," said Dr. Deichhardt. He rose ponderously, surveyed his fellow publishers, and turned to Randall. "We are in agreement. Too much is at stake to entertain disbelief or sentimentality. Yes, Mr. Randall, go ahead. You can set your trap at once."

IT HAD BEEN a long day, and now, at eleven twenty in the evening, Steve Randall was glad to be returning to his rooms in the Amstel Hotel.

Slouching in the rear seat of the Mercedes-Benz limousine, he was conscious of the folded single sheet of paper tucked with his wallet in the inside breast pocket of his sport jacket. On that sheet he had personally typed the names of Christ's twelve disciples, which had been used in the twelve copies of the memorandum that he and Jessica Taylor had prepared. After each disciple's name had been typed the name of the member of Resurrection Two who had been sent that copy of the memorandum.

He pondered the length of time it would take the betrayer in their midst to send the memorandum itself, or convey its contents, to the Dominee Maertin de Vroome. His earlier memorandum on the staging of the announcement had reached de Vroome within three hours of its release. This memorandum, each version typed by Jessica, had gone out forty-five minutes after he had left the meeting with the publishers. The copies had been hand-delivered by Heldering's security personnel, to recipients still at work in the Krasnapolsky or to those who were in their own hotels or apartments in Amsterdam. Signatures of the recipients had been required, and Randall had waited in Heldering's office until he had been assured that all twelve had received their memorandums and signed for them.

That had been more than five hours ago. If the contents were going to be relayed to de Vroome, Randall was certain that the cleric had the information in hand by now. Randall could only hope that their own spy, planted inside de Vroome's operation, would remain undetected, vigilant, and would report the exact version of the blue memorandum that the enemy had received.

Again, Randall tried to deduce which of their own, for motives of love or money, was selling them out.

He could not begin to imagine. He could only pray, pray that the impostor be caught and removed before he laid hands on their precious secret, the advance edition of the International New Testament that Herr Hennig would soon deliver from Mainz.

While still in his office, Randall had telephoned Angela to ask her to join him for a late dinner. Although fatigued, he had been unable to resist seeing her this evening. They had dined quietly together in the elegant restaurant of the Hotel Polen, and exchanged reminiscences of their own lives. Afterwards, even though he was tired, Randall knew that it would have been impossible for him to part from this girl were it not for the fact that he would be seeing her again in the morning. He had dropped her off at the Victoria Hotel, and even now, returning to his own place, he could still feel the lingering softness of her lips on his own.

His car was turning left, and a minute later, having bade Theo good night, Randall stood on the sidewalk before the Amstel.

About to go into the hotel, he heard someone call out to him. He stopped, turned around, as the man hailing him emerged swiftly from the shadows of the parking island.

"Mr. Randall!" the man called out a second time. "One moment, please!"

The man striding toward him became fully visible in the illumination from the hotel.

Cedric Plummer.

More angered than surprised, Randall started to turn away, but Plummer grabbed him by the arm.

Randall yanked his arm free. "Beat it," he said. "We've got nothing to talk about."

"It's not for me," the Englishman pleaded. "I won't bother you. I've been sent by someone else—someone important—who wants to see you."

Randall was determined not to be taken in. "Sorry, Plummer. I can't think of anyone you know I'd have any interest in seeing."

He moved toward the stone steps, but Plummer stayed with him. "Mr. Randall, wait—listen. It's Dominee Maertin de Vroome—he's the one who just sent me."

Randall halted in his tracks. "De Vroome?" He eyed the journalist suspiciously. "De Vroome sent you to find me?"

"Yes, absolutely," said Plummer, bobbing his head.

"How do I know this is not some kind of trick you're playing?"

"It's not, I swear. Why would I lie? What have I got to gain?"

Randall teetered between distrust and an excited desire to believe. "What would de Vroome want to see me about?"

"I haven't the faintest notion."

"I'm sure you haven't," said Randall sardonically. "And what reason would de Vroome have for using you, a foreign journalist, as his go-between? He could simply pick up the telephone and call me himself."

Encouraged by Randall's question, Plummer responded eagerly. "Because he does everything by indirection, obliquely. He is circumspect in all personal contracts. A man in his position has to be wary. He would not chance calling you, nor would he desire to see you or be seen with you in public. If you knew Dominee de Vroome you'd understand his behavior."

"And you know him?"

"Quite well, Mr. Randall. I'm proud to call him a friend."

Randall remembered Plummer's sensational interview

with de Vroome for the *London Daily Courier*. It had been an exclusive and lengthy firsthand interview. Somehow, for Randall, it lent credibility to Plummer's claim of friendship with the Dutch cleric.

Randall considered a meeting with de Vroome. It offered many pitfalls, offsetting the advantages. But an irresistible factor prodded Randall. The only shadow that had fallen across Randall's future and the success of Resurrection Two had been the shadow of the enigmatical de Vroome. It was not often that one had the chance to come face to face with the enemy who had cast the shadow. Truly irresistible, this opportunity. Dominee de Vroome was big game, the biggest.

Randall stared at the anxious journalist. "When does de Vroome want to see me?" Randall asked.

"Now, right now, if it is convenient for you."

"It must be urgent if he wants to see me at this late hour."

"I can't say whether it is urgent. I know he's a night person."

"Where is he?"

"In his office at the Westerkerk."

"Okay, let's find out what the great man wants."

Minutes later they were driving in Plummer's five-year-old Jaguar coupé along the darkened Prinsengracht—the Canal of the Princes—which snaked around the western perimeter of Amsterdam's central city and the Dam. Sunk low in a bucket seat of the sport car, Randall studied Plummer's profile—the thinning hair, small eyes, colorless complexion enlivened only by the tuft of beard—and he speculated on just how close the British journalist was to the powerful leader of religious radicalism.

"Plummer, I'm curious about de Vroome and yourself. You called him your friend—"

"That's right." Plummer kept his eyes on the road.

"What kind of friend? Are you his press propagandist and in his pay? Are you working for his reform movement? Or are you merely one of his many spies?"

Plummer's ring-laden fingers left the wheel and waved several times in a gesture of dismissal, a gesture peculiarly effeminate. "Heavens, no, my dear chap, nothing quite so melodramatic as that. To be the soul of candor, I would say that the Dominee and I have found a common interest—namely, your new Bible scheme up there behind the walls of the Grand Hotel Krasnapolsky. We both have our different reasons for wishing to learn what we can of it before your Dr. Deichhardt spoon-feeds it to the masses. I've found that I can help Dominee de Vroome in this respect, in small ways, turning in to him oddments of information, tidbits, the droppings a journalist is always able to come across. In return, I rather expect the Dominee will help me in one large way—giving me the exclusive story to write for the world market before you get to announce it." He offered Randall a sickly buck-toothed smile. "Sorry, old boy, if this rubs you wrongly, but *c'est la guerre.*"

Randall was more amused than annoyed at his companion's frankness. "You're rather sure your friend de Vroome can serve our heads up on a platter for you, aren't you?"

Plummer offered his furtive smile again. "I'm sure."

"Well, at least you've given us fair warning."

"The playing fields of Eton and all that." Then he added, without a smile, "Whatever else you may think of me, I am a gentleman, Mr. Randall. And so is Dominee de Vroome."

"Yes, de Vroome," said Randall. "I know only a little about him. What is he officially? Head of the Dutch Reformed Church?"

"There is no official head of the Nederlands Hervormd Kerk—the Dutch Reformed Church. The four to five million Protestants here, in 1,466 parishes in eleven provinces, elect fifty-four representatives, some ministers, some elders, to the synod. You might say the synod heads the Dutch church, but actually it doesn't. Its members are witnesses, not bishops. Dominee de Vroome likes to say that the synod is not the authority but rather the conscience of the church. The church here is very community-centered, almost anarchistic to an Englishman or an American. The Dominee was elected by the church council of this community to head one individual local church, the most important one in Holland, true, but still one church. He has told me time and again that he has no special authority even in his own church. His only power derives from his personality. His sole duties are to speak well and listen well, and never to forget that his church is really the people's church. I mention this so that you will understand the man you are about to meet."

"You make him sound like a simple neighborhood pastor," said Randall. "I've heard he's the leader of the Radical Reform Christian Movement, with legions of clerical and lay followers throughout the world."

"That is true, also," agreed Plummer, "but it doesn't contradict what I was saying. On a local level he carries no more weight than a peasant. And this very fact—that in practice he is what he preaches, the incarnation of a relevant people's faith—is what makes him a king abroad. As for being branded a radical, the word is made to sound so ominous. A radical is simply someone who wishes to make immediate fundamental and drastic changes in the existing order. In that sense, yes, Dominee de Vroome is a radical church leader."

Plummer pointed over the steering wheel. "There it is, his headquarters, the Westerkerk, consecrated in 1631, built like a cross in neoclassic style, probably the highest tower in Amsterdam. Ugly pile, eh? But it is Holland's first church—Dutch royalty is married there—and de Vroome's presence probably makes it Protestantism's first church."

They parked in the Westermarkt, and Randall waited in the square while the Englishman locked his Jaguar.

To Randall, the house of worship ahead resembled an oversized Dutch house crowned by a stark steeple reaching for the sky. This combination made it appear both friendly and forbidding, exactly like its main tenant, Randall suspected. Examining the façade more carefully in the lamplight, Randall could see that it was constructed of small bricks that had aged from red to brown, and now looked like dried blood. Randall decided that the total look was really forbidding, as was probably Dominee de Vroome himself.

"What does Dominee mean?" Randall asked Plummer, who had come up alongside him.

"Master," said the British journalist. "That's from the Latin *dominus,* and the equivalent here of Reverend. Incidentally, when you address de Vroome, you call him Dominee too."

As they started toward the church, Randall said, "De Vroome sent you to invite me here. He didn't know whether I'd accept. Do you think he's expecting me?"

"He's expecting you."

"And you're positive you don't know what he wants to talk about?"

"I wouldn't expect him to tell me. He'll tell you." Plummer paused. "Of course, I can guess."

"He's not going to try to force some information out of me, is he?"

"My dear chap, the Dominee isn't as crude as all that. He may be persuasive, but he's a pacifist. I'm afraid you've been conditioned by those endless violent films you have on your American television. Or is it that you've heard about those corpses beneath the Westerkerk?"

"What corpses?"

"Oh, you didn't know? In old times, the parishioners were buried beneath the church. This created such a stench that worshipers brought along bottles of eau de cologne when they attended services. In fact, some of the elderly still bring along their bottles of perfume today, although the smell has long since been controlled. No, Mr. Randall, you won't be laid out among those corpses." He gave a toothy grin. "At least, I don't think so."

Randall had an impulse to speak of the hoodlums who had attacked him his first night in Amsterdam at a section of the very canal that ran past the Westerkerk, but he thought better of it.

They veered away from the massive dark Spanish door that fronted the church, and walked toward a small, homey Dutch bungalow, painted green, the windows covered with white voile curtains, that adjoined the church.

They went up four steps to the bungalow door which bore one word: COSTERIJ.

"The main church entrance is locked," Plummer explained. "This is the guardian's house."

The door was unlocked, and they were in an entry hall.

"Let me find out where the Dominee is," said Plummer. He continued into the bungalow, and disappeared. Randall heard his voice and a feminine voice, an exchange in Dutch, and then Plummer reappeared and gestured toward a large door. "He's inside the church."

Randall followed the journalist into the church. The interior was vast and cavernous, and only one of the four bronze chandeliers hanging from the vaulted ceiling was lit, leaving most of the church hidden in darkness. Except for the red strip of carpeting which covered the plank floor up the middle aisle, and formed a cross with an intersecting strip of carpeting at the center of the church, one had the impression of severity and austerity. Instead of pews, there were rows of chairs covered in green velvet, attached to one another so that they seemed like benches, and all the rows faced toward one prominent roofed balcony constructed between stone columns at the center of this place of worship. This, Randall guessed, was the preacher's rostrum.

Plummer had been scanning the interior, and now he pointed toward the center. "There he is. In the front row, across from the pulpit."

Randall focused his eyes, and finally made out the solitary figure of a clergyman, swathed in black, hunched forward in a chair, elbows on his knees, head buried in his hands.

"He is meditating," said Plummer in a respectful whisper.

The distant figure moved. The head lifted, turned in their direction, but the lighting was too poor for Randall to be certain that they had been noticed.

Plummer touched Randall. "He knows you're here. Let's wait in his office. It'll only be a minute or two."

They returned to the entry hall of the guardian's house, climbed a short staircase. At the top were two signs. The one on the left read: WACHT KAMER. The one on the right read: SPREEK KAMER.

"The Waiting Room and the Speaking Room," said Plummer, directing Randall to the right. "The Speaking Room is his office. See the light over the door. It shines red when he doesn't wish to be disturbed."

The office surprised Randall. Despite what Plummer had told him, he had expected an office befitting an internationally known prince of the church. The master's office was unpretentious and cozy. There was a sitting arrangement: a couch, coffee table, two fauteuils. There were a fireplace, a simple desk and straight-back chair, a range of books on shelves, a painting of several rows of coats of arms, and a modern oil painting of *The Last Supper*. The office was brightened by a half-dozen lamps.

Randall refused to sit. Tension had finally taken hold of him. He worried whether this interview might not be considered foolhardy by Deichhardt and Wheeler and the other publishers. Certainly, Inspector Heldering would not have permitted it. Randall had no idea how much or how little his host knew of Resurrection Two. That he knew something, from his spy or spies, was obvious. Whether he knew the contents of the International New Testament or the details of Professor Monti's discoveries was an unknown factor. That he might attempt to trap Randall into some revelation was also a danger to be guarded against.

Perturbed, regretting having come to the lair of the enemy, Randall moved restlessly to the window near the desk. That moment, the door creaked open, and Randall spun around.

Dominee Maertin de Vroome stood inside the door fondling two brown-marked Siamese kittens.

His size and his apparent age were unexpected. He was tall, at least six feet three, and he was relatively young for his station, surely no more than forty-five or forty-eight. He was draped in a long-straight-cut black talar or cassock, which was without adornment. His hair was unusual, flaxen, almost saffron, thick and long. The facial features were ascetic and cadaverous, a high, lined brow, hooded eyes that were disarmingly powder-blue, sunken cheeks, a nearly lipless mouth, a lantern jaw. Although his body was cloaked in the cassock, Randall guessed that the frame beneath was sinewy and spare.

From across the room, Plummer, reduced to an unctuous Uriah Heep, had stammered, "Dominee—this is Mr. Steven Randall. Mr. Randall—Dominee de Vroome."

Unceremoniously, de Vroome dropped the cats to the rug, stepped forward, lank arm extended, and he shook Randall's hand quickly, briefly.

"Welcome to the Westerkerk," he said. His voice was subdued, but throaty and vibrant. "It is generous of you to come at this hour. I will try not to keep you too long. I had heard of you, of course. I thought a meeting might be to the advantage of both of us. I would suggest you sit on the sofa. It is the most comfortable place in the room. It may even tend to lower your resistance."

A cool customer, Randall thought, as he sank down on the couch. Cool, urbane, formidable.

"What makes you think I have any resistance to lower?" asked Randall.

Dominee de Vroome did not reply. He made a gesture toward Plummer that told the journalist he could remain in the office. Plummer lowered himself nervously into a chair against the bookcases and seemed to melt into the books. Dominee de Vroome glanced at his desk top, as if checking for messages. Then, satisfied, he came to a chair directly facing Randall, gathered his cassock about him, and sat down.

He addressed himself to Randall. "I would assume that as a new member of Resurrection Two—whatever that idiotic code name may mean, although I believe I can conjecture a correct answer—I would assume that you have already been carefully briefed about me, about my role as an opponent to the religious orthodoxy your employers represent. Therefore, having heard only one side of it, and out of a natural loyalty toward those for whom you work, you would have to regard me as the Devil incarnate. Your guard is up. You are understandably resistant."

Randall could not help but smile. "Wouldn't you be, too, Dominee? I am in the business of keeping a secret. You are dedicated to finding out that secret."

De Vroome's lipless mouth formed an indulgent smile. "Mr. Randall, I have means other than using you to uncover the purpose of Resurrection Two and the exact contents of its newly translated New Testament. You are my guest, and I have no intention of making you uneasy by probing for what you have pledged to keep concealed."

"Thank you," said Randall. "Then may I ask, what can you possibly want of me?"

"Mainly, your ear. To what end, you shall learn shortly. First, it is vital that you know what I stand for and what your employers and their lackeys stand for. You believe that you already know, when in fact you do not."

"I'll try to be open-minded," promised Randall.

De Vroome's bony fingers flickered. "No one can be fully open-minded. Everyone's brain is a jungle of prejudices, taboos, folk tales, deceits. I cannot expect that you will open your mind entirely to let all that I say go in. I request only that your mind not remain entirely closed to me."

"It is not closed," said Randall, wondering what difference it made, one way or another, to de Vroome.

"What I believe in, what millions in every land who believe as I do stand for, demand, insist upon, is a new church, one meaningful for and relevant to today's society and its needs," said de Vroome. "This requires, beforehand, a new understanding of the Scriptures, which must be read in the light of our scientific knowledge and progress. Dr. Rudolf Bultmann, the German theologian, sounded the first call to arms in our nonviolent revolution. To him, it was time-wasting to seek an earthly Jesus. To Dr. Bultmann, what mattered was seeking the essence, the deeper meanings, the truths, of the early church's faith—the kerygma—by demythologizing the New Testament, stripping, as he said, the gospel message of its nonfactual elements. To reunite modern man with reli-

gion, Dr. Bultmann believed, we must rid the New
Testament of the Virgin Birth, the miracles, the Resurrection, the unscientific promises of heaven or threats
of hell. As the heirs of all the investigators from Galileo
and Newton to Mendel and Darwin, we find it implausible
to accept, as Alan Watts has pointed out, 'the inheritance
of Original Sin from Adam, the Immaculate Conception of
Mary, the Virgin Birth of Jesus, the Atonement for sin
by his Crucifixion, his physical Resurrection from his death,
his corporeal Ascension into Heaven, and the resurrection
of our bodies from death on the morning of the Last
Judgment, which will consign us both physically and
spiritually to everlasting bliss or everlasting torture.' In
order to believe, what modern man wants and can
accept as plausible is a message from a wise man or
teacher, who might have been named Jesus, a message
that helps modern man to contend with the reality of
existence—or, as one Oxford theologian summarized Dr.
Bultmann's thinking, to give every person a message 'by
which he can face up to his being one who is going to
die and so begin to live authentically.' In short, to para-
phrase something said of Renan, we have to produce a
person who is not possessed by faith, but who possesses
faith. Do I make myself clear, Mr. Randall?"

"You do, Dominee."

"We have reached the stage where I believe it necessary, for our time, to revise the Scriptures more radically,
if the gospel is to be a useful instrument in assisting and
saving modern man. Belief in Jesus Christ as a Messiah
or as a historical being is of no importance to religion
today. What is of importance is rereading, in new depth,
the social message of the early Christians. It does not
matter who spoke the message or who wrote it. It does
matter what meaning the message can have today, especially when the message is freed of its supernatural and
mythical elements, and strained and purified to leave its
residue of love of man for man and its belief in brotherhood. Which brings me to the conservatives, the keepers of
the old Christ and the old myths, whom you are prepared
to represent—"

"How do you know they are that conservative?" Randall interrupted. "How can you be so sure they are not also prepared for drastic change?"

"Because I have known them personally, each and every one, and I know what they stand for. I will not speak of your five publishers, the promoters of a new Bible. They are beneath contempt. Their interests are selfish, commercial, and their only Scripture is their profit ledgers and their only religion is their individual gross national product. To survive, they need the support of your Trautmanns, Zacherys, Sobriers, Riccardis, Jeffries, as well as the old-fashioned church councils and Bible societies. These are the ones whose belief in Christ, whose husbanding and protecting of their Lord, has stultified and retarded religion and the church for centuries. They know the basic reason for religion is death. And so they preach false fear and false hope at one and the same time, and they drop a curtain of ritual and dogma between themselves and the real problems of real human beings. True theology, we've been told by Tillich, is about that which concerns us ultimately—the meaning of our existence, the significance of life. Yet those orthodox theologians ignore this. As my friends at the Centro pro Unione in Rome say, these are the ones who wish only to preserve the old religious club, the orthodox status quo, from the inevitable process of dissolution. Unless they reform, or give way to us who would reform, the world will consist of new generations without religion, without faith, without the heart for survival that can grow only from faith."

"You've spoken of a purging of the Bible," said Randall. "But how would you reform the organization of the church itself?"

"You mean in a practical way?"

"Yes, in a practical way."

"To put it concisely—" said de Vroome. He absently patted the Siamese cat rubbing against his leg as he considered what he would say before speaking again. "The new church I advocate will be one church, Protestant and Catholic as one. It will have Christian unity. An ecumenical spirit—one world in one church—will prevail. This church will not promote a blind faith, miracles, celibacy and irrefutable authority for its clergy. This church will reject riches, will spend its money on its people and not on massive cathedrals like the Westerkerk, Westminster Abbey, Notre Dame, St. Patrick's in New York. It will work in the community, through small groups which will not suffer sermonizing but will enjoy spiritual celebrations. It will integrate minorities, it will acknowledge the equality of women, it will promote social action. It will support birth control, abortion, artificial insemination, psychiatric help, sex education. It will oppose governments and private industries that are in the business of killing, oppressing, polluting, exploiting. It will be a church of social compassion, and its clergy and its members will act out, will live, not merely mouth, the Sermon on the Mount."

"And you don't feel the theologians and publishers at Resurrection Two want that kind of Christianity, too?"

De Vroome's mouth curved into a lipless smile again. "Do you think they want what I want, what the great mass of people want? If so, you ask them. Ask why they oppose my movement, if it is not merely to preserve their traditional ways and their hierarchy. Ask them why, in matters of Christian ethics, they always vacillate from compromise to obdurate fanaticism. Compromise is laziness. Fanaticism is excess of zeal, and therefore lack of love. There is a third solution—that of the hour—that of solving the immediate needs of our fellows and neighbors. Ask your associates whether they are prepared to give up dogmatic church teachings for free discussions. Ask them what they are doing—*now*—about race relations, poverty, the unequal distribution of wealth. Ask them whether they are prepared to surrender their fat institutions for a universal Christian community, where the minister or priest is not a special person, not a dignitary, but simply a servant who can bring to those who employ him a spiritual life. Ask them these questions, Mr. Randall, and when you have their answers, you will understand what they will not understand. That the main problem of life is not to prepare for what comes after life is ended—the main problem is how to provide heaven right here on earth today."

Dominee de Vroome paused, stared at Randall for several seconds, and he resumed, measuring each word.

"As to this secret Bible your friends are readying—whatever is in it, whatever good tidings it has to offer, whatever sensation it creates—it is not a product of love. The motives behind its publication are both unsavory and sinful. For the publishers, the motive is pure profit. For the orthodox theologians, the motive is largely to divert millions of people from earthly reform, to mesmerize or frighten them into returning to the old hopelessness of the ritualized mystical, dreamland church. I assure you, with that new Bible of theirs they expect to kill my movement and wipe out the underground church. With that Bible, they mean to revive the religion of the hereafter and put an end to the religion of now. Yes, Mr. Randall, their motives are unsavory and sinful—"

Randall had to protest. "Dominee, if I may interrupt. I honestly think you are going too far. You may have a valid complaint about the publishers, although I feel you're judging them too harshly. Anyway, I won't try to vouch for their motives. But I've met the rest of the staff involved in this project, and I believe these people are devout, honest, and sincere defenders of what they regard as divine revelation. Take Dr. Bernard Jeffries, at Oxford. He was the first of the theologians I met. I believe his dedication to the project derives solely from his devotion to scholarship and spiritual—"

Dominee de Vroome held up a hand. "Stop right there, Mr. Randall. You say—take Dr. Bernard Jeffries. Let me take Dr. Jeffries as a perfect example of what concerns me. That he is a man of scholarly pursuits I will not deny. That he may be a man of religious conviction I will not question. But those are not the main motives for his participation in producing your new Bible. There is another motive, and it is entirely political."

"Political?" repeated Randall. "I cannot believe that."

"Can't you? Have you ever heard of the World Council of Churches?"

"Of course. My father is a clergyman. I've heard him speak of it."

"Do you know anything about it?" de Vroome persisted tenaciously.

Randall hesitated. "It's—as I recall—it's an international organization that includes most Protestant church groups. I can't recall any details."

"Allow me to refresh your memory, and in so doing, paint you a clearer picture of your unselfish Dr. Jeffries." The Dutch cleric's countenance had, in Randall's eyes, frosted over. The vibrant voice had become harder. "The World Council of Churches in Geneva is composed of 239 Protestant, Orthodox, Anglican churches from ninety nations. These churches possess 400,000,000 members throughout the world. The World Council is the only religious organization outside of Rome with a potential of authority and control that matches the Vatican. Yet, since its formation in this city in 1948, and to this day, it has in no way resembled the Vatican. As the first general secretary announced at the first assembly, 'We are a Council of Churches, not *the* Council of one undivided Church.' And as the third assembly proclaimed from India, 'The World Council of Churches is a fellowship of churches which confess the Lord Jesus Christ as God and Saviour according to the Scriptures.' In short, the Council is a loosely knit body of varied churches with different social and racial backgrounds, seeking interchurch communication, seeking Christian unity, striving for a consensus of faith and common social action. Between its assemblies, held every five or six years, its policy is implemented by a Central Committee and an Executive Committee. Now, the two most active positions in the organization are those of the general secretary, who has a full-time paying job, and the chairman, who has an honorary job. Of this pair, the general secretary, who heads the Geneva staff of two hundred persons, who is the liaison officer between member churches, who speaks for the Council to the

outside world—this general secretary has the greater influence."

"Yet, he is not an authority figure?"

"Definitely not, as things stand today," said de Vroome.
"The general secretary has no judicial power. I repeat,
he has influence, and a potential to wield power. Which
brings us to your scholarly, spiritual, unselfish Dr. Bernard Jeffries. The hierarchy of the orthodox church—the
senior ecclesiastics, the entrenched conservatives—has a
plan afoot today to overwhelm the next assembly of the
World Council of Churches, to make Dr. Jeffries the next
general secretary in Geneva, and through him to restruc-
ture the World Council into a protestant Vatican, with
Geneva its headquarters. Thus, the conservatives will rule
by edict and proclamation, and direct the adherents of
all churches backwards toward blind faith and end all
hopes of a living, breathing, vital people's faith. And
how will the orthodox cabal accomplish this? Through
the excitement, the propaganda, engendered by the new
Bible being prepared by your crowd at Resurrection Two."

Listening, Randall had a vague recollection of hearing
Dr. Jeffries' name linked with the World Council before.
He tried to recall where he had heard this. Then he remembered. From Valeri Hughes, Dr. Knight's fiancée, in
London. But there had been some logic in that earlier
reference to Dr. Jeffries as a candidate for general secretary of the Council. Now, in de Vroome's version, the
motives behind the candidacy shed a different and uglier
light upon it.

Randall spoke what was next on his mind. "Does Dr.
Jeffries know of this plan?"

"Know?" said de Vroome. "He's at the forefront of the
scheme, actively collaborating and politicking in secrecy
to promote himself to general secretary. I have documentation—copies of correspondence between Jeffries and his
conspirators—to support every word I have told you."

"And do you think he can make it?"

"He can make it if your new Bible gives him enough
publicity, distinction, and stature."

"Let me reframe and pose my question again," said Randall. "Do you think Dr. Jeffries *will* make it?"

"No," said Dominee de Vroome flatly. The lipless smile once more. "No, he will not make it, and they will not make it."

"Why not?"

"Because I intend to stop them. I intend to stop them by demolishing Jeffries' springboard to power—your new Bible—by discrediting and destroying it before you can announce it and circulate it among the public. Once that is done, there will be another general secretary for the World Council of Churches. You see, Mr. Randall, I intend to be the next general secretary."

Randall showed his amazement. "You? But I thought you were against ecclesiastical authority and—"

"I am," de Vroome said brusquely. "That is why I must be the next general secretary of the World Council. To protect it from the power-hungry. To preserve it for Christian unity. To make it even more responsive to social change."

Randall felt bewilderment. He could not perceive whether the Dominee was honest in the virtues he professed, or he was himself as ambitious and political as those he opposed. And there was something more. De Vroome had just spoken of the need to destroy the new Bible. Randall felt that he must confront the Dominee with the unreasonableness of his determination to destroy.

"I can't comment on who should be the next general secretary of the World Council," said Randall. "But I feel I can and must comment on an attitude you've taken toward a revised version of the New Testament that you have never seen, never read, know little about. Political advantages aside, I really can't see how you can wish to destroy—that was your word, *destroy*—a Bible that may provide millions of people with comfort, with new faith and new hope, a work that may promote brotherhood and love, the very ends you seek with your movement. How do you find it morally defensible to destroy the Word when you know nothing of its message?"

De Vroome frowned. "I don't need to know its message

beforehand," he said sternly. "Because I know its messengers."

"What does that mean?"

"I know everything that needs to be known about the persons involved in the discovery, the authentication, the production, and the promotion of your Bible."

For the first time, Randall began to lose control of his temper. "What are you insinuating?" he said with an edge to his voice. "I've met the important personnel on the project. And, as I've told you, I've come to know some of these people quite well. Most of them, I am positive, are decent, sincere, honest, and most of them have integrity and are filled with good purpose. You can't know them half so well as I do."

"Really?" said de Vroome with amusement. He stood up. "In that case, let's find out what you know—and what I know—about your devoted and faithful flock."

Infuriated by the clergyman's overweening self-assurance, Randall tried to contain himself as he watched Dominee de Vroome go around to the back of his desk. From inside his cassock, de Vroome brought out a key, opened a desk drawer, pulled out a file folder, opened it and laid it on his desk.

He sat down, took out a thick sheaf of papers, riffled through them, deliberated a moment, and held up the pages for Randall to see. "My dossier on the personnel connected with Resurrection Two," said de Vroome. "Too much for you to read." He dropped the sheaf on the open folder, rested his elbows on the edge of the desk, and cupped his chin in the palms of his hands. "I can tell you all that you need know about your flock in a few minutes."

"You may be telling me lies."

"You need only go to each person I speak of to verify what I've told you. In fact, I invite you to do so."

"Go ahead," said Randall tartly.

"We've disposed of your selfless Dr. Bernard Jeffries," said Dominee de Vroome. His tone remained calm and matter-of-fact. "Let us examine several others in your circle. Let us take George L. Wheeler, your wealthy American religious publisher, who hired you for this project. What do you know of him? Do you know that this captain of industry was on the verge of bankruptcy when he arranged to sell out his firm to Mr. Towery, president of the cartel Cosmos Enterprises? Yes, it is true. But the deal has not yet been consummated. It is contingent on the successful publication of your new Bible. For Wheeler, the new Bible must be a success if he is to survive in business and retain his social station. As for Towery, his only interest in taking over Wheeler's publishing house is to acquire the prestige his connection with the new Bible will give him in his prominent Baptist circle. That is the reason Wheeler hired you—to satisfy Towery and to save himself by making sure the new Bible becomes the most famous one in history."

"You're telling me nothing I didn't know already," said Randall, intensely annoyed with de Vroome's arrogance, and unwilling to admit that he had heard something new. But he had not known that Wheeler's entire business survival depended on the success of the International New Testament.

"I've told you nothing you didn't know already?" repeated de Vroome. "Perhaps I can improve my record. Let us take the new Bernadette of Lourdes, your plain little secretary, Miss Lori Cook. You were at the hospital this morning, the Free University Hospital, and you witnessed the results of a miracle, did you not? Your Miss Cook has been a cripple since childhood, but yesterday she had a vision, and today she can walk normally. Imagine! I am sorry for you and for her, because the fact is—Miss Lori Cook could always walk normally. She is neither a traitor to your project nor a cheat. She is only a sick, neurotic, pathetic fake. It was easy to check her story in America, if one only looked. A phone call to a cleric in our movement, in Miss Cook's home vicinity, produced the truth, and the documentation is on its way. We have evidence of Lori Cook's athletic prowess in secondary school, a prowess which demanded sturdy legs. Her true affliction was that she was unattractive, never received attention or love, and she made up her mind when she enlisted in your project to play the cripple and win the affection of pity. Recently, she saw that she could gain more attention and indulgence by playing Bernadette, so now she is playing this new role. She is cured, she is attended, she is loved. Soon she will be legend. But, Mr. Randall, do not make her legend in order to promote your Bible. If you do, we shall be forced to expose her —and you—in public. I would not want to hurt the poor child. I won't ask you to believe me, or my word here—"

"I don't," said Randall, shaken by de Vroome's disclosure.

"—I will only ask you not to be foolhardy enough to use Lori Cook in your promotion. Should you do so, you will regret it." De Vroome lifted a cat to his lap, and then sifted the papers before him. "Which of your flock would you like me to discuss next? Ah, perhaps those you met on your journey this past week—the ones you believe you know so well and trust? Shall we speak of them?"

Randall said nothing.

"By silence, you give consent?" asked de Vroome. "Briefly, then. You were last in Mainz, Germany. You spent the day with Karl Hennig. An excellent, forthright fellow, this German printer of yours, is he not? A lover of Gutenberg and of fine books, is he not? He is also more. He is the Karl Hennig who, on the evening of May 10, 1933, joined thousands of other Nazi students in a torchlight parade through Berlin, culminating in a mass celebration at the square on Unter den Linden. There Karl Hennig and his fellows, so admired by Dr. Goebbels, consigned twenty thousand books to a bonfire, books by Einstein, Zweig, Mann, Freud, Zola, Jack London, Havelock Ellis, Upton Sinclair. Yes, Karl Hennig, beloved Bible printer and Nazi book burner. For this information, I give credit to my friend"—De Vroome gestured behind him—"Mr. Cedric Plummer."

Dazed by what he was hearing, Randall had almost forgotten Plummer was still in the room.

He saw Plummer smirking with gratification, heard him

saying, "It is true. I have the negative of an old photograph of young Hennig throwing books into the bonfire."

For Randall, the events in Mainz and Frankfurt yesterday were coming into focus. Hennig had probably refused to see Plummer in Mainz until he learned the reason for the journalist's visit. After that, Hennig had met with Plummer in Frankfurt. Now the reason for the meeting was clear: blackmail.

"Why in the hell discredit Hennig?" Randall blurted out to Plummer. "What have you got to gain by it?"

"A pristine advance copy of your new Bible," said Plummer, grinning. "A cheap price to pay to recover the negative of an old photograph."

Dominee de Vroome moved his head in assent. "Exactly," he said. "A copy of the new Bible is our price."

Randall sank back into the couch, unable to speak.

"Just two more and we will be done," Dominee de Vroome went on relentlessly. "Let us consider your remarkable and objective man of science, Professor Henri Aubert, with his carbon-14 dating process. You were in Paris with Professor Aubert. He told you, I am sure, that the discovery he authenticated restored his faith, his humanity, his desire to give his wife the child that she had always wanted, did he not? He told you she is with his child, did he not? He lied to you. Professor Aubert lied to you. He is physically incapable of giving his wife a child. How so? Because years ago, he underwent a successful vasectomy. He believed in birth control, and he chose to be sterilized by a surgeon, had the vas deferens which carried the sperm from his testicles to his seminal vesicles—the tubes that carried the sperm for procreation —severed and tied off. Your Professor Aubert is not to be trusted. He deceived you. He cannot give his wife a child."

"But he did!" Randall exclaimed. "I met Madame Aubert. I saw her. She is pregnant."

De Vroome's smile was once more indulgent. "Mr. Randall, I did not say Madame Aubert could not be pregnant. I said only that she could not be pregnant by Professor Aubert. She is pregnant? Of course she is pregnant—but by her lover, by Monsieur Fontaine—yes, the very same, your spotless French publisher of Bibles. As for Professor Aubert, obviously he has shut his eyes to this. Not because he wishes a child, or wishes to keep his wife, but because he wishes no scandal at a time when he and a colleague have been nominated for a Nobel Prize in chemistry for a discovery unrelated to carbon dating that they have been developing for many years. Your Professor Aubert puts honors above pride—and veracity. Surely, you do not expect me to trust the word of a man like this on any matter, do you?"

Randall did not want to believe de Vroome, but he no longer had the strength to challenge the Devil's advocate. He waited.

"I save the most meaningful and personal bit of information for the last," said de Vroome. "Painful as it is to both of us, I must now speak of Miss Angela Monti, of Rome, your new love."

Randall wanted to spring up and leave. Yet, he knew that he must hear whatever must be heard.

"Of course, you have met her father, Professor Augusto Monti, who provided information for the new Bible, have you not?" said de Vroome. He did not wait for a reply. "Or perhaps you have not met him, as others have not recently? I think you have not met him. And why not? Because he is always sent away, to the Middle East, to anywhere, on new excavations by those superiors who are jealous of him? Is that not what Angela tells everyone, yourself included? Forgive me, but Miss Monti lies. Where is Professor Monti then? He is in Rome, in a suburb of Rome somewhere in hiding, in disgrace, his retirement enforced by his government. Why? Because the Italian government learned that Professor Monti, in preparing to make the excavation that led to whatever he discovered, behaved with impropriety. Instead of leasing the site for his excavation, he swindled the poor peasants who owned the land and got title to it himself, so that he could retain fifty percent of the value of his find instead of dividing it with the ones who owned it. He cheated the peasants, and after Professor Monti made his find, the former owners went to the Ministry of Public Instruction with their story. They were reimbursed. The scandal was hushed up. Professor Monti was quietly removed from his post at the University of Rome and put out of sight, forced into hiding and into a disgraceful retirement."

Randall sat upright, shaken with anger. "That's a pack of lies and I don't believe a word of it."

Dominee de Vroome gave a short shrug. "I am not the one for you to be furious at. Angela Monti is the one with whom you should be angry. She has kept the truth from you, not merely to protect her miserable father but also to use you to promote her father's name. If she can seduce you into making her father's the most renowned name in the project, she could feel he would be important enough to defy his government and come out of retirement to reap his glory. And the Italian government would be too intimidated to reveal the scandal, or act punitively in any way. Miss Monti lies to you. And she uses you. I am sorry, but it is so."

"I still don't believe it."

"Ask Miss Monti, if you wish."

"I intend to," said Randall.

"Do not bother to ask her to confirm or deny what I have revealed," said de Vroome. "She would only lie to you again. Instead, ask her to bring you to her father."

"I wouldn't stoop to that," snapped Randall.

"Then you may never know the truth," said de Vroome.

"There are many truths, as there are many points of view, many interpretations of what is seen or heard."

Dominee de Vroome shook his head. "In the case of each person I have mentioned, there is only one truth, I fear. For, as Pontius Pilate inquired of Our Lord in the myth, *'Quid est veritas?'*—'What is truth?'—and in this instance, were I to reply to Pilate, I would convert the letters of his words into an anagram, *'Est vir qui adest'*—which translates, 'It is the man who stands before you.' Yes, Mr. Randall, the one who stands before you in this office—Maertin de Vroome—holds the truth. If you will investigate as I have, if you will seek truth as I have, you will learn to trust and to believe in me. If you do, you will appreciate why I asked to see you this night."

"Yes, I've been waiting to hear that," said Randall. "Why did you invite me here tonight?"

"To attempt to show you the sincerity of our cause, and to show you the sincerity of those in Resurrection Two. To let you see that you are being misinformed and ill-used and duped. To make you understand you are being employed as a tool, you and many others as well, by a commercial syndicate of publishers and a band of inflexible wrong-minded religionists. I brought you here to win you to my side and our cause. Instead, in my effort to open your eyes, to make you see light, I fear I have only antagonized you."

"What do you want of me?" Randall insisted.

"Your services, and your genius in your specialty. We need you here, on our side, the just side, to help us counter the propaganda of Resurrection Two and to promote our own effort at restoring religion and faith to the people of the world. It is a generous offer I am making you, Mr. Randall—the opportunity to leave a sinking ship for a sound one, the chance to preserve your future and your integrity, the chance to believe in something. As for the cash of the realm, my associates and I can offer you as much as Wheeler and his cohorts have given you. You have everything to gain, and nothing to lose."

Randall came to his feet. "From what I've heard—I have nothing to gain—and everything to lose. I have faith in the people I'm working with. I have no faith in you. I've heard gossip, not fact. I've heard overtones of blackmail, not words of decency. As for your cause, it is mere promise. As for Resurrection Two, it is actual performance. As for you yourself—"

Randall gazed at the man seated motionless behind the desk. The cleric's face was as unflinching as an iron mask. Randall wondered whether he dared go on, and then he went on.

"—I think you are no less selfish or ambitious than those I now work for. But you, Dominee, I believe you are more fanatical. You may see it as a necessity, and for a good end, but I could not work for a man so righteous, so unbending, so certain he alone knows truth. I could not become a turncoat, and help you destroy the very thing I have finally come to believe in—the Word—yes, the Word which we are going to give to the world. It is a message you know nothing about, and if I have my way, will not know anything about until it safely belongs to the world. Good evening, Dominee. I can wish you good evening, but I cannot wish you good luck."

Breathless, waiting for thunder, he was disappointed to find that there was none. De Vroome was merely nodding, and for a moment Randall felt that he had been overly melodramatic, and he would have felt foolish except for one thing that rankled. De Vroome had savaged defenseless people—Jeffries, Wheeler, Lori Cook, Hennig, Aubert, even Angela and her father. The Dominee had shown himself to be ruthless and vindictive, and so Randall was not ashamed of his outburst.

"Fair enough," de Vroome was saying. "I will not try to convince you—tell you how wrong you are—about me, about my cause—or how wrong you are about those you so loyally defend. We have each had our say tonight. We will let it stand for now. But remember this. I have alerted you to some facts about your colleagues and what they represent. I have asked you to seek the truth for yourself. When you do, you may wish to see me again. You may look upon me and my aims more kindly and with more charity. Should this occur before your Bible is published, as I believe it will, know this—my door will still be open to you. Our cause can use you."

"Thank you, Dominee."

Randall had turned to leave, when he heard the other speak again.

"Mr. Randall, one last bit of advice."

At the door, Randall turned back, and saw that Dominee de Vroome had released his cat and was standing, as was Plummer behind him.

"And an admonition for you and your colleagues." De Vroome was unfolding a piece of paper. "Do not waste your time with foolish and childish tricks in an effort to entrap me." He held up a sheet of blue paper. "I refer to this memorandum, this so-called confidential memorandum, that you circulated among your staff and consultants late today."

Randall swallowed, and waited.

"You pretended this was a serious memorandum about your promotion effort," continued de Vroome. "You were obviously testing your personnel, to learn whether one among them was disloyal and passing on each step of your operation to us. Your hope was that if I saw this memorandum, as I have seen it, I would act upon it publicly, anticipate and counter it, and thus somehow reveal to you where the breach in your security is concealed, so that your Heldering might know which of your personnel to eliminate in order to plug the leak. But you made one mistake—two actually—because you are an amateur at theology and so your knowledge of the New Testament is faulty. The contents of your memorandum are such a palpable impossibility that any knowledgeable scholar—one thoroughly versed in the gospels, in Christian lore, such as I am—would see through this nonsense at once, would not for a moment accept it as fact, let alone publicize it and fall into your ridiculous trap. Don't play these games with me again. Or if you must try, leave the games to your experts."

Randall felt the blood rising to his head. De Vroome had not detected the real trap. There was still a chance. "I haven't the faintest idea what you're talking about—" he began.

"You haven't? Let me be more explicit." De Vroome looked down at the sheet of blue paper. "Let's see what you wrote. 'Confidential. The royal palace announcement of our publication will be on a day dedicated to honoring the Resurrection of Jesus Christ. It has been decided that the twelve following days will be successively dedicated to the twelve disciples mentioned by name in the New Testament.' Then you mention the twelve disciples, including Judas Iscariot." De Vroome shook his head. Tensely, Randall waited for the Dominee to resume, to read the last sentence, the sentence with the code name that would reveal the traitor in Resurrection Two. But de Vroome read no more. He lowered the sheet in his hand, and shook his head again. "Foolishness."

Randall feigned bewilderment. "I simply do not understand—"

"Your foolishness? Would you expect anyone to believe you were serious about a promotion that honored a new Bible by dedicating twelve days to twelve disciples and making Judas Iscariot one of them? Judas—the historic synonym for traitor, the betrayer of Christ?"

Randall winced. That *had* been foolishness. He had not discussed each disciple by name with the publishers. He had looked them up himself and had dictated the damn memorandum in too great haste, and distributed it without bothering to have any of the experts check it over.

"And your second error," de Vroome went on, "was in stating that the New Testament mentions twelve disciples by name, when any theologian—if he were attentive—would know that it mentions thirteen. For, after Judas had betrayed Him, Christ replaced him with Matthias, the thirteenth named disciple. Had your memorandum credited Christ with having thirteen disciples, and suggested dedicating twelve days of promotion to twelve of them, substituting Matthias for Judas, you might have deceived me, and your trick might have succeeded. But this"—he slapped the blue sheet with contempt—"this kind of child's play will gain you nothing." He smiled at Randall. "Do not underestimate us. Respect us, and you will ultimately be with us."

Hungrily, Randall's gaze held on the blue sheet of paper. The last sentence. He must see that last sentence. His heart was palpitating. He was sure its beat filled the room. Desperately, he sought for something, anything, that would make de Vroome reveal the last sentence.

"Dominee," he said, trying to keep his voice controlled, "I appreciate your little lecture in public relations and scholarship, but I'm afraid it is lost on me. I did not write this memorandum."

Dominee de Vroome gave a snort of impatience. "You

are obstinate. You still play games. Would you recognize your own signature?"

"Certainly."

"Is this your signature or is it not?"

Dominee de Vroome thrust the blue memorandum across the distance of the desk toward Randall.

Barely able to cross the room, his legs weak, Randall moved to the front of the desk.

He peered down at the memorandum. The last sentence, above his signature, leaped up at him.

The first of the twelve days will be dedicated to the disciple Matthew.

Matthew.

Randall lifted his head, trying to disguise the triumph that swelled within him. He worked his features into an expression of sheepish apology.

"You win, Dominee," he said. "Yes, that is my signature. I quite forgot that memo was to go out today."

Dominee de Vroome nodded, satisfied, withdrawing the memorandum and slowly folding it. "Forget whatever else you will, but one thing do not forget. We will know everything there is to know about the new Bible before you can hypnotize the public with it. We will prepare the public to withstand your assault and to repel it. If you wish to be on the victorious side, you will come here and work hand in hand with us. . . . Now, Mr. Plummer will return you to your hotel."

"Thank you, but I'd prefer to get some air," Randall said hastily.

"Very well."

De Vroome led Randall to the door, and without another word, he ushered Randall out of the office.

Minutes later, with the guardian's house and the towering church behind him, Randall made his way through the shadows of the thick trees surrounding the Westermarkt, and stumbled toward the nearest shining streetlamp in the lifeless square.

One name, one only, beat against his eardrums, echoing and re-echoing through his head.

Matthew.

He had no patience to find a taxi now. This was the time for truth. Only one of the twelve who had received the memorandum he had distributed this afternoon bore the code name of Matthew.

Who had received the notice with the incriminating appellation *Matthew?*

Who?

Beneath the yellow streetlight, Randall fumbled inside his jacket for the list of the twelve disciples and the twelve persons of the project matched to them.

He had his list. He opened it. His eyes ran down it.

Disciple Andrew—Dr. Bernard Jeffries
Disciple Thomas—Rev. Zachery
Disciple Simon—Dr. Gerhard Trautmann
Disciple John—Msgr. Riccardi
Disciple Philip—Helen de Boer
Disciple Bartholomew—Mr. Groat
Disciple Jude—Albert Kremer
Disciple Matthew—

Disciple Matthew.

The name opposite that of Matthew was the name of Angela Monti.

VII

It HAD BEEN a sleepless night, and now it was midmorning of the blackest Friday that Steve Randall had known in his entire life.

He had ordered Theo to drive him, not to the Grand Hotel Krasnapolsky, but to the five-story building alongside it on the Dam, to de Bijenkorf, the largest department store in Amsterdam.

He had telephoned Angela Monti twenty minutes earlier from the Amstel, had missed her at the Victoria Hotel, but his next call had caught her just as she was entering the cubicle adjacent to his office where she was preparing to replace Lori Cook as his secretary.

The phone conversation had been one-way, his way, and brief. "Angela, I've got to see you about something urgent. Not in the office. Somewhere outside. You've said you've been to Amsterdam many times before. What about that department store on the Dam? Has it got a snack bar or coffee shop, anywhere we can sit for a few minutes?" It had a coffee shop on the ground floor and one on the top floor, the fourth floor. "Okay, make it upstairs. I'm starting right over. Meet me there."

He entered de Bijenkorf from the Dam side. Since the hour was early, the mammoth emporium was not yet swarming with shoppers. He asked an English-speaking salesgirl, in handbags and hats, for the elevators, and she directed him straight ahead to the center of the store.

He hastened between the counters and showcases, with their piles of costume jewelry and artificial flowers and stereo records and towels, not seeing much, not caring,

369

trying to concentrate on his confrontation with Angela
Monti.

She was possibly a liar, almost certainly a traitor. At
first he had doubted de Vroome's intelligence that Professor Monti was in disgrace and Angela had both lied and
used her body to shield and promote her father. And even
after possessing the proof that Angela was collaborating
with de Vroome to destroy Resurrection Two, Randall
had found it hard to believe. Why should she want to
help ruin a project when its destruction would, in turn,
also totally ruin her own beloved parent? Unless—and this
was a real possibility, Randall perceived—unless Angela's
parent was anything but beloved to her. For all Randall
knew, Angela might really hate her father, and have
looked forward to an opportunity to sabotage the project
built on his discovery.

At any rate, whatever her motive, the sickening fact
remained: The trap that had been sprung last night had
undeniably exposed Angela as the informer within Resurrection Two. Once that was clear, there seemed no more
reason to doubt de Vroome's statement that she was a
fraud and a cheat. Yet, only yesterday noon, and the night
before, he had been more intimate with her than he had
ever been with any woman, and he had loved and trusted
her as he had no other woman. It was impossible to
believe that she had betrayed not only the project but his
own love for her. Yet, it was also impossible to explain
away the cold evidence that she had done that very thing.

In minutes, he would know. He dreaded the truth, but
he must have it, even if he had to wring it out of her.

He wanted to strangle her for sabotaging the little
faith he had so recently acquired. But to do that meant to
commit suicide himself. This confrontation was a hopeless one. There would be no survivors.

The elevators were all in use. Not many yards away he
saw customers mounting an escalator. He could not wait.
He hurried to the escalator, caught the first step, and
held the moving rail as it ascended.

Leaving the last escalator on the fourth floor, he

searched right and left, until he saw the sign reading: EXPRESBAR/EXPRES BUFFET.

He went through a turnstile, accepting a yellow ticket from a preoccupied matron—the ticket a bill or check to be punched to show what he had ordered. Ahead of him, at a long food bar, he caught sight of Angela with a tray in her hand. She was inspecting the menu hanging on the wall behind the counter: *warme gerechten, koude gerechten, limonade, koffie, thee, gebak*.

He came up behind her. "Please make mine plain tea, nothing else. I'll find a place for us to sit."

Before she could greet him, he turned away, so that he would not have to see her face. The Formica-topped tables in the center of the snack bar were filled. On the other side, there was a curving snack counter with high stools, and there was plenty of room. He hoisted himself up on a stool, his back to the food bar, and by peering over the narrow counter he could look down the gaping store well which exposed the activity on the first floor far below.

The wait seemed interminable.

"Good morning, darling." It was Angela.

"Good morning," he said coldly. He took the tray, with its tea, coffee, buttered toast, from her, kept it between them so that he would not have to kiss her, and held it awkwardly until she had lifted herself onto the stool beside him. He set the tray down on the counter, and busily sugared and stirred his tea, unable to meet her eyes.

"What's wrong, Steve? You are very strange this morning."

He met her eyes, the beautiful, now puzzled, green eyes that hid the deception and betrayal behind them.

He felt sick, plain sick in his gut, and he did not know where or how to begin.

"Steve?" she persisted. "Why do you look at me that way?"

"What way?"

"So cold."

This could be ended only by making a beginning. He began. He knew that his voice was shaky. "Angela, I learned something last night, something about you, and I have to confront you with it." He inhaled, and then made his first accusation. "You lied to me about your father."

Unmistakably, the color rose on her cheeks. "I lied to you? Who says that? What crazy thing have you been told?"

"You made me believe that your father was being kept away from Resurrection Two because of the jealousy of his superiors, and because of politics. You said the reason he couldn't see me or cooperate with members of our project was that he was constantly being assigned to distant archeological digs, to Pella, to Egypt. You said your father was forced to undertake those trips to hold on to his teaching chair at the University of Rome. Last night I heard something else."

Angela's voice was as tremulous as his own had been. "What did you hear? Will you please tell me?"

"That your father was never sent on any of those archeological digs you spoke about. That your father was dismissed from his position at the University of Rome. That he was ordered into retirement, and now lives, secluded and in semi-hiding, somewhere in the suburbs of Rome. He's there now and he has been there for most of the years since his discovery."

He hesitated about the rest of it, but she would not let him hold anything back. "Steve, what else did you hear?"

"That your father was forced into retirement by the Ministry because, in acquiring the land for his excavation near Ostia Antica, he swindled the owners out of their property, so that by owning the property instead of leasing it, he could keep fifty percent of the worth of whatever he found instead of only twenty-five percent. This came out after the dig was concluded. The Ministry hushed it up to avoid tarnishing the find itself and to keep it out of the sensational press. The owners of the property were reimbursed—in fact, bought off by the Ministry—not only to rectify what your father had done to them, but to ensure their silence. Your father was disgraced, and was forced to leave the University of Rome. He went into retirement, and to keep his pension, I suppose, he agreed not to associate himself with Resurrection Two and to stay out of sight. To protect his name, you, as your father's daughter—you lied to everyone about his activity. This part of your lying is understandable to me. It's the other part that is not understandable—and is unforgivable, Angela."

"What is the other part?"

"You avoided, as much as you could, cooperating with the project until I came along. I was the big publicist the syndicate had hired, the one retained to promote and bring fame to the project. In me, you saw the one who could make the distinguished Professor Monti so well-known everywhere, so celebrated, so acclaimed, that the Italian government would no longer be able to keep him in virtual exile and would not dare ever mention his scandal again. Publicity and fame would clear your father, liberate him, restore him. To reach this end, you deliberately set out to use me, lie to me, manipulate me."

She stared at him. A gulf of silence separated them.

"You believe I used you, Steve?" she said.

"I don't know. I've got to find out."

"You believe I made love with you, in your bed, and in my room, let you enter my body, because I wanted to seduce you into being a puppet to aid my family?"

"Look, Angela—"

"Who told you that I lied to you, that I used you? Who told you my father was disgraced because he committed a swindle, a crime? Who told you these things?"

"I saw Dominee Maertin de Vroome last night."

Randall was watching her carefully, trying to detect from her reaction how close she was to de Vroome. Her reaction was one of surprise. He could not make out whether she was surprised that de Vroome would see him or surprised that he had got to her collaborator.

"De Vroome?" she murmured.

"Yes, last night. The Dominee sent for me, and I saw him. The outcome of our meeting can wait a moment. The point is that de Vroome wants to destroy us. Toward that end, he has collected dossiers on certain key personnel in Resurrection Two. He had a very complete dossier on your father and you. He divulged some of the contents of that file. Now you know his facts, Angela. I might not have accepted them as facts, except for something far more serious that I learned."

"Something more serious? What?"

"In a moment. First, I must have an answer to the question you still have not answered. What de Vroome told me—true or untrue, Angela?"

"Untrue, absolutely untrue," said Angela, her voice shaking. "If I lied to you at all, the lies were small lies, unimportant ones, white lies I had to make, until I knew you better. But what de Vroome told you of my father— that my father committed a crime—absolutely untrue. That is a slander invented by those who would traduce my father, by Dr. Tura and his colleagues, by de Vroome himself."

"If what I learned is untrue, then what is true, Angela?"

"You know Italy's archeological law on excavations. While the government owned most of the Ostia Antica site, it did not own or control a parcel of land along the old coastline, the land where my father wished to dig. This area of several acres was in private hands. My father offered the landlords, two brothers and a sister, their choice—to rent from them or buy from them."

"Did your father tell the landlords what he was looking for?" asked Randall.

"Of course. The landlords thought that he was crazy. They wanted no part of his gamble. They were eager to get rid of this useless property and they were delighted to sell the land to him outright. They even overpriced their land, and it was a strain for my father to raise enough lire to purchase it."

"Then where did de Vroome get the idea that your father's action was irregular?"

"From Dr. Fernando Tura, of course. When my father made his great discovery, Dr. Tura was wild with jealousy. He even informed the previous owners of the land about the fortune that their outright sale of it had cost them. He goaded them into going to the Ministry and protesting that my father had misled them, swindled them, had pretended he wanted the land for something other than an archeology excavation. The members of the Ministry were compelled to make a thorough investigation, and they held a closed hearing. They found that everything my father had done had been proper, correct, and the charges were groundless. My father was found innocent on all counts. There is evidence of this, if the government will declassify it and show it to you."

"And your father, Angela?"

"He was pleased to be vindicated. But he is a high-strung man. The pressure of the investigation, mainly the fact that those who had been his friends would even consider the charges against him, investigate him, try him, and have such distrust in him for so long, was more than he could bear. Even before he had been cleared, he resigned from his chair at the University of Rome, and went into voluntary retirement. He wanted no more to do with professional politics. He had achieved his life's goal and it was enough."

"He's in retirement now?"

"Yes. He lives the life of a recluse, devoting himself to writing and studying. He is bitter about his treatment and will have nothing to do with those in his academic circle, or even those who have developed his discovery. He feels that the announcement of his achievement will speak for itself and for him. But Dr. Tura, to justify his own behavior and protect his own position, has never ceased his innuendoes and whisperings of a scandal. No doubt, de Vroome heard them and saw Dr. Tura and chose to accept the slanders as facts for his dossier. Why not? As you have said, Steve, de Vroome is out to destroy the project and everyone connected with it. Why did I bother to see you in Milan, after I refused to see members of your staff? Simply to see that you had the accurate story of my father's role. If, as my father believes, the announcement of the discovery will speak for him to the world, then I, as his daughter, should see that the announcement is complete and correct."

"Why did you come to Amsterdam to work as a consultant?"

There was a ghost of a smile on Angela's face. "Not to use you. There was no need to use you. You invited me. I accepted. I accepted not to be sure my father would get more publicity. He will get enough. His position is secure. I accepted because—because I had immediate affection for you—and wanted to be near you."

Randall was moved, yet he could not allow himself to soften. His far graver charge was still to be made. The instant that he fired his shot, their relationship would be dead forever. She was Matthew, she was the traitor, and she must be informed of what he had discovered before he went to Inspector Heldering, Dr. Deichhardt, George Wheeler, and the others.

What had she just said? Yes. That she had come to Amsterdam to be near him.

"Angela," he said, "can you think of any other reason you joined the project?"

"Any other reason? No, there is no other." She knit her brow. "What other reason could there be?"

"Like wanting to do something for someone else besides your father or me."

"Someone else? What are you—?"

There was no way to cushion the blow. The hit had to be direct.

"Angela, why are you working inside our project as an undercover informer for Dominee Maertin de Vroome? Why are you passing our secrets on to our enemy?"

He had never seen a face more stunned. Not frightened or fearful. Plain stunned. Her mouth worked silently, before her first word was uttered. "What? What did you say?"

He repeated exactly what he had said. He added, "I have irrefutable evidence that you're on de Vroome's side."

"Steve, what are you talking about? Have you gone out of your mind?"

He would not be turned aside. "Late yesterday afternoon I sent a confidential memorandum to twelve persons on our project. One of these copies reached de Vroome. It was your copy that went to de Vroome. I know that for a fact, Angela. There's no denying it."

Her bewilderment appeared genuine. "Memorandum? I gave *what* memorandum to de Vroome? You're making no sense at all. I don't know de Vroome. I've never set eyes on him in my life. I do not intend to. How would I? Why would I? Steve, have you gone mad? Whatever are you saying?"

"I'll tell you what I'm saying. You listen carefully."

Bluntly, he told her of the first secret memorandum that had been leaked to Dominee de Vroome, of the second confidential memorandum he had created as a trap, and of seeing a copy of the memorandum with her code name, Matthew, in de Vroome's office the night before.

"The memorandum containing the name of Matthew was hand-delivered to you, Angela. I have the receipt initialed by you. Now do you remember it?"

"Yes," she said, "I do recall it. I received it—let me think—yes, I napped for quite a while at the hotel after you left. When I woke up and saw how late it was, I was distressed, and rushed to the Krasnapolsky to try to get some work done. I went to the office Miss Dunn had originally assigned me, and began cleaning out my files— there wasn't much yet—to move things to your secretary's office. The security guard came—yes—I got the memorandum from him, glanced at it to see if it was important. It did not seem to be. I put it in one of my manila file folders and carried them to Lori's office. There was an empty drawer in the second cabinet. I refiled the folder containing the memorandum, and the others, in that drawer. I put it there. I distinctly remember doing that. It must still be there."

Randall weighed what she had told him. Either she was being perfectly honest or she was the most brazen liar he had ever encountered. The case for her honesty was weak. "Angela," he said, "there was only one memorandum with the name Matthew in it. You're telling me it's in your file. I'm telling you I saw it in de Vroome's office. That one sheet of paper couldn't be in your office and in de Vroome's at one and the same time."

"I'm sorry," she said, "I can't explain further. I'll show you my copy right now."

"Okay, let me see it."

As they came off their stools in the snack bar, Angela faced him squarely. "You do not believe me, do you?"

"I only know what I know—that de Vroome showed me your copy of the memorandum."

"Steve, can't you see my assisting that horrible de Vroome makes no sense? He wants to wreck Resurrection Two and discredit the International New Testament. I want to help the project and further the acceptance of the new Bible. If not for your sake, then certainly to see that my father's name and discovery are honored. Why should I collaborate with a man who, in effect, would destroy my father with everyone else?"

"I don't know why. There may be a lot I don't know about Professor Monti or Angela Monti. For all I know, you may despise your father."

"Oh, Steve," she said in despair. She picked up her purse as he took the restaurant tickets to pay them. "I'll let you see I still have your memorandum."

Silently, they rode the elevator to the ground floor of de Bijenkorf, left the department store, and ten minutes later they had returned to Lori Cook's office which Angela now occupied.

As Randall stood grimly by, she unlocked the second of the two metal cabinets, opened the third file drawer, and crouched down beside it. "It is under P," she said. "The tab of the folder has on it *Public Relations Memoranda*." She fanned back the dividers, dipped her hand behind the one labeled P, and looked up puzzled. "There's nothing here. But I'm sure I—" Frantically, she started examining the manila folders behind every divider. "I must have misfiled it. Wait, I'll find it in a second."

Minutes passed, and she had not found it.

She came to her feet, panicky, at a loss.

Randall's suspicion of her honesty remained. "Are you sure you filed it?"

"I think I did," she said uncertainly. "After I moved, these folders were piled on the desk here. I started filing—"

"Did anyone come into your office before you finished and locked the cabinet?"

"Did anyone—? Why, yes. I didn't mention them at dinner last night because the visits seemed unimportant." She went to the desk. "Several people came in looking for you. I—let me see—I tried to be efficient, write down the name of each person who came by or called—" She opened the center desk drawer, pulled out a shorthand pad and turned to the first page. "Jessica Taylor dropped by briefly. She said she'd been working with you, and wondered if you needed her for anything else. I told her you were out, and I had no idea where you were."

"I was downstairs with Heldering checking to see if all the memos had been delivered." He gestured toward her shorthand pad. "Who were the others?"

Angela flipped the page. "Elwin Alexander and—" She stopped abruptly. "I remember! How stupid to forget. His name is here. I wrote it down. Look, Steve, you can see—"

Her finger ran down the shorthand pad until it pointed to the penciled-in name of Dr. Florian Knight.

"Knight?" said Randall.

"It was Dr. Knight," said Angela with relief. "Thank God that's cleared up. Now you will believe me. Yes, Dr. Knight came when I was filing. He wanted to see you. He said he'd been to a publicity conference you had, and afterward you promised him some material so that he could brief himself on the kind of information you would want from him. You did tell him that?"

"Yes."

"When you weren't here, he saw my folders on the desk and said maybe he could find what you'd told him about. He showed me his security was a high grade, like mine and other consultants', so there was no reason to refuse his request. He went through the folders, and said that most of what he needed was probably in your office, but for now he'd like to borrow your recent memoranda, just because he had joined the project late and he wanted to know your plans. He said he'd return the file material to me in the morning when he'd look in on you again."

"Did he return it this morning?"

She cast about the desk, troubled. "Apparently not. He must still have it."

"No, he doesn't have it," said Randall grimly. "Maertin de Vroome has it." He struck the palm of his hand with his fist. "Dr. Knight. Dammit. I should have known."

"Known what?"

"Never mind."

"It was wrong of me to let him borrow it?"

"That's not important now. You couldn't have understood it was wrong."

"Steve, but now you know I had nothing to do with de Vroome. Now you'll believe me. Come, I'll go with you to Dr. Knight's office. He'll verify what I've told you in front of me, and maybe have an explanation."

"I won't need an explanation from him," said Randall with bitterness.

Inwardly, Randall cursed his own sentimentality. At the time that he had heard of Knight's hatred of Dr. Jeffries and Resurrection Two, from Knight's fiancée, Valerie Hughes, in that London pub, he had realized that he should not encourage the Oxford don to join the project. From the outset, Knight was the weak link, the one most likely to sell out to recover the money that he felt the new Bible had denied him. Randall recalled that he had worried about Knight even yesterday, had purposely not sent him a copy of the memorandum, in the vain hope that the real saboteur might be someone else. But the saboteur was Dr. Florian Knight after all. Dammit.

Angela was waiting. "Should we go see him?"

"There's no need for you to go," he said. He tried to smile. "Angela, forgive me for distrusting you. I can only say—I love you."

She went into his arms, eyes shut, and pressed her lips against his. As the kiss ended, she whispered, "I love you more, much more than you are capable of returning love to me."

He smiled. "We'll see," he said. He disengaged himself. "Now, to Dr. Knight. I want to see him alone."

Quickly, Randall went down the hall to Dr. Knight's office.

Dr. Knight was not there.

The secretary was apologetic. "He telephoned to say he will not be in today."

"Where is he?"

"In his hotel working. The Hospice San Luchesio."

"The San what?"

"I will write it down for you. San Luchesio. It is at Waldeck Pyrmontlaan Number 9. Almost all of our project clergymen and theologians stay there. It is a strange hotel."

Randall had no time to ask her what was strange about it. He took the address from her and started for the door.

"Should I phone Dr. Knight that you are coming to see him?" the secretary called out.

"No. I'd prefer to surprise him."

IT WAS, indeed, a strange hotel.

The first sight of the San Luchesio was deceptive. It looked like an ordinary apartment building, a modern five-story building, in a wide street.

The San Luchesio was something that Randall had never heard about before—a small hotel built exclusively for transient Protestant and Roman Catholic clergymen and their families, and for nuns.

Theo, who had been driving Randall to the showdown with Dr. Florian Knight, had been a fount of information. In the past year Theo had ferried innumerable clergymen —as well as secular theologians connected with Resurrection Two, who had been given special permission to live in the hotel—from the San Luchesio to the Krasnapolsky, and back again, and one question to Theo had brought Randall a deluge of detail.

The San Luchesio, named after the first follower of St.

Francis of Assisi, had been built in 1961. The ecclesiastical hotel had thirty-four rooms with fifty beds. The cost of a bed and breakfast was fourteen guilders—about four dollars—a day. Off the lobby, Theo had explained, there was a large many-windowed double-duty hall. During regular hours it was used as a prayer room; during mealtimes it was transformed into a dining room. This hall was furnished with movable brown seats, each seat with its own table. If a guest wished to pray or meditate, he could make his movable seat turn to face the holy pictures on the wall. At mealtimes, the occupant could switch the direction of his seat back to the center of the room and dine at his table. Off the lobby, according to Theo, was the hotel's own chapel, with a stained-glass window. Two cassocks hung near the window, one for Catholic priests, the other for Anglican ministers, and a central cabinet held the paraphernalia needed for Mass.

Theo had brought his Mercedes-Benz limousine to a halt in front of the San Luchesio, and Randall stepped out, traversed the walk, and went inside.

The lobby did not have the appearance of a hotel lobby at all, but rather resembled the parlor of a cheerful, immaculate private residence. The surrounding walls had horizontal strips of wood with upholstered cushions buttoned to them, and Randall saw that these served as chair backs when a visitor sat on the stools beneath them. There were lively pictures on the wall, biblical scenes appliquéd on cloth, giving a wonderfully colorful effect. Ahead was the single hotel touch: a reception desk, which was presided over by a top-heavy lady in her fifties.

The whole scene exuded purity and goodness.

It was a helluva place, Randall thought, to confront a theologian and to expose him for what he was, a son of a bitch and a goddam traitor.

Randall went directly to the desk. "I'm here to see Dr. Florian Knight. We work together."

The portly receptionist put her hand on the telephone. "Is he expecting you?"

"Possibly."

"I'll try his room. May I have your name, please?"

After giving his name, Randall wandered nervously to the entrance of the convertible prayer hall and dining room, absently looked at the brown wooden chairs and tables, and came back to the desk just as the receptionist was placing the receiver back on the telephone.

"Dr. Knight is in," she said. "He is on the fourth floor. He will meet you at the elevator."

He was in the corridor, waiting, when Randall emerged from the elevator on the fourth floor. Dr. Florian Knight was the same gaunt Aubrey Beardsley figure that Randall had seen as recently as yesterday here in Amsterdam, and yet he was not the same. For the first time since Randall had met him, Dr. Knight was not jumpy, jittery, angry. He was uncharacteristically calm and at ease. He was also, as he walked Randall to his single room, deeply preoccupied and detached.

Knight's hotel room was even smaller than the cramped bedroom of his London flat. The room was clean and austere—a bed, a washbowl, a folding table, a garment cupboard that probably could hold no more than two suits. There was a lone armchair beneath the high-set window.

"You take the chair," said Knight, his tone more hospitable, less supercilious, than usual. "I'd offer you a drink, except that alcohol in any form is strictly verboten in this Franciscan hostel. Otherwise, I find the place quite comfortable. The good brothers run the place as if St. Francis of A. were its executive director, and since St. Francis was rather keen on speaking to birds, the servants go about twittering to the inmates. All most charming."

As he sat on the edge of the bed, Knight added, "I'm sorry you had to come out of your way like this, Mr. Randall. I intended to be back at the Kras tomorrow, and again be at your service. At any rate, you're here. Anything special?"

"Yes, something quite special," said Randall emphatically. "And it concerns you."

"Well, then, here I am, sir."

Randall decided not to waste words. He would give it

to him straight. "Dr. Knight, at the end of yesterday's working day you borrowed a file of material from Miss Monti, my secretary. The file contained a confidential memorandum I had prepared. Several hours later, that confidential memorandum was in the hands of Dominee Maertin de Vroome, the sworn enemy of our project."

He paused, expecting some strong reaction from Knight, one of either surprise or disavowal. Instead, the Oxford don displayed no emotion. "I'm sorry to hear that," said Dr. Knight calmly, opening a tin of Altoids and offering Randall a peppermint, which Randall ignored, before popping one into his own mouth. "But I can't say I'm surprised."

Taken aback, Randall stared at the scholar. "You're not surprised?"

"Well, while I hadn't expected it to get to de Vroome, the possibility was always there. I'm only surprised you found out. Are you certain de Vroome has that memorandum?"

"You're damn right I'm certain. I met with de Vroome last night. I saw the memo in his hand."

"And you are positive it is the very one I borrowed from Miss Monti?"

"One and the same," said Randall harshly, still disconcerted by the scholar's matter-of-fact acceptance of his role of traitor. "I'm going to tell you how I traced the theft to you."

Quickly, Randall disclosed the code names used in the copies of the memorandum, and followed this with some details of his meeting with de Vroome and the confrontation with Angela Monti. When he finished his recital, his gaze remained fixed on Knight. The British scholar continued to suck his peppermint, although now the hand holding the Altoids was unsteady. "What do you have to say to this?" Randall demanded to know.

"Very clever," said Dr. Knight with admiration.

"And very unclever of you, in fact downright stupid," said Randall. "I considered you a poor security risk from the moment I learned your book, *Christ Plain*, would be rendered unpublishable by the appearance of the International New Testament. I should have known someone so embittered by our project—so desperate for money—would go to any length to obtain what he felt was justly his."

The tin in Dr. Knight's hand was trembling more visibly. "So you know all that about me?"

"I knew it from the start in London. But I was so impressed by your credentials, by your potential value to the project—that, coupled with Valerie's plea on your behalf—"

"Ah, Valerie."

"—that I put down any doubts I had and persuaded myself that you were and would remain trustworthy. I was wrong. You betrayed us. I'm going back to report what I know. You're through."

"No," Dr. Knight said quickly, almost frenziedly.

His cool British façade had cracked, begun to disintegrate. He was, in life, the picture of Dorian Gray, changing, grown old, before Randall's eyes.

"No, don't tell them," he pleaded, "don't let them sack me!"

"Don't let them?" said Randall, astonished. "You've admitted you gave the confidential memo to de Vroome—"

"I gave nothing directly to de Vroome, believe me, nothing. If I was weak, betrayed you at all, it was in small ways, harmless ways. But that has changed. I can be trusted now, completely. I am dedicated to Resurrection Two. It is my life. I can't allow myself to be separated from its work."

He came to his feet, agitated, and started to pace, wringing his hands.

Astounded, Randall watched him. The contradictions in Knight's behavior and speech made absolutely no sense. He was sick, Randall decided, sick, a hysteric. Randall determined to jar him back into rationality. "Dr. Knight, how can you say you're dedicated to Resurrection Two on the one hand, and on the other, just minutes ago, admit you gave away our secrets to Dominee de Vroome? Do you expect us to keep on a traitor?"

"I'm not a traitor!" Dr. Knight shouted vehemently. He moved toward Randall, stood over him. "Can't you understand? I intended to be one. I started to be one. But I couldn't—once I knew the truth—I couldn't. And now you must permit me to stay. I'll kill myself if I can't stay."

"What in the hell are you talking about?" exclaimed Randall. "You're not making sense. This is ridiculous. I've had enough—"

He started to rise, but Knight clawed at his shoulder, holding him down. "No—no—wait, Randall, give me a chance. I'll explain, I'll tell you the whole thing, and then it'll make sense. I was afraid to, but I see that I must or all is lost. Please listen to me."

Not until Randall sat back did Dr. Knight move away from him, pacing past the bed, trying to control his agitation, trying to work out what he must say. At last, with some semblance of calm, he returned to the side of the bed, sat down, stared abjectly at the floor, and resumed speaking.

"When you came here, I tried to brazen it out. I thought my very frankness would disarm you, and lead the way to an understanding—well, enable me to satisfy you that I had participated in some wrongdoing, but that it was behind me, that I had changed and could be depended upon. But I see that you still regard me as a turncoat, that you actually mean to have me sacked. Now I see there's no way to avoid confessing the whole truth. I suppose there's no reason for me to protect the others—"

The others. Randall sat up. He listened intently.

"—and no reason to fear revealing to you what took place last night and this morning." He looked up. "If you still think I'm not making sense—"

"Go on," said Randall.

"Thank you. About my bitterness, my anger toward Dr. Jeffries, that is quite true. It was indiscreet of dear Valerie to tell you about that, but I can forgive her. Valerie's avocation is her effort, always, to save me from myself and"—he gave up a fleeting smile—"and for herself. But I remain devoted to her. Yes, she begged me to join Resurrection Two. I agreed, but not for the reasons she thought. I came here, as you suspected, with feelings that made me untrustworthy. I knew Resurrection Two had its enemies. I knew who they were. I had read Plummer's interview with Maertin de Vroome, and the two articles he has since published in a similar vein. I had no plan, but in the back of my mind lurked the thought that through my membership in Resurrection Two, I might find my own salvation."

"You mean money."

"Well—yes. If we must be frank, I had thought money my only salvation, money that had been denied me because the International New Testament was about to be published, money to restore my hearing, money to enable me to marry and support Valerie and live the life proper to a deserving young British scholar."

"And so you sought out Cedric Plummer?"

"It wasn't necessary," said Dr. Knight. "It was Plummer who sought me out. Or to be more precise, it was someone who represented Plummer."

Randall's eyebrows shot up. "Someone else? Someone in the Krasnapolsky?"

"Yes."

Randall reached into his coat pocket and pulled out the miniature tape recorder. "If you don't mind—?"

"You want to record me? To what purpose?"

"If others have been involved with you—"

"I see. This will help acquit me?"

"I won't guarantee that, Dr. Knight. If you have a legitimate defense, it's to your advantage that I have it on tape, should it be needed. If I'm not satisfied with your story, I'll turn the tape over to you—and you can tell the publishers your story firsthand."

"Fair enough." He waited as Randall adjusted the recording volume on the miniature machine and placed it on the floor between them. Dr. Knight considered the recorder. "My jury," he said. "It will inspire me to make my confession and defense as full and impassioned as possible."

"You were saying that when you arrived here, checked

into the Krasnapolsky, you were approached by someone other than Plummer," Randall prompted him.

"Someone who somehow knew about my personal situation, about my unpublished book on Christ, about my handicap, about my anger and needs and yearnings. It was suggested that there might be a way for me to recoup the money that should have been mine. I held off. I could not bring myself to betray a trust. I could not see myself as Sir Roger Casement. Still, in the short time I've been here, I've made a habit of copying whatever secret materials I've received or could lay my hands on. I've been careful to listen to whatever could be heard and make notes and hide them. I did nothing until I was approached again. I wanted to determine what my services were worth. In turn, I was asked what I could offer. Impulsively, testing, I handed over my small hoarding of Resurrection Two papers to the party who had approached me, and immediately after that I was brought to meet Plummer. He graciously informed me that what I had given them was useful."

"Is that how they learned the date of our announcement and our plan to broadcast from the royal palace by Intelsat?"

"Yes. All useful, Plummer told me, but not enough. They would want to continue to receive any more notes and memoranda I could pick up, but most important they must have an advance copy of the new Bible or at least a précis of the unique contents of the new Bible, meaning the Petronius and James material, which I had worked on but had not seen fully. Plummer said that they had other means of obtaining the material—"

"Hennig," said Randall.

"What?"

"Never mind. Go on."

"—but they could take no chances. They wanted to be doubly certain. Then, Plummer named the price. It was —it was overwhelming. The sum could be the solution to my every problem. It was irresistible. I agreed to get them the new Bible, or at least transcripts of the new discoveries that were in it. I promised to deliver it to them yesterday."

Once more, Randall showed his astonishment. "How could you hope to lay your hands on a copy? The book is under lock and key at the printer's. All the advance proof pages are in the vault."

Dr. Knight wagged a finger. "Not quite. But let me not digress from my chronology. I tried to obtain a copy of the new Bible the day before yesterday, but failed. As I was unable to deliver it, I was eager to mollify my—my contact and prove my goodwill. I searched for a few oddments I could give them, and among these was your Matthew memorandum."

"I see."

"Of course, they were not satisfied. They wanted the Bible itself. I felt positive I could lay my hands on a copy that evening, meaning last night."

"But you couldn't," said Randall.

"On the contrary. I could and I did."

Randall came forward. "You got hold of the International New Testament?"

"With little difficulty. You see, Mr. Randall, all of the bound proof editions are not in the vault. Each head theologian has his own copy. Dr. Jeffries has a copy. Don't forget, our relationship is still close. He has a large room down the hall. I have access to it to share his reference books. I knew that he kept his International New Testament locked inside his briefcase. He has a combination lock on it. But he is absentminded, and makes it a practice to write everything down. I searched his room for the combination. As I expected, it was written down. I memorized it. I had to get to his briefcase when he was out. He planned to go out for the evening the night before last, but postponed the date. I knew that he was going out last night. I waited for him to leave. Then I entered his room. I opened his briefcase. I removed his bound galleys of the International New Testament. I smuggled the book out of the hotel and took it to a photo-copying shop I had found earlier, one that would be open in the evening. I noted the new material, the translation of the Petronius Parchment and the Gospel According to James, and I had these pages copied. I went back to Dr. Jeffries' room, returned his Bible to his briefcase, locked it, and went to my room with my photocopy."

Randall was breathless. "You've turned it over to them?"

Dr. Knight wagged his finger once more. "I was about to. I was about to lift up the telephone and call my contact and arrange to turn it over last night in exchange for my thirty pieces. But you know, I am what I am—a scholar, a curious scholar, before being a practical businessman. So I could not resist reading the Gospel According to James before giving it up to them."

"You read it," said Randall slowly. "What happened next?"

"The miracle," said Dr. Knight simply.

"The what?"

"My communion with Our Lord and the miracle that followed. Mr. Randall, if you knew me well, you'd know that I am deeply interested in religion but I am not an intensely religious man. I've always viewed Christ, His mission, from the outside, objectively, as a scholar. I've never got close to Him or admitted Him into my heart. But last night, I read James and last night I sat here, as I sit now on this bed, and I wept. I saw Jesus plain for the first time, felt His compassion for the first time. I was gripped by the strongest emotional turmoil I have ever known. Can you understand?"

Randall nodded and kept his silence.

"I fell back on the bed and closed my eyes," Dr. Knight said with growing intensity. "I was suffused with a love of Christ, by my overflowing belief in Him, my desire to be worthy of Him. I must have slept. In my sleep, or perhaps in some waking interlude in the night, I saw Jesus, touched the hem of His garment, heard Him speak to me—*to me*—some of the words that His brother James recorded. I begged Him to forgive me my sins, committed and as yet uncommitted, and I promised to devote my life to Him. He, in turn, blessed me and ordained that everything would henceforth be right for me.

You think the episode, the dream or waking dream, shows me up for a madman, a lunatic? I would have thought so, too, except for what followed."

Briefly overcome, sinking into some introspection, Dr. Knight had ceased speaking. Randall, caught in the other's emotion, tried to bring him back. "What followed, Florian?"

Dr. Knight blinked. "The incredible," he said. "I awakened early this morning, the sunlight streaming through the window above you. I was drenched in perspiration. I felt purged of every meanness. I felt peace. I lay still, and then I heard a sweet, a lovely sound, a bird chirping on the windowsill. A bird, I heard a bird break into song—I, who had not heard a bird in years—I, who could barely hear a human being unless he stood beside me and literally shouted—I, who had been deaf for ages—I heard a bird, and without my hearing aid—I had not worn my hearing aid to bed. See it there, on the bedside table. Just where I left it last night. I don't have it on—you hadn't noticed—but I've heard every word you've spoken in this room, clearly, easily, with no effort. This morning, I was crazed with excitement. After hearing the bird, I leaped from my bed and turned on my transistor radio, and the music swam over me. I rushed to the door, flung it open, and the maids were chattering down the hall. I could hear. I had offered myself to Christ, and He had forgiven me and restored my hearing. He had healed me. That is the miracle. Do you believe me, Randall?"

"I believe you, Florian," said Randall, deeply touched. He wondered what would come next. He did not have to wait long.

"When I had recovered my equilibrium, I made my telephone call. I spoke to my—my contact. I told him I was prepared to see him. Instead of going to work, I met with him in his secluded residence in a suburb of Amsterdam. I advised him forthwith that I had been unable to obtain the new Bible for him. I told him that I regretted making the promise and even regretted turning over those minor materials I had already given him. In fact, I requested the return of what I had given him yesterday, your Matthew memorandum. He said he could not return it, that it was in other hands. Presumably, it had already reached de Vroome, although I didn't know it."

"Yes, it had."

"Then, this person—my contact—he urged me to continue trying to get the Bible for them. I said the idea was repugnant to me. He said he was certain they would pay me more than had been agreed upon. I said I wasn't interested in bartering. Then he became threatening, said unless I cooperated he would expose my involvement to date. I told him I couldn't care less, and I left him. I came back here, destroyed the photocopy I'd made of the International New Testament pages, to insure that the contents would be safe from de Vroome, and shortly afterward I learned you were here to see me. Now you understand what I owe to the new book, to James, to the project, and why I am praying that you won't have me dismissed. I must stay on. I must help in the good work."

Randall had been listening and thinking. There was no question that, by whatever means, miraculous or psychological, Dr. Knight's hearing had been restored. In a sense, yes, this was a true miracle. Whether Lori Cook's miracle had been a fraud or not no longer mattered. Dr. Knight's miracle was evidence enough of the power of the message in the new Bible. But this miracle, Randall told himself, was one he personally would never reveal to the publishers, let alone permit it to be exploited to sell the International New Testament. And he would advise Dr. Knight to go along with him, and continue wearing his hearing aid until the Bible was successfully launched. That Dr. Knight's trustworthiness was now beyond reproach, that his sincerity was unquestionable, was self-evident. Only one thing remained.

"Florian," said Randall, "if you want to stay with us and help in our good work, as you've put it, you can begin by telling me about the real informer in our midst, the one who first approached you, the contact man who is a friend of de Vroome's."

"He's not really a friend of de Vroome's," said Dr. Knight. "I'm not sure he even knows de Vroome personally. He's a friend of Cedric Plummer's. That was clear the first time he took me to Plummer. We met inside the Fantasio nightclub. We sat on a bench, in there, and the two of them smoked pipes of hash. They seemed very close. I am sure my contact man gave our secrets to Plummer and he, in turn, must have passed them on to de Vroome."

"That's right," said Randall. "Now the name of Plummer's man, the traitor in Resurrection Two? You'll have to tell me."

"Our Judas?" said Dr. Knight. "Hans Bogardus, the project librarian. He's the one we'd better get rid of—if we don't want to see our Christ crucified again and forever."

BACK ON the first floor of the Grand Hotel Krasnapolsky, Steve Randall headed straight for his office.

In the secretary's cubicle, Angela Monti looked up from her typing questioningly. "Was it Dr. Florian Knight?"

"No."

"I'm glad. Who was it, then?"

"Not now, Angela. We'll discuss it later. Get me Dr. Deichhardt on the phone. If he's not in yet, get me George Wheeler."

Randall continued into his office. He took his tape recorder from his pocket, ran the cassette tape backwards several minutes, played it, ran it backwards again, listened to it once more, stopping and starting it to erase certain secret information. Satisfied, he set the machine, shoved it into his briefcase and waited for Angela to buzz him.

At last, impatient to get it over with, he picked up his briefcase and returned to Angela's office just as she was hanging up the phone.

"I am sorry, Steve," she said. "They are both out of the city. Dr. Deichhardt's secretary says the publishers are in Germany, in Mainz, for a meeting with Mr. Hennig this morning."

"Did she say when they'll be back in Amsterdam?"

"I asked. She could not say. She does not know."

Randall cursed under his breath. He would have to do the dirty work himself. He knew that the critical encounter with Bogardus could not wait. There was too much at stake.

"Okay, Angela, thanks. See you later."

He strode up the corridor, turned right, and stopped before the door to Kamer 190. On the door was painted the word LIBRARY in five languages, and beneath these, in cursive writing, *Hans Bogardus*.

Randall steeled himself, and went inside.

Hans Bogardus, seated at a wide table piled high with reference books, was bent over an open volume, making notes from it. His long blond hair fell forward, obscuring his face. At the sound of the door's opening, closing, his head jerked up. His effeminate young features showed surprise. He started to rise, but a gesture from Randall kept him in his chair.

"Stay where you are," said Randall, taking the seat in the chair directly opposite him.

As Randall plumped his briefcase on the table, and began to open it, he looked directly at the young Dutch librarian. As ever, Randall found Bogardus repulsive. Except for the froggy eyes and thick lips, the librarian's face was almost flat, two nostrils seemed to represent a nose, and the complexion was pallid, almost albino.

"How are you, Mr. Randall?" he said in his falsetto.

"I have something for you," said Randall.

The librarian's attention shifted eagerly to the briefcase. "The final printed Bible from Mainz—it has come in?"

"It's not come in," said Randall. "But when it does, you're not going to be one of the ones who see it, Hans."

Bogardus' pale eyelashes fluttered warily. He moistened his fat lips. "What—I do not—what do you mean?"

"This," said Randall. He held up the miniature tape machine. With deliberation, he set the machine down on the table between them. He pressed the *Play* lever. "The first voice you'll hear is that of Dr. Florian Knight. The other is mine. The recording was made less than an hour ago."

The tape started revolving. Dr. Knight's voice came on with unmistakable fidelity. Randall leaned forward, turned the volume up slightly, then sat back in his chair, arms crossed on his chest as he watched the listening librarian.

Gradually, in the painfully slow seconds that followed, as Dr. Knight's confession filled the book-lined room, Hans Bogardus' colorless face began to take on color. Blotches of pink surfaced on his immobile cheeks. He made no movement. Only the sound of his quickened breathing could be heard as counterpoint to Dr. Knight's speech.

The tape had almost run out. Dr. Knight's solemn— now relentless—concluding accusation rose above the table.

Our Judas? Hans Bogardus, the project librarian. He's the one we'd better get rid of—if we don't want to see our Christ crucified again and forever.

After that, the soft purr of the rubbing tape. Randall reached out, stopped the machine, returned it to his briefcase.

Icily, he met Bogardus' blank stare. "Do you care to deny this in front of Dr. Knight and the board of publishers and Inspector Heldering?"

Hans Bogardus did not reply.

"All right, Hans, you've been found out. Fortunately for us, what you've turned over to your friend Cedric Plummer, for Dominee de Vroome, has been of small value. You'll get no more, and certainly not the advance copy of the Bible. I'm going to have Heldering send a security guard up here to keep you under surveillance— until I reach Deichhardt or Wheeler in Mainz today, and report to them, and have them fire you."

Randall waited for the hysterical outburst, the belated denial, the wild scene of defense.

It did not come.

An evil, almost vicious, grin split the young Dutchman's

flat face. "You are a fool, Mr. Randall. Those bosses of yours—they will not fire me."

This was something new, unexpected, this brazening it out. "You think not? Suppose we just—"

"I *know* not," Bogardus cut in. "They will not dare to fire me, when they hear what I have learned. I will remain in my job until I choose to go. I shall not leave until I have the Bible to take with me."

The young Dutchman was insane, Randall decided. It was no use trying to talk to him. Randall pushed back his chair. "Okay, let's find out whether you're fired or not. I'm going to telephone Deichhardt and Wheeler in Mainz—"

Bogardus pushed against the table, still grinning at Randall cockily. "Yes, do that," he said. "But be sure of one thing, when you do that. Tell them that Hans Bogardus, with his genius, has discovered in their Bible what all their scientists, textual scholars, and theologians were too blind to see. Tell them that Hans Bogardus has discovered a fatal flaw in their Bible, one which can destroy it, reveal it as a fake, and ruin them completely, if he chooses to disclose this flaw to the world. And disclose it I shall, if I am forced to leave here."

Definitely mad, Randall felt certain. Still, the young Dutchman spoke with such shrill conviction—he has a mind like a computer, he can find anything, Naomi had once said—that Randall did not leave his chair. "A fatal flaw in the new Bible? How could you find one in a book you haven't seen, let alone read?"

"I have read enough," said Bogardus. "I have kept alert for a year. I have looked, I have listened, bits of this, pieces of that. I am the reference librarian. Requests come to me to research a word, a sentence, a paragraph, a quotation. The inquiries are guarded, but I have seen many separate pieces of the puzzle. Much has been kept from me, from others here, it is true. I do not know the exact title of the new Bible. I do not know the exact contents of the discovery. I do not know ninety percent of the new text. But I do know it concerns material heretofore not known about Jesus Christ, with details of an extended ministry. I do know, for a certainty, that Jesus is put in many places outside ancient Palestine, and one of them is Rome."

Randall was impressed, and more respectful of the librarian now. "Okay, Hans. Suppose the little you claim to know is accurate. Do you want me to believe that this little could give you enough information to find what you call a flaw—"

"A fatal flaw."

"—very well, a fatal flaw that the world's greatest experts overlooked, men who have had the entire text, who have translated it and studied it for years?"

"Yes," said Bogardus, "because they have tunnel vision, see only what they wish to see, because they look with the narrow eyes of faith. I tell you, it has happened here in Amsterdam before. Between 1937 and 1943, six new and unknown Vermeers, painted in the seventeenth century, were discovered by a man named Hans van Meegeren and sold to the greatest museums and collectors in the world for eight million gulden—over three million dollars, American. The critics and experts hailed these Vermeers as authentic. The critics and experts would not see that the hands of Christ in one portrait were modeled after van Meegeren's own hands, the chairs in one painting were painted from chairs in van Meegeren's modern studio, the oil used on the canvases contained synthetic resin, which did not exist until after the year 1900, whereas Vermeer had died in 1675. The Vermeers were hoaxes, and later exposed. But anyone with the eyes of truth would not have had to see an entire forged Vermeer canvas to find the flaw. One quarter of an inch of the canvas, with its synthetic resin, would have been enough. So, in the same way, I have seen enough. I have seen one quarter of an inch of the entire canvas of your Bible and I have seen enough to call it a fake."

Having heard him this far, Randall decided to play along a bit farther. "And this so-called flaw—you've passed it on to Plummer and de Vroome?"

Bogardus hesitated. "No, I have not. Not yet."

"Why not?"

"That—that is a personal matter."

Randall flattened his palms on the table and rose to his feet. "Okay, now I'm positive you're lying. If you'd found anything wrong with the Bible, you'd have delivered it straight to Plummer. He's paying you for that, isn't he?"

Bogardus jumped to his feet. His face was a mass of outraged pink. "Cedric pays me nothing. I do this for him out of love!"

Randall stood stock-still. That was the connection, he realized. Bogardus and Plummer a devoted twosome. He'd touched a homosexual nerve end.

Bogardus had turned his head away. "I have kept to myself what I know, I have held it back from Cedric. I know its value to him. It would be more important even than the new Bible. If he wrote about the flaw, made it public, he—he would be famous and rich. But I have kept it for—what do they say in the American cinema?— my ace in the hole. Because lately, lately Cedric has not been so kind to me, and—and I know, even though he does not know I know, he has been unfaithful to me. Someone who is still younger, more, more attractive. Cedric has told me, when this is over, he will take me on the trip to North Africa for a holiday. He has promised it, after I bring him the new Bible. Yes, the new Bible will be enough to keep him for me for now. But if something should go wrong, I hold onto my ace, my private discovery that will undermine all that is here."

Randall had winced at the pitiful desperation in the distraught Dutchman's voice, the desperation of one afraid of losing another. Now, Randall wondered how much validity there could be to the librarian's claim that he knew of something in the International New Testament that would discredit it. Bogardus had to be promoting a lie, anything to frighten the publishers into retaining him and surrendering the text of the new find to him. There was no choice but to challenge the traitor.

"Hans—" Randall called out to the Dutchman.

Bogardus, immersed in his own wretchedness over Plummer, barely seemed to remember he was not alone.

"Hans, you've given me no reason not to report you to the publishers and have you fired immediately. You boast that you've found an incongruity in a passage of the new Bible. I presume that's what you mean by a flaw. If you've found such evidence, this is the time for you to put up or shut up. For my part, I don't think you've found a damn thing to prevent me from having you thrown out of here."

"You think not?" said Bogardus fiercely.

But he added nothing more.

Randall hesitated. "I'm waiting."

Bogardus, licking his thick lips, remained silent.

"Okay," said Randall, "now I'm positive—you're not only a traitor but a phony, and I'm going to tell them to get rid of you."

He pivoted and started for the door.

"Listen!" Bogardus suddenly shouted. He came with a rush to block Randall from leaving. "You can tell them to get rid of me, but you'd better not stop there. It does not matter if they know. It is too late for them, anyway. You tell them to look at Papyrus Number 9, the fourth line from the top. No one has ever realized what that means but me. If I give that out to Cedric, to the world, that is the end of Resurrection Two. But"—he gasped for breath—"I will promise never to reveal it, if they will give me their Bible immediately. Otherwise, they are completely lost."

"They're going to throw you out of here today, Hans," said Randall.

"Tell them Papyrus Number 9, fourth line. You will see."

Randall pushed past him, opened the door, and went out.

All right, he would see.

AN HOUR LATER he had seen.

Randall was at his desk, the telephone receiver caught between his ear and shoulder, waiting for the switchboard operator in the Karl Hennig works in Mainz to locate George Wheeler for him.

Still waiting, Randall once more reviewed the sheet of typed notes in his hands. These notes represented what he had been able to learn of Bogardus' "fatal flaw" in Papyrus Number 9, line 4, of the Gospel According to James.

It had been difficult to acquire this information. For one thing, Randall was no scholar. For another, he had no access to the original fragments in the vault. For yet another, he could not read Aramaic. The last became the stumbling block when he had remembered possessing a complete set of Edlund's photographs of the papyri, the only set of prints existing, in the confines of his security file.

He had studied the glossy close-up of the fragment captioned Number 9, and it had been utterly indecipherable and meaningless, with its antlike curlicues and characters and dots, many impossible to make out clearly, marching across the picture. But the print was accompanied by a list of chapter headings and paragraph numbers showing where each Aramaic line appeared in the translations of the Gospel According to James. Papyrus Number 9, line 4, would be James 23:66 in the English edition of the International New Testament.

Since he had not been permitted to retain the copy of the Bible that he had read, Randall had tried to figure out who might have a copy at hand. The publishers were out of the city. Dr. Knight had destroyed his own photocopy. Then Randall had remembered. Dr. Knight had used the galley pages in Dr. Jeffries' briefcase.

Randall had located Dr. Jeffries in his office. The British theologian had been more than pleased to cooperate. Umm, James 23:66, umm, let us see. Randall had come away with the translated line. "And Our Lord, in his escape from Rome with his disciples, had that night walked across the abundant fields of Lake Fucinus, which had been drained by Claudius Caesar and cultivated and tilled by the Romans."

Simple, straightforward, innocent.

Where was the fatal flaw to which Bogardus had pointed?

The Jews had been driven from Rome in 49 A.D., and Jesus among them, and it was the year that Jesus had died, the last year of his life, according to James. What was wrong with that?

Without giving away what he was after, Randall had recruited Elwin Alexander and Jessica Taylor to find out for him whatever they could about the Emperor Claudius, the expulsion of the Jews from Rome in 49 A.D., and this acreage of cultivated soil that had once been Lake Fucinus or the Fucine Lake near Rome. His researchers had ransacked the writings of the ancients—Tacitus, Suetonius, Dion Cassius, the group who had written the *Historia Augusta,* and modern historians as well, before and after Gibbon. In short order, Randall's publicity team had returned with photocopies of the material they had found.

Helplessly combing the material, Randall had suddenly been struck by a date, and in moments he recognized the so-called fatal flaw to which Bogardus had referred.

Lake Fucinus had been a landlocked lake near Rome. It had no outlet. Regularly, when the seasonal rains came to ancient Rome, the waters of Lake Fucinus would rise, overflow, and swamp the countryside. Emperor Claudius had assigned his engineers to drain the lake permanently. They had developed a plan. It was a formidable task. A three-mile tunnel was to be dug from Lake Fucinus through the rock of an adjacent mountain and this would lead into the Ciris River beyond. Claudius had commanded thirty thousand laborers to toil for over a decade to excavate and construct the tunnel. When completed, he had released the waters of Lake Fucinus through the tunnel, drained and emptied the lake entirely of its water, and converted the dry lake bed into farmland.

Jesus had walked across the farmland of what had formerly been Lake Fucinus in 49 A.D. This, according to James.

Claudius Caesar had not drained the water from Lake Fucinus and converted it into farmland until 52 A.D. This, according to Roman historians.

The flaw, the Bogardus flaw.

Jesus, in flight, had hiked across a dry lake bed in 49 A.D., despite the irrefutable fact that the lake still existed in that year and would not be emptied of water until three years after Jesus Christ's death.

The anachronism, in the Gospel According to James, was there, for all to see. Possibly no one would ever notice it, as no one had seen it up until now, save one Dutch librarian. Yet, if it were to be underlined, broadcast to people everywhere, the public would be disturbed, just as Steve Randall was disturbed this moment.

There must be an explanation for this slip.

Still waiting on the line to speak to George Wheeler in Mainz, Randall felt that the publisher would have no trouble resolving the problem. With that out of the way, Bogardus could be fired at once, and Resurrection Two would finally be safe from Dominee de Vroome.

The German telephone operator at the Hennig switchboard was speaking again. "Herr Wheeler has been notified. He is coming to the phone."

There was a series of clicks, followed by Wheeler's voice breaking like a thunderclap against Randall's eardrum.

"Hello! Who is this—Steve Randall?"

"Yes, George, I had to—"

"They pulled me out of a critical meeting. Said it was an urgent call. What's so damn important? Can't it wait until I get back?"

Despite Wheeler's irritation, Randall persisted. "No, it can't wait, George. It is important. We've got a problem here."

"If it's got to do with publicity—"

"It has to do with the whole project, with the Bible itself. I'll fill you in fast. I saw Maertin de Vroome last night."

"You what? Saw de Vroome?"

"That's right. He sent for me. I was curious. So I went."

"Dangerous business. What did he want?"

"I'll go into that when I see you. The main thing—"

"Steve, look, we can talk about it tomorrow." Wheeler sounded harried, under stress. "I've got to get back to the other publishers and Hennig. Something came up, an emergency. I'll see you—"

"I think I know all about your emergency," interrupted Randall. "You've just found out Plummer and de Vroome are trying to blackmail Hennig. They've got evidence that Hennig was a Nazi book burner in 1933."

There was an exhalation of surprise from Mainz. "How did you know that?" asked Wheeler.

"From de Vroome."

"That bastard."

"What are you going to do about it?" Randall wanted to know.

"We're not sure yet. De Vroome has negatives and some prints, but pictures can lie. In this case, the photograph misrepresents the truth. Karl Hennig was just a kid at the time, just starting prep school, and to him they were having fun in the streets, and he joined in the fun. What kid doesn't want to throw his textbooks into a fire? He wasn't a Nazi, either. Didn't belong to the Hitler Youth or anything like that. But if it got out, was distorted, sensationalized—well, you're a publicity man—you know—"

"It would look bad. I know. It would hurt sales."

"Well, it's not going to get out," said Wheeler flatly. "We've got several plans to shut them up. One thing for sure. We're not paying de Vroome's price. We're not giving up our secret beforehand to de Vroome for any price."

"That's what I'm calling you about, George. Because I've just run into a similar blackmail situation right here at the Krasnapolsky. And I want to know how far—"

"What blackmail situation? What's going on there?"

Briefly, Randall told him how, through the meeting with de Vroome, he'd been able to learn the identity of the traitor in their project.

"Who is it?" Wheeler broke in.

"Our librarian. Hans Bogardus. I confronted him an hour ago. He confessed. He's been passing on our—"

"He's fired!" Wheeler barked. "You told him that, didn't you?"

"No, wait, George—"

"You go in and tell him this second. You say Dr. Deichhardt and George Wheeler authorized it. You get Heldering and his guards upstairs, and have them throw that sonofabitch Bogardus out on his ass."

"It's not that simple, George. That's why I had to call you."

"What do you mean?"

"He's trying some extortion of his own. He claims to have found a piece of evidence that challenges the authenticity of the Gospel According to James. He says he'll turn the evidence over to his boy friend, Cedric Plummer —yes, that's the way it is—and they'll blow us sky-high, if we attempt to fire him."

"What in the hell are you talking about, Steve? What evidence?"

Randall picked up his sheet of notes and read Wheeler the passage from James and the research on Lake Fucinus.

"Ridiculous!" Wheeler exploded. "We've had the greatest experts on earth—experts in carbon dating, in textual criticism, in Aramaic, in ancient Jewish and Roman history. It's been years of work. Every word, phrase, sentence of James has been under a magnifying glass, scrutinized by the keenest eyes and minds in the world. And they've all, unanimously, without a single exception, approved it, authenticated it. So who's going to listen to some fag librarian squeaking about an error?"

"George, they may not listen to a fag librarian, a nonentity, but the whole world will listen to Dominee Maertin de Vroome, if he picks it up."

"Well, he's not picking it up, because there's nothing to pick up. There is no error. Monti's find is real. Our Bible is foolproof."

"Then how do we explain that our New Testament has Jesus tramping across a drained lake in Rome three years before it was drained?"

"I'm sure either Bogardus or you have got it wrong,

have fouled it up. No question about that." He paused. "All right, all right, just to set your mind at ease, read me that material again—slowly. Wait, let me get my pen and a piece of paper. All right, read me that nonsense."

Randall read it to him slowly. When he had finished, he said, "That's it, George."

"Thanks. I'll let the others see it. But it'll come to nothing. You can forget it. Just proceed as usual. We've got to solve our problem here."

"Okay," said Randall, feeling reassured. "I'll go ahead, then, and fire Hans Bogardus. And I'll have Inspector Heldering escort him out of the hotel."

There was the shortest of silences on the other end. "About Bogardus, yes, of course we have to get rid of him. But on second thought, Steve, maybe we should do it ourselves. I mean, an employee like Bogardus isn't your responsibility. Hiring and firing is our responsibility. Dr. Deichhardt likes to be very correct in matters like that. Those Germans, you know. Tell you what. You forget about Bogardus for today. You do your job. Tomorrow, when we all get back to the office, we'll do our duty. I think that's best. Now, I'd better return to Hennig and our immediate problem. Uh, and by the way, Steve, thanks for your vigilance. You've plugged that leaking dike in Amsterdam. You deserve a bonus. And as for that—that Lake—whatever it was—Fucinus, forget it." Wheeler was gone.

Randall hung up.

Yet, five minutes later, still in the swivel chair behind his desk, Randall had not been able to forget it.

He tried to zero in on what was disturbing him.

He zeroed in.

It had been the change in George Wheeler's tone and his attitude about the firing of Hans Bogardus. The publisher had first wanted Bogardus thrown out of the Krasnapolsky immediately. After learning of the librarian's find and threat, Wheeler was suddenly less insistent about firing him immediately.

Odd.

But something else was even more troubling to Randall. It was the casual way in which Wheeler had brushed aside the anachronism Bogardus had found. Wheeler had not refuted it with any new facts. He had simply kicked it under the rug. Of course, Wheeler was no theologian, no scholar, so real answers could not be expected from him. But someone, Randall decided, had better find an explanation soon.

He straightened in his chair. He himself was one of the Keepers of the Faith, the new Faith. Both as a publicity man and as a human being, he could not sell something to the world (or, in truth, to himself) if there were questions about it that could not be answered.

Here, on his desk, was one question. The Bogardus flaw. The very credibility of the project might be destroyed if the question could not be answered.

It was a small thing, true. Yet . . .

An old, old adage by someone, by Herbert, George Herbert was it, or perhaps Benjamin Franklin, jogged through his head. *For want of a nail the shoe is lost, for want of a shoe the horse is lost, for want of a horse the rider is lost.*

Well, this rider was not going to get lost.

He was going to nail this one down.

Randall reached for the telephone and pressed the buzzer. "Angela, call Naomi Dunn. Tell her I'd like to get a flight to Paris in the next two hours. Tell her to arrange an appointment for me with Professor Henri Aubert in his lab for late this afternoon."

"Another trip? Is something the matter, Steve?"

"Just research," he said, "a little more research."

ONCE MORE, Randall was in Paris, in the Centre National de la Recherche Scientifique on the Rue d'Ulm where Professor Aubert had his office and laboratories.

Now, on opposite ends of a Louis XVI sofa, they faced one another as Aubert opened the file folder that had just been delivered to him.

Before considering the contents, Aubert massaged his furrowed brow, and his beaky features reflected his bewilderment. "I still cannot understand, Monsieur Randall, why you wished me to review our test results of the Monti papyri a second time. I can report to you nothing different than I reported at our first meeting."

"I just want to be reassured that you overlooked nothing."

Still, Professor Aubert was not satisfied. "There could be nothing to overlook. Especially in the instance of these Monti papyri." He studied Randall. "Is there something that is particularly troubling you?"

"To be truthful," admitted Randall, "there is some confusion about a translation made from one leaf called Papyrus Number 9." Randall reached down beside the sofa, unlocked his briefcase, and extracted the photograph of Papyrus Number 9 taken by Oscar Edlund. "This one," he said, holding it up for the French professor.

"A beautiful specimen." Aubert gave a resigned Gallic shrug. "Very well. Let me review our test of the papyri."

Randall returned the photograph to his briefcase, filled his pipe, and smoked, as he observed Professor Aubert thumbing through his test reports. Aubert pulled out two pieces of yellow-colored paper, and read them carefully to himself.

After an interval, Aubert looked up. "The summaries of our carbon-14 tests confirm what you already know. The papyrus in question is absolutely authentic. It derives from the first century, and could logically be placed in 62 A.D., when James wrote on this pressed fiber."

Randall had to be doubly certain. He had done some homework en route to Paris and this meeting. "Professor," he said, "there have been some authorities who have been critical of radiocarbon testing. G. E. Wright had a single piece of ancient wood tested three different times, and came up with three different dates as far apart as 746 B.C. and 289 B.C. And after Dr. Libby reported on his testing of the Dead Sea Scrolls in 1951, someone writing in *The Scientific American* a year later thought there were many 'puzzles, contradictions and weaknesses' about radiocarbon dating and that it was still far from being 'as

straightforward as an electric dishwasher.' Have you allowed for such a margin of error?"

Professor Aubert chuckled. "Of course I have. And,
of course, the critics were right, those you've mentioned,
who spoke of a rather wide margin of error back in the
1950's. In those days, through our tests, we could narrow
an object to within fifty years of its origin. Gradually, with
improvements, with favorable conditions, we have been
able to pinpoint an ancient find to within twenty-five years
of its life." He cast aside his folder. "If you possess any
further apprehensions about the authenticity of Papyrus
Number 9, you can divest yourself of them. I have my
test reports, and I have my long experience in interpreting
such reports. It is enough. In fact, in all due modesty, my
word should be sufficient to put you at ease. You can
trust me, Monsieur Randall."

"Can I?" said Randall. He had not meant to blurt it
out, but there was too much at stake to camouflage truth.
"You are sure I can trust you completely?"

Professor Aubert, who had begun to rise, preparing to
terminate the meeting, sat down again. His beaky features
had become more rigid. "Monsieur, what are you suggesting?"

Randall realized that he was in too deep to make any
retreat. He plunged on recklessly. "I am suggesting that
you may have been something other than truthful with
me, when we were together last time, about what you
told me of yourself."

Professor Aubert regarded Randall a moment, and
when he spoke, it was cautiously. "Of what do you
speak?"

"You made much of your new faith in the future. You
told me that you had finally given your wife the child
she had always wanted. Since then, I have learned from
a certain source that you underwent a vasectomy, that
you had voluntarily arranged to have yourself sterilized
some years ago, so that you would be—and are—incapable of impregnating women."

Aubert was visibly shaken. "Your source, monsieur.
Who gave you such information?"

"Dominee Maertin de Vroome, who seems to have closely investigated many persons connected with our project. He gave me this gratuitous information about you."

"And you believe him? After all, monsieur, you saw my wife, Gabrielle. You saw for yourself she is in an advanced state of pregnancy."

For Randall, this conversation was becoming increasingly difficult. Nevertheless, he determined to see it through. "Professor Aubert, I didn't say your wife could not have a child. I said that according to de Vroome, you could not give her one, although you told me that you had." He hesitated, and added, "I mention this only because we were discussing trust."

Professor Aubert nodded, almost to himself, and he seemed to relent slightly. "Very well. You are right. If you are to depend upon my word, you must believe in it, without exception. Very well, it is true. What your informant told you is true. I did have the surgery, the vasectomy, foolishly, long ago. I am sterile. I am incapable of impregnating a woman. Still, this is something one generally does not speak of, and certainly nothing by which my word or integrity should be judged. What is important is what I told you about the effect Petronius and James had on me and my return to faith. In both those matters, I spoke the truth. What is also true is the fact that I had informed Gabrielle that I wanted a child as much as she did, perhaps even more. And so—I told her to find the means to become pregnant."

Randall felt ashamed for having brought the whole thing up, and he felt loathing for Dominee de Vroome for having programmed him to distrust his colleagues. "I'm sorry, Professor Aubert. I'm sorry to have questioned your word for even a moment."

The French scientist tried to smile but failed. "It is understandable under the circumstances. But now you are satisfied?"

"I'm entirely satisfied," said Randall, getting ready to leave. "I wanted to assure myself that the writing on the papyrus came from the time of Christ, and you've assured me about the writing."

Professor Aubert had become alert and professional once more. "Pardon, Monsieur Randall, but I think you misunderstood me. I did not guarantee that the *writing* on the papyrus came from the time of Christ, but only that the papyrus itself came from that period. Our radio-carbon dating process can authenticate the papyrus, but not what appears on it. Our tests show that the material used for the Gospel According to James—including in this instance the material used in Papyrus Number 9—is what it has been represented to be. As for the message written on the papyrus—while I am certain it is also authentic, still, that is not in my field and not within my scientific province."

The distinction, which had never occurred to Randall, now gave him pause. "Well, whose field is it in then? Who authenticates the writing?"

"That process requires any number of specialists. There would be two more scientists involved. One would examine the papyrus before an ultraviolet lamp to see whether there were any traces of earlier writing, to learn whether someone had acquired an ancient piece of erased papyrus. Another scientist, a chemist, would make a chemical analysis of the pigments in the ink itself. For example, in his writing, James the Just used a reed, cut on a diagonal to make a sharp edge, for his pen. He dipped it in ink made of *noir de fumée*—lampblack—which had been blended with an ancient form of glue. This ink can be analyzed to learn whether it belongs to the general 62 A.D. period."

"But who tests what is written, the writing itself?"

"Experienced scholars, theologians, textual critics. The textual critics would compare this Aramaic fragment with other existing Aramaic writings known to be authentic. The scholars would see that the text was written on the right side of the papyrus, not the verso or back. But the most important criterion would be the quality and style—or usage—of the ancient language, to authenticate the Aramaic itself." Professor Aubert managed a smile. "But all of this was done, all of it, in authenticating the Gospel According to James. Teams of experts were employed to verify the writing. I can see no reason for you to doubt them."

"You're right, of course," said Randall. "However, let's say I'm unreasonable and stubborn. Let's suppose I still entertained the smallest doubt. How would I go about dispelling such a doubt?"

"Very simply. By consulting with the leading Aramaic expert in the world. More than that you could not do."

"Who is the leading Aramaic expert in the world?"

"One Aramaic scholar stands above all others," said Professor Aubert. "There are many fine ones, of course, like Dr. Bernard Jeffries, of Resurrection Two, or the Reverend Maertin de Vroome, of the opposition faction. But head and shoulders above these there is one other. He is the Abbot Mitros Petropoulos of the monastery of Simopetra on Mount Athos."

"Abbot Petropoulos," said Randall, wrinkling his forehead. "His name isn't familiar to me. Nor is Mount Athos. Where is that?"

"One of the last truly quaint places left on earth," said Professor Aubert with relish. "Athos is a monastic community, on its own remote peninsula in Greece, about a hundred and fifty miles north of Athens directly across the Aegean Sea. It is a small self-governing territory with twenty Greek Orthodox monasteries, ruled by a Holy Synod at Karyes composed of one representative monk from each monastery. It was established over one thousand years ago, probably in the ninth century by Peter the Athonite, and was the only Christian center to survive Islamic or Ottoman rule. At the turn of our century there were, I believe, almost eight thousand monks on the hilltops of Athos. Today, there are perhaps three thousand."

This was all new to Randall, and sounded bizarre. "Those monks—what do they do there?"

"What do monks do anywhere? They pray. They seek ecstasy, a oneness with God. They seek divine revelation. Actually, on Athos, there are two sects. One sect is cenobitic, orthodox, austere, rigid, conforming to vows of poverty, chastity, obedience. The other sect is idiorrhythmic, more lax, more democratic, permitting money, personal possessions, comforts. Of course, the Abbot Petropoulos is a cenobitic monk. Still, his great reputation in Aramaic has made him more worldly. He studies as much as he prays, just as others also teach, paint, or garden, when not involved in their devotions."

"Have you met the abbot?" asked Randall.

"No, not personally. But I once spoke with him on the telephone—incongruous, but several of the monasteries possess phones—and I have corresponded with him. You see, Mount Athos is a storehouse of ancient manuscripts —at least ten thousand ancient manuscripts are in their libraries—and several times, when forgotten medieval parchments have turned up, the Abbot Petropoulos has sent them to me for testing. But I know him to be, from what I have heard, the final authority on the Aramaic of the first century."

During the last, Randall had searched his briefcase, and located the restricted directory of personnel who had worked or were working at the Hotel Krasnapolsky in Amsterdam. He went hastily through the list of international language experts and translators on the project. He could not find the Abbot Mitros Petropoulos' name among them.

Randall looked up. "Well, this is odd, to say the least. The abbot's name isn't listed as a past or present language consultant on Resurrection Two. Here we have the most important archeological and religious discovery in history. It is written in Aramaic. And here we have you speaking of the world's foremost expert in Aramaic. Yet the expert was never a part of our project. Would you have any idea why he was never used?"

"I am sure he was consulted at one time or another," said Professor Aubert. "It would be unthinkable for a find like the James papyri not to have passed before his eyes. There must be some explanation."

"What explanation, I wonder?"

"Speak to your Dr. Deichhardt or Mr. Wheeler. They employed the translators. They will know. Or see Professor Monti. He would surely know."

"Yes," said Randall uncertainly. But he realized that it would be impossible to get to Wheeler, or any of the other publishers, in Mainz. Professor Monti, in retirement in Rome, would be equally difficult to reach. Suddenly, Randall had another thought. "Professor Aubert, I've just had an idea how I might clear up this business of Abbot Petropoulos. Do you have a phone available?"

Professor Aubert came off the sofa and indicated the telephone on his desk. "You can use my phone and have privacy. I want to put away this file of our tests, and check what is going on in the laboratory. I shall be back in ten minutes. Do you wish my secretary to place your call?"

"If you don't mind. I'd like her to put through a collect call to our project headquarters in Amsterdam. I'd like to speak to Miss Angela Monti."

HE HAD BEEN speaking to Angela on the telephone a few minutes. His pretense had been to find out whether there had been any important business during the day that required his attention.

Now, almost casually, he introduced his question. "By the way, Angela, there's one more thing I wanted to ask you. After your father made his discovery, did he submit the James papyri to any leading Aramaic experts— or was that done only by the publishers after they leased the papyri?"

"But certainly my father had the papyri examined by Aramaic experts. My father could read Aramaic well enough to know the value of what he had discovered, but he could not trust himself. He had to go to the foremost scholars in Semitic languages."

"In Rome? Or did he consult scholars elsewhere?"

"Everywhere. It was necessary. You know the results." There was a short silence. "Why do you ask, Steve?"

"I was just curious."

"Just curious? By now I know you better than that, Steve. Why are you concerned about the Aramaic?"

There was no reason to keep it secret from her, he decided. She had proved herself completely truthful and trustworthy this morning. "Well, I don't have time to go into details. I found the informer in our project. Not Dr. Knight. Someone else. Through that person, I learned there may be a—a mistranslation from the Aramaic—something that creates an inexplicable discrepancy in the text."

"Oh, there can't be! Too many Aramaic specialists, the best alive, have studied the text in the papyri."

"Well, that's what is bothering me," Randall said. "That all of the best specialists may not have been consulted. I've just learned here in Paris, from Professor Aubert, that the foremost Aramaic scholar in the world is the Abbot Mitros Petropoulos, head of one of the monasteries at Mount Athos in Greece. I don't find his name among those who worked on Resurrection Two. Does his name mean anything to you, Angela?"

"Abbot Petropoulos? Of course. I have met him personally. My father knew that the abbot was the outstanding scholar in Aramaic, and five years ago my father and I went to Mount Athos to see the abbot. He was most hospitable to us."

"Your father showed Abbot Petropoulos the papyri?"

"Exactly. Requested the abbot to examine and authenticate the Aramaic text. It was an unforgettable experience. The monastery—I forget which one—was so picturesque. The abbot took much time to inspect and analyze the writing. My father and I had to stay overnight—eat that horrible food—I think there was cooked octopus—until the abbot completed his examination on the second day. The abbot was thrilled by the discovery. He said there was nothing on earth comparable to it. He assured us of its authenticity completely."

"Well, that's good to know, believe me," said Randall, relieved. "The only thing that puzzles me is why Dr. Deichhardt didn't employ Abbot Petropoulos instead of Dr. Jeffries to supervise the final translation. I should think the abbot would have been the first scholar they would have hired."

"But they did try, Steve. My father recommended the abbot, and the publishers wanted him. The obstacle was

Abbot Petropoulos himself. He had entered into a prolonged period of fasting, and this, on top of the limited
diet in the monastery, the unsanitary conditions, the pol-
luted water, weakened him and he became severely ill.
He had looked frail enough when my father and I saw
him. Anyway, when the translating work began, the abbot
was too ill to leave Mount Athos and come to Amsterdam.
The publishers could not wait for his recovery. They had
to be satisfied with the abbot's verification of the papyri.
For the translation, they felt that they could proceed with
the other scholars, who were just about as able."

"That explains it," said Randall.

"Now will you stop the unnecessary worrying and come
back to me?"

"You bet I'll come back to you. See you tonight, darling."

After hanging up, Randall felt better. If Abbot Petropoulos had authenticated the writing on the papyri, as
Professor Aubert had authenticated the papyrus material
itself, there was nowhere else to turn and nothing more to
question. If Hans Bogardus had found a flaw in the text,
it must be a minor one resulting from some shading of
translation. Randall would leave further examination of
that to the publishers and their theologians. For himself,
he had done enough, and he felt reassured that the International New Testament—and his own fresh faith—
would be protected from the enemy.

Five minutes later, briefcase under his arm, he was
waiting outside Professor Aubert's office to thank the
scientist for his generous giving of time and cooperation.

When Professor Aubert returned, Randall thanked him.
"I'm heading back to Amsterdam," he said. "It's all
cleared up now."

"*Ah, bon,* I am pleased," said the scientist. "Let me
see you to the door." As they started walking, Professor
Aubert said, "So you learned from Miss Monti that Abbot
Petropoulos did work for the publishers on the project?"

"Not exactly for the project," said Randall. "But earlier, five years ago, the abbot did see and examine the
papyri containing the Gospel According to James, and he

fully authenticated it. In fact, Professor Monti and his daughter, Angela Monti, traveled to Greece and spent two days with Abbot Petropoulos at his monastery on Mount Athos while the abbot studied the Aramaic."

Professor Aubert looked at Randall sharply. "Did I hear you say, Monsieur Randall, that Miss Monti went with her father to call upon the abbot?"

"That's right."

"They visited Mount Athos together?"

"Yes, Miss Monti and her father were there."

"Miss Monti told you that?" Professor Aubert said incredulously.

"Yes, she told me that."

Professor Aubert threw back his head and burst into laughter. *"Pas possible."*

Randall stopped in his tracks. "What's so funny about that?"

Professor Aubert tried to contain his amusement. He placed an arm around Randall's shoulders. "Because she was having a joke with you, Monsieur Randall. She was —what is the expression?—she was pulling your leg."

Randall was unamused. "I don't understand."

"You will understand. You see, anyone who knows anything about Mount Athos would know that Miss Monti could never have visited Mount Athos. She could not have set foot upon that peninsula, five years ago or today or ever. Did I not mention it to you before? It is the reason Mount Athos is among the unique sites in the world. No woman is allowed to cross the border of this monastic community. In a thousand years, no woman has ever been permitted to be there."

"What?"

"It is true, Monsieur Randall. From the ninth century, because of the vow of chastity, in order to reduce sexual temptation, women have been barred from Mount Athos. In truth, except for insects and butterflies and the wild birds which cannot be controlled, the female of every species is banned. On Mount Athos, there are roosters but no hens, bulls but no cows, rams but no ewes. There are cats and dogs but none of the female gender. The population is entirely male. No child has ever been born there. Mount Athos is the land without women. So I assure you, when she spoke of being there, your Miss Angela Monti was only teasing you."

"She was dead serious," said Randall in a voice barely audible.

Observing Randall's face, Professor Aubert sobered. "Perhaps she meant that Professor Monti alone went to see Abbot Petropoulos."

"Neither of them saw the abbot," said Randall grimly, "and the abbot never saw the Aramaic on the papyri." Randall paused. "But he will. Because I'm going to show it to him. Professor Aubert, how do I get to Mount Athos?"

VIII

ALMOST TWO DAYS LATER, incredibly, Steve Randall found himself deposited into the Middle Ages.

It was an early, sunny Greek afternoon, and he had arrived at his destination, the monastery of Simopetra, an old, old edifice of stone and wood and outdoor galleries and cantilevered balconies that clung to the side of a cliff, twelve hundred feet above the Aegean Sea.

Carrying a lightweight overnight bag filled with a change of clothes and some toilet articles that he had purchased in Paris, and his securely locked briefcase, he was wearily plodding across a dusty courtyard. Ahead of him strode the guestmaster, Father Spanos, a purple-robed, middle-aged monk who had met him when he had arrived by mule with his cross-eyed, foul-smelling young native guide, Vlahos.

"Follow me, follow me," Father Spanos chanted over his shoulder in his thickly accented English, and Randall, already short of breath, followed the agile monk inside the monastery of Simopetra and up steep, rickety wooden steps.

From below there rose the heavy, resounding thud of slow hammering, except that the echo was more like that of a dulled but throaty bell ringing out.

Randall paused, startled by the sound. "What is that?" he asked.

Arriving at the top of the stairway, Father Spanos called down, "The second summons of the *semandron*. It is from the wooden hammer against the cypress plank, to bring our one hundred to their prayers. The first summons is midnight. The second, now after the noon meal, is for the singing of the hours and the liturgy. The third and last comes before sunset."

Randall had reached the top of the stairs. "How long does this second prayer last?"

"Three hours. But no fear, you will not have to wait so long for Abbot Petropoulos. He is expecting you. His devotions will be brief." The monk bared his serrated teeth. "You are hungry, no?"

"Well——"

"Your meal is prepared. By the time you are finished, the abbot will be ready. Come."

Randall was trudging behind Father Spanos again, along a broad, dank, whitewashed corridor broken by chipped Byzantine columns and occasional frescoes of saints with gouged-out eyes. Finally, they entered the cell-like reception room with its recently gray-painted walls. In the center of the room stood a long table and two polished wooden benches. There was a single place setting, a pewter plate and a pewter jug with a green apple as a stopper, a tin fork of doubtful cleanliness, and a large wooden spoon.

Father Spanos directed Randall to the place set at the table.

"You will eat now," the guestmaster said. "After the repast, the abbot will receive you in his office, the next room."

"How is the abbot? I've heard he's been quite ill the last five years."

"He has been sick. Intestinal disorder. A period of the typhoid fever. Yet, the abbot has much resistance. The climate, the spiritual life, the medicinal dried herbs, and the power derived from touching of the holy icons have given Abbot Petropoulos back his strength. He is recovered."

"Has he traveled outside the community in recent years?"

"No. Except to Athens twice. But he plans to travel outside of Greece most soon." Father Spanos wheeled, and clapped his hands loudly. "An acolyte will serve you now."

"Before you go," said Randall, "one more question. I've heard no women are permitted to enter the holy communities of the peninsula. Is that true?'

Father Spanos bowed his head slightly and said in a solemn tone, "The edict was made ten centuries ago. Nothing female, human or animal, has ever defiled our communities. Three exceptions. Once, in 1345 A.D., a Serbian king brought his wife on shore. In more recent times, Queen Elizabeth of Romania approached a monastery, as did Lady Stratford de Recliffe, wife of a British ambassador, but both were turned away. Beyond such attempts prompted by the Devil, no female has been here. Example. In 1938, there died here our good brother, Mihailo Tolto, at the venerable age of eighty-two. He lived and died without ever having seen a woman in all of his entire life."

"How was that possible?"

"Father Tolto's mother died in childbirth. He was brought to us as an infant, four hours old. He grew to manhood, to old age, never leaving here, never once setting his eyes on a woman. One more example." The monk's serrated grin reappeared. "A Greek gynecologist, overworked by his female patients, wanted to be certain to escape them for rest and peace. He came to Athos for his vacation. Here, he knew, no woman patient could reach him or bother him. It is true. We suffer no temptations of Eve. Only the brothers and God. I hope you will enjoy our humble fare."

No sooner had Father Spanos departed than a shy acolyte, garbed in a cassock, began to serve Randall his lunch. The meal was simple: a lumpy gruel, pieces of white fish, imported sheep's cheese, vegetable marrow, black bread, Turkish coffee, an orange. Angela, as well as his guide Vlahos, had prepared him for cooked octopus, but he was grateful there was none. And the jug of strong red wine made what he ate more flavorful.

Yet, Randall's mind was not on this meal but on what had transpired two days ago in Paris.

Angela Monti had betrayed his trust. She had lied to

him. She had told him of her visit to Mount Athos, the one place on earth she could not possibly have been.

Throughout his arduous journey, he had been filled with inner rage, all of it directed toward her. He had loved and believed in this Italian girl. When he had thought her a traitor and a liar last week, she had proved to his complete satisfaction that she had been neither. And then he had loved and trusted her even more. Now—this ultimate and indefensible lie.

In his worst moments, en route from France to Greece, in his angry dialogues with her inside his head, he had lashed out at her, savagely called her an unscrupulous, double-crossing bitch. He hated characterizing any woman in those terms. But that was the expression of his rage, his towering disappointment in the girl he had hoped worthy of his new-found faith and belief in others.

At journey's end—ironically in a land that admitted no women—this one woman still dominated his thoughts. If she had never been here, he had brought her here, and gradually, remembering her, his anger had decreased. He tried to invent excuses for her lie, because he loved her still, but he could find no excuses, not one.

He determined to exorcise her from his brain.

He reviewed the events of the last three days that had brought him to this isolated and alien one-sex peninsula.

Late the preceding Friday afternoon in Paris, after Angela's lie—dammit, expel her, exorcise her, be free, concentrate—he had, on impulse, made up his mind to submit the Bogardus anachronism in the James papyrus to the final judgment of the world's leading Aramaic expert.

Then, while still in Paris, he had given over Saturday morning to the formalities of obtaining an invitation, then a permit, to visit Mount Athos. Without the prestige and political power of Professor Aubert, it would have taken weeks. With Aubert on the long-distance telephone, it had taken no more than a few hours. The Ecclesiastical Section of the Greek Ministry of Foreign Affairs had granted Randall his *diamonitirion,* his special passport to the independent republic of Athos, and promised it would be waiting for him in Salonika. Aubert had contacted a colleague at the University of Salonika, who in turn had contacted Abbot Petropoulos in Karyes on Athos for an appointment. The abbot had agreed to receive Randall at the monastery of Simopetra. After that, the complex travel arrangements had been hastily made.

Once his itinerary had been set, Randall had placed two telephone calls to Amsterdam. He had telephoned the Hotel Victoria to leave word for Angela Monti that he would be away on a special mission for five or six days. Next, he had tried to telephone George L. Wheeler at the Hotel Krasnapolsky, but had learned that the publisher was still busy with Hennig in Mainz, and Randall had left no more than a cryptic message that he was off to meet with Abbot Petropoulos on the Bogardus flaw and would return within days to prepare their publicity campaign for the announcement day.

Yesterday, Saturday, he had taken an Olympic Airways jetliner from Orly Airfield in Paris to Salonika in Greece. The flight had taken less than four hours. Riding up Salonika's wide avenues between Greco-Moorish houses and innumerable Byzantine churches, he had picked up his Athos passport at the American consulate, checked out the final reservations for the remainder of his journey, and spent a restless night in the Hotel Mediterranean.

Early this morning, he had taken a dirty, oil-caked coastal steamer from Salonika eighty miles to Daphni, the official port for Mount Athos. There, in the red-roofed police station, an officer, wearing a velvet cap with the Byzantine double eagle on it, white skirt, and pompoms on his shoes, had stamped his passport. Next, in the customs shed, long-haired monks had inspected his bag and briefcase, and one dour monk had actually—actually!—felt and prodded his chest, explaining, "To be certain you are not a woman disguised as a man."

Having passed through customs with his baggage and sex approved, Randall had been met by his guide, who had been notified in advance to expect him. The Greek youth, Vlahos, both guide and muleteer, was plainly dressed except for shoes made of strips of automobile tires, which he wore to make climbing easier. Vlahos had already hired an *engaze,* a private boat, to transport them the short distance by sea to the landing for Simopetra. The private boat had proved to be a light skiff of questionable seaworthiness, yet with the slightly intoxicated owner at the tiller and Vlahos and himself shaded from the sun beneath a ratty tarpaulin, the chugging single engine and rocking craft had brought them safely across the water to the boathouse wedged in between the boulders at the foot of the Lhasa-like monastery perched high on the pinnacle above the sea.

There Vlahos had bargained for the rental of two mules, and astride these, they had labored upward, ascending the precarious trail which twisted around the sheer cliff toward the peak of the aerie. After twenty minutes, they had rested at a shrine which held an icon depicting the Virgin with St. Joachim and St. Anne. While they took water from their canteens, Vlahos had explained that Simopetra meant Silver Rock, and that the monastery, their destination at the summit, had been founded in 1363 by a hermit with a vision.

Randall's only vision had been one of escaping the dangerous path, the jolting mule, the enervating sun, and finding safety and solidity, Paradise enow, at the end of the trail. Fifteen exhausting minutes later, they had reached the top, and beyond the cabbage patches soared the vertical wall of the monastery with its rotting, plankfloored balconies, and from a doorway of the building the guestmaster was hastening to meet them.

All this exotic nightmare, Randall had thought, just to learn how Jesus, according to James, had been able to cross the allegedly drained bed of a Roman lake that would not be drained until three years after His crossing!

It was crazy, quixotic, this quest. He wondered why he had undertaken it. But he knew. He wanted to keep his newborn, barely animated faith alive.

"Mr. Randall—"

He turned on the bench to find Father Spanos standing next to him.

"—if you please, the Abbot Mitros Petropoulos will see you now. It is usual to address him as Father."

Willingly, Randall surrendered his overnight bag to the monk, retained his briefcase, and allowed himself to be led into the abbot's office.

The room he had entered was surprisingly spacious and brightly lit. The walls were covered with vivid but crudely wrought religious frescoes. Icons with representations of the archangel Gabriel, Christ, the Virgin enthroned, abounded. An impressive pewter chandelier suspended from the ceiling, and numerous brass oil lamps everywhere, bathed the office in unrelieved yellow. At a round table, which held lighted tapers and was scattered over with bulky medieval books, stood a patriarch of surely seventy years or more.

He wore a fezlike black hat, a heavy black robe with a small skull-and-crossbones sewn into the habit, and crude peasant's shoes. He was a smallish, frail Greek, with patches of parchment-thin brown skin showing through his long hair, despite his bushy white moustache and beard. Odd rimless square spectacles sat low on his thin nose.

Father Spanos introduced the patriarch, and was gone. This was the Abbot Mitros Petropoulos.

"Welcome to Simopetra, Mr. Randall. I hope you did not find the journey too tiring." His tone was gentle, soothing.

"I'm honored to be received here, Father."

"Do you prefer to conduct our conversation in French or Italian, or will my English satisfy you?'

Randall smiled. "English, by all means—although I wish I knew Aramaic."

"Ah, Aramaic, it is truly not so formidable as you may imagine. Of course, it is difficult for me to judge any longer. I have devoted a lifetime to its study. Do join me." He had lowered himself into a ladder-back chair at the round table, and Randall quickly sat down beside him. "I expect," the abbot went on, "you will wish to spend the night before returning to Salonika."

"If I may."

"We enjoy our infrequent guests. Of course, you may find some shortcomings in our accommodations. For one thing, I must warn you, the bathtub is unknown in our monastery. We like to say, 'Who is once washed in Christ needs not to wash again.' But you will find your mattress fumigated and without fleas or other bugs."

"My only interest, Father Petropoulos, is in Aramaic."

"Yes, of course. The language of Our Lord. A humble language, without beauty in itself, yet some of the greatest wisdom on earth was couched in its speech. Yes, Aramaic. A Semitic language. It derives from Aram, the name of the highlands of Syria and Mesopotamia, where it was spoken by the Aramaic people. These people were nomads who began to settle in northern Palestine, which included Galilee, after the fifth century B.C. It was the common speech of the poor in Galilee when Christ grew to manhood. Hebrew, itself, was generally confined to the educated. In Christ's time, Hebrew was used by priests, scholars, and judges, whereas Aramaic was used by the masses, as well as those involved in commerce and trade. Yet, Hebrew and Aramaic are very close. One might say they are cousins."

"In what way do they differ?"

"It is not easy to explain," said Abbot Petropoulos, stroking his beard. "How can I put it? Hebrew and Aramaic have the same alphabet of twenty-two written characters or signs. But these are only consonants. Neither language has signs for vowels. But when spoken aloud, each language has more phonetic sounds than its alphabet allows for. So when the spoken languages are written down, the missing sounds or vowels are indicated by marks attached to the nearest consonants. A person writing in Hebrew and another writing in Aramaic would put down the same consonants for the same word—but each would add different, slightly different, marks for any vowels. For example, if James had written *My Lord* or *My God* in Hebrew, it would come out *Eli*—whereas in Aramaic it would come out *Elia*. Do I make myself clear?"

"We-ll," said Randall, "I think I have some understanding."

"It is of little importance," said the abbot. "What concerns you here, I gather, is ancient Aramaic?"

"Exactly."

"So let us proceed. I must say, Mr. Randall, except for the scant information from Salonika that you wished me to examine a papyrus bearing writing in first-century Aramaic, I know nothing more of the reasons for your visit."

"Father, have you heard of Resurrection Two?"

"Resurrection Two?"

"The code name for a Bible-publishing venture which has been taking place in Amsterdam. A group of publishers have banded together to put before the world a new version of the New Testament based on a momentous archeological discovery made outside Rome a half-dozen years ago—"

"Yes, of course," interrupted Abbot Petropoulos. "It comes back to me now. The biblical scholar in Great Britain—Jeffries, Dr. Jeffries—tendered an invitation for me to collaborate in the translation of the Aramaic find. He was not too explicit, but the little he wrote me sounded intriguing. Had I not been so ill at the time, I would have been tempted to accept. But it was impossible. Are you able to reveal, Mr. Randall, what it is about? I shall hold it in confidence."

Without hesitation, in the next five minutes, Randall unfolded the high points contained in the Petronius Parchment and the Gospel According to James.

When he had finished, the abbot's eyes shone. "Can it be?" he muttered. "Can it be, such a miracle as this?"

"It can be, and it is," said Randall quietly, "depending upon your judgment of one puzzling fragment of papyrus found in the excavation."

"This is the Lord's work," said the abbot. "I am His servant."

Randall lifted his briefcase to his lap, unlocked it, and sought Edlund's photograph of Papyrus Number 9. As he did so, he said, "This discovery was made in an ancient resort near Rome by Professor Augusto Monti, the Italian archeologist. I was given to understand that Professor Monti and his daughter called upon you five years ago to authenticate his find. I've since learned it would be impossible for his daughter to have visited Mount Athos—"

"Utterly impossible."

"—but I've wondered whether Professor Monti himself actually came here to consult with you."

The abbot's great beard moved from side to side. "No one, no one by that name, has ever called upon me. At least . . ." His voice drifted off, and the corners of his eyes wrinkled, as he tried to remember something. "Monti, you said? Was this the one from the University of Rome?"

"That's right."

"I do recall an exchange of correspondence, I definitely recall that. It may have been four or five years ago. Perhaps even earlier. This professor in Rome wished me to be his guest, to pay for me to come to him in Rome to authenticate some Aramaic papyri. He was too busy to visit me in Athos. Later—another thing I recall—Dr. Jeffries, in inviting me to collaborate in the translation, did refer to an Italian archeologist as the discoverer of two remarkable first-century documents. But as to meeting Monti personally here in Athos or anywhere—no, I have never had the good fortune to meet him."

"I thought not," said Randall, concealing his bitterness. "I only wanted to be sure." He lowered his briefcase to the floor, but held the photograph of the crucial papyrus, as well as a copy of the final English translation of the Aramaic. "This is what I have come to Athos to show you. But before I show it to you, Father, let me explain the problem that has arisen, the one I am hoping you can resolve."

Omitting details about Bogardus and his role at Resurrection Two, Randall briefly explained that someone, even as the International New Testament was on the presses, had stumbled upon an anachronism, a discrepancy, in the translation of the passage describing Jesus' flight from Rome across a fertile valley where Lake Fucinus had once existed.

"Yet, according to Roman historians," concluded Randall, "Lake Fucinus was not drained of water until three years later."

The abbot understood. "Allow me to see the translation," he requested.

Randall handed it to him. "See the fourth and fifth lines."

The abbot read the translation to himself, then reread the fourth and fifth lines, half aloud. "Our Lord—mmm —'that night walked across the abundant fields of Lake Fucinus, which had been drained by Claudius Caesar and cultivated and tilled.' " He rocked thoughtfully. "Yes. Now if you will permit me to see the Aramaic from which this translation was made."

Randall handed the photograph to the abbot. The Greek elder glanced at the photograph, grimaced, and looked up. "This is merely a reproduction, Mr. Randall. I must see the original papyrus."

"I don't have it, Father. They would never let me, or anyone, travel with it. The papyrus is far too valuable. They keep it under security in a special vault in Amsterdam."

Abbot Petropoulos was plainly disappointed. "Then the task you assign me is doubly difficult. To read Aramaic, those tiny characters, is difficult enough. But to examine them in a reproduction, and try to translate them accurately, is nearly impossible."

"But this photograph was taken with infrared, to bring out the most faded characters and—"

"No matter, Mr. Randall. Reproduction is a second state, and almost always—to my aging eye—unsettling."

"Can you at least try to make out what's in the photograph, Father?"

"I intend to. I certainly intend to." He rose with a grunt, hobbled over to a lamp table, opened a drawer, and withdrew a large magnifying glass.

Randall watched intently as the abbot bent, holding the photograph of the papyrus beneath the lamp, and studied it through the magnifier. For several minutes, the abbot continued to inspect the photograph with deep concentration. At last, he set the magnifying glass on the table, and shuffled back to his chair, where he picked up the translation and read it once more.

Wordlessly, he returned the translation to Randall, and stroking his full white beard, he appraised the photograph. "You know, of course, Dr. Jeffries and his colleagues had the advantage of working from the original papyrus. With this in mind, it is likely their translation is excellent. If it is, then the codex or scroll this fragment represents must certainly be regarded as the most astounding and thrilling discovery in Christian history."

"I have no doubt about that," Randall agreed. "But I do doubt that—or at least wonder whether—the translation from the Aramaic was exact?"

Abbot Petropoulos scratched beneath his beard, lost in thought. "As far as I can make out from the photograph, the translation is quite accurate. I could not swear, give an oath, that this is so. Many of the Aramaic characters, as you can see for yourself, are faded, almost washed out, blurred by the passage of centuries. Several words, in the lines you question, are barely legible."

"I know, Father, but still—"

Ignoring Randall, the Greek elder went on. "It is always so with these ancient manuscripts. A layman does not comprehend the problems. First, we are dealing with the physical material, the papyrus. What is the papyrus that was used in a manuscript like this one? This writing paper was manufactured from the pith in the stem of the papyrus plant, found in the Nile region of Egypt. The pith was sliced into strips, and two layers of these strips were glued together crosswise. The resulting papyrus paper was no more durable than our modern cheap bond paper, and certainly not meant to survive nineteen centuries of time. In damp climates, papyrus disintegrated. Under dry conditions, it survived longer, but became extremely brittle, likely to crack or crumble into dust at the touch of a finger. This papyrus fragment you have shown me in a photograph is probably so brittle, so worn, that the writing on it is almost obscure. Further, in the first century, Aramaic was written in square-shaped script, each letter or character set down separately on this pith paper. As a result, individual words were not connected. One might think this would make them easier to distin-

guish and read. Quite the opposite. It is far easier to read
a word in which the letters are connected in cursive or
running hand, but unfortunately, connected words, cursive writing, did not come into being until the ninth century. Such are the obstacles, made greater to overcome
when one is considering them in a reproduction."

"Yet, this Aramaic was read, was fully translated."

"It was, just as the thirty-one hundred ancient fragments and manuscripts of the New Testament, which exist
around the world—and eighty of them on papyrus and
two hundred of them in uncials, that is, in capital letters
—were also successfully translated. But they were translated after enormous difficulties."

Randall persisted. "Apparently, in these papyri also,
the difficulties were overcome. The Gospel According to
James was translated. You've said you believe that it
may be an accurate translation. Then how can you explain
the incongruity in the text?"

"There are several possible explanations," said the
abbot. "We do not know whether James, in 62 A.D., was
literate enough to have been able to write this gospel in
his own hand. He may have been. More likely, to save
time, he dictated it to an amanuensis, a practiced scribe,
and only affixed his signature. This papyrus may represent what the scribe first wrote down, or an extra copy—
one of the two other copies James said he had sent to
Barnabas and Peter—set down by a scribe. In listening
to the dictation, the scribe may have heard something
wrong, misunderstood it, transferred it to his papyrus
incorrectly. Or a copyist, because of a tired hand or eye,
or a mind given to wandering, may have copied a word,
several words, a phrase, incorrectly. Remember, in Aramaic, a mere dot over or under a word, or a dot placed
in the wrong position, can entirely change the meaning
of that word. For example, there is a word in Aramaic
that can mean 'dead' or can mean 'village,' simply depending on where a dot is placed. Such a minor error
might very well account for the anachronism. Or, indeed,
in writing or dictating this biography of Christ, thirteen
years after Christ's death, James's own memory may have

been faulty about where or how Our Lord departed from Rome."

"Do you believe that?"

"No," said the abbot. "This material was too precious, even in its time, to permit slipshod human error."

"What do you believe?"

"I believe the most probable explanation would be that the modern translators—with all due deference to Dr. Jeffries and his colleagues—made a mistake in translating the Aramaic into English and into our other contemporary languages. The mistake may have occurred because of either of two reasons."

"And those reasons?"

"The first is simply that we do not know today all the Aramaic words that James knew in 62 A.D. We do not know the entire Aramaic vocabulary. No dictionary existed for that language, and none came down to us. So, while we have successfully defined many of the words, each newly discovered papyrus gives us unknown words we had not seen before. I remember one discovery made in the grotto of Murabba'at, a wadi in the Judean Desert, that I was called upon to help translate. The discovery consisted of legal contracts in Aramaic written in 130 A.D. and two letters written in Aramaic by the Jewish rebel chief, Bar-Kokhba, who was responsible for the 132 A.D. revolt against Rome. There were numerous Aramaic words I had never seen before."

"How could you translate them then?"

"The very way Dr. Jeffries and his colleagues translated some of the unknown words they surely encountered in the James papyri—by comparison to known words in the text, by trying to understand the meaning and sense the writer was striving for, by similarity to familiar grammatical forms. What I am saying is that it is often impossible to express an ancient language in modern words. At such times, translation becomes more a matter of interpretation. But this kind of interpretation can lead to mistakes."

The abbot patted his beard thoughtfully, and then continued. "The second pitfall, Mr. Randall, is that each

Aramaic word may have several meanings. For example, there is one Aramaic word that means 'inspiration' and 'instruction' and 'happiness.' Which definition, a translator would have to decide, had James meant to use? The translator's decision is both subjective and objective. Subjectively, he must weight the juxtaposition of the various words in a line or several lines. Objectively, he must try to see that a dot or stroke that may have once existed has now faded away. It is so easy to overlook, to miscalculate, to blunder. Human beings are not all-knowing. They are susceptible to misjudgments. The translators of the King James Version of the New Testament worked from ancient Greek texts, and they referred to Jesus as 'his Son.' Actually, ancient Greek had no word like 'his.' This was corrected in the Revised Standard Version to read 'a Son.' This change was probably more accurate, and it alters the meaning of the reference to Jesus."

"Could that have happened in this translation?"

"It could have. The Aramaic was translated to read that Our Lord 'walked across the abundant fields of Lake Fucinus, which had been drained.' If you substitute 'fields around' or 'fields near' for 'fields of' and 'which would be' for 'which had been,' the meaning is entirely changed."

"You believe it is possible those words were mistranslated?"

"I believe that is the most likely explanation."

"And if they were not mistranslated? If this is an accurate translation?"

"Then I would regard the entire authenticity of the Gospel According to James as suspect."

"And if this was merely mistranslated?"

"I would regard the new gospel as accurate and the most momentous discovery in man's history."

"Father," said Randall, leaning forward in his chair, "don't you feel it would be worth any effort to find out whether this gospel is, indeed, the most momentous in man's history?"

Abbot Petropoulos appeared confused. "What are you trying to say?"

"I am suggesting you return with me to Amsterdam tomorrow morning, and there examine the original papyrus yourself, and once and for all tell us whether we have a true discovery or a possibly spurious one."

"You want me to go to Amsterdam?"

"Tomorrow. Your expenses would be paid. A generous contribution would be made to your monastery. But most important, your authentication could place the International New Testament above suspicion."

Abbot Petropoulos nodded thoughtfully. "The last *is* the most important. It would, indeed, be God's work. Yes, Mr. Randall, such a trip is possible. But not tomorrow."

"Wonderful!" exclaimed Randall. "When can you make it?"

"I have long been planning to attend, as representative of our monastic republic of Mount Athos, an ecclesiastical council of the Greek Orthodox Church, which will be presided over by my superior and friend, His Holiness the Patriarch of Constantinople. It is imperative I attend the sessions along with the metropolitans of the church. We must make every effort to bind our eight million faithful closer together. The opening session of the council takes place in Helsinki seven days from today. I have been scheduled to leave Athens for Helsinki five days from now."

The old abbot slowly came to his feet. Randall felt sure there was a smile hidden behind the full beard.

"So, Mr. Randall," the abbot continued, "I have just been considering leaving here one day earlier, in four days from now, and making a brief detour. After all, Amsterdam could be considered on the route to Helsinki, could it not? Yes, I will be there to set eyes upon your original papyrus, and to tell you whether we have been visited by a miracle or a hoax. . . . Now, Mr. Randall, you must rest before dinner. We are preparing our favorite delicacy for you. Have you ever tried boiled octopus before?"

* * *

RANDALL HAD EXPECTED, upon returning to Amsterdam and his job at the Hotel Krasnapolsky three days later, to find George L. Wheeler and the other four publishers furious with him for his truancy.

Instead, Wheeler's reaction had taken him completely by surprise.

Actually, Randall had returned the evening before—he had left Mount Athos at daybreak of Monday morning and arrived in Amsterdam on Tuesday night—and he had meant to confront Wheeler immediately, and follow that scene by one more showdown, the one with Angela Monti. But the return trip, the treacherous descent of the mountainside on a mule, the private boat, the coastal steamer, the jetliner from Salonika to Paris, the changeover in Paris, the plane to Amsterdam, the taxi ride from Schiphol Airport to his hotel, had been more grueling than his first trip.

He had come back to his suite grimy and staggering with fatigue, and in no condition for a confrontation with Wheeler or with Angela. He had been too exhausted even to shower. He had fallen on his bed, and slept straight through until early this morning.

Going to his office in the Krasnapolsky, he had decided that he was not yet ready to have it out with Angela. First things first, he had told himself. There were two testings of faith to be made, that of the validity of the Word, and that of Angela's honesty, and it was the Word that must be faced first.

From the reception room of the publishers' offices, he had made an interoffice call to Angela, had greeted her, had deflected her warm welcome, had explained that he would be tied up with the publishers the entire day (and because he had known he would not be, and had not wished to see her when he returned to his office, he had given her a research assignment at the Netherlands Bijbelgenootschap, the Bible Society). As for a date this evening, he had been evasive. He might still be tied up, he had said, but he would let her know.

That done, he had marched into Wheeler's office, prepared for the worst, and he had been surprised.

He had impulsively spoken out at once, not giving the publisher a chance to interrupt, revealing where he had been and what he had been doing in the past five days.

Wheeler had heard him with benign interest, and had responded in a manner almost congratulatory. "No, I'm not worried that you've neglected your promotional work. None of us is. I think it is far more important that you convince yourself there is nothing wrong here. After all, we can't expect you to put your heart into the selling of a product, unless you believe in it one hundred percent."

"Thank you, George. Once Abbot Petropoulos has seen the fragment, and approved, I'll be totally converted."

"That's another thing I may say we're grateful for. We've always wanted to get Petropoulos out of his hermitage, merely to double-check the translation, and we've always failed. You've succeeded where we've failed, and we can only be thankful for your initiative. Not that we've ever had any doubts about the papyrus. But it'll be a feather in our caps to have the abbot associated with the project, and it'll be a pleasure to see him dispel your last worry."

"That's good of you, George. I'll make up the work. We'll be ready on announcement day."

"Announcement day. We'll all feel relieved when that's come and gone. Meanwhile, although we have to remain vigilant, I think we can all breathe a little easier now."

"How so?" Randall had wondered.

"On the Hennig side, I think we've got a feasible plan to protect him from Plummer's blackmail. As for our office Judas, that bastard Hans Bogardus, we fired him. We threw him right out of here the minute we came back from Mainz."

"You did?"

"Oh, he put up a fuss, threatened us with exposure as he'd threatened you, warned us that he'd point out his so-called fatal flaw to de Vroome and Plummer and they'd ruin us the minute the new Bible was made public. We told him they could go ahead and try, but his friends' efforts would avail them nothing. Once they saw the

Bible, they'd see it was invincible. Anyway, we threw Bogardus out of here."

Randall had never been more impressed. That the publishers had been unafraid of Bogardus, and were ready to welcome Abbot Petropoulos' examination of their papyrus, had almost restored Randall's faith in the project completely.

There had been one last request to make. "George, I have the photograph of Papyrus Number 9 in my briefcase—"

"You shouldn't be lugging anything as precious as that around. You should keep it under lock and key in your fireproof file."

"I will, after this. But I wanted to compare it with the original papyrus fragment in the vault. I wanted to see whether the original is really easier to read. In other words, I'd like to know what the abbot will have to work with."

"You want to have a look at the original? Certainly, if it'll make you happy. No problem. Let me ring Mr. Groat in the vault and tell him to take the original out and have it ready. Then we'll go down to the basement, and you can see for yourself. I warn you, there won't be much to see. Trying to make out anything on an ancient piece of papyrus is almost impossible, unless you're an expert like Jeffries or Petropoulos. Still, you'll get a kick out of it, just seeing it—a piece of manuscript from 62 A.D. bearing the words, the actual words, written by the brother of Jesus. It'll be something you'll want to tell your grandchildren one day. Very well, let me get hold of Mr. Groat, and then we'll go downstairs."

All that had occurred before ten o'clock this morning.

Now, at eight minutes after ten, Randall and Wheeler were in the elevator, descending beneath the Hotel Krasnapolsky to the basement where the specially constructed vault safeguarded the treasures that had made Resurrection Two and the International New Testament a reality.

The self-service elevator came to a smooth, gentle stop, the automatic door slid open, and Randall followed Wheeler into the basement, where they acknowledged the salutation of the armed security man seated in a folding chair.

They clattered across the cement floor of the gloomy basement, their heels sending reverberations through the underground passage. Turning a corner into a second corridor, they were met by a dazzling square of fluorescent light shining at them from the far end.

"The vault," explained Wheeler.

Nearing the square of light, Randall could make out the massive fireproof vault door, with its silvery latch and black-and-white combination safe dial, as it stood ajar.

Suddenly, from the recesses of the vault, burst the stocky figure of a man. He catapulted through the doorway and came on a run toward them.

Startled, Randall and Wheeler stopped, and Randall gaped at the man whose flat toupee was askew, his brush of a moustache dancing, his dark suit coat flying open to reveal his bobbing gun holster. This was Mr. Groat, the vault curator.

He skidded up before them, panting so heavily that he was unable to utter the words he was trying to speak.

Wheeler grabbed him by the shoulders. "Groat, what in the hell's the matter?"

"Mijnheer Wheeler!" Groat cried out. *"Help! Ik ben bestolen! Politie!"*

Wheeler shook him hard. "Dammit, man, speak English! *Spreek Engels!"*

"Help—we need help," the stocky Dutchman gasped. "I—we—we have been robbed. The police, we must call the police!"

"Dammit, Groat, this whole place is filled with our police," said Wheeler angrily. "What's happened? Pull yourself together and tell me what's happened."

Groat broke into a spasm of coughing which he finally brought under control. "The papyrus—the Papyrus Number 9—it is missing—gone! It has been stolen!"

"You're crazy! It can't be!" bellowed the publisher.

"I have searched everywhere—everywhere," whispered Groat. "It is not in its assigned drawer—even the other drawers—it is not in them—it is not anywhere."

"I don't believe it," snapped Wheeler. "Let me look for myself."

Wheeler started ahead, going fast, with the terrified curator at his heels.

Randall followed slowly, trying to understand, to put it together in his head.

Reaching the open entrance to the vault, Randall scanned the fireproof, burglarproof chamber. It was at least twenty feet deep and ten feet wide, constructed of steel-reinforced concrete against which were fastened tiers of metal drawers, and all of these, Randall had heard, were asbestos-lined. Four fluorescent lights set in the concrete ceiling shone down on a long rectangular table covered with white matting on which rested a dozen or so oblongs of flat glass.

Randall's attention was drawn to the activity of Wheeler and the vault curator.

Groat was pulling out one wide, low, glass-topped drawer after another, as Wheeler examined its contents. The pair moved from one drawer to the next, and the publisher appeared increasingly frustrated and apoplectic.

Wondering whether there could be any other areas in the chamber where the papyrus might have been misplaced, or even hidden, Randall examined the vault once more. There were two air vents high on the left wall, and beneath them, at eye level, a series of dials and switches, no doubt to control the humidity for the priceless brittle papyrus and parchment. The stone floor was clean.

Randall stood back, as the publisher, his face dark and worried, and the dumbfounded, burly curator came toward him.

"It's impossible, but he's right," croaked Wheeler. "Papyrus Number 9 is missing."

"Just that one?" asked Randall incredulously. "What about the others? Are they still there?"

"Just the one," said Wheeler, trembling with mingled rage and frustration. "Everything else is in place." He pushed between Randall and Groat to inspect the lock of the massive steel door. "No marks, no paint chipped off. It hasn't been jimmied."

Randall addressed himself to the curator. "When did you last see Papyrus Number 9?"

"Yesterday evening," said the frightened Groat, "in the evening when I shut the vault to go home. I check each drawer for each specimen every night before I leave, to be sure it is there, to study its condition so that I know the humidifier is preserving it properly."

Wheeler spun around. "Have there been any visitors down here since last night?"

"None, not one," said Groat, "until you and Mr. Randall arrived."

"What about the guards that Heldering keeps on duty down here?" Randall wanted to know.

"Impossible for them," said the curator. "They would have no means to break in. They do not have the intricate safe dial combination."

"Who knows the combination?" demanded Randall.

Wheeler stepped between them. "I can tell you who has access. There are seven persons only. Groat, of course. Heldering. The five publishers—Deichhardt, Fontaine, Gayda, Young, and myself. That's it."

"Could someone have stolen the combination numbers?" said Randall.

"No," replied Wheeler flatly. "The combination's never been put to paper. We've each memorized it." He shook his head. "This just couldn't happen. It's incredible. The damnedest mystery I've ever come up against. There's got to be a simple solution to this. I say again, it couldn't happen."

"It happened," said Randall, "and to the one piece of papyrus—by coincidence—we are concerned with, the one we came down to see."

"I don't give a damn which papyrus it is," Wheeler barked. "We can't afford to lose a fragment. My God, this could be a disaster. We don't even own the materials. They belong to the Italian government. They are national treasures. After our lease expires, we've got to return them. And that's not the worst of it. The worst of it is we've got to have every single one of the original papyri to back up, to prove the validity of our International New Testament."

"Especially Papyrus Number 9," said Randall quietly. "That's the one in question."

Wheeler frowned. "Nothing's in question."

"Plummer and de Vroome will tell the world this one is, and the whole Bible because of it, unless the Abbot Mitros Petropoulos can see it and give us the answer."

Wheeler slapped his forehead. "Petropoulos! I forgot about him. When is he checking in here?"

"Tomorrow morning."

"Well, hell, you'll have to delay him or postpone him. Cable him. Tell him his examination has to be postponed. Tell him we'll be in touch with him in Helsinki."

Randall's heart sank. "George, I can't do that. He's on his way to Amsterdam already."

"Dammit, Steve, you have to! We have nothing to show him. Now, let's stop wasting time. I've got to notify Heldering and his staff, and Deichhardt and the others. Our main job is to find out where that papyrus fragment is and recover it."

"The Amsterdam police," said Groat, "we must call the police."

Wheeler turned on him. "Are you crazy? If we let that whole damn city police force in on this, we'd be dead. The end of our security. De Vroome would know everything. He'd be off and running. No, that's out. We have our own police force. I'm getting Heldering right on it. Everything on two legs inside Resurrection Two—and this has to be an inside job—is going to be third-degreed to a fare-thee-well. Every office, every desk is going to be turned inside out. Even the quarters where our personnel live, everything searched, until we recover that missing papyrus. Groat, you stay right here at the vault, you stand by. The security guard, too. Me, I'm going straight upstairs to sound the alarm. And you—you, Steve—notify Petropoulos we can't see him, at least not now."

Ten minutes later, when Randall returned to his

office, still deeply troubled, he found an envelope propped against the calendar on his desk.

It was a cablegram sent from Athens.

It was signed Abbot Mitros Petropoulos.

He was, indeed, already on his way to Amsterdam and eager to examine the fragment. He would arrive tomorrow morning at 10:50.

Randall groaned inwardly. The expert of experts, the restorer of faith, was on his way. There was no stopping him anymore. And there was no Bogardus flaw to show him now, nothing to show him, nothing at all.

Randall felt sick. Not from frustration—but from distrust.

THE FOLLOWING MORNING, having come to Schiphol Airport a half hour early, Steve Randall sat at the snack bar of the coffee shop awaiting the arrival of Abbot Mitros Petropoulos on the Air France flight he had transferred to in Paris.

Sipping his hot coffee—the third cup of the morning—Randall stared glumly at the festive quintet of white globular lamps rising from the counter.

He felt more depressed than ever. He had no idea what he could tell the abbot, except the truth about the disappearance of Papyrus Number 9, which the publishers did not want known. Randall could think of no lie, so he had decided that he must tell the truth and tender endless apologies for bringing the elderly priest out of his way. He could imagine the abbot's dismay at the news of such a loss. He wondered, also, whether the abbot would entertain any suspicions, the same suspicions that had been eating away at his own innards since yesterday.

For yesterday's long hunt for a clue to the missing papyrus had drawn a total blank.

Heldering and his security agents had interrogated every person working in Resurrection Two on both floors of the Grand Hotel Krasnapolsky. They had also poked through every nook and cranny of every office and conference room. They had made a list of every member of the project not on the premises and sought each one out, from Dr. Knight toiling in the San Luchesio clergymen's hotel to Angela Monti at the Victoria Hotel, after she had returned from her research assignment. They had even searched Mr. Groat's apartment and, Randall had overheard, slipped into Hans Bogardus' rooms while the former librarian was absent.

Inspector Heldering and his agents had learned nothing and found no trace of Papyrus Number 9.

The publishers, who had refused either to panic or to give up, had shut themselves in with Heldering until midnight. For everyone concerned, the mystery had deepened. For Randall, only his suspicions had deepened.

Last night, he had retired, alone, to his suite in the Amstel to brood. He had taken one call, from Angela, had evaded her questions about what was going on and why she had been so brusquely interrogated, had pretended that he was about to confer with members of his staff in the next room, had promised to see Angela the following night, which was tonight. The encounter with Angela tonight was another misery-making event, and one he knew that he could no longer put off.

Yes, he had brooded last night, and he was brooding still, sitting here in the coffee shop of the Schiphol Airport. It was just too much of a coincidence, this sudden disappearance of a dubious papyrus on almost the eve of its final testing for authenticity. He hardly dared conjecture how the disappearance might have come about. He had to remind himself, constantly, that the loss of the papyrus was as damaging to the five publishers as it was to his own faith. Without that fragment, they were vulnerable, just as without that fragment, he could no longer have belief. The disappearance simply could not be an inside job. Yet, in no way could it be an outside job, either.

Defying all logic, the shadow of distrust, of suspicion, remained with Randall.

From above, a voice crackled through the airport loudspeaker again, and this time it was paging him. "Mr. Steven Randall. Will Mr. Steven Randall please come to *inlichtingen*—to the information desk."

What could it be?

Hurriedly, Randall paid his bill, and hastened out of the coffee shop toward the main information desk in the Schiphol Arrival Hall.

He gave his name to the first pretty Dutch girl behind the desk.

She found a message slip and handed it to him.

It read: "Mr. Steven Randall. Call Mr. George L. Wheeler at the Grand Hotel Krasnapolsky immediately. Most urgent."

Within the minute, Randall was on the telephone, waiting for Wheeler's secretary to connect him with the American publisher.

Randall clamped the receiver tightly to his ear, not knowing what to expect, knowing only one thing with certainty: that Air France Flight Number 912 from Paris, bearing Abbot Petropoulos, was arriving in exactly four minutes.

Wheeler's voice came through the receiver, not a drone, not a bark, but a bell, jubilant as a bell.

"Steve, that you? Great news! The greatest! We found it—we located the missing papyrus!"

His heart jumped. "You did?"

"Would you believe this—it wasn't stolen—it wasn't taken out of the vault. It was right there all the time. How do you like that? What recovered it was a desperation move, actually. We didn't know where to turn. An hour ago, I suggested we try the vault one more time. But this time I wanted all those metal and glass drawers dismantled, pulled out and disassembled. So two carpenters went to work. And when we got Drawer 9 out and on the floor, we found it, we found the missing papyrus! What happened was the back of the drawer had become loose and dislodged, and the piece of papyrus and its flexible protective sheets of cellulose acetate had somehow slipped back and through the opening in the rear of the drawer and slid down out of sight, and got pinned back against the vault wall. We recovered it, dangling there, and thank the Lord it was intact, no worse for wear. How do you like that, Steve?"

"I like that," Randall gasped. "I like that very much."

"So bring on your Abbot Petropoulos. The papyrus is sitting here waiting. We're ready for him."

Randall hung up, and laid his arm and head against the telephone, weak with relief.

He heard the loudspeaker.

"Air France Flight Number 912 has just landed from Paris."

He started toward the waiting area where passengers emerged from customs.

He was ready for the abbot, for truth, and—once more —for faith.

A CURIOUS SCENE, Randall reflected.

They were inside the vault, all of them, in the basement of the Hotel Krasnapolsky, and they had been gathered there, at hushed attention, for at least twenty minutes. Their collective concentration was focused on the only seated figure in the chamber, that of Mitros Petropoulos, abbot of the monastery of Simopetra, Mount Athos.

The abbot, wearing his fezlike black hat, swathed in his black robe, his white beard brushing the table's edge, was hunched low over the brown papyrus leaf which had been removed from its cellulose folder and was now pressed flat between two plates of glass. He was totally engrossed in his analysis of the faint black Aramaic characters written in narrow columns on the rough papyrus pith. Occasionally, almost absently, he would grope for his thick magnifying lens, bring it before his eyes, as he bent lower over the table. Several times, he consulted rare reference books, then sought the fountain pen at his elbow, and jotted a note on the scratch pad nearby.

Behind him, at a respectful distance, Dr. Deichhardt, George Wheeler, Monsieur Fontaine, Sir Trevor Young, and Signore Gayda kept a tense and nervous watch. Beyond the publishers, Mr. Groat, solemn and somewhat soothed, waited.

Randall, surrounded by Dr. Jeffries, Dr. Knight, Professor Sobrier, Monsignore Riccardi, stood just inside the vault, absorbed in the suspenseful one-man show.

Randall wondered, fleetingly, whether they were all part of a death watch. He noted the time. Now, twenty-five —a tick—twenty-six minutes had passed.

Suddenly, Abbot Petropoulos moved. His frail frame straightened. He sat back in his chair. "Very well," he said firmly. He clutched his beard, twisted to address the publishers. "I am satisfied."

The silence was broken, yet no one else spoke.

Abbot Petropoulos resumed. "The discrepancy can be explained. There has been a minor error, an understandable error, but an error nevertheless, in the reading of the original Aramaic and in the translation of it. Once the correction is made, no one can question the text. It is authentic beyond doubt."

The drawn, tight faces of the five publishers, as one, opened up, shining, beaming with relief.

They crowded in on the abbot, reaching for his hand, each shaking it with thanks and self-congratulation.

"Wonderful, wonderful!" Dr. Deichhardt crowed. "Now to the error you have discovered—?"

Abbot Petropoulos found his scratch pad. "The troublesome sentence in the Aramaic had originally been read by your translators to mean, 'And Our Lord, in his escape from Rome with his disciples, had that night walked across the abundant fields of Lake Fucinus, which had been drained by Claudius Caesar and cultivated and tilled by the Romans.' Several of the almost invisible writing strokes, curlicues, hooks, must have been overlooked, but when detected, they offer different words and change the meaning. Correctly read and rendered, the Aramaic sentence actually translates as, 'And Our Lord, in his escape from Rome with his disciples, had that night walked across the abundant fields near Lake Fucinus, which would be drained by Claudius Caesar and cultivated and tilled by the Romans.' You see, 'walked across the abundant fields near' had been mistaken to read, 'walked across the abundant fields of,' and 'which would be drained' had been mistaken to read, 'which had been drained.' "

The abbot laid down the pad. "So your mystery is solved. All is well. Gentlemen, I might add, I regard seeing this James papyrus as one of the most moving moments in my long life. The entire discovery is a high point in the spiritual history of man. This text will alter, for the better, the course of all Christendom. I thank you for the opportunity to enter so close to the person of Our Lord."

"Our thanks, our thanks to you!" Dr. Deichhardt exclaimed. He and Wheeler helped the abbot to his feet. "Now," the German publisher announced, "we will go upstairs to a joyous luncheon in celebration. You, Father, must join us before we send you off to your council in Helsinki."

"I am honored," said the abbot.

Wheeler had snatched up the abbot's scratch pad. "I'll be a little late. I'd better phone Herr Hennig in Mainz. We've got to stop the work at the bindery. We've got to have the translations corrected and the entire page reset and rerun for each edition."

"Yes, yes, it must be done immediately," agreed Dr. Deichhardt. "Tell Hennig we can have no delays. We will pay the extras for the plant costs and for the overtime of his workmen."

As they began to leave the vault, Randall and his group parted to make way for the abbot and the publishers. Passing Randall, the abbot halted briefly. "You can see now, Mr. Randall, what I meant when you showed me the photograph of the papyrus at Simopetra. The photograph was not so clear. For one thing, it had no dimension of depth, and revealed no indentations pressed into the papyrus. Most often, for one like myself who has lived among these ancient documents, the original will offer what no reproduction can make plain."

"Yes, I'm glad you were able to see the original, Father," said Randall. "You've certainly helped solve a big problem."

The abbot smiled. "You will share the credit with me."

With that, the abbot and the publishers departed, followed by Sobrier and Riccardi. And Randall found himself alone in the vault with an upset Dr. Jeffries, a beatific Dr. Knight, and a bustling Mr. Groat.

"One second, Mr. Groat," Dr. Jeffries called out. "Before you put that papyrus away, let me have another look at the confounding thing."

Dr. Jeffries shambled toward the piece of papyrus pressed between glass plates, and Randall and Knight went along with him.

Dr. Jeffries was obviously distraught. The responsibility of heading the team of translators and settling upon the final translation, Randall realized, had been entirely Jeffries' own. To have been caught in such an error had been a heavy blow to his ego. At the moment, he showed it, running his fingers through his shaggy white hair, wrinkling his pinkish nose until it turned crimson. He had brought his pince-nez to his eyes, and was glaring down at the papyrus.

Randall, who had not yet seen the controversial original papyrus, closed in to have a look. It was a rather large leaf of ancient brown paper, wrinkled, mottled, thin, frangible, its edges flaked. There were two uneven holes in it, as if silverfish had nibbled away at the strands of pith. Most surprising was the clarity of the Aramaic script. With his naked and untrained eye, Randall could actually make out complete portions of the crowded columns.

"Umm—umm—I don't understand," Dr. Jeffries was muttering. "I will never understand how I could have misread that sentence. Now, as I look at it now, it seems so distinct, so clear, so right to have translated it as the abbot did. A few smears, of course, but still, I should have seen the words correctly." He shook his head sadly. "It must be my age, my age and my eyes—"

"Had you translated this section?" Randall asked.

"Yes," sighed Dr. Jeffries.

"But there were four others on your committee who checked the translation after you, Dr. Jeffries. They misread it, also."

"Mmm—true. Still, the fault—"

"The fault," said Dr. Knight with wry amusement,

"is that colleagues who work with someone as eminent as Dr. Bernard Jeffries are apt to be intimidated by him. If he gives out an opinion, it becomes a decree, a commandment which lesser scholars fear to contradict or countermand. I say this only out of high respect for Dr. Jeffries' scholarship."

Dr. Jeffries snorted. "Scholarship requires keen eyesight. My own is no longer keen. I shall undertake no more such projects. In fact"—he turned toward his protégé— "the time has come for younger men, with younger eyes and more agile minds. Florian, I may be relinquishing my chair at Oxford shortly. I may. be moving to Geneva to assume other responsibilities, quite different. When I resign I will be asked for my recommendation for a replacement. I shall remember my promise to you, Florian. Besides, I can think of no one more qualified."

Dr. Knight bowed his head. "Your good opinion of me is all that I wish, Dr. Jeffries. An auspicious day, this." He indicated the papyrus. "What matters, truly, is the marvel and portent of this find. As the abbot remarked, it will change the course of Christendom."

Randall pointed to the flattened papyrus. "Dr. Jeffries, these are the lines the abbot just translated, aren't they?"

"The troublesome lines?" Dr. Jeffries said. "Yes, those are the ones."

Randall brought his head down inches above the papyrus. He strained to examine the tiny characters. "Amazing," he said. "They're so much more distinct, easier to read, than the photograph I have of them." He looked up. "Why should that be? I thought infrared photography restored ancient writing that could not be deciphered, made it much clearer than the original. Isn't that so?"

"I hesitate to generalize." Dr. Jeffries was no longer interested.

"I thought I heard that from Edlund once. If that's so, then actually the photograph should be clearer and easier to read than the original here."

"For accuracy, one always goes to the original," said Dr. Jeffries impatiently. "No distortion. Well, enough of this bloody business. Let's go up and have lunch, with a generous portion of crow for me."

The three rode up in the elevator to the first floor where Randall, having decided to skip the luncheon, left the two Oxford scholars and made his way back to his office. Entering the secretary's room, he was uncomfortable at the thought of having to face Angela before this evening. But her desk was bare and the room was empty, and then Randall recalled that last night he had given her a second assignment at the Netherlands Bible Society.

Solaced by the thought that he could be alone—free of Angela and Wheeler and the others for the time—he went into his office, stripped off his jacket, loosened his tie, lit up his pipe, and began to pace slowly around the room.

In Zaal G, the dining room, the publishers were having their celebration.

Alone in his office, Randall was in no mood for celebration, not yet.

A scruple, a misgiving, still nagged him, and he wanted to define it better. Hans Bogardus had clouded the project by exposing a flaw in the Gospel of James, and now an unimpeachable expert from Greece had explained away the flaw and proclaimed the new Bible as pristine and authentic once more. All this was true. Yet, what had happened in between was what bothered Randall.

At Mount Athos, the abbot had been reluctant to pass judgment on a photograph of the questionable papyrus, but he had thought at the time that it was accurately translated. If this was so, he had admitted that the entire New Testament must be held suspect. Now, a few days later, the abbot had studied the very same papyrus, in the original, and had passed absolute judgment that the Aramaic had *not* been accurately translated, and therefore the New Testament was above suspicion.

What had changed the abbot's judgment? A new view of the papyrus—or—a new papyrus to view?

That was the crazy part of the business, the disappearance of Papyrus Number 9, the incredible disappearance, at the very moment when it had become vital to see it. Coincidence, right? Okay. Then the next crazy business, the reappearance of the papyrus, the incredibly fortunate recovery of it, just in time for the abbot's arrival. Another coincidence, right?

Well, maybe.

Maybe.

It was strange about faded Aramaic on an ancient papyrus, strange how the merest millimeter of a squiggle here or there could make the difference between unholy hoax and divine truth. The mere location of the minutest squiggle, not seen before, seen now, resurrected the fortunes of five religious publishers. How much of men's fortunes and futures depended on how little.

The photograph was what bothered Randall most of all. If the abbot had been unable to distinguish the characters forming the words in the photograph, he should have found it even more difficult to do so in the original. Goddammit, this simply made no sense, Randall told himself. He was almost certain that infrared photography brought to a photograph what could not be seen clearly in an original. Yet, the words in the photograph had been infinitely more blurred and faded than the original he had just observed.

No, it made no sense. Or, possibly, it made too much sense.

Randall stood before his fireproof file cabinet. He unlocked it, slid loose the security bar, and pulled out the cabinet drawer where he had finally deposited his photograph of Papyrus Number 9 at Wheeler's insistence.

The manila folder containing Edlund's pictures of the Monti find—the only set in the building—was right in front. Randall reached in for the first photograph, and pulled it out. It was not Number 9, but a shot of Number 1. Disconcerted—he had thought when he returned Number 9 to the folder, he had filed it first—Randall peeled through the set of pictures. The photograph of Papyrus Number 9 was the last one, the one at the very back.

He decided that this was no cause for suspicion. He

had been careless about filing before. He had probably just stuffed the photograph of Papyrus Number 9 into the folder without regard to where he was placing it.

He brought the enlarged, glossy, eleven-by-fourteen-inch photograph of the papyrus back to his desk, and sat down in his swivel chair to study it.

Dr. Jeffries had verified which were the controversial Aramaic lines when they had been in the vault together. Now, Randall sought those lines and found them quickly. His eyes fastened on them, as if mesmerized.

The same as before, those lines, yet somehow, in some way, not the same.

He blinked. They were clearer, more distinct than he remembered their being when he had examined them on Athos. Or so it seemed. Hell, they were as legible as, more legible than, even the original papyrus he had just seen in the vault. If this had been the photograph he had shown Abbot Petropoulos on Athos, the abbot would have been able to read the characters easily, in fact more easily than he'd been able to decipher the original.

Randall threw the photograph on his desk and rubbed his eyes.

Were his eyes deceiving him? Was this the same photograph it had always been? Or was his old cynicism, the cynicism that his wife Barbara, that his unhappy father, that he himself, always hated, was this cynicism, this self-destructive disbelief in anything of value, returning and spreading through him again like a cancerous growth? He weighed his feelings.

Was the misgiving that persisted within him an honest desire to find truth or a rotten habit of rejecting faith?

Did he have reason for renewed suspicion or was he indulging himself in his familiar, cheap and unfounded skepticism?

Goddammit, there was one way to find out.

He came off the swivel chair, grabbed up the photograph, and went for his jacket.

One person would have the answer. One person, and only one, had taken this photograph. Oscar Edlund, the photographer for Resurrection Two. And it was Oscar Edlund he was going to see right now.

A HALF HOUR LATER, Randall turned away from the taxi that had brought him to Edlund's address, and found himself viewing a nineteenth-century, three-story Dutch house located on a quay known as Nassaukade.

This was the house, Randall had learned, that had been leased by Resurrection Two as living quarters for some of the men on the project. Albert Kremer, the copy editor, and Paddy O'Neal and Elwin Alexander, the publicists, were among the tenants occupying the eight bedrooms. Here, also, Edlund had his lodgings, as well as his darkroom.

Randall's taxi had been unable to drop him off directly in front of the house. That parking space was taken up by an official-looking red sedan, with a driver in an unfamiliar uniform waiting at the wheel. As Randall approached the house, he studied the red sedan, trying to figure out what the gilded crest on the door meant. It bore the words: *Heldhaftig, Vastberaden, Barmhartig.*

The driver seemed to read Randall's mind, for as Randall came abreast of the car, the driver leaned across the front seat and called out good-naturedly, "You are American? The words, they mean Heroic, Determined, Helpful. It is the motto of the Amsterdam fire brigade. This is the commandant's—the fire chief's—staff vehicle."

"Thank you," Randall called back, and immediately wondered what the fire chief was doing here.

Randall turned toward the house entrance just as the front door opened and Oscar Edlund, his acne-scarred features more melancholy than ever, emerged with a heavyset officer, the commandant no doubt, who was attired in black-visored cap with a red shield in its center, and a gold-buttoned navy blue uniform with four gold stripes on the jacket sleeve.

Although absorbed in conversation, Edlund saw Randall, and held up a finger to tell him to wait a minute. Randall waited, still wondering, and finally Edlund was shaking hands with the fire brigade official, who then briskly took his leave. Passing Randall, the official gave him a friendly nod, climbed into the staff car, and moments later it was off.

Puzzled, Randall started toward the house, and was met halfway by the Swedish photographer.

"I should have phoned first to find out whether you were busy," Randall said apologetically. He gestured over a shoulder in the direction of the departing red car. "What's going on?"

Edlund ran his fingers through his mussed carroty hair. "Trouble, nothing but trouble," he said unhappily. "Pardon me if I am distracted. The gentleman you saw is the commandant of the Amsterdam fire brigade. He just came by to give me the report. His *onderbrandmeester*—"

"His what?"

"His assistant firemaster and some aides were here until dawn making the inspection." He looked at Randall quizzically. "You do not know? I am sorry. We had a sudden flash fire in the rear of the house last night—"

"Was anyone hurt?"

"No, nothing like that. The house was fortunately empty when the fire broke out. Everyone was at the Kras for a special night meeting that was called."

"A special night meeting? What was that about?"

"The publishers called it, but only Dr. Deichhardt and Miss Dunn represented them. To speak to us of the need for faster work. It was unimportant, a pep talk."

"And while you were away, this fire broke out?"

"Yes," said Edlund gloomily. "A neighbor saw the smoke rising and called the central alarm station in the Nieuwe Achtergracht. A fire engine and ladder truck arrived in minutes. By the time Paddy, Elwin, and I returned, the blaze had been put out, but I had to remain awake for hours while the firemaster and his crew tried to determine the origin."

Randall surveyed the building. "Your house looks none the worse for wear."

"The fire was contained where it originated. The flash fire came from my darkroom and workshop. It was controlled there before it spread. But it did do severe damage to both my darkroom and workshop."

"You mean your photographic workrooms were burned and nothing else?"

"Just that. About half of the darkroom destroyed, and some of the rest. Let me show you."

They went through a narrow entry hall, pungent with kitchen smells, continued through the high-ceilinged living room with its green velvet couches and carved cupboard, where there hung a distinct aroma of smoke, and presently they arrived at an isolated room in the rear where the stench of smoke was more pronounced.

A heavy oak door, shattered by axes, with a battered combination lock similar to the one that protected the Krasnapolsky vault, the wood of the inner door scorched and blackened, stood open.

"My darkroom and workshop, or what is left of them," said Edlund. "You cannot see much until the electricity is restored. The red lights do not work now. But this part of the room is for developing the pictures, and hanging and drying them. Those are tile walls, and on the Formica-top table I open my film. And those tanks are for—well, that is of no interest to you. But can you see? The right wall and the equipment there are charred. The wall ahead is almost burned out. The curtain separating this from my adjoining rooms was burned away. If you will come after me'"

Edlund stepped gingerly through the foul-smelling darkroom, with Randall behind him, past a machine with a foot pedal that had been grotesquely melted by flame, and into another room where the remains of cameras, reflectors, and a gutted file cabinet added to the devastation.

Helplessly, Edlund surveyed this second room. "It started in here, apparently. What a mess. A bad time to happen. I will have to work twenty-five hours a day to make up for the loss."

"What started the fire?" Randall asked.

"At first, the assistant firemaster insisted that it was vandalism. I showed him how that was impossible. This darkroom was—actually both rooms were—very specially designed and constructed in the remodeled part of this old house, to protect the area for security purposes. You see, there is no way to break in—those hooded air vents are too small—except through the heavy, fire-resistant, oak door. You saw it. The fire brigade had to smash it, break it down, to get inside with their hoses. It was not touched before that by vandals. No arsonist could solve the combination lock to open the one door."

"How many persons know the combination?"

"I have the combination, of course," said Edlund. "No one else uses this office." He thought about it. "Well, I suppose others in Resurrection Two must know the combination, since they built this darkroom for me. I suppose Inspector Heldering would have the dial numbers. Maybe, also, Dr. Deichhardt and the other publishers. I do not know. I finally convinced the assistant firemaster it could not be vandals. They would have no way to get inside."

"What if the vandals obtained entrance through someone in Resurrection Two?"

Edlund glanced at Randall. "I considered that, also. But it has no logic. Why should anyone in our project wish to destroy our work?"

"Why should anyone, indeed," said Randall, half to himself.

"So the fire brigade went on with its inspection, and just now, as you came, the commandant of the brigade gave me the report. While the report is not absolutely conclusive, the commandant believes the fire originated through the accident of a faulty electrical connection." Edlund pinched his nose. "It stinks here. Let's get out."

They left the darkroom, and emerged into the hallway beyond the battered oak door. The harassed photographer offered Randall a cigarette, and when Randall declined, Edlund took one for himself and lit up. "I am sorry to burden you with my minor trauma," he said, "especially when you have been so kind as to come to see me in my place for the first time. I am a poor host. You have some business to discuss, Steve?"

"Very little. Only one thing." He indicated the manila envelope he was carrying. "I wanted to have a look at the negative of one print you made for me—the negative for your picture of Papyrus Number 9."

Edlund reacted with complete dismay. "But that was part of my loss. You saw the inner alcove with the ruined machinery and file. My entire set of negatives, each and every one—they all went up in smoke with the rest. They are ashes. So, you see, I cannot accommodate you today. But that is not so serious. I have already arranged to shoot new photographs of the papyri and parchment in the vault tomorrow. The day after, I will have the new negatives, and I can show you the one you wish to see. So that is no loss for you. You have no worry."

"I'm not worried about that," said Randall cautiously. "I have a complete set of prints taken from your original negatives. I just wanted to compare the print I have here of Papyrus Number 9 with its original negative—to see whether the print had brought out everything on the negative."

Edlund was bewildered. "But of course everything that was on the negative is in your photograph. Why should it not be? I do my own developing and printing. I take great care—"

"Oscar, don't misunderstand me," Randall interrupted quickly. "I'm not questioning your work. It's just that, well, in going over the entire set of prints before we determined how to use them in our publicity campaign, we found there was one, just one, that did not seem to have the same quality—well, of clarity, precision—as the others."

"Which one? The Number 9? That cannot be. They are all the same, of the same quality, done in the same manner. The photograph, you have it with you? Let me see it."

Randall removed the eleven-by-fourteen-inch glossy print of Papyrus Number 9 from the envelope and handed it to Edlund. "Here it is."

The Swede gave his photograph the briefest examination. "Nothing wrong with it," he said. "Same quality as the others. Everything in it is clear. Sorry, Steve, but this is no different from the other prints I made."

"You used the infrared technique in making this photograph, didn't you?"

"Certainly."

"Tell me, why infrared?"

"I thought you knew about that. When you have to photograph an item that is, at least in part, illegible, you subject it to infrared photography. Ordinary methods would not bring out what cannot be clearly seen. Infrared will. The papyrus reflects infrared radiation falling on it and becomes—well—becomes illuminated, more legible."

"And that's how you shot the photograph you're now holding?" Randall hesitated. "Or did you shoot that photograph? Take another look at it, Oscar. Would you swear you shot that?"

Instead of looking at the photograph again, Edlund stared at Randall. "What are you talking about, Steve? Of course I shot this picture. Who else on earth would be permitted to do so? I am the only photographer on the Resurrection Two project, the only one with clearance, the only one hired to produce the artwork for your department. I shot all the photographs and made all the prints. What makes you even suggest I didn't prepare this picture?"

"Just that it appears different from the others. It doesn't have the same quality or—or style."

"Quality? Style? I do not know what you are driving at." With slight annoyance, he held up the photograph again, angling it above his eyes to catch the best light in the hallway. This time he inspected it with care.

"Oscar, concentrate on lines four and five of column one," urged Randall.

"Yes, all right. They are perfectly fine. Perfectly legible."

"That's my point," said Randall. He wondered whether he could reveal to Edlund his true concern, that the first time he and Abbot Petropoulos had studied the photograph, those lines had been indistinct, as they must have been on the papyrus itself, and now, mysteriously, they were perfectly distinct in both the photograph and the papyrus. He decided not to speak of this yet, but rather to pretend that he had seen the papyrus itself earlier. "Oscar, when I first saw the papyrus, those lines were among the most difficult to read, almost indecipherable. You could hardly make out the squiggles or tails in the Aramaic. But here in the photograph, you can make them out clearly. It doesn't make sense."

"To you it makes no sense. To a photographer it makes good sense. When I am given something like a fragment of papyrus which may have two or three areas that are very faint, blurred, stained, I employ what is known as the dodging technique. If I used a greater exposure to bring out the faint lines or areas, I would overexpose the rest of the Aramaic on the papyrus. So what I do is prevent my photoflood light from hitting certain sections during the copying procedure. I block out the distinct sections of the papyrus which need only one third of the exposure that the blackened, blurred portions need, and by this dodging technique, I obtain a fairly uniform, fairly legible negative and print. So there you have the technical explanation of why what you saw illegible on the papyrus is fairly legible in the photograph. Let me show you."

He held the print up closer to Randall.

"There, you can see how my dodging brought up the faint Aramaic in the fourth and fifth lines and made it so clear. There was another area of this papyrus, I recall, equally blackened and illegible until I . . ." His voice trailed away, and he stood blinking at the lower fringe of the Aramaic column. "That's odd," he muttered.

"What's odd, Oscar?" prompted Randall.

"This other lower area. It's overexposed. Somewhat overexposed. It's not undodged, but—but not well dodged. The paddle held up to block the light, cut the exposure—it—it just isn't like me to do it so sloppily, so poorly. I am sure—or at least I was sure—I kept my exposures balanced and even throughout. I am sure I did. I've seen these pictures a hundred times, and I have always been satisfied. Yet, here it is, an overexposed section. I mean, to the naked eye, to anyone else, it would not be noticed, perhaps. But to my eye, it is apparent. I cannot understand this."

Randall gently took the photograph from him. "Maybe you didn't make this print, Oscar?"

"I made it, because I made them all," he said doggedly. "Still, such poor craftsmanship is not like me. It's strange that this happened."

"Yes," said Randall. "A lot is strange that's happened on the project lately."

Randall wanted to add that it was strange how a few lines of the photograph that had been blurred to the eye on Mount Athos had become less blurred in Amsterdam. And that it was strange how a certain papyrus had disappeared the very day he wanted to see it, only to reappear conveniently the following day. And that it was strange how a negative he had wanted to compare to this print, supposedly taken from it, had been consumed by a fire only hours earlier. And that it was strange how Edlund's dodging technique had been amateurishly applied by him in only one photograph, this photograph of Papyrus Number 9.

For Randall, there were questions, but no satisfactory answers. Certainly, Edlund, without the crucial negative, and with the unshakable conviction that he was the project's one and only photographer, could provide no answers.

Randall surmised that unless there was someone, somewhere, to support his doubts, or allay them for all time, he would have to devote himself to Resurrection Two on blind faith. He also knew that it was difficult, almost impossible, to possess blind faith when your eyes had been opened. But opened to what?

That instant, a thought struck him, and his eyes were opened to a possible solution he had completely overlooked, the most obvious one of all.

"Oscar, do you mind if I use your phone?"

"There is one right behind you on the wall. Go ahead. Now, if you will excuse me, I have much cleaning up to do."

Randall thanked the photographer, waited for him to

leave, and finally he went to the telephone and dialed Resurrection Two.

He told the switchboard operator that he wanted to speak to Abbot Petropoulos. In moments, he was connected to Dr. Deichhardt's secretary.

"This is Steven Randall. Is the Abbot Petropoulos still there?"

"Yes, Mr. Randall. He just returned from lunch with the publishers. He is conferring with them in Dr. Deichhardt's office."

"Could you buzz inside? I'd like to speak to him."

"I am sorry, Mr. Randall, but my instructions are there are to be no telephone calls or interruptions."

"Look, nobody'll mind. They know I'm responsible for the abbot's being here. Just break in on them. This is important."

"I cannot, Mr. Randall. Dr. Deichhardt's order was exact. No interruptions."

Exasperated, Randall took a new tack. "Okay, how long will the abbot be there?"

"Dr. Deichhardt will accompany the abbot to the airport in forty-five minutes."

"All right. I'll be back in less than thirty minutes. Can you take a message and see that Abbot Petropoulos gets it the minute he comes out?"

"Of course."

"Tell him—" He deliberated over his message, and then he dictated it slowly. "Tell him that Steven Randall would like to see him briefly before he leaves for Schiphol. Tell him I'd be grateful if he would come to my office. Say I want to—to thank him again personally and to say good-bye. Have you got it?"

She had it. Satisfied, Randall hung up. He hurried outside to find a taxi.

Twenty-five minutes later he had returned to the first floor of the Hotel Krasnapolsky, eager to show Abbot Petropoulos the puzzling photograph of Papyrus Number 9.

He had entered his office, prepared to wait for the

abbot to come by, when he realized that he was not alone.

Standing across the room was George L. Wheeler, a Wheeler that Randall had never seen before. The ruddy moon face of the publisher was devoid of its cheerful salesman's guise. Wheeler was fuming. His hefty frame advanced and planted itself in front of Randall.

"Where in the hell have you been?" he barked.

Intimidated by his employer's unexpected aggressiveness, Randall hesitated. "Well, I wanted to get together some publicity photographs and—"

"Don't give me that crap," said Wheeler. "I know where you've been. You've been out to Edlund's. You were just there."

"That's right. He had a fire in his darkroom and we—"

"I know all about that goddam fire. I just want to know what you were doing snooping around there. You didn't go there to get any publicity prints. You went there because you're still Mickey Mousing around about that Papyrus Number 9."

"I had a few more doubts, and I wanted to check out something."

"With Edlund. And when he couldn't help, you decided to bug Abbot Petropoulos again," said Wheeler angrily. "Well, I'm here to tell you that you're not seeing the abbot today, not today or any day. He left for the airport ten minutes ago. And if you have any cute ideas about contacting him in Helsinki or on Mount Athos for a replay, forget it. He's been advised to see no one, speak to no one, including our own personnel, about anything involving the Gospel According to James. He's wholeheartedly agreed. He, too, wants to preserve God's work from those on the inside, as well as those on the outside, who want to make trouble."

"Look, George, I'm not out to make trouble. I'm only out to make doubly certain that everything we support is authentic."

"The abbot is satisfied it is authentic, and so are we. So what in the hell are you trying to do?"

"I'm only trying to satisfy myself. After all, I'm part of this operation—"

"Then, goddammit, act like it!" Wheeler's features were livid. "Act like one of us and not like one of de Vroome's demolition squad. You brought your own man here to check the papyrus, and he checked it and confirmed it was genuine. What in the hell else do you want?"

Randall did not answer.

Wheeler's bulk came forward a step. "I'll tell you what *we* want. We want to replace you, that's what, but we know replacing you would create delays. So we agreed that if you'd stick to your business, and keep your nose out of our business, we'd go along with you. We took you on, at a fat fee, to pitch our Bible to the public. We didn't hire you to investigate our Bible. It's been investigated a thousand times over by qualified men who know what they're doing. We didn't hire you to play Devil's Advocate, either. There are enough de Vroomes out there without your giving them aid and comfort. You're here for one thing only. To sell our Bible. And I've been chosen to remind you of your real job, and you'd better do it—do your job and nothing else."

"I intend to," said Randall evenly.

"I'm not interested in intentions. I'm interested in results. What we need is results. You listen to me. We know who tried to destroy Edlund's darkroom. We know it was some of de Vroome's hoodlums—"

"De Vroome? How could he or any of his people get into that place?"

"Never mind how. Just remember who. It was de Vroome, and you accept our word for it. Now then, we're not taking any more chances with that radical bastard. He's getting desperate, and he's capable of anything. We've decided to beat him to the punch. We've moved our announcement up one last time. We're making it right away. We're making it in eight days, on Friday, on July fifth. I've been with your staff for the past hour. We've changed the dates for the royal palace and for Intelsat. We're getting up the telegrams and cables, invitations to the press. We're rushing out pre-announcement stories, so that the press can alert the public to watch for a big event a week from tomorrow. We've ordered Hennig to bring in unbound books for your staff the minute he has them ready. We want the publicity staff—and that means you, too—on the job day and night, right through announcement day. We want every release ready by the time we march into the royal palace to tell the world about our Bible. You hear me, Steve, nothing is to interfere with your job from this minute on."

"Okay, George."

Wheeler stalked to the office door, opened it, pivoted. "Whatever you're after, Steve, take my word, you're not going to find it. Because it doesn't exist. So quit chasing phantoms, and trust us."

He was gone.

And Randall was left with his questions and without his answers. Suddenly, he was left with something else. One more phantom.

One more. The last one who might have the answers.

For the first time, he looked forward to seeing Angela Monti tonight.

HE HAD WORKED late with his staff, and it was not until ten o'clock in the evening that he had finally been able to leave for his long-delayed meeting with Angela Monti.

Much as he had wanted the reunion, he had dreaded it. Since learning in Paris how Angela had deceived him —since the journey to Mount Athos, during which he had raged inwardly at her—so much else had happened that his anger had diminished and receded with the passage of time. But a residue of distrust lingered on. If he had had a choice, he would have continued avoiding her and their moment of truth. He'd known that he had no choice—that he must see her. There was too much at stake.

When Randall had reluctantly rapped on the door of Room 105 in the Victoria Hotel, he had made up his mind to handle Angela coolly, dispassionately, directly. Yet, when the door had opened to reveal her, the tousled black hair, the seductive green eyes, the voluptuous body

outlined beneath her white negligee, he had almost
forgotten his resolutions. He had returned her embrace,
tingling at the scent of her perfume, the pressure of her
full breasts against his chest, the warmth of her being.
He had responded even as he tried to regain control of
himself. After brushing her cheek with his lips, he had
finally pulled away from her and entered the comfortable
hotel room.

Some awkward small talk had followed—her research
for him, his heightened activity because of the new dead-
line—and she had mixed a double Scotch with water for
him, and poured a cognac for herself. He had been unable
to plunge straight into *J'Accuse,* and each passing moment made the attack on her honesty—and what it must
lead to—more and more difficult to initiate.

He had tried to confine their conversation to business.
Not easy. But there had been one long shot he did want
to play. Photographs. He had brought up the problem of
photographs. A great variety was needed for the promotion campaign. He had expected Edlund to fill his require-
ments. Unfortunately, Edlund had suffered a misfortune.
Randall told her about the darkroom fire. She had been
sympathetic. Then, Randall had reminded her of their
first meeting in Milan, when she had spoken of a collection of pictures she possessed, pictures taken by and of
her father during the Ostia Antica dig.

"Do you have those pictures with you?" he had asked.
"I'm especially eager to see any photos your father may
have taken of the James papyri when he found them, or,
better yet, close-ups of the actual papyri after they were
treated and put under glass."

Yes, she had brought with her to Amsterdam a varied
selection of photographs. She had gone to the armoire,
pulled out a cardboard box, opened it, and dumped the
dozens of pictures on the green carpet in the center of the
room.

Now, a half hour later, they were seated on the floor
together, he coatless and cross-legged, examining each picture she handed him.

For Randall, the visual recording of the excavation was

fascinating. Among other things, they offered him his first glimpse of Professor Monti, a short, portly, elderly man, with the kind, cherubic face of an Italian organ-grinder. There were Italian workmen, sweating in the trenches of the excavation under the hot Roman sun. There were several posed shots of Angela, and of her older sister Claretta, taller, thinner, less beautiful than Angela, with their father in the field after his triumph. There were some photographs of Professor Monti displaying his discoveries, but the Aramaic on the papyri was lost in the distance between the subject and the camera. There was everything, except the one thing that Randall sought.

He finished with the last of the photographs. He looked up. "Fine, Angela. Many of these will be useful for our publicity campaign. I'll go through them again on the weekend, and we'll reproduce the best in quantity."

Her eyes held on him. "You don't sound too enthusiastic."

"Oh, they're good. I guess I'd hoped—well—I rather hoped you might have some close-ups of the papyri."

"There were some, if I remember correctly," she said. "My father used to sit and examine certain pictures by the hour. This was before his find was authenticated, and leased by the Italian government to the publishers. My father even had himself tutored in Aramaic, so he could read the papyri as well as he could read Italian or German or English. He practically memorized them, every bit, every character, he was so proud and in love with them."

"Where are those close-ups today?"

"I don't know. I tried to find them, to bring them with me when I came to Amsterdam. I could not find one. I asked my father, but he's the typical absentminded professor. He could not remember what had happened to them. I guess he didn't care. He had already photographed them in his brain. But I think perhaps he gave them to the Ministry, and the Ministry probably turned them over to Dr. Deichhardt." She looked hopeful. "Maybe you could ask Dr. Deichhardt."

"Yes, I suppose I could."

"Anyway, I thought you had a set of your own from Mr. Edlund."

"I have, only—well, it's not important. I just wanted to see some other shots."

She was watching him inquisitively. He evaded her gaze, and busily occupied himself by gathering together the scattered photographs and returning them to the cardboard carton.

When he had completed the task, he realized that Angela was still studying him.

"Steve," she said quietly, "why have you been avoiding me?"

"Have I been avoiding you?"

"Yes. Something has happened. When will you love me again?"

He could feel the muscles behind his neck go rigid. "When I can believe in you again, Angela," he said.

"Don't you believe in me now?"

"No," he said bluntly. "No, I don't, Angela."

There. It was out at last. He felt relieved, and once more angry and righteous in his anger. He met her eyes frankly, prepared for her protests. She did not speak, nor was any reaction visible. Her beautiful face, except for the moving eyelashes, remained immobile.

"Okay," he said, "you asked for it. So let's get it over with."

She waited in silence.

"I don't believe in you, because I can't believe you anymore," he said. "You lied to me last week, Angela. You'd lied to me before, but that was a small lie and unimportant. This time it was a big lie and it might have been important."

He expected a response, but still there was none. She seemed more sad than upset.

"You lied to me about Mount Athos," he went on. "You told me that you went with your father to Mount Athos to see Abbot Petropoulos. You told me the abbot had studied the papyri and authenticated them. Do you remember that? Those were blatant lies, Angela. I know.

Because I went to Mount Athos myself. Do you know I went to Mount Athos last week?"

"Yes, Steve, I know."

He did not pursue her knowledge of this. He would not be diverted. "I was there at Mount Athos. But you weren't. No woman, no female, has been permitted on the Athonite Peninsula in over one thousand years. Women are banned from that place. You were never there, and your father was never there, either. And the abbot never set eyes on your father—or on the papyri, either, until this morning. Can you deny that?"

"No, I can't, Steve. I won't." Her voice was barely a whisper. "I did lie to you."

"Then how can you expect me to believe in you—to trust you—to believe anything else you tell me?"

She closed her eyes, passed her hand over them, then looked at him with anguish. "Steve, I—I don't know whether I can reach you. There is so much of you that is head and not heart. Only your heart could understand that sometimes a lie is the truest thing one can speak for one's own heart. Steve, when you phoned me from Paris, my heart could hear the part of you, feel the part of you, of your nature, that worries me most and that I like the least."

"And what's that?" he said aggressively.

"Your cynicism. Your irrational, defensive, self-protective cynicism. Maybe it is self-protective for you, Steve, and keeps you from hurt. But it is also anti-life, and it stands between you and life, prevents you from accepting or giving deep love, true love. A person without faith cannot love. I heard you on the phone from Paris. I perceived you were again doubting the authenticity of my father's find. I saw you losing the little trust you had gained. You were becoming again the Steve Randall who could not be close to his parents, his wife, his child, to anyone. There you were, in the face of one-hundred-per-cent evidence of authenticity from the most respected and experienced scholars and Bible experts in the world, trying again to discredit the miracle my father unearthed at Ostia Antica. In Paris—in Athos—always searching for anyone, even the Devil, who would agree with you to justify your cynicism. Well, I couldn't stand it anymore. I wanted to put a stop to it. Not for my father's sake, believe me, but for your sake. So I said the first things that came to my mind. I remembered the name of Abbot Petropoulos at Mount Athos. I had typed the letters when my father corresponded with him. But I knew nothing about Mount Athos, so I fell into a stupid, blundering lie. Yes, I lied, I was ready to lie, to say we had been to Athos, anything, to prevent you from trying to ruin the one last thing that could give meaning to your existence. It was as if you were neurotically obsessed by the idea of doing what de Vroome has failed to do—to destroy Resurrection Two, my father's lifework, new kindled hope for mankind, and finally our relationship and your own self. That's what I tried to prevent, Steve. Obviously, I failed. You went on to Athos, compulsively you went on, and when the abbot disagreed with you and supported all of us, still you were not satisfied. Whatever the facts, proved and proved again, still you must go on. I don't know what you are after this time. But I could see just now, you are not really interested in these photographs. You are after something else—whatever it is—something to tell you that you are right to remain disbelieving, not trusting. I would lie again to stop you. I would lie a thousand times to stop your self-destructiveness."

She was breathless and weak.

She reached out for his hands, clasped them wordlessly, searching his face for some understanding.

At last, she spoke again. "Steve, I love you. I would do anything in the world to make you love me—to make you have faith, faith in me and what I believe in—in the project. With such faith you could know love—not only for me, but for yourself. Is it possible for you?"

He stared at her steadily. "It is possible," he said.

"How? What can I do? I've told you I'll do anything in the world you ask."

"Anything?" he said softly. "Very well. I want you to take me to Rome tomorrow."

"To Rome?"

"I want to meet your father."

"My father," she echoed in an undertone. "That is important to you?"

"I want to meet the man who found the Word. I want to show him a photograph, ask him a question. He's the last one, the end of the line. After I've met him, I'll have to stop. It's what you want, isn't it? For me to stop? For me to have faith? So now it's up to you, Angela. It's in your hands. Will you bring me to your father?"

"That—that would resolve any doubts you have about me?"

"Yes."

She took a deep breath, held it, and then exhaled. "Very well, Steve. It—it is a mistake, but it must be done. We will fly to Rome tomorrow. You will meet Professor Augusto Monti. You will meet him face to face. Perhaps that will solve everything."

IX

AFTER THE Alitalia jetliner from Amsterdam set them down on the runway of the Leonardo da Vinci Airport some distance from Rome this late Friday morning, and as they walked across the cement field and up the wide reddish ramp toward the *carabinieri* controlling customs, and the sign reading *Controllo Passaporti,* there had been one satisfying thought uppermost in Steve Randall's mind.

Angela had delivered.

They had followed the blue-shirted porter carrying their bags—Randall had retained his precious briefcase—through the glass enclosure of the air terminal, swarming with noisy passengers and visitors, out beneath the mammoth metal overhang. They had hailed a taxi, and going past the huge bearded statue of da Vinci, past the blue signs emblazoned ROMA, past the billboards advertising Pepsi-Cola, Ethiopian Airlines, Visit Israel, Telefunken, Olivetti, past the green umbrella pines and the outlying fields of zucchini and broccoli, past the food market known as Cassa del Mercato, past the apartments of the San Paolo suburb and the dog-racing Cinodromo and the broken slabs of the Forum and the Colosseum—and throughout the half-hour ride to the Hotel Excelsior—Randall was filled with a growing sense of excitement.

This ancient and new place, he kept thinking, this is where it began. Here, people would remember centuries later, was where Resurrection Two had started and where the rebirth in faith had had its beginning. Here was where hope had once more been given to a sorry materialistic world. All this was possible—Randall had prayed it was possible—if this last black doubt could be erased by the

470

one person on the project who, until now, had eluded everyone.

Leaving Angela with her suitcase on the walk of the inner driveway of the Hotel Excelsior, Randall had hastened into the lobby to register for his overnight stay. Once he had deposited his own bag in the large double room, Room 406, assigned him, he had gone downstairs with his briefcase to join Angela and accompany her to the Monti family villa where her recluse father would be waiting for them.

Emerging from the hotel, crossing the inner driveway toward Angela, who was now on the Via Vittorio Veneto beckoning to him, he felt as if he had walked into a red-hot blast furnace. It was high noon, and Rome was simmering beneath the intense summer sun.

Angela had hired a driver and car. The driver was a grinning, compact, ageless Italian in white ducks, who introduced himself as Giuseppe. His car, a large, sleek Opel, was blessedly air-conditioned and shuttered at all windows.

Settling into the rear seat, Angela, unsmiling, watched Randall close the back door. "You are ready?" she said. "We will now go to my father."

"Again, Angela, thanks."

She spoke rapidly in Italian to the driver. She gave him their final destination in English. "The Villa Bellavista, which is just after you enter the Via Belvedere Montello."

With that, they spun off into the traffic of the Via Veneto, and were on their way to see Professor Augusto Monti.

At last, thought Randall.

The ride took forty minutes, perhaps forty-five. Randall caught the names of some of the squares and streets they traveled through. Piazza Barberini. Via del Tritone. Piazza Cavour. Viale Vaticano, skirting Vatican City. Via Aurelia, leaving Rome. Via di Boccea, the countryside, with only scattered buildings and communities.

A sharp right turn. The Via Belvedere Montello. The Opel was slowing. The Opel braked to a halt.

"Here it is," said Angela. "Villa Bellavista."

Randall looked out the car window. Behind a green iron fence on a pink-yellow stone base, set back beyond a rolling lawn and a garden, partially hidden by cypress and pine trees, rose a rust-colored, two-story mansion.

Angela spoke to the driver, and he shifted gear, and the Opel moved slowly along the iron fence until it reached a gate being held open by a grizzled gatekeeper. The keeper waved, and Angela waved back, as Giuseppe swung his car onto a drive. Seconds later they were before the steps leading to the terrace and the recessed front door of the mansion.

Giuseppe had gone around the car swiftly to help them out. Randall, taking his briefcase, as well as his mixed emotions—anticipation, apprehension—with him, ascended the steps with Angela. At the front door, she did not bother with a key. The door was unlocked. She opened it, nodded over her shoulder at Randall, and he followed her inside.

They were in an entry hall, the floor composed of glazed bricks. To their left was a staircase. To their right was a living room. They went into the living room, an enormous room, with a vaulted ceiling and more glazed red bricks for flooring. The furnishings included two grand pianos, numerous groups of furniture, and an assortment of lamps.

A lot of house for a lone, retired scholar, Randall thought.

Angela led him to the nearest seating arrangement, a green velvet couch, coffee table, several cream-colored chairs. At the couch, Randall did not sit. He stood rigid, staring off. Two strange and confusing sights held his attention.

Ahead, the picture window jarred him. It was barred from top to bottom.

Ahead, also, from a side door, two young women had entered the room. They were attired identically, in starched headgear, white collars, and aprons over navy-blue uniforms.

Bewildered, Randall turned to Angela. Her eyes were on him. She gave a short nod.

"Yes, my father lives here," she said. "It is an insane asylum."

FIFTEEN MINUTES LATER, alone and pacing in the living room—reception room, really—of Villa Bellavista, Steve Randall had still not recovered from the initial shock of Angela's disclosure.

Until today, it had seemed perfectly logical to believe that Professor Monti had gone into seclusion and retirement outside Rome for political reasons. Even upon their arrival here, Villa Bellavista had deceptively resembled a private residence, the perfect luxurious hideaway for a onetime eminent archeologist who had made a priceless discovery. As a matter of fact, this building had once been some wealthy Roman's suburban mansion before being sold to a group of Italian psychiatrists who had converted it into a *casa di cura*, a sanitarium for the mentally disturbed. The doctors had seen to it that the building retained, as much as possible, its homey residential furnishings and atmosphere in the belief that this would have a salutary effect upon the patients.

But it was, plain and simple, to use Angela's jolting words, an insane asylum. And Professor Monti was, and had been for more than a year, its most prominent and unpublicized patient.

All of this Angela had revealed to Randall in the emotional moments following her first disclosure.

"Now you will understand my evasions and lies," Angela had said. "My father was perfectly well and normal, his mind perfectly keen, until a little over a year ago. Overnight, he suffered a complete mental collapse. He became withdrawn, disoriented, uncommunicative, and has been cared for here ever since. I could not tell anyone, not the publishers, not even you, Steve. If the news had gotten out—had been distorted by my father's enemies or enemies of the project—it might have placed a stigma, cast a doubt, on all his work, on his discovery, on the project itself. I could not let this happen. So I stood between my father and those who wished to see him. But last night, I knew I could no longer prevent you from

finding out. I was tempted to tell you and have it done
with. I was afraid you might still think I was lying. So
I did as you wished. I brought you to Rome, to Villa
Bellavista, to see for yourself. Now, you will trust me,
Steve?"

"Always and forever, darling." He had taken her in his
arms, shaken and ashamed. "I'm sorry, Angela, I'm truly
sorry. I hope you will forgive me."

She had forgiven him, because she had been able to
understand his suspicions. She had said one more thing.
"Besides, I brought you here to meet my father for another reason. He is usually in what appears to be a catatonic state, but sometimes, rarely, very rarely, he must
have brief intervals of lucidity. Always, when my sister
and I see him, he is completely out of touch with any
reality. But sometimes, there is a glimmer, a flash, of his
normal self. I hoped, for your sake, when you showed
him the photograph and spoke to him, it might touch some
memory in his past. In that way, it would remove your
last uncertainty about the Gospel According to James."

"Thank you, Angela. But you don't really expect any
recognition from your father, do you?"

"It is most unlikely. Yet, one never knows. There are
so many mysteries about the human mind. Anyway, I will
go in now to see him alone. You wait. I shall not be
long. After that, I will have someone take you in to meet
him."

With that, she had gone.

Randall continued his pacing, trying to fathom how a
brilliant professor like Monti—with a mind so alert all his
life—could overnight lapse into insanity. Randall no longer looked forward to contending with that mind. He had
never had to deal with a mentally ill person before. He
had no idea of what to expect or how to behave. Still,
clinging to a small hope that the professor might—with
some word, some sign—put to rest his concerns about
Papyrus Number 9, Randall knew that he must go through
with the meeting.

He realized that Angela Monti had reappeared.

She was not alone. She had entered the reception room

accompanied by a tall, rawboned, young nurse. While the nurse held back at the opened door, Angela, drawn, strained, came toward Randall.

"How is he?" Randall wanted to know.

"Quiet, polite, serene," she said. She swallowed, and added, "He did not recognize me."

She fought tears, but they came, and hastily Randall put an arm around her shoulders, trying to comfort her. She fumbled for a handkerchief in her purse, dabbed at her eyes, and finally looked up at Randall, forcing a tiny smile. "It—it's always this way. Never mind, I'll be all right. You can go in and see him now, Steve. Don't worry. He's harmless. Calm. I tried to tell him about you. I do not know whether he understood. But you try. Go with the nurse—Signora Branchi. She'll show you the way. I'll keep myself occupied. I've got to call home, tell Lucrezia—she's our housekeeper—my sister is coming from Naples today with the children to see me."

Randall left her, introduced himself to Signora Branchi, and together they went into an antiseptic corridor. Halfway up it, Signora Branchi removed a ring of keys from the pocket of her navy blue uniform.

"This is Professor Monti's room," she said. Then noticing that the door was ajar, she became instantly concerned. "It is supposed to be locked." She stuck her head into the room, and turned back to Randall with obvious relief. "It is the maid. She is inside collecting his lunch tray." Seconds later, the maid, in a different uniform, headgear, and a white apron over a pink dress, emerged carrying a tray with the luncheon remains.

Signora Branchi whispered a question in Italian, and the maid replied in an undertone, and padded off down the corridor. Signora Branchi glanced at Randall. "I asked how he is. She says he is as usual, sitting by the window, staring. We can go inside. I will simply present you and leave you alone with him. How much time will you need?"

"I don't know," said Randall nervously.

"Dr. Venturi prefers visits not to exceed ten to fifteen minutes."

"Very well. Give me fifteen minutes."

Signora Branchi opened the door wider, and led Randall inside. To Randall's surprise, it was not a hospital room at all. He had somehow expected a room such as the one his own father had occupied in the Oak City hospital. Instead, this room had the appearance of a combination sitting room-library-bedroom in a private apartment.

Randall's immediate impression was of a sunny, comfortable, even cozy, enclosure, pleasingly air-conditioned. On one side of the room was the bed, and next to it a table and lamp. A partially opened door revealed a large bathroom with a blue tiled floor. At the opposite side of the room, beneath a modern oil painting, stood a decorative desk and leather desk chair, and lined up on the desk were framed photographs of an older woman with heavy earrings (probably the deceased wife), portraits of the patient's daughters, Angela and Claretta, as well as those of his grandchildren. In the center of the room were an overstuffed armchair, a table with a green plant, two sturdy straight chairs. Through the broad window was a restful view of the gardens. Only the thin iron bars on the window marred the serenity of the vista and, along with the white-painted walls, reminded one that this was a psychiatric clinic.

At the window, mechanically swinging forth and back, almost lost in the depths of a rocking chair, was a small, remote elderly man, his face still plump, wisps of white hair, tufts of gray eyebrows, blank watery eyes fixed on the flowers outside. Less portly, more wasted, the man, than in the photographs Randall had seen last night, photographs taken six years earlier.

Signora Branchi had gone to the rocker, touched the sleeve of the occupant's brown sport shirt. "Professor Monti," she said quietly, speaking to him as one awakening a person from sleep, "you have a visitor here from America."

She crooked a finger at Randall, as she groped behind her to drag one of the weighty straight chairs up before the rocker. "Professor, this is Mr. Randall. He is interested in your work."

Professor Monti watched the nurse's moving lips with mild interest, but he made no acknowledgment of Randall's presence by expression or speech.

Signora Branchi turned away. "I'll leave you two, Mr. Randall. If you need me, there is a buzzer hanging down from the headboard of his bed. Otherwise, I'll be by for you in fifteen minutes."

Randall waited for her to leave, listened to the door lock being bolted, and finally lowered himself into the hard chair across from the small figure in the rocker.

Professor Monti had at last become aware of his visitor, and now regarded him silently and without curiosity.

"I'm Steve Randall," said Randall, introducing himself again. "I'm from New York. I'm a friend of your daughter Angela. You just saw Angela. I believe she told you a little about me."

"Angela," said Professor Monti. He repeated the name without accent or punctuation, with neither recognition nor a question mark. He had simply repeated the name as a child tests the oddity of a new plaything.

"I'm sure she explained to you about my connection with Resurrection Two, and the work I'm doing to promote your discovery," Randall continued, somewhat helplessly.

He felt as if he were addressing the white wall beyond Monti's rocker. He had an impulse to buzz for Signora Branchi and run. Nevertheless, compulsively, he went on talking, relating how George L. Wheeler had hired him and brought him to Amsterdam. He spoke of the excitement that he and the others on the project felt as they neared the announcement day when the professor's discovery at Ostia Antica would be given to millions of people around the globe.

As Randall pressed on, Professor Monti became more attentive. Although withdrawn, unable or unwilling to speak, he appeared to be inwardly responsive to what Randall was telling him. He seemed as alert as any slightly senile, elderly person might be to a monologue from a stranger.

Randall took heart. This could be that long-awaited

lucid interval, possibly brought on because Randall was treading familiar ground. This might be a lucky day.

"Let me tell you exactly why I am here, Professor Monti," Randall said.

"Yes."

"Your discovery has been authenticated. The revised New Testament has been translated into four languages. The Bible is almost ready for release, except—" He hesitated, then went ahead bluntly. "One problem has arisen. It's my hope that you can solve it."

"Yes."

Randall observed the professor's face. There was genuine curiosity in it, or so it seemed. Randall felt definitely encouraged.

About to resume, Randall reached down into his briefcase, turned on his tape recorder, and next extracted the crucial photograph.

"Several of us found a baffling error—at least what we think to be an error in the translation. Now, I'll tell you what troubles me." Randall considered the photograph. "I have here a photograph taken of Papyrus Number 9, one of the papyri you found near Ostia Antica. What troubles me is that this photograph isn't like the first photograph I saw of Papyrus Number 9. My worry is that Papyrus Number 9 has been altered by someone, or another papyrus has been substituted for it."

Professor Monti tilted forward in his rocker. "Yes?"

Heartened, Randall went on. "There is no longer any way to learn whether this photograph represents the original papyrus you found or if it represents an altered papyrus. The negative of the original picture has been lost in a fire. However, Professor Monti, Angela says you lived so close to each precious fragment that every character, every Aramaic squiggle, every dot, is imprinted on your mind. Angela feels that you would know almost immediately whether this picture really is a true reproduction of the papyrus you excavated—or if it represents an altered or substitute leaf. It is of utmost importance, Professor Monti, that we know the truth. Can you tell me whether this is a picture of the papyrus you discovered at Ostia Antica?"

He handed the print over to Professor Monti, who took it carefully with both quivering hands. For several seconds Professor Monti ignored the photograph, as his gaze remained fixed on Randall, and he continued to rock silently.

At last, seeming to remember what was in his hands, his eyes shifted to the photograph. Slowly, he lifted it, adjusted it at an angle, so that the sun streaming through the barred window shone upon it. A gradual smile formed on the round face, and Randall, watching, felt a surge of hope.

Muted seconds passed. Professor Monti brought the photograph down to his lap, eyes still upon it. His lips began to work, and Randall strained to catch his words, slurred and barely audible.

"True, it is true," Professor Monti was saying. "I wrote this."

He raised his head to meet Randall's eyes. "I am James the Just. These events I witnessed." His lips worked again, and his voice was louder. "I, James of Jerusalem, brother of the Lord Jesus Christ, heir of the Lord, eldest of the Lord's surviving brethren and the son of Joseph of Nazareth, am soon to be brought before the Sanhedrin and the head priest Ananus charged with seditious behavior because of my leadership of the followers of Jesus in our community."

Randall slumped back in his chair.

My God, he said to himself, the old man believes he is James of Jerusalem, brother of Jesus Christ.

Professor Monti had lifted his eyes toward the ceiling. He was going on, his cracking voice more fervent. "The other sons of Joseph, the Lord's surviving brethren and mine own, are Judah, Simon, Joses, Jude, and all are beyond the boundaries of Judea and Idumaea, and I remain to speak of the firstborn and best beloved son."

Professor Monti was reciting, in his accented English, an early portion of the Aramaic papyri that had been included in the Gospel According to James in the

International New Testament. But there was something unexpected, almost weird, in the recitation, and Randall caught it at once. Professor Monti, in listing the names of the brothers of Jesus and James, was filling in a missing part of the third papyrus, a part that had crumbled or dissolved and disappeared after almost two thousand years.

This was inexplicable, except for one possibility—that Professor Monti was, or had been, so steeped in Bible lore that he had recalled the names of the brethren from other sources, from the Gospel According to Matthew, from Acts, from the early church historian Eusebius, and filled them in and incorporated them in his recital.

"I, James the Just, brother of Our Lord—"

Professor Monti was going on and on with his demented declamation.

Overwhelmed by sadness for the hopeless old man, for poor Angela, Randall sat and listened and grieved.

Professor Monti's words had become indistinct. He lapsed into silence, and stared out the window at the gardens.

Gently, Randall removed the photograph from the old man's lap and returned it to his briefcase. He shut off his tape recorder, and noted the time on his wristwatch. Signora Branchi would be back in a minute or two.

He came to his feet with his briefcase. "Thank you, Professor Monti, for your time and cooperation."

To Randall's surprise, Professor Monti rose courteously from the rocker. He appeared smaller than before. He shuffled past Randall to his desk. He settled behind his desk, seemed momentarily to have forgotten his purpose, then opened a drawer and found a sheet of blank paper and the stub of a yellow pencil.

He made several strokes on the paper, noted his handiwork, added another stroke, and appeared pleased with himself. He took up the paper and offered it to Randall.

"For you," he said.

Randall accepted the paper, wondering what Monti had drawn upon it.

"A gift," mumbled Professor Monti. "It will save you. A gift from James."

Randall looked down at the sheet of paper in his hand. There was a crude drawing.

As best Randall could make out, it was a childish, primitive and enigmatic sketch of a fish with a spear driven through it.

This was the gift from James, a talisman that would save Randall, the professor had promised. It made no sense whatsoever to Randall. He wondered what had been its meaning in Professor Monti's clouded mind. Randall sighed. He would never know, and it didn't seem to matter anymore.

Randall heard the door of the room opening.

Quickly, he folded the drawing, stuffed it into his jacket pocket, thanked Professor Monti for his memento, and again thanked him for his time, and then he left Angela's father at the desk and went to Signora Branchi in the doorway.

Reaching the corridor, he watched while the nurse locked the door. As she came to him, she said, "I'll take you back to Signorina Monti now."

But Randall was not ready to leave. He had one more thought.

"Signora Branchi, I was wondering—is there one physician or psychiatrist on the premises who is in charge of Professor Monti's case? I mean, one doctor who has worked closely with the patient?"

"Yes, of course. We have seven doctors on our staff, but the director of the staff is Dr. Venturi. He has overseen Professor Monti since the professor was admitted to Villa Bellavista. He has his office upstairs."

"Would it be possible to see him, even briefly?"

"Wait here. I will find out whether he is free."

DR. VENTURI proved to be free.

The staff director was a semibald, slender Italian, with sympathetic, limpid dark eyes, arched nose, and busy hands. He did not look like a physician at all, and Randall decided that this was because he was wearing a lively checked suit jacket, instead of a white coat.

When Randall asked about the white coat, Dr. Venturi good-naturedly explained, "The usual clinic coat puts a distance between the doctor and the patient, and we do not find this desirable. We wish our disturbed patients to feel equality with their doctors. It is important for us that every patient—Professor Monti included—should not feel different from us. We wish our patients to trust us, to relate to us as friends."

Dr. Venturi's office was as unmedical as his own person. Seated in a floral-patterned chair across from the physician's Empire desk, Randall found himself in the middle of a room furnished with modern sofas, lush plants, abstract paintings.

Randall, in a last desperate effort to seek some clue to the mystery of Papyrus Number 9, had been reporting to Dr. Venturi on his unsuccessful meeting with Professor Monti. He had just finished relating Monti's delusion that he was James the Just, brother of Jesus Christ.

"Has the professor behaved this way before?" Randall inquired.

"Frequently," said Dr. Venturi, picking up a letter opener, putting it down, picking up a pencil, dropping it. "And it is most puzzling to us. The behavior is inconsistent with his general symptoms. You see, one who feels he is a messiah—or the brother of Jesus in this case—is usually a paranoiac with a superiority complex. Professor Monti, on the other hand, has loss of memory and catatonic symptoms related to hysteria and based on guilts. It would be clinically understandable for him to suffer delusions, but ordinarily a patient in his condition would not believe himself to have the identity of an exalted person like Jesus or James, but rather someone who feels guilt for perhaps having done harm to Jesus or James. His behavior with you today, performing as the brother of Jesus, remains incomprehensible to me. But, of course, we know little of Profrssor Monti's inner past, his psyche, and it is unlikely that we shall ever have an opportunity to learn more."

Randall stirred in his chair. "You mean you know nothing about Professor Monti's professional background and his archeological excavations?"

"Ah, Mr. Randall, then *you* know about Monti's discovery outside Ostia Antica? I could not speak of it until—"

"I'm part of the project, Dr. Venturi."

"I was not sure. I was sworn by his daughters never to speak of it to strangers. I have kept my word."

"How much do you know of the professor's work?" asked Randall.

"Very little, in fact. When I was called into the case, Professor Monti's name was already familiar to me, of course. His name is well-known in Italy. From his daughters, I learned he had made an excavation near Ostia Antica that would have great importance in the fields of biblical history and theology. I was told it would form the cornerstone of a new Bible."

"But you don't know the substance of his discovery?"

"No. Are you implying that if I knew, I might better understand his delusions about being James, brother of Christ?"

"It might shed some light, Doctor. And yes, what Professor Monti uncovered will lead to a momentous new Bible."

"I suspected that. Recently, in our Rome daily, *Il Messaggero,* I read a three-part series by a British journalist —I forget his name—"

"Cedric Plummer?"

"Correct, Plummer. The articles were vague, long yet short on facts, about secret preparations in Amsterdam for

publication of a new Bible, a version based on new findings and supported by church conservatives to maintain
the status quo. It was intriguing, but so marked with hearsay and speculation that I found it difficult to take seriously."

"You can take it seriously," said Randall.

"Ah, then that is the forthcoming Bible for which our
patient is responsible?" Dr. Venturi absently turned a
page of his desk calendar, then turned it back. "Too bad
Professor Monti will not be able to enjoy the fruits of his
labors. As to his delusions, while this Bible may clarify
them for us, I doubt if this clarification will have any
medical significance for him. Did anything else take place
during your meeting downstairs?"

"I'm afraid not," said Randall. Then he remembered,
and reached into his jacket pocket. "Except for this." He
unfolded the sheet of paper, and showed it to the physician. "Professor Monti drew this for me as I was leaving.
He said it was a gift that would save me."

"Ah, the fish," said Dr. Venturi knowingly.

He did not take the drawing from Randall, but instead
searched among the folders on his desk, and opened one.
He extracted several sheets of paper, and displayed them,
one after the other, six in all, for Randall. Each bore a
variation of the speared-fish sketch that Randall held in
his hand.

"You see, Mr. Randall, I have my own private collection
of Professor Monti's art," said the physician. "Yes, he does
these sketches as occasional gifts for me or for his nurses.
I am afraid that his art is limited to this single subject—
the fish. He is obsessed with it. He has never been known
to make a drawing of any other object since he has been
in our care. Just the fish."

"It must have some meaning," mused Randall. "Have
you theorized about what he is trying to communicate?"

"Naturally, but I cannot imagine precisely what, except
that the fish also relates closely to his delusion about
living in the first century. As undoubtedly you know, the
first followers of Christ, the early Christians, when persecuted and hunted, employed the symbol of the fish to

identify themselves secretly to one another. The origin of this visual password is interesting. To His pioneer disciples, the Messiah was known as 'Jesus Christ, Son of God, Saviour,' which, translated into Greek, the language used by Roman occupation forces, was *Iesous Christos, Theou, Uios, Soter*. The initials of those five Greek words which used to be spelled I-CH-TH-U-S, we now spell out *ICHTHYS*—the word for *fish* in Greek. Even today, we call the study of fish ichthyology. So, you see, the initials of Jesus Christ's name and titles spelled out *fish*—the symbol of identification of the beleaguered cult of Christians to one another."

"Fascinating," agreed Randall. He examined Monti's drawing once more. "But the spear. That wasn't part of the symbol, was it?"

"No," said Dr. Venturi, returning his own collection of drawings to their folder, "no, that appears to be an addition entirely Professor Monti's own. The spear—or javelin or harpoon—whatever it is—would seem a negative symbol. Still, who can guess what is truly in his mind? In thinking himself James, the brother, is he revealing sibling rivalry toward Jesus, the fish, by stabbing Him? Or does he feel that the spear driven into the symbol of his brother is a weapon driven into his own person? We cannot say. I am afraid that this symbol, like so many things connected with Professor Monti, shall remain a mystery."

Dr. Venturi located an aged meerschaum pipe and a pouch of tobacco. "Do you mind—?" he said.

Randall indicated his own straight briar, and after they had exchanged tobacco blends, and were smoking, he returned to the subject of Professor Monti. Only now, Randall decided to step backwards in time.

"Doctor," he said, "when was Professor Monti first confined to this clinic? And, if you feel free to tell me, what were the circumstances under which he was committed here?"

"The circumstances?" Dr. Venturi puffed smoke steadily. "Of course, the case history is confidential, but when Angela Monti advised me she was bringing you here, she also requested that my staff be open and frank with you about her father's condition."

"She's in the waiting room," said Randall hastily. "If you wish to consult with her again——?"

"No need." Dr. Venturi sucked thoughtfully on his meerschaum, and finally placed it in a ceramic ashtray. "My own involvement in the case began—let me recollect—about a year and two months ago. I was notified by a colleague of mine—he happened to be the Monti family physician—that my services were urgently required for one of his patients, who was in the Policlinico, a hospital on the university grounds. The patient proved to be Professor Augusto Monti. He had suffered a sudden, acute, nervous breakdown. I called upon him at once, examined him, and diagnosed his condition."

"What was it that put him into the hospital?"

Absently, Dr. Venturi picked up his pipe, set it down, sought a pencil, and began to doodle on a note pad. "You wish to know the circumstances leading to the confinement? Two days before Professor Monti's breakdown, as I subsequently learned, he was observing his usual routine at the University of Rome. He was teaching his classes in the Aula di Archeologia. He was consulting with members of his faculty staff. He was making an application for a grant to allow him to undertake a new excavation in Pella. Also, on that day, as on most of his busy days, he was keeping a schedule of appointments and receiving visitors."

"What kind of visitors?"

"The usual kind a prominent archeologist would see. At times he might see colleagues and fellow professors from other countries, or government officials. Perhaps salesmen of field equipment, graduate students or editors of archeological journals. I do not know his exact activities that day. His daughter may be able to tell you more. I know only that he had been in the university most of the morning, had gone out once or twice on appointments, had returned to the university again to do some more work. By evening, when he had not returned home for dinner, his daughter Angela telephoned to request an usher on duty at the school to remind her father to come home. The usher went upstairs to the director's office in the archeology department. The usher rapped, but received no response. He thought this unusual, since the lights were on. He took the chance to go inside. There he found Professor Monti at his desk—the desk in disorder, a lamp overturned—incoherently babbling, talking without sense, the kind of talk you just heard from him. He was entirely disoriented. Then, he fell into a stupor. The frightened usher called his daughter and an ambulance was summoned immediately."

Randall shuddered at the scene, reliving what must have been Angela's own horror. "Was Professor Monti coherent—or rather, did he ever make any sense after that?"

"Not once in the year and months since," said Dr. Venturi with a sigh. "Something had simply snapped, so to speak, in his brain. He had literally, to use the vernacular, lost his mind. He has been out of touch with reality ever since."

"There is no hope of bringing him back?"

"Who can say, Mr. Randall? Who knows what the future will give us in science, medicine, psychiatry, or the advances to come in the biochemistry of mental abnormalities? For the present, there is nothing. You may be sure, we have tried everything. After several days, I had Professor Monti moved here to the Villa Bellavista. We undertook various forms of treatment—psychotherapy, pharmacological medication, electroshock under anesthesia. To no avail. Today, our efforts are to keep him comfortable, at peace, able to sleep. We also encourage him to be occupied. We encourage him to go to our atelier regularly, participate in webbing—similar to weaving—or to use our swimming pool, but he has little interest in these. Mostly, he will sit at the window staring outside or listen to music or sometimes watch television, although I do not think he absorbs what he views."

"Angela—Miss Monti, that is—thought that he had an occasional lucid moment."

Dr. Venturi shrugged. "She is his daughter. If it makes her happier to think that, we do not contradict her."

"I see," said Randall thoughtfully. "And visitors? Does Professor Monti have any visitors other than his two daughters?"

"His daughters, his grandchildren on holidays, and on his birthday, the housekeeper."

"No outsiders?"

"None are admitted," said Dr. Venturi. "A few have asked permission to visit him. They have been denied. The professor's daughters made the decision that his presence here, and his unfortunate condition, must be kept secret, as far as possible. Only Professor Monti's immediate family, or those accompanying them, may call upon him."

"But the outsiders," Randall persisted. "You spoke of a few who requested permission to visit the professor. Do you recall who they were?"

Dr. Venturi waved his meerschaum. "I would not remember the names. Some of the professor's old cronies and colleagues from the university. They were advised merely that he was suffering a nervous disorder, and must have rest. Several tried in the first months, and were turned away. They have not been heard from again."

"Anyone else?" asked Randall. "Any attempts by anyone else in recent months to see him?"

"Well, now that you mention it—there was one, and I recall this because it was recent and his name is so well-known."

"Who was it?" Randall inquired with interest.

"An eminent cleric, the Reverend Maertin de Vroome, made a written request to visit Professor Monti. I must say, I was impressed. I had not known that he and Monti were friends. I was advised, shortly after, that they weren't—were not friends. I had hoped a visit from him might stimulate my patient, so I passed the Reverend de Vroome's request for admission on to the daughters. They rejected it, and rather firmly, I might add. So I informed the Reverend de Vroome that no visitors were permitted. As a matter of fact, you are the first outsider allowed to see Professor Monti since his confinement here." He eyed the clock on his desk. "Do you have any other questions, Mr. Randall?"

"No," said Randall, rising. "There's nothing more to ask —or to learn."

THE RIDE back to Rome, in Giuseppe's air-conditioned Opel, was gloomy.

In the rear seat, with Angela huddled against him, a reluctant Randall was forced to repeat what had transpired during his meeting with her father and then with Dr. Venturi.

Angela reminisced briefly, wistfully, about her father as he was in earlier years, of the alertness and keenness of his mind. It was a pity, she said with infinite sadness, that her father would never know the marvels his discovery would surely lead to.

"He knows now," Randall reassured her. "He knew from the moment that he made his find. He knew and enjoyed the full pleasure of what he was able to give to the world."

"You are sweet." She kissed his cheek. "You are very sweet."

She invited him to join her sister, and her sister's children, at their family home for dinner. He was tempted, considered it, but then thought better of it.

"No, I think it would be best for you to be alone with your family," he said. "We'll have plenty of time together after this. Besides, I should get back to Amsterdam. The big push is on. As it is, Wheeler'll blow his stack because I was out of the office today."

"You are flying back tonight?"

"Maybe late tonight. I've simply got to catch up on some personal correspondence while I'm here. Once I return to Amsterdam, there'll be no chance. I'm behind on letters to my father and mother, and my daughter. Also, some business things. Like Jim McLoughlin, the Raker Institute fellow. You know the one. My lawyer hasn't been able to locate him yet. So I thought I'd write McLoughlin a personal letter, which might be forwarded to him. That sort of thing. Yes, I'll probably be taking the last flight back."

"Let Giuseppe drop you off at the Excelsior first," said Angela. "After that, he can take me to my home."

Randall gave the driver the instructions, and turned to Angela once more. "Will you be coming back to Amsterdam in the morning?"

She gave a teasing smile. "In the evening tomorrow, if my boss will not fire me. I hoped to go shopping with my sister, and take my nieces to the Borghese Gardens, and maybe visit some friends. You will have your secretary back tomorrow night, if it is all right?"

"It's not all right, but I'll be waiting."

She was studying him. Her smile had disappeared. "One thing I wanted to ask, Steve—"

"Yes?"

"Once we are in Amsterdam again, what will you do next?"

"Next? Work, of course. Work like a beaver to put the project over." He saw her intent face, and he understood. "Oh, you mean—am I going to continue trying to find out more about the papyrus fragment—the photograph? No, Angela. Your father was the last stop. Dead end. Even if I wanted to, there's no place to go. I'm putting my deerstalker cap and magnifying glass into storage. I'm putting all my Sherlock Holmesing into retirement among the beehives. I'm back in the business of promotion. I'm devoting myself totally to selling the Word."

"Even if you have doubts?"

"Angela, I've come to this, here in Rome. I'll always have doubts about the mysteries, as I'll always have a degree of faith. Do you know Ernest Renan's prayer? 'O Lord, if there is a Lord, save my soul, if I have a soul.' That's me, today."

Angela laughed. "You can live with that?"

"I have to. I have no choice." He squeezed her hand. "Don't worry. I'll go ahead. . . . Here we are at the Excelsior. Okay, darling. One more kiss. See you tomorrow."

After he had left the Opel with his briefcase, and

watched the car depart, he started into the cool lobby of the Hotel Excelsior. Pausing at the concierge's desk for his key, he crossed the lobby to the elevators.

One of the elevators had just reached the ground floor and was disgorging its passengers. He stood aside until it was empty, entered the elevator, half turning to press the button for the fifth floor. As he did so, he realized someone else had entered the elevator directly behind him, and was now reaching over his shoulder to press the button for the fourth floor. The arm over his shoulder was draped in clerical garb.

As the doors closed on the two of them, and the elevator slowly started to rise, Randall came around for a view of his companion.

He sucked in his breath.

Towering above him, cloaked in a black cassock, the cadaverous face offering the slightest lipless smile, was the Dominee Maertin de Vroome. "So we meet again, Mr. Randall," said Dominee de Vroome. "I trust you had a successful visit with our Professor Monti this afternoon?"

Utterly disconcerted, Randall blurted, "How in the devil did you know I saw him?"

"You came to Rome to see him, just as I myself did earlier. Simple. I have made it one of my holy duties to keep a watchful eye on you, Mr. Randall. Since our last occasion together, I've observed your every subsequent move with increasing interest and growing respect. You are, as I guessed from the start, a seeker after the truth. There are not many. You are one. I am another. I am pleased to know our quests are the same, and that our paths have converged. Perhaps the time has come for us, here in the Eternal City, to have one more private talk."

Randall had stiffened. "About what?"

"About the forgery of the Gospel According to James and the forgery of the Petronius Parchment."

"What—what makes you so damn sure they are forgeries?"

"Because I have just seen the forger himself and I have learned all the details of the hoax. . . . Well, here we are, my floor. I trust you will be getting off here, too, Mr. Randall?"

IN THE SPLENDOR of the vast, plush sitting room of Dominee de Vroome's Hotel Excelsior suite, Steve Randall sat stunned.

Utterly stupefied by the clergyman's matter-of-fact announcement, Randall had docilely tagged after him from the elevator, across the richly carpeted landing into the large entry hall and finally into the suite itself.

Randall wanted to believe that this was a trick, a lure, some kind of game de Vroome was playing with him. Even though he had been so skeptical of the project, so filled with doubts, Randall wanted to doubt the project's enemy now. He could not. Something in the ring of de Vroome's voice as he spoke in the elevator had told Randall that he was at the brink of truth at last.

He sat deep in the brown velvet armchair, wordless still. He did not take his eyes off Dominee de Vroome. The clergyman had inquired whether he wished a snack, some hors d'oeuvres, sent up by room service. He had recommended the caviar Beluga or the prosciutto di Parma. Randall had shaken his head, incredulous at his host's casualness.

"Then certainly a drink," said Dominee de Vroome, "you will want a drink."

The clergyman had moved silently across the Oriental rugs to what proved to be a wood-faced refrigerator between the marble fireplace and the antique mahogany desk. He examined the bottles on the tray atop the low refrigerator.

His back still to Randall, he inquired, "What will you have, Mr. Randall? I am pouring myself a cognac and water."

"Scotch-on-the-rocks, please."

"Very well."

As he prepared the drinks, de Vroome resumed speaking. "Most of the personnel behind the production of the International New Testament—yes, Mr. Randall, I know the title now—they are decent people, men of deep spirituality, as you have pointed out. They believe in the essence of the Word, as do I. But so eager are they to see a renewal of universal faith that they have submitted to those who would manipulate them. They have allowed themselves to be blinded by those who are the commercialists, as well as the power-hungry, of religion, those who would use any means to survive." He paused. "Even forgery."

De Vroome stepped away from the makeshift bar slowly, a drink in each hand.

"Entertain no doubts, Mr. Randall. You have been on the right track. There is a forger. We have heard him. We have seen him."

He reached the small, dark, wooden coffee table, set Randall's glass of Scotch before him, and settled himself comfortably on the cushion of the brown couch nearest Randall.

He held up his cognac and offered a toast and a wry smile.

"To Truth," he proposed.

He sipped his cognac, noting that Randall had not touched his own drink, and he nodded understandingly.

He placed his cognac on the table, wrapped his black cassock around his legs, and faced Randall squarely.

"The facts," he said. "How did we locate the forger? We had no means of locating him, although we were certain that one existed, or had existed. No, we did not find him. He found us. The bait, unintentionally, was Cedric Plummer's series of articles concerning the schism in the Christian churches, concerning my efforts at reformation, concerning the preparations of the orthodox hierarchy to maintain themselves by publishing a drastically revised New Testament based on some unannounced new discovery in Italy. Mr. Plummer's articles, as you know, were syndicated internationally, and one of the major newspapers to carry a translation was *Il Messaggero,* the widely circulated newspaper here in Rome."

So far, the sound of truth, Randall thought. No more than an hour ago, Dr. Venturi had mentioned reading the Plummer articles in *Il Messaggero*.

"As you may imagine," Dominee de Vroome went on, "Mr. Plummer received a considerable number of readers' letters in response to this highly sensationalized series. One of these letters, written by hand on cheap stationery, was mailed to Mr. Plummer in care of the Rome daily, which in turn forwarded it with other letters to Mr. Plummer in care of his home newspaper, the *London Daily Courier*. Plummer's editor in London automatically sent on the pack of mail once more, to Cedric Plummer at his hotel in Amsterdam. While our British journalist friend may have many shortcomings, disrespect for his reading public is not one of them. As is his practice, Plummer read every letter addressed to him—and one particular letter, postmarked Rome, he read and reread several times, before bringing it to me at the Westerkerk. This particular— and highly provocative—letter was written by a gentleman who introduced himself as a Frenchman who had dwelt for many years as an expatriate in Rome. He did not sign his letter with his real name, but with an amusing and self-deprecating pseudonym. He signed himself—Duca Minimo. Are you acquainted with the Italian language, Mr. Randall?"

"I am not," said Randall.

"Duca Minimo is Italian for Duke of Nothing. A fine counterpoint to the contents of the letter which were something, something, indeed. I might add, the correspondent gave Plummer no address, except for *Fermo Posta, Posta Centrale, Rome*—General Delivery at the main post office in Rome. Now to the contents of the letter—"

Dominee de Vroome took another sip of his cognac before continuing.

"—which seemed too good to be true. This French expatriate in Rome wrote that he had read Plummer's articles with great interest. His very words. Great interest, indeed. An understatement unmatched by any in my memory. In his letter, he went on to say that this new Bible—the International New Testament, he believed it would be called—was based on an excavation made by the Italian archeologist, Professor Augusto Monti, of the

University of Rome, at the perimeter of the ancient town of Ostia Antica, about six years ago. The excavation had produced an extraordinary discovery, a new gospel written in Aramaic by James the Just, brother of Jesus, and purported to be earlier in date than any gospel in the existing canon. Along with this new fifth gospel, Monti had also found scraps of an official ancient Roman parchment sent from Jerusalem to Rome, a document containing a terse account of the trial of Jesus. Based upon this discovery, wrote the Duca Minimo, the International New Testament had come into being. But, wrote the one signing himself Duca Minimo, the entire basis for the new Bible was a lie, the Monti discovery no more than a carefully and scholarly contrived forgery which had been years in preparation. The new find was a forgery, the Duca knew, because he himself had been the forger, and he was proud to say that its authentication and acceptance placed him in the front rank of literary hoaxers, exceeding anything done in the past by Ireland, Chatterton, Psalmanazer or Wise."

Dominee de Vroome's guarded eyes sought a reaction from Randall, but there was none.

"A learned gentleman, our correspondent, to say the least," added de Vroome.

Absorbed as he was, Randall held his tongue to hear what would come next.

"To conclude with the contents of the letter," de Vroome went on. "This French expatriate wrote Plummer that he was ready to reveal his entire role in the hoax and to make the forgery public on the eve of the appearance of the new Bible. He wrote that if Plummer wished to know the details of the forgery, and to know the price he would place on offering proof of his handiwork, he was ready to meet and negotiate with Plummer on neutral ground. For this preliminary meeting, he was prepared to receive Plummer alone, on a certain date at a certain place in Paris, if Plummer would send him air fare from Rome to Paris, and return, as well as what amounted to a mere pittance for food and a night's lodging. This,

Mr. Randall, was the letter that Cedric Plummer brought to me."

Randall picked up his glass of Scotch. He was in need of it at last. "And did you believe the contents of that letter?" Randall asked.

"Not at first. Of course not. The earth is teeming with religious crackpots. Normally, I would have ignored such a letter. However, the more I studied it, the more I saw the possibility that its author might be speaking the truth. I think it was one piece of internal evidence, in the letter, that gave it a semblance of veracity. The writer spoke of Professor Monti's discovery near Ostia Antica. Until then, Monti's role had been known to us, but the exact site of his discovery had been a carefully guarded secret at Resurrection Two. All of us on the outside knew a discovery had been made in Italy that related to the new Bible. None of us, I among the others, knew the precise location of the find. This was impressive, and something that could be verified, and which I was able to verify at once, through certain associates I have here in Rome. Once I could give them the actual name of the excavation —a dig near Ostia Antica—my associates were able to confirm that the vicinity of Ostia Antica had, indeed, been the place where Monti had made an important—if still secret—biblical discovery. Also, the title of the new Bible for the first time, which I have since verified as accurate. At any rate, here was inside information which until that time only the inner circle of your project had access to. Perhaps others, on the outside, might have known about it—but an obscure French expatriate in Rome? This was something I could not ignore. Even if this Duca Minimo had not been the forger, even if he had acquired his inside information secondhand, still he was knowledgeable enough to be taken seriously. If he was not the source for this knowledge, then he certainly had contact with someone who was. He was definitely worth seeing, especially considering the modest financial investment involved. So I instructed Cedric Plummer to write him care of General Delivery in Rome, evince interest in hearing the self-styled forger's story, agree to the date, time, site of the meeting, and to send him his round-trip ticket and his expense money. Plummer replied as instructed, and on the agreed-upon date, he flew to Paris for the rendezvous."

"You mean—Plummer actually met this man?"

"He met him."

Randall took a big swallow of Scotch. "When?"

"One week ago today."

"Where?'

"At Père-Lachaise in Paris."

"Where's that?"

"Le Cimetière du Père-Lachaise—you have not heard of it?" said Dominee de Vroome with surprise. "It is the celebrated cemetery in Paris where so many great figures of the past—Héloïse and Abélard, Chopin, Balzac, Sarah Bernhardt, Colette—are buried. Our forger had written that he would be waiting for Plummer at exactly two o'clock in the afternoon before the Jacob Epstein sculpture that stands over the grave of Oscar Wilde. A theatrical touch, all that, admittedly. Yet, not without reason. For a notorious person, a confessed forger, it was safely out of the way, and there would be privacy. I once visited Père-Lachaise. Vast, quiet, isolated, hillocks, paths, forests of poplar and acacia trees. Perfect, and very intriguing to a sensationalist like Plummer."

"And they met there, Plummer and the forger?" Randall prompted.

"They met there," said de Vroome, "but not at Wilde's burial site, as originally had been planned. When Plummer arrived at the cemetery, a guard asked his name, and handed him a sealed envelope someone had left for him. The envelope contained a scrawled note from the Duca Minimo. He had changed the rendezvous point. He advised Plummer to proceed to the grave of Honoré de Balzac. It appeared there was too much traffic around the Oscar Wilde site. Plummer found this touch especially poetic. Balzac had attracted to his pen countless scoundrels and rogues. And now, he had attracted the man who was possibly history's greatest forger. Plummer purchased a tourists' map of the cemetery, marked off the route to Balzac's tomb, and had no difficulty finding it. And there, also, he found the forger."

Dominee de Vroome stopped, finished his cognac, and considered his glass as well as Randall's empty one.

"Another, Mr. Randall?"

"No more of anything—except your story. What happened?"

"As ever the dedicated journalist, Cedric Plummer made extensive notes after the encounter. I have read them. The essence of the notes? This. The real name of our self-proclaimed forger is Robert Lebrun. Plummer found him to be an old man—eighty-three years old, as it turned out—but not senile, perfectly alert, clear-headed. Hair dyed brown. Gray eyes, a cataract growth over one eye. Steel-rimmed spectacles. Pointed nose. Long jaw. Loose full dentures. His face deeply wrinkled. Probably of medium height, Plummer thought, but seemingly shorter because his posture is stooped. Walks with an odd gait, a roll or limp, because he is an amputee, has an artificial left leg which he dislikes discussing. His background gives some foundation to his story."

"Where is he from?"

"Paris. Born and raised in Montparnasse. He did not tell Plummer too much. They were standing there, near Balzac's tomb, in the sun, and Lebrun was quick to tire. In his youth, he had worked as an engraver's apprentice. He was impoverished, and wanted money for himself, his mother, his brothers and sisters, so he toyed with simple counterfeiting. He found that he had a gift for such forgeries. He started by forging passports, moved on to faking small-denomination currency, graduated to historical letters, rare manuscripts, illuminated medieval Bible fragments done in minuscules. Then, he overreached. He undertook to forge a government document without sufficient preparation. I do not know the details. He was exposed, arrested, tried, and because there were minor offenses on his record already, he was sentenced to imprisonment in the notorious penal colony of French Guiana. There, in the penal colony, life was impossible for young Lebrun. The prison authorities made no attempt to rehabilitate him.

He became more recalcitrant than ever, and he suffered for this, and was almost broken. At one point, after confinement on one of the three islands off the coast that were later known as the Devil's Island group, Lebrun was on the verge of suicide. It was then that he was befriended by a French Catholic curé, a priest of the order of the Congregation of the Holy Spirit, who came from St. Jean to visit the penal colony islands twice a week. The priest took great interest in Lebrun, turned him toward religion and faith and spiritual reading, and gradually Lebrun's life gained purpose and scope. Finally, after three years in the Guiana penal colony, Lebrun was presented with some kind of opportunity to receive a pardon. Plummer was unable to learn the details of it. But whatever it was, the opportunity turned into a betrayal, and Lebrun became more embittered and antisocial than ever. Especially against religion."

Randall was confused. "I don't understand," he said.

"Forgive me for not clarifying this crucial point. Actually, I know little about it. All that Lebrun would disclose was that this priest he had trusted, this man of the cloth, brought him a proposal from the French government. If Lebrun would volunteer for some dangerous venture or experiment, and survive it, he would be granted amnesty and be freed from the penal colony. Lebrun was reluctant to volunteer, but encouraged by the priest, he did so. He survived the venture with the loss of his left leg, but freedom was worth even this price. But freedom did not come to him. The amnesty that the priest had promised Lebrun, on behalf of the French government, was not granted. Lebrun was thrown back into his tropical hell-hole. From that black day of betrayal onward, Lebrun vowed to have his revenge. Against the government? No. It was against the priesthood, the clergy, all religion—because of the deception he had suffered at the hands of religion—that he vowed to have his revenge. Thus, in his angry heart and head, he conceived his warped plan, one that would mock the Christ-believers and strike a fatal blow against clergymen of every denomination."

"A forgery of a new gospel," murmured Randall.

"That, and a forgery offering a pagan source for the trial of the Christ he had come to abhor. He would dedicate what remained of his life to preparing the hoax, getting the public to believe it, and finally to exposing it, thus showing the falsity of religious faith and the gullibility of the foolish faithful. Between 1918, when he was thrown back into his Guiana island cell, and 1953, when France brought to an end its notorious penal colony, Robert Lebrun prepared his revenge. He steeped himself in the Bible and biblical lore and the history of Christianity in the first century. Finally, after thirty-eight years of confinement, his imprisonment ended with the elimination of the Guiana penal colony by the French government. Lebrun was returned to France, liberated, a free man, but also an ex-convict obsessed with vengeance against the church."

"And he undertook his master forgery?"

"Not at once," said Domineee de Vroome. "First, he wanted money. He resumed the underground life of a counterfeiter, becoming an illegal one-man factory for fake passports. He also resumed his studies of the Scriptures, of Jesus, of early Christian times, of Aramaic. He was, obviously, a brilliant, self-educated scholar. At last, he saved enough money to acquire the ancient materials he required. With these materials, and his knowledge and his hatred, he left France to take up residence in Rome and to develop secretly on papyrus and parchment what he hoped would be the most successful forgery in history. He completed it, to his satisfaction, a dozen years ago."

Randall was totally mesmerized, too intrigued to sustain disbelief any longer. "And Monti?" Randall asked. "Where does Professor Monti enter into it? Did this Lebrun know Monti in Rome?"

"No, Lebrun did not personally know Professor Monti in the beginning. But, of course, in his studies of biblical archeology, Lebrun had become acquainted with Monti's name. And then one day, after he had finished the forgery, and while he was puzzling over where and how to have it buried and excavated, he came across a radical paper that Monti had written for an archeological journal."

Randall nodded. "Yes, the controversial article Professor Monti wrote projecting the possibility of finding the missing Q document in Italy instead of Palestine or Egypt."

"Exactly," said Dominee de Vroome, impressed. "I see you have done your homework well, Mr. Randall. But of course, you have an excellent tutor in Professor Monti's daughter. Well, to go on. In the Biblioteca Nazionale, one day, Lebrun read this Monti paper and at once the loose threads of his plot were pulled together. Of the places suggested by Monti for a possible future find, one was the site of the ancient ruins buried along the old coastline near Ostia. After a meticulous study of the site, Robert Lebrun managed to entomb his forgery deep beneath the earth among the ruins of a first-century Roman villa."

Randall's skepticism surfaced. "How could he possibly do that without being detected?"

"He did it," said the cleric firmly. "I do not know how, and he did not tell Plummer his means. I do think Lebrun was and is capable of anything. Above all, as you must be aware, he was always a man of infinite patience. Once his sealed papyrus and parchment forgeries were buried, he allowed a number of years to pass to permit the sealed jar and stone block to become part of the covered ruins, to absorb the ravages of time from without and to appear as aged as the contents within. During this period, the Italian government had authorized further excavations in Ostia Antica proper, and Lebrun watched and hoped that his forgery would be uncovered accidentally. But these diggings were not extensive enough. Meanwhile, Professor Monti was continuing to publish his radical papers, promoting his views about the possibility of a Q document in Italy, and as a result Monti was being severely castigated and ridiculed by his more conservative colleagues. Reading of this, hearing of this intramural controversy, Lebrun guessed that Professor Monti must be smarting under the attacks of his academic critics and bursting to

prove that his projections were not fanciful. The time for
action, Lebrun decided, had come. So seven years ago, as
Lebrun told Plummer in the Paris cemetery, he made up
his mind to call upon Professor Monti at the University
of Rome. And, as it turned out, Lebrun's psychologizing
had been correct."

"You mean, Monti was receptive?" said Randall, bewildered. "But to what?"

"To a small fragment of papyrus with Aramaic on it
that Lebrun brought with him," said Dominee de Vroome.
"Lebrun must not be underestimated. He is diabolically
clever. From Papyrus Number 3 of the Gospel According
to James, he had removed two pieces of the materal, jagged
sections, to make the buried papyrus leaf appear eaten
away and real. One of these two pieces he saved intact,
and the other one he reshaped and wrote upon. This was
the fragment he unwrapped and displayed to Professor
Monti. Lebrun anticipated that he would be asked how
it had come into his possession. He explained that he was
an amateur student of Roman history of the first century,
and had long been preparing a book about Rome and
its colonies in that period of antiquity, and it was his
weekend avocation to visit the ancient sites involved with
early Roman commerce. Since Ostia had been an active
seaport in the time of Tiberius and Claudius, Lebrun had
spent countless weekends foraging about the outskirts
and trying to envision the port as it had been almost two
thousand years ago, all this to be grist for his book. At
least, so he told Monti. Lebrun explained that he had become a familiar figure in the area, and one Sunday afternoon—so he said—an Italian urchin shyly approached
him with a souvenir for sale. It was the very fragment
that Lebrun had brought to Monti."

"Wasn't Monti curious to know how the boy got hold
of the fragment?" Randall interrupted.

"Of course. But Lebrun had an answer for everything.
He explained that the urchin and his young friends, when
playing, enjoyed digging caves in the mounds and hills,
and the week before they had uncovered a small sealed
piece of earthenware, which broke into bits when they

tried to dig it out. There were some old pieces of paper in it, many of which crumbled to dust when exposed, but several remained intact. The wild youngsters, in their play, used these for toy money and finally threw them away. However, this one boy saved a single fragment, thinking it might be worth a few lire to an amateur scholar. Lebrun claimed he acquired the fragment from the lad for a paltry sum, being uncertain of its value, then returned to his rooms in Rome, and examined the faded papyrus minutely. Almost immediately, from his own deep knowledge of ancient manuscripts, he saw its possible significance. And now he was bringing it to Professor Monti, director of archeology at the University of Rome, for authentication. According to Lebrun, Monti was skeptical but interested. He requested that Lebrun leave the papyrus fragment with him for a week, so that he could look into it. You can imagine what happened next."

Randall had been listening carefully. As he had so long questioned Resurrection Two's story, he now questioned Lebrun's exposé of that story. Both were equally pat. Still, one of the versions had to be true. "What I'm interested in, Dominee, is what Robert Lebrun imagined next."

De Vroome's eyes held him. "You are still skeptical, as Professor Monti was originally." He smiled. "I believe you will be convinced, as was Professor Monti in the week that followed his receipt of the papyrus fragment. For when Lebrun returned to the university a week later, Monti received him royally and closeted him in his office. Monti did not hide his elation. He was, Lebrun recalls, beside himself with excitement. Monti announced that he had studied the fragment thoroughly and he was more than satisfied as to its authenticity. This fragment appeared to be a piece of an early New Testament codex and could predate any known to exist. It could even predate the earliest known gospels, that written by Mark attributed to 70 A.D. and that by Matthew thought to have been written in 80 A.D. If this fragment survived, there must be more. If more fragments were found, they might represent the

most incredible biblical discovery in history. If Lebrun
would direct him to the site of this find, Monti was prepared to obtain the necessary permissions and begin his
search. Lebrun was ready to cooperate on two conditions.
First, he demanded that, if the excavation proved successful, he be given half of the money Monti derived from it.
Second, Lebrun insisted that he must remain a silent partner, his own role be kept secret, his name neither discussed nor recorded by Monti, since he was an alien
in Italy, with an undeserved record as a juvenile offend-
er in France—he did not, of course, reveal to Monti
the true extent of his criminal record—and he wanted
no publicity which might bring up his background as a
youth and get him expelled from his adopted homeland.
Professor Monti was amenable to both conditions, and
the agreement between the two was made."

"And Monti started his excavation outside Ostia Antica?"

"Yes, at the site to which Lebrun directed him, mapped
out for him. After a half year of preparation, Professor
Monti began digging. Three months later, he came upon
the hollow statue base containing the so-called second
sealed jar, the one that held the Gospel According to
James and the Petronius Parchment. And six years
later, today, the world is about to receive its fifth gospel
and its historical Jesus in the International New Testament."

"Dominee," said Randall, sitting up, "I think I'll have
another drink."

The clergyman rose. "I think I had better have another, too."

As de Vroome took the empty glasses to the refrigerator, Randall nervously tamped fresh tobacco into his
pipe bowl. He had been searching for this door to truth,
and now that it had been opened, he still could not see
clearly inside. "That can't be all of the story," he insisted. "There are many—"

"By no means is that all of the story," de Vroome replied from his position at the drink tray. "There is still
the denouement to come—actually, two denouements

—one relating to Lebrun and Monti, the other to Lebrun and Plummer and myself."

The clergyman finished pouring the drinks, and returned with Randall's Scotch and his own cognac and water. Settling back into the corner of the couch, Dominee de Vroome took up the story once more.

"According to Robert Lebrun, after the discovery was authenticated and sold to the publishers of Resurrection Two, Professor Monti dutifully gave him half of the earnings from the find. But Lebrun's original goal was not money, remember. His real purpose remained to have the discovery accepted by the church, and then expose the hoax and enjoy his final vengeance. Year after year, he waited for the publication of the International New Testament, and whenever this patient criminal lost his patience, he was reassured by Monti that the find was being translated or proofed or set in type, and that it would be made public soon. That was the moment Lebrun awaited. The moment when the discovery was made public, and then he would prove to the public it was a lie and the church a fraud. But last year, something significant happened to Lebrun. He had gambled away most of his Ostia money, spent it recklessly on street women, and he was nearly penniless. Since he was accustomed to being penniless, this was not enough to inspire his next act. What inspired a new meeting with Monti was a real love affair. In his foolish old age, Lebrun had fallen in love with one of the prostitutes who populate the Borghese Gardens. She was a young, silly, shrewd girl, I am certain, and she had no use for this old man unless he could provide her with comforts, even luxuries. Lebrun frankly confessed to Plummer that he was desperate to possess her. He saw only one solution. That was blackmail."

"Blackmail? Whom did he want to blackmail? Professor Monti?"

"Correct. Recent years had not mellowed his obsession to expose religion, the church. But a new obsession had taken its place beside the old one. The need for money,

money to buy love. And so, sometime last year, he arranged a private meeting with Professor Monti—"

"When last year?"

"I am not certain."

A year and two months ago, perhaps, Randall calculated. "Could it have been in May of last year?'

"That sounds about right. At any rate, he met with Professor Monti somewhere outside the university. He insisted upon knowing when the discovery was to be published. By this time, the translation was being readied for printing by Hennig in Mainz. Monti was able to assure Lebrun that the Bible would be made public in the following year, that is to say, this year. He even told Lebrun the name of the Bible. Satisfied about that, Lebrun unleashed his thunderbolt. Lebrun told Monti that he desperately needed more money, lots of it as soon as possible, and he expected Monti to give him this money. Apparently, Monti was nonplussed. He had no money to spare, but even if he did, he saw no reason to dole it out to Lebrun. They had made their bargain. Monti had fulfilled his part of it, paid Lebrun what he had asked. There was no reason to give him more. 'There is plenty of reason,' Lebrun told Monti. 'If you don't give me more money, I will ruin you and ruin the Bible that those publishers are preparing. I will expose your entire discovery for what it is—a forgery—a hoax and forgery invented in my brain and perpetrated by my hand.' Can you visualize the effect this had on poor Professor Monti?"

Randall removed the pipe from his mouth. "Surely Monti didn't believe him?"

"Of course Monti did not believe him. There was no reason he should. Besides, how could he? But Lebrun told Plummer that he had been prepared for this. He had brought with him absolute, incontrovertible proof of his forgery."

"What proof?"

"He would not reveal this to Plummer," said Dominee de Vroome. "But apparently he had proof, real proof, of forgery. Because when Professor Monti saw it, he was stricken, almost went into a state of shock. Lebrun told him, 'If you give me the money I want, I'll turn this evidence of forgery over to you, and your career and reputation will remain safe and the International New Testament will remain authentic. If you refuse, I shall make this evidence public and expose James and Petronius as forgeries. What do you say?' What Monti said was—he would find a means of getting up the money somehow, some way."

"Did he?"

"He never had the chance, as you very well know, Mr. Randall. He went back to his private office and his desk at the university. You can imagine his feelings as he sat there alone, in a state of petrification, suffering the knowledge that he had been duped, and that his entire life's work would be brought down in ruins around him and that he would be disgraced, even as those in Resurrection Two and the world church, who trusted him, would be made bankrupt. He suffered a total mental collapse, a complete breakdown. When Lebrun tried to reach him several days later, for the blackmail payoff, Lebrun learned that the professor was too ill to speak to anyone. Lebrun distrusted what he heard, so he made further inquiries at the university and learned that Monti was on an extended leave. Still unsure, Lebrun one afternoon followed Monti's daughters to the Villa Bellavista outside the city. When he found out their destination was a sanitarium for those suffering mental disorders, he was forced to accept the fact that Monti could no longer be of use to him."

"Did he make any attempt to speak to Monti's daughters?" Randall wondered.

"Not to my knowledge," said de Vroome. "After that, as he confessed to Plummer, Lebrun considered several other victims for his blackmail. He weighed the idea of going to the Italian Ministry of Public Instruction and extorting money from them to hush up the scandal. But he had sense enough to realize that he was no match for a government, which would merely arrest him, confiscate his evidence of forgery, and get rid of it. He thought of going to Amsterdam and confronting the publishers with his evidence of hoax. He felt that they might do anything to protect the millions of dollars they had invested in the project. But he feared them, too. He feared they would find a means of arresting him, taking away his evidence, putting him in jail. He even thought of going to the press. But he was afraid the press would regard him as a madman, and reveal his unsavory background. His only recourse, he concluded, was to come upon someone, some private person, with spotless credentials, who wanted to destroy Resurrection Two as much as he did. And then he came across Cedric Plummer's series of articles, and he felt that he had found his man and his one hope. And he was right. He had."

With a trembling hand, Randall took a long swallow of Scotch. "Well," he said, "what was the outcome of that meeting between Plummer and Lebrun in the Paris cemetery? Did you pay him off and get the evidence of forgery?"

Dominee de Vroome frowned, stood up, sought a cheroot from a box on the lamp table. "The second denouement," he muttered, lighting the cheroot, "and more bizarre than anything that preceded it."

He remained standing, twisting the cheroot in his fingers. "Yes, Plummer negotiated an arrangement with Lebrun as they strolled out of Père-Lachaise Cemetery together. Lebrun had left his proof of the forgery hidden in some secure place in the vicinity of Rome. He agreed to return to Rome, retrieve it, and wait for Plummer to join him there. They arranged this second meeting—Lebrun set the time, the date, the hour, and the place, an obscure, out-of-the-way café he occasionally frequented. There, Plummer would be permitted to examine Lebrun's proof of forgery, and for this and a written account of the hoax, Plummer would exchange a relatively modest sum of money."

"How much?"

Dominee de Vroome stood puffing on his cheroot from his great height. "Lebrun wanted fifty thousand dollars in American currency, or its equivalent in Swiss or British

currency. Plummer bargained with him. Lebrun settled
for the sum of twenty thousand dollars."

"Well, was the meeting held?"

"In a manner of speaking, yes. But first let me fill you
in on one change in the plans. When Plummer returned
to Amsterdam and related to me what had transpired
between Lebrun and himself, I was—let me put it this
way—I was extremely hopeful and exhilarated. I made
up my mind at once that the transaction was too vital to
our cause to be handled by Cedric Plummer alone. He
is an enthusiast and a journalist, but he is not an expert
on papyrus, on Aramaic, on textual criticism. I am an
expert on all of these. I was certain that Lebrun's proof
of forgery would be the other fragment he had snipped
out of your Papyrus Number 3 and kept intact. Or something similar. I expected it would also contain some
undeniable evidence that it was not genuine but counterfeit. I was qualified to make a judgment of such proof,
far more so than Plummer. So I accompanied Plummer to
Rome."

"When was that?"

"Three days ago. We drove to the rendezvous point in
the city here—"

"Where in the city?"

Patiently, de Vroome indulged Randall. "It was a cheap
little students' café or bar across the narrow thoroughfare
that enters into the Piazza Navona. The café itself was
on the corner of the Piazza delle Cinque Lune—the
Square of the Five Moons—and the Piazza di S. Appol-
linare. Not at all as picturesque as it sounds. The café
is called the Bar Fratelli Fabbri—the Bar of the Brothers
Fabbri. Unprepossessing. Four outdoor tables with wicker
chairs in front of the establishment and a weatherworn
green awning to protect habitués from the hot sun. Two
entrances curtained with blue plastic streamers or strings to
keep out flies—the kind of entrance streamers one associates with an Algerian house of ill repute. Plummer and
I were to meet Robert Lebrun there at one o'clock in the
afternoon. We arrived fifteen minutes early, with our
twenty thousand dollars, and we took an outdoor table

and ordered Carpanos and waited with considerable tension, you may well guess."

"Did he show up?" Randall asked anxiously.

"At five minutes past one, as we began to wonder and worry, a taxi suddenly swung into the Piazza delle Cinque Lune and skidded to a halt directly across the wide street from the café. The back door opened, and a rather stooped, elderly man stepped out, and limped over to the taxi driver to pay him. I remember Plummer's gripping my arm. 'That's Robert Lebrun, that's him!' Plummer jumped to his feet and called out, 'Lebrun! I'm here!' Lebrun spun around, almost falling because of the artificial leg, and squinted at our table, and he was immediately transformed. He seemed to become very agitated, very angry. He squeezed one hand into a fist, and shook it at us. He shouted crazily to Plummer, 'You broke your word to me! You don't mean to publish it! You are going to sell me out to them!' And he pointed a finger at me. As he did so, I realized for the first time that I was still wearing my clerical garb, my cassock. An idiotic blunder. I'd worn it to a service, and had not bothered to remove it. The old man was sure that Plummer had been fronting for the church, was trying to get his hands on proof of forgery for the church, which would get rid of it. Plummer tried to shout back, to push through a rush of traffic, and reach him and explain my presence. It was too late. Lebrun had stumbled back into the taxi, and the taxi raced off with him, and there was no hope of catching up with him, no hope whatsoever. We never saw him again, nor were we able to locate him. There is no Lebrun in any Rome phone book or directory or city record. He vanished completely."

"So you have nothing," said Randall.

"Except what I have related to you in this room. Yet, I've revealed to you all that has happened, exactly as it happened, all of our secrets, because I knew that you've had the same suspicions about the new Bible that I have had, and because you were able to accomplish one thing that I could not. You alone, Mr. Randall, got to see Professor Augusto Monti today. And it is Monti—the only

one left—who would know the real name of the forger
and his address. Monti, and only Monti, could lead us to
Lebrun and final proof of the forgery. Do you think Professor Monti would help you?"

Randall put away his pipe, took up his briefcase, and
came to his feet. "You know Monti suffered a nervous
breakdown. You know he is in a sanitarium. What help
could he be?"

"But his colleagues at the university inform us he is
suffering only a temporary mental disorder."

"That's what they have been led to believe. It's not
true. I was with Monti. I tried to have a rational conversation with him. I failed. Professor Monti is hopelessly
insane."

Dominee de Vroome seemed to sag. "Then we are
hopelessly lost." His eyes met Randall's. "Unless there is
something more you know that could help us. If so, will
you help?"

"No," said Randall. He started to cross the living room
toward the door, but as he came abreast of Dominee de
Vroome, he halted. "No, I can't help you, and if I could,
I'm not sure I'd want to. I'm not sure such a person as
Robert Lebrun exists. If he does exist, I'm not sure he
could be believed. Thank you for your courtesy, and for
your confidence, Dominee, but I'm going back to Amsterdam. My search for truth has ended here in Rome. I
have no faith in your Robert Lebrun—or in his existence.
Good night."

But leaving de Vroome's suite, entering the landing of
the fourth floor, and starting up the staircase to his own
room on the fifth floor, Randall knew that he had not been
honest with the Dutch cleric.

Randall knew that he had deliberately lied.

He had no doubt whatsoever that a man named Robert
Lebrun existed somewhere in this city, and that this Lebrun must have some kind of proof of forgery. It was
logical, fitted perfectly into the sequence of events that
Randall had already learned.

What remained was to locate Lebrun and obtain the
proof. He was not going back to Amsterdam yet, not

yet. He was going to make one final effort to search out the truth. For now, he had a clue, a clue that might lead him to Robert Lebrun.

It would all depend on one thing. It would depend upon the success of a telephone call that he was about to make to Angela Monti.

X

LATE THE following morning, another glaring yellow, suffocating Rome day, Steve Randall waited in the cool living room of the Monti home for the housekeeper to bring him what he so eagerly sought.

Everything that might follow had hinged upon his call to Angela Monti the night before. She had been away from home with her sister, and had not returned his call until after midnight.

He had decided to withhold from her the news of his unexpected meeting with Dominee de Vroome in the Excelsior, and the revelation by the clergyman that her father's historic discovery might be a forgery. He had felt there was no reason to upset Angela with de Vroome's shocking disclosure, especially since it had not yet been proved.

"So you are leaving for Amsterdam in the morning?" Angela had asked.

"Probably in the afternoon, early afternoon," he had replied. "There's one more thing I want to do in the morning. However, it'll require your cooperation." He hesitated, and went on as casually as possible. "Angela, the day your father had his breakdown—actually, in the period afterwards, after you took him to the hospital—what happened to his papers, all the effects on and inside his desk at the university?"

"A week after we confined my father to Villa Bellavista, Claretta and I went to the university, to the office —I still remember how painful it was to do this, when someone you love has become helpless—and we removed

513

everything from his desk, and from around the office, and packed it all into small cartons."

"You saved everything?"

"Every scrap of paper, every kind of supply. In case he should recover someday, which we knew was unlikely, but it made us feel better. Also, we were in no mood to sort out everything. We just filled the cartons, and had them moved with the file cabinet to our house. We still have them in a storage room. I've not had the heart to look at them since."

"I can understand that, Angela. Look, would you have any objection to my going through those cartons, the ones holding the things from your father's desk? It's something I'd like to do in the morning, before leaving Rome."

"Why, no, there is no objection. There is not too much. You can see it." She had paused. "What are you looking for, Steve?"

"Well, since your father can't be part of the announcement-day ceremonies, I thought I might find some notes he made that could speak for him in Amsterdam."

Angela had been pleased. "What a nice idea. Except, I won't be here in the morning. My sister and I will be out with the children. If you'd prefer to wait until I return—"

"No," he had interrupted hastily, "I'd better not lose any more time. I can do this by myself if someone will let me in."

"I will instruct Lucrezia to admit you. She's the housekeeper—she's been with the family forever. The only problem . . ." Her voice had drifted off.

"Is what, Angela?"

"The only problem is that you won't be able to read my father's notes. He knew so many languages, but he always made his notes in Italian. I thought if I were here —but you don't want to be delayed, do you? I know what —Lucrezia can translate fairly well from Italian into English. So if there is something that interests you, something that looks important, then you can simply ask her. Or take it back to Amsterdam, where I'll help you with it when I return. What time do you want to be here in the morning?"

"Would ten o'clock be all right?"

"Fine. I'll tell Lucrezia to expect you, and to bring out for you the cartons with my father's effects from his desk. Do you want to see the file, also?"

"Any idea what's in it?"

"Carbon copies of his lectures, speeches, published papers."

"What about his personal correspondence?"

"He cleaned it out just weeks before his breakdown. He needed more space, so he threw it all out. But the rest in the file, especially his published papers, might be useful for your publicity."

"It could be. But it would take too much time right now. Maybe later, after the announcement date, we can go through that material together."

"I would be happy to help you. So tomorrow you only wish to see the cartons?"

"Yes. Just the stuff from the desk."

Hanging up on Angela, he regretted his lie. But he knew that he couldn't tell her what he was after, at least not yet. Only one thing mattered. He had to find Robert Lebrun.

Yesterday, listening to de Vroome, it had all come together, and the shape it had taken was the possibility of a real Lebrun and a clue that might locate him.

Dr. Venturi had unwittingly provided the first half of the clue: that often Professor Monti made appointments to meet people outside the university, and on the day of his breakdown, he had returned from an appointment with someone.

Dominee de Vroome had provided the second half of the clue: that Professor Monti's appointment, on that fateful day, had been with a person named Robert Lebrun.

Brought together, the two pieces of information formed a lead. A slight one, built on hearsay and conjecture, but a lead nevertheless, and the only clue to Lebrun's whereabouts—and to possible truth.

And now it was morning, and Randall waited in the living room of the Monti house near the Piazza del Popolo. It was an old house—more like a two-level apartment in size—and it had been remodeled and cheerfully decorated. The living room was furnished with green-and-gold-painted Venetian pieces, expensive and comfortable. The housekeeper, Lucrezia, a proprietary, motherly-bosomed retainer well advanced in years, attired in an aquamarine-colored smock that covered her like a tent, had welcomed him in her quaint English with the warmth she bestowed upon one of Angela's prospects. She had brought him coffee and cakes, and handed him an Italian-English dictionary and phrase book that Angela had left behind. Then she had bustled off to find the cartons holding the contents of Professor Monti's desk.

Randall moved to the round table that held the serving tray and poured his coffee. The crucial fact, he reflected, was that Angela and her sister had preserved their father's effects, untouched since the night he had been found deranged at his desk. Now, there would be critical questions. Had Professor Monti, on that day in May one year and two months ago, actually left his university office to meet with Robert Lebrun on the outside? And if so, had Professor Monti, a busy man with many appointments, made a record of this appointment with Lebrun? Or had he neglected to do so? Or been afraid to do so?

Randall had begun to drink the coffee when Lucrezia reappeared carrying a sturdy cardboard carton. Randall put down his cup to help her, but before he could do so, she had deposited the carton at his feet.

"You look this one," grunted Lucrezia. "I go for one more, another."

She left the room, and Randall lowered himself to the carpet, and sitting cross-legged on the floor, he folded back the corrugated carton flaps. Slowly, he began to remove the contents.

He was not interested in the blue folders filled with research papers, or the onyx pen holder and pen, or the blank yellow scratch pad.

A professor with many personal appointments would

normally list them, note them in some way, on something like a desk calendar or special appointment sheet. Randall had no idea what was used in Italy—he had not wished to ask Angela—but there had to be something, some record, even a note from a secretary, unless Monti had kept everything in his head.

More papers, the last typescripts of lectures or speeches undelivered, and correspondence unanswered and never to be answered.

Carefully, Randall dug deeper into the carton, almost halfway down, and now in his hand he held a leather booklet, maroon-colored, with a large paper clip that caught together the cover and a thickness of inner pages. On the cover was a title imprinted in gold and in Italian. The title read: *Agenda*.

Randall's heartbeat quickened.

He opened the appointment book to where the paper clip was set.

The date read: *8 Maggio*.

On the lined page were listed the hours of the morning, afternoon, evening. Several lines were filled in, apparently in Professor Monti's hand with his black pen.

Randall's eyes went slowly down the page of the appointment book, studying each of the notations:

10:00 . . . Conferenza con professori
12:00 . . . Pranzo con professori
14:00 . . . Visita del professore Pirsche alla Facoltà.

He checked the key words in the Italian-English dictionary, but there was no clue so far, so far on that fateful day only a staff conference, a lunch with some faculty professors, and Monti's receiving a foreign professor (apparently German) in his office.

Randall's eyes continued to go down the page, and suddenly stopped:

16:00 . . . Appuntamento con R. L. da Doney.
Importante.

Randall sat stock-still.

He translated.

16:00 meant four o'clock in the afternoon.

R. meant Robert. *L.* meant Lebrun.

Doney meant Doney's world-famous outdoor restaurant-café—the *gran caffè* of Roma—on the Via Vittorio Veneto, outside the Hotel Excelsior.

Appuntamento con R. L. da Doney. Importante meant —Appointment with Robert Lebrun at Doney. Important.

With a thrill of discovery, Randall realized that he had found what he was searching for.

On a late afternoon in May of last year, Professor Monti had noted that he was to meet with Robert Lebrun at Doney's café. It was there, according to de Vroome, that Lebrun had revealed his alleged forgery to Professor Monti, and it was there that Monti had begun his dark retreat into insanity.

A slim lead out of the recent past, but a real one, a very real one.

Randall replaced the appointment book in the carton, hurriedly packed the other articles on top of it, and leaped to his feet.

Lucrezia was coming into the living room with a second carton. "This box, it has only the scientific books, the periodicals, no more," she announced.

Randall went quickly across the room toward her. "Thanks, Lucrezia, I won't need to see it. I found what I was looking for. Thanks so much."

He pecked a kiss at her plump cheek, and left her wide-eyed and startled, as he rushed to the door.

RANDALL ABANDONED his taxi at the driveway to the entrance of the Hotel Excelsior. He strode past the front of the hotel, past the group of idle chauffeurs gossiping in the sun, and stood on the sidewalk surveying the scene where Robert Lebrun had made his shattering disclosure to Professor Monti a year and two months ago.

Doney's café-restaurant was divided into two sections.

The restaurant part was indoors, an extension of the ground floor of the Hotel Excelsior. The café itself, whose tables were all outdoors, occupied the remaining length of the street on the Via Vittorio Veneto from the edge of the hotel's driveway to the distant corner.

Doney's café consisted of two long lines of tables and chairs. On one side, rows of tables backed against the wall of the indoor restaurant, on the opposite side, rows backed against the parked automobiles and traffic on the forever-crowded Via Veneto. The sidewalk bisecting the padded blue chairs and tables was for strollers and for the café's waiters.

As he stood in the sweltering heat, contemplating the café, Randall was grateful that Doney's was shaded from the sun by two fringed blue awnings. At this hour, just before Saturday noon, it looked inviting, if not yet promising for Randall's hunt.

There was only a handful of scattered customers at the tables—mostly tourists, Randall guessed. The scene was almost a still life, and those who moved seemed to move in slow motion. It was the goddam torridity of Rome in late June, Randall thought, which tended to liquefy both ambition and initiative.

With the scant information he now possessed, Randall considered how he should proceed. A year and two months ago, he recalled, it was Robert Lebrun who had summoned Professor Monti to meet with him. Therefore, Lebrun must have been the one to name the Doney as the place for their appointment. If he had selected Doney's, which was hardly an out-of-the-way café, was in fact extremely popular, it must have been because Doney's was familiar to him. If this was true—it just as likely was not true, but *if* it was—then Robert Lebrun must himself have been familiar to those who worked in Doney's.

Randall studied several somnambulant waiters. They were outfitted in white jackets with blue epaulets, high stiff collars holding dark blue bow ties, black trousers, and were accessorized with lavender menus or empty trays. Near the opening between the rear tables that led into the restaurant, hands clasped behind him, was an older Italian with an air of authority. He was formally attired—bright blue dress jacket, starched collar and bow tie, tuxedo trousers—and he looked alive. The table captain, Randall decided.

Randall moved up the sidewalk, felt the relief of the sudden shade, and settled himself in a chair at an unoccupied table facing the thoroughfare. After a brief interval, a waiter took notice of him and ambled to his table, placing a lavender menu before him.

Opening the menu, Randall asked, "Is the table captain around?"

"Si." He called off to the formally attired older Italian. "Julio!"

Julio, the table captain, advanced quickly, his order pad and pen poised. "Your pleasure, sir?"

Randall absently scanned the menu. Everything was listed twice, once in Italian and then in English. His eye held on *Gelati,* then beneath it fixed on *Granita di limone* —Lemon sherbet—500 lire.

"I'll have the sherbet—lemon," said Randall.

Julio noted this. "That will be all?"

"Yes."

Julio ripped off the order sheet, handed it to the hovering waiter, and retrieved the menu.

"Actually," said Randall, "there is something else I want. It has nothing to do with your menu." Randall had his wallet out, and he extracted three large 1,000-lira bills. "I'm an American writer, and I need some information. Perhaps you can help me."

The professional stone face of the table captain showed fissures of interest. His eyes held on the lire in Randall's hands.

"If it is possible," the captain said, "I will be very glad to help you."

Randall folded the bills, and pressed them into the captain's warm hand. "How long have you worked in Doney's, Julio?"

"Five years, sir," He slipped the bills into a pocket, murmuring, *"Grazie,* sir."

"Were you working here—I mean, not on vacation or anything—in May of last year?"

"Oh, yes, sir." He was eager now, gracious, friendly. "It is before the tourist season, but busy, very busy."

"Then you were probably on the job. I'll tell you what I'm after. I'm doing some research, and there is someone I'd like to see who I'm told often comes to Doney's. A friend of mine met this person here a year ago May. I was told the person I'm looking for is a regular at this café. Do you recognize the regulars?"

Julio beamed. "But naturally. It is not only my job, but it is inevitable I become acquainted with our faithful customers. I know each by name, and come to know something of each one's character and life. It is what makes my occupation so rewarding. Who is the one you wish to know about?"

"He is a Frenchman, but a resident of Rome," said Randall. "I have no idea how often he comes to Doney's, but I am told he does come here." Randall held his breath, and then he spoke what he prayed was his open sesame. "Robert Lebrun is his name."

The captain looked blank. "Lebrun," he repeated slowly.

"Robert Lebrun."

Julio was racking his brain. "I am trying to think." He faltered, as if fearful of having to surrender his tip. "It does not register. We have no regular customer I know by that name. I would surely remember."

Randall's heart fell. He tried to recall Dominee de Vroome's description of Lebrun. "Maybe if I told you what he looked like—"

"Please."

"In his eighties. He wears glasses. Very wrinkled face. Kind of hunchbacked. About your height. That gives you Robert Lebrun. Does that help?"

Julio was aggrieved. "I am sorry, but there are so many—"

Randall remembered something else. "Wait, there is one thing you would have to notice. His walk. He walks with a limp. He lost one leg long ago, and he has an artificial leg."

Immediately, Julio brightened. "We have one like that. I have not known he was French, because his Italian is perfect, he is the perfect Roman gentleman. But his name is not Lebrun. Actually, I do not know his real name, except what he tells us. When he has too much Pernod or Negroni, he makes fun and tells us his name is Toti, Enrico Toti. It is a local joke. You do not understand it?"

"No."

Julio pointed off. "When you drive into the Borghese Gardens, and through the parks, there are many statues, and there is one, a very huge sculpture of a heroic nude man on a square stone base, and this man has one leg. He is leaning on a rock, one leg outstretched and the stump of his left leg resting on the rock. At the base of the statue it says *Enrico Toti,* and it tells when he died in 1916. This man Toti, even though he had only one leg, he volunteered for the Italian Army in the Austrian-Hungarian War, and was rejected, of course. But he volunteered again, still again, and they could not refuse, so they took him in the Italian Army with his one leg and his crutch and he fought and was a great hero. So this one-leg customer of ours, he joked that many years ago he was a hero and his name was Toti. So that is the only name—"

"Toti?" said Randall. "Well, that doesn't sound like Lebrun, does it? Of course, maybe he has many names." He became aware that the captain had broken out in a grin, and he wondered why. "What is it, Julio?"

"Another name, it just comes to me. It is foolish, but—"

"You're saying this Toti does have another name?"

"Foolish, very foolish. But the girls who walk the streets —you know?—they gave him this name because he is so intellectual and pretending to be elegant when he is so poor and pitiful. They call him"—Julio chuckled—"Duca Minimo, which means Duke of Nothing. It is the nickname they tease him with."

Randall grabbed the captain's arm in excitement.

"That's it, that's one of his other names? Toti alias Duca Minimo alias Robert Lebrun. He's the one I'm looking for.

"I am happy," said Julio, his three thousand lire now secure.

"Does he still come to the Doney?" Randall wanted to know.

"Oh, yes, most faithfully, almost every afternoon when the weather is fine. He comes for his *aperitivo* promptly at five o'clock in the late afternoon, before the rush, and he has his Pernod 45 or his Negroni, and makes his jokes, and reads his newspaper."

"Was he here yesterday?"

"Yesterday I did not work on that shift, although today I do. Let me find out—"

Julio went over to where three waiters were standing out of earshot, questioned them, and two of them laughed and nodded vigorously.

The captain returned, smiling. "Yes, this Toti—your Lebrun, as you call him—he was here for an hour at his usual time yesterday. Most probably, he will appear today at five."

"Great," said Randall, "absolutely great." He dug for his wallet and pulled out a 5,000-lira bill. Shoving it at the overwhelmed captain, he said, "Julio, this is important to me—"

"Please, thank you, sir, thank you very much. Anything I can do, I am happy to do."

"Do this. I'll be down here at a quarter to five. When Toti or Lebrun comes, point him out to me. I'll take care of the rest. If he should happen to come earlier, phone me in my room. I'm staying right here in the Excelsior. My name is Steven Randall. You won't forget? Steven Randall."

"I will not forget your name, Mr. Randall."

"One more thing, Julio. Our friend Lebrun—how does he come to Doney's every day? I mean, is he brought by a taxi or does he walk?"

"Always he arrives by foot."

"Then he must live in the neighborhood, in the vicinity.

He wouldn't walk a long distance with an artificial leg, would he?"

"It is improbable."

"All right, said Randall, rising. "Thanks for everything, Julio. I'll see you at four forty-five."

"But, sir, your lemon sherbet."

"All yours, with my compliments. I've had my dessert for today."

HE HAD spent a restless five hours in his double room on the fifth floor of the Hotel Excelsior.

He had tried not to think about what lay immediately ahead. He had thrown his suitcase on the bed, opened it, and taken out his correspondence files. At the glass-topped table beside the room's single window, he had tried to catch up on his letters.

He had written a routine interested-son letter to his mother and father in Oak City, including regards to his sister Clare, and to Uncle Herman. He had written a brief note, more touristy than fatherly, to his daughter Judy in San Francisco. He had started a letter to be forwarded to Jim McLoughlin of The Raker Institute, explaining that Randall Associates had been trying to locate him for weeks to let him know that due to circumstances beyond their control (he would not mention Towery or the Cosmos buy-out,) the firm would not be able to take on the Raker account. But he had been unable to finish that letter, and in the end had torn up what he had written.

Because he had been remiss about responding to his attorney's letters, he had considered phoning Thad Crawford in New York, but finally realized he lacked the patience for it. Although not hungry, he had called room service and ordered what was intended to be a light lunch, but which turned out to be cannelloni with mushrooms and stewed chicken with tomato sauce and peppers, and which he compulsively ate because of his growing anxiety.

He had considered letting Angela know that he was still in Rome, but decided against the call as one that would

either force him into another lie or fill her with apprehension. He had considered calling George L. Wheeler in
Amsterdam to explain his truancy, since the announcement of the International New Testament was only six
days off, but he had determined to postpone that call—
and Wheeler's inevitable wrath—until he had met Robert
Lebrun.

As much as he'd meant to keep Lebrun out of his
thoughts, he had found it impossible. He had paced his
hotel room, until he knew every inch of the pattern of the
Oriental rug, every nick in the marble-covered bureau
with its bowl of flowers, every drawn line in his own
countenance as it was reflected again and again in the
oval mirror above the dressing table.

He had come to Resurrection Two in Amsterdam a little
over two weeks ago to do a vital job and to learn for
himself the meaning of faith. Yet, he had spent half his
time, and had made his way to a climactic moment in
Rome, in an effort to annihilate the one thing in which
he might believe.

It had begun with the Bogardus flaw. Perhaps it had
been kept alive, this quest to exterminate, because of the
Randall flaw. His flaw, as Angela had pointed out, as
everyone close to him had told him at one time or another,
was that of unrelenting cynicism. So this hunt was mad-
ness, unless his own rationale was honest. And his rationale was that to have faith one must not rely on
unquestioning mystical belief. One must know tangible
reality.

And so, finally, it all came down to the person of
Robert Lebrun. One way or the other, with Lebrun lay
the last answer.

Those had been his thoughts in his hotel room upstairs.
They were still his thoughts now, as once more he sat at
a table in Doney's café, fretful and uneasy. He no longer
knew whether he wanted Lebrun to turn up or not. He
was only certain that he wished this excruciating encounter were over with and done.

For at least the tenth time in the past quarter of an
hour, he checked his wristwatch, those slow, slow moving

hands on the dial. It was six minutes after five o'clock. He took another sip of his Dubonnet, and as he did so, from the corner of his eye he saw the captain, Julio, gliding toward him.

Julio spoke in an undertone. "Mr. Randall, he is here."

"Where?"

"Behind me, in this row, at the third table behind me. You will recognize him."

Julio stepped aside, and Randall turned his head.

There he was, just as de Vroome had described him, but more so in every way. He seemed smaller, more hunched than Randall had expected. Neat brown hair, surely dyed. The skeletal features, all eroded by age, all tiny ridges and ravines. The round steel-rimmed spectacles with tinted lenses. A threadbare gabardine suit-coat draped loosely over his shoulders, with the empty sleeves hanging free, in the style of fashionable Italians and aspiring young actors. He looked hoary and antiquated, but not feeble. A lone drink rested on the beige tablecloth before him. He was absorbed in a newspaper.

Quickly, Randall left his table.

Reaching his destination, he took the free chair across from the occupant of the table and deliberately sat down in it.

"Monsieur Robert Lebrun," he said, "I hope you will allow me the pleasure of offering you a drink and introducing myself."

Lebrun's creased face showed over the top of the newspaper, and his hollow gray eyes were wary. His wet lips, slavering, worked over his ill-fitting dentures. "Who are you?" he croaked.

"My name is Steven Randall. I'm a publicity man and writer from New York. I've been waiting here to meet you."

"What do you want? Lebrun, you said. Where did you hear that name?"

The Frenchman's manner was anything but cordial, and Randall knew that he must work fast. "I understand you were once a friend of Professor Augusto Monti, that you had a partnership in an archeological enterprise together."

"Monti? What do you know of Monti?"

"I'm a close friend of one of his daughters. As a matter of fact, I saw Monti himself yesterday."

Lebrun was instantly interested, but guarded. "You saw Monti, you say? If so, tell me where you saw him."

Okay, thought Randall, the first test. "He's at the Villa Bellavista. I visited him, talked to him, and spoke to his physician, Dr. Venturi." Randall hesitated, and then presented himself for the second test. "I know something of your collaboration with Professor Monti, of the discovery at Ostia Antica."

The sunken eyes fixed hard on Randall. The flabby mouth was working wetly. "He told you about me?"

"Not exactly. Not directly. As a matter of fact, his memory is impaired."

"Go on."

"But I was given confidential access to his private papers, all the papers in his possession at the time he met with you here in Doney's over a year ago."

"So you know about that."

"I do, Monsieur Lebrun. That, and more. My curiosity, as a publicist and writer, was understandably aroused. I made an effort to trace you. I wanted to speak to you, in friendship, in the hope that what I have to say would prove to be of benefit to both of us."

Lebrun pushed his spectacles higher on the bridge of his nose, rubbed the stubble on his long chin, as he tried to reach some decision about this stranger. He seemed impressed, but cautious. "How can I be sure you are not lying?"

"About what?"

"That you saw Monti. There are so many charlatans everywhere. How can I be sure?"

This was an obstacle. "I don't know what evidence I can give you," said Randall. "I saw Monti, we spoke at length—meaningless as most of it was—and I came away with . . . well, what can I repeat?"

"I must be sure you saw him," insisted the old man doggedly.

"But I *did* see him. He even gave me—"

Suddenly remembering what he had stuck into his jacket pocket when he had left his room, Randall brought the sheet of paper from his pocket, unfolded it on the table. He had no idea what this would mean to Lebrun, but it was all he had of Monti. He pushed the paper in front of Lebrun. "Monti drew this picture for me, a speared fish, and gave it to me as a farewell gift. I don't know whether it means anything to you, but he drew it for me, gave it to me. That's the only thing I can show you, Monsieur Lebrun."

The drawing seemed to have a salutary effect on Lebrun. Holding it a few inches from his eyes—from one eye, actually, for now Randall saw that the old man's other eye was filmed by a cataract—Lebrun examined it, and returned it. "Yes, it is familiar."

"Then you are satisfied?"

"I am satisfied this is a drawing I often used to make."

"You?" said Randall, taken aback.

"The fish. Christianity. The spear. The death of Christianity. My wish." He ruminated briefly. "I am not surprised Monti has taken it up. His last memory. I betrayed Christianity and Monti. The death of me. His wish. That is, if he drew this."

"How would anyone else know about this?" pleaded Randall.

"Perhaps his daughter."

"She has never seen him sane since his last meeting with you."

The Frenchman scowled. "Maybe. If you saw Monti, did he make any reference to me—or to my work?"

Randall felt helpless. "No, he did not speak of you. As for your work—you mean the Gospel According to James and the Petronius Parchment?"

Lebrun made no answer.

Randall said hurriedly, "He thought he was James, the brother of Jesus. He started reciting, in English, word for word, what had been written in Aramaic on Papyrus Number 3, the first of the pages with actual writing on it." Randall stopped, trying to recall the contents of the tape recording that he had made at Villa Bellavista and replayed several times this afternoon. "He even filled in a missing portion of the third papyrus."

Lebrun showed signs of increased interest. "What was that?"

"When Monti discovered the Gospel According to James, there were a number of holes in the papyri. In the third fragment, there is an incomplete sentence that reads, 'The other sons of Joseph, the Lord's surviving brethren and mine own, are'—and then the next is missing, but the text picks up with—'I remain to speak of the firstborn and best beloved Son.' Well, Monti recited that, but he also filled in the missing portion."

Lebrun leaned forward. "What did he fill in?"

"Let me see whether I can remember." He tried to replay the tape in his head. "Monti said to me, 'The other sons of Joseph, the Lord's surviving brethren and mine own, are Judah, Simon, Joses—' "

" 'Jude, and all are beyond the boundaries of Judea and Idumaea, and I remain to speak of the firstborn and best beloved Son,' " Lebrun concluded for Randall, and sat back.

Randall stared at the old man. "You—you know it."

"I should," said Lebrun. His lips curled upward, so that his mouth became one more wrinkle on his face. "I wrote it. Monti is not James. I am James."

For Randall, it was a terrible moment, this moment he had sought and had not wished to find. "Then it's all a lie—James, Petronius, the entire discovery."

"A brilliant lie," amended Lebrun. He glanced to his left, then to his right, and added expansively, "A forgery, the most magnificent in history. Now you know." He studied Randall. "I am satisfied that you met with Professor Monti. I am not satisfied about what you want of Robert Lebrun. What do you want from me?"

"The facts," said Randall. "And your proof of forgery."

"What would you do with this proof?"

"Publish it. Expose those who would preach false hope to a gullible public."

There was a long silence, as Robert Lebrun sat deliberating. Finally, he spoke. "There have been others," he said softly, almost to himself, "others who have wanted the evidence of hoax and who gave their solemn pledges to expose the inner rottenness of the church and the sordid side of religion. They turned out to be agents of the clergy itself, trying to lay their hands on the truth and bury it so that they might preserve their myths forever. Their money would not be enough if I could not trust them to expose the Word. How can I trust you?"

"Because I was hired to publicize Resurrection Two and promote the new Bible, and I was almost taken in, until I began to have doubts," said Randall frankly. "Because my doubts made me search for truth—and perhaps I have found it in you."

"You have found it in me," said Lebrun. "I am less certain I have found it in you. I cannot surrender the truth about the work of a lifetime, unless I am certain —positive—that it will see the light."

For the first time Randall had met another, besides de Vroome, whose skepticism matched, if it did not exceed, his own.

The man was being exasperating and frustrating beyond endurance. Since the Plummer fiasco, Lebrun was probably unable to trust any fellow human being. Who on earth had sufficient character, and the faultless background needed, to convince this old man that his investment of years would be repaid, that his so-called proof would be given to people everywhere? Then, Randall thought of one. If young Jim McLoughlin were here in Randall's boots—McLoughlin with his fierce integrity, with his admirable record of investigation of hypocrisy and chicanery, with his Raker Institute dedicated to truth seeking and damn the consequence—he alone might win the trust of Robert Lebrun.

That instant, it struck Randall.

Jim McLoughlin and The Raker Institute *were* here, right here in Rome, minutes away.

With a surge of confidence, Randall said, "Monsieur Lebrun, I think I can convince you that I deserve your trust. Come with me to my room upstairs. Let me submit my proof. Then, I am sure, you will be ready to submit yours."

THEY WERE in Randall's room on the fifth floor of the Hotel Excelsior.

Robert Lebrun, with his uneven, stiff gait, had avoided the soft armchair and footstool and made his way to the straight chair beside the glass-topped table that Randall had earlier used as a desk. Once he was seated, his eyes followed Randall's every move.

Now, Randall had his suitcase open on the bed again and was rummaging through it. He came up with the legal-sized manila file folder bearing the typed label: *The Raker Institute*.

"Can you read colloquial English?" Randall asked.

"Almost as well as I can read ancient Aramaic," said Lebrun.

"Okay," said Randall. "Have you ever heard of an organization in the United States called The Raker Institute?"

"No, I have not."

"I suppose not," said Randall. "It hasn't been widely publicized as yet. In fact, I was asked to handle its first big publicity campaign." He went around the bed toward Lebrun, holding out the folder. "This is an exchange of correspondence between me and a man named Jim McLoughlin, head of The Raker Institute, prior to his meeting with me in New York. This also contains notes of our meeting. You will hear more of McLoughlin in months to come. He is the latest in the great tradition of American dissenters, crusaders who have exposed evil, men like your own Zola—"

"Zola," murmured Lebrun in a voice that was almost a caress.

"We have always had them. They have been few, and they have often suffered in the hands of the powerful. But they have never been silenced or made extinct, because they have been the voices of public conscience. Men like Thomas Paine and Henry Thoreau. And more

recent crusaders like Upton Sinclair, Lincoln Steffens,
Ralph Nader, who exposed the deceptions practiced on the
unsuspecting public by corrupt captains of industry. Well,
Jim McLoughlin and his investigators in The Raker Institute are the newest and latest in this line."

Robert Lebrun had been listening attentively. "What
do they do, this man and his Institute?"

"They have thoroughly investigated an unwritten conspiracy by certain American industries and corporations
to keep certain inventions and products from the public.
They have unearthed evidence that big business—the oil
industry, the automobile industry, the textile industry,
the steel industry, to name a few—has bribed, has even
committed violence, to withhold from the public a cheap
tablet that can replace gasoline, a tire that will almost
never wear out, a cloth that can survive a lifetime of use,
a match that would last forever. And that's only the
beginning. In this next decade they will go after conspira-
cies against the public practiced by the telephone
companies, by banks and insurance companies, by arma-
ment manufacturers, by the military and certain other
branches of government. McLoughlin believes that the
public is endangered by unregulated free enterprise. He
also believes that the public, not only in a democracy but
under communism as well, has representative government
—but no representation. He is out to expose every plot
perpetrated against the public. And, as you will see, I am
the one publicist he has called upon to aid him."

Randall laid the folder on the table before Lebrun.

"Here it is, Monsieur Lebrun, the only good character
reference I have in this matter of exposing the lie and
seeking the truth. Read it. Then decide whether you wish
to trust me or not."

Lebrun picked up the folder and opened it.

Randall headed for the door. "I'll leave you alone for
the next fifteen minutes. I'm going down to the bar to get
a drink. Would you like one?"

"I may not be here when you return," said Lebrun.

"I'll take my chances."

"A whiskey sour, strong."

Randall left the room.

He carried his rapidly diminishing bravado, and an inner prayer, to the bar downstairs.

Nearly twenty minutes had passed before he returned to the fifth floor and his room. As he entered, followed by a waiter carrying his Scotch and the whiskey sour on a tray, he wondered whether he would have one drink—or both—for himself.

But Robert Lebrun was there, still seated at the table, the folder closed beside him.

Randall dismissed the waiter and offered the whiskey sour to the old man. Lebrun accepted the drink. "I have made up my mind," he said in an oddly remote voice. "You are my last chance. I will tell you how I wrote the Gospel According to James and the Petronius Parchment. It is not a long story, but there has never been one like it before. It is a story that must be made known—and you, Mr. Randall, shall be its apostle to carry the truth about the lie, the lie of Christ's new coming, to the entire world."

HUNCHED IN THE CHAIR beside the table, addressing himself in an unemotional monotone to Randall, who was seated on the edge of the bed across from him, Robert Lebrun had been recounting the events of his youth before he had been condemned to the French Guiana penal colony.

For a half hour he had spoken of his impoverished and mean childhood in Montparnasse, of discovering early his skill at counterfeiting and creative forgery which led him into a life of petty crime in Paris, of his numerous arrests and sentences for these petty crimes, of his effort to secure permanent comfort and independence by undertaking the forgery of a government document, and of his final detection by the French Sûreté, and of his being found guilty after a trial before the Tribunal Correctionnel.

Although Randall had heard some of this already, he listened with fascination because Lebrun was the source. Randall did not let his hard-won confidant know that not twenty-four hours before, he had heard a small part of Lebrun's story from Dominee de Vroome, who in turn had heard it from Cedric Plummer. He pretended that he was learning of it for the first time, and waited for what he had not yet been told and was eager to know.

"And so," Robert Lebrun was saying, "because I had already been imprisoned four times in France for lesser crimes, I was automatically categorized as an incorrigible, beyond grace or rehabilitation. I was sentenced to spend my life in the penal colony of French Guiana in South America. The entire colony became popularly known by one name—Île du Diable—Devil's Island—but actually, there were five separate prisons there. Three of these were islands, and only the smallest, no more than one thousand meters in circumference, not quite twelve hundred yards, was Devil's Island itself. This island was reserved for political prisoners only—like Captain Alfred Dreyfus, who had been wrongly put there for supposedly selling military secrets to Germany, and at no time did this small Devil's Island ever have more than eight prisoners in its shacks. The two other islands nine miles off the shore of Guiana were Royale and St. Joseph. The two prisons on the mainland, some distance from the city of Cayenne, were St. Laurent and St. Jean. I was sent to St. Joseph Island."

Lebrun's dry voice had begun to crack. He brought the whiskey sour to his lips, took a long swallow, and cleared his throat.

"What year were you sent to French Guiana?" Randall asked.

"Before you were born," Lebrun cackled. "In the year 1912."

"Was it as bad as has been written?"

"Worse," said Lebrun. "Convicts who escaped to write about it would write of the cruelties, and their sufferings, but somehow they tended to romanticize it as an adventure. It was nothing like that, no glamorous hell. Only the known cliché describes it exactly—the dry guillotine, where you were executed every day but could not die. Torture and pain without end, I learned, are worse than mere death. Prometheus was a greater martyr than St. Peter. I was shipped to Guiana in 1912 on *La Martinière,* confined not to a cabin but to a steel cage with ninety others on the starboard side of the hold. Originally, the penal colony had been meant as a place where convicts might be rehabilitated and redeem themselves. Can you believe the official name for these islands was Îles du Salut—Salvation Islands? But, like all man-made organizations, its purpose was corrupted. When I was sent there, the penal philosophy was—once a man is a criminal, he is always a criminal, he is beyond redemption, a beast, so let him suffer and rot to death and never be permitted to bother society again."

"Yet, you are here."

"I am here because I willed myself to be here," said Lebrun fiercely. "I had reason to survive, as you will soon see. But not in the beginning. In the beginning, when I thought I was still a man, and tried to act like one, they set out to remind me that I was an animal, less than an animal. How can I explain the first two years? To say the life was brutalizing—to call it inhuman—mere tea-cup words. Listen. In the day mosquitoes, in swarms, feeding on the sores covering your broiling naked skin, with jiggers burrowing under your nails, and red ants biting your feet. In the night, bats, vampire bats, sucking your blood. Always dysentery, fever, blood poisoning, scurvy. Look."

Mouth open, Lebrun retracted his lips, baring the raw bluish-red gums above the cheap dentures. "How did I lose my teeth? They rotted from *scorbut,* a kind of scurvy. I spit them out, two, three at a time. With more than four convictions, as a lifer, I was classified with the *relégués,* one of those who would never leave the colony. On St. Joseph Island, I hammered rocks in the sun from daybreak to nightfall, and if I protested, I was thrown into solitary. Do you know what solitary meant on St. Joseph? There were three cell blocks—the regular prison, the solitary, and the lunatic asylum—and the most inhuman was solitary. I would be thrown into a cement pit twelve by eight feet. No roof. Just iron bars above. In the cell a wooden bench, a latrine bucket, a blanket that could be changed only once in two years. The stink of the foul air and human dung made you choke. In solitary, I would every day spend twenty-three and a half hours in that cement pit, with a half hour outdoors in the courtyard for air. The regular prison was not much better. Sometimes worse, especially at night when you tried to sleep on your wooden cot, and the perverts, the homosexuals, attacked you. Day in, day out, the food was the same, coffee, nothing else, for breakfast. A pint of hot water with mashed vegetables called soup, a crust of bread, three ounces of putrid beef for lunch, and either dried beans or moldy rice for dinner. I was worked to a bag of bones, beaten, whipped, kicked, tortured by the guards, who were mostly vicious Corsicans, brutal ex-Foreign Legionnaires or former *flics,* and my only dream was of suicide, of the relief that would come with death and with being laid to rest in the Bamboos, the convict cemetery in St. Laurent. Then, one day, a miracle happened—I thought so, anyway—and there was a reason to live."

The priest, Randall remembered. De Vroome had mentioned a French Catholic priest who had befriended Lebrun in his darkest hour.

"About ten miles from St. Laurent-du-Maroni, near the Maroni River, the penal colony had a clearing surrounded by malarial swamps and the densest jungles," Lebrun went on. "Here were administrative offices, guards' shacks, a sawmill, a hospital, a concrete prison, and one special hut, and this area was called the Camp of St. Jean or St. Jean Prison. For the three hundred convicts there, with their sores, lesions, empty eyes, it was a terrible place. They slept on concrete floors covered with pus and excrement. They were fed only mash soup and unripe bananas. They slaved from six in the morning until six at night, chopping down trees in the jungles and being harnessed like horses to pull the wood into the village. It was there, to St. Jean, that I was sent, and that was the miracle that gave me reason to live."

"You found reason to live? In a hellhole like that?"

"Yes. Because of the special hut in the clearing," said Lebrun. "I mentioned a special hut, did I not?"

"You did."

"It was the camp church—the only church I knew of in the penal colony, not counting the unused chapel on Royale Island," said Lebrun. "This church hut was set on pilings. Except for the sloping wooden roof, it was built of stone, with five windows in each side wall. It was not for the use of prisoners, of course, but a place of worship for the foreign guards, and French administrators and their wives. There was also a dedicated priest—" Lebrun broke off, conjuring up a memory of the clergyman, and finally he spoke again. "His name was Paquin, Père Paquin, a slight, anemic and very devout French father from Lyons, and he was in charge of the St. Jean church. He also visited prisoners in the hospital, and occasionally at the other mainland prison and those on the islands."

"You mean he was the only clergyman in the entire penal colony?"

"The only one," said Lebrun. He reflected a moment, and corrected himself. "No, when I first arrived, there were others. You see, the Guiana penal colony existed for a century, and in the beginning there were Jesuits, but later they were supplanted by the French Order of the Congregation of the Holy Spirit from Paris. When I came to Guiana there was an apostolic vicar, like a bishop, who resided in the capital, in Cayenne, and he was answerable to the Vatican. The vicar had under him curés who conducted religious activities in the eleven parishes of French Guiana. But three years later, in the time I speak of, they were all expelled, except one. Only Père Paquin remained."

"Why were the clergymen thrown out?"

"Because, as the curé once told me, they determined to help Guiana's disinherited sheep—that is what they called us—by starting an international crusade of prayers to bring to attention the plight of the convicts. The French government was antagonized, and recalled the clergy, opposed religious activity, permitting just one curé to stay on."

"Your Father Paquin?"

"Yes," said Lebrun. "And he had his church hut in St. Jean. Since this church hut was undecorated and unfurnished except for the altar and some wooden benches, the curé Paquin one day decided to improve it. He wanted to put in stained-glass windows and have holy paintings on the walls to make the sanctuary more spiritual and attractive. He required an artist, and he heard I was the only former artist to be found among the eight thousand prisoners in the penal colony. So he requested my transfer from St. Joseph Island to St. Jean on the mainland. Of course, I was no artist and never had been, except for engraving portraits of La Belle France on counterfeit banknotes. But the fact that I was known to have forged an illuminated medieval Bible made the officials recommend me. My change from being in the custody of the brutal island guards to my assignment to assist this curé was so great that I found it unbelievable."

"In what way?" asked Randall.

"Père Paquin, aside from his religious fanaticism, was a reasonable man, and good to me and appreciative of my creative talents. I was no longer terrorized. I was treated with kindness. I was given medical attention, fresh prison clothes, slightly better food. Since I was not really an accomplished artist, I suggested that the new windows be decorated with quotations in Greek or Latin from the New Testament, and that the walls of the church hut be painted with ancient Christian symbols like the fish and the lamb, and many more. The curé was enthusiastic, and obtained a considerable library of research books for me, various versions of the Bible, Latin and Greek and Aramaic grammars, illustrated histories of the first church, similar volumes. I pored over every book, absorbed every word, not once or twice, but endlessly. I spent a year decorating the church. It drew much praise from visitors, and Père Paquin was proud of it and of me. All through this period, almost unknowingly, I was being converted to Christ. Under the curé's guidance, I was taught that the only hope and peace for me was in God, in His Son, in goodness and in love. For the first time in three years of injustice in hell, I had a glimpse of decency on earth and wanted to live and see my homeland again and become a human being again. But I was committed to the penal colony until death—yet, because of this priest, I wanted to live. Then the opportunity came."

"The opportunity for what?"

"To be pardoned. To be free."

Lebrun paused to take another swallow of his whiskey sour and then he resumed speaking.

"It was 1915, and all of Europe was locked in combat, in the early bloodshed of the First World War," Lebrun was saying. "The director of the Penal Administration assembled the *condamnés,* the convicts with shorter sentences, and some of the *relégués,* the lifetime ones, the incorrigibles, but the ones who had shown good behavior, and I was one of these since I had been under the patronage of the priest. We were told that if we volunteered for a special battalion of the French Army, to serve as infantrymen on the Western front in Europe against the Hun, we would be given consideration and leniency after the war. It was all ambiguous, unspecific, and few offered themselves. When my curé, Père Paquin, could not understand why I had not taken advantage of this opportunity, I told him I had discussed it with the men and none of us wished to risk having our heads blown off without a guarantee of reward. My curé friend consulted with the authorities, and he returned to me with a positive offer. If I would volunteer to fight for France, and if I would persuade my fellow convicts to do so, the French Ministry of War would guarantee us amnesty and freedom the week that the war was ended. 'In fact,' Père Paquin promised me, 'as a servant of Our Lord, in the name of Jesus the Saviour, you have my personal pledge to stand behind the government's promise. You have my word that if you volunteer to fight, you will be pardoned and be restored to citizenship and freedom. I give you my word, not only on behalf of the French government, but in the name of the Church.' This was enough for me—and, partially through my persuasion, for the other. The government was one thing. But the curé and the Church were infallible and trustworthy. So, with other convicts, I volunteered for service."

To Randall, this was incredible. "Monsieur Lebrun, are you telling me that the Devil's Island penal colony had a special unit that was sent back to France to fight the Germans?"

"Exactly."

"But why haven't I ever read about it in any history book?"

"You will understand in a moment why it is not widely reported," said Lebrun. He massaged his thigh, where the stump fitted into his artificial leg, Randall supposed, and he started speaking again. "Inspired by our curé, we signed up as infantrymen. We sailed from French Guiana, and in July 1915 we disembarked in Marseilles, and touched the soil of our beloved France once more. Our regiment was formed. Our officers were our guards from Devil's Island. We had all the privileges of soldiers, save one. We were never permitted a leave while in the army. We were called the Devil's Island Expeditionary Force, under the leadership of none other than General Henri Pétain."

"Were you sent into actual combat?"

"Directly into combat, into the trench warfare in Flanders. We remained on the front lines, without relief, for three years. It was wretched and bloody beyond imagining. Casualties climbed, but it was better than what we had left behind, and, inspired by the freedom my priest had guaranteed us, we stayed on and fought like tigers. Because we were in the vanguard, and never given relief, two thirds of our eighteen hundred men died in battle. Those of us who survived fought on. Six months before the end, my left limb was shattered by shrapnel from a German artillery explosion. The leg was amputated, but I was saved. It was a big price to pay for freedom, but when I woke up in the military hospital I decided it had been worth the cost. By the time I had healed, and learned to walk with a primitive artificial leg of wood, the Armistice came and then peace, and the war was ended. I was a young man. My new life was about to begin. With six hundred other survivors of our Devil's Island Expeditionary Force, I celebrated the ride back to Paris, where we were to wait for our proclamation of amnesty. Upon our arrival, we were marched to Santé Prison. The prison stay was unexpected, and I sent for my curé—Père Paquin had been an army chaplain at a command post behind the lines—and I asked him what was happening. He blessed me and thanked me for my sacrifice, even embraced me like a son, and assured me in the name of the Saviour that Santé Prison was only temporary quarters before our release and that our freedom would be granted within the week. I was so relieved that I wept with joy. A week passed, and suddenly one morning our old Corsican guards from French Guiana, reinforced by countless new guards, with rifles and bayonets unsheathed, tramped into Santé Prison, surrounded us, herded us into trains, and transported us to Marseilles. There, we were thrown prison clothes and we were informed that, for reasons of national security, we must all be returned to *le bagne,* the convict settlement in Guiana, to serve out our sentences. It was impossible to riot. There were too many guns at our heads. I had a glimpse of Father Paquin. I cried out to him. He offered no sympathy. He only shrugged. And I remember the last thing I did before we were marched aboard the convict ship. I shook my fist at him and I shouted, *'Fumier et ordure*—garbage and manure—on the Church! *Merde* on Christ! I will have my vengeance!' "

Randall shook his head in disbelief. "That actually happened?"

"It happened. Yes, it happened. It is recorded today in the archives of the Ministry of Justice or the Ministry of National Defense in Paris. And so back we went to the mosquitoes, the jiggers, the ants, the heat, the swamps, the hard labor, the beatings, the brutality of Devil's Island and Guiana. But this time I had a better reason to live, to survive. There is no stronger motivation for a mortal than revenge. I would have revenge. Against the heartless government? Against the lying, double-crossing clergyman? No. I would have my revenge against all the deceit of religion—truly the enemy of life—the drug, the opium that oppresses—with its false prattlings about a kindly Saviour. My faith was as shattered and crippled as my body. And it was while still on the convict ship that disembarked us at St. Laurent-du-Maroni that I conceived my masterstroke—the coup de grâce against all Christ-salesmen—my deception that would even the score with the Church hierarchy for its deception against me. I conceived, in its rudimentary form, the Gospel According to James and the Petronius Parchment. From 1918, when I was returned to the Guiana penal colony, until 1953, when the colony was shut down and abandoned by the French Committee of Liquidation because of the bad reputation the conditions there were giving France around the world, I made the careful preparations for my coup."

Horrified and enthralled, yet his feelings overlaid with sympathy, Randall continued to hear the old man out.

An exemplary prisoner, Lebrun had been given more latitude than the others. By carving coconuts and novelty trinkets and preparing gift scrolls for sale in Cayenne, by a certain amount of thievery, by forging medieval manuscripts (mailed to Paris by a cooperative guard who took a thirty-percent commission), which were sold to dealers through his criminal contacts, Lebrun acquired the money to pay for additional research books on religion. He was also able to buy materials to counterfeit banknotes, which in turn were peddled at discount prices and gave him income to obtain still more costly religious books to research his project.

During the thirty-five years of his second incarceration, Lebrun had made himself into an expert on Jesus, on New Testament lore, on Aramaic and Greek, on papyrus and parchment. In 1949, because of his good record, his status was changed from *relégué*—lifer—to *libéré*—freeman, one who no longer need stay in the prison itself but who must remain in the vicinity of the penal colony. Exchanging his striped prison garb for the coarse dark blue outfit of the *libéré,* Lebrun moved into a shanty on the Maroni River a short distance from St. Laurent, and he continued to support himself by making souvenirs and forging manuscripts. In 1953, when the Guiana penal colony was closed, the *relégués* were sent back to France to continue serving out their sentences in government prisons, and Lebrun, with other *libérés,* was returned to Marseilles on the S. S. *Athesli* and set free on the soil of France, at last.

Making his home in Paris once more, Lebrun resumed his underground counterfeiting of banknotes and his forging of passports, to get hold of money for sustenance and for the expensive materials required to perpetrate his long-planned hoax. When he was ready, he turned his back on France forever. After smuggling a trunk crammed with a forger's materials into Italy, he followed it, found quarters in Rome, and began to create his awesome biblical forgery.

"But how could you even begin to dream of fooling the scholars and theologians?" Randall wanted to know. "I can see where you might learn enough Greek, but I've been told Aramaic is a real brain twister, besides being an extinct language—"

"Not quite extinct," said Lebrun with a smile. "A present-day form is still spoken by Moslems and Christians in a border area of Kurdistan. As for Aramaic's being, as you put it, a brain twister—it is, it was, but I gave over four decades of my life to studying it, far more time than I ever devoted to learning the refinements of my native French. I studied scholarly journals in philology, etymology, linguistics, which published the technical papers written by the foremost authorities from Simopetra's Abbot Petropoulos to Dr. Jeffries of Oxford. I studied textbooks, such as the German one, *A Grammatic of Biblical Aramaic* by Franz Rosenthal, which I found in Wiesbaden. Most important, I obtained and studied in reproduction—and copied out by hand hundreds of times, so that I could write the language easily— the ancient Aramaic manuscripts of the Book of Enoch, the Testament of Levi, the Apocrypha of Genesis, all of which exist today. A difficult language, it is true, but with application I mastered it."

Impressed, Randall wanted to know more. "Monsieur Lebrun, it's the authenticity of the papyrus that puzzles me the most. How could you possibly manufacture papyrus that would pass our complicated scientific tests?"

"By not attempting to manufacture it," said Lebrun simply. "To try to reproduce ancient paper would have been foolhardy. Actually, the papyrus, the parchment also, they were the least difficult elements of the forgery. The most dangerous, perhaps, but the easiest. As you know, Mr. Randall, I had been not only a counterfeiter but also a thief. My friends in the underworld were criminals and thieves. Together, over a period of two years, we acquired my ancient writing materials. Through my studies, I knew the location of every catalogued first-century scroll and codex, as well as the as yet uncatalogued finds. I knew the public and private museums and libraries where these were stored or displayed, and I knew the private millionaire collectors as well. Many scrolls are blank at the beginning or at the end, while many codices have unused leaves, and I stole these."

The audacity of the man was amazing to Randall. "Can you be specific? I mean, which collections—where?"

Lebrun shook his head. "I prefer not to recite to you the exact sites from which I liberated papyrus and vellum, but I do not mind telling you of a number of collections we—uh—surveyed, and some of these were among the ones we eventually visited again with more serious intentions. We called upon the Vatican Library and the Turino Museum in Italy, the Bibliothèque Nationale in France, the Oesterreichische Nationalbibliothek in Austria, the Bodmer Library near Geneva in Switzerland, and numerous repositories in Great Britain. Among the latter were the Beatty Collection in Dublin, the Rylands Library in Manchester, and the British Museum in London."

"You actually committed thefts in those places?"

Lebrun preened himself. "Yes, we did, in some of them, not in all—because all did not possess papyri and parchments dating exactly to the first century. The British

Museum was particularly fruitful. A most tantalizing source, the museum, offering as it did a first-century papyrus roll with blank areas, a Samaria papyrus with a fair portion of it blank. Best of all, a great amount of the British Museum's papyri, again with batches of them blank, was unorganized and uncatalogued, due to lack of personnel and maintenance funds, and therefore they were relatively unsecured. Then, of course, there was a treasure trove in my native Paris, in the Bibliothèque Nationale. The Bibliothèque Nationale has hoarded many thousands of these manuscripts in storage, untranslated, unpublished, uncatalogued. What a pity, such a waste. So I availed myself of a few of the blank first-century parchment leaves and put them to good use. You understand me, monsieur?"

"I certainly do," said Randall. "But how in heaven's name did you pull it off?"

"By going ahead and doing it," said Lebrun ingenuously. "By proceeding boldly but with care. Some museums I entered well before dawn, and others I hid in until after closing time. In either case, once I had dismantled the alarm systems, I performed the robberies myself. For heavily protected museums, I used more practiced colleagues whom I paid well. In two instances, I negotiated. Those poor museum and library guards are pitifully underpaid, you know. Some have families, many mouths to feed. Modest bribes open many doors. No, Mr. Randall, the small amount of papyrus and parchment that I required was not hard to come by. And mind you, all pieces were authentic, the parchments no earlier than 5 B.C. and the papyri no later than 90 A.D. For the ink, I used a formula used from 30 A.D. through 62 A.D., which I reproduced with a special aging ingredient added to lampblack and vegetable gum, the very ink employed by first-century scribes."

"But the contents of your Petronius report and your James gospel," said Randall. "How could you dare invent what you did? How could you possibly imagine two such documents would be acceptable to the most learned theologians and scholars in the world?"

Lebrun's mouth formed a toothy grin. "First, because there was a desperate need for two such documents. There were those in religion, greedy for money or power, who wanted such a find to be made. The religious leaders were ready for it. They desired it. The climate and times were ripe for a resurrected Jesus. Also, because not one idea or action I set down in the name of Petronius and James was fully invented by me. Nearly everything I used had been suggested at least once by Church fathers or historians or other early gospel writers in the years following the first century. Everything was there, moldering and neglected or completely ignored, except by latter-day theorists."

"What was there?" Randall demanded. "Can you give me some examples? Let's take the Petronius Parchment. Was there actually a person named Petronius?"

"The Lost Gospel of Peter says there was."

"The Lost Gospel of Peter? I never heard of it."

"It exists," said Lebrun. "It was found in an ancient grave near the town of Akhmim on the Upper Nile in Egypt during 1886 by French archeologists. The Peter gospel is a parchment codex that was written near 130 A.D. It differs from the canonical gospels in twenty-nine ways. It says Herod—not the Jews, not Pilate, but Herod —was responsible for the execution of Jesus. It also says the captain heading one hundred soldiers in charge of Jesus was named Petronius."

"I'll be damned," said Randall. "You mean the Peter gospel is for real?"

"Not only is it real, but Justin Martyr—who became a Christian convert in 130 A.D.—tells us that in its day, when it was being read, the Peter gospel was more respected than today's four gospels. Yet when the New Testament was assembled in the fourth century, the Peter gospel was not admitted, was cast aside, relegated to the Apocrypha—that is, the writings of doubtful authority."

"Okay," said Randall. "In your Petronius Parchment, you have Jesus tried as a subversive and a rebel who considers himself above the current Caesar. What made you think that would be swallowed?"

"Because many of the Bible scholars on earth believe it to be true," replied Lebrun. "I need only quote to you from that challenging but iconoclastic work, *The Nazarene Gospel Restored* by Graves and Podro: 'There is no doubt that Jesus was anointed and crowned King of Israel; but the Gospel editors did their best to conceal this for political reasons.' "

"And your forgery of the Gospel According to James," said Randall. "The various sayings you attribute to Jesus. Fact or fiction?"

Lebrun's eyes glistened behind his steel-rimmed spectacles. "Let us put it this way, monsieur—fact was the basis for my fiction. The Logia, the Sayings of the Lord, presented very few problems. Once more I consulted the Apocrypha, the ancient documents of questionable accuracy. Let us take, as an example, one ancient document that was excavated—the *Epistula Jacobi Apocrypha*—the Apocryphon of James, a collection of remarks attributed to Jesus. I borrowed some of them, merely revising or improving upon them. In the Apocryphon, when Jesus takes leave of James, it reads, 'After He had said this He departed. But we knelt down, and I and Peter, we gave thanks and sent up our hearts toward the heavens." In the Revised Version According to Lebrun, I put it, 'And he bade us remain, and blessed us, and with his staff in hand he went off and disappeared in the mist and the darkness. Then we knelt down and gave thanks and lifted up our hearts to the heavens.' "

Self-satisfied, Lebrun squinted at Randall, awaiting his reaction.

Once more, Randall shook his head at the audacity of it, and gave a grudging approval. "I see what you mean," he said. "Fact serving fiction. I'd like to know more. What about James's description of Jesus? Didn't you expect that this Jesus, with narrow eyes, elongated nose, face disfigured by scars and blemishes—didn't you expect this to meet resistance?"

"No. Again, there were ancient hints of His having an unattractive appearance. Clement of Alexandria, when

chastising followers preoccupied with good looks, reminded them that Jesus was 'ugly of countenance.' Andrew
of Crete wrote that Jesus had 'eyebrows which meet.' Cyril
of Alexandria recorded that Christ possessed 'a very ugly
countenance,' but added that 'compared to the glory of
the divinity, the flesh is of no worth.' It was enough for
me to go by."

"But what did you have to go by to justify your writing
that Jesus survived the Cross?"

"There is a long tradition that Jesus did not die when
He was crucified. Ignatius, who became bishop of Antioch in Syria during 69 A.D., stated that Jesus was 'in
the flesh' after His Resurrection. According to Irenaeus,
the respected Papias—who was the bishop of Hierapolis
—personally knew the disciple John, and this Papias
stated that Jesus did not die until He was fifty. The
Rosicrucians have always claimed that they possess ancient documents proving Jesus escaped death on the Cross
in Jerusalem. A Rosicrucian historian wrote, 'When they
entered the tomb, they found Jesus resting easily, and
rapidly regaining strength and vitality.' These sources also
state that the Essene sect hid Jesus. Incidentally, Essene
means not only 'holy one' but also 'healer.' An Essene
may well have healed Jesus. That was the contention of
Karl F. Bahrdt and Karl H. Venturini, who wrote a life
of Jesus in the late 1700's. They theorized that the
Essenes had staged Christ's miracles, staged the Resurrection, and that He was removed from the Cross not dead
but merely unconscious, and was revived by an Essene
healer or physician."

"And this business of bringing Jesus to Rome?"
prodded Randall.

"Rome," said Lebrun, repeating the word lovingly.
"My greatest risk, but why not? The Jewish-Pharisees of
the second century strongly believed that the Messiah
would appear in Rome. Peter saw Jesus in the flesh on
the road to Rome. The Roman historian, Suetonius,
blamed Christ for creating disorders in Rome. In fact,
there is a tradition which reports James as telling his

followers that if any of them should wonder where their God is, he can assure them, 'Your God is in the great city of Rome.' " Lebrun paused, considering what he had just said. He seemed satisfied. "I think Rome was logical enough."

"Apparently it was."

"You see, Monsieur Randall, almost every concept in my forgery was based on some ancient clue. These are the same clues that have tempted modern-day theologians and New Testament scholars to try to reconstruct Christ's life, fill in the gaps, through deduction and logic, through interpreting the background of the time and theorizing. The modern biblical experts know that the present four gospels are not factual history. The four gospels are largely a series of myths strung together, although these myths may have been based on actual occurrences. This has challenged many modern experts to speculate on what might have really happened early in the first century. They would like nothing more than to be proved right by the discovery of a lost gospel—one they have always believed existed as the primary source for the four accepted gospels. So I knew that whatever resistance the James and Petronius stories might meet, there would still be hundreds of theologians and scholars alive to say, 'At last, the actual evidence of what we have so long theorized must have happened.' "

"Your assumption proved right, Monsieur Lebrun. The most respected international experts have studied your James gospel and Petronius trial report and approved them."

"I never doubted the outcome for a minute," said Lebrun complacently. "After I had safely buried my forgery—and that, in some ways, that second to last step was the most difficult—"

"How the most difficult?" Randall interrupted.

"Because once I was forced to use the area of Ostia Antica as the site for the discovery, in order to support Professor Monti's ideas and to involve him later, I was faced with difficult problems."

"In what way?"

"To have secreted my handiwork in some cave in Israel or Jordan, or in some storage room in a monastery in Egypt, would have been easier, more logical. Most major finds have been made in those dry areas. But Ostia Antica—dreadful. One could not imagine a more unlikely place for papyrus to survive nineteen to twenty centuries. There was the water problem. Ostia's elevation was so low in ancient days that it was seasonally flooded by waters from the Tiber. No papyrus or parchment could be expected to have endured this recurrent flooding. Then I had to grapple with another historic fact. In the second century, Hadrian Caesar demolished Ostia and rebuilt it a meter higher in elevation to neutralize the flooding. I overcame the problem by deciding to encase the manuscripts in a stone block."

"Wouldn't that be suspect at once?"

"Not in the least," said Lebrun. "I knew that many wealthy merchants once lived in villas on the coast near Ostia Antica—and if one of these merchants, a Jew secretly turned Christian, had wanted to preserve valuable manuscripts brought in from the colony of Palestine, he would have done it in just this manner."

"So to preserve them you used an ancient stone block?"

"Not easy," said Lebrun. "All stone in Italy does not protect against water. I experimented with many. Tufa stone is common but proved too porous. Clay, which might do in the Dead Sea climate, was too fragile for a seaport area like Ostia. Even marble breaks down under water. I finally settled upon one of the twenty-five varieties of gray granite, a durable granite, one without feldspar which swells and exfoliates in groundwater. I got a chunk of this ancient granite, and squared it up to resemble a base stone that could have supported some ancient statuary. I sawed the granite block in half and chiseled it out. Then I wrapped the James gospel papyri and the Petronius Parchment in oiled silks, stuffed them inside a pottery jar, sealed the jar, and placed the jar inside the hollowed-out granite block. That done, I rejoined the two halves of the granite block, sealed it with pitch, aged it further, and buried it in an unexcavated area where there were thought to be second- and possibly first-century ruins below the ground. I waited several years for the buried stone to become one with the soil and overgrowth. Then I approached Professor Monti with a fragment I had held out, and I pretended it had been discovered in another jar in that area. Once I had Monti on my side, I never worried again."

It was diabolical, the whole thing, Randall decided. To have undertaken it, this old man was either crazy or a perverted genius. That is, if he had undertaken it at all, and was not fantasizing. "And now you are ready to expose your hoax of the Gospel of James and the Petronius Parchment to the world?"

"I am ready."

"You've tried to expose it once or twice before, I believe you said."

"Yes. Last year I met with Monti, because I needed money. I threatened to make the forgery known, if he did not give me additional money, which I deserved. Of course, I confess, had he given me the money, I would have kept my word for only a short time, that is, suppressed the forgery for a while. But I would have held on to part of my evidence so that later I could make the hoax public. Because, money or no money, I could never let the church escape my revenge. Then, more recently, I entered into negotiations with another interested party, but I withdrew when I realized this party was acting on behalf of the church itself, which wants to acquire my exposé and suppress it to save their faith and their fake Bible."

"You are prepared to sell it to me if I expose the whole story?"

"I am, for the proper monetary consideration," said Lebrun with delicacy.

"What do you regard as a proper monetary consideration?" asked Randall, adding hastily, "That is, allowing for the fact that I am a mere individual and not a bank."

Lebrun finished the last of his drink. "I will be reasonable. If it is in American dollars—"

"In American dollars."

"Twenty thousand dollars."

"That's a lot of money."

"It can be made in two payments," said Lebrun. "After all, what I give you will make you rich and famous."

"What will you give me in return for the money?"

"Proof," said Lebrun, "incontrovertible and unimpeachable proof of my forgery."

"What is this proof?"

"First a papyrus fragment that fits into the lacuna, the gap or hole in Papyrus Number 3 that you referred to in the Doney. This fragment bears the missing section Monti recited to you, the one where James lists the brethren of Jesus and himself. It is irregularly shaped, and measures roughly 6.5 by 9.2 centimeters in size—2½ by 3¾ inches—and did fit perfectly into the hole in the so-called original."

"But the experts may say it is authentic, as real and authentic as the rest of the papyrus in Amsterdam."

Lebrun offered up a malicious, supercilious smile. "I had long ago anticipated that possibility, Mr. Randall. This fragment I kept back bears in its pressed pith, drawn with invisible ink right over the text that can be seen, half of a speared fish. The other half is on your Papyrus Number 3. The fragment I kept back also bears my own contemporary signature, and a sentence in my hand saying this is a forgery. No, you would not be able to bring out the invisible ink by any childish method—it is not written in milk to become legible when held over heat. No, nothing like that. The ink is based on a formula used by Locusta—"

"By whom?" Randall interrupted.

"You have not heard of Locusta? She was Emperor Nero's official poisoner shortly after the time I arranged for Jesus to be driven out of Rome. Locusta taught pupils her poison recipes, and experimented with her concoctions on human slaves. Under orders from Nero's mother, Locusta administered poison in a mushroom stew to the Emperor Claudius. She is said to have killed ten thousand people. Naturally, she often had to communicate with Nero in secret. So she became adept at devising invisible inks. I came across one of her more sophisticated and little-known formulas."

"Can you tell me what it is?"

Lebrun hesitated a split second, then bared his discolored dentures. "I will tell you nine tenths of her formula, and supply the remaining tenth when we conclude our deal. Actually, Locusta derived her formula from the writings of one Philon of Byzantium, a Greek scientist. He had invented, around 146 B.C., an invisible ink made up of gallotannic acid extracted from gall nuts. If you wrote with that ink, what you wrote could not be seen. To make what had been written visible, you applied a solution of what is now called copper sulfate mixed with one other ingredient. Very esoteric. You shall know the entire formula, and be able to bring out my invisible name and writing and drawing on the papyrus and disprove the authenticity of the entire James gospel. For my delivery of this formula and the missing fragment I've just described, I will expect the first half of the twenty-thousand-dollar payment. If you are satisfied, I will then give you the remaining and most conclusive evidence of my forgery in return for your second payment."

"What will that be?"

Lebrun continued to smile. "Additional fillers, one for each lacuna in the James gospel. Mr. Randall, you have worked at jigsaw puzzles, have you not? You know how neatly a jagged or crooked piece of the puzzle can fit in to complete the entire puzzle, do you not? That is it. In Amsterdam, the publishers have twenty-four pieces of papyrus, some of the pieces with one or two portions missing, nine small missing portions in all. I have those nine missing portions. Each irregular piece, removed from a Resurrection Two papyrus, will fit neatly back into it, perfectly into it, as the missing pieces of a jigsaw puzzle fit. When these missing parts are used to fill in perfectly the holes in the papyri, the evidence of forgery and hoax will be obvious and irrefutable. I have eight of these parts. The first missing piece is the one I showed Monti, but the remaining eight are protected in an eighteen-inch iron box and safely hidden. Would these items be enough to satisfy you that the International New Testament is based on a forgery?"

"Yes," said Randall. He could feel the goose pimples creeping up the flesh of his arms. "Yes, that would do it. When can you deliver this evidence?"

"When would you like it?"

"Tonight," said Randall. "Right now."

"No, I couldn't possibly—

"Tomorrow, then."

Lebrun still seemed doubtful. "Not tomorrow, either. I have naturally secreted the two items. I hid them last year after my final visit with Monti. Very recently, I almost removed them from their hiding place for an interested buyer—but then, because I had certain misgivings about the buyer, I decided to delay producing the evidence until I had a second meeting with him, in order to reassure myself of his intentions. My misgivings proved justified. So you see, Mr. Randall, my proofs of forgery remain where I concealed them over a year ago. As a result—I cannot explain further—retrieving the items for you will take a little time. They are outside Rome—not far, but still I would need most of tomorrow to recover them."

Wondering what it was about the hiding place that complicated the delivery of the evidence, Randall decided not to press for an explanation. "Very well," he said. "If you can't make it tomorrow, then the next day will do. Let's say the day after tomorrow. Monday."

"Yes," said Lebrun. "I can deliver what you want the day after tomorrow."

"Tell me where you live. I'll be there."

"No," said Lebrun. He came slowly to his feet. "No, that would not be wise. We will meet in Doney's café at five o'clock in the afternoon. We will make our exchange. If you wish, we will then come here to your room to see that you are satisfied."

Randall stood up. "Okay, Doney's café, Monday at five."

As they walked to the door, Lebrun cast him a sidelong

glance. "You will not be disappointed, this I promise you. Au revoir, my friend. It is a happy day."

Watching Lebrun limp toward the elevator, Randall wondered why he himself was anything but happy on this happy day.

Then, observing the forger enter the elevator, he knew. Faith had fled.

THERE WAS one task left, one uncomfortable obligatory scene to be played, before Randall began his forty-eight-hour vigil.

There was a long-distance telephone call to be made. Now he made it to the Grand Hotel Krasnapolsky in Amsterdam, person-to-person, to George L. Wheeler.

Wheeler was still in his office at Resurrection Two, and his secretary quickly put him on the line.

"Steve?" Wheeler barked.

"Hello, George. I thought I'd—"

"Where in the hell are you this time?" Wheeler interrupted. "Did I hear my secretary say—?"

"I'm in Rome. Let me explain."

"In Rome?" Wheeler exploded. "Goddammit. In Rome? Why aren't you here at your desk? Didn't I make it clear to you everyone's got to buckle down, work twenty-four hours a day, to get ready for the press conference at the royal palace next Friday? I was sore enough when Naomi told me you'd skipped out of town yesterday on some research. I expected you back last night—"

"I intended to be back yesterday," Randall cut in. "But something important has come up—"

"There is only one thing important, and that's that you haul your ass back here and get on with your job, once and for all. We've got to be ready for the announcement—"

"George, listen to me," Randall implored. "There may be no announcement. I'm sure you won't want to hear this, but you'll be grateful to me in the end. I think you'd better postpone the announcement—maybe the whole publication of the International New Testament."

There was an interval of shocked silence on the Amsterdam end, and finally Wheeler's voice came grating back. "What in God's name are you talking about?"

Randall girded himself. It was going to be rough. But he had to spill out every nasty detail. There was no choice. "George," he said, "you can't publish that Bible. I've learned the truth about it. Professor Monti's discovery —the Petronius Parchment—the Gospel According to James—they are outright forgeries."

Once more the dead silence. Then Wheeler's flat statement, hard and low. "You're crazy."

"This moment, I wish I were. Believe me, I'm not. I've found the forger. I've spoken to him. He has the proof. Now will you hear me out?"

"You're wasting your time and mine." Wheeler's tone was irate. "Go ahead, if it makes you feel better."

Randall wanted to say it did not make him feel better. It made him feel lousy. But this was no time to bother with his feelings. This was the critical moment to make the publisher face up to the facts.

"Okay," said Randall grimly. "Here's what I came across in Rome."

He went on relentlessly. He told about coming to Rome and forcing Angela to take him to her father. He told Wheeler where he had found Professor Monti. He told him how he had found Monti, of the archeologist's mental condition, of the subsequent conversation with Dr. Venturi. Next, Randall spoke of Dominee de Vroome, of the Dutch clergyman's lying in wait for him at the Hotel Excelsior, and of the meeting in de Vroome's suite. He repeated concisely what he had heard from de Vroome, no details, not even the name of the forger or a mention of the forger's confession to Plummer, only the bare facts of a forger's contacting Plummer from Rome, and of their rendezvous in Paris, when Plummer and the forger had bargained over the evidence of the hoax.

Here, George L. Wheeler stopped him. "So it was de Vroome—de Vroome and Plummer—who came up with a convenient forger," said Wheeler furiously. "And you fell for it? I should have known they'd try anything at the last minute. So they've hired a forger to try to sabotage us?"

"No, George," Randall protested, "it's not like that at all. Will you please listen to me?"

He went on quickly. He explained how Plummer had tried to see the forger in Rome, to acquire the evidence of hoax, and how the forger had been frightened away by the unexpected sight of Dominee de Vroome.

"That's when I decided to make an attempt to find out whether there really was a forger," Randall went on, "and if there was, to locate him, and hear firsthand what he had to say."

Randall recounted how he had hit upon the idea of examining Monti's papers, and had come upon the date and place of the appointment with the forger a year and two months ago. He told how he had gone to Doney's café, and how he had come face to face with the forger.

"George, the forger left my hotel room just a half hour ago," Randall said. "He's a French expatriate who went by the name of Robert Lebrun in Paris, but who took an Italian name, the name of Enrico Toti, here in Rome. He's an elderly man, over eighty, and he's devoted most of his life to creating the James papyri and the Petronius document. Do you want to hear how he did it?"

Randall gave the publisher no time to reply. He plunged into the story of Robert Lebrun. But not all of it, not now. Instinctively, Randall had decided to withhold the information about Lebrun's upbringing, his youth, his criminal activity in Paris, his arrests, his deportation to the French Guiana penal colony, his disillusionment with the Church, even his obsession to revenge himself on the world's religious community. That bad character material, Randall discerned, would merely reinforce Wheeler's refusal to suffer the essential facts.

Randall stayed with the essential facts.

Revealing how Lebrun, motivated by some unexplained bitterness toward the Church, had made himself into an expert on New Testament lore, Randall spoke of the decades Lebrun had spent preparing his foolproof forgery.

Then Randall spoke of the manner in which Lebrun had arranged for Professor Monti to make his discovery.

"I'm sorry to have to bring this to you, George," Randall concluded with compassion, realizing that the publisher must be in a nearly suicide state. "But I knew you and Dr. Deichhardt and the others would want the truth."

He waited for Wheeler's response. There was none. The line from Amsterdam to Rome was mute.

"George," said Randall, "what are you going to do?"

Wheeler's voice came cracking over the line. It was savage in its intensity. "I know what I should do. I should fire you, just as I should have fired you before." He paused. "I should fire you here and now for being the goddam fool you are. But I won't. Time is too short. We need you. As for the rest of that bull, you'll come to your senses fast, once you realize how de Vroome has taken you in."

The captain going down with his sinking ship, Randall thought. It was the last thing he had expected. "George, didn't you hear me? Despite what you've got at stake, isn't it clear to you that the whole thing is a hoax—a hoax pulled off by a warped genius? I know what a loss it will be for you to jettison the whole project. But think of the loss of credibility and cash if you bring out the Bible, and it is exposed after publication."

"There's nothing to expose, you fool! De Vroome staged the whole thing to win you over, to use you to panic us, cause dissension among us."

"Go to de Vroome. He'll confirm it."

"I wouldn't dignify that bastard's duplicity. You've been taken in by a trick—a vicious lie. Be man enough to admit it, and screw your head on right, and come back to your job while we're still in a charitable mood."

Randall tried to hold his temper. "You really don't believe it?"

"I don't believe one iota of it. Some psychopathic liar in the pay of de Vroome—you expect me to believe him?"

"Okay, you don't have to," said Randall, fighting to

keep his tone reasonable, "you don't have to, until I have the proof to show you."

"What proof?"

"Lebrun is delivering the evidence of his forgery to me the day after tomorrow—Monday afternoon—at Doney's downstairs."

It was as if Wheeler had not heard this. Suddenly, he was speaking again, his rage repressed, his tactics revised. He was addressing Randall in a tone that was almost conciliatory, in a manner that a father might use when mildly chiding an errant son.

"Let me tell you something, Steve. I'm a God-fearing man, you know that. I've accepted Jesus as my personal Saviour. I think a lot about Our Lord and what He can do for us. Yet, I have always felt, in my heart, that if Jesus Christ returned to earth again, as He has now by the grace and miracle of His brother's gospel, there would always be someone lurking to betray Our Lord a second time for another thirty pieces of silver. This Robert Lebrun, he's a sick Christ-hater, that's what he is. If Christ sat with us, He would be inspired to say once more, 'One of you shall betray me,' and when asked who this might be, Our Lord would say again, 'He it is, to whom I shall give a sop, when I have dipped it.' And Christ would dip the sop and hand it to your Robert Lebrun—and perhaps to de Vroome and you as well."

It was weird, Randall thought, hearing Christ's performance and words at the Last Supper being reenacted by an American businessman Bible publisher on a long-distance call from Amsterdam.

"Steve, take my advice," Wheeler was continuing, "don't be part of that cheap betrayal. The real Christ is among us. Let Him live. Don't let Lebrun be His twentieth-century Judas. And you, Steve, don't be His Pilate. Don't ask again what is truth—when we have the truth."

"But what if Lebrun has the truth? What if he comes to me on Monday—"

"He will not come to you, Steve," the publisher said flatly, "not on Monday or any other time. We have the authority of the world's most respected biblical scholars on our side. And you, what have you got? The cock-and-bull story of a demented ex-convict out to assassinate God and His Son. Think about that, Steve."

The phone banged in Randall's ear, and then he did as his employer had instructed him. He thought about it.

And what he thought about was almost the last thing Wheeler had said. *And you, what have you got? The cock-and-bull story of a demented ex-convict. . . .*

Ex-convict.

How did Wheeler know that Robert Lebrun had once been a convict? Randall had been careful, very careful, not to mention it, not to speak a word about Lebrun's past.

Yet, Wheeler knew that Robert Lebrun was an ex-convict.

It was strangely ominous, and Randall shivered, and for a moment, that moment, he felt a foreboding for what was not known and could therefore be evil.

XI

IT WAS LATE Monday afternoon, at last, a warm day, not
hot, the sun already low, and Steven Randall sat in
Doney's café on the Via Veneto waiting for Robert Lebrun.

Absently, he toyed with the untouched glass of Campari on the table before him, and his head continued to
turn from left to right and from right to left, as if he
were at a tennis match, as he inspected the ceaseless flow
of pedestrians coming and going on the sidewalk between
the rows of tables.

It was tiring, being so intensely expectant, and he told
himself that Lebrun would be here when he had promised
to be here, and he tried to relax. He massaged the back
of his neck, the muscles as tight as wire cables, and he
gave himself the brief luxury of allowing his mind to
wander.

The marking of time, from his parting with Lebrun on
Saturday evening, until this hour of their reunion on this
late Monday afternoon, might have been unendurable, had
not Randall driven himself to occupy almost every hour
with work. He had not worked on Saturday night, it was
true. After Lebrun's departure, but especially after the
conflict with George L. Wheeler on the telephone, he had
been too agitated to do anything meaningful. Instead, he
had eaten a snack in his room, and pondered the immediate future. What if—despite Wheeler's mockery of the
possibility of forgery—Lebrun did deliver absolute proof
of forgery? What would be Randall's next step? Would he
go to Wheeler and Deichhardt and the other publishers,
and lay it out for them, and make them accept what they
would no longer be able to deny? On the other hand,

what if they willfully rejected the truth? What then? It was unlikely that they would ignore any real evidence of forgery, but if they did?

There were other alternatives, and these Randall had pondered over and seen as possibilities. The only thing he had been unable to see was what there would be in this for him, except the satisfaction of having uncovered the truth. A bleak satisfaction, this prospect of truth accompanied by the destruction of his revived faith, but bleak or no, it would somehow give his inner being a new dimension.

Yesterday, the entire day and most of the evening, he had actually worked at his job. He was still on the payroll of Resurrection Two, and he felt it his duty to make his expected contribution. But it was slow going, slogging enforced labor, the collating of research and the writing of press releases extolling the miracle of the International New Testament. It was dreary because it was preparation for glorifying what he now regarded as a lost cause, a fake that would never see the light of day.

Also, off and on yesterday, he had been on the telephone to Amsterdam, a half-dozen times at least, collaborating with his public relations staff. Oh, they were all there on Sunday, dedicated and beavering, O'Neal, Alexander, Taylor, and de Boer. They had read him their releases, and he had offered suggestions, corrections, and given them last-minute directions. In turn, he had dictated to them his own releases for final editing and mimeographing.

At one point, Jessica Taylor had told him, almost as a casual aside, that Angela Monti had returned from Rome, checked in, been surprised he was not there, and had made inquiries about him. Hearing this, Randall had asked Jessica to let Angela know that he was still in Rome, some appointments, some interviews, but that he would be back by Tuesday. Anything more to tell her? No, nothing more, except to go on manning her desk and attending to his telephone.

Unlike Wheeler, not one member of his staff had asked

him what in the hell he was doing in Rome at a busy time like this.

Two more things, yesterday. The first, vital; the second, in its way, crucial.

The vital thing. He had telephoned his attorney, Thad Crawford, awakened him in his apartment in New York, and ordered him to call the bank early Monday morning and use his power of attorney to transmit $20,000 to Randall in Rome. And to see that it was available in American dollars and in cash.

The crucial thing—crucial only because Wheeler had unnerved him about Lebrun's veracity, or lack of it—was to be more certain about the ex-convict he would be dealing with shortly. An old friend of Randall's—they had broken into the publicity field together—had long ago given up public relations to return to his first love, journalism, and he had been a fixture in the Paris bureau of the Associated Press, in the Rue de Berri, for many years. This was Sam Halsey, sharp, undulled by routine, whose friendship Randall cherished and enjoyed renewing in extended drinking bouts whenever Sam came through New York on home leave.

So the second thing had been to locate Sam Halsey in Paris yesterday, and luckily, Randall had found him at once, tied to the lonely night desk at Associated Press, as cheerful and profane as ever.

Randall had stated that he wanted a favor, some research checked out, with the answers required before the following late afternoon. Did Sam have anyone around who could do this? Sam had asked what it was that Randall wanted. Randall wanted to know whether the French Army had formed a regiment called the Devil's Island Expeditionary Force in 1915. Also, Randall wanted to know whether there was any record in the files of the Ministry of Justice concerning a young Frenchman named Robert Lebrun who had been arrested and tried for forgery in 1912, and had been sentenced to Devil's Island. Intrigued, Sam Halsey had volunteered to do the research himself the next morning and to call back.

Today, this Monday morning and the last half of the

afternoon, Randall had not worked for Resurrection Two. Quite the contrary, as Wheeler might have pointed out, had he known, Randall had worked against his deluded employers at Resurrection Two.

Thad Crawford had come through with what Wheeler —Wheeler again, damn him!—would have characterized as the thirty pieces of silver. Randall had eventually picked up the $20,000 at American Express near the Piazza di Spagna. The cash, in bills of large denomination, lay in his safe deposit box at the Excelsior, ready to be turned over to Lebrun in exchange for evidence of his forgery.

Before that, there had been two telephone calls from Sam Halsey in Paris. The first call had been to report that after much weight-throwing and arm-twisting in the press section of the Ministry of National Defense, its spokesman had reluctantly given Sam permission to examine classified papers in the Service Historique de l'Armée at Vincennes. There, the curator had been cooperative. Going over old documents with Sam, he had confirmed that there had indeed been a regiment of convict volunteers from French Guiana in 1915 who had fought as the Devil's Island Expeditionary Force under General Pétain. One disappointment, though. In its roll of enlistees there had been no "Lebrun, Robert." The closest to that name, under L, had been one "Laforgue, Robert." But Sam was not through. He was heading over to the Ministry of Justice to do some more poking around, and he would get back to Randall within a few hours.

Sam Halsey had called a second time, in less than an hour. The dusty 1912 files of the Ministry of Justice had produced no criminal named "Lebrun, Robert," either. But with his reporter's nose picking up a scent, and just for the hell of it, Sam Halsey had checked for that other similar name, the name "Laforgue, Robert."

"And, Steve, the jackpot—a counterfeiter, a forger with five aliases, and one had been—hear this, my lad —'Lebrun, Robert,' sentenced to the penal colony of French Guiana for life and in 1912."

So Lebrun had leveled. Despite Wheeler, Lebrun had

not been caught in a single falsehood, not yet. Randall's belief in the story of the forgery, and the forthcoming evidence, had been fully restored.

With confidence, Randall had come down to Doney's café ten minutes before five o'clock to await the appearance of Robert Lebrun.

Randall brought his mind back from its wanderings to the present and to the immediacy of his quest. He looked at his watch, and was unsettled and instantly made anxious by what it showed him. The time was exactly five twenty-six. He cast about, searching again. The sidewalk was crowded, so many strangers, so many different faces, but not one of them the face and person branded indelibly on his brain.

It was a half hour past the time Robert Lebrun had unmistakably set for their meeting.

Randall concentrated on the continuing parade of moving pedestrians, on the men, on the elderly men, anticipating the leap of excitement he would feel when he laid eyes on the hunched old one, with his ungainly walk, the dyed brown hair, the metal-rimmed, tinted spectacles, the crafty features corroded and eaten by time and crinkled as a prune, the one bringing two salable objects, first a small package with a devastating missing fragment bearing the scream of hoax in invisible ink, and the other a bulkier package with a small iron box containing the devastating missing parts of an ancient jigsaw puzzle and the requiem for James the Just and Petronius the centurion.

Minutes ticked away, gobs of minutes, and there was no such one to be seen anywhere.

The untouched Campari on Randall's table was touched at last, the glass drained to the very bottom.

Still, no Robert Lebrun.

Steadily, Randall's heavy heart sank. His high hopes had become a landslide, an inner disaster, and at five minutes after six o'clock, his hopes hit rock bottom.

Wheeler had warned him: *He will not come to you, Steve.*

And Lebrun had not come.

Randall felt crushed, and then cheated and indignant.

What had happened to that son of a bitch? Had he feared giving up his thunder and changed his mind? Had he decided he could not trust his new partner and withdrawn from the deal? Or had he bargained elsewhere for a better offer and received it? Or had he known that he was merely perpetrating another swindle and had last-minute misgivings about going through with it?

Whatever the answer, Randall had to know why Robert Lebrun had reneged on their deal. If Lebrun would not come to him, then dammit, he would go to Lebrun. Or, at least, he would *try* to go to Lebrun.

Randall threw 500 lire and a tip on the table, stood up, and went to find his Lebrun specialist, his personnel director in Doney's, Julio, the café captain.

Julio was standing in the open doorway between the outdoor café and the inner restaurant, adjusting his bow tie. He greeted Randall with warmth. "Is everything working out, Mr. Randall?"

"Not exactly," said Randall grimly. "I was to meet our friend here—you know, the one you call Toti or Duca Minimo—Robert Lebrun. We had made a business appointment for five o'clock. Now it's after six. He hasn't shown up. Could he have possibly come by before five?"

Julio shook his head. "No. There were few in the café. I would have noticed him."

"The day before yesterday you told me that he always comes to Doney's on foot, as far as you know. You agreed that because of his artificial leg, he could not walk a great distance. That would mean he probably lives somewhere nearby."

"It would be my guess that he does."

"Julio, think back. Can you remember ever hearing where he might live?"

The captain appeared distressed. "I have never heard. I have not even an idea. After all, Mr. Randall, there are so many customers, even the regular ones." He tried to be helpful. "Of course, there are no private residences, at least not many, in this immediate neighborhood, and if

there were, Toti—Lebrun—Signore Lebrun surely could
not afford one. It is my impression he is poor."

"Yes, he is poor."

"So then, he could not afford to live permanently in
a hotel, either. There are a few less expensive hotels in
the district—mostly the girls who walk the streets use
them—but such hotels would still be too much for our
friend. It is my belief he must keep a small apartment.
There are many lower-class ones not so far away, within
walking distance of the Doney. But the question, which
address? I cannot say."

Randall had reached for his wallet. Even in Italy,
where natives were generally more gracious and helpful
to strangers than anywhere else, the lire often served as a
spur to creative cooperation. Randall pressed 3,000 lire
into Julio's hand. "Please, Julio, I need more of your
help—"

"This is very kind of you, Mr. Randall," the captain
said, pocketing the bills.

"—or perhaps there is someone you know who can
help. You got me to Lebrun once. Perhaps you can again."

The captain's forehead had furrowed in thought.
"There is one small possibility. I cannot promise. I will
see. If you will be so good to wait."

He stepped quickly down the aisle to the sidewalk,
snapped his fingers imperiously at several waiters to his
right, calling out, *"Per piacere! Facciamo, presto!"* He
swung to the left, and repeated the summons.

Waiters from both directions came on the trot, con-
verging on their captain. Randall counted seven of them.
Julio was speaking animatedly to them, gesticulating, pan-
tomiming a stiff walk to describe Lebrun's artificial leg.
When he finished, several of the waiters reacted with
exaggerated shrugs of their shoulders. Two or three
scratched their heads, trying to think. But all remained
dumb. At last, Julio lifted his hands helplessly, and
dismissed them. Six of the waiters started back to their
posts. Only one waiter lingered, chin cupped thoughtfully in one hand.

Julio had begun to turn back to Randall. Julio's swarthy

features bore the expression of a sad bloodhound. He was about to speak when suddenly the waiter behind him sprang alive.

"Julio!" the waiter exclaimed, grasping his captain's elbow. Julio bent sideways, his ear close to the waiter's mouth, as the waiter whispered to him intently. The waiter lifted one arm, pointing across the street, and Julio kept nodding, his face gradually wreathing into a smile. *"Bene, bene,"* said Julio, clapping the waiter on the back. *"Grazie!"*

Randall stood in the doorway, mystified, as Julio hastened back to him.

"It is possible, it is possible, Mr. Randall, but one can never tell with these women," said Julio. "The waiters, our waiters, they know most of the Italian girls who walk the streets, the young prostitutes. Like everywhere in Europe, they are throughout Rome—in Pincio Garden, in the Carcalla Park, on the Via Sistina by the Piazza di Spagna—but the most pretty ones, they come to the Via Veneto to make smiles at the passersby and make business. At this hour, many come to sit for the *aperitivo*—some here in the Doney, but more across the street where is the Café de Paris, our competition—sometimes it is livelier there. So Gino, this waiter who speaks to me, he remembers that Toti—your Lebrun—he is friends with many of the prostitutes. Gino says he was even once going to marry one."

Randall nodded eagerly. "Yes, I'd heard that."

"So Gino says the one Lebrun was to marry when he made much wealth, this one has a friend she lives with in a room, and this friend always makes her place in a special table in the Café de Paris at this hour. Her name is Maria. I, too, know the one. Gino thinks she can tell where Lebrun lives. She may not tell, but"—he rubbed his dry fingers together—"a little money, it loosens the tongue, no? Gino thinks she is there now. We will see. I will take you."

"Can you do it now, Julio?"

Julio grinned. "For an Italian to talk to a pretty girl, leaving work, it is no problem. It is pleasure."

Julio started up the crowded sidewalk, with Randall behind him. They went past the Hotel Excelsior to the corner, and waited for the traffic light to change. Across the way, parallel to Doney's, Randall could see the red awnings carrying the lettering: CAFÉ DE PARIS RESTAURANT. The tables partially hidden by the plants and shrubs seemed more fully occupied than those at Doney's.

The traffic light had changed. As they started across the street, skipping out of the path of charging cars swerving in from the intersection, Julio said, "I will introduce you only as an American friend who wishes to become acquainted. I will then leave you. It is best. You can explain to her what you want. They all speak English. Maria, also."

When they reached the magazine kiosk on the other side, Randall held Julio back for a moment. "What should I offer her?"

"For Italian men, a girl like this Maria, who is a better-class girl, she would charge ten thousand lire—around fifteen dollars—but for a tourist, especially the American, who is dressed more expensively and does not know how to bargain, she will maybe ask twenty thousand lire—thirty dollars—and maybe with bargaining it could be less. The sum is for a maximum of one half hour in the bed—some side-street hotel, maybe. You pay for time. If you wish only to talk, it is the same. But"—Julio winked—"sometimes you can talk, and also make love. These girls, they are proud they can make fast turnover. The half hour is usually ten minutes. They can take care of a man in ten minutes. They are clever. So, we will see if she is in her place."

Julio elbowed past the browsers congregated about the kiosk, halted under the red awning, and faced the rows of tables backed against the Via Veneto. Randall had followed, but kept a short distance behind. Julio was surveying the occupants at the tables, when his face lit with recognition. He waved, beckoned Randall, and slipped between two tables toward the rear, with Randall trailing a few feet behind.

She was a pretty young thing, swishing the toothpicked olive in her martini glass, now holding out a hand to welcome Julio. She had long black hair that framed most of the Madonna-like face, the picture of purity and innocence, contradicted only by the sheer summer dress cut low in front to reveal half of each ample breast and by the shortness of the tight dress that was pulled high on her full thighs.

"Maria," Julio had murmured, and made the gesture of kissing the back of her upraised hand.

"Signore Julio," the girl responded with pleased surprise.

Julio stayed on his feet, bending close to her, addressing her in an undertone in rapid Italian. Listening, she nodded her head twice, and gazed frankly up at Randall, who was standing by, feeling awkward and uncomfortable.

Julio reached back and drew Randall forward. "Maria —my friend here from America, Mr. Randall. You will be nice to him." He straightened and grinned at Randall. "She will be good to you. Please, sit. *Arrivederci.*"

The captain was gone, and Randall took a chair beside Maria, still uncomfortable, wondering whether any of the other customers were staring at him. But no one seemed to be paying attention.

Maria moved closer to him, and the mounds of her partially bare breasts trembled provocatively. She recrossed her legs and tendered a half smile. *"Mi fa piacere di vederla. Da dove viene?"*

"I'm afraid I don't speak Italian," Randall apologized.

"Forgive me," said Maria. "I was saying I am delighted to meet you and where is your home."

"I'm from New York. I'm pleased to meet you, Maria."

"Julio says you are also a friend of the Duca Minimo." Her smile broadened. "That is so?"

"Yes, we are friends."

"A nice old man. He wanted to marry my best friend, Gravina, but he could not afford it. Too bad."

"He may have some money soon," said Randall.

"Oh? It is true? I hope so. I will tell Gravina." Her eyes held on Randall's. "You like me? You think I am pretty?"

"You're very pretty, Maria."

"Bene. You want to make love now? I do everything for you. Good love. Regular love. French love. What you like. You will be happy. It is only twenty thousand lire. Not much to have good love. You want to come with Maria now?"

"Look, Maria, apparently Julio didn't tell you—but there's something more important I need from you."

She blinked at him as if he were crazy. "More important than love?"

"At the moment, yes. Maria, do you know where Lebrun—the Duca—Duca Minimo—do you know where he lives?"

She was instantly wary. "Why do you ask?"

"I had his address. I lost it. I was supposed to see him an hour ago. Julio thought you could help me."

"That is all you have come to me for?"

"It is very important."

"To you, yes? Not to me. I am sorry. I know his address, but I cannot give it. My girl friend and I, he has sworn us never to give it. I cannot change my oath. So now maybe you have time to let Maria love you."

"I've only got time to see him, Maria. If he's your friend, I can tell you I want to see him to help him." Then he remembered, and tugged the wallet out of his inner jacket pocket. "You said you'd make love for twenty thousand lire. Okay, is it worth twenty thousand lire if you can make me happy in a different way?"

He was extracting the large-denomination bills from the wallet, when she glanced around nervously, and pushed the wallet away. "Not here, please."

"I'm sorry." He returned the wallet to his pocket, but kept the lire wadded inside his fist. "It's worth it to me. You don't have to do a thing. Just show me where he lives."

Maria contemplated the money half hidden in Randall's

hand. She looked at him shrewdly. "I am sworn not to tell. But you want to help him. To make him rich?"

He was ready to agree to anything. "Yes."

"If it is for him, I will myself show you where he lives. His apartment is near."

He gave a sigh of relief. "Thanks."

Without delay, he paid her check, got up with her, and together they left the Café de Paris. They went past the kiosk to the corner, caught the green light, and scrambled across the Via Veneto to the corner of the Hotel Excelsior.

She indicated the wide street running along the side of the hotel. "Via Boncampagni," she said. "He lives on this street, not far. Three or four blocks. We can walk."

She linked her arm loosely in Randall's arm, and they started at a brisk pace up the Via Boncampagni. She hummed as she walked, but at the end of the first block she stopped abruptly. She held out the palm of one hand. "You pay me now," she said.

He released the wad of lire into her hand. She removed her other arm from his own, and carefully counted the bills. Satisfied, she stuffed the money into her white purse.

"I take you to your friend," she said.

She started walking again, resuming her humming, and he walked along beside her.

Entering the third block, he said, "How do you know where the Duca lives?"

"I will tell you. Do not repeat to him. He has great pride. But sometimes, when Gravina or myself, one or two of the other girls also, when we cannot get a room in a hotel, when it is filled, we make an arrangement with the Duca to use his room to service our clients. We pay him half our earnings to use his room. We do not care. He is kind. It helps him for his rent."

"What is his rent?"

"For one room, bath, tiny kitchen, fifty thousand lire a month."

"Fifty thousand? That's around eighty dollars. He can afford that?"

"He lives here many years, he says. Since he was rich."

They were crossing an intersection, the Via Piemonte, and starting into the fourth block. "When was he rich?" Randall asked.

"Maybe four years, five years ago, he says."

It added up, Randall thought. Five years ago he received his share of Monti's bonanza for the discovery at Ostia Antica.

"Here it is," Maria announced.

They had come to a halt before a six-story apartment building of indeterminate years, the dingy stone façade caked in soot. The building entrance stood between the Iranian Express Company and a shop with a sign, BAR-BIERE, with a barber's pole beside its entry.

Chiseled into stone above Lebrun's apartment building was a single word: CONDOMINIO.

Beneath were two massive wooden doors, flung open, and beyond this opening was a glass door, and an entry hall with some kind of booth, and beyond that a courtyard.

"I leave you here," said Maria, extending her hand. "I must return to work."

Randall shook her hand. "Thanks, Maria, but where do I—?"

"You go inside. The booth you see on the right is where the *portière* puts the mail. On the left is the elevator and there is also a stairway. But you must see the *portière* first, to say you want to see the Duca. If he is not in the booth, you go to the courtyard. On one side are the windows with plants in front where the *portière* and his wife, they live. You call there. They will take you to your friend. *Buona fortuna.*" She started to leave, but had an afterthought. "Mr. Randall, when you see him, do not tell him Maria brought you here."

"I won't, Maria. I promise."

He watched her go toward the Via Veneto, her un-girdled full buttocks and her white purse swinging, and at last he turned back to the apartment building.

Robert Lebrun, he thought. Finally.

He strode from the sidewalk, across a cobblestoned area, across the entry's dirty marble floor, opened the high glass door, and went inside. The *portière's* booth was empty. Randall continued into the dusky courtyard.

A spread of rubber plants filled the center of the court, and to the left, from an open window, a youngish man, quite dark, of Sicilian cast, was watering a line of plants on the sill. He stopped watering to consider Randall with curiosity.

"Hello," called Randall. "Do you speak English?"

"*Si.* A little."

"Where can I find the *portière?*"

"I am the *portière.* You want something?"

"A friend of mine lives here. I'd like—"

"One moment." The *portière* disappeared from the window, and seconds later reappeared through a side door leading into the courtyard. He was a small, jaunty man in a blue work shirt and patched blue jeans. He confronted Randall, hands on his hips. "You want to see someone?"

"A friend." Randall wondered which name to use. He regretted not asking Maria what name the old man went by. Probably the Italian. "Signore Toti."

"Toti. Sorry, no. There is no Toti."

"He has a nickname. Duca Minimo."

"Duca—?" The *portière* shook his head vigorously. "No one here with such name."

Then it must be Lebrun, Randall decided. "Well, actually, he's a Frenchman—most of us know him as Robert Lebrun."

The *portière* stared at Randall. "There is a Robert—a Frenchman—but not Lebrun. Could you mean maybe Laforgue? Robert Laforgue?"

Laforgue. Of course. It was the name Sam Halsey, of Associated Press in Paris, had found Lebrun listed under in the Service Historique records. It was Lebrun's real name. "Yes!" Randall exclaimed. "That's the one. I always get his last name twisted. Robert Laforgue is the one I want to see."

The *portière* was looking at Randall strangely. "You are a relative?" he asked.

"I'm a close friend. The signore is expecting me. He is waiting to discuss an important business matter with me."

"But that is impossible," said the *portière*. "He was in a bad accident yesterday at noon in front of the Stazione Ostiense. He was crushed by a hit-and-run automobile driver. He was killed immediately. My sympathies, signore, but your friend is dead."

A COOPERATIVE YOUNG police officer had led Steve Randall outside the Questura, the Rome police headquarters, had flagged a taxi for him, and had instructed the driver, "Obitorio, Viale dell' Università," and rattled off something more in Italian, repeated the word "Obitorio" and had specified the exact address, "Piazzale del Verano 38."

The taxi driver quickly made the sign of the cross, shifted gears, and now they were off, speeding toward the large university complex in Rome where the city's morgue was situated.

Rocking from side to side as the taxi veered and rattled around corners, Randall was still numb from shock but gradually recovering.

Most persons, Randall reflected, suffer few moments of shock in a lifetime. Yet, in little more than a month, he had endured shock—the impact of surprise or horror, the sudden jarring of the senses or emotions—time and again. There had been his father's stroke, Barbara and the divorce, Judy's drug problem. And on the heels of these there had been the instance when he had been led to believe that Angela was the traitor in the project, and the time when he had learned of the Bogardus flaw. There had been the recent moment when he had learned that Professor Monti was confined in an insane asylum, and the moment in the elevator when Dominee de Vroome had revealed that he had just seen the forger of the James and Petronius documents. There had been other instances as well, when a piece of information made the head spin and the heart and the blood freeze. For him, it was as if shock had become a way of life.

But on no occasion had he suffered a blow greater than that which he had endured two hours ago when the apartment *portière* had told him that Robert Lebrun was dead.

The blow had been so unexpected that it had left him almost dumb. Yet, horrified, he had survived the news, had even regained his composure, because his experiences with Resurrection Two had conditioned him to these assaults on his sensibilities.

He could remember—it was still as if in a dream—how the *portière* had gone on to tell him of the events of Sunday afternoon, which was just yesterday. The police had appeared at the apartment on Via Boncampagni to ascertain whether a Signore Robert Laforgue was a resident there. Assured that this building was indeed where Laforgue—Lebrun—lived, they had informed the *portière* that he had been killed in an accident three hours earlier.

The victim had been crossing the square from the Pyramid of Caio Cestio to the Porta San Paolo railroad and metro depot, actually heading toward the small station known as Stazione Ostiense, when a large black automobile—one witness had thought it to be an American Pontiac, another witness had believed it to be a British Aston Martin—had plummeted into the square, struck the victim head on, thrown him at least ten meters, and in the confusion had kept on going, to disappear from sight. The victim, his body badly crushed and mangled, had been killed instantly.

To the *portière*, the police had explained that while the victim's personal effects carried the name Robert Laforgue, and this address, there had been nothing more on his person to indicate the name of a relative or friend or insurance company. Did the *portière* know of any relative or friend who should be notified, or could take over disposal of the body? The *portière* had been unable to think of the name of anyone close to the victim. Routinely, the police had gone up to Lebrun's flat in search of some clue. Apparently, there had been none.

Randall recalled that he had requested permission to

see Lebrun's rooms. Like a sleepwalker, he had followed the *portière* into the elevator. There had been a slot for coins in the elevator—anyone who uses the electricity must pay for it, the *portière* had muttered—and the *portière* had deposited a 10-lira piece in the slot and pushed the button for Floor 3.

On the third floor, to the left of the elevator, the *portière* had unlocked a green door. Inside, an entry, once green also, now faded and soiled and flaking, a single room with a sagging daybed, two standing lamps with ugly beige shades, a worn chiffonier, a radio, a cracked mirror, a portable refrigerator still humming noisily (the *portière* had immediately disconnected it), a few shelves propped on bricks and holding well-thumbed French and Italian paperbound books (mostly nonfiction politics and novels, not one dealing with theology or antiquity, in either ancient Palestine or Rome). Overhead, a cheap fixture with a dim bulb. Adjacent to the single room there had been a cramped pantry, hardly a kitchen, with a wooden counter holding a hot plate and a sink, and beyond that a tiny bathroom.

With reluctance, under the watchful eye of the *portière,* Randall had scoured Lebrun's rooms, gone through Lebrun's pitifully few belongings—two threadbare suits and a shabby trench coat, some clothes in the drawers, the ragged books. Except for several unpaid grocery bills and a blank tablet, there had been neither personal papers nor cards, not even correspondence, to give any clue to Robert Lebrun's contact or association with any other human being on earth.

"Nothing," Randall had said wearily. "No photographs, no notes, no writings in his hand."

"He had a few lady friends outside. Otherwise, he lived like a hermit," the *portière* had said.

"It's as if someone had been here and swept the place clean of his identity."

"There have been no visitors, to my knowledge, except the police and you, signore."

"So what remains of Robert Lebrun is the corpse," Randall had said mournfully. "Where is the corpse?"

"The police only advised me, should someone turn up, a relative or a friend, that they will hold the body for one month in the Obitorio—"

"The morgue?"

"*Si,* the morgue—they will hold it for a month to wait if someone will claim it and pay cost for a burial. If no one does, they will bury the body in the Campo Comune—"

"Campo Comune? You mean, like a potter's field?"

The *portière* had nodded. "Where the unclaimed are laid to rest."

"I think I'd like to see the corpse, just to be sure," Randall had said. The police had found identification on the body, yet someone else might have been carrying papers bearing Lebrun's name. Randall had to see for himself. He had to be positive. "How do I go about that?"

"You will first have to go to the Questura, the police headquarters, for a permit to view the corpse and make identification."

And so Randall had gone to Rome's police headquarters and applied to see the remains of Robert Laforgue, alias Robert Lebrun. Placed in the charge of a young Italian officer, Randall had given Lebrun's various names, a description of the Frenchman, the victim's age, and a few other particulars. He had then given his own name and background, and made up a story of his friendship with Lebrun, of having known him in Paris and of calling upon him whenever he visited Rome. He had filled out four pages of the *Processo Verbale,* some kind of official report, and that done, he had been given written permission to view the body, identify it, and claim it if he wished. Because he had appeared confused, the young officer had put him in the taxi and directed it to the city's morgue.

The taxi had slowed, and Randall peered out the window. They were cruising between the buildings on the grounds of the Città Universitaria. They had reached the Piazzale del Verano, and the driver braked his vehicle. He pointed to a yellow-brick three-story building behind a wall with double iron doors painted blue. "Obitorio," the driver whispered.

Randall paid him, adding a generous tip, and the driver crossed himself again, waited for his passenger to leave, and sped away.

Pushing open an iron door, Randall found himself in a small courtyard surrounded by buildings. Over the entrance to the nearest and largest building was a sign illuminated by an outdoor lamp. It read UNIVERSITÀ DI ROMA, ISTITUTO DI MEDICINA LEGALE E DELLE ASSICURAZIONI, OBITORIO COMUNALE.

Obitorio Comunale. A hell of a place for the climactic meeting with Robert Lebrun.

Just inside the main building there was a guard in a nondescript uniform. Several doorways confronted Randall. He offered his police permit to the guard, and was directed into a room to his right where a flabby and thickly moustached Italian official, a red collar on his charcoal uniform, stood checking papers behind a long marble counter.

He lifted his head as Randall approached, and he made some kind of inquiry in Italian.

"I'm sorry, but I speak only English," said Randall.

"I speak English, not very well, but also," said the morgue official. His tone was hushed, the professional and respectful hush common to funeral directors and morgue officials the world over.

"My name is Randall. I've come to identify a body, a friend. His name is Robert Lebrun—no, Robert Laforgue. He was brought here yesterday."

"You have the permission from the police?"

"I have." Randall handed over his pass.

The uniformed official examined it, pursed his lips, took an intercom speaker from beneath the counter, spoke rapidly into it in Italian, placed it back beneath the counter, and came around it to meet Randall.

"If you will please follow with me," he said.

They returned to the entry hall and made for another door with milky glass and the lettering INGRESSO È VIETATO, which Randall took to mean that entry was forbidden. The official unlocked the door, and as Randall stepped into the corridor beyond, he was assailed by a sickening stench. The smell was unmistakably that of cadavers, and he was overcome by a wave of nausea. His instinct was to turn and flee. This identification was pointless. Survival was all that mattered, but the official had him firmly by the arm and was propelling him up the corridor.

At the far end, a policeman stood on duty before a door that bore a sign: STANZE DI RICONOSCIMENTO.

"What's that?" inquired Randall.

"Rooms of Recognition," translated the official. "It is here you identify."

The policeman held the door open, and Randall, hand covering his nostrils, forced himself to go inside. It was a small room with modern fluorescent lighting. Two doors in a glass wall on the opposite side of the room had been thrown back, and an orderly was efficiently wheeling in a cot on which a body lay, draped over from head to foot with a white sheet.

The official jerked his head toward the cot, and like an automaton, Randall went with him to the cot.

The official took the edge of the sheet and lifted it partially back. "Is this the one—your Robert Laforgue?"

Randall's stomach had come up into his throat, as he bent forward. One glimpse, and he recoiled. The wrinkled ancient face, with the dead skin like a piece of papyrus, bashed and bruised and purplish on bloodless brown, belonged to Robert Laforgue, alias Lebrun.

"Yes," Randall whispered, fighting down nausea.

"You are positive of the identification?"

"Positive."

The official dropped the sheet, waved his hand at the orderly to remove the cot, and turned to Randall. "Thank you, signore. We are finished here."

As they left the identification ward, and went into the corridor, what Randall could scent now was not merely the fetid odor of death but the foul smell of coincidence.

This new malodorous smell engulfed him. When he had wanted to view the original Papyrus Number 9 in Amsterdam, it had disappeared by coincidence. When he had wanted to see Edlund's negative of the papyrus, the photographer's negatives had been lost in a fire by coincidence. When he was ready to receive the evidence of hoax in Rome, the forger had been killed in an accident the day before by coincidence. By coincidence—or by design?

The morgue official was speaking. "Signore, do you know of any relative to put claim to receive the body?"

"I doubt that there is any."

"So, since you are the only one to appear to make the identification—there have been no other ones—it would be legal for you to make disposition." He glanced hopefully at Randall. "If you wish."

"What do you mean?"

"Since identification is made, we must now dispose of the body. If you make not the claim, the body it goes to be buried in the Campo Comune—"

"Oh, yes, I heard. Your potter's field."

"If you wish the responsibility, we can arrange for the private funeral company to take away the body, to embalm, to put it in the chapel and to bury in the Catholic cemetery, the Cimitero Verano, with proper services. Also, a gravestone. We make this respectable church burial, if you pay. Whichever you like, signore."

They had arrived at the entry hall, and turned into the room with the marble counter. Randall did not hesitate. Lebrun, whether phony or legitimate, had been prepared to cooperate with Randall. Even though he had not had the chance, he did deserve something in return. Human respect, at the very least.

"Yes, I'll pay all funeral expenses," said Randall. "Give him a proper burial. Only one thing—" He could not help smiling slightly, remembering Lebrun. "No religious services and no burial in the Catholic cemetery. My friend was a—an agnostic."

The morgue official made a gesture of understanding, and stepped behind his counter. "It will be done as you wish. After the funeral company embalms, the burial will be in the non-Catholic cemetery—the Cimitero Acatolico. There are many nonbelievers, foreign poets, in peace there. It will be most proper and correct. You will pay now, signore?"

Randall paid now, accepted a receipt, signed one final document, and was glad to be done so he could leave.

As he started to go, the morgue official called after him. "Signore! A moment—"

Wondering what now, Randall returned to the marble counter. The official had placed a plastic bag between them. "Since you have made the claim, you may possess the victim's estate."

"You mean the stuff in his apartment? You can give everything to some nonreligious charity."

"It will be done—but, no, I speak of what is in this sack—his personal effects, taken from the body when he was brought here." The official loosened the drawstring of the plastic bag and turned the bag upside down, and Lebrun's last possessions clattered on the counter. "Take what you wish for the memento." A telephone began ringing at the rear of the room. "Excuse me," said the morgue official, and he hurried to answer the phone.

Randall stood silently at the counter with the last of Robert Lebrun.

There was little enough, and what there was made his heart ache. He picked up each item and put it aside. A bent metal watchcase, with the hands of the watch stopped at twelve twenty-three. A half-empty package of French Gauloise cigarettes. A matchbox. Some Italian 10-lira coins. Finally, a cheap, scuffed, brown imitation-leather wallet.

Randall held the wallet, opened it, began to empty it of its contents.

An identification card.

Four 1,000-lira bills.

A crisp piece of paper, folded.

And a pink oblong railroad ticket

Randall threw the identification card and money on the counter next to the emptied wallet. He unfolded the fresh piece of paper. From the center of the sheet, the drawing of a fish, a fish with a spear driven through it, leaped up at him. The fish was similar to the one

Monti had drawn, but rounder, done by another hand, possibly Lebrun's own. In the lower right-hand corner of the page, minutely lettered in ink, were the words: *Cancello C, Decumanus Maximus, Porta Marina. 600 mtrs. Catacomba.*

Now the pink railroad ticket. It was in three parts. The squares were bordered with thirty-one numbers, each obviously representing a day of the month. The top square read: ROMA S. PAOLO/OSTIA ANTICA. The bottom square read: OSTIA ANTICA/ROMA S. PAOLO.

Randall's temples began to throb.

The morgue official had returned to the counter. "Many pardons," he said. "You have found anything?"

Randall displayed the pink ticket. "What's this?"

The official squinted. "The ticket for the railroad. It is punched for use yesterday. The top section is from the Rome San Paolo station to take the train to Ostia Antica, where we have the famous seaside resort and many ancient ruins. The next section is for the return—it is round trip, same date—from Ostia Antica to Rome. The third section is the receipt. It was bought for yesterday, but not used, because the piece to go and the piece to return have not been torn off."

Randall's head continued to throb, and in the chaos of his mind he tried to reconstruct Sunday's scene: Robert Lebrun had gone to the San Paolo railroad station yesterday, purchased a ticket that would take him to Ostia Antica and back again, all in the same day. He had been too early for his train, and had probably limped out into the square to find a place to enjoy the sun before leaving. Later, crossing the square back to the station, he had been run down and killed, the unused ticket still in his wallet.

He had been going to Ostia Antica, the site of Professor Monti's great discovery, to recover the evidence and proof that this discovery had been his own forgery.

Randall slipped the ticket into his jacket pocket, and studied the drawing of the fish and the cryptic words in the lower right-hand corner of the paper. He looked up. "What is the Porta Marina?"

"Porta Marina? It is also Ostia Antica. At the far part of the ruins of Ostia Antica—the Baths of Porta Marina —very interesting, very antiquity, you must see."

You bet I'll see, Randall vowed to himself.

He folded the paper and pressed it into his pocket with the ticket. "Keep the rest," he told the official.

"Thank you, thank you, and my condolences for your loss of a friend, signore."

Yes, condolences for the loss of a friend, Randall thought, as he left the morgue. But thanks, also, to a friend, for a small legacy and a small hope.

Going into the warm Roman night, Randall knew that he must finish the journey that Robert Lebrun had begun. The pink ticket in his pocket had not been used. In the morning there would be another pink ticket in his pocket, and this one would be used, from Rome to Ostia Antica and from Ostia Antica to Rome.

And after that? Tomorrow would tell.

Too SLOWLY, last night's tomorrow had become today.

The new pink ticket was in his pocket, the dates bordering the ticket punched at 2, and here he was, on the late Tuesday morning that was July 2, on the rickety commuting train rumbling closer and closer to the half-buried ancient seaport where, under Professor Monti's spade, Resurrection Two had begun and where, through Robert Lebrun's covert testimony, Resurrection Two might end.

Last night had been a busy night for Steve Randall. He had ascertained, through the concierge at the Hotel Excelsior, the departure times of the morning trains leaving Rome for Ostia Antica. A mere twenty-five-minute ride to Ostia Antica, he had been advised. After that, following leads, he had gone down into the Via Veneto district to search out several Italian bookstores, with English language sections, that would be open until eight or later. He had found two, and in them he had found what he wanted: used copies of the authoritative volumes on Ostia by Guido Calza, who had directed some of the earliest twentieth-century explorations of the ruins, and by Russell

Meiggs, who had written the most thorough historical record of the rise and fall of the ancient city.

To supplement the books, Randall had acquired a tourist map which showed the plan of the city in early Roman times and in modern times, and a guidebook which described those ruins unearthed in the past century. There had been no references to Professor Augusto Monti at all —understandable, since the map and the books predated Monti's find of six years ago. Besides, Randall remembered, Monti's discovery had been kept a well-guarded secret, and would not be made public until the end of the week.

Throughout last night, and for two hours after midnight, Randall had pored over these books, and the map with its ancient and modern plans, studying them with the care he had never given any test in high school or college so many years ago. He had almost committed the sights and saga of Ostia Antica and its environs to memory. He had delved into the layout of the typical patrician Roman villa of the first century, such as the one that Monti had excavated. The typical one had a vestibule, an atrium or open court, a *tablinum* or library, a *triclinium* or dining room, bedrooms, an *oecus* or main salon, a kitchen, servants' quarters, a number of latrines —and yes, by God, sometimes even a *catacomba*.

On the slip of paper in his wallet, Robert Lebrun had jotted—after *Porta Marina,* after *600 mtrs.*—the word *catacomba,* and last night, in his reading, Randall had pursued it. He had learned that numerous excavations in Italy had revealed that an occasional villa, owned by a secret Christian convert, would have its own *catacomba,* the private subterranean family burial chamber.

Having finished with the books, Randall had taken from his suitcase the folder of research notes, his own and Angela's, made on Professor Monti's excavations in the seaport area six years earlier. Summoning up every last word Robert Lebrun had confessed to him in their single meeting, he had added them to the brief notes he had already made. Finally, eyes bleary, brain fatigued, he had gone to sleep.

This morning, armed only with the map and the single sheet of paper with its drawing of the speared fish and its cryptic notes in the lower right corner, he had taken a taxi to Porta San Paolo.

It had proved to be an undistinguished depot, some stone columns outside, marble floor inside, and past the cafeteria and newspaper stand, a row of ticket windows. With his punched pink ticket in hand, he had been directed to the platform of the station and to his train, and to a day coach painted white and blue, and just moments after he had boarded it, he and the other passengers had been on their way.

Now, checking his watch, he had been seventeen minutes on his way. A mere eight minutes separated him from his destination.

Normally, he would have found the trip unbearable. The passenger seats were hard wooden benches, neither dirty nor clean but merely old. The coach was crowded and suffocating, packed with poorly dressed, simple Italians, who were returning to their villages and towns from the big city. There was much chattering, whining, complaining—or so it sounded—and most of those around him were wet with perspiration, as the merciless sun beat through the grimy windows. From the start, the electric lights overhead had been left burning, which had been beyond comprehension until they had passed through their first mountain tunnel, and then another and another.

Watching the scenery roll by outside the window, Randall could make out nothing of interest. There were many dilapidated apartment buildings, some laundry flying from the tiny balconies, and here and there, the dull conforming bungalows of housing developments. The train had jerked to stops before neglected-looking small town stations—one Magliana, another Tor di Valle, after that Vitinia.

Now, they were leaving Acilia. The scenery was improving. The skyline offered olive groves, farms and meadows, watercourses running into the Tiber, and a modern highway, the Via Ostiensis, Randall guessed, visible on a parallel line.

All this had once been the majestic road from Rome to the port developed by Julius Caesar and Augustus Caesar and improved upon by the later Caesars, Claudius and Nero, the port that had been a fortress against invaders and eventually had filled the granaries in Ostia, the bread-basket of the capital.

Yet, Randall did not really care about what was outside the window, or about the heat and stifling conditions within the coach. His entire focus was on what lay ahead, on the possibility that Robert Lebrun's dead hand would lead him to the evidence of forgery that had obviously been secreted somewhere beyond the government-con-trolled excavations of the ancient seaport—most probably somewhere in the vicinity of the spot where Lebrun claimed to have planted his hoax for Monti to find.

Randall knew the odds against him. They were the odds placed against finding that needle in the haystack. Still, he had a clue, a shred of confidence, and he felt impelled to play out this final act. Somehow, nothing seemed more important than to know whether the message in the Gos-pel According to James and the Petronius Parchment, being given to the world by Resurrection Two in a few days, was the Word—or the Lie.

The train was clacking more slowly, actually grinding to a halt. Randall glanced at his watch. Twenty-six min-utes since Rome. He peered outside in time to see the white lettering on the black sign. It read: OSTIA ANTICA.

He jumped up, squeezed in with the dozen or more sweating passengers crowding the aisle, and shuffled with them to the end of the coach and to the exit.

After leaving the platform, the passengers were stream-ing toward an underpass. Randall followed them. Down the stairs he went, through the blissfully cool concrete tunnel beneath the railroad tracks, and up more steps into the small, heat-baked station. He hurried past a headless piece of statuary beside the ticket window and emerged outdoors.

Trying to ignore the scorching heat, getting his bearings, he was agreeably surprised. It was as if he had been

dropped into a rural paradise. Ahead of him were palm
trees and fig trees, and beyond them he could see stairs
climbing to a bridge. His fellow passengers had evaporated. He was alone in this quiet and peaceful place—
and yet, not quite alone.

A taxi driver, a comical-looking, grinning, stunted native, with a broad-brimmed gondolier's hat tilted on his
head, a tattered gondolier's shirt, a scarlet sash, and flapping trousers, was rapidly intercepting him.

The sunburned driver touched the brim of his hat respectfully. *"Buon giorno, signore.* I am Lupo Farinnaci.
Everybody in Ostia, he know me. I have taxi. Fiat. You
want taxi?"

"I think not," said Randall. "I'm just going to the excavations—"

"Ah, *scavi, scavi,* excavations, *si.* You walk. It is a
near walk. Over the bridge over autostrada to the iron
gate."

"Thank you."

"You no stay long. Too hot. You want cool ride maybe after, to Lido di Ostia, beach for Rome, Lupo take
you in taxi."

"I don't think I'll have the time."

"Maybe, you see. If you need taxi, Lupo here—Lupo
at restaurant named To the Landing Place of Aeneas—
Lupo also sometimes by fruit stand far side. Maybe you
see."

"Thanks, Lupo. If I need you, I'll find you."

Roasting, he started for the bridge, and by the time
he had crossed it and descended near an open field and
a cluster of pine trees, his soaking shirt was pasted to his
skin. Map in hand, he identified the fifteenth-century
castle of Giuliano della Rovere, who became Pope Julius II, and after that he spotted the unique country
restaurant with the strange name, Allo Sbarco di Enea—
To the Landing Place of Aeneas, Lupo had called it—
where, under a roof composed of climbing vine, he could
see people dining. The main entrance to the ruins—the
map called it Cancello A, Porta Romana—must be near.

A short walk farther, and the open iron gate loomed,

fronted by a yellow sign which announced in black:
SCAVI DI OSTIA ANTICA.

Once he was through the gate, everything was again
transformed, as if by magic, into wonderland. Ahead of
him stretched a park, or what appeared to be a park, with
green pine trees that gave off a cool and pungent scent,
and from the ocean a few miles away a slight breeze
curled around him and heightened his mood of anticipation.

To his left, he saw a miniature pavilion, and inside it
an elderly fat lady observing him. She held up a roll of
tickets, calling out, *"Bisogno comprare un biglietto per
entrare, signore!* You must purchase the ticket, mister!"

Acknowledging her, Randall went and purchased a ticket
to see the ruins. Pasteboard in hand, scooping up his
change, he spotted another yellow sign in Italian. He
looked at the ticketseller inquiringly.

"It say from the superintendent, do not go near to excavation, not allowed," she explained. "Ruins you see, not
excavation. It say beware from difference in level of soil
when walk to protect the legs."

"I'll be careful," Randall promised her.

Again following his map, he sought the Decumanus
Maximus, the ancient main street that went straight
through all that had been uncovered of Ostia Antica. He
had no difficulty finding the road, but from his first steps
he knew that he would have difficulty traversing it.

The main street, this day as it had been in its heyday
in the second century, was paved with separated
slick rounded stones, and going over them you slid, stumbled, twisted your ankles. At last, because the slippery,
erratic surfaces were impeding his progress, Randall took
to the side of the road, where there was grass, and he
picked his way through the grass and patches of ground
and ancient debris as he continued through this corpse of
a Roman city.

Here, his map told him, were the broken walls of a
second-century granary, and there, the columns of a theater that had been alive in 30 A.D. Here, the remains of the
Guild Temple, and there, the Forum Baths. But, impa-

tient with the map, he preferred to feast his sight on the total scene, viewing the exposed layers that revealed the overturned marble urns with their elaborate carvings, the section of an apartment with its painted interior walls, the dried-up fountain basins, the imposing remains of arches, and a large boulder inscribed *Decumanus Maximus.*

He was two-thirds through the ruins of Ostia Antica, and the area was utterly desolate, not another soul in sight, and he was beginning to feel lost.

He moved beneath the shade of a pine, sat on the edge of a shattered stone wall, and unfolded the sheet of paper taken from Lebrun's wallet.

He reread the cryptic notation in the lower right corner: *Cancello C, Decumanus Maximus, Porta Marina. 600 mtrs. Catacomba.*

Studying this for the hundredth time, Randall was less certain that it meant what he had thought it meant yesterday. He had believed this to be Lebrun's intended destination on Sunday, a record of the area where he had secreted the evidence of his forgery. Now, Randall suffered his first doubts.

Still, there was no choice but to go straight ahead. According to his map, Cancello C—which, according to his Italian-English dictionary, was Gate C—or the Porta Marina lay around the curve of the road, at the very end of the Decumanus Maximus and at the outer boundary of the ruins of Ostia Antica.

He pocketed both the folded paper and map, pushed off from the stone wall, struck out into the sun, and headed for the curve in the main thoroughfare.

In five minutes, he reached the end of the bumpy cobbled road, and before him were the tumbled stones of the Baths of the Porta Marina. To his right, past the excavated garden houses of the Hadrian era, lay an expanse of hilly field, its cropped grass yellowing and wilting in the blazing sun.

Hand over his eyes, squinting at the area between the meadow and the Baths of the Porta Marina, he made out an open booth, a tourist stand selling fruit juices, and then he made out something else. A human figure that was growing larger by the second as it scrambled toward him, hailing him.

He waited, and the runner proved to be a skinny, brash youngster, thirteen or fourteen, a mop of jet-black hair, dark eyes like saucers. shirtless and all ribs, wearing only khaki shorts and torn tennis shoes.

"Eh, signore!" he shouted, racing up to Randall, placing his hands on his hips as he tried to catch his breath. *"Lei è inglese, vero?* You are an Englishman, no?"

"American," said Randall.

"I speak English," announced the boy. "I learned in school and from many tourists. I will introduce myself. My name is Sebastiano."

"Well, hello, Sebastiano."

"You want a guide? I am a good guide. I help many Americans. I show them every sight of Ostia Antica for one hour for one thousand lire. You want me to show the principal ruins?"

"I've already seen the principal ruins. I'm looking for something else now. Maybe you can help me?"

"I will help you," said Sebastiano enthusiastically.

"I understand that there was another excavation around here, about six years ago, on some private property near by. Now if—"

"Scavi of Augusto Monti?" interrupted the boy.

Randall showed his surprise. "You know? I'd heard it was still secret—"

"Yes, much secret," said Sebastiano. "No one hears of it, no one comes to see it. The sign says restricted area because there are still holes and trenches, and no one is allowed by the authority. The government has made it a historic ground and now supervises it. But my friends and I live close by here. play in the fields, so we see everything. You want to see *scavi* of Augusto Monti?"

"But if it is restricted?"

Sebastiano shrugged. "No one watches. No one looks. You want to see for one thousand lire?"

"Yes." He remembered Lebrun's note in his pocket.

"The part I want to visit is six hundred meters from the Porta Marina."

"Easy to do," said the boy. "You come. I will count six hundred meters as we go. You are an archeologist?"

"I'm a geologist. I want to examine the—the soil."

"No problem. We start. I count six hundred meters in my head. It is before the swamps and sand dunes. I know where it brings us."

Where it brought them, ten minutes later, was to the entrance of a deep trench, a central trench which split off into many trenches and gaping holes, largely covered over with wooden planks that rested on heavy beams which served as roofing.

Beside the main trench opening stood a cracked and flaked, weatherbeaten sign. Randall poked a thumb at the sign. "What does it say?"

Sebastiano knelt down beside it. "The sign, it reads, I translate—*Scavi,* it is difficult for me—I remember—'Excavations of Augusto Monti. Danger. Restricted area. Do not enter.' " He stood up, beaming. "As I told you."

"Good." Randall peered into the trench. Five or six wooden steps had been built to climb down inside this underground passage. "Is there any light down there?"

"From the sun only. But enough. The roofing is not tight together. The light shines through. This trench leads to big excavation of ancient villa, only half dug up. You want me to show you?"

"No," said Randall quickly, "no, that won't be necessary. I'll be down there just a few minutes." He found a 1,000-lira bill and pressed it into the boy's palm. "I appreciate your wanting to help, but I'd prefer that no one bother me while I'm checking things over. Do you understand?"

Solemnly, the boy made a pledge with his raised hand. "I will tell no one. You are my client. If you need me again, to see more, I am by the fruit stand."

Sebastiano turned, loped off through the field, waving back once, and dropped out of sight beyond a mound of grass. Randall waited until he was gone, and swung back to the entrance of the covered excavation.

He hesitated. Suddenly, it was foolish, quixotic, this ridiculous venture. What in the hell was he, one of America's leading public relations men, the publicity director of Resurrection Two, doing here in the middle of nowhere, beside this isolated and abandoned dig?

But it was as if an unseen hand were pushing him. Robert Lebrun's hand. Had not Lebrun been heading for this spot two days ago?

Immediately, he stepped down until his foot rested on the first shaky wooden step, and then he gradually backed down, step by step, lowering himself between the earthen banks until his foot had touched the hard soil at the bottom of the trench. He came around, and saw that the narrow excavation went on at least twenty yards ahead, and that the underground darkness was dispelled by numerous shafts of sunlight filtering through the planks and beams above.

He began to advance cautiously. Here and there, on the sides, the earth was partially shored up, to prevent cave-ins, and at intervals there were vertical posts, like wooden columns, to support the plank roofing and occasional pieces of sheet metal above. At one point the earth had been dug away to reveal an ancient mosaic floor in a short cross tunnel, and after that there were many boxes, some empty, most half filled with chunks of red rock, pieces of marble, a portion of what resembled a marble trough, and chipped yellow bricks.

Approaching the far end of the trench, before it fanned out toward the larger excavations, Randall could see that the planking overhead had been dislodged, or some of the boards removed, so that his path was considerably better lighted.

Again, inspecting the sides of the gouged-out slit, he found himself facing a section of the wall of the excavation that was curiously different—it was recessed, seemed to be composed of limestone, and appeared to be the remains of one side of a grottolike room—and then Randall abruptly stopped in his tracks.

On the recessed wall to his right, for the first time, graffiti.

On the surface of the rock-hewn wall—could this be the family *catacomba?* the ancient subterranean burial chamber?—faintly etched into the porous rock known, he remembered, as *tufa granulare,* were primitive pictures, drawings of the first century, the graffiti of the hunted early Christians of apostolic times.

There were not many, and they were not distinct, but their outlines could be seen.

Randall moved close to the tufa wall. He made out an anchor. The secret early-Christian anchor masking the Cross of Christ. He made out the Greek letters χ and ρ, the first two letters of the Greek word Christos. He made out a crude dove and an olive branch, symbols of the early Christian sign for peace.

Randall crouched down alongside the wall. He made out what resembled a—yes—a whale, the pioneer Christian sign for the Resurrection. And then, in the crumbly red rock the vague outline of a fish, another fish, and a third primitive fish, carved small as minnows, the symbols of the word I-CH-TH-U-S, whose letters were the initials of the Greek words for Jesus Christ, Son of God and Saviour.

Definitely the wall of tufa hid a subchamber, a concealed basement vault, where a Roman family converted to Christianity had once stealthily buried its dead and had left signs of its belief and faith on the rock.

Randall backed off, eyes carefully scanning the surface for more graffiti, eyes going across this wall, and up and down that wall, and then suddenly—way down low, a mere foot above the trench floor, he saw it.

He lunged forward, dropping to his knees, to see it close up, to be sure, to be absolutely positive. His eyes held on this one of the graffiti, more distinct, far less ancient, than any of the others.

Into the tufa rock had been carved the drawing of a fish, a fat fish, a fish with a spear driven straight through its middle.

Randall's hand groped for the paper in his pocket, unfolded it and with both hands he flattened it against the wall.

The speared fish that Robert Lebrun had drawn on the sheet of paper was the exact replica of the speared fish laboriously cut into the tufa wall of Monti's old excavation.

Breath came hard. Randall fell back on his haunches, and he whispered to himself: By God, I found it, by God, I may be at the grave of Resurrection Two.

His next move.

He thought it out carefully, and when he was satisfied, he came hastily to his feet and began retracing his steps through the excavation.

Climbing up out of the cool tunnel into the blaze of early afternoon, he went swiftly through the field, over the hillock, until the fruit stand was in view and within reach of his voice. He caught sight of the boy, his recent guide, Sebastiano, dribbling a ball on the ground, and another person, the driver with the perpetual grin and the old Fiat, Lupo, who was enjoying some kind of drink at the counter.

Randall called out to the boy, tried to attract his attention by waving both arms, and at last Sebastiano saw him, threw aside his ball, and came to him on the run. Randall had wanted to ask Sebastiano for as much equipment as possible—a pickax, a shovel, a wheelbarrow—but these, he decided, would be beyond the boy's immediate resources, and even if they were not, any pursuit of them might arouse suspicion.

Randall was waiting with three 1,000-lira bills, and he held up two of them. "Sebastiano, how would you like to earn two thousand lire?"

The boy's eyes bugged out.

"I'm anxious to test some soil in the trench, take a few samples of it," Randall said quickly. "I need a sharp pointed spade, a strong one of any kind, for a little while, for an hour maybe. Know where I can borrow one?"

"I can bring you a spade," Sebastiano promised eagerly. "There is one in the back of our house for gardening."

"I just want to borrow it," Randall repeated. "I'll return

it before I leave. Would it take you long to bring it to me?"

"Fifteen minutes, most."

Randall handed the boy the 2,000 lire, and then dangled a third bill over his palm. "And another thousand lire if you will keep all this quiet, positively between us."

Sebastiano clutched at the third bill, also. "*È il nostro segreto, lo prometto, lo giuro.* It is between us, our secret. I promise you, I swear," he pledged, enjoying the conspiracy.

"Hurry up, then."

Sebastiano streaked off, galloping across the field, not toward the fruit stand, but toward the road to the right of it.

Randall waited impatiently in the field, smoking his pipe, staring at the ruins of Ostia Antica, trying not to think of the Monti excavation behind him. In less than fifteen minutes, Sebastiano reappeared with a small pointed iron spade, an excellent one, the kind soldiers used to dig slit trenches, and Randall thanked the boy, muttered something again about silence, and promised to return the spade to him at the fruit stand in an hour or so.

After the boy had left him, Randall hurried to the Monti excavation, carefully backed down into the trench, and made his way to the far end where the sun still fell on the tufa wall of ancient graffiti. Removing his jacket, leaving it on the floor of the trench with the spade, he went to the spot where he had seen boxes lined up. He selected three that had once contained artifacts, boxes crusted with dirt and clay but now empty, and he dragged them one after the other to the place of his own work.

Scratching a large square around Lebrun's speared fish, he began to hack at the tufa, breaking into it with the metal tip of the spade, demolishing the speared fish (no destruction of surviving antiquity, after all), defining and hollowing out the square. The surface facing was more ossified, less penetrable, than he had anticipated, and it took all his muscle and strength to chip away and break it. But once the solidified catacomb wall had begun to crack, flake away, disintegrate, the tufa became less resistant and crumbled more easily, and his task became less discouraging. Digging steadily, shoveling the clumps of stone into three boxes, he felt he was making real progress.

Heady with anticipation, he drove his spade deeper and deeper into the porous stone.

AN HOUR had gone by, and during almost every minute of that time, ceaselessly, he had been digging.

Now rivulets of sweat streamed steadily down his cheeks, and chest, and sides, and his shoulders and spine ached. He slammed the iron spade once more into the gaping hole of the catacomb wall, came out with another shovelful of lumps of soft rock, and dumped it into the nearly filled box beside him.

Panting, he stopped to rest, leaning on the spade handle, and then pulling out his already filthy handkerchief to wipe the perspiration from his forehead and eyes.

There were crazy people everywhere, Randall reflected as he stood there, possibly some of the fanatics running the project in Amsterdam, certainly Monti in Rome, maybe Lebrun in heaven or hell, but of them all, he himself must be the craziest.

What would his own father in Oak City say if he could see him now? What would George L. Wheeler and Naomi say? Worst of all, what would Angela Monti say?

Their verdict would be unanimous. He was crazy, either that or the devil embodied in flesh.

Yet, he had been unable to ignore the fantastic clue offered him by the shade of Robert Lebrun—the speared fish in the hand, and the speared fish on the wall.

After discovering it, one of his first thoughts had been to get in touch with the Higher Council for Antiquities and Fine Arts in Rome, and to explain everything to them and summon their aid. He had held the thought, and banished it. He had feared that the powers-that-be in Italy might be in collusion with the powers-that-be at Resurrection Two. Unlike himself, they might not wish truth, only profits and success, and harboring this distrust of them, Randall had been able to understand for the first time something of Robert Lebrun's paranoia about his enemies, both churchmen and government authorities.

And so, out of this paranoia, although his decision had about it an element of childishness, immaturity, even impractical romanticism, Randall had determined to do what could be done alone. In fact, to do what Lebrun might have done had he lived to revisit this site forty-eight hours ago.

The speared fish cut into the catacomb wall had been an invitation to dig. So dig Randall would.

He had tested the catacomb wall, the portion of it caught in the afternoon sun and bearing the ancient graffiti. He had learned about this reddish rock, this tufa, in his researches. It was porous, crumbly, broke fairly easily under pressure, when it was in darkness and dampness. For this reason, the first- and second-century Christians had found it perfect, in the catacombs, for digging out grave shelves. Yet, when the tufa was exposed to light, to sunshine and fresh air, it automatically hardened, became almost unbreakable rock, as resistant as marble. These were facts that Randall knew, and they were what had made his amateur archeological enterprise possible.

For the wooden planks above, parted or dislodged, had allowed strong sunlight to fall on this wall for months, and the thin outer crust of tufa had hardened like marble and further preserved the ancient graffiti. But down low, the bottom fourth of the catacomb wall was not exposed to the sun or the light, and there, in the area around the speared fish, the tufa had not hardened but had remained accessible for digging. Perhaps that was the reason Lebrun had secreted his evidence—if, indeed, he had—down at the damp bottom. And that was why Randall had been able to consider digging at all.

Now, an hour later, he could survey a formidable hole in the lower part of the wall, a hole that had produced nothing but shards and particles of rock.

The most disheartening part of all this obsessive labor had been the persistent nagging fact that he did not know exactly what he was hoping to find.

Sweat-drenched and weary, resting on his shovel, Randall tried to remember what Robert Lebrun had promised, as evidence and proof of forgery, in the Excelsior Hotel room—

First, a papyrus fragment that fits into the lacuna, the gap or hole in Papyrus Number 3 . . . the missing section Monti recited to you, the one where James lists the brethren of Jesus and himself. It is irregularly shaped, and measures roughly 6.5 by 9.2 centimeters in size—2½ by 3¾ inches—and did fit perfectly into the hole in the so-called original. . . . This fragment I kept back bears in its pressed pith, drawn with invisible ink right over the text that can be seen, half of a speared fish. The other half is on your Papyrus Number 3. The fragment I kept back also bears my own contemporary signature, and a sentence in my hand saying this is a forgery. . . .

I will then give you the remaining and most conclusive evidence of my forgery . . . the publishers have twenty-four pieces of papyrus, some of the pieces with one or two portions missing, nine small missing portions in all. I have those nine missing portions . . . eight are protected in an eighteen-inch iron box and safely hidden.

I have naturally secreted the two items . . . retrieving the items for you will take a little time. They are outside Rome—not far. . . .

Outside Rome, not far, that was clear enough, Randall thought. Retrieving the items will take a little time. That was damn clear.

The second part of the evidence, in a small iron box— that was also clear enough, Randall thought.

But the first part of the proof, the first part that Lebrun had promised to deliver for the first payment, the single papyrus fragment, irregularly shaped and roughly 2½ by 3¾ inches in size—that part was not clear. Lebrun had neglected to describe the kind of container in which it was secreted, and Randall had neglected to ask him, and now it was too late.

Still, it must be in some protective container, and surely that would be recognizable, if it could be found. Randall gazed down at the heaps of tufa in the boxes. He had not passed over any foreign object. He had broken up every clump of tufa. He had not come upon any container of any kind. He wondered if he ever would or if, in fact, it existed at all outside of the ex-convict's imagination.

He straightened, gripped the wooden handle of the spade, and he resumed digging.

More tufa, more detritus, more nothing.

As he continued the excavation, as the minutes crawled past, he began to realize that his main obstacle was not his running out of time but out of strength.

In went the shovel, and out.

In again, and—clang—he struck something hard—a boulder? Dammit, if he had run into granite, the dig was ended. He knelt with a groan, and peered through the sweat running into his eyes, trying to make out what he had come up against in the hole. It looked like just another rock, and yet it did not. He dropped the spade, and reached into the hole, clawing for the obstacle, running his fingers over it to feel its size. At once, he realized, sensed, felt from his fingertips and from the sensation beneath his skin, that it had form and shape. It was a man-made object. Maybe an ancient artifact. But—

Maybe not.

His fingers, deep in the hole, tore away at the object, trying to dislodge whatever this was from its position between the layers of tufa. Back in with the spade, manipulating the point of the spade beneath it, above it, around it, trying to move it.

Then by hand again. In minutes it loosened, and it was coming free, and he had it in both hands, dragging it out of the hole.

It was some kind of pottery, a squat clay jug or jar, no more than eight inches high and twelve inches in circumference. It was sealed on top with some kind of thick, solid black substance, probably pitch. Randall tried to break through the black top, with no luck. He brushed away the clinging dirt, and a thin black band of pitch around the middle of the jar became visible. Apparently, it had been in two halves, and was glued together by this pitch.

Randall placed it on the floor of the trench, backed away on his knees, and with the handle of the spade, he struck down at the middle of the jar. Instantly, under the sharp blow, it cracked open, the two halves falling apart, one of them partially shattering.

Randall pounced on the splinters of baked clay, separating them, and at once the contents lay before him. A single object, a ratty gray leather pouch.

He picked up the pouch, held it gingerly, almost unable to bring himself to open it.

Slowly, he pulled the top apart, reached carefully inside, and his calloused fingertips became alive at the cool touch of what felt to be some kind of fine fabric. Gently, he began to extract the fabric, removed it, a square of oiled silk which had been folded over many times. He began to unpeel it, opening it, until what it contained was revealed.

Hypnotized, he stared down at what could have been a brittle brown maple leaf, yet was a fragment of papyrus —Lebrun's precious papyrus. It was covered with Aramaic characters, several lines of faded Aramaic written in ancient ink. It was the missing portion of Papyrus Number 3 that Robert Lebrun had described, the first piece of the evidence that he had promised to deliver.

Here it was, Randall told himself, this piece, either the evidence of a modern forgery that would explode the validity of the International New Testament and prevent the resurgence of faith the world over—or a piece of an authentic ancient papyrus that Monti had overlooked or one that Lebrun had got his hands on and held back, that would further support Resurrection Two and expose Lebrun as merely a boastful and psychotic liar.

Yet, somehow, Lebrun had led him to this, and had reminded him that within its pith the papyrus fragment carried invisible proof that the Gospel According to James was a hoax and a lie.

Randall was too exhausted to feel any emotion.

Yes, here it was, and possibly here was truth.

With care, Randall wrapped the papyrus fragment in its oiled-silk protective cover once more, and his stiff fingers slipped it back into the dirty gray pouch.

His instinct was to leave with his treasure this very moment. But memory of the second part of the evidence of forgery, the small iron box with its additional eight fragments, challenged him. With this first part discovered, could the second devastating proof of hoax be far away? If this also existed, it should also be here, and likely in the same area, perhaps within the depths of the same hole.

Wearily, Randall came to his feet holding his spade, staring at the hole. Momentarily, he wondered how an old man like Lebrun had possessed the strength for this labor—unless he had been more vigorous than Randall had imagined or unless he had used a younger accomplice or a paid helper in the vicinity. Well, speculation was pointless now. Lebrun *had* managed the feat. Randall questioned if he himself could do as well, presuming there was more to be unearthed.

Calling upon almost the last reserves of his stamina, Randall determined to dig on. He drove his spade into the hole, farther and farther, enlarging it, coming upon nothing but tufa, and wondering constantly whether Lebrun had put all his eggs in one basket or had hidden the small iron box elsewhere. No matter, he must continue to dig.

He had brought out one more shovelful of porous rock, dumped it, when he heard a ringing in his ears that sounded like human voices. He must be getting lightheaded, he decided. About to turn back to the hole, he heard the ringing again, the voices more distinct now, and he paused and listened, head cocked.

Definitely voices, or a voice, a woman's voice.

He dropped his shovel, and flattened against the opposite wall of the trench. There was no mistaking it. A distant voice floating from far across the meadow above. He started to spin toward the direction of the tunnel opening, meaning to climb outside and learn where the sound was coming from. But an intuition, more a reflex for self-preservation, kept him from exposing himself at the only entrance.

Still, he must know who—or what—was out there.

Since the trench rose three feet above his head, there was no way to peer over its edge or pull himself up through an opening in the planked roof. His glance fell on the boxes filled with debris at his feet. Quickly, he stooped, and with effort born of urgency, shoved them across the trench floor. Straining, he lifted one box on top of the other to form shallow crude steps.

Cautiously, fearful of his footing, he went up his self-made staircase, and with effort pushed the overhead planks farther apart. Then, ever so slowly, he raised his head until his eyes were above the edge of the trench, and his view of the field and the hillock stretching toward the periphery of Ostia Antica and the fruit stand and the highway was clear.

He saw the source of the voice, now become voices again, at first glance.

They were still at a distance, the three of them, and they were advancing in his direction, striding rapidly down the hillock, and they were agitated and noisy. There was a woman, an Amazon of an Italian woman, between two companions, a boy and a man. She had a meaty hand on the boy's arm—the boy was Sebastiano—and with her free hand she was gesticulating, threatening to strike him, berating him in a shrill voice, the individual words as yet inaudible. And Sebastiano, he was protesting, as she half pushed and half dragged him toward the Monti excavation.

Randall's attention focused on the other person, and this was more alarming. For the other person resembled the law, no sword, no fancy hat, like the *carabinieri,* but an olive-green summer shirt and trousers, a visored hat with a badge, two white bands crisscrossing on the shirt, and a white belt with a pistol in a white holster. Definitely, a member of the *polizia,* the rural police.

They were coming nearer, approaching fast.

Randall tried to figure them out, and sensed at once what was happening.

The woman was Sebastiano's mother. She must have missed her goddam spade or shovel, or somehow got wind of the fact that her son had removed it. She had shaken the truth out of the boy, and then she had told the local policeman about Randall. Immediately, the issue had become more than the shovel. A stranger, a foreigner, had secretly invaded private property, was digging without permission in a government-controlled archeological site. *Pericolo!* Danger, danger to the state! *Fermi quell'uomo!* Stop that man!

They were coming to find him, possibly to arrest him.

Randall ducked down from his improvised steps. Whether his speculation was or was not accurate no longer remained the issue. There was real risk here, a real trap, and trouble. He must not be caught with the pouch and its papyrus fragment. The pouch! He bent, retrieved it and his jacket, and the hell with everything else. Only one thought now. Escape. If caught with the pouch, he'd never be able to explain it, not in a thousand years.

He climbed up the boxes again, and peeked over the trench.

They had veered off now, the three of them, the police officer, the woman, the boy. They were coming not directly toward him but toward the entrance to the main trench of the dig. They were passing his vision, about a half block away, almost arrived at the entrance. The instant they reached it, began to disappear from his sight, descend into the trench at his rear, he would move.

"Lei dice che lo straniero è sceso da solo qui?" the mother was scolding the boy. And she was screaming at the policeman, imploring him *"Dovete fermarlo! È un ladro!"*

Desperately, Randall wondered what she was saying. Certainly something about a stranger going down here alone, using her shovel. Certainly something about catching him, catch the thief.

They were disappearing from sight, first the policeman, next Sebastiano, then the raucous mother.

He could hear their chattering resound through the underground tunnel.

Randall moved fast. He ascended to the uppermost debris-packed box, carefully set the pouch on the dirt bank and flung his coat over the side, took a good hold of the edge of the trench, and with what strength was left in him, hoisted himself over the top, falling forward on the grass above. Then, rolling fully out of the trench, fully free, snatching up his jacket and holding tightly to the leather pouch, he staggered to his feet.

He began running, stumbling and running, fast as his weak legs would carry him. He went up the slope, espied the fruit stand by the roadside in the distance, and he made for it, racing downhill toward it, gasping for breath, slowing into a trot as the land leveled off and the fruit stand grew closer.

Then, choking, gulping for air, he recognized the grinning little Italian who had been talking to the proprietor of the fruit stand, and was now departing, starting for his tiny Fiat.

"Lupo!" Randall shouted. "Lupo, wait for me!"

The taxi driver wheeled around, startled, and when he saw Randall advancing, his grin flashed on. Pressing his gondolier's hat on his head, he looked hopefully at Randall.

"I'm hiring you," gasped Randall. "I need your taxi."

"To the railroad station?" said Lupo, his gaze still fixed on his customer's disheveled appearance, the dirty face, stained shirt, filthy hands.

"No," snapped Randall, grabbing the driver firmly by the arm and pulling him toward the Fiat. "I want you to drive me straight to Rome, fast as possible. I'll pay you well to take me, and also for your gas and the time it takes you to return here. Can you make it fast?"

"We are practically there!" chortled Lupo. He yanked open the rear door of his taxi. "You enjoyed the antiquities of Ostia Antica, signore? It makes a restful day, no?"

AT LAST, he was safely inside the confines of his room at the Hotel Excelsior.

In the lobby, where he had been a sight to behold, he

had requested the worried concierge to make a reservation for him on the first available flight from Rome to Paris. In the lobby, still, he had telephoned Professor Henri Aubert in Paris. Aubert had been out of the office, but his secretary had carefully taken down the message. Monsieur Randall would be in Paris before the dinner hour. *Oui*. Monsieur Randall must see Professor Aubert at the laboratory at that time on a matter of greatest urgency. *Oui*. Monsieur Randall will telephone to confirm the meeting upon his arrival at Orly Airport. *Oui*.

Now, in his room, Randall saw that there was barely time for one more call and a quick shower before checking out.

One more call.

Presuming that Aubert proved the piece of papyrus in the leather pouch to be genuine, a product of the first century, there was a last step, a more critical test. As Aubert himself had once pointed out, the authenticity of the papyrus did not guarantee the authenticity of the document itself. In the end, it was the Aramaic text that mattered. And in this instance, Randall knew, there was something else. The invisible writing which Lebrun had mentioned.

Whom to speak to?

There was a temptation, almost filial, to contact George L. Wheeler or Dr. Emil Deichhardt, and reveal to them what he had in his possession, and have them bring in Dr. Jeffries and Dr. Knight, their experts in Aramaic, as well as some of the project's experts in Roman history. But tempting as this was, easy as it might be, Randall resisted it.

Unless Wheeler and Deichhardt were either masochistic or suicidal, they would not appreciate Lebrun's evidence of forgery. They could not be trusted. Nor could Dr. Jeffries, who had his eyes on the leadership of the World Council of Churches, and whose stepping stone to that leadership was a successful International New Testament —no, Jeffries could not be trusted, either. Not even Dr. Knight, dear Dr. Knight, his hearing restored through the miracle of the new find. He could have no unbiased judgment, either. Nor, indeed, could anyone else at Resurrection Two, Randall realized. They all had too much at stake.

What he wanted, he knew, was someone as skeptical, and yet as objective about seeking truth, as he had tried to be in his own search.

There was only one.

Randall picked up the telephone, got the long-distance operator. "I want to place a person-to-person call, most urgent, to Amsterdam. No, I don't have a number. It's the Westerkerk in Amsterdam. That's a church. The person I want to speak to is Dominee Maertin de Vroome."

"Please hang up, Mr. Randall. I will try to locate your party, and call you right back."

Hastily, Randall emptied drawers, cleaned table and bureau of his effects, shoved them into his suitcase, holding out only a fresh shirt and a pair of slacks. He stripped down to his shorts, tossed his dirty shirt and trousers into the traveling bag, and finally, and with care, slipped the gray leather pouch into the suitcase. He closed it, and locked it.

The telephone rang. He snatched up the receiver.

It was the hotel operator. "We have your party in Amsterdam, Mr. Randall. You can go ahead now."

The line was clear.

Randall instinctively lowered his voice as he spoke into the mouthpiece. "Dominee de Vroome? This is Steve Randall. I'm calling from Rome—"

"Yes, the operator said the call was from Rome." The Dutch cleric's tone was suave as ever, and attentive. "How very kind of you to remember me. I thought you had turned your back on me."

"No, I followed through. I guess I believed all that you told me. But I had to find out for myself. I went after Robert Lebrun. I found him."

"You did? Really, you met him?"

"In person. I heard his story. Substantially the same as Plummer reported to you, only more of it. I can't go into details now. I'm catching a plane shortly. But I made a deal with Lebrun."

"Did he deliver?"

"In a way, he delivered. I'll tell you about it when I see you. The fact is, I have his evidence of forgery right here in my room with me."

The listener in Amsterdam emitted a long thin whistle. "Wonderful, wonderful. Is it a missing portion of one of the papyri?"

"Exactly. With Aramaic writing on it. I'm bringing it to Paris. I'll be arriving on Air France at Orly Airport at five o'clock. I'm going straight to Professor Aubert's laboratory. I want him to check out the papyrus."

"Aubert is unimportant to me," said Dominee de Vroome. "But I can understand that he is important to you—and to your employers. Of course, he'll find the papyrus genuine. That would have been the easiest part for Lebrun. It is what is written upon the papyrus that will give proof of forgery or not."

"That's why I'm calling you," said Randall. "Do you know anyone we can trust"—he realized that for the first time he had used *we* with de Vroome—"anyone expert enough to examine the Aramaic, and tell us—"

"But I've told you before, Mr. Randall," the cleric interrupted, "there are few others, anywhere, more familiar with Aramaic than myself. In a matter as delicate as this, I think you had better place your trust in me."

"Gladly," said Randall, relieved. "I was hoping you would help. Now, one more thing. Have you ever heard of a woman named Locusta?"

"Emperor Nero's official poisoner? Of course."

"Dominee, are you as conversant with ancient Roman history and customs as you are with Aramaic?"

"Even more so."

"Well, just to make certain there could be no question about his forgery, our friend Lebrun drew upon an ancient Greek formula Locusta used for writing in invisible ink, which could later be made visible, and he applied this formula to the fragment I have as conclusive proof of his forgery."

Dominee de Vroome chuckled. "A positive evil genius. Has he given you the formula?"

"Not all of it," said Randall. "I know this invisible ink consists of gallotannic acid taken from gall nuts. To make the writing come out, a mixture of copper sulfate and one other ingredient is applied. I don't have the name of the other ingredient."

"No matter. That nonsense will be no problem. So, Mr. Randall, thanks to you, we finally have on hand what we always suspected existed. Very good, excellent. My heartiest congratulations. Now we can put an end to the sham. I shall leave Amsterdam at once. I will be at Orly to await your arrival. Five o'clock, you said? I shall be there, ready to proceed. You know, we must work fast. There is no time to lose. Are you aware that your publishers have moved up their worldwide announcement of the new Bible to this Friday morning? It is to take place from the stage of the Netherlands Royal Palace."

"I'm well aware of that," said Randall, "only I don't think it's going to take place, not from the royal palace or anywhere else, not after that stick of dynamite in my suitcase is set off on Thursday. See you at five."

NOT UNTIL his jetliner touched down on the rain-slicked runway of Orly Airport outside Paris did Steve Randall feel safe.

His experiences in Italy had been disturbing and threatening. Now, that was all behind him. His plane was disgorging its passengers down the ramp and onto the soil of France. And though Orly was beginning to be shrouded in fog, and was swept by a steady drizzle, it was France and it was beautiful. France meant freedom. He felt liberated and relieved for the first time in days.

He took up his precious suitcase—he had not permitted it out of his sight while boarding this plane in Rome, and he had been allowed to keep it with him as hand baggage—and he joined the others leaving the jetliner.

In minutes he would be with Dominee Maertin de Vroome, an ally, his one dependable ally, and together they would go to Professor Aubert's laboratory to open the leather pouch. With that, the forces of light would have their weapon, and their day, against the recently dominant forces of superstition.

Quickly, efficiently, Randall was transported to the disembarkation hall, and directed through it by the French hostess to the floor above. Falling in line with the other passengers, he stepped on the moving walk that ran the interminable length of the transit corridor, and stepped off it beneath the illuminated sign that read: PARIS.

Here, the activity was intense. There were the desks and red Formica stalls he had seen before, each manned by a *police de l'air,* an airport policeman wearing visored cap with a winged insignia, light blue shirt and blue trousers. This was what the French called the Police Filter or passport control. Immediately beyond, and underneath another sign, DOUANES, or Customs, installed in beige boxes, were the French customs officials, each also attired in a uniform, with only his visored hat with the insignia of an exploding grenade over a hunting horn, and navy blue jacket with silver buttons visible. After that, past the turnstile or swinging gate—Randall could not make out which—he could see the congregated mass of visitors and tour guides awaiting the arrival of relatives, friends, business associates, and tourists.

Falling in for passport control, Randall craned his neck for a glimpse of the tall, imposing person of Dominee de Vroome and his familiar black clerical cassock. But the waiting crowd was too dense. He could not find de Vroome, at least not from this distance.

Now, he was before the desk, and an unsmiling, bored *police de l'air* was holding out his hand. Randall released his suitcase momentarily, sought the green United States passport inside his breast pocket, and presented it with his *carte de débarquement.* The policeman turned a page or two of the passport, considered Randall's photograph (he had been fifteen pounds heavier in that photograph and he hated it), compared it with Randall's own countenance, checked a mysterious row of square pink cards arrayed on holders at the desk front, glanced at Randall a second time and finally nodded. Retaining the yellow disembarkation card, he returned Randall's passport and gestured him toward the customs boxes. This done, the policeman stood up, and began to leave his stall over the protests of the other passengers waiting in line.

Suitcase once more in his grip, and with his free hand tugging the declarations form from his jacket pocket, Randall moved on to the nearest customs box and uniformed official, as he continued to survey the crowd of visitors for Dominee de Vroome.

Still holding his suitcase, he handed the form to the official, eager to get through this formality and plunge into the critical business of the evening. But the customs official, accepting his form, was inattentive, distracted by one of his colleagues behind him. At last, the official turned back, ready to give Randall's declaration his undivided attention.

The official looked up. "You have no other baggage to claim downstairs, monsieur? This is your only baggage?"

"Yes, sir. Just the one piece I have with me. I was away for just a few days." He disliked himself for these nervous explanations, but customs agents, not only here but in the United States, made you feel guilty when there was nothing to feel guilty about. "It's merely my overnighter," he added, raising his suitcase higher.

"You have not exceeded the 125-franc import limit? No goods purchased, or gifts received, or valuables in Italy above that amount?"

"Exactly as I stated in the form," said Randall with a trace of annoyance. "I have only my personal effects."

"Nothing to declare?" the official persisted.

"Nothing." Randall's irritation was increasing. "You have my declaration. I've made it clear. I've sworn to it."

"Yes," said the customs official, rising. He called off, "Maurice!" He stepped out of his box, waited for another younger customs man to replace him, and came up alongside Randall. "Please follow me, monsieur."

Bewildered, Randall was at the customs official's heels as they went through the exit, and pushed through the parted mass of visitors. Again, Randall tried to seek out de Vroome, enlist his help to overcome this red tape, but de Vroome was still nowhere to be seen.

The customs official beckoned to Randall, who caught up with him, angered by the continuing delay. Suddenly, Randall realized that another official had flanked him, and he recognized the wiry, phlegmatic airport policeman he had talked to in passport control.

"Hey, what's going on here?" Randall protested.

"We will go downstairs," the customs official explained levelly. "A mere formality."

"What formality?"

"Routine baggage check."

"Why not do it right here?"

"It would impede the flow of traffic. We have special rooms off the baggage-claim hall." He led the way to the escalator. "If you please, monsieur."

Randall hesitated, glaring at the official, then appraised the airport policeman looming over him, and he thought better of resisting. Carrying his suitcase, he started to walk between them, and descending on the escalator, he had his initial premonition of danger, the apprehension that he thought he had left behind in Italy had begun to creep over him in France.

As they crossed the busy ground floor of the terminal, heading toward the sign reading SORTIE, Randall protested once more. "I think you're making a mistake, gentlemen."

The officials did not reply. They led him into the vast hall where passengers were recovering their luggage from revolving belts, and guided him toward a series of empty rooms with open doors which unobtrusively, almost discreetly, were ranged along the far wall. At one open door, a gendarme—*agent de police* or Sûreté Nationale, Randall could not discern—stood on guard, his club and pistol butt plainly visible. He nodded as the customs official and airport policeman escorted Randall into the room.

"Now, will you tell me why I'm here?" Randall demanded to know.

"Place your bag on the stand there," the customs man said quietly. "Please open it for inspection, monsieur."

Randall lifted his suitcase onto the stand. He went through his pockets for his key. "I've already told you there's nothing to declare," he insisted.

"Open it up, please."

The airport policeman had retreated unobtrusively into the background, while the customs official stood close to Randall, observing him as he unlocked his bag and unsnapped the latches. Randall lifted the lid of his suitcase. "There you are. Go ahead and see for yourself."

The customs official moved past Randall, and stood over the suitcase. With professional efficiency, his hand slid around the interior of the suitcase searching for hidden pockets or a false bottom. He began to go through the shirts, shorts, socks, pajamas. He removed several manila folders, riffled through them, put them back. He rummaged deeper inside, found something, pivoted and dangled it before Randall.

It was Lebrun's soiled gray leather pouch.

"What is this, monsieur?"

"A cheap souvenir from Rome," Randall said hastily, trying to repress his concern. "It's worthless to anyone except me. A facsimile of a piece of Bible manuscript. I'm a collector."

The customs official seemed not to be listening. He had opened the pouch, drawn out the folded silk wrapping, slowly unfolded it, and now he looked at the fragile leaf-like fragment of papyrus. His gaze went past Randall. He asked, *"C'est bien ça, Inspecteur Queyras?"*

The airport policeman came forward. He nodded. *"Je le crois, Monsieur Delaporte."* He was holding one of the pink cards Randall had seen on his passport control desk. He glanced at the pink card, and addressed himself to Randall. "Monsieur Randall, it is my duty to inform you that our Service of Investigations has been alerted by the Republic of Italy to be on the lookout for you. We have been notified by the Italian judiciary that you have appropriated a priceless national treasure from Italy, without permission of the government to remove it or the legal right to possess it. Such an act is forbidden by the Italian law, and you will be subjected to a heavy fine if ever you should return to Italy. However——"

Randall listened, petrified with disbelief. How could anyone in Italy possibly have known what he had in this luggage?

"——the concern of the government of Italy is not precisely the concern of the government of France," the airport police officer, Inspector Queyras, went on in faultless English. "Our concern is that you committed a *flagrant délit,* which is to say you hid in your luggage an object of great value, failed to declare it to our customs, and, in fact, attempted to smuggle it into France. This is a misdemeanor under our law, monsieur, and punishable——"

"I hid nothing!" Randall exploded. "I declared nothing, because I had nothing of value to declare!"

"The government of Italy appears to take another view of this papyrus," the inspector said calmly.

"Another view? There is no other view. What do they know about that scrap of papyrus? I'm the only one who knows. I tell you—listen to me, don't make fools of yourselves—that scrap in the pouch is worthless in terms of money; it is an imitation, a forgery that pretends to be an original. It has no value to anyone, except to me. In itself, intrinsically, it's not worth a sou, not a penny."

The police officer shrugged. "That remains to be seen, monsieur. There are experts in these matters, and we are in contact with one of them already, to make a study and give an opinion. Meanwhile, until this is done——"

He reached out past the astounded Randall and took the fragment of papyrus from the customs official. He again enfolded it in its silk covering, and then slipped it back into the pouch.

"——until an examination is made, Monsieur Randall," the airport police officer concluded, "we are confiscating this object."

Leather pouch in his palm, he started out of the room.

"Wait! Where are you going with that?" Randall demanded.

The inspector half turned at the door. "That is our concern, not yours."

Randall felt an uncontrollable rage begin to rise inside him at this injustice. To lose the papyrus now, his precious proof, the evidence of hoax, to those stupid bureaucrats! It must not be, it could not be!

"No!" he insisted. He leaped forward, grabbing the airport officer by the arm and swinging him around. "No, dammit, you can't have it!" He reached for the pouch. The inspector tried to fend him off, but Randall smashed his forearm against the officer's throat, and caught the pouch with his free hand as the inspector dropped it.

Staggered, clutching his throat, the officer reeled backwards, shouting, *"Bon Dieu, attrape cet imbécile!"* Randall had the pouch safely in his grasp, but that moment the customs man lunged at him. Frenzied, Randall sidestepped the customs man, lashing out to drive him off. The customs man cursed, and came at Randall again, grappling for one of his arms, and suddenly, there were more of them, two more, the Sûreté guard from outside and the airport police officer, piling in on Randall, wrestling with him, bullying him bruisingly against the plaster wall, pinning both his arms.

Blindly trying to fight back, to struggle free of them, Randall saw someone's knee come up at him. He tried to twist aside, but the knee smashed into his groin. The pain, instantaneous, excruciating, fanned outward from his testicles, searing through his intestines and over his body. He moaned, shutting his eyes, trying to double up, feeling the pouch loosen and float from his fingers. He slid down, down, almost in slow motion, to the floor, and curled there, panting like a wounded animal.

"Ça y est, il ne nous embétera plus," he heard a French voice say above him. "No more trouble. He is finished."

Two of them had hooked him beneath the armpits, and were hoisting him up off the floor to his feet.

They pressed his arms behind him, and they were holding him rigidly. His eyes gradually regained their focus. The grim airport police officer unblurred. He had the pouch once more. He was striding out of the doorway with the pouch.

Randall's eyes followed him. Another figure, a familiar one, still at a distance, was coming into view, a tall, austere man in a black cassock. It was Dominee de Vroome, at last.

"De Vroome!" Randall shouted. "De Vroome, I'm here!"

But the Dutch clergyman did not seem to notice. He had come face to face with the airport police officer, who was speaking to him, and showing him the leather pouch. De Vroome was nodding, listening and nodding, and then, with the airport police officer, he began to turn away.

"Wait, please, let me go, I've got to see him," Randall cried out in desperation to the customs official and guard who held him. "De Vroome's expecting me. I sent for him."

"You did?" said the customs man with amusement. "I hardly think so. Because we are the ones who sent for him."

Randall stared at the customs man without comprehension. "I don't know what you're talking about. I must see him." He made one frantic effort to break away, straining to free his arms, and that instant he felt the sharp cut of metal on his wrists crossed behind him. Then he knew. He was handcuffed. "I must see him," Randall pleaded.

The customs man nodded agreeably. "You will see him tomorrow when you are heard before the Paris *juge d'instruction,* the examining magistrate, Monsieur Randall. Right now, you are placed under arrest for the customs infraction, not declaring and attempting to smuggle into France an object of great value. Also, you are under arrest for disturbing the public peace and for committing assault on an officer of the law. You must go to jail."

"But the papyrus," Randall protested.

"Its worth, and your future, monsieur, will be decided tomorrow in a court of the Galerie de la St. Chapelle at the Palais de Justice."

XII

It was morning finally, an overcast, forbidding Paris morning as seen through the barred cell window high above.

At least, Randall reflected bitterly, sitting on the edge of the straw sack on his cot and buttoning his fresh shirt, at least he had not been treated like a common criminal.

Now, completely awake and refreshed, despite his insomnia through most of the night spent in this isolated and barren cell of the detention Dépôt connected with the Palais de Justice, Randall tried to analyze what had happened to him and to anticipate what was about to happen next.

He was still perplexed. He had been arrested for smuggling an object of value into France, as well as for assaulting an officer, that much for sure. Following the mad episode in the Orly air terminal last night, he had been hustled into a *panier à salade*—French slang for police van, he gathered—and transported to the complex of buildings known as the Palais de Justice on the Île de la Cité.

He had been hurried inside a building called the Petit Parquet. There, in an overly bright room, he had been confronted by a stern, unsmiling Frenchman who had introduced himself as *le substitut du procureur de la république*—frightening, until the interpreter, also on hand, had explained that this was merely the deputy public prosecutor.

There had been a short interrogation, and finally the formal charges. He had committed an *outrage à fonctionnaire dans l'exercice de ses fonctions*—an outrage

617

against a civil servant in the performance of his duties, the interpreter revealed—and attempted to smuggle undeclared valuable goods into the country. The *substitut* had signed a paper which made his arrest official.

Because of special circumstances—what special circumstances? he had wondered—the Minister of the Interior had arranged for his case to be heard without a delay. In the morning he would appear before a *juge d'instruction*—a judge of the procedure—for full examination. Until that time he would have to be kept in short-term police detention in the Dépôt of the Palais. One last thing before incarceration. He was entitled to retain the services of an attorney for tomorrow's examination. Did he desire to telephone an attorney or telephone a friend who could find him one?

Randall had weighed this. He knew no lawyers in Paris. He thought of, and rejected, the idea of calling the American Embassy. The whole incident was so humiliating to him—and one so difficult to explain—that he didn't want to risk exposing his predicament to some supercilious compatriot who might spread the tale as gossip before all the facts were in. He thought of Sam Halsey, over at Associated Press in the Rue de Berri. Sam would certainly be able to provide a competent criminal defender. But then, an enthusiast in Sam's office might get wind of Randall's dilemma and leak a garbled and incomplete version of the story to the press, making him appear absurd. Besides, the very idea of retaining legal counsel for an open-and-shut case like this—the papyrus fragment could easily be proved a fake, and that's all there was to it— seemed pretentious and ridiculous.

When Randall had inquired about the necessity of counsel, he had learned that there was no necessity other than giving him every protection possible. He had also learned that acquiring an attorney would certainly delay his case for three or four days. That had helped him make up his mind. Since Resurrection Two would be given to the world in forty-eight hours, he wanted no postponing of his examination, and therefore no attorney. He would be satisfied to speak in his own defense.

With the matter of an attorney settled, Randall had been taken out in the night drizzle and through the courtyard and open grilled gates of the Palais de Justice and across the Boulevard du Palais to the Préfecture de Police. Led into the anthropometry section of the Préfecture, he had been fingerprinted and photographed—both *de face* and in profile—and after that he had been again interrogated to learn whether he had any previous criminal record and to obtain his version of the trouble in the Orly air terminal.

This done, Randall had once more been taken out into the rain by two *agents de police,* returned to the courtyard of the Palais de Justice, and finally escorted here to the Dépôt, in a building adjoining the Palais. He had been locked in this jail cell—solitary, no other inmates—and it was anything but comfortable. Yet, he had known more disagreeable quarters during some of the darker, drunken nights of his life.

The Dépôt cell, with its barred window, with its clanging iron door bearing a peephole for the guards, had offered such conveniences as a cot with straw mattress, a washbowl with only cold water, a toilet that could not be flushed (it flushed itself automatically every fifteen minutes). Yet, Randall had been given some back copies of *Paris Match* and *Lui* to read, and his pipe, a disposable lighter, and his packet of tobacco to enjoy. He had been interested in nothing except this opportunity to think, to work out how he would be able to reach de Vroome and Aubert and make the facts of the forgery known, before the public announcement of the International New Testament occurred in a little more than two days.

He had been unable to think, because the day had been so long and emotional, from Ostia Antica to Rome to Paris to this cell in the Palais Dépôt. But then, he had been unable to sleep either, because of overfatigue and the ghostly images dancing through his brain: Wheeler and the other publishers, and Angela, and de Vroome, and always the memory of old Robert Lebrun. Somewhere during the blackness, he had slept, fitfully and terrified by recurrent dreams, but he had slept.

Now, morning. The warden had been kind enough to

him, no complaint. Apparently, because he was a special
case—certainly a generous gratuity hadn't hurt—the warden had sent along, besides the usual prison breakfast of
black coffee and bread, fruit juice and two eggs. Further,
from Randall's suitcase, he had brought his razor, shav-
ing mug, and comb, and a fresh change of undershorts,
socks, shirt, and a clean necktie. Finally, almost dressed,
Randall could think.

He tried to recall what he had been told was ahead of
him this morning. A trial or a hearing? He could not
remember which. So much confusion last night. He
thought that he had heard the deputy public prosecutor
speak of an examination before a *juge d'instruction*.
What in the devil did such an examination consist of?
He recollected being told something about a questioning
process, by the magistrate, of himself, of witnesses. He
had inquired what witnesses? Well, there was the assault
charge, the public disturbance, to be taken care of, but
that was the lesser offense. More important, the smuggling
of an undeclared national treasure from Italy into France.
No treasure, he recalled shouting again, but a fake, a
nothing, a phony, a fake. Therefore, the witnesses, he had
been reminded, the experts to determine the authenticity
and value of the fragment of papyrus.

Most confusing, to Randall, was de Vroome's role.
The Dutch cleric had appeared at Orly as he had promised. He had been there to assist Randall. Yet, the idiotic
customs man had insisted that de Vroome's appearance
had been at the behest of French customs. It made no
sense to Randall.

Another mystery, a darker one, the most threatening
one of all: Who had informed upon him to French customs?

Plainly, someone had set out to trap him. But who
even knew that he had the missing piece of papyrus in
his possession? There were, of course, the boy Sebastiano
and his mother, and that Italian policeman from Ostia.
Yet, they would not know his identity, even if they had
realized that he had removed something from the trench.
There was the taxi driver, Lupo, who had driven him

from Ostia to Rome. But the driver could not have known who he was or what he had on his person. There was Professor Aubert, for whom he had left an urgent message to meet him last night. But Aubert could not conceivably have divined the reason for the requested meeting. Finally, there was Dominee de Vroome, whom he had telephoned from Rome, the only one who knew everything. Yet, de Vroome was the single person on earth knowledgeable about Resurrection Two who would have absolutely no motive for betraying him. After all, by bringing in the evidence of forgery, Randall would be handing de Vroome the very weapon he sought to destroy Resurrection Two and promote his own position of power.

There was no logical explanation, save one.

If Robert Lebrun had not been killed by accident, but had been deliberately murdered, then the person or persons who had somehow learned what Lebrun was doing for Randall would also have been able to find out what Randall was doing in Rome and Ostia Antica.

That was the one possibility, and it was meaningless, vaporous, because the suspects were faceless and nameless.

Dead end.

He had finished knotting his tie, when the cell door rattled and swung wide.

A strapping young man in red-banded visored kepi and navy-blue uniform, with a St. Cyr military college look, stepped briskly into the cell.

"You had a satisfactory night's rest, Monsieur Randall? I am Inspector Bavoux of the Garde Républicaine. I have been directed to escort you to the Palais de Justice. The examination will begin in one hour. The witnesses will be assembled at that time. You will have every opportunity to be heard."

Randall came off the cot, and pulled on his sport jacket. "I requested Dominee Maertin de Vroome of Amsterdam to testify on my behalf. Is he among the witnesses who will appear?"

"Most certainly, monsieur."

Randall gave a sigh of relief. "Thank God. . . . Okay, Inspector, I'm ready for them. Let's go."

THEY WERE GATHERED in a small, functional hearing room located in the Gallery of the Judges of Instruction, on the fourth floor of the Palais de Justice.

As he headed into the building of the Palais, and turned left into the Galerie de la St. Chapelle, Steve Randall found that his confidence had been reinforced by the inscription over a staircase entrance. It read simply: LIBERTÉ, ÉGALITÉ, FRATERNITÉ.

Fair enough, he had thought.

Now, still standing rigidly in the defendant's box set against one wall, Randall noted that twenty-two minutes had passed since the surprisingly informal proceedings had begun. He knew that his time to be heard was near. He felt no anxiety. He felt calm and reassured. He would be called upon merely to lay the groundwork for his belief that the scrap of papyrus he had taken out of Italy and brought into France was a forgery, and of no monetary value. Once his belief was supported by expert testimony, by the unimpeachable opinion of the authoritative Dominee Maertin de Vroome, he would be vindicated. Everything before and after de Vroome's appearance was legal window dressing. With de Vroome's pronouncement of forgery, Randall knew, the magistrate could do nothing but fine him for assault and free him.

From the corner of his eye, Randall took in the witnesses once more. He had hardly been surprised by their presence when he first entered the modern chamber. Their lives and reputations, as well as their fortunes in dollars, pounds, francs, lire, marks, were at stake in the outcome of this hearing.

There were five rows of benches. In the first row, like figures sculptured in granite, sat Wheeler, Deichhardt, Fontaine, Young, Gayda. Behind them, solemn and attentive, sat de Vroome, Aubert, Heldering. In the back row sat Naomi Dunn, tight-lipped, impassive. The earlier witnesses were no longer present. Upon completion of their testimony, they had been dismissed.

There were no outsiders, no members of the press, no idle spectators. The magistrate had clarified this at the outset. The proceedings were closed to the public owing to, as the magistrate had so nicely put it, "the discretion required by the subject to be discussed."

Star Chamber, Randall thought.

He wondered who had made the arrangement for the session to be secret. The cabal of publishers, of course, with their powerful ecclesiastical connections that reached into the Vatican and the World Council of Churches. France was, after all, responsive to the wishes of the Church. Then, too, there were Monsieur Fontaine, and his alter ego, Professor Sobrier. Also, there was Signore Gayda and his influential Monsignore Riccardi. Men like these were involved not only in religion but also in politics. They would count for much here. They had wanted secrecy, and had got their wish.

Randall did not mind, because he had de Vroome, and with de Vroome there would soon be truth and a pipeline to the public.

Half listening to the witness still being interrogated, Randall reviewed the events that had taken place before this moment.

The *juge d'instruction*—his name was Le Clere—had entered the chamber and seated himself behind one of two oversized steel desks facing the witness chair and those in attendance on the benches. Unexpectedly, he had been attired not in the traditional black toga with white bib, but in ordinary civilian clothes, a skimpy conservative brown suit. He had the anemic, dwarfish, indoor look of the typical civil servant or petty bureaucrat, with stand-up hair that resembled a wire wig, and a disconcertingly piercing voice.

He had called the proceedings to order. From a third desk, placed at a right angle to the magistrate's pair, the *greffier,* the court clerk, rose from his typewriter to read aloud the bill of charges against Randall in French and then in English. Impatiently, the *juge d'instruction* had stated that he had dispensed with the services of an interpreter (except for those witnesses who spoke only

French), in the interest of saving time. This was possible because, out of justice to the defendant, the hearing would be held in English. What had followed he had kept moving at a fast pace, as if time were money, or as if he had an early lunch date he did not wish to miss.

The opening witness had been the customs official from Orly Airport, Monsieur Delaporte, who had detailed the horrendous behavior of the defendant. The second witness had been the Sûreté Nationale guard, Gorin by name, an inarticulate protector of the public safety, who had been alerted in advance by the security force of Orly that a smuggler might have to be searched and might become violent, and Gorin had participated in subduing him.

The third witness had been the inspector of the *police de l'air,* the officer of the airport police named Queyras, who testified that he had been informed by the head of the *carabinieri* in Rome that an American, one Steven Randall, had illegally acquired a Christian treasure of great antiquity and had taken it from Rome without permission and would be attempting to bring it into Paris. Queyras had prepared one of the pink cards—describing criminals who were wanted—and when Randall had come through, Queyras had confiscated the leather pouch with its papyrus fragment, and had joined in subduing the intractable visitor. After entering his pink "wanted" card into evidence, Queyras had been dismissed along with the previous two witnesses.

The next witness, a new face to Randall, had been Dr. Fernando Tura, former superintendent of the Ostia Antica region and recently elevated to membership on the Higher Council of Antiquities and Fine Arts in Rome. He had come here on behalf of the Ministero della Pubblica Istruzione. A swarthy, officious, bantamweight Italian, with furtive eyes and handlebar moustache. Randall had disliked him at once, and for good reason: This was the man, according to Angela, who had obstructed and slandered her father from the beginning.

Dr. Tura had been the next witness. He had been questioned.

No, Dr. Tura had never laid eyes on the defendant

before. He had learned about Signore Randall only yesterday: that the American signore had by some means,
and without permission of the Ministry, obtained a missing papyrus fragment, which belonged to the codex of
the Gospel According to James, a discovery made in Ostia
Antica six years earlier by Professor Augusto Monti, of
the University of Rome, with the cooperation of Dr. Tura.
The defendant had made the effort to remove this national treasure from Italy. No, Dr. Tura had no idea
precisely how Signore Randall had obtained the valuable
fragment, whether he had stolen it or whether it had been
a fortuitous find, but in either case he had broken the
law.

Dr. Tura had translated the Italian law. "Archeological
objects found in Italy belong to the state, based on the
principle that anything underground is state property. Only
the Minister of Public Instruction may grant permission
for execution of archeological researches, and no excavation may be made without license."

The defendant had outrageously defied this last principle of the law, and more than that, had not reported
his find, had in fact removed it from Italy. The Italian
government wished to recover the fragment in order to
turn it over to a syndicate known as International New
Testament, Incorporated. This syndicate had leased all
of the documents discovered by Professor Monti, of which
this fragment was an integral part, for the purposes of
publishing a revised version of the New Testament.

It was this earnest Dr. Tura who was the current witness, and was now concluding his testimony.

With a start, Randall realized that Dr. Tura was leaving the witness chair, and that the magistrate was addressing Randall himself.

"Monsieur Randall, I am now prepared to receive
your testimony. State your profession."

"I am the head of a public relations firm in New York."

"What were the circumstances that brought you to
Rome?"

"Well, that's a long story, your Honor."

"If you please, make it a short story, monsieur," said

Magistrate Le Clere curtly and without humor. "Come straight as possible to the fact of your appearance in Orly Airport yesterday."

Randall was stumped. How to turn a mountain into a molehill? He must try. He must prepare the way, as clearly as possible, for de Vroome. "It all started when I was summoned to a meeting in New York by a well-known religious publisher, Mr. George L. Wheeler." He glanced at Wheeler, who was concentrating on the toes of his shoes, refusing to acknowledge this mention of his name. "Mr. Wheeler wished to engage my services to publicize a new Bible. He represented an international syndicate of publishers of religious books—men who are present in this room—which was preparing a revision of the New Testament based on a startling archeological find. If you would like to know the contents of this find—?"

"Not necessary," said Magistrate Le Clere. "I have a deposition from Monsieur Fontaine summarizing the contents of the International New Testament."

Ah, Randall thought, our good judge has already been briefed by the gentlemen from Resurrection Two.

"You were hired to direct the publicity of this new Bible?" the magistrate asked.

"Yes, sir, I was."

"Did you believe in its authenticity?"

"Yes, sir, I did."

"Do you still regard the added contents of the International New Testament as authentic?"

"I do not, sir. Quite the contrary. I regard the added contents as blatant and outright forgeries, as I do the contents of the leather pouch taken from me at Orly Airport yesterday."

The magistrate produced a handkerchief and blew his nose loudly. "Very well, monsieur. What brought about your disenchantment?"

"If I may explain—"

"Do explain, but confine yourself to facts relevant to this hearing and the indictment."

There was so much Randall wanted to relate now, the compounding of so many suspicions, the mounting of so.

many coincidences, yet he knew that these would not be accepted in evidence and would not bolster his defense. He searched his memory for hard facts, but they eluded him and it surprised and disconcerted him how few there were.

"Well, to be brief, sir, in my hotel room in Rome I met with the admitted forger of the James and Petronius manuscripts. He was a French citizen named Robert Lebrun. He—"

"How did you come upon him, monsieur?"

"I first learned of him through Dominee de Vroome."

"Had Dominee de Vroome met this alleged forger?"

"Not exactly, your Honor."

"Either he met him or did not meet him. Which?"

"The Dominee told me he saw him, but he did not meet him. He did know about him through a friend."

"But you yourself met the alleged forger?"

"I did. Through a clue found in the papers of Professor Monti's estate, I was led to Lebrun. I persuaded Lebrun to tell me how he had forged the Gospel According to James and the Petronius Parchment. He told me he spent long years plotting and preparing his hoax. He was an incomparable biblical scholar and a genius at counterfeiting. He related every step of his preparation to me. I was convinced that he spoke the truth."

"And you obtained the fragment found in your suitcase from this Lebrun?" asked the magistrate.

"No."

"You did not? He did not sell it to you?"

"He was prepared to, and I was prepared to buy it, to prove to the publishers that their new gospel was a fraud and that they dared not put forth their International New Testament. However, Lebrun was prevented from delivering his evidence of forgery—this fragment your police took from me—into my hands."

"He was prevented? How was he prevented?"

"He was killed, exterminated, in a so-called accident on the day he was to deliver it."

Magistrate Le Clere glowered at Randall. "Are you

telling me, monsieur, this Lebrun is not alive to corroborate your testimony here?"

"I'm afraid he's not. Lebrun is dead."

"So we have only your word?"

"You have more, your Honor. You have Lebrun's evidence of forgery in that fragment your officials confiscated at the airport. You see, sir, dead men do tell tales. Because, in a manner of speaking, Lebrun himself, even after his death, led me to find his proof."

Randall recounted how the personal effects he had examined in the Roman morgue had led him to the Monti excavation outside Ostia Antica.

"Once I unearthed Lebrun's evidence," Randall concluded, "I had to be positive it was, indeed, a fake. From Rome, I telephoned Professor Aubert's office to make an appointment. I wanted him to do a radiocarbon test of the fragment. Next, I telephoned Dominee de Vroome and requested his cooperation in determining whether the Aramaic text in the papyrus—and the invisible writing Lebrun had added to the fragment—supported Lebrun's confession of forgery. There was no doubt, in my mind, about the hoax. But I knew that I must have a more scholarly opinion to convince the publishers that it was a fraud and should be abandoned. So quite naturally, I left Rome and arrived in Paris with this piece of papyrus, knowing it was no national treasure, was utterly worthless except as evidence for stopping the Resurrection Two project. When the airport officer tried to confiscate my one piece of proof, I instinctively tried to recover it. I did not intend violence. I meant only to preserve a shred of evidence that could save the public from one more lie, and the publishers from making a grave mistake."

"You are finished, monsieur?"

"I am."

"You will remain in the dock. We will continue with the final two witnesses." He considered a slip of paper beside him, and looked up. "If Professor Henri Aubert will please come forward?"

Professor Aubert, with his pomaded pompadour and fastidious attire, was impressive as he settled in the witness chair. He had passed Randall stiffly, without a glance, and now he was ready to read from his written report.

His testimony was the shortest, requiring no more than a minute, and for Randall his summation was not unexpected.

"The ordinary radiocarbon test can be accomplished in one to two weeks. Through use of a newly modified counting apparatus, my assistants and I, working into the night, were able in fourteen hours to test a minuscule portion of the papyrus fragment submitted to us by the judiciary last evening. I have here the result."

He unfurled a piece of yellow typescript. He read from it. " 'According to our measurement made of the papyrus fragment in question, after due testing in our radiocarbon dating apparatus, the date of life of the papyrus may be reasonably placed in the year 62 A.D. As a result, the single fragment of papyrus submitted to us as of late yesterday may be considered authentic by scientific standards. Signed, Henri Aubert.' "

The magistrate seemed impressed. "The fragment brought into this country, then, by the defendant in the dock, it is of unquestioned authenticity?"

"Absolutely." Aubert held up a finger. "I must add, I limit verification to the age of the papyrus fragment itself. I cannot speak of the authenticity of the text. That decision I leave entirely to the judgment of Dominee de Vroome."

"Thank you, Professor."

As Aubert left to return to his seat in the second row, Dominee de Vroome rose and waited in the aisle.

The magistrate addressed him. "If Dominee Maertin de Vroome will come forward to conclude the testimony in the hearing, the court will be honored."

Eagerly, Randall watched the imposing Dutch cleric stride to the witness chair. He hoped to catch de Vroome's eye, but the theologian's frosted profile was all that Randall could see.

Standing beside the witness chair, formidable in his unadorned black cassock, he faced the *juge d'instruction*.

Magistrate Le Clere undertook his examination immediately. "Is it true, Dominee de Vroome, that the defendant, as stated in his testimony, telephoned you from Rome and requested you to render an opinion on a missing portion of Papyrus Number 3 which he claimed was evidence of forgery?"

"It is true."

"Is it true that you were also requested by a branch of the Sûreté Nationale, through the good offices of the Louvre's special laboratory, to make a study of this fragment to determine its value?"

"Yes, that is also true."

The magistrate was pleased. "Then the judgment you render will satisfy both the prosecution and the defense."

Dominee de Vroome offered a lipless smile. "I doubt that my judgment can satisfy both sides. It can satisfy only one."

The magistrate also smiled. "I will rephrase. Both the prosecution and the defense are satisfied with your credentials for passing a judgment on this matter."

"It would appear so."

"Therefore, I will waive any inquiry into your qualifications as an Aramaic scholar and a textual expert in Christian and Roman history. All parties will accept your judgment. You have studied this papyrus fragment confiscated from Monsieur Randall?"

"I have. I have examined it with minute care through the night and this morning. I have studied it in its context, against the entire collection of the Monti papyri, which was made available to me by the proprietors of the International New Testament. I have inspected it, also, in the light of information given by one Robert Lebrun and by the defendant, Steven Randall, with regard to the Aramaic text's being a forgery and the papyrus leaf's containing invisible writing and a drawing—done in ink prepared from an ancient Roman formula—used by Lebrun to prove the gospel was of his own making."

Magistrate Le Clere bent closer to the witness. "Dominee de Vroome, were you able to come to an absolute decision on the value of this papyrus fragment?"

"I was able to do so. I have come to a judgment."

"Dominee de Vroome, what is your judgment?"

Dominee de Vroome, every inch the apostle of God, permitted a theatrical interval to pass before his vibrant voice resounded through the hearing chamber. "I hold only one conclusion. It is my unqualified judgment that the fragment of papyrus the defendant brought out of Italy yesterday is *not* a forgery—is beyond question an authentic and inspired work from the pen of James the Just, brother of Jesus—and as such it is not only a national treasure of Italy, but one of all mankind, and a fitting part of the greatest discovery in the two-thousand-year saga of Christianity. I congratulate the proprietors of the International New Testament on being able to add it to the inspired work they are about to give to the world!"

With that, without waiting to hear the response from the magistrate, Dominee de Vroome turned and briskly strode toward the seats where the publishers were on their feet according him a boisterous ovation.

De Vroome's pronouncement burst upon Steven Randall like the explosion of a hand grenade. He recoiled, shattered, stricken speechless by this unexpected turn of events.

As Dominee de Vroome went past him, Randall wanted to scream out: de Vroome, you conniving, double-crossing, dirty, sonofabitch.

In the uproar, he could hardly comprehend what followed.

But he was unable to utter a word, a sound. He had fallen back against the wall—impaled, as if an invisible spear had been driven through him.

Magistrate Le Clere was saying, "The court is ready to render a verdict—unless there is more testimony to be heard. Does any other party present wish to be heard?"

A hand went up. George L. Wheeler, waving an arm to gain attention while his colleagues gathered around de Vroome, was requesting permission to be heard. "Your Honor, I request a brief recess to speak to the defendant privately before the verdict is rendered."

"Your request is granted, Monsieur Wheeler. You have

the court's permission to speak to the defendant in privacy." He rapped his gavel sharply three times. "The hearing stands recessed. We will reconvene in precisely thirty minutes to deliver the verdict in this case."

"GODDAMMIT," barked George L. Wheeler, "I don't know why I'm even bothering about you."

"You're bothering about me," said Randall calmly, "because you want your new Bible to appear pristine and above mortal doubt, and I represent a source of defection and potential dissent, and you don't want that."

They were together, alone, in the windowless anteroom adjacent to the hearing chamber, both doors shut tight. Randall, his rage at de Vroome having subsided into his familiar cynical distrust of all men, sat in one of the two straight chairs in the cubbyhole, his legs wearily outstretched, as he steadily puffed at his pipe.

He continued to observe the American publisher marching back and forth before him, and despite the distaste he felt for Wheeler, he also regarded him with a new and grim respect. After all, this shallow, mealymouthed peddler of Bibles had somehow managed to turn a more intellectual, infinitely superior enemy, the Dominee de Vroome, into a turncoat and a subservient member of the orthodox religious establishment. Randall realized, with regret, how badly he had underestimated this commercial buffoon. Wheeler was capable of a legerdemain, a diabolism, Randall had not suspected before. He wondered whether Wheeler would try to cast a spell over him. Else, why did the repulsive sorcerer want to see him in privacy?

Wheeler had ceased his pacing to come to a halt before Randall.

"So that's what you think," he said, "that I'm here to convert you, so there won't be any dissent? You're an awful smart-ass, Steve, and for all your pretensions of high-mindedness and brain power, you're goddam stupid. Listen to me. Your opposition would mean nothing to us, would amount to no more than the inaudible croakings of a small frog in a big pond. No, you're a thousand-percent wrong about my motives. Considering the way you tried to sabotage us, I should let you go down the drain. But I can't. For one thing—and you won't believe this because you're still a smart-ass—I happen to have affection for you, fatherly affection. I've come to like you. And I can't stand being wrong about where I put my affection and my trust. For another thing—and I'm not ashamed to admit it—I'm a businessman, and proud of it, and I can use you. Not just for the announcement ceremony. That's under control. This minute, radio and television stations, newspapers, in every corner of the world, are alerting the public to an international broadcast to be made on Friday heralding a biblical discovery of a momentous nature. So that part of it has begun to roll. But I never let myself forget that our selling campaign only starts with the official announcement ceremony taking place the day after tomorrow. And I want you in on my continuing campaign, because you know the project as few others do, you know what we're after, and you can be of tremendous help. I'm here speaking to you like this, because I'm banking on one thing. That you've learned your lesson."

"What lesson, George?" inquired Randall blandly.

"That you're utterly in the wrong about the authenticity of the James and Petronius documents, and we're in the right. And that you're ready to be man enough to admit it, and rejoin the team. Listen to me, Steve, if an important figure, a famous churchman and scholar like the Dominee Maertin de Vroome, whose skepticism exceeded that of all others, could be man enough to see the light, admit to error, and offer himself in our support, I don't see why you can't do the same."

"De Vroome," said Randall, relighting his pipe. "I was going to ask you about de Vroome. How'd you pull that one off?"

Wheeler drew himself up, offended. "You just won't let go, will you, Steve? Everyone is crooked—"

"I didn't say *everyone*."

"Of course not. You were excepting yourself." He

poked a finger at Randall. "Stop being a smart-ass and listen to me. No one, but no one, could bribe or buy out a human being with the integrity of a de Vroome. He had to come to his final judgment of our project using his own good conscience. And he did. Until now, when he was sniping at us, trying to subvert us, he never knew exactly what we were trying to do or the details of the magnificent documents we had in our possession. But when he came to us to be shown—and since it was the eve of the announcement, we felt he could be shown—he dropped his antagonism and resistance at once. He saw that we had the real thing, the real Christ, and that mankind would be the benefactor in receiving Him through the International New Testament. De Vroome capitulated immediately. He wanted to be on the side of the angels and the Holy Ghost, just as he was minutes ago in this French courtroom."

"So now he's supporting you all the way," said Randall.

"All the way, Steve. He'll be on the platform beside us in Amsterdam when the Good News is broadcast to the four corners of the earth. It was not easy for him, Steve, a big man like that, to confess error, to change his thinking. But as I said, and I repeat it, Maertin de Vroome was man enough to do just that. And Dr. Deichhardt and the rest of us, we understood how difficult this was for de Vroome, and in turn, we showed our charity in our own fashion. Indeed, to prove to you we're not the villains you make us out to be, I can tell you we met de Vroome halfway."

"Halfway?" said Randall. "Where's that, George?"

"That's where mature men try to iron out their differences, work together to present a solid front. Since de Vroome was prepared to support us, we were prepared to support him. We've withdrawn our backing of the candidacy of Dr. Jeffries to throw our united support behind Dominee de Vroome for the next general secretary of the World Council of Churches."

"I see," said Randall.

He saw. He knocked the ashes out of his pipe—ashes

THE WORD 635

—into the standing ashtray beside him. Yes, he saw. Everything.

"And what about Dr. Jeffries?" said Randall. "Where does that put him?"

"It puts him in another job, the job of chairman of the Central Committee of the World Council."

"An honorary job. You mean he doesn't mind becoming a figurehead?"

"Steve, Dr. Jeffries and the rest of us take a different view of these matters than you do. We do not think of our own vanity. We have a cause held in common. Unity is what it is all about. Small sacrifices are expected. The important thing is that with de Vroome on our side, we have unity."

"You certainly have," said Randall, trying to subdue the vitriol in his tone.

"Now, with everything settled, with a dynamo like de Vroome heading the World Council," Wheeler went on, "and with unanimous ecclesiastical backing of the International New Testament, we are assured of the greatest return to religion and revival of faith since the Dark Ages. The next century will become known as the Age of Peace."

Hiding his disgust, Randall straightened in his chair. "Okay, great, George, good work. Just satisfy me by explaining one thing. I've talked to de Vroome. I know what he stands for—stood for. Just tell me how a radical reformer like that managed to compromise all he represented to go along with your conservative orthodoxy?"

Wheeler looked hurt. "You have a mistaken opinion of us. We're anything but hidebound fundamentalists. We've always been ready to accommodate the shifts and changes necessary to fill the spiritual and earthly needs of humanity. That's the miracle of the Man from Galilee. He was flexible, understanding, compromising. And we are His children. We are flexible, also, in order to serve best the common good. Steve, we know compromise is never one-sided. When de Vroome accepted our discovery, was prepared to end his opposition and rebellion, we were prepared to make him the head of the World Council with everything that entails. That means we were prepared to go along with him on a certain amount of reform, not only in interpretation of the Scriptures, of liturgy, but also in areas of social reformation and efforts to make the church more responsive to human needs. As a result of this compromise, this healing of a dangerous schism, we now go forward not only with a new Bible but with a new and dynamic world church."

Randall sat very still, staring at this sanctimonius double dealer.

It's the ruthless, happy club, Randall thought. The power club. Like a giant anteater, with a snout called compromise, giving a little, taking a lot, it lapped up all resistance. It was invincible. Like Cosmos Enterprises. Like munitions cartels. Like big governments. Like worldwide banking. Like one orthodox faith, played by the numbers. He saw, clearly, at last, how this latest amalgamation had come about. He, Randall, had been the unwitting catalyst. He had found the weapon to destroy what was truly cynical and anti-people, the weapon that would bring an end to Resurrection Two. He had passed it on, in trust, to Maertin de Vroome. With this weapon, de Vroome had the instrument and leverage to force the leaders of Resurrection Two into a compromise. Recognize me and I'll recognize you. Resist me, and with Randall's weapon I'll fight you, and ultimately destroy you. And in the end, de Vroome had preferred not extended civil war to achieve total victory, but immediate compromise for instant half-victory. Once installed as general secretary for the World Council, he would be a Judas goat leading the faithful into Wheeler's fold.

And in this big scheme of things, Randall could see, only one person had been left high and dry. Himself.

The point was obvious. Resistance by one alone is impossible. Hang together, or hang alone. Together, only a suffering of the soul; alone, death.

"What do you want of me, George?" he asked quietly. "You want me to be a man like de Vroome. Is that it?"

"I want you to face the facts, as de Vroome did. The facts, and nothing more. You've indulged yourself in your reckless games, pursuing foolish suspicions, consorting with criminals and crackpots, and you've produced nothing but further substantiation of the International New Testament—and a pack of trouble for yourself. Now admit that you've been wrong."

"And if I admit it, what then?"

"Then we might be able to save you," said Wheeler carefully. "You're in deep trouble in that courtroom. I'm sure the magistrate will throw the book at you. You'll wind up in the Bastille for God knows how long, and in disgrace, and you'll have gained nothing. The market for dissenting martyrs in the near future will be very poor. When you go back in there to hear the verdict and the sentence, request a final statement. We'll see that you're permitted to give one. Monsieur Fontaine has great influence here. Our project is much respected here."

"What statement should I make, George?"

"A simple one, made forthrightly and humbly, retracting your previous testimony. State that you heard an authentic fragment of papyrus, a missing portion of James, had been found in Rome. As a devoted member of Resurrection Two, you set out to recover the fragment for its rightful owner. In Rome, you found the fragment in the possession of a hardened criminal, Robert Lebrun, who had stolen it from Professor Monti. You bought him off for a pittance. You had no idea the Italian government would object to your taking that fragment out of Italy. You simply considered it to be a part of the James papyri in Amsterdam. You carried it to France quite openly for routine authentication. You made no attempt to smuggle it in. When you were found out, you panicked. You hadn't known you'd broken a law, and you got scared. You pretended the fragment was a forgery, worthless, merely to prove you weren't handling a national treasure, and you made up that story to protect yourself. It was a mistake caused by ignorance of the law and overenthusiasm for our project. Say you are sorry, and you beg the forgiveness of the court. That's all you have to say."

"And if I do that, what will the magistrate say?"

"He'll consult with us, with the five of us and the Italian government's representative, and there'll be no more problem. The magistrate will accept our recommendation. He'll reduce your fine and suspend your sentence, and you can walk out of here a free man, your head held high, and join us once more in producing the great press show and an unforgettable historic drama the morning after tomorrow from the royal palace in Amsterdam."

"Sounds appealing, I must admit. However, what if I refuse to retract?"

The smile disappeared from Wheeler's face. "We wash our hands of you. We leave you to the mercy of the court. We will be unable to keep your behavior a secret, even from Ogden Towery and Cosmos Enterprises." He waited. "What do you say, Steve?"

Randall shrugged. "I don't know."

"After all this, you don't know?"

"I just don't know what to say."

Wheeler frowned, and looked at his gold wristwatch. "Ten minutes to make up your mind," he said grimly. "Maybe you'd better spend those ten minutes with someone who has more influence on you." He started for the door. "Maybe you'll find something to say to her." He opened the door, beckoned to someone outside, and glanced back at Randall. "Your last chance, Steve. Take it."

He went out the doorway, and a moment later, Angela Monti came through it, hesitating, closing the door behind her.

Randall rose slowly to his feet. It seemed a lifetime since he had seen her last. She looked disconcertingly like she had looked when he had first set eyes upon her—ages ago, by emotion's calendar—in Milan. She was wearing a silk blouse, sufficiently sheer to reveal her white lace half-bra, and a wide suede belt, and a short summer skirt. She removed her sunglasses, and her green almond eyes studied him worriedly, as she waited for a word of welcome.

His first instinct had been to catch her in his arms, embrace her, pour out his heart.

But his heart was corroded with distrust. Wheeler had

said that he could spend his ten minutes with someone who might influence him. Angela was here to influence him.

He did not welcome her. "This is a surprise," he said.

"Hello, Steve. There is not much time. But I was allowed to see you."

She came across the gloomy room. Since he still made no effort to greet her, she went to the chair across from him and, poised, she sat down on the edge of it.

"Who sent you here?" he asked harshly. "Wheeler and the rest of his Galilee Mafia?"

Her fingers tightened on her suede purse. "Nothing has changed, I see. Except you are more bitter. No, Steve, I came here from Amsterdam at my own request. I heard what had happened. Last night, after you were arrested, Naomi phoned me for some information, and she told me about your trouble. Apparently, Dominee de Vroome had called the publishers from Paris. They were all leaving immediately to join de Vroome. Since Naomi was also going, I asked whether I could come along."

"You weren't in the hearing room."

"No. I didn't want to be there. I am no Mary. I have no taste for Golgotha. I suspected what might happen. Late last night, after Mr. Wheeler finished meeting with de Vroome, he visited me and told me everything he and the publishers had heard from de Vroome. Then, a little while ago, when Mr. Wheeler was with you, Naomi filled me in on what had taken place during the hearing."

Randall sat down. "Then you know they're trying to crucify me. Not only Wheeler and his cohorts, but de Vroome as well."

"Yes, Steve, as I said, I was afraid it would happen. And now, from what Naomi has told me, apparently it did."

"Do you know Wheeler just asked the heretic to recant, so that he could be free to rejoin Resurrection Two?"

"I am not surprised," said Angela. "They need you."

"They need unanimity. They don't want troublemakers." He saw that she was uncomfortable, and he wanted to challenge her. "What about you? What do you want?"

"I want you to know that whatever you decide, my feelings for you will not change."

"Even if I continue to attack your father's discovery? Even if I succeed in exposing it and destroying it—and with it, your father's reputation?"

The beautiful Italian face had grown taut. "My father's reputation is no longer the issue. The issue is the life or death of hope. I know you found and sided with Robert Lebrun, as did de Vroome at first. It did not turn me away from you. I am here."

"Why?"

"To let you know that even if you have no faith—no faith in what my father found, in those who support it, or even faith in me—you may still find the right way."

"The right way?" Randall repeated angrily, voice rising. "You mean like Dominee de Vroome found it? You mean you'd like me to sell out like de Vroome did?"

"How can you be so certain that de Vroome sold out, as you put it?" She was trying to be reasonable. "Don't you believe de Vroome is a man of decency and faith?"

"He may be that," Randall conceded, "but he still got his price—the World Council of Churches. Sure, you can call him decent if you feel that any means is justified by a worthy end, no matter what."

"Steve, do you not believe that also? Do you not believe the end is what really counts—if the means used to reach it harms no one?"

"No," he said firmly, "not if the end is a lie. Then what is achieved will harm everyone."

"Steve, Steve," she pleaded, "you have no evidence, not one iota of proof, that the James and Petronius stories of Christ are a lie. You have only your suspicions. You are alone in this."

He was becoming agitated. "Angela, if I had not been there alone in Rome—if you had been beside me those last days—you'd be beside me right now. If you could have met and heard Lebrun, and experienced what happened after, you'd have had your eyes opened and your faith would no longer be blind. You'd have asked yourself hard questions, as I did, and you'd have found hard answers. How could Lebrun, a man who had survived every kind of brutality, who had reached his eighties alert and vigorous, who lived in Rome for so many years, wander in front of a hit-and-run driver and be accidentally killed the very day he was to retrieve the evidence of his forgery for me? I can guess how that happened now. Wheeler and the publishers, or de Vroome—I can speak of them as one now—kept an eye on me. Just as de Vroome knew I'd seen your father at the asylum, he had the means to know I might try to find Lebrun. I was probably shadowed. My meeting with Lebrun in Doney's and the Excelsior was probably reported. Lebrun was probably followed from the Excelsior to his home. And the next day he was mercilessly run down and liquidated. Angela, we don't live in a sweet, kind fairy-tale world when the stakes are so high. The life of an obscure ex-convict would be expendable if his extinction might promote the glory of Christ, save the church, enhance the sale of millions of new Bibles, and raise a new conspirator to the highest seat in the Protestant hierarchy."

"Steve—"

"No, wait, hear me out. One more question—in fact, several more. Who knew I had gone to Ostia Antica, who knew I had found the papyrus fragment, and who got the Italian government to tip off customs in Paris that I was carrying this evidence of forgery? The answers are obvious now. De Vroome knew Lebrun had such a fragment. Then, from me, de Vroome learned I had the fragment in my possession. De Vroome went back to Wheeler, Deichhardt, Fontaine, the others, and made his deal—or clinched his deal—and they set out to grab me at Orly and eliminate the evidence of forgery, and eliminate me, as well, in the process. Those are the questions. Don't tell me they don't bother you, either, Angela?"

For several seconds, she fiddled with her sunglasses. "Steve, how can I speak to you? We speak two tongues—yours the language of skepticism, mine the language of faith—and so our answers to the same questions translate differently. Lebrun's death on the day he was to help you? Is it so unusual for an old man of over eighty, wandering our busy streets of Rome, to be struck by an automobile? Steve, I am a Roman. I read and hear of that happening in our city. The drivers are the most wild and reckless in Europe. That one should run down an old man? An ordinary occurrence, a familiar accident, not a conspiracy, not a murder. De Vroome, Wheeler, Dr. Jeffries murderers? It is absurd to imagine. As to your being caught in customs? The Italian government has many agents and spies around its national treasures. You were seen fleeing from Ostia Antica. It would have been enough to alert someone. But even if it had been those in Resurrection Two who arranged for your arrest. Is that bad or illogical? They had to see what you had uncovered, before you jumped to conclusions and misused it. They had to confiscate and test and examine it. Had it been evidence of forgery, I have no doubt they would have given in to you and postponed or stopped the pub- lication of the International New Testament. But when they learned, from the very one you had selected as an expert, that your piece of evidence was as authentic as the papyri that had already been discovered by my father, they had to stop you, proceed against you to prevent an undeserved scandal. Steve, don't you see? The language of faith provides different answers."

"Does it provide an answer to the one question I haven't asked?"

She looked puzzled. "What is it? Ask it."

"How did a certain Professor Augusto Monti come to dig at Ostia Antica?"

She appeared confused. "Because somebody found a piece of papyrus outside the ruins six years ago and showed it to him."

"You did not know it was Lebrun who brought the clue to your father?"

"No. I never heard his name until Mr. Wheeler men- tioned it last night."

"Didn't you know Lebrun met your father at Doney's last year on the day your father—your father had his breakdown?"

"No. I never knew that until yesterday when Mr.

Wheeler told me you claimed to have seen a note of such a meeting in my father's appointment book."

"And you see nothing unusual about that? Nothing suspicious?"

"No. My father dealt with many different people that day and in the days before."

"All right, Angela, let me test your faith. Would you be ready to tell the magistrate that your father met with Lebrun in Doney's last year? It would establish the relationship between your father and Lebrun. It would cast further doubts on the case, and might lead to a new search for the final truth. Do you have faith enough to do that?"

She shook her head. "Steve," she said, "I have already revealed what I know to the magistrate, in the deposition given him by the heads of the project. Last night, I called Lucrezia in Rome and had her read us my father's notation in his appointment book. Everyone, the magistrate included, felt that the initials 'R.L.' were hardly conclusive evidence. But even if the initials meant Robert Lebrun, what would this prove in fact? Nevertheless, I wanted the magistrate to know about it. You see, Steve, I am not afraid. When one has faith, one is not afraid of truth."

The wind had gone out of him. He sat, at a loss. One last gasp. "Would you be ready to offer that information to one other person?"

"Who?"

"Cedric Plummer. Would you be ready to confirm what Plummer had only heard from Lebrun—that your father actually met with Lebrun?"

She threw up her hands. "Steve, Steve, he, too, already knows it. Plummer knows everything. He would see nothing suspicious in it. When Dominee de Vroome joined Resurrection Two, then Plummer also joined. He was converted, so to speak. He laid aside his poison pen, and will now write the exclusive history of the entire project from six years ago to today."

Randall sank back in his chair. It was too much. Every inch of enemy territory had been invaded and occupied. Which meant Herr Hennig's neck was saved. Plummer's blackmail of Hennig, in an attempt to obtain the International New Testament in advance and expose it, had been made unnecessary.

He looked off. Someone had been rapping on the door, and now it opened. The court clerk put his head in. "Monsieur Randall, it is time for the verdict."

Randall stood up. "Half a minute," he said. Angela had come to her feet across from him. He confronted her once more. "You want me to retract, don't you?"

She put on her sunglasses. "I want you to do what you must do, no less and no more." She considered saying something else, and finally she said it. "I really came here to tell you, whatever you are, whatever you will become, I could love you—if you could learn to love in return, to love yourself first, and to love me. But you cannot learn to do this until you have faith, in humanity and in the future. I am sorry for you, Steve, but more, I am sorry for us. I would sacrifice anything for you—except faith. I hope someday you will understand. Now, you will do as you wish."

She hurried from the room, and he was alone.

"YOU DESIRE to make a final statement before the verdict, Monsieur Randall?"

"I do, your Honor," he said to the magistrate. "I've reviewed in my own mind the testimony I already gave in this hearing room. I want to say that I went to Rome with no intention of undermining Resurrection Two or the International New Testament, but with the sole motive of verifying, for myself and for the directors of the project, that they had found, beyond a shadow of a doubt, the real Jesus Christ."

He saw that Wheeler, the other four publishers, even Angela, had leaned forward in their front-row seats.

Randall faced the magistrate. "What I heard in Rome, what I saw with my own eyes, has convinced me that the papyrus fragment I was led to and which I brought into France, as well as the entire collection of papyri and the parchment that serve as the basis for the International New Testament, is a modern fabrication, a sham and a fraud, produced by a master forger's hand. I believe the products of Professor Monti's find are worthless, and the Jesus offered by James the Just and Petronius is a graven image and a spurious Christ. Despite earlier testimony to the contrary, I still maintain the evidence I had on my person upon entering France was a forgery—worthless, I repeat—and therefore I committed no crime. I trust the court, taking into consideration my own firsthand knowledge and investigations, motivated by no personal gain, will find me innocent. Moreover, I pray the court will return to me the missing portion of Papyrus Number 3, which is in a sense a legacy left to me by Robert Lebrun, so that I may have its contents assessed and examined by more objective experts elsewhere in the world. I have nothing further to add."

"You are finished, Monsieur Randall?"

"I am."

"Very well. The defendant has been heard. The verdict in his case will now be rendered." Magistrate Le Clere rustled a sheaf of papers on his desk. "There are two counts in the indictment. The second count of public disturbance and criminal assault is hereby dropped, in consideration of the defendant's heretofore law-abiding record as a citizen in his own country and in consideration of the unusual circumstances and provocation surrounding his physical arrest. As to the first count, that of conveying into France, without proper declaration, an ancient document of inestimable value and in itself the treasure of the nation from which it was transported—"

Randall held his breath.

"—the court finds the document authentic, and the defendant guilty as charged."

Stonily, Randall waited.

Alone, he thought.

"Sentence will now be passed," the magistrate continued. "The defendant, Steven Randall, is fined five thousand francs and sentenced to jail for three months. In view of the defendant's seemingly sincere claim that he did not break the law deliberately, and in consideration of a certain request made to this court by the defendant's clients, the fine is hereby waived and the sentence of three months is suspended. However, to protect his clients, and to prevent another public disturbance, the defendant will be remanded to his temporary prison cell, there to serve two days' incarceration, until the announcement of the International New Testament has been made public. After forty-eight hours—namely at noon of Friday, the day following tomorrow—the defendant will be escorted from his prison cell under police guard to Orly Airport where he will be placed, at his own expense, on a flight to the United States, and therefore, expelled from France."

The magistrate cleared his throat.

"As for your request, Monsieur Randall, that the papyrus fragment in question be returned to your possession, the request is denied. Since authenticity has been established, the confiscated papyrus will be turned over to its present leaseholders, the directors of the International New Testament, Incorporated, otherwise known as Resurrection Two, to do with as they please."

He slapped both palms on his desk.

"The hearing stands adjourned."

From somewhere, two *agents de police* had appeared. Randall felt the cold metal on his wrists, and saw that he was manacled.

His eyes went to the rows of benches, avoiding Angela, holding on the jubilant Wheeler, Deichhardt, Fontaine, as they gathered around Dominee de Vroome.

As Randall watched, one thought entered his mind. Sacrilege or not, it had entered his mind and remained there.

Father, forgive them; for they know not what they do.

Father, he amended it, forgive them not for what they are doing to me, but for what they are doing to the Holy Spirit and to unsuspecting, helpless, gullible humanity throughout the world.

ONE OTHER BAD MOMENT—not bad, actually, but shocking, incredible, and somewhat bizarre—and that a half hour later when he had been returned to the Dépôt.

He had been sentenced to expulsion from France, at his own expense, as an undesirable element. Inspector Bavoux, of the Garde Républicaine, had requested money from him to pay for his one-way ticket back to New York. Randall had searched his wallet and traveler's checks and was dismayed to learn that he did not have the necessary sum with him. He was advised that he had better raise the money somewhere at once.

He remembered that he had not brought with him the $20,000 he had placed in the safe deposit box in the Hotel Excelsior in Rome. Before leaving for Paris, he had arranged with the hotel's cashier to have it transferred back to his New York account. Since he lacked that money, his first notion was to telephone Thad Crawford or Wanda and arrange for one of them to cable him the necessary sum, but once again he recollected that he had a close friend in Paris.

And so, from the warden's office, he telephoned Sam Halsey, at the Associated Press.

Without going into the whole complicated business of Resurrection Two and the International New Testament and Lebrun's papyrus fragment, he told Halsey that he had been arrested at Orly yesterday for bringing an undeclared art object through customs. It was all a mistake, but nevertheless he was being detained at the Dépôt of the Palais de Justice.

"I need some money, Sam. I happen to be short at the moment. I'll pay you back from the States in a few days."

"You need money? How much? You name it."

He named it.

"I'll send it right over," said Halsey. "Hey, wait a minute, Steve, you haven't told me—did you plead guilty or not guilty?"

"Not guilty, of course."

"Well, when's your trial set for?"

"I've already had my trial. I was tried this morning and found guilty. I was sentenced and fined, both suspended. My goods were confiscated. I'm being expelled from France. That's why I need the money."

There was a prolonged pause on the other end of the

line. "Let me get this straight, Steve," said Halsey. "You were arrested—when?"

"Last night."

"And tried and sentenced this morning?"

"That's right, Sam."

"Hold it, Steve—now maybe one of us is crazy, but that can't be—I mean, that can't be, it doesn't work that way in France. You'd better tell me what happened this morning."

Simply, briefly—conscious of his guards hovering over him—Randall related to Halsey what he could of the session before the *juge d'instruction,* the final verdict, the sentence.

Nonplussed, Halsey was stuttering at the other end of the phone. "But—but that can't be—can't—it makes no sense. Are you positive it happened just the way you've told me?"

"Sam, for Chrissakes, that's exactly what happened. I went through the whole thing in the past few hours. Why should I make it up?"

"My God!" exclaimed Halsey. "My God, in all my years here—well, I've heard rumors of duplicity, kangaroo trials—but this is the first time I've heard it firsthand from anyone."

Randall was utterly bewildered. "What do you mean? What was wrong about it?"

"What was right about it, you mean! Listen, Steve, my sweet innocent abroad, you've been taken, you've been railroaded. Don't you know anything at all about French legal procedure? Sure, you're booked for an offense. Sure, you go before a *juge d'instruction* to be heard. But that's only a preliminary examination. A *juge d'instruction* has no judicial power whatsoever to render a verdict and pronounce a sentence. He can only decide whether it's a nonsuit, and if it is, charges should be dismissed—or he forwards the case for prosecution to the Parquet. If you're to be prosecuted, it takes six to twelve months before you go on trial in front of three judges of the Tribunal Correctionnel. Then there's a real trial, prosecution and defense attorneys, the works, before a verdict is rendered.

The one exception to that procedure, a rare one, is when you're caught *en flagrant délit,* caught in the act of the crime, and there are no doubts whatsoever. Then, and only then, can you be put on immediate trial before the Tribunal de Flagrant Délit—which would be more like what you just went through, except it would still be heard by three judges and there would be a deputy public prosecutor and a defense attorney. But you didn't go through that, apparently—"

"No. I definitely didn't."

"What you went through—it seems to be a bastard combination of both procedures—but it has nothing to do with French law, at least as I understand it."

Yet, Randall recalled, the police had offered him the opportunity to find an attorney, probably to disarm him, avert any suspicion. Then, he recalled, they had made it difficult for him, telling him his case would be delayed if he retained legal counsel. But, he asked himself, what if he *had* obtained an attorney? The answer seemed obvious. The ones in control would have changed the scheduled proceedings into something that conformed to French law, even if it meant unwanted publicity. But either way, Randall realized, the result had been preordained. The verdict had to be guilty.

"No question about it," Halsey was saying, "that was a kangaroo court, and you were beautifully railroaded." He paused. "Steve, this sounds as if somebody high up, very high up, wanted to get you out of the way pretty badly, get you out of the way quickly and quietly. I don't know what you're involved in, but it must be damn important to someone."

"Yes," said Randall dully, "it's damn important to someone, to several someones."

"Steve," said Halsey urgently, "do you want me to get into this?"

Randall considered his friend's intervention. At last, he said, "Sam, do you like working in France, in Europe?"

"What do you mean? I'm mad about it."

"Then don't get into this."

"But justice, Steve—what about justice?"

"Leave that to me." He paused. "I appreciate your love, Sam. Now send the money."

He hung up.

Justice, he thought.

Liberté, Égalité, Fraternité, he thought.

Then he realized that those words were only the promise of France. But he had not been tried by France, a mere government power. He had been tried by a super-power. He had been tried by Resurrection Two.

IT WAS EVERYWHERE this bright Friday morning, this morning of his release from prison. It was the greatest story Randall could remember in his lifetime.

In all his years on earth, he was sure there had been nothing that exceeded the coverage and attention given this event. Certainly the announcements of the Japanese attack on Pearl Harbor, the fall of Berlin and death of Hitler, the launching of Sputnik I into outer space, the assassination of John F. Kennedy, the first step on the moon by Neil Armstrong, had been momentous—but to the best of Randall's memory the public sensation each had generated had been matched by the electrifying and thunderous news from the royal palace in Amsterdam that Jesus Christ had undeniably lived on this earth, as both human being and as spiritual messenger of the Maker.

For so many days, Randall had been so absorbed in the technicalities and dilemmas of authenticity and truth, and in his own survival, that he had half forgotten the impact that the Gospel According to James and the Petronius Parchment might have on the millions and millions of frail and questing mortals.

But throughout the drive from the Dépôt of the Palais de Justice to Orly Airport outside Paris, Randall had observed evidence of reaction to this historic miracle on every street corner, in every café, at every shopwindow. Frenchmen and foreigners alike had turned out into the open, snatching up newspapers, glued to transistor radios, massed around storefront television sets, caught up in the passion.

In the police Citroën in which he rode with three blue-uniformed French law officers, Randall was a neglected minor player in the drama already under way.

He had sat in the rear seat wedged between two of the officers, Gorin, of the Sûreté Nationale, and an *agent de police* named Lefèvre, handcuffed to Gorin, who was on his left. Both officers had been lost in their special editions of *Le Figaro, Combat, Le Monde, L'Aurore,* virtually half the front pages given over to The Event. Randall glimpsed two of the giant headlines. One read: LE CHRIST REVIENT PARMI NOUS!—CHRIST RETURNS AMONG US. The other read: LE CHRIST RESSUSCITÉ PAR UNE NOUVELLE DÉCOUVERTE! —CHRIST RESURRECTED BY NEW DISCOVERY. Beneath the giant headlines were photographs of three of the original James papyri, the Petronius Parchment, the excavation site outside Ostia Antica, the revised portrait of Jesus as He had actually appeared in His life, the cover of the International New Testament.

In the front seat of the police car, the officer chauffeuring them had been silent all the way, spellbound by the preliminary commentaries that preceded the main announcement being broadcast in French from Amsterdam.

Occasionally, the officers on either side of Randall had read some piece of information aloud to one another, and sometimes, aware of Randall's inadequate French, they had translated it into English. From what Randall could make out, the newspaper accounts about the International New Testament, with its story of Jesus by His brother and its story of the trial by a centurion, were based on a limited advance release issued to the world press after midnight. The full details were being presented from a stage in the Burgerzaal—the vast Citizens' Hall—of the royal palace in Amsterdam. The complete revelation was being made before two thousand members of the press, who had been summoned to the auditorium from every civilized nation on earth, as well as to several billion television onlookers in every corner of the globe to whom the news was being transmitted via Intelsat V, a 1,900-circuit solid-state communications satellite orbiting the earth along with earlier sister satellites and relaying the picture images and commentaries.

Only once, in their ride, had the police officer named Lefèvre had a personal exchange with Randall. He had paused in his reading, looked at Randall incredulously, and said, "You were actually a part of this, monsieur?"

"I was."

"But then why do they deport you?"

"Because they are crazy," Randall had said. He had added, "Because I did not believe."

Lefèvre's eyes had widened. "Then you are the one who must be crazy."

They had drawn up before the Orly terminal, and the officer named Lefèvre had opened the back door of the vehicle, stepped down, and tried to help Randall out. Because he had been handcuffed to Gorin, Randall had been forced to back out, bruising his wrist and being painfully reminded of who he was and what was happening to him.

The ground floor of the Orly terminal, always noisy, was now hushed. As a convenience for passengers and visitors, and their own personnel, Air France had posted large-screen television sets the length and breadth of the main reception area. Around these sets, people were jammed ten to twenty persons deep. Even at the ticket and information counters, customers as well as service personnel absently went about their business while they concentrated on handy television screens.

The police officer, Lefèvre, went to pick up Randall's one-way transatlantic ticket that was being held for him, and confirm the boarding time. While he was gone, Gorin edged toward a cluster of people to watch the nearest television set, and Randall, linked to him at the wrist, was forced to go along.

Peering between the heads of the packed viewers, Randall tried to see the images on the screen as he listened to the commentator, speaking first in French, then in English, the two official languages used on this announcement day.

A camera was panning the interior of the Burgerzaal, the Citizens' Hall of the royal palace in Amsterdam. Row upon row of the press corps and visiting dignitaries were being shown, followed by intimate close-ups of the majestic setting. There were the vaulted windows, with brown shutters, each bearing an identical stylized gold flower in its center. There were the six crystal chandeliers above, originally colza oil lamps left behind by the Emperor Louis Napoleon. There were portions of the marble floor visible, inlaid with curving bands of brass representing the celestial globe. There were endless groups of statues, and it was only upon seeing the last group—Righteousness trampling Greed and Envy (Greed as Midas, Envy as Medusa)—that Randall lost his equanimity.

Greed, he thought bitterly, and almost as if on cue, the camera panned the platform, and there they all were, Randall's bêtes noires, each one.

The camera revealed each in his plush velvet chair, and the commentator identified each one. In the semicircle onstage, reverent, spiritual, otherworldly: Dr. Deichhardt, Wheeler, Fontaine, Sir Trevor, Gayda, and Dr. Jeffries, Dr. Knight, Monsignore Riccardi, the Reverend Zachery, Dr. Trautmann, Professor Sobrier, Dominee de Vroome and Professor Aubert, Hennig, and finally the only one who was a beauty among the beasts, Angela Monti (representing her ailing parent, Professor Monti, the Italian archeologist, explained the voice of the European Broadcasting Union.)

Dr. Deichhardt was coming forward to the podium, to the pulpit draped in satin decorated with a woven cross.

Dr. Deichhardt was reading aloud the full, detailed announcement of the discovery of the James gospel and the Petronius trial report, and giving a summary of their contents, and displaying a copy of the International New Testament that was being officially published on this history-making day.

Randall felt a hand on his arm. It was the police officer, Lefèvre, brandishing the ticket. "Do not lose it," he admonished Randall, "or you will be back in jail." He shoved the air flight ticket into Randall's jacket pocket. He

reached out and tugged at his colleague. "Gorin," he
whispered, "we have fifteen minutes before we put him on
the plane. Let's watch this up in the lounge where we
can sit."

Minutes later, entering the third-floor cocktail lounge
that teemed with people transfixed by the blaring television sets, Randall stood amazed. He had never witnessed
a scene such as this. There were spectators not only at
the tables, seated cross-legged or kneeling on the floor,
crouching in the aisles between tables, but spectators
standing, ringing the room, all of them riveting their attention on the dozen television sets.

But there was something more going on. Many of the
viewers, perhaps most of them, were behaving like pilgrims witnessing a miracle at Lourdes. Some were praying
to themselves, others praying aloud, yet others repeating
in undertones the words coming out of the television sets.
Some were weeping, others rocking back and forth, and in
a distant corner there was a sudden commotion. A woman, nationality undeterminable, had slumped into a faint,
and was being attended.

There was no place to sit, yet in minutes the maître
d'hôtel of the airport lounge had set up a table and
located three chairs for them. There was always a place,
Randall reminded himself, for the police.

Awkwardly, he sat next to his Siamese twin, Gorin,
and he glanced around the room, wondering whether any
of the people present had noticed his handcuffs. But no
one immediately surrounding him was interested in anything except what was being shown on the television
screens.

Randall brought himself to peer at a nearby screen,
and instantly he realized the motivating power for the
emotional reaction engulfing the lounge.

The ascetic countenance of Dominee Maertin de
Vroome, his lean frame garbed in an embroidered talar,
filled the screen. From the pulpit of the royal palace,
from the pages of the International New Testament opened
before him, he was reading aloud in French (while a bat-

tery of interpreters rendered instant translations into other
languages for audiences around the world) the Gospel
According to James in its entirety. His sonorous reciting
of the Word resounded through the lounge, as if it were
the voice of the Lord Himself, and even the praying and
weeping became muted.

From a distance, the incongruous, tinny public address
system intruded the announcement of a flight about to
leave, and the police officer, Lefèvre, crushed out the
butt of his cigarette and nodded to Randall. "Time to go."

On the way, from every direction, the persistent sounds
of television sets and transistor radios ambushed Randall
and the two police officers who flanked him.

At the boarding ramp, passengers were flowing into
the overseas jetliner. While Gorin held Randall back,
Lefèvre went into a widespread consultation with a passenger agent. He returned, explaining, "Our instructions are
that you must be the last to board, Monsieur Randall.
It'll be only a few more minutes."

Randall nodded, and glanced to his left. Even here,
at the point of departure, a portable television set was
in operation, with its own coterie of followers, most of
them transient and pausing for a last morsel before leaving land for their flight. Randall tried to make out the
varied scenes flashing on and off the screen.

There were quick cuts of world leaders in high places,
each with a comment or brief congratulation to mankind
for having received the marvel of Jesus Christ Returned.
There was the Pope from the balcony of St. Peter's overlooking the Vatican piazza, and the President of France
in the courtyard of the Élysée Palace, and the panoply
of royalty in Buckingham Palace, and the President of
the United States pretaped in the Oval Office of the White
House, and later in the day there would be presidents and
premiers in Bonn, in Rome, in Bucharest, in Belgrade,
in Mexico City, in Brasilia, in Buenos Aires, in Tokyo, in
Melbourne, in Capetown.

The scene had shifted back to the inside of the royal
palace in Amsterdam, and the camera was moving in on
the assembled theologians, as their spokesman, Mon-

signore Riccardi, was stating that the next twelve days would celebrate—a day set aside for each disciple of Christ (Matthias in place of Judas, of course)—the appearance of the corporeal Jesus Christ in the pages of the International New Testament.

On Christmas Day, Monsignore Riccardi was announcing, the pulpits of every church throughout Christendom, Protestant and Catholic alike, would be dedicated to the greater glory of Christ Revived, as preachers and priests would deliver their sermons on the new fifth gospel, now the first gospel and now the best hope of mankind.

Christmas Day, Randall thought, the day he had always (except in the last two years) returned to Wisconsin, to Oak City, to the steepled white church where Nathan Randall addressed his flock. Fleetingly, he thought of his father and his father's protégé, Tom Carey, and how and where they might be watching and listening to this satellite program, and what it would be like at Christmas, with James the Just a part of every worshiping family.

Randall's gaze returned to the screen. There were shots of Angela Monti, of Professor Aubert, of Dr. Knight, of Herr Hennig, as the commentator explained that these persons involved in the discovery, authentication, translation, and printing of the new Bible would shortly come forward to reply to spontaneous questions from the assembled members of the press.

The camera had moved in on Monsignore Riccardi, once more, as he was concluding his talk.

Randall was distracted by the passenger agent who was frantically signaling them from the gate leading to the boarding ramp. "*Voilà,* everyone is on the plane," said Gorin. "You are the last, and now we will escort you inside."

The two policemen prodded Randall toward the gate, as Lefèvre brought out a ring of keys, and inserted one key into the handcuffs linking Gorin and Randall. The handcuffs came apart, and Randall pulled his hand and arm away, and massaged his wrist.

They had reached the boarding ramp.

"Bon voyage," said Lefèvre. "Sorry it had to be this way."

Randall nodded wordlessly. He was sorry, too, sorry it had to be this way.

He craned his neck for one final glimpse of the satellite show from Amsterdam. The television screen was hidden from his sight. But the audio portion could still be heard. Randall moved away from his guards, but Monsignore Riccardi's apocalyptic voice trailed after him.

"As John had written, 'Except ye see signs and wonders, ye will not believe.' And now James has written, 'I have, with mine eyes, seen signs and wonders, and I can believe.' Now all mankind can echo: We do believe! *Christos anesti!* Christ is risen! *Alithos anesti!* He is truly risen! Amen."

Amen.

He entered the cabin of the plane, as the solemn airline stewardess firmly shut the door behind him.

There was only the roar of the jet engines.

He took his seat. He was ready to go home again.

FIVE AND A HALF months had passed.

Incredibly, he was home again.

Another Christmas Day in Oak City, Wisconsin, and yet like no other before it, he knew in his heart.

Steve Randall sat snug and relaxed in the front pew of the First Methodist Church, surrounded by those of his blood and his past, those he cared for and who cared for him. From the scarred oaken pulpit off to the right above him, the Reverend Tom Carey was launching into his sermon, a sermon drawn from a living vision of Jesus Christ and His Calvary in the crisp pages of the International New Testament, a sermon being echoed and reechoed from thousands of similar pulpits in similar houses of worship girdling the globe this Christmas season. Tom Carey's speech, like his very person, had taken on a new confidence, a new conviction and force, rebrought on by the message of hope found in the person, flecting the revival and strengthening of his belief

the ministry, the social and spiritual parables of the Resurrected Christ.

Half listening to the story and the message that by
now had become so familiar to him—to him most of all,
among the hundreds jammed into his father's old
church—Randall glanced down either side of the pew.

He sat on the ash wood seat between his mother, Sarah,
her smooth, pudgy face blissful as she hung on every
utterance from the pulpit, and his father, Nathan, the
elderly gentleman's features partially restored to a semblance of his onetime vigor, the light blue eyes dancing
after the cadence of his protégé's words from the pulpit.
Only the cane propped beside him and the thick slowness of his speech reflected the remnants of the stroke
he had survived. Beside his father, Randall could see Clare,
his sister, and next to her, Swedish jaw thrust forward, Ed
Period Johnson. Shifting slightly on the bench, Randall
inspected those who were sitting beyond his mother, first
Judy, her long corn-silk hair covering much of her angel
face, his alert, clear-eyed daughter, and then Uncle Herman, fatter but less vacuous than in earlier times.

They were all intent, entirely devoted to the Reverend
Tom Carey's sermon, hearing what was still fresh to them,
the sign, the wonder of Christ risen.

But Randall, he had heard it, he had heard it, lived
with it, bought it, questioned it, doubted it, fought it, been
defeated by it, and now his attention wandered. None here
had known that he, the prodigal son, had been part of
Resurrection Two, and they did not know it yet. Randall
had resolved to tell them after the services, his father
first, the others later. He would relate to them his purpose
abroad, and some of what had transpired. How much he
could reveal to them, he did not know. That remained
unresolved in his mind.

Randall stared above the now bowed heads, at one of
the towering stained-glass windows of the church, at the
shadows thrown by the branches of the trees outside,
barren of leaves but still heavy with the fresh whiteness
of last night's winter snowfall. He searched for a glimpse
of his past, the innocent years, but they were too distant,

and all he could perceive clearly in the eye of his mind
was the more recent past, the restless, angry, agonizing
past of the last five and a half months.

He sank deeply into the slough of introspection, and
that recent past, so tortured in memory, became more real
than the present.

He lived it once more, those weeks after he was severed from Resurrection Two and deported from France.

Back to New York, he remembered, to the offices of
Randall Associates, Public Relations, to the comfortable,
efficient presences of Wanda, his devoted secretary, Joe
Hawkins, his bustling assistant, Thad Crawford, his clever
attorney, and the rest of them, his staff, who depended
upon his creativity and energy.

Briefly, Randall had gone through the motions, the routine, where the telephone became your fifth limb. But he
had no energy, because he had no interest, and he was
listless, because he had no goal.

He wanted to escape, and for three of the five and a
half months he did. Thad Crawford had a summer place
in Vermont, a farm with a caretaker, livestock, a brook
winding through the ten acres, and a comfortable, restored Revolutionary War house that was unoccupied.
Randall had gone there to lay the ghost, the ghost that was
a nightmare collage of Amsterdam and Paris and Ostia
Antica and Wheeler and de Vroome and Lebrun and
James the Just. He had taken his tapes, his notes, his
recent memories, and a portable typewriter. He had tried
to live the recluse, and had almost succeeded. The telephone was operative, and he had maintained a tenuous,
thin line to the outer world, to decisions required by his
office subordinates, to his daughter Judy in San Francisco, to his parents in Oak City. But mostly, he had
given his waking hours to the book he was writing; the
anti-Good Book, it was wryly coded in his brain.

Not the best of times, the weeks of those months. He
was confused, wrathful, self-pitying, but mostly confused.
He wrote and he drank and he tried to get the venom out
of his gut. He wrote pages, reams of pages, spilled it out,
the entire exposé of Resurrection Two, told of his involve-

ment with it, of the denouement with Lebrun in Rome, of
the treachery of the mighty de Vroome, of his own expulsion from France, all of it, everything, except Angela.
He spared her.

Writing it down, he sometimes felt that he was writing
the greatest detective story of all time. On other days, he
was certain that there had never been an exposé of religious mendacity, double-dealing, treachery, like the one
his de Sade fingers flagellated out of the typewriter. On still
other days, he was positive that he was producing the
most naked self-portrait of a sick and cynical paranoiac
yet put to paper.

He drank and he wrote, and the book floated to its
conclusion on a river of Scotch.

When he was finished, the catharsis had drawn every
last drop of venom from him. What remained was the
hollow shell of his aloneness and his undiminished confusion.

Moving out of the farmhouse in Vermont, as the au-
tumn front chilled the grass and earth, he returned to
New York City with his manuscript. He placed it in his
office safe, the combination known only to Wanda and
himself. He did not know whether he would leave it as
part of an unpublished corpus that represented his effort
to exorcise the satanic forces that had resided within him,
or would finally publish it to counteract the Frankenstein's
monster that had the entire country, and half the world, in
its grip.

In the long saga of modern literature, he was sure,
there had never been a success as complete as that of the
International New Testament. Wherever you looked, this
Book of Books confronted you, tried to proselytize and
enmesh you, tried to engulf you. The radio stations, the
television screens, day and night, it seemed, were filled
with it. They seemed to Randall to spew out little else.
The newspapers and magazines were never a day without full pages of feature stories or picture layouts, or
advertisements. If you went shopping, visited a bar, dined
in a restaurant, attended a party, you heard it discussed.

The drums beat, and the charismatic new Christ was gathering souls again, souls without number. The decrease in violence was being attributed by some to the return to Christ. The improvement in the economy was being credited by others to Christ. The drop in drug usage was owing to Christ. The end of this war, the beginning of that peace talk, the general well-being and euphoria and brotherhood sweeping the earth were heralded by the recently awakened as the work of Christ.

At last report, Randall noted, the International New Testament had sold three million copies in hardback in the United States, and an estimated forty million copies around the world. All of this in hardly more than three or four monhs.

He began to think that he should publish his exposé. It might be a pebble bouncing off Goliath. Or, whipped from a slingshot generated by his own publicity campaign, it might strike the hulking monster a stunning blow, and bring him down, and slay him, slay the lie.

It was at this time, while considering this act, that Randall received the long-awaited telephone call from Ogden Towery III, head of the conglomerate Cosmos Enterprises. The contracts had finally been prepared for the take-over of Randall's firm and the guarantee of his future security, and they were only awaiting signatures, Towery's signature and his own. There had been an unaccountable delay. Crawford had tried to get through to Towery's battery of attorneys, and had failed. Crawford could not understand what was going on. Randall suspected that he knew. Wheeler, friend of Towery, had warned Steven Randall in Paris: Fall in line with Resurrection Two or suffer the consequences.

Then, Towery had telephoned, had called Randall directly, person-to-person.

A brief conversation, no wasted words, to the point, unfriendly.

"Randall, I've heard from George Wheeler. Remarkable success he's having. He tells me he owes none of it to you. He says you did everything you could to prevent it.

He says you tried to sabotage the project. What do you say to that?"

"I tried to stop it because I had evidence it's a fake."

"Heard about that, too. What's bugging you, Randall? You an atheist or Communist—is it something like that?"

"I can't sell what I don't believe in."

"Listen to me, Randall, you leave what to believe in or not to believe in to men like Wheeler and Zachery and the President, and you do your job. Now I got those contracts on my desk. Before I sign them, before I take you into our Cosmos family, I got to know where you stand."

"Where I stand?"

"What are you going to do in the future about the International New Testament? Are you going to try to sabotage it again, make more trouble, do something subversive, or what? I mean, like making speeches or writing and publishing garbage against the new Holy Book? I want to know, and Wheeler wants to know. If you've got any such notions, I want nothing more to do with you. If you're smart enough to behave like a decent, God-fearing son of a clergyman, the way you're supposed to, the way that would make your daddy proud, then I'll buy you. But I'd want it put in writing first, an addendum to the contract, before I sign. Legally, in the contract addendum, you will not be permitted to speak out or publish anything subversive against the International New Testament. If I have that assurance, you have my assurance Cosmos will take you in. What's your answer—yes or no?"

"Maybe."

"What in the hell does that mean?"

"Mr. Towery, it means maybe yes, maybe no. It means I never make important decisions without thinking about them."

"Well, you think fast, young man. I expect your answer by the last day of the year."

He hung up, and there it was, and Randall was scared. To have been dropped by Resurrection Two was one thing. To permit himself to lose the deal with Cosmos Enterprises was quite another, much more serious, because the sellout, the take-over, was where he lived, his last safe route from the rat race, his future security and independence. But the new condition was sick-making, and he felt ill and depressed and tried to weigh the contracts on Towery's desk against the exposé manuscript in his safe, and in balance he did not know which outweighed the other.

Several weeks later, another telephone call had come, one that accentuated his confusion more than ever. For months, Randall had tried to reach Jim McLoughlin, to inform him that for reasons that could not be disclosed (Towery and Cosmos again), Randall would have to renege on their handshake and would not be able to handle The Raker Institute account. McLoughlin had been away on his extended secret trips, and had been out of touch in all that time.

"Now he's back and on the other line," Wanda informed him, "calling from D. C. Says he returned to find a ton of messages and letters from Thad Crawford and you, and he's sorry to have been so neglectful, but he's been off in some remote place working twenty-five hours every day. Now he's eager to talk to you, and make plans for going ahead on your handling of his first white paper against big business. Shall I put him through?"

Randall had no stomach for telling McLoughlin what had to be told. "No, not today, Wanda, I'm not up to it. Look, Wanda, tell him I just left for the airport, I'm off to Europe again on some emergency business of my own. Tell him I'll be back next month and I'll call him, I'll call him before the end of the year."

The best way to solve problems, he had decided that day, was to ignore them. If you did not face them, maybe they'd go away. If they went away, they'd no longer exist. At least, not until the end of the year.

Yes, the best way to solve them was to ignore them and to drink.

And so he drank, through the last of October and all of November and much of this December, he drank, as in the old times. He took alcohol straight, gallons, as an antidote against problems of conscience and business, against confusion, against desolation. The only trouble was, you had to wake up. Then you were sober. And then you were lonely.

He had never felt more alone in his life, in or out of bed.

Well, he remembered the old-fashioned remedy for that, also, and he took it in heavy doses.

The girls, the women, the ones who looked best horizontal and naked—they were everywhere, and they were easy to come by for a successful, free-spending big shot, and he came by them. The actresses with big tits, the neurotic society chicks, the taut liberated career broads —the ones who came to his office on business, the ones he found in bars or discotheques or through referrals (ask-her-if-she's-got-a-friend)—they all got stoned or drunk with him, and undressed with him, and copulated with him, and when you finally reached the moment before sleep, you knew that you were still alone.

This was noninvolvement, and in desperation, he sought involvement.

Human contact with meaning. Not just sex.

One night, loaded, he decided to call Barbara, in San Francisco, and see what might come of that, if that could be patched up. But when the housekeeper answered, "This is the Burke residence," Randall remembered, through the fog of drink, that Barbara had married Arthur Burke a couple of months ago, and he dropped the scalding receiver back on its hook.

Another night, loaded again, terribly so, feeling maudlin and auld-lang-syne, he had thought of putting in a call to his last girl friend, that swinger, great lay, Darlene —Darlene Nicholson—where the hell was she?—yes, Kansas City, and beg her forgiveness, and bring her back to his bed. He had no doubt that she would abandon her boy friend, that kid Roy Ingram, and come running. But as he began to reach for the phone, he remembered that silly Darlene had wanted to get married, that that was what their breakup had been all about in Amsterdam, and he had not reached for the phone but for the bottle instead.

He had even, in his sick searching, risked losing his gorgeous secretary of three years, Wanda, by propositioning her one night before leaving the office, feeling high and miserably low, and wanting her, someone . . . tonight her. And she, gorgeous, big-bosomed, independent black girl who knew him so well, and did not fear him, she had said, "Yes, boss, I'd been wondering when you'd ask."

She had joined him in his bed nightly, that magnificent ebony body, long arms outstretched toward him, red nipples pointed toward him, huge fleshy thighs parted for him, and she had loved him and loved him for a month of nights. She had coupled with him—mindless, perspiring bouts—not for a desire to retain her job, not for any female adoration that she held for him, but out of a deep, touching, human understanding of his want and his condition, and so her love had been pity. After a month, perceiving this, ashamed yet with gratitude, he released her from his bed and kept her at her desk as friend and secretary.

Finally, last week, there had come the envelope stamped *posta aerea* with the postmark stamped ROMA. Inside was a delicate holiday card—Merry Christmas, Happy New Year—and on the blank side of the card a note. His eye went down to the signature of the sender. The sender was simply "Angela."

She had thought about him often, wondering what he was doing, prayed that he was peaceful and well. Her father was as before, alive and dead, totally unaware of the marvel his spade had wrought. Her sister was fine, and the children also. As for herself, she was busy, so busy now that the Bible was out, occupied answering hundreds of letters pouring in for her father, occupied writing articles and holding interviews in her father's name. Anyway, she was being brought to New York for a week by Wheeler to do television. She was arriving the morning of Christmas Day. She would be at The Plaza. "If you feel any purpose would be served, Steve, I would be glad to see you." Then, simply, "Angela."

He had not known what to answer her, and so he had

not replied, not even to explain that he would be out of
New York, that he had promised to see his parents
during the week between Christmas and New Year's, and
visit with his daughter, who was coming from California
to meet him in Wisconsin, and it was impossible for him
to see her in New York, even if he wanted to—or dared
to.

Angela's note had been the first sobering thing to happen to him in five and a half months. The second had
been his return home to Oak City last night, to join with
the family around the glittering pine tree and sip the traditional eggnog mildly laced with rum and to exchange
and open the gaily wrapped gifts and to listen with Judy
to a group singing Christmas carols in the snow outside
the front door.

And the third sobering moment had occurred here in
the front pew of the First Methodist Church.

Suddenly, Randall realized that he was in the pew
now, and that Tom Carey's sermon was over, and those
on either side of him, his dear ones, family and friends,
were rising from their seats.

What he saw, in this illuminating moment, was their
eyes, all of their eyes, shining bright with hope—his mother, grateful and happy, and his father, transported and
beaming, both parents younger than he had known them
to be in recent memory, both thrilled to have lived long
enough to see and hear the Word; his sister Clare, more
resolved and self-reliant than he had ever seen her, with
renewed faith in her decision not to crawl back to her
married lover and employer and his payoff job and to go
her own way toward something and someone new; his
daughter Judy, composed and thoughtful and transformed
by an insight gained from the sermon which had given her
a maturity that Randall had not seen in her before.

He looked behind him. The eight hundred or more
parishioners, in twos and threes, in groups, streaming
out of the church. He had not seen fellow human beings
like this in his lifetime, not seen them so warm, so kind,
so comforted and self-assured about themselves and assured about one another.

This beginning was the end which justified any means, Angela had told him their last time together.

The means did not matter. The end was all.

This she had said.

To this he had said No.

Now, this instant—because it was Christmas, because it was home, because it had been the most sobering moment of any in these months, witnessing the sight of heaven on earth mirrored in those many hundreds of eyes —this moment he might be inclined to say to Angela, to say Maybe—Maybe the end was all that mattered.

He would never, never be sure.

He leaned forward and kissed his mother. "Wonderful, wasn't it?" he said.

"To think I lived to see this day, son," she said. "If there is never another day like it, for your Dad or for me, it will be enough."

"Yes, Mom," he said. "And Merry Christmas, again. Look, you go back to the house with Clare and Uncle Henry and Ed Period and Judy. I've got a rented car outside, and Dad and I'll drive back together. We'll take the long way home, like when I was a kid and he used to drive the flivver, remember? But we won't be long, Mom. We'll be there while the food's still hot."

He turned to his father, who was leaning on his cane, and he crooked an arm under his father's armpit to give him added support, and guided him toward the red-carpeted aisle.

His father smiled at him. "We owe Our Lord our hearts, our souls, our trust, for His goodness in revealing Himself to us on this day, and for bringing us together in health and fullness of spirit to receive His message."

"Yes, Dad," Randall said gently, relieved that his father was now able to talk almost as clearly as before the stroke.

"Well, now, son," the Reverend Nathan Randall said with a spark of his former heartiness, "I guess we've had enough churching for one day. It'll be a treat driving home with you. It'll be like old times."

* * *

IT WAS LIKE OLD TIMES, their drive, yet Randall sensed that it was a new time.

The long way home, on the gravel-and-dirt road now frosted with fresh snow, skirted the lake which everyone called a pond, and was only ten or fifteen minutes longer than the short way through the business district of Oak City.

Randall drove slowly to savor this nostalgic interlude.

They both looked funny, Randall thought, like two large stuffed cherubs. In the church vestibule, aware that the temperature had dropped, that the glare from the partially hidden sun was deceptive, they had bundled into their overcoats and scarves and pulled on their fleece-lined gloves. Now, in the rented car (the heater not working, naturally), they were insulated from outdoor chill and comfortable.

As in times gone by, his father talked, an occasional word slurred due to his infirmity, but talked with an energy rekindled, and Randall was pleased to be silent and listen to him.

"Look at Pike's Pond out there," his father was saying. "Is there a prettier or more restful natural sight on earth? I've always told Ed Period that Thoreau would have liked it more than Walden Pond had he come out our way. Glad he didn't. We'd have suffered tourists' leaving their paper plates and empty beer cans forever after. But now it's still as it was when you were a boy of ten or twelve. Do you recollect those days, Steve?"

"I remember, Dad," said Randall quietly, gazing out at the lake, cupped in by the thick wooded areas all around, the water no longer visible. "It's frozen over."

"Frozen over," repeated his father. "Whenever it got frozen over like that, the ice on top maybe six inches thick, solid, we used to come here and go ice fishing. Remember ice fishing, son?" He did not wait for an answer. "Each of us would dig several holes in the ice, straight through to the clear water underneath. Then we'd set up our traps and lines, only five to a person according to the law. Been a long time since I made one of those. You'd take the stick, carve a notch on top, set and fasten the metal rod into the notch, with your line and hook and minnow on one end and your red flag on the other. We'd plant the stick in the ice at the edge of the hole and drop the line with the bait down in the water. Then we'd all go back near the car parked on the ice or to the shore, clapping ourselves and each other with our mittened hands to keep up circulation, and we'd build a fire and we'd sit around joking and singing as we watched those flags. Suddenly, out there in Pike's Pond there'd be a bite, a flag would fly straight up, and we'd whoop like red Indians and go scrambling out on the ice to see who'd be the first to haul in a black bass or pickerel. You were the first usually, when your legs got longer after you started growing up."

Randall recalled it vividly, with a pang. "You ought to do it again sometime, Dad."

"No more. Not in the winter. There are some things you shouldn't do again in the winter. But I'll tell you this. Dr. Oppenheimer says I'll be well enough to go fishing again when the weather's better. Ed Period and I were discussing it just last week. When spring comes, we were talking about taking a fishing trip up round the Dells. Still pretty country up there."

They lapsed into silence once more as Randall turned the wheel and headed up the narrow road winding away from the lake.

After a while, his father resumed talking. "Just thinking how the past is never gone, always part of the present. Just realizing how much enhanced and more meaningful my past has been made—my youth, my life with your mother, my service to God—because of that new Bible. I keep dwelling on that discovery, that new gospel. Your mother and I, we've read it and reread it, at least a dozen times. Remarkable, the revelation. Jesus tending His sheep in the pasture. Jesus standing over Joseph's grave, speaking as He spoke. I've heard nothing more meaningful. Even if you were a nonbeliever, you would have to believe. You would have to know God's Son is among us, and you'd gain strength. It gives life meaning."

"If it does, Dad, that's important."

"Nothing more important, Steve," said his father fervently. "To quote Coleridge—I *believe* Plato and Socrates. I *believe in* Jesus Christ. I'll tell you what I was thinking in church this morning, during Tom's sermon. I've never faltered in my faith, so don't misunderstand what I'm saying. But I've suffered the last years, seeing how the young—not the young alone, their parents, also—were abandoning the church and the Scriptures. They were turning away to false idols, to the Show Me and Prove It of science, as if visibility were all that verified truth, as if science itself were without abstractions and mysteries. People were gorging themselves on what they could touch and hold, but still, in each pause, they wanted purpose and meaning in life. Don't you think that was happening, son?"

"I do."

"They couldn't find their answer in God and His Son, because they couldn't see Christ through faith alone, so they couldn't accept a message from One in whom they did not believe. So they turned their backs on Him. I think it happened to you, Steve. It certainly happened in varied degrees to the majority of families in our parish."

"I know. I discussed it with Tom Carey when you were ill."

"Well, I feel personally blessed to know that's over with. I truly think Christ knew what was happening. That's why He reappeared in the nick of time. The discovery at Ostia Antica could have been no accident. It was divinely inspired."

Ostia Antica, Randall thought. No, it was no accident. How difficult it was going to be to tell his father about it.

"Now we can answer, to the satisfaction of all, the two questions of our creed," his father was saying. "Do we confess Jesus Christ as our Saviour and Lord and pledge our allegiance to His kingdom? Do we receive and profess the Christian faith as contained in the New Testament of Our Lord, Jesus Christ? Those who could not answer affirmatively before can finally answer Yes. Thanks to James the Just, they can answer Yes today. For them, there is—by scientific criteria—visible proof of the Saviour. For me, my selfish trial is over. I see my church safe. I see Tom Carey sound again and my pulpit in good hands and restored to respect. I see a haven for the wandering young, like my granddaughter Judy, like my daughter Clare. You can see the difference in them, can't you, Steve?"

Randall nodded. "I'm pleased for them. I can't tell you how pleased."

"For myself, I was never afraid to leave when my time came. I always retained profound faith in a heaven above —not a heaven of golden spires and streets, but a heaven where the redeemed, in mind and spirit, in the eternal soul, might be received by God and His Son. That was always my heaven above—but now, I've lived to the day when I see the possibility of a heaven on earth, when goodness will overcome poverty and violence and injustice. Henceforth, goodness in the ecumenical sense, that of peace and love embracing the entire world, will prevail. This Resurrection will make our two hundred Protestant sects as one, and will make us one with the Catholics, and bring us closer to our Jewish brethren, for each of us like the Lord himself was a Jew in the beginning." He paused, loosening his scarf. He said, "How you've let me ramble on. Winter does tend to make one more garrulous. Enough. I want to hear about you, Steve. You said you were going to tell me about your summer."

"It was unimportant, Dad. Perhaps another time."

"Yes, we must talk again."

Randall glanced at his father, and saw that he had leaned his head back against the seat and that the old man's eyes were heavy-lidded. Not Spinoza, but Nathan Randall, the truly God-intoxicated man, Randall thought.

"You must be tired, Dad," he said, as he wheeled the car into their street. "You deserve some rest."

He slowed, going past the snowbanks.

"I merely feel peaceful, son," he heard his father mur-

mur. "I've never felt such divine peace. I hope you can find it now, too."

Randall drew up before the house, parking at the curb, and shutting off the ignition. He turned away from the wheel to tell his father that he believed he would find peace, also, somehow, in the same way or in another way, but somehow, and to tell him that they were home.

But his father's eyes were closed in sleep, and there was an infinite stillness about him.

Even before Randall took his father's hand, and touched his pulse, he had the premonition, and then he knew that his father had died. He moved nearer the resting old man, and it seemed impossible. His father didn't look dead. The gentle smile on the reposeful face was as alive as ever.

Randall brought the limp body to him, inside his arms, cradling the old gray head against his chest.

"No, Dad," he whispered, "don't go away, don't leave me." He rocked his father in his arms, and the voice of his childhood pleaded out of the past. "Stay, Pa, please, you can't leave me alone."

He clutched his father closer and closer, refusing to accept it, trying to will him alive.

The old man couldn't be dead, simply couldn't be, but after a while he knew that he wasn't and never would be, and then he released him, at last.

THE FUNERAL SERVICES in the chapel of the funeral home had ended, and the last of the many mourners had filed past the open casket and were gathering outside in the snow, and now Randall, supporting his mother, led her away from the casket and at the exit turned her over to Clare and Uncle Herman.

He kissed her on the forehead. "It'll be all right, Mom. He's at peace."

He lingered a moment, watching them lead her outside to where Judy, Ed Period, and Tom Carey were waiting beyond the hearse.

Alone in the chapel, he looked around the sanctuary of last farewell helplessly: the rows of seats now empty;

the minister's lectern abandoned; the organ quiet; the family room vacated. But echoing still in his heart were snatches of the service. He could hear the opening hymn, "God of Grace, God of Glory." He could hear Tom Carey's reading, "Jesus said, 'I am the resurrection and the life; he who believes in me, though he die, yet shall he live, and whosoever lives and believes in me shall never die.'" He could hear all present chanting in chorus the Gloria Patri, "Glory be to the Father, and to the Son, and to the Holy Ghost; as it was in the beginning, is now, and ever shall be, world without end. Amen."

His eyes fell on the open casket resting before the bank of flowers.

Almost involuntarily, as one mesmerized, he moved toward the casket, and stood over it, staring down at the mortal remains of his father, the Reverend Nathan Randall, lying in his final sleep.

He thought: You can't be a man until your father has died. Who was it who had said that? He remembered: Freud had said that.

You can't be a man until your father has died. He stared into the coffin. His father had died, definitely died, yet he did not feel like a man at all, only like a son, the son who had been a boy, the little boy lost.

He fought it, remembering he was a man, but still the tears came down, and he tasted their salty wetness on his mouth and felt the hot choking dryness in his lungs, and uncontrollably he began to sob.

After long minutes, the sobbing grew less and ceased, and he wiped his eyes. He was not a boy, he knew, he was in fact a man, like it or not, yet inexplicably he was pervaded by the same warmth of hopefulness and believing and assurance that he had known as the boy stranger he had left behind so long ago.

One last look. Rest in peace, Dad, rest up there in your heaven of the mind and spirit and soul with God and the Jesus Christ you just saw and know so well. I leave you, Dad, but I leave you not alone until that day we are all together again.

Then, after a moment, only a little afraid, Randall left

the casket to join the others in the concluding rite of passage.

The next hour, at the cemetery, he lived through in a daze.

At the graveside, standing before the closed coffin and the heap of dirt, he recited the prayer for his departed parent.

"Father of all mercy, seeing eyes and hearing ear, oh listen to my plea for Nathan, the old man, and send Michael, the chief of your angels, and Gabriel, your messenger of light, and the armies of your angels, so that they may march with the soul of my father, Nathan, until they bring him to you on high."

Not until they had left the cemetery in the two limousines, heading back to the house to receive friends and family coming to pay their respects, did Randall recall with a start the familiar graveside prayer again and realize its source.

It was the prayer read by Jesus at the graveside of His father, Joseph, and reported in the Gospel According to James.

A prayer as reported by James the Just or by Robert Lebrun.

Somehow, for Randall, it didn't matter anymore, not one goddam bit. The words would comfort his father on his last journey, and whatever their origin, they were sacred and they were right.

His head had cleared and the constriction had gone from his chest. A half mile from the house, he requested the driver from the funeral parlor to stop and let him out.

"Don't worry, Mom," he said. "I just want some air. I'll catch up with you and Clare and Judy in a few minutes. I'll be fine. Just see that you take care."

On the sidewalk, he waited until the limousine was out of sight, then avoiding a youngster flopping on a sled, Randall removed his gloves, thrust his hands in the pockets of his overcoat, and started to walk.

Five blocks later, as the gray wooden-and-stucco house came into view, the snow began to fall again, light, thin flakes fluttering downward, cooling his cheeks and celebrating life.

By the time he had arrived at the white front lawn, he felt restored and ready to reenlist in the community of men. There was some unfinished business left in this unfinished year, and it had to be completed. He started toward the front porch, and through the bay window he could see that the living room lights were on and dozens of callers were surrounding his mother and Clare, and he could see Ed Period serving punch and Uncle Herman circling around with the sandwich tray, and he knew that his mother would be all right. He would join her shortly. First, as a son who had become a man, he must settle something for himself.

He veered away from the porch, and headed for the sidewalk running along the house to the back door. Quickening his pace, he reached the rear door, went inside to the kitchen, and climbed the backstairs to the bedrooms.

He found Wanda in the spare bedroom, packing the last of her belongings into her overnight bag. He had telephoned her in New York yesterday to tell her what had happened and to say that he would not go back to the office until the day after New Year's. She had simply turned up last night, not as his secretary but as his friend, to be near him and help him in any way she could. Now, she was preparing to go back.

He came up behind her, pulled her around, hugging her as he kissed her cheek. "Thanks, Wanda, thank you for everything."

She held him off and studied him worriedly. "You going to be all right? I called for a taxi to take me to O'Hare, but I can stay longer, if you need me."

"I need you in New York, Wanda. There are some things I want you to do. I want them done before New Year's Day."

"I'll be in the office tomorrow. You want me to write them down?"

He smiled slightly. "I think you'll remember them. To begin with, you know that book I told you I wrote up in Vermont, the one I put away in the safe?"

"Yes."

"It's in an old ream paper box with a label reading *Resurrection Two*."

"I know, boss. I typed the label."

"Okay, you have the combination to the safe. Tomorrow, take the box out, and keep it handy. I'm going to get rid of it."

"You mean that?"

"Old bridges are for burning, Wanda. I don't need them. I'm not turning back. I want to go ahead—"

"But after all that work on the manuscript, boss?"

"Hold it, Wanda. I didn't tell you yet how I'm going to get rid of it. You'll know that in a few minutes. Now, next, I want you to call Thad Crawford. He knows that Ogden Towery and Cosmos are waiting to hear from me before New Year's Day. Have him tell Towery I've made my decision. The answer is, Mr. Towery, get lost. I'm not selling out to Cosmos. I have something better in mind."

"Wow, boss!" exclaimed Wanda, embracing him. "Even sinners' prayers are sometimes answered."

"Now, one more thing. You can do that right here. Do you know where to locate Jim McLoughlin?"

"I spoke to him last week. He wanted to know when you were coming back."

"Okay, locate him." He pointed to the telephone on the bedside table. "Tell him I'm back. I want to speak to him right now."

Presently, he was on the long-distance phone to Washington, D. C., with Jim McLoughlin.

The young man was saying, "About time, Mr. Randall. I thought we'd keep missing each other until it was too late. Things are really humming with us. We've got the facts on all those thieves and hypocrites and phonies. We're going to make free enterprise really free again, and not a minute too soon, believe me. The next step is up to you. Are you ready to tell the whole world about The Raker Institute? Are you ready to go ahead?"

"On two conditions only, Jim. And my name is Steve."

"Steve, sure." But the voice on the other end was troubled. "What conditions, Steve?"

"The first. While I was in Europe, I had a little chance to play at your game. I got involved in probing, trying to track down, a certain matter—a business matter, in a sense. I was trying to find out whether something—you might call it a consumer product—was a fraud, a deception foisted upon the public, or if it was an honest enterprise. I had reason to think it a fraud, but I could never fully prove it. The people involved in selling this product most likely believe it to be honest. They may be right. However, there is reasonable doubt. Anyway, I've written up a long account of my involvement in the project, and I'm having my secretary send it to you tomorrow. You'll receive a box bearing the label *Resurrection Two*—"

"*Resurrection Two?*" McLoughlin interrupted. "What did you have to do with that? Want to tell me about it?"

"Not now, Jim. Besides, the manuscript will tell you all that you need to know for the time being. Then, we can talk. Anyway, if you decide to pick up where I left off— look into the whole thing one day, resume the search for truth if you think it's in the public interest, whatever it leads to—fine. My only concern is that you consider it. After that, you're on your own."

"First condition met and accepted. No sweat." McLoughlin hesitated. "What's the second, Steve—your second condition for handling The Raker Institute?"

"I'll take you on, if you take me on," said Randall simply.

"What does that mean?"

"It means I've decided to go into the business of truth, also. You've got the investigative arm, but no voice. I've got no arm, but I've got a stentorian voice. So why don't we join forces, merge, work together to try to clean up the country and make life better for everyone? Right now, and right here on earth."

Jim McLoughlin gave a mighty shout. "You mean that, Steve? You really mean it?"

"You're damn right I mean it. We go together, or I don't go at all. You can stay president. I'll settle for vice-president—V.P. in charge of voice. You hear me?"

"I hear you, man! You've got a deal! What a Christmas present!"

"For me, too, Jim," Randall said quietly. "See you at the barricades."

When he returned to Wanda, and took her bag from her, he could see that her cheeks were wet and her face was glowing. "Oh, Steve, Steve—" she said, and choked up.

"You get back to your typing, girl," he said gruffly, "and leave the foolishness to me."

He saw her downstairs and into her taxi. As the car started, she rolled down the rear window.

She put her head out. "Just wanted to say I like your two girls, boss, I like them very much. A winning parlay for sure. Play it. They're in the backyard making a snowman. Happy New Year, boss!"

The taxi sped away.

He turned back to the house, considered going inside, but there was time enough for that.

There was still some unfinished business, the last of it, and it was in the backyard.

He walked slowly alongside the house, brushing the soft snowflakes from his cheeks.

He knew that he had finally found for himself the answer to Pilate's classic question, the one that had haunted him all the summer and since.

Pilate's question: What is truth?

He had thought it a question for which there was no answer. Now, he knew that he had been wrong. There was an answer.

Enjoying the melting snow on his face, he mouthed the answer to himself: Truth is love.

And to love, one must believe: in self, in others, in the underlying purpose of all living things and in the plan behind existence itself.

That is truth, he told himself.

He arrived at the expanse of white snow behind the house, for the first time feeling as his father had always wanted him to feel, at peace, unafraid, and not alone.

Ahead, there loomed the huge, funny snowman, and

his daughter was reaching up patting its snowball nose into place.

"Hi, Judy," he called out.

She half turned, and waved gaily, calling back, "Hi, Dad," and she resumed her play.

Then he saw the other girl, a jaunty ski cap on her dark hair, emerge from behind the oversize figure made out of snow, busily trying to shape it and make it into a man.

"Hello, Angela," he called to her. "I love you, you know."

She came running, plowing through the snow, toward him. "Darling," she called back, "my darling!" And then she came into his arms at last, and he knew, he knew that he would never let her go.